PHOENIX GREEN EARTH
Book Two

The two Warrens, Liz and Ted are travelers. Even though they during a few short, hectic, sort of peaceful years resided in the ancestral home in London, they spent most of their lives Journeying across the vast reality of the world… beyond… on their long and hard path to a terrifying and remarkable destiny.

Novels published by Midnight Fire Media

Your Own Fate
Night on Earth
Dreams Belong to the Night
Alarums of Reality
Afterglow Dust
Black Dragon
Falling
Thunder Road - Ice and Fire
Season of the Witch
Afterglow Rain
Forsaken
Afterglow Fire

Anthology: Red Shadow and Other Stories

The Janus Clan series:

The Defenseless
The Slaves
Birds Flying in the Dark
At the End of the Rainbow
Lewis of Modern York
The Werewolf of Locus Bradle
ShadowWalk
Phoenix Green Earth book 1 and 2

Poetry:

Amos Keppler: Complete Poems 1989 – 2003
Secrets - Descriptions of what cannot be described

(A few of the) novels to be published:

The Nine: Catching the Wind
The Valley of Kings
Fangs and Claws of the Earth
Fallen
Resurrection Dreams

Phoenix Green Earth
Book Two

by

Amos Keppler

«The Second Twenty Years»
1988 - 2008

Midnight Fire Media

2021

Midnight Fire Media

http://midnight-fire.net/mfm
For more about Phoenix Green Earth and The Janus Clan:
http://midnight-fire.net/sw

E-Mail:
Amos13@midnight-fire.net
manofhood@yahoo.com

Cover, text, design, premedia, art and photos Amos Keppler

ISBN 978-82-91693-33-0

Part two:
The Three Years of the Wanderers

I am the Bennu, the soul of Ra, and the guide of the gods in the Tuat; let it be so done unto me that I may enter in like a hawk, and that I may come forth like Bennu, the Morning Star.

Transformation - The Phoenix

– But we are alive and free, and much more, she whispered in triumph. – And we're going to drown their world in flames.

Elizabeth Stevens - AKA Betty Morgan

CHAPTER TWELVE
NIGHTS OF FUTURE PAST

ASCENSION
BIRTHPLACE EARTH
1ST NIGHT Year One AV (After Venus)

Her body rose ninety degrees, standing upright, levitating effortlessly in the air above the bed from one moment to the next. She stared at the open-mouthed people in white lab coats with black, opaque eyes. They all saw her eyes. It didn't matter if they saw her front or back or sides. The exposed skin began glowing in a bluish shadow, even her hair, reaching below her feet. The people standing closest to her began gasping, as waves of pain, of power washed over them. And then, in a matter of seconds they turned to dust before shocked colleagues' eyes. One second, two later the effect had spread to the entire room. Dust and empty clothes followed the brief, horrible death-cries. Her clothes changed, turning into a hood and a robe. Her face changed, turning into dark ash.

Two lonely people remained, standing frozen before the regal figure. Her voice, when she spoke didn't sound rusty at all, but soft as a warm wave of water and air, as thunder and fire, a thousand echoes washing over them.

– Do you know why, she snarled, – why you aren't dust with the rest?

Sick realization hit them, as they failed to look at each other in horror, as their attention was looked on her, as they began feeling the effects of her initial, invasive probing.

And, unable to speak, unable to voice the savage joy she invested in them, they knelt in reverence to their Queen, their Goddess.

An impatient sign from her, and they rose, and then, in a flash she was right there in front of them. She... entered them, and began learning about them, things even they didn't know, and in a second, two, she had learned it all. They both convulsed as their bodies and minds began changing, as they began displaying their true selves, what they had repressed their entire lives. She let them see themselves through her eyes, and they gasped in fear and helpless fascination. They knew beyond knowing that she hadn't really done anything to them, except brought forward what had been hidden inside them for so long... waiting for release.

– Martha, Victor, she said softly. – Behold yourselves. Rejoice. This is who you are.

Their old lives were gone, by the snap of her fingers. They hardly even remembered their life before these moments anymore, as the seconds passed. When they glanced at the dust and clothes on the floor it didn't seem important at all, in any way they could identify.

She rose slightly in the air, reaching outwards, constantly probing and prodding. Speech is a barrier. She spoke in their minds. Come with me. Join with me.

And it was an order, not a request, and not even that. It was merely a confirmation of a fact already established.

Distant screams, a multitude of choking echoed it in their minds. It didn't really faze them.

I feel it, you know, she told them, she shared with them. I feel every soul on Venus dying.

And that fazed them. They cried as she cried, wept as she wept, raged as she raged. And they became like her, a Storm, a moving fire spreading across and beyond the world.

They watched as a wand and a sword appeared from nowhere, into her left and right hands, and they gasped in yet more awe. She nodded and smiled to herself, her dark ashen face hardly changing expression.

A large hole opened in the ceiling above. Victor had eagerly, with his tongue hanging out communicated the direction to the elevator to her, but the Goddess didn't care about such trifles. She rose, and they rose with her, through all the levels of the giant compound. Dust and clothes and blood rained down on them, but didn't touch them, didn't faze them. Every level on their way up came to be littered with the remains of people. They glimpsed hordes of soldiers, before they, too were dust. Others joined them as they ascended. Lillith's group grew, changed like them, transformed like them, eagerly following the Queen Goddess on her Journey.

The winds didn't faze her.

The figure, the robed figure, a shadow in bright day floated through the air from far away, above a half-faded road in the desert. Desert mist floated with it. A hood covered its head, and concealed its face. It's coming, the Fates cried, and fearful people sought close to each other in their tiny homes below the ground. In one hand it held a wand, with a skull on top, and in its other hand it held a sword, a black blade burning in fire, an irresistible unmoving force closing in on people's flesh and souls.

The Nightraven wandered through a landscape of hot mist and searing heat. For every step forward, it got that much closer, even if it was still far off. A creature without face, and body and soul and blood.

She was Lillith, now, inside and out. Very little remained of Stacy Larkin, of Jill Stafford, except what was Forever.

And that was Everything.

Waves of Power kept surging through her and grew, as she sucked up the lifeforce of the crowds she killed.

Behind her, in her slipstream, ran, flew and strived her brood, a growing number of people, of kin, of mutants she picked up on her way,

Except for them, in her wake, she left nothing but dust, but ashes.

2

The Great Migration began.

Some would argue that it had begun much earlier, in the nascent years of Space travel, but that wasn't really the case. This was the day, the moment mankind left

Earth behind, and began spreading across the Universe.

As the remains of Venus were fired through space, so was mankind. Hundreds of people, even thousands escaped the vicious attack on their lives that fateful night. Some of the small ships were tracked down and the people onboard were mercilessly executed on the spot. Most weren't, as they were willing and able to defend themselves viciously and return the aggression in kind. They spread to the outskirts of current civilization, the unofficial colonies around Jupiter and Saturn and the frontier in the asteroid belt. They also made autonomous colonies of their own. Where there previously had been only one place for the persecuted and harassed to go, there were now many.

Lillith moved west, crossing what was left of the North American continent in that direction. She moved towards the Spaceport. It was so clear in her mind. She was already there.

Clouds and whirlwinds of air danced around her. It was her. She was it. One blink and the cold, dark Space surrounded her. She was out there, spreading, spreading outward with each successive breath.

The Spaceport was underground, like basically everything these days, protected by a thick metal cover. She could sense them down there, the panic and the confusion and bewilderment, the absolute horror of what was coming, coming for them. They scurried down there, like rabbits in a hole. And they were.

They were.

She scanned them, every single one of them, in a matter of seconds, briefly allowing herself to marvel at what she had become, before pressing on.

A large hole opened in the ground. One moment it wasn't there. The next it was. She grabbed those of her brood that couldn't fly, surrounded them, embraced them all in her protective bubble, and descended the rabbit hole.

She sensed that she was starting to leak, becoming «full». Her brood writhed in pain and joy as they were bathed in the sea of her energies. She still had limits, even though they were far above what they had once been. The Homo Sapiens in the rabbit hole survived her instant close proximity, now.

Kill them, she commanded. Kill them all!

And the slaughter began.

People were being ripped apart. They died consumed by flames, in a thousand ways in the confined space, where there was no place to run. She experienced it all closeup, as if she herself made every kill, caused every scream and painful death. All of it sustained her and strengthened her, and a serene, transcendent pleasure lit her face.

She didn't need these people, didn't need any of them. There were already engineers and technicians and relevant scientists aplenty among her brood.

Information downloaded itself into her cerebral cortex, into the deepest recesses of her brain every microsecond, in a continuous flow, and she could take it all. Her mind, like all of her expanded in a thousand directions, and kept growing exponentially in every subject she cared to accept. It was a rush beyond rushes, beyond anything she had experienced before, and she smiled.

Dead and mangled bodies decorated the floor and walls everywhere. The ruckus died off slowly, as the bloodlust faded and Lillith's people began reorienting themselves towards other pursuits, and as always, she spurred them on, granting them purpose and life, and joy filled their hearts.

They walked to the technical equipment, to the computer screens and machines, and began operating them with immediate, growing confidence. Some just stood there, letting their minds do the jobs for them, and it felt far easier than doing it with their hands. They kept growing into their new lives with ease, with painful ease, kept adapting to the new demands put on them, and the joy felt by the Goddess' approval, the Mother's grace knowing no bounds.

The space shuttle at the center of the adjacent hall, decorated by blood and limbs and guts, and pieces of flesh was filled slowly, as all necessary tasks were quickly and efficiently completed. The ceiling above their heads began sliding away, revealing the not very restful sky. The wind picked up immediately, as the desert sand began mixing with the previously so stale, hermetic air.

The shuttle rose, up through the hole and into the battering winds. Lillith sensed the powerful engines, so much improved in the time she had slept, yet no more than a distant rumble, compared to the Universe she experienced. It was practically impossible to see anything through the windows, and even the instruments had great difficulties reading anything useful, but she had no problems reading anything. The shuttle rose, in no time at all, through the agitated atmosphere and into dark, illuminated Space, dead, cold, alive Space. Her Shadow embraced the shuttle, even though she was painfully aware of the fact that not even her powerful flesh could survive out here unprotected. But Space kept revealing itself to her, like everything did. She looked at Eva, the pilot, looked at her deliberately with her eyes.

The buzz surrounding their flight filled her and excited her. Communications were livid practically everywhere where there was communication. She saw everything, experienced it all in her mind's eye and beyond. It was as if she had become the entire scene, everything moving and/or breathing in the vastness surrounding them. They tried to fire at them, but she swatted them like flies, and they stopped. It was that easy, beyond easy. She smiled.

The Space Station, the giant, illuminated construct loomed in the distance, growing larger in their vision by the second. It was the seventh of its current kind, and the biggest and most sophisticated in history… And it had been completed two days ago.

Lillith knew this, just as she knew the names of the people on the Earth Council, and many other things.

She had already caught up with this brave, new world, but it would never, ever catch up with her.

Several other half-completed constructs loomed around them. They were far away, but so big that they rivaled the Earth in their eyes. This, this area was a factory, and what it produced was wayfaring space stations, traveling machines in Space.

It had been coined the grandest project ever undertaken by mankind. The newsvids spoke about it constantly, spoke of desperate hope to the huddled masses back on Earth, about the new world, new life awaiting them out there.

Lillith made a gesture, dramatic, unnecessary, and suddenly it was her face showing up on the vidscreens, her voice speaking to humanity from afar.

– You want to know the truth? You want to know the fate most of you will suffer out here, anywhere?

She snapped her fingers, and everyone saw scenes from the mining societies in the asteroid belt and elsewhere, saw people suffer and die in confined and poisonous spaces.

– You will be serfs, she cried contemptuously, – even more than you already are. When are you going to wise up? Your masters are such accomplished liars, and you such accomplished dupes. When are you going to wake from your slumber, and take responsibility for your own lives?

– I won't come and rescue you. No one will. You'll have to do that yourself, the way you should have always done. I won't come for you, but I will come… If only one single mutant is killed or injured or even bothered, we will come for that community and obliterate it.

She smiled into the Vid.

– I will come!

She didn't really pause, but they experienced it that way, as her image, her imprint was frozen at their mind's eye forever.

– Members of the new Nazi-organization that has become so popular in recent years can count their days. I will come to each and every one of your «centers» and remove them from the face of existence. It will take time and effort, but it will be done. My will be done. The time for pussyfooting around you despicable racists is over, and you better face up to that fact. Every community housing such a center will be destroyed. If you're unable to rid yourself of them on your own, I will come and do it for you, and you won't like me as a houseguest. You won't care for my visit at all…

The demonic face turned even more terrifying, and it was as if Lillith leapt from every Vidset there was, and at the jugular of those watching.

Space Station 7 loomed above them, or so it seemed, at least to some of them, but not to her. To her it felt small, like a trinket she held in the palm of her hand.

They docked smoothly. She made sure of that, even though she didn't really have to do anything. The evacuation had long since begun, and continued in a somewhat orderly manner. She projected herself onboard, on all the levels of the space arc, on all the ports, and the remaining fleeing crewmembers pointed at her in terror and fled in panic. Lillith, the Demon Mother was everywhere, also in the minds of those fleeing her presence… forever.

She stepped onto the landing bridge, as she entered the enormous ship in the flesh, as she had earlier entered it with her mind. There was gravity here, fairly similar to that of Earth. The difference was only notable to someone with her enhanced senses. She pressed on, further inside the construct of steel and wires and electricity. Her brood followed her with wide eyes. They walked, somewhat slowly, now, as she did.

This is our home, now, she told them, and will be for quite a while, while we stake our claim on the Universe.

She turned to one of them, before he managed to speak up, knowing well that he would do so before he knew himself.

But they're watching us like hawks, My Lady, he pointed out nervously, anxiously. I know you can protect us, but you will need to rest sooner or later.

I won't need sleep. I've slept enough. But when the time comes when I choose rest, choose brief sleep, we won't need to be cautious any longer, at least not more than moderately so.

She stared pointedly at them all, as she appeared before each and every one of them.

Come, my children, she called. We have much work ahead of us, in this and later brief homes, enough to last a thousand lifetimes.

She raised her arms and cried out, and her voice made the walls shiver and shake.

– I NAME THIS PLACE ATLANTIS. MAY IT SERVE THE PEOPLE LONG AND WELL

Wild cries rose from the gathering, the hailing of the Queen Goddess.

And they followed her, eagerly, passionately, as Atlantis once more came alive around them, as its thousand lights and countless shadows sparked and burned.

3

It took six hours to fire up the enormous, powerful engines. Lillith sensed their buzz, their glow. It was nothing to her. It took two days to start all the systems, and make sure everything was up and running without a glitch, among them the hydroponics and the gardens left behind, making sure there were no hidden beyond hidden traps.

It was like seconds to her.

Traps were a concern. Even though she was able to read electronics, the beyond advanced technology surrounding them, to perceive it pretty much the way she perceived everything, she lacked the ability to properly interpret it. She had to do that by proxy.

Will… Venus Bombs be a problem, My Lady?

No, she shook her head. They don't have that many of them left, and I can identify and swat them easily. They're nothing to me. Homo Sapiens will have to come up with something new, totally new, and even though they possess a kind of desperate ingenuity, it will take time, time we won't grant them.

I'm lessened, she thought, closing a part of her off from her peers. I'm not whole.

She had been, briefly. Surrounded by death, by tons of quickly decaying flesh, the moment before Death had filled her to the brim, she had been one with her surroundings, with Existence itself.

Atlantis broke free of its boundaries, as it left the port, left Earth behind, and set out in the Universe.

Ships followed them for a while, but not for long. She appeared on their bridges.

That was all the incentive they needed to stay away. This far, she told them, but no further.

Years followed, and they were nothing to her. She observed and taught her brood, until they became accomplished fighters, until they were almost as lethal, as much a death dealer as she had become. As she had sworn, they paid visits to the Earth Council's many outposts, and left each and every one of them in ruins. There were deaths also among her people, and she allowed that, because it hardened them, prepared them for what was to come, and she made sure they understood that.

She healed them, and gained their praise. She stood and let them die in agony, and increased their fear. Years passed like quicksilver.

The frozen lake and the castle was a magnificent sight, as she stood on its north shore, on Titan, one of Saturn's moons. This place of magick would always be warmer than the rest of this planet. Titan was warming slowly, very slowly, by the heat introduced into its atmosphere centuries earlier.

She faced Bianca, one of her oldest living kin, at the edge of the forest. Bianca was a sentry, guarding the treasure between the trees.

– I won't let you hurt him, she said, tight-lipped.

Lillith smiled. Bianca's lips trembled, and Bianca crumbled before her.

– I won't hurt him. I need him.

They walked, between the living, breathing trees, reaching the edge of the forest, walking the frozen, endless waste, for hours and hours, a few seconds of her time.

She heard the loud, monotonous voice from far away, finally with her ears, like she had for so long with her mind.

– I've been waiting for you.

Again and again and again:

– I HAVE BEEN WAITING FOR YOU

She spotted the hut on the low rise, a valley away. It didn't look far, but in this treacherous wasteland she suspected it was, and she proved herself right, as she struggled to walk behind her descendant.

– I bring him food once a day, Bianca told her in her frosty voice. – Sometimes he feeds, but often he doesn't.

The cries grew incessantly louder, until it periodically overwhelmed any other sound, even the near ice-river, where the giant pieces gnawed at each other and created a noise of another world. But the piercing voice echoed through space, through eternity, gnawing at Lillith's sanity, speaking about what was still out of her reach.

The man in rags sat, somewhat at the center of the hut. There was no door, no protection against the cold. The entire creature seemed frozen, undead. A trickle passed down Lillith's spine.

– I've been waiting for you, David Warren said in a perfectly normal voice, chilling Lillith to the bone.

– I'm here, she confirmed.

The frozen fireeyes moved and saw and sensed, as it focused on her. What burned inside him wouldn't let itself be extinguished by anything. She suspected that even

13

the frozen void of Space wouldn't keep the carcass before her from breathing. Or perhaps it didn't need to breathe. Perhaps the burning ravaging his mind solely fueled him.

The two women entered the hut, and the present and the image they saw burning in David Warren's mind became one.

He rose on unsteady feet, looking at her with an old man's face.

– I went catatonic, he said. – Not because of Venus' fate, but because of you.

– I know, she said softly. – And now you're awake, and ready to serve your Goddess.

She walked, and he walked with her. Bianca took two steps outside the hut, and stopped, indecisive, looking at her great grandmother and her lover like a lost soul.

Lillith walked a few more steps, before turning, signing to her.

– You, too, will advise me, she informed Bianca.

– On what? The woman snarled in her fear and spite.

– On all matters your Queen Goddess deem necessary. He's boundless knowledge without consideration. You're consideration, strategy without knowledge. You balance each other perfectly, like all true beloveds should.

– I HATE YOU! Bianca shouted. – I'll spit on your grave!

Two pair of eyes met. The eternal black pool drowned the fire in the other's flickering eyes.

Can you match eternity? Lillith snarled. Have you even touched it at your fingertips? Have you seen even a glimpse of what I've seen?

Bianca fell on her knees with a loud wail, baring her neck to the strongest. She began crying, softly, soundlessly, feeling like a girl again, waiting for the adult's scorn.

Lillith walked. Bianca choked and rose, and ran, until she, too, with bowed head, walked in The Queen Goddess' slipstream.

There were beasts roaming the waste and the forest. Before the wail from the hut had kept them away. Now, Lillith did. She heard them, felt their fangs gnaw at her bones. One, too bold, got too close, and she snarled, and it whimpered, and it dissolved in fire and ashes, and its life force leapt into her, and she was content.

She frowned, focusing on David. He noticed instantly, drawing something from his pocket.

– All of us carry one, he said, filled with sorrow. – It's all that is left of...

... of Wolf, of Venus. Lillith touched the stone before returning it to him. She sensed echoes of Carla. It was like the piece contained a part of her very spirit, her essence. Both heat and cold coursed through Lillith.

They returned to the castle, the Fire Lake, Lillith did. She walked inside, facing the others across a horrible gulf of time. There was Samhain, almost as much in his pure form as she was. There were fires, and mist and shadow. She faced Anubis at the base of the staircase leading to the attic. He stared at her with his lupine eyes, vibrant and alive, and she felt the pleasant stirrings within.

She smiled at him, and knew that she melted something, somewhere inside him, in his hardened heart.

14

Time flowed; both off and on the ice-world she made her home. She walked on yet another world she couldn't recall the name of, among fires, mangled bodies and pools of blood. An arm moved, drawing her attention. She fixed her stare on the ruined form below. She was Full, and didn't consume it.

Bianca drew her sword, her magnificent ceremonial sword, shining in brilliant red. Lillith stayed her hand with a small move of her index finger.

– We… knew what was going on, the man gasped. – But we were unable to do anything about it. We were victims ourselves.

She witnessed the culling, the endless torture and atrocities, through his and others' minds. Her wrath knew no bounds.

– But now you know better, don't you?

– Yes, he coughed, only a heartbeat or two away from death.

The Queen Goddess healed him, as an afterthought, with no effort whatsoever, and it was nothing to her. He sat up, staring at her, at his hands, as she and her entourage walked on.

– They will come to you, David told her, standing at her right side, as she sat on her throne. – I'm not exactly sure of when. I see multiple images. But they will come, and they will bow and kneel in your presence.

She nodded. She saw it herself, in her moments of clarity and dream visions, but never as clear as she saw in his incredibly astute mind.

Mars loomed in the distance, and thereby also Earth, as her army amassed more and more people, more and more ships, power at the Queen Goddess' command, as the Hunger also grew, as she constantly tasted blood on her tongue.

One day she noticed a call from one of the aides in the constant buzz of her mind. She walked to the communication room. They greeted her there, her servants, her cohorts, with their excited and happy childish faces.

A face, an image parted with the many Vids in the air, gaining her attention. It spoke, and she listened, half-heartedly, as triumph swelled within.

– The Earth Council is no more, the man on the Vid stated. – It has been overthrown, its influence reduced to insignificance everywhere. The business conglomerates across the Solar System have pledged themselves to our cause. I've been authorized by my peers to sue for a just peace.

«A just peace». She hid the contempt behind a mask of indifference.

– Granted, she nodded relaxed, patronizing. – Go on.

– We will grant your people full citizenship, he continued angrily. – Not you and others among you, which presence is deadly to us, but all the rest. We will enforce rigidly any racist attack, any prejudice or any undue exploitation against anybody, anywhere. Children will be taught this, taught respect for your kind from an early age, and granting the High One's mercy The Burning Times will never occur again.

She paused for effect, but her dazzling smile spoke volumes, making him blush, and even he, with his limited awareness knew what she was going to say before she said it.

– Granted…

That was it, really. There were still kinks and stuff to work out, but this was the crux of it. Within another year or so the details were worked out, and the mingling of the two offshoots of humanity began once again.

She stood before the mirror, the very unnecessary mirror in her bedroom, as she was being dressed by Bianca and the other maids, as she saw herself far more clearly through their eyes than she would through any mirror.

The garb reminded her a bit, just a bit of the one she had worn in ancient Egypt. The stray thought made her shudder, shudder just a bit.

It was flashy and bright, and beautiful, signaling confidence and power, worthy of her stature. She shrugged.

Please, Goddess, one of the maids begged, both passionate and devoted and fearful, in her jumble of thoughts. Please stand still or we can't do the job you've charged us to do, can't do your godly presence justice.

Lillith acknowledged her. The Goddess' presence, always in her mind, increased just a little. She stepped back, casting her eyes to the floor, waiting for the shoe to drop. Lillith smiled and petted her cheek, and the girl melted in her hand.

Don't fear, dear Juana, you will be rewarded, not punished for your devotion. I'll be good.

Uncertain laughter, both loud and in the mind echoed in the room.

They brushed and braided her hair in smooth, skilled moves. It felt so pleasant, very, very pleasant. Lillith closed her eyes, even though it did her no good. They put on her hat, the physical proof of her stature. It was the kind surrounding her head, hiding her hair in front, making it flow like water down her back, displaying her face prominently to those beholding her.

She stood before them, beholding herself, the garb, the dress, hiding her skin, revealing her skin, the sword in her right hand, the wand in her left.

– This is exactly the symbolic effect I wanted, she nodded, speaking aloud. – Thank you, my faithful.

Juana, Bianca and the others curtsied gracefully in their gratitude and bliss.

She sheathed the sword, but held on to the wand, as she left the room.

Drums heralded her entry into the great underground hall. She walked there with Bianca and David at her sides, the same long, long stone path down she had walked centuries earlier. The throne awaited her between the pentacles, a place brimming with power. She sat down on it. Circe had made it for her. It fit her perfectly. She sat there, nodding, smiling, and accepting the accolades from her subjects.

The regal figure rose, walking to the edge of the stone, raising a hand. It turned quiet, expectancy rising in the great hall.

– We've done it! She cried it out in triumph. – We've taken our place in the Universe, and we've done so on our own terms.

The reply was a thousand raw voices filling the room.

She walked off the edge and levitated to the floor below. David and Bianca followed two steps behind her. She walked to the giant round table at the center of the hall. The sea of people split before her. They touched her as she passed them. Bursts of power flared as skin touched skin. They gave willingly of themselves to their Queen Goddess, and she was grateful.

16

Three vacant seats awaited her and her aides. They took their place around the table. It was still quiet. It didn't really have to be, for everybody to hear her voice, but was quiet anyway.

– We did it! She spoke quietly. – We won, and our enemies are in tatters. There will be no more persecution, no more bad treatment of those who are born different. We're entering a golden era, where variety is the norm, not the rare exception.

She sensed hesitation in part of the assembly, and nodded towards a young woman, leaving it to her to express what many felt.

– I still don't trust them. We left the inner planets pretty much intact. Perhaps we should have finished the job and taken the war all the way to Earth?

Lillith smiled, pleased that grievances had been voiced, and they all smiled with her.

– They still outnumber us, ten thousand to one, she explained patiently, as if to children. – We achieved what we set out to do. Time will do the rest.

And clarity was mirrored in their faces, their eyes, as they raised their fists, as the buzz grew in their minds, and their One voice rose at the high ceiling. Lillith smiled wider, showing her fangs fully, and no longer sensing fear in her children.

There were dance and song and enjoyment of beverages and spices inside the warm and cozy mountain. The sounds and acts between the cold walls resonated both within and without, spreading like wildfire beyond Titan itself.

The first few members of the People traveled openly, brazenly to the distant realms of Mars and Earth, volunteers sticking their neck out. There were stares and touches of hostility, but nothing happened. The Earth Council was indeed no more, and its eager supporters were either in jail or had fled to their own distant corners of the Solar System. The hostility and distrust remained, though, at least for a while. It was a slow, slow process, but Lillith didn't mind. She had time.

Integration happened over night. There were occasional skirmishes, aggression on both sides, but they were dealt with, in a somewhat frank and open manner. Lillith observed it all, from her throne room and the giant ship she used to travel Space. And when it was needed she took action, but those times grew increasingly rare, and she stayed at home, in her castle more and more.

She sensed Titan changing, turning more hospitable, turning fairly warm, turning eternal winter into seasons, and with it the Universe itself, or at least humanity's tiny corner of it. It happened over night in her new, eternal perspective. She saw everything change one afternoon resting in her pleasant hammock. It practically moved itself. She imagined, in moments of weakness a happy, thirteen-year-old girl by her side.

Weary eyes opened, watching Bianca, sweet, still innocent Bianca approach her and take her place in the left hammock.

The Queen Goddess walked around in her castle when she was being awakened by the cries of a newborn. Something stirred within her. She walked to the nursery. Everybody looked up, startled. It was common that Lillith greeted the newborns, but this was clearly a special occasion.

She walked straight to the crib. The boy stared up at her with bluish, deep eyes.

She nodded to herself. The long wait was done. Another Dreamweaver had been born.

In a blink of her eyes he grew to adolescence. She saw him crawl, saw him run on unsteady legs, saw his run turn steady and strong. The river broke, finally, as ice turned to water, and its slow run turned rampant. She made sure he impregnated many females the moment he was able to. But she didn't treat him any better than the other children. He was given the same, harsh upbringing, the same, hard preparation for adult life, perhaps even a bit harsher. She sensed it the day the air shifted around him, recognized the shimmer like a sore gut.

He sat alone on a rise above the river. She walked to him. He shook when he discovered her, and quickly knelt, shivering in her presence.

– Come, she commanded him, reaching out a hand.

He took her hand, and she pulled him on his feet.

– Move! She bade him. – Use your gift. Please your Goddess.

And just like that… it happened. The Shadow World hadn't exactly been closed to her all these years. There were other, harder ways to access it, but this was different. This was like slipping inside. She guided him, steered him, even though she allowed him to go where he wanted to go this one time on their many travels together. They ended up on the roof of the castle. He was breathing hard. She was hardly breathing any harder. And then she almost stopped breathing, seeing the world, its raw beauty through his eyes and senses. She smiled to him. Her love smothered him, and he reeled under its onslaught.

The day dawned, when he grew able, with her aid to teleport aboard Space Station 7 looming in geo-stationary orbit above the castle, above Raven's Court. They startled everybody when they appeared out of nowhere, and she was pleased. The People needed to be kept on their toes.

– Leave us! She bid them.

And they were gone.

The two of them stood there, on the command deck, staring into Space.

– Is the Goddess pleased with me? He asked hoarsely. – Do I perform to her expectation?

There was a hint of sarcasm in his voice. Lillith… liked that.

– So far, she replied lightly, smiling, dazzling him, making him bare his neck.

– So, are any of my… my offspring taking after me?

– No. She shook her head. – Can't you tell?

It was a rhetorical question. She didn't expect a reply, and didn't get any.

– But I didn't expect that either. Your kind is rare. To my knowledge there have been less than ten of you in the entire history of mankind. I wanted to maximize the potential in future generations. And when they come, and they will, I will breed them extensively as well.

Why? He asked, without asking.

Look out there, she bid him, and he obeyed. What do you see?

He shook his head, without shaking his head, staring into the emptiness, exasperated because he didn't fathom her and her intentions, and he wanted to,

18

desperately.

– I see Life, she stated. – I see it everywhere. And I see this clumsy ship. Humanity has survived its childhood. I want us to survive our maturity as well. I want us to survive.

And more, she bid him. There is always more.

She procured the little rock from her pocket, the kind she and each and every one of them always carried with them. It had become the sign of adulthood, of maturity among them. She saw it through his eyes, saw it glow and pulse, and she saw him understand.

They traveled wide and far in the coming decades, searching for the glowing stones. The two of them floated in cold Space, protected by her ever-stronger force field. Mario had become skilled, now. With her aid he was able to do incredible things, including catching the big rock in his net of mist and shadow, and they brought it home, to the growing heap below what had once been known as Frazer Hill. It became a hill itself, and even a mountain.

And they traveled to distant worlds, in an ever-wider circle, working themselves slowly outwards, ever outwards, planting the seeds, the seeds of Life.

She levitated before the mountain with closed eyes, focusing more than she had ever focused, and then she sensed it, sensed the first stirrings of a revived consciousness, and she let out a cry of wild joy, so powerful that it almost made her fall.

The river broke in spring, like it had for many seasons, now. The thunder kept them awake at night, like it did every year. She took many of The People to bed, the large bed, swimming in the heap of bodies, of warm, energetic bodies. And life rose within them all. The sound of thunder faded to obscurity in their ears.

Lillith Raven Moonstar awoke in the midst of nude and warm bodies, awoke to a baby's cry. She walked to the nursery followed by her children and their eager, excited chirping.

Mario handed her the girl. She received the small, warm body, and she sensed what rested inside it immediately, and it grew the moment she took the tiny life in her arms. She looked into the crystal-clear eyes, and was cast a thousand years back in time. Tears fell from the corners of her eyes, and her happiness was echoed in sighs and gasps all over the castle and beyond.

– Ellen, the Raven nodded. – She's Ellen for now. We'll see, in time what she will call herself.

Time slowed to a crawl. Raven noticed every year, as Ellen grew to adulthood. She saw her play with the other children, saw her walk into the wilderness among the beasts, and she wasn't worried.

Lillith sat on her throne, observing through her extended senses what happened outside, as the ice broke, and the river flowed, and the children shouted in joy.

Bianca entered the hall, levitating the long distance, landing at the spot at the Goddess' left side, standing there a moment before speaking.

– Is Lillith pleased? The centuries-old woman wheedled like a girl. – Is Lillith happy?

– Lillith is pleased. The regal figure frowned. – Her will is done, and she is pleased.

She sat among the children, in the shadow of Raven's Court, speaking about the past, the present and the future.

The girl returned from her mound, her hill, her mountain.

– Venus is late, another girl cried, with both excitement and venom in her voice. – Venus is idle.

– I know, Venus said out of breath. – I'm sorry.

– We're all late, sometimes. Lillith coaxed them. – And we shouldn't be afraid to be idle. We've got time, all of us.

She didn't treat Venus any different from the rest of them, but the others still perceived it that way. She sighed.

It was the height of summer, and the past returned to her, with its poisonous tail.

– We are the People, she said. – Our tale is long, and wrought with hardship, with joy and ache, and pain, and that is also how it should be. We are everything Human, and thus we'll remain, until the end of time and beyond.

There was a classroom of sorts, where the little tykes were taught basic technology and skills, but it was no ordinary class the way Stacy Larkin recalled it. It was far too random, far too casual and idle for that. The children learned because they wanted to learn, and they were never pushed. Not in that.

And Lillith was pleased.

People floated above the water, in the water, those among them able to do so. The others excelled in other ways.

Lillith noticed Bianca's pointed stare. She began breathing faster. Bianca walked inside, into the cool shadows of the castle, and Lillith followed her there.

Followed her to the lavish bedroom with the large bed where there were still imprints of the many bodies that had enjoyed their bodies the night before. Bianca undressed, posing before the Goddess, and Lillith saw straight through her nudity to the far more naked soul beneath. Lillith nodded, as much to herself as the shivering bundle of desire awaiting her pleasure, and she, too, began undressing. She took her time, caressing Bianca with her mind, as Bianca began doing the same, and they both shivered in heat long before they actually touched skin to skin.

Bianca kissed her lips, a pointed charge sending shivers through Lillith's body. Lillith closed her eyes and smiled content, in boundless anticipation. Lips touched, hands touched, hands and lips touched skin, and it was even better than the initial Distant Touch. Lillith grabbed Bianca, holding her up, studying her with infinite hunger in her eyes. Bianca didn't resist, but let herself be appraised, be judged. She smiled sweetly to the Demon Mother, relaxing her body to the point of turning limp, surrendering to the other's mercy.

They tumbled down on the bed, stood kneeling on it face to face. They embraced and they kissed. The kiss turned sweet and hungry. Bianca was skilled, very skilled. Lillith was pleased with her, so very pleased.

Bianca sucked on the nipples, licked them eagerly and pleasing. Her tongue felt good, and even more so as she descended Lillith's body and began exploring her

20

already wet hole.

– You're such a great pet, Lillith mumbled, breathing, breathing, breathing, her eyes increasingly filled with mist and hazy clouds. – I've trained you well.

– The Goddess is… pleased with me?

– Very pleased, child. You're a treasure.

The girl moaned as the Goddess touched her, in her rough, demanding, unable-to-resist way. They touched each other with their power and with their skin, all combining into flaming desire. This was how the gods made love, power without guilt, no morality, not thought, nothing but the need burning within them both.

Bodies joined, thoughts joined, desire joined, to become one creature. Lillith saw all of Bianca, and she saw nothing. No thoughts, no response betrayed her or exposed her. She was so good, so devilishly skilled… an assassin of the first order. Lillith moaned, a long, wailing howl, and let go, let go more and more and more…

Lillith grabbed her wrist, her wrist holding the black blade; Moonstar's dark pools of eyes suddenly clear as steel.

– I wondered what had become of it.

Bianca snarled at her, while two wills did battle, and it was no contest at all.

Lillith turned the blade that had been pointing at her, and pushed it into Bianca's Chakra center. Bianca gasped once, gasped twice, while The Goddess held her in her ruthless grip, and then… then she erupted in flames.

And Lillith felt it, felt the pleasure, the glory, as she bathed in the other's energies, as they truly became a part of her, as she soaked it up far better than any sponge.

David stood at the center of the room. He was screaming, screaming his heart out, like a little baby lost.

She silenced his vocal chords with a thought, and the scream in his mind with a little more effort.

– How does it feel? She asked him softly. – How does it feel to hurt, *Jahavalo?*

He stared at her in mute horror, at the pile of ashes on the bed.

– Yes, I knew who you were all the time, she told him, – but you didn't, not until this very moment. You knew everything about the rest of us, but nothing about yourself. So, I guess you knew nothing at all, then?

The shaking bundle of a human being attempted to speak, but nothing but a few, stuttering noises escaped the flickering lips.

– You wanted Power, My Lord, so I gave it to you, all you can ever choke on. I wanted you to understand what you've wrought, on us all, on mankind, what your legacy is.

– The… the wax dolls, he whimpered.

She studied him without mercy in her black wells.

– THE WAX DOLLS, he screamed.

And fell on his knees.

And his tears, they were blood.

The fireeyes turned dull and empty as he sat there, as his tears silently hit the floor.

Circe was summoned, and she came, followed by two aides, two that was also rock shapers.

– Throw him in a cell, Lillith shrugged. – I want him out of my sight.

Filled with sorrow and shock they obeyed, and grabbed the close to lifeless husk, and carried it away. They carried it to the depths of the castle, where they made a cell for him, one seamlessly woven and with no exit. They left him there.

He began screaming after a few hours, and he kept doing so, without pause, in the years and decades to come.

– THE WAX DOLLS, he screamed.

– THE WAX DOLLS, he screamed.

– THE WAX DOOOOLLS.

They didn't really hear his voice, except as a faint echo, and in time they also learned to close off their mind to the mindless scream. Except at night, during one particularly bad nightmare. He was present, in their midst, now, and until the end of time.

Lillith Raven Moonstar sat on her throne, while people rushed back and forth, making the final preparations for the festivities.

A thousand years, she mused. A thousand years since Venus' destruction, since my awakening, since I set out on my… path. Since my life began.

Lillith smiled.

Venus approached her, warily, until she knelt in the Goddess' presence.

– So, is it finally coming back to you?

– I remember p-pain and l-loss, Venus said. – And the rest, too, but so faint, like it wasn't me at all.

– It will come back to you, Lillith said. – You have all the time in the Universe. Now, get up. It isn't appropriate for you to kneel, not for anybody.

– So, the Queen Goddess doesn't want me to show her respect?

Lillith frowned at the thin, shaky and submissive voice.

– No, get up.

Venus rose, but her eyes stayed lowered, cast to the floor.

She waited, waited for the woman on the throne to once more acknowledge her.

– Yes? Lillith snapped impatiently.

– Perhaps Lillith in her wisdom can tell me why I shouldn't kneel for her, why I shouldn't grovel at her feet? After all, it is Your Highness that saved us from extinction. It is Lillith's vision that is propelling us forward, her will that is shaping us, shaping and polishing the People to her expectations.

Lillith rose abruptly. Everybody else in the room jumped.

– Leave me, she commanded Venus.

– As the Queen Goddess desires.

– But return later. You are hereby appointed my new advisor. I'm a little short in that respect, and have been for a while.

Venus curtsied, and obeyed Lillith's command, in mind as well in body. Lillith sensed it and felt a familiar sadness pass through her mind.

But she shook it off, and focused, as she had for so long, now, on today, on tomorrow.

The day dawned. Venus stood at Lillith's side as the festivities began. So did several representatives of both older and younger generations.

They sent her thoughts of support and devotion. She knew they were with her, knew it with every fiber of her being. They knew her, knew her to her very bones, and they loved her. She was their mother. She had even become the Mother of those souls older than her or of her age. And if there was a bit of fear, and even terror, it was muted, delegated to a place remote in their consciousness. And fear was a good teacher. They were *with* her, and she was pleased.

Thoughts flooded her from all the worlds The People had spread, and they were with her. The time had come for the great game, for it to truly begin. She knew that, and the knowledge burned within her, and in that moment, she saw, in bright, dark flashes beyond even their residing universe, allowed herself to believe, to hope she would accomplish everything she had set out to do…

And she was pleased.

4

The People reentered Homo Sapiens' society, entered their boardrooms, their workplaces, their other governing bodies. It happened slowly, hesitatingly at first, but the trickle eventually turned into a flow, inevitable, like time and change. As the hot wind blew on Titan, so it did all over the solar system penetrating everything and everyone.

The now well-known mutants, no longer living in secret, common as grass are sucked into the greater human society, slowly becoming human society, becoming humanity. The mutants, struggling for millennia to survive countless attempts at genocide are finally ascending. Evolution is taking its toll.

Inevitably.

Another Dreamweaver was born. Lillith noticed it not long after conception this time. She recognized the child's signature, its emanation, as she was growing increasingly attuned to it.

It was a girl. Lillith stood with the little bundle in her arms and once again felt the tiny pangs of disappointment.

– You're scouring the Universe for her, for them, all of them, aren't you? Venus said. – But they're nowhere to be found.

Lillith nodded, the catching in her throat not going away.

She traveled the Solar System, both with her ship, with Atlantis, and without it. It was a small task for her to guide her Dreamweavers from world to world. She had to guide them for their first visit to a place or a planet. They had problems with traveling where they hadn't been before in the flesh, without a distinct sense of that particular spot. She provided that.

But she also enjoyed traveling slowly. She had time. And she eventually visited every planet, every settlement in the solar system. Except…

– Except Earth, Venus said. – Why not?

– Would you go there? Lillith snarled, – now, when you don't have to anymore? You became free of its chains when you became Venus.

She stared into the vastness through a window on the command bridge of Atlantis, the new and improved and so much faster Atlantis.

– It sickens me, she mumbled. – Merely the thought of it makes me want to throw up.

And she shared with them all her memory of the blue planet as it had been, juxtaposing it with what it had become.

– It's done, she mumbled. – Let it be.

The entire metal vessel shook around them, as she shared her revulsion with them, as she shared everything.

They landed on Mars close to two thousand years after her birth, her most recent birth. She wasn't quite certain precisely what year it was. They tended to blur to her these days. The welcoming committee met them at the spaceport. Of course, they did.

– Welcome, Honored Mother. The woman at the head of the procession curtsied before her.

The Queen Goddess nodded, allowing their bowing and submissive acts. Irritation riddled her, as they made their way outside. The woman and her court noticed her foul mood, of course, but they were actually unable to define its cause.

They show respect, Venus pointed out, good humored.

They're just bureaucrats, Lillith snarled, baring their neck for the superior power. This is not it. This is not what it was all for.

Crowds met them on Mare Ter, the biggest city on the once red planet. The thicker atmosphere had made the skies fairly blue, like they had been on Earth. Crowds of The People, but also countless mundanes, anxious at first, but when nothing happened they relaxed and loved her as much, if not more than her brethren did.

Don't worry, my children, she thought. I've fed, and fed well. I can be merciful. You know my mercy, like you know my mercilessness.

You're born with me in your thoughts.

Crowds made her stronger, now, not weaker, like they once had done.

She could hardly recall that time, that person. The memory was dim, like mist at a long-passed spot on a trail.

– We will go where no one has gone before, she shouted, and they heard her, heard her far better than they would have done if she had merely spoken to them through the numerous speakers. – We will spread across this galaxy and beyond. There will be no end to us. When this universe is done, we will be there to close its gates, ready to move on.

Most of them didn't understand what she meant, but some did. They felt the non-visual images and sensations she grew in them, and the boundless Hunger rose from their depth, even stronger than before.

They knew, beyond knowing what she was about.

Jahavalo was found in his cell one morning without his head. Its remains were splashed on the walls. They all sensed it, sensed something, those in Lillith's court. The five with her outside the cell, when Circe opened the wall looked at her.

24

– He wanted to go so much, she said. – I don't know how many years he has focused on doing this one act.

– So, do you know where he is? Samhain wondered.

– No, she shrugged. – I let him go. I had to, sooner or later. It was growing tiresome keeping track of him, anyway.

– So, now he's out there, roaming somewhere? Morningstar stated, a clear touch of anger in his voice.

– Yes. Lillith smiled. – Just like all the rest of us. I can't say I'm not worried, okay. But I would be more worried about myself, if I had kept him on a leash another millennia.

And there was relief, as they looked at her, as they realized something, as they looked at her, and knew she hadn't forgotten.

Giant ships left their home world, and set course out of the solar system, to the great unknown.

– They and their many children will roam the Universe forever, Lillith told the circle around the fire. Some of them will be stopped or reach a dead end, but some of them won't.

They were sent in both planned and erratic patterns, leaving the local system in all directions. A few had Dreamweavers with them, but all had Dreamweaver family members in their crew, carrying the seed, the potential means to transcend time and space.

– So, this is your great game? Jason bowed in acknowledgement to her. – It took me a while until it dawned on me actually. Not too shabby.

He was the same. He was different. Like she was.

He had always been, and would always be one of the few beings in existence able to understand her, to at least partially fathom her motives.

She had sensed that about him long ago, and sensed their kinship, their mutual trust, or lack of distrust.

And so had he, about her.

She returned to the castle. It was a castle, now, through and through, but she knew that in a thousand years it could be something completely different. The image of him staring out at the vast lake, the infinite sea was the way she would always remember him.

– Stacy! He called.

She turned, and waved, and smiled, before entering the cool shadows of the castle.

Venus came to her later that day, bringing refreshments, like Delphi, like Gabi had used to do long ago.

– It's time, Carla said.

She was fully Carla, fully Wolf again, now, having freed herself from the cobwebs of time. Lillith nodded, without being fully conscious why.

– It can be argued that you were a force of nature, that you, after your awakening were like the wind or the storm or the fire of the Universe, but things - and you - have settled, now, and that isn't so anymore. It's time to move on. If you stay and don't leave your children to solve their own affairs, you will be no better than

Jahavalo was.

Lillith hesitated, pondered deliberately, to gauge Venus and her own reactions.

– I think you're correct, she finally said, bringing a big smile to the other woman's face. – Humanity has reached too far and grown too numerous for me to retain any semblance of control of it, anyway.

– Exactly as you planned, Venus nodded. – We have Hyperspace technology. We have the Dreamweavers. And we will spread to every corner of this universe. Sooner or later, one way or another we will find a way to transcend time and space, time/space itself.

– You knew, huh? Lillith shook her head.

– I knew, Venus and Earth confirmed, and that very thought brought tears to Lillith's eyes. – My ability to sense my surroundings has only grown, and I feel the Wrongness.

They heard something, sensed something. Whatever it was, when they turned Everett stood there, looking almost, almost normal.

– So, where is Jason these days?

– He took off, Stacy replied. – I don't believe we will see him again for quite some time.

There was silence between the three of them, their shared destiny poignantly beating their hearts.

– So, when do we leave?

Anubis asked.

Lillith closed and opened her eyes, smiling a bit.

– Not quite yet.

– And what about Jason?

– We won't need him.

More years, more seasons, both short and long passed by, while Lillith and her close circle once again waited.

And waited, and waited, and waited.

Until one day, yet another cry from a newborn, a very special boy filled the castle, and chased across Fire Lake, and through its forest.

– He is More, Lillith said. – He is what we need.

Word had gotten out by now, about her decision, and once it had, she felt kind of good about it. They would and should say goodbye.

The People and also others, clearly distraught and needy came to Titan and Ravenscourt from all over the solar system to pay their respect, and to persuade her from leaving. Seeing the sadness and desperation in their eyes and mind just made her more determined to go through with her plans, both for theirs and her own sake.

The castle began humming. She heard it, and perhaps some of the others did, too. It called to her. Memory called to her, like it had done before.

Like it had done many times.

She didn't even remember all of them, except during the flashes, the moments, the slices of time, but now she did. Or she was at least getting there. Memory rose within her, like a slow-building volcanic eruption.

They gathered around her, her twenty and one. Those she had chosen to accompany her, that had chosen themselves. They turned as one towards Fire Lake, towards the castle.

– Leave, now, she said, speaking with her voice, with both her voice and her mind. – The rest of you leave. We will see each other again, once, under a blue moon. Paths that cross will cross again.

They, those dismissed by the Goddess walked through the forest while the beasts were howling, and when they turned and looked back they could no longer see the lake and the castle.

But yet they did. Even in the far-reaching fields below the hill and the Venus-mountain they were able to see the lake, the castle and the twenty-two people walking through its gates. Even without using their powers they saw it. They saw the castle from the outside, and glimpses of those inside it. A long time, minutes, days, years passed by without anything happening. The castle began glowing in that eerie light they all knew so well. The entire hill glowed. It pulsed and glowed ever stronger. The humming from the twenty-two inside the castle, in its endless depths grew to a howl. The Hill faded from the onlookers' view, forever imprinted on their memory. And then they looked up, startled, at the brilliance of Shadow surrounding the starship Atlantis, as it started humming, becoming alive, being born, fading from view.

– I cannot sense them anymore, Eleanor said, – cannot sense them anywhere.
– But they are yet here, another said, she couldn't tell who.
– They will always be here, she said.

Come darkness, come night many fires were lit, across the entire night half of Titan, a vigil, a celebration of what had been, what would be.

They joined with the seekers out there, in the many ships, in humanity's many spearheads into the Unknown, into the blackest of nights.

When the night's lights faded at the rusty dawn, they knew they woke up to a new world.

The two with glowing eyes watching it all from eternity's viewpoint saw and experienced it all. They saw through the eyes of millions, as they sought and found and died, and lived through the generations, as they spread from what had practically been one single point to a number of points too vast to be counted.

They saw Lillith for a while, as she visited strange new worlds, as she moved on, as she kept moving on, never quite content, never quite there, always driven by the compulsion to move on. The two pairs of eyes lost contact with her, as many lines slowly became one, as they followed one branch of the Warrens through the ages.

They saw the tapestry, they saw it collapse on itself, saw it unfold, and collapse and unfold again.

On Titan the many furnaces of the human heart faded and still celebrated, as the rust of dawn caught up with them, as the eternal shadow never left them. They bathed in the warm sunlight, but their spirit roamed out there, in the eternal night.

Humanity roamed the Galaxy. They traveled west, towards the galactic core. But after some time, their descendants traveled back east. They traveled down. After a while they traveled back up… or in and out, out and in. Paths crisscrossed each other, until no one knew the original path anymore, and what was first and last became quite the debatable issue.

The small ship floated through Space. It was one single craft, which was kind of rare these days, a slick, fast carrier of souls.

They had looked everywhere, time and time again, and not gotten anywhere, at least not anywhere near where they wanted to go. The glowing Dyson Sphere rested behind them. Once more, for the hundredth or thousandth time they set a new course. They cruised in the free space beyond the left-behind solar system's outer planet, pondering their options.

– There is no Path ahead, Jasper the Dreamweaver said, – only back.

«Back» was dozens of systems, a trail of failures and broken dreams.

– So, it's the Rocky Road, then? Jenna, the pilot said.

The Rocky Road was Hyperspace, a nightmare of lethal buffering and dangers.

Based on the works of Miguel Alcubierre, Francisco Lobo, Matt Visser, Eric Lentz, among others did on a «warp drive» during the early years of space travel, Stanislaw Mechinski and colleagues devised a way of traveling through space, traveling on the "rocky road" circumventing the light speed limit, virtually without moving. This initially somewhat flawed or incomplete interpretation had become the theoretic foundation of Hyperspace travels.

– The Rocky Road it is, Jeff nodded.

They all sat down, and strapped themselves in. Jasper, too.

– I'm blind in this place, he said. – There's no shadow realm here.

No humans had ever come this way, leaving the residue of their shadows, creating the very familiar realm of mist and pale darkness.

Except in the ship. The path ahead was empty to him, but the ship was filled with a confusing whirlwind of past, present and future, with specters all speaking to him simultaneously. He could see the ship's monitors, the Vidolo environments surrounding them, like they would be, and he saw the red glare on them, and he shivered imperceptibly, his careful masking of his worry totally in vain, as always.

They knew him, like he knew them. They Saw through him, not as good as he Saw, but enough to know bits of the reason for his concern.

– Nothing good can come from this, he said, to the air.

They knew him, knew he was prone to depressions. Powerful Dreamweavers and other powerful Seers had been known to suffer from that since the early days and nights of The People's existence. They didn't ignore him, but they nodded to each other, beyond despair, beyond stubbornness, and pushed on.

Everybody sat down and strapped themselves in. Jasper did, too. Their powers worked everywhere, also in what was still popularly called Hyperspace, but they, both they and their powers, were like Nothing there, like everything and everyone was.

Jenna began glowing. She didn't use her hands, even though there was that possibility on the console in front of her. The ship's hum changed to a deeper pitch and reality began blinking out around them, around their vessel. They moved. They stood still. Reality inverted itself, and kept doing so, in an insane, totally unpredictable pattern. The now so familiar pain cut through them. This environment, if it could be called that, anything like that, was lethal to them, hostile to all life. The envelope of the ship shielded them, but only to a point. Only the remarkable healing power that was part of their inheritance kept them somewhat intact, both mentally and physically. The ship fell apart by the second. Jasper held it together, somewhat, enveloping it and them in his power.

The Rocky Road wasn't red. They saw nothing even resembling color. There was nothing there. Everything was one big Nothing, and they couldn't understand how anything or anyone could exist here at all.

Hyperspace was a blink. Traveling from one spot of the Universe to another was like a snap of the fingers, or it should be, in theory, but sometimes, like now, the fingers were cold, frozen, and they just didn't work. They didn't move, not an inch, or so it seemed and felt. Jeff looked for the ship's afterburner, and there wasn't any. Nothing suggested they would ever move forward at all, but they did.

They slipped through Unfolded Space, and for a moment it was like they ceased to exist, and then life once again *was*, and they appeared a million miles from where they had been just a few seconds ago, speculatively speaking.

Pain attacked them like a million angry wasps, and then eased, and they sat there gasping, breathing sweet life, their skin slowly, so much slower than it normally did knitting itself.

This Dyson Sphere was old. It glowed in red, imperfect and incomplete. It was clearly one of the first ever made. Hope and anxiety warred within them all.

– Do you think? Jenna turned to Jeff, like she always did.

– It's too early to tell, he replied cautiously.

– We've seen dozens of these, Justin growled.

– But only dozens, Jeff reproached him softly, humorously.

He nodded to Jenna and she brought them further towards the veil-like borderline of the Sphere, of the solar system ahead. He couldn't tell exactly when they breached its confines. It was always a subtle process, one hardly definable even to the keenest observer. They knew, at some point they weren't in open Space anymore.

Jasper froze. Jeff noticed, and just the fact that he noticed told him something, something vital.

– The Dust fills this Sphere, Jasper cried out.

They all sensed it, one way or another, the sting of old and forgotten memories. It was crowded in here. Human beings had been all over the place. The enormous and uncharacteristic empty spaces spoke to them, sang to them, of despair and hope, love and hate, and everything else.

– The old charts... do they fit?

Everybody noticed Jeff hoarse voice.

– Hard to tell, Jenna frowned. – There are similarities, but a lot of the ancient points of reference are gone, but... yes, I would say they do.

Jenna would know. She had been taught navigation since she had been one.

Exhilaration grabbed them, even though it had grabbed them before, quite a few times during their Quest. The familiar fatigue claimed them, as they ventured further into the red glow. Giant structures, what had certainly been made from giant planets hovered «above» them as they pulled towards the distant sun.

Jeff looked at Jolanda.

– There are no major population centers left here, she said, pain in her voice. – Not anywhere.

He had half expected that, but he had allowed himself to hope. Jolanda could smell life, sniff her way to it like the keenest tracker.

– There is life, she said, – but scarce, faded, like a dream. No major populations, not of any species.

Exactly like a dream, Jeff thought. But he kept that thought from the others, even though they knew he did it, and they looked astonished and hurt at him.

– There is something ahead, she said. – I don't know exactly what it is, but it is powerful beyond belief.

– One of the ancients, perhaps? Jenna cried excitedly.

And hope once more rose in their hearts.

– Perhaps. Jolanda frowned. – But if it is I can no longer recognize him from Memory.

Him? Jeff looked at her.

– It is, Jasper stated solemnly, and they all shivered by the shiver in his voice.

There was a planet ahead. An actual planet. They saw it on the Vidolo, as well with their power of perception.

– This one is on our charts, Jenna said, and now the excitement and anxiety were evident in her voice and mind. – It's called Steron. My brothers and sisters, we're in humanity's birth system.

Jeff looked at the information, the images and sensory input on the Vidolo environment surrounding them.

– It is fertile and glowing with life, Jeff said excitedly, before frowning, looking at the representation of the planet in their archives and then at the dark and foreboding place ahead. – Or it was, once.

– This is the second terra-formed planet, Jenna told them. – It was called Mars then.

There was an atmosphere down there, scant but breathable. They saw, sensed that easily, all of them, when they got close.

– That means...

– Yes, she responded, interrupting him.

The ship slipped into the atmosphere, without the shaking and buffering usually connected with it. If Steron, or Mars had ever been able to offer much resistance to a starship that was of the past. That, too.

30

– He's down there somewhere, Jasper stated solemnly. – He doesn't want us here.

– There's something wrong with it, Jolanda said, – with the entire planet. I can sense major tectonic activity.

– This is his Kingdom, Jasper stated in his dead voice, – And its last day has come.

– No, Jeff whispered under his breath. – Not now, when we're so close.

They didn't really have to look for the spot. It pointed to itself, in a way they all sensed. There was an eerie glow at the rise. They didn't merely see it, but it spoke to them, to their Memory in a way that couldn't be denied.

There were buildings here and there, but they were hardly more than ruins, hardly more than remains, remnants of what once had been.

The lone figure stood by a fire, at the center of the field. The low gravity and thin atmosphere made the fire flicker and reach tens of lengths in all direction. It didn't seem to touch him or disturb him the slightest, even though it occasionally surrounded the small form. The eerie glow centered on him. It wasn't really a glow at all, but more like a shift, a twist in reality. Their eyes saw the tiny form of a man. The glow in their mind perceived a giant, indistinct figure.

The ship landed, somewhat elegant not far from him. He didn't seem to notice. The travelers left the ship and approached cautiously. They all studied him with curiosity mixed with fear, both emotions too powerful to be denied.

– Greetings! Jeff called to him.

There was no reply. They almost stopped, in reverence, in fright, but Jeff pushed them on. There was just a minute walk or so from the ship, but it seemed much longer, as if they didn't really move at all, but floated in a mist of dense air.

They stopped before him, in a half moon circle, and then he did notice, did acknowledge them, and they shook, and shook hard.

– Company? At this late hour?

His voice was coarse, clearly rusty, seemingly unused for decades, perhaps centuries.

– We're weary Travelers, sir, Jeff said, – looking for a brief-home. My name is Jeffrey War'n, and these are my pack mates, and our brother Carl Lark'n.

– I'm Jason, the creature welcoming them said.

He took them into his embrace, and it made them gasp and heave.

– Are you *that* Jason? Jolanda asked him. – Are you Him? Are you… S-samhain?

– I am, he replied calmly.

They fell on their knees before him, sore afraid.

He made an irritated gesture, and they hurried up again. Another gesture and he shrunk the fire to a more manageable size. Seconds, minutes passed into hours as they gathered with him around the campfire.

They looked at him, under lowered eyes. He was old. They knew that. Compared to him the oldest among them was an infant. But he didn't look old. In spite of the long hair and beard, and the indeterminate signs of age, he hadn't aged a day. They would guess he looked exactly or fairly the same physically as he had in his youth.

– How long have you been traveling? He asked them.

Jeff spoke on their behalf, like he usually did.

31

– We don't know exactly. Jonas on your left was born after we started on our Quest, but we don't know exactly how old he is. It's hard to keep track of time on the Path. We did celebrate his hundredth year many years ago.

– I can imagine, the giant before them shrugged.

– What happened here? Jolanda cried in despair. – With this planet?

– You know! He grabbed her with his fireeyes, and didn't let go, and she was helpless.

She nodded in despair.

– This was once a fertile and lush globe, he said. – But humanity destroyed it, like they destroy everything. I saw a film once…

They looked blank at him.

– It was what they used to call Holovids, he said patiently. – Or is that Vidolos, now.

He grinned and looked almost human.

– It was about an alien invasion of… of *Earth*. Their behavior was like that of locusts…

– *Tasre*, Jeff explained to the others, – flying insects digesting crops, moving from one field to another, leaving nothing in its wake.

– *We* have become like Locusts, Jason declared passionately. – We move from planet to planet, leaving nothing but death and destruction in our wake. We arrive at a given point, terra-forming it or not, start using its natural resources without caring about the consequences. We move on, leaving it a dead husk, and we never *stop*.

Silence grabbed them, like ice.

– We're looking for Earth, sir, Jeff said.

– Why? Jason asked him instantly, flatly.

Startled, they stared at each other.

– We want to see the Birthplace, Jenna said stubbornly. – The origin of us all.

He looked at her, and she felt his eyes like insects crawling her veins.

– But we can't *find* it. It isn't on any current chart. Even here, so close, we have no change of locating it. That's why we came to Steron, to Mars, in the hope of finding some records, any records predating the Migration.

Jason mumbled something, but they didn't get what.

– Ashamed, he repeated. – I think they're ashamed, even after all this time.

He paced a bit. They didn't dare disturb him.

– Your ship, he finally said, casually. – It's… fast, isn't it?

– Not really, Jeff replied. – It's a fairly old model and…

– It's fast, Samhain nodded. – It only takes hours to cross the system, on a journey that used to take years. I felt you, you know, from the moment you entered the Sphere.

– What did you feel? Jolanda whimpered.

– I felt Destiny's Hand, Jason said.

And the joy and fear grew a bit more within them.

– I can take you to Earth. With your ship it's only minutes away from here. At least it will be, after we've eaten. You need to feed, to replenish yourselves.

– But…

– Didn't you hear what I just said? He corrected her, he sneered at her. – You're weary travelers, and you need to rest.

The skull on the left side of his face became more pronounced, and they shook in awe and horror, and bowed to his might.

It washed over them in waves, and it was all they could do to resist it, and not cringe like rodents in his presence.

He led them into the nearest building, one of the few left with a roof. There was a kitchen, an actual old-fashioned kitchen leaping from the history Vidolos. They looked wide-eyed around the dusty room. The lamps and electricity buzzed off and on endlessly. He made dinner mechanically, somewhat efficiently. It didn't take long, less than a minute after he had made the proper preparations. He put the smoking plates on the table. They sat down on the quirky chairs.

His social skills are a little rusty, Jenna grinned fearfully to Jeff on their intimate, private mode, fearing he would hear her. But they're still there.

– You'll have to forgive me, Jason told the group. – My social skills are a bit rusty. Centuries of isolation will do that to you.

He began eating with his hands, and his guests did as well.

– This is unprocessed food, Carl exclaimed.

– Yeah, I can't stand the modern shit, Jason nodded.

– It, all this is almost… Carl began.

– Exhilarating? Jason finished for him.

– Precisely, sir. Carl said eagerly, munching a suspicious piece of meat. – Society has become so ordered, so structured that anything out of the ordinary like this is… refreshing.

– Even in our travels we hardly experience much beyond the… the mundane, Jolanda said. – Even life on the frontier worlds quickly becomes *boring*.

– You're children in need of direction, Jason told them. – In need of growing up, of a purpose, and I will give it to do. I will be your Destiny's Hand.

A wide range of emotion once more surged through them.

– Do you know? He said deliberately. – Do you know what a Dyson Sphere is?

They looked uncertain at him, at each other, aware that he passed them a rhetorical question, but unable to grasp his meaning.

– It's wanton destruction, he said. – Large machines are cannibalizing the giant gas planets. All comets and meteors and asteroids in a given system are used as well. It's a *rape,* pulling all life up by the root, very inductive of the mindset of any people using such a horrible «tool».

They fed, both digesting his food and his words. It bounced within them, and grew as they pondered their meaning. The weariness faded as the meal ended and the nourishment strengthened their bodies and mind.

Thoughts, words without words bounced back and forth among them, and among them and Him. He rose. They did as well.

– You've chosen me as your Teacher, he told them. – The teaching will be cruel and invasive. I've waited a thousand years on this place. I knew you, or someone like you would come, even though I didn't know exactly when.

Jolanda stepped forward, her entire being glowing in desire, in sudden, abrupt need. She began undressing in slow, lazy movements, revealing herself to him, and then there was no need, because he *looked* at her, and in that single glance he saw everything that was to know about her.

– The others will become my students, he told her, told them, – but you will become more. You will become my apprentice.

– Yes, Jason, she replied in a daze, slurring on every word. – Please teach me, teach me the secrets.

The apprentice of Death? Jenna said to Jeff. No!

He held her back.

Samhain stared down at the girl below him from a thousand different angles, and she sighed in both fear and anticipation.

– My very touch will hurt you, he said. – There will be great pain, at least initially, until you grow powerful enough to resist it.

A momentary anger flared in her eyes.

– I know pain, My Lord, she said angrily, besieging.

– No, you don't, my pet, my apprentice, he countered, making her shrink before him, – but you will. You all will.

And then she heard him in his mind.

No, you don't, he snarled. – *But you will.*

And she gasped, even before he Touched her, and the moment he did, she howled in pain, and Jeffrey was absolutely certain her howl would wake any dead unfortunate enough to hear her.

Samhain placed her on all fours and took her, ravaged her right there, before them. They couldn't help but respond to it, to become aroused, to become desire, just like the sister in Death's throes.

And the helpless cries of pleasure that ended their «joining» felt even worse, really. They experienced it all, through her, and even by proxy, like this, it shook them, shook them like ragdolls, and they felt torn apart in the Storm.

They crouched there, afterwards the lot of them, in each other's arms, somewhat comforted, but Samhain brought their sister with him, leaving the house, taking her into the vast wilderness surrounding the village. They didn't see her again, hardly even felt her for hours after that, and when they did they hardly recognized her. But they sensed him, as they, too, felt his touch, and that slight touch was enough to make them cringe in horror, and they couldn't imagine what she went through.

The two suddenly stood there, in the doorway. He towered above her, as he held her in front of him. Saliva flowed from her mouth, and her previously expressive and alive eyes had turned into vast and empty pools.

– She's mine, now, he snarled at them, – and lost to you Forever.

She was only a shade after that, trailing Samhain's shadow. They saw her only in glimpses. Almost like she didn't even exist anymore, except like a stray thought in Samhain's mind.

– Come, he said, – Earth and Destiny await us!

34

The ship didn't feel the same. He filled it with his presence. They didn't feel the same. He filled them.

He held a crystal in his hand, a mechanical storage unit clearly not current, but it was compatible with current technology. They knew that when he put it in a vacant spot at the panel, and a revised chart filled the room. They saw the eight planets, like they had been. Neptune, Uranus, Jupiter, Saturn, Mars, Mercury, Venus… and Earth.

– It's so easy, Jenna, said dizzily. – It's right there. So easy.

And it was. They saw it. They saw it not.

– I'm Open, Jolanda droned on, in a beyond creepy voice. – Open, open, open. I can see everything.

She kept mumbling, kept droning on, sometimes unintelligible, sometimes lucid. Sometimes they understood her. Most of the times they didn't, and it bothered them, bothered them terribly.

– What do you see, my love? He stood behind her, with his hands on her shoulders, and even that touch hurt her.

– I see insects, she said dreamily. – I see cockroaches. Where nothing else can live, they do. I see amoeba and pools of fluids and poison.

A scarred, dark and ruined ball and its equally shrunken satellite entered their line of vision.

It was basically two interconnecting rocks in Space, and that was all.

– W-what is that? Jeffrey choked.

– That is Earth, Jason pointed out, quite unnecessary, uncannily filled with rage and sorrow. – The result of millennia of abuse and destruction. An old friend of mine, a painter and artist, I can no longer recall his name, painted a famous image called the World Grinder. This is slightly worse than even his nightmare vision, though.

They stood there, just stared at the horror below. Their far-sensing powers saw just as good what the mechanical probes picked up, a globe practically devoid of life. Mars had, for some reason, been left somewhat intact, but this… this was beyond anything.

– This is humanity's ultimate nightmare vision come alive, Jason told them uncannily softly, – every possible Armageddon-prophecy fulfilled, squared.

Jeff fell to his knees, right there. They all did, all the youths, except Jolanda. She kept staring ahead with an excited smile brightening her face.

They hardly noticed that Jason walked off. Their ship and themselves kept hovering above Dead Black Earth like vultures.

But they did notice when he returned, with his hair cut and beard shaven off, when he looked more alien than ever.

Jeffrey's eyes cleared. He rose, with an effort, turning towards his pack mates, the people he had led through what they had believed had been centuries of hardship, without truly knowing anything about what hardship truly was.

He strived to speak, made several wasted efforts before one, final attempt succeeded.

– We have found what we were looking for, he told them angrily. – We have found the *truth*. We can use that to make others see it as well.

He walked to Jasper, grabbing him and shaking him.

– You mumble and turn restlessly in your sleep, and in the morning, you never speak about it. What is it?

– You mean about the wax dolls? Jasper whimpered. – I can't really remember much when I woke up, except that it is all unsettling, very unsettling.

– It's the Tachiti, isn't it? They will return one day, with a vengeance?

– Y-yes. Jasper stuttered. – Every Seer since time immemorial has had that dream, in one form or another, but I don't' know what it *means*.

– It means we better be prepared, prepared for them, too.

Jeffrey turned towards Jason. He nodded.

– They will come, he stated, – and they will continue their relentless work of making slaves of us all.

He saw through Jasper's mind, saw Jolanda's belly grow big, saw glimpses of the future. It was enough. When he turned towards his brethren, he saw that they were with him, saw them respond favorably to the initial thoughts of Tomorrow forming in his feverish mind. They were with him. They were all with him.

– You! He pointed without pointing at Justin. – You will be our scribe, our chronicler. You will write everything down, be a witness to our beginnings.

Justin didn't protest in any way. There was nothing left of his previously so grumbling nature. He looked beaten, like they all did, but Jeffrey sensed the same defiance in him, like he did…

In them all.

He smiled.

And turned to Samhain. He didn't kneel, but he bowed his head, leaving their lives and future in the ancient's hands.

And they all felt the sigh of Destiny, good and bad, move through them, the weariness and despair, so grounded in them, now that it was actually changing, changing into something new and different, and fresh and eager. They had been waiting, looking for something for so long, something they had been unable to define, to name their entire lives. And now the waiting was done. Now… they had found what they had been looking for.

Now, life stood in their midst, and rose from their core like the Storm it was.

6

FROM THE ANNALS OF ALLASEE WAR'N

I'm Allasee, Albert in the old language. I'm the current chronicler, scribe of this War'n clan. That honor was passed on to me by Alanor, my great grandmother. She was eight hundred and nine when she decided to do other things, to move on, on her quest for knowledge. We are Jason's children, his legacy. He found our ancestors in their deep despair, and took that despair, and turned it into something else, into the fire and Shadow that is our birthright. He stayed with us until we were his children no more, until we could walk on our own. This is that day, and it's a day both of sorrow and excitement.

Today is a momentous moment. He left us, early this morning, cloaked in mist and Shadow, like Lillith, our Great Mother did millennia ago.

Jason left us today. After centuries of training us, guiding us in the purpose he set out for us, he gave us these parting words:

«I leave you nothing, except the fire inside. Whatever happens you won't go silently into the night. You won't be Indians».

And he was gone, just like that, and we grieve because he isn't with us anymore. We can no longer sense him anywhere. He left us, just like I've been told Lillith did millennia ago. We have to be grateful, I guess. He doesn't want us to be his eternal children. He leaves us to give us a change to stand and live on our own.

The Indians, the natives of one of Earth's old continents, were a diverse set of tribes being overwhelmed by invaders with superior technology and purpose, and eventually numbers. Millions of people were eradicated in a mere century. Yes, it would be wise of us to heed Jason's parting words, to heed them even more than all the other words and thoughts he imparted in us.

The Tachiti is coming. All Seers, signs and portents tell us that. Our common sense tells us that. They will come, like the Europeans came to the Mayans, to the American natives and to countless other people, destroying them all.

Jason tells us we won't just roll over and play dead, and that makes me very, very happy.

7

FROM THE ANNALS OF ANALIN WAR'N BORN 11831

Something momentous happened today. It finally happened.

The sky was filled with ships, filled on a thousand worlds. The Tachiti is here. That fact fills me with dread and with purpose. They are here, and humanity's final test has come.

They look very much like us, evidently being of the same stardust as we are. The writings of an ancient Oracle and Dreamweaver tell us of the second-generation stars exploding and seeding the Universe with life. Life came to Ancient Earth that way, and related seeds came to the Tachiti home world. They have been very forthcoming in providing us with genetic samples. We share the same base code DNA. The similarities are many, though not many enough to make us the same species by far. Even though we see a parallel evolution they are further from us than any plant or beast originating on Ancient Earth.

But it's hard seeing that by looking at them. They look and feel very much like us. They have been very forthcoming.

8

Liz and Ted opened their eyes from the dream after having slept twelve thousand years.

They had shared a history not their own, one that had now become their own.

So much to take in. So much to digest. A flow of information, beyond pure information, even beyond experience. Six hundred generations lived in the blink of an eye, in the eternity of the Universe, one night of Dream and Desire.

They sat by the table, the round table without a head, the one Phoebe, Analin, Kerron and all the rest sat around, boiling in their hearts and minds.

Analin stood up, raising the cup.

– We are Jason's People, she said. – Or the Cult of Samhain, like spiteful tongues call us.

She turned without turning to the two newcomers or rather firstcomers, love and passion glowing in her eyes, and in her ring.

– You have Shared with us. You have become one with us, have become us, but in a sense, in a vast number of senses you already were. He was your son, at least in his latest incarnation. It makes sense. It makes very much sense.

She handed the cup to Ted, for him to drink first. He shook his head. She smiled and drank, and so, a moment later did he and Liz. When one drank, they all did, anyway. Analin was the Storyteller, her power of projection clearly the strongest among their host.

– It's only been a hundred years since the Tachiti arrived, and they are already very much running things.

Kerron spoke with aggression accentuated in his very voice. It echoed among the tribe. They kept staring at the living history in their midst with hope and longing in their eyes.

– Where are we heading? Liz wondered.

She already knew, or knew just after she had asked the question. She wasn't sure.

– Montan, she stated slowly. – A planet, a wonder of wonders and one brief-home for the weary traveler.

Her voice, the recitation of Memory was laced with irony, an approach finding favorable response in all those present.

– It has one thing going for it, Analin said. – It's a kind of… of free port, I guess you would say. It's considered being outside «official» Tachiti territory.

– That's good. Ted nodded. – That's a very good thing.

The assembly sighed around him. He realized his eyes were glowing again, and they could never have enough of that. Phoebe kept staring at him, unashamed, with endless love. There was something… a rapport echoing in him, a vision of blood and a river. He realized startled that she was pregnant, pregnant already. And the moment he realized it, the others did as well.

One of the boys, one of the girls circled the table, pouring wine into the glasses, taking another round to yet another sigh of the senses, dropping their blood into the mix of wine and spices.

So much emotion, Liz thought, Liz said, so much boundless passion.

38

There was a pause, one of hesitation and apprehension.

And then she rejoiced, and the room exploded with her, exploded in fire.

Analin raised her glass in excitement and anticipation, her glass of wine and blood, the blood of the gods.

– What was prophesized, what was promised has become mortal truth, she said softly. – Our loved ones have returned to us. Across a gulf of Space and Time they have come, to bring Life and Freedom to us all, to return to us what was lost, was misplaced.

Outside, in the Space liner's murky corridors and bright halls everybody felt it, felt its poignancy and Power. Analin smiled in glee and triumph, and wild, wild anticipation.

– To new life, she cried. – To Change.

She spoke with both her mind and vocal chords, as did they all, and they drank.

Liz didn't have to close her eyes. She saw the planet below, saw Montan, «The Hopeful» without trying, its rivers and seas, its waterfalls and mountains and forests, and the hopes and dreams of its one billion people. It was all there, at the tip of her tongue, and her eyes glowed, beyond ashes, even beyond fire.

We never went to California, Ted, the Ted from long ago said in her Memory. We never set foot there.

She remembered, like splinters in the mind's eye, flashes of fire in the gut.

She remembered it all. As if it had just happened. And it had. As if it was still happening.

And it was.

CHAPTER THIRTEEN
RAVENSCOURT

NORTHFIELD, MASSACHUSETTS
UNITED STATES OF AMERICA
NOVEMBER 15, 2005
(western, christian timeframe)

Linsey Kendall stares at his eyes in the mirror. They are changing, finally changing, after all these years. They used to be brown, dark brown, but they are not anymore. Slowly, explicitly they become bonfires in the night, strands of night and fire. He rejoices. He feels fear.

Time flies, flies like the wind, and no one can catch it, catch its breath.

«The Three Years of the Wanderers» began.

They came from far away. They all came from far away, to this place of antiquity and mystery.

The Black Dome faded before the morning sun. It had filled the horizon, but on this day, it dissolved into nothing, as if it had never been. For days and weeks, it had mystified and terrified the world. Now its physical properties vanished, but its effects lingered, multiplied and reinforced themselves moment by moment in this new age, this world of Magick and Twilight.

Many times before, the world had appeared to have changed, but really hadn't. But now it had, explicitly.

The change was no longer superficial, but deep down, at its very foundations.

More Special Forces from the Unites States Army, accompanied by international «observers» broke what had been the perimeter of the dome and invaded it from all sides, joining those presumably there already. They had to walk or run. No vehicles, no machines worked within or in close proximity to what had been the Black Dome. With them were hungry and apprehensive, so called «embedded» representatives for national and international media, public and private government.

One special group, though, entered the city of Northfield, Massachusetts almost unseen, unnoticed. They walked through the ruckus with a purpose, with fire glowing in their eyes. Shadows danced around their bodies.

Another walked from a dark, secret place within what had been the Black Dome.

In a quiet, secluded spot in the eye of the Storm the two groups met. The bright sunlight didn't seem to quite reach them. They walked and moved in Shadow. All the ravens flapped their wings and cried their cry, and landed on the new arrivals' shoulders.

– Welcome, Arthur. Welcome, Guinevere, the tall, dark Stacy Larkin cried, holding the wand with the skull on top in her left hand.

– Thank you, Merlin, Elizabeth Warren chided.

– I have here another, rather small addition to your ranks of knights, Stacy said softly.

– Small, perhaps, but crucial, Ted Warren said.

– You're not wrong, Stacy nodded. – There is autumn and there is fall, and it is all the same.

Ted and Liz realized that they were able to hear people's thoughts, to listen to them without aid. At some stage, in there in the shadow world they had added yet another power or level of power to their arsenal.

They felt everybody present and it wasn't overwhelming in any way, but like a warm breeze, the warm autumn breeze here, now.

The spirits of the dead surrounded them and danced in the air.

– And on that note, Stacy said, – let's all go somewhere else, let's begin the beguine.

She wasn't the tallest among them, but clearly the most enigmatic and imposing. Her frame was cast in shadow, and that shadow was glowing and casting its ebony light at them all. The change from only three weeks ago, what to her was only a week was startling. She was everything she had been then… and so much more. It was as if she wasn't the same woman, and that was both true and false.

They followed the thrice-born witch in between the tighter growing bushes and what was fast becoming a forest, just a few steps… to the sword in the stone.

The sword casting a shadow shine. The blade wasn't black, but it looked like it was at certain angles. Everybody stared at it, even Stacy herself, pondering everything with her black eyes.

– I'll need a few volunteers, she grinned darkly.

Almost all of them stepped forward.

– Now, now, there is no need to get excited…

Many attempted to draw the sword from the stone. The excitement prevailed no matter how many failed. The physically strongest pulled and pulled and pulled, to no avail.

Ted and Liz waited until the end.

They exchanged glances.

– Be my guest, she said graciously.

He took two steps forward and unceremoniously grabbed the tilt, and pulled.

Nothing happened. He tried again, pulling real hard, and then he released the hilt and stepped back.

Liz hesitated, glanced at him, at them all, before finally committing to it. She circled it like a vulture, studying it almost like she would a lover or an enemy.

– That's mighty fine workmanship, she commented casually.

It looked kind of ethereal, like it wasn't truly of this world, and recalling the sight from Jahavalo's defunct kingdom in the shadowland, she suspected that it could be true.

She grabbed the hilt, steeled herself and pulled, pulled hard… and almost pulled herself off balance and fell.

Everybody looked accusingly at Stacy. She looked completely unfazed.

– Now the two of you together, she said casually.

41

They stared astounded at each other and felt stupid because they hadn't considered that.

Two right hands grabbed the hilt and pulled, and the sword slipped from its resting place in the stone, and they didn't feel stupid anymore. They raised the sword above their heads and made a slow, deliberate 360 degree turn to face the entire circle of flesh and blood surrounding the stone. Waves of excitement and a range of emotions they couldn't possibly identify hit them like a velvet glow sledgehammer tempered at the center of the sun.

2

– Welcome to Raven's Court, Raven grinned wolfishly.

And the house that was a castle, the castle that was a house welcomed them, embraced them like rain, like moonlight, like home after a long Journey. And it was the Journey, the very Tapestry dancing on the misty wall. They heard it sigh, and scream and howl.

– It tickles, Liz said amazed.

The others, also those standing at the other side of the large room could practically see the gooseflesh break on her arms. In a place where only shadows lit the walls and the floor and the ceiling and the yard outside, there was a row of paintings making the term «gooseflesh» totally obsolete.

Inside the first frame there was only a brief text, written in big, delicate letters:

«To the witches following me on the path to madness: This is
this centennial, as I see it. Young friends, young rivals, beware of
the future hidden in your depths, beware of the beast inside».
Alan Rachine 1904 AD

– This held a special significance to me, Stacy said. – I guess it holds a slightly different meaning to the two of you.

Her very words held meaning, of course, but also the quality of her words got to them, evoking a poignant reality stabbing them deep. She spoke to them with her every movement, with every little nuance shift of her body and twinkling eyes.

She was older than they were, and she emanated some of the same ancient nature as Carla and Jahavalo, and Martin Keller and Lillian Donner, Everett Moran and Jason Gallagher and others present besides, but also different, more poignant, far more so, in fact, enough to stagger them.

They knew her, in ways they could never know others.

Rachine had painted what was his future, his unique, unmistakable take on it. It did something to them, to them all.

– Why are all his paintings inscribed with Self ar 1904? Lydia giggled. – They weren't all painted that year, were they?

The fresh, young soul of Lydia Warren had turned seventeen, and she had come of age.

William Carter Lafayette stared at the paintings. He could, in fact hardly take his eyes off them. The brain cells and their wiring began firing in his skull.

They walked upstairs, up the long, broad stairs to the hall of mirrors and open windows. Ted and Liz, and also several of the others recognized the place from a thousand dreams.

In every shadow, in every corner of the eye they spotted a reflection of something half forgotten, half vivid, memories of impossible events. White turned black, and black the most exquisite of images, colors not of this world.

They were all together, at last, all the angels of the Abyss. Even the laughter sounded different, layer upon layer of complexity. When they looked at a given face they didn't see merely one, but an endless row simultaneously. They laughed and joked like old friends.

And it was such an inadequate description.

– It's like sitting up all night, waiting in vain for inspiration, William said. – And suddenly there it is.

Ted caught a glimpse of Stacy, among the sea of faces. He saw her sneak up the stairs, and he followed her further up, all the way to the roof, where they could see the world.

– It's sufficient that you are here, to hear what I have to say, she stated. – What you hear she hears.

This was such a strange place, even by their standards. It, both the air and roof seemed to be alive, and he sensed close and distant lands. He looked into her black eyes, her pools of shadows.

– I feel close to death, he said.

– It's not strange that you should feel close to death, face to face with proof of your eternal existence, she said.

Liz cocked her head below, and heard her, her words and her meaning.

– Death has always been close, he said. – Even with our powers, it's a «miracle» we've made it so far. Almost everybody from my first time in London, my time in Denver is dead.

– She told you, Stacy said softly. – «These are your first soldiers, Phoenix. With them you will fail, succeed and fail again».

He looked astonished at her, and she was astonished to actually see a glimpse of a tear in his eye's edge.

– You're not wrong. She nodded. – We've met before, and we will meet again. We're connected with a thousand strands of the tapestry's web. Delphi told me you were coming, and I knew, even though I didn't know that I knew.

– We looked for Delphi for years, he pondered, – but we couldn't find her.

– Because you looked for her too early, misled by your perception of the nature of time.

– We looked for Laurie, too…

– It wasn't her fate to be found.

She was slightly taller than him, now, when she was doublesouled, now, when she was herself, was Whole. Her form seethed and frothed in his eyes, like his was burning and fizzling in shadow in hers.

– Fate? He queried ironically.

Lillith smiled to him with affection and malice, slightly different from what he remembered, even more enigmatic and dangerous.

– I rode the wings of time back to see Jahavalo when he was Zarathustra, she said softly. – I showed him he would be very close to victory, but not that he would win. I showed him his destiny, but not his fate. He's dust, now, like Laurie. Their spell is broken. They will never regain their dominance over mankind.

– It is strange hearing you not speaking about them in the past tense, he mused

– No, it isn't, she stated. – You know there's no death. Once, in the cauldron that is the Tapestry, that is the Universe, we created ourselves out of nothing, and thus we remain and grow forever.

She looked down at the roof. Her hands glowed slightly. The fabric of the roof seemed to dissolve, and he could see down below, as he could anyway, without her aid.

– And here, now, Guinevere is your warriors, your true fighters in shadow.

He laughed out aloud, and they heard him.

– You were always so funny, Merlin, he noted. – I can remember that clearly.

He remembered this place, remembered Ravenscourt, as it once had been, and for a brief moment, it was as if no time had passed since then at all.

– «King» Arthur and the «knights» did exist, she said, – but in a form quite removed from the silly and distorted christian version. We fought the christians, fought Jahavalo's armies, and he corrupted even that.

He remembered. In that moment, it was crystal clear in his memory.

There was a... disturbance on the outskirts of his mind. He sensed the soldiers and the establishment's representatives roam the city below.

– Look at them, she mused, – how they encroach on our domain, how hard they strive to be important, to be relevant. They scurry down there, not knowing themselves and the world.

She turned to him, taking his hands.

– We do. We finally do, know all exquisite pain and pleasure of existence, and it's ours to command.

There was a jolt as she offered her powers to him, and he took it, and shared it, shared himself with everybody below, and they reached out to the soldiers, the soldiers of the established order, making them turn away from The Hill, never venturing up there at all, only believing they did, finding nothing but forest and wild, wild nature scaring them to death and leaving a pervasive memory of discomfort and fear at the back of their minds.

The soldiers, the countless investigators descending on the town, never came near them, any of them, never more than touched the surface of the mystery shrouding Northfield. They spoke to Stacy and others, but they didn't truly. Everything just slipped through their fingers, and they would eventually leave, more confused and befuddled than ever.

Hours passed, not in a daze, but in bright burning memory, as every seeker

44

descending on the town earned an ever stronger, ever more powerful sense of who and what they were.

The soldiers and the other intruders remained, but they didn't really incur on the people of The Hill. The city kept *breathing*, as plants kept growing at an excessive rate, and eventually, in not that many days every piece of metal, of concrete and forged compounds would be covered in green and brown.

– This is truly the place to live for the children, Ted said.

He stood with Liz and Stacy in the hall of mirrors and open windows. The wind was blowing. The wind, too, was stronger than ever.

– I concur, Stacy said. – We should go and fetch them immediately.

A hole appeared in the very air. Gabrielle Asteroth stepped through it.

Ted and Liz stared at Gabi, instantly, slowly grasping the implications, the endless possibilities.

– Yes, Phoenix, the girl nodded. – I know I can be of endless use to you, a powerful tool in your mighty hands, and that fact makes me very proud.

She opened another hole, and the four of them stepped through it, and Liz and Ted found themselves back in the house in London.

– I can go anywhere I've been, she stated proudly, – and anywhere I'm showed a clear image of in my head. Stacy relayed the location from your minds, and here we are. With a telepath's timely assistance, I can basically go anywhere on Earth.

– And bring as many as you want? Liz asked sharply.

– Yes, My Lady, Gabi replied, bowing her head, a bit taken aback by the woman's intensity.

Some of the children and current guardians were in the room. They gasped, shocked at first, but quickly smiling in joy and rushing the arriving party. The loud shouts attracted everybody, and they approached, a little apprehensive, cautious, until they saw who the arrivals were.

– How long can you keep open a portal? Ted asked.

– Until I decide to close it, Gabi replied, a little less awed. – I know it stays open, even if I should be asleep or unconscious. The shadow world is my domain or at least my province.

She was so articulate, such an excellent conveyer of the subtlety of language. Ted had to smile.

The shadow world wasn't their domain, at least not yet. They had felt something, a growing connection after the battle, but not more than that… yet.

– She has a power similar to Judith, Liz said, – except it's far superior in reach and strength.

– Actually, I think my control and understanding of it exceeds that of Jahavalo, the girl stated calmly. – And I'm yours to command.

The children in the London residence were brought over to Northfield. They left most of the others. It was an amazing event that brought a lot of chatter on the grapevine, both on and off the Internet. Speculation ran rampant when journalists and others discovered that the children were gone, seemingly vanished into thin air, right under the noses of the selfsame vigilant journalists. Ted and Liz and bunch reached the headlines again. Their legend grew to yet new and unprecedented heights, and the number of recruits joining the movement rose to record-high figures.

Yet another skillful public relation campaign by Phoenix Green Earth, commentators concluded.

But the uncertainty in their voice and demeanor was noticeable, at least to those able to see straight through their façade of arrogance.

The wildest stories spread from those leaving Northfield, among those being present during the Samhain ritual and not staying, but no one took them seriously, and establishment journalists wrote their tales off as hallucinations, due to «the massive amounts of drugs being ingested».

The children appeared in the library, a place now becoming a true library. Each child carried books. The adults moved back and forth for a while, bringing the shelves and other stuff. They didn't abandon the London branch, but consciously reduced it in importance.

– Is this home, now? A child asked.

– Yes, Ted replied, – it's the «safe» haven our kind has always yearned for. During the eons, when we've been away, we've always wanted to return. We've missed it, even if we haven't known what we were missing. As long as we don't make it our own prison, we'll be okay.

And just like that, moving day was done.

Not long afterwards the sound of loud, happy children echoed across Fire Lake, as they swam and played. The adults, too, undressed and threw themselves into the lake with the pure water. They could smell and taste it, the purity stemming from another Earth where there was no civilization. Ted and Liz, and a few others journeyed there, through the portal below the lake.

The water turned cold. The day on that other Fire Lake was gray. It was raining hard, and even they got cold quickly. This was the natural climate this time of the year this far north, probably even a bit warmer than average. There was no snow or frost, but winter wasn't far off.

They ran to the edge of the Hill there, looking down on the valley below, seeing and sensing nothing but forest and the eternal wilderness everywhere, and it felt good, felt so incredibly good.

– This is such an inspiration, Michelle said. – Isn't that so, father?

He nodded, a little concerned on her behalf.

– It's a model of how it should be everywhere, he stated firmly.

They returned to Ravenscourt, and the heat struck them like a wall. Floating there, in the pleasant water made them even giddier with excitement and expectation. They dived down below again, deep down, almost to the area where the divide, the boundary between worlds was. Ted frowned and Liz frowned, noticing something simultaneously. They were two and sixteen, the same fourteen that had been with them physically on The Long Walk to Boston after the storm, and then there was Andrea Natchios and Sally Regehr. The circle of people formed, practically by itself. Bubbles grew out of the water around their bodies, as if boiling in heat.

Energy passed between everybody. Liz and Ted sensed that easily, Andrea and Sally became part of the circle, the growing circle surrounding the two at its center. They knew Andrea and Sally, like they knew the others, deep down on levels impossible to properly determine. One glance had been enough, had been all it took to form a bond with the latest arrivals. It, not blood, not power, whatever it was tying them together grew in complexity and strength.

They returned to the surface, allowed themselves to float back up. It was so pleasant. They didn't have difficulty breathing at all. Eighteen pair of eyes and ears dipped up and down, there in the water, so astute and aware.

Strong, vigorous limbs returned them to shore, to the ground surrounding the castle. Stacy and bunch waited for them there, waited to take them deep below, down the stairs, to the lower kingdom, into the ceremonial hall. Torches flared, as they entered the vast underground complex.

They all sought to the center of the floor, driven there by their own, inner fire and determination and powerful longing. Stacy nodded to Circe, to Morgana Rae. The blonde South American native stepped forward, stepped away from the others. She bent down and touched the rock bed, and virtually instantaneously a loud rumble shook the ground. Stone grew like vines before her, as she seemed to become stone herself. The vines thickened and joined, and turned into one, single mass of gray, flowing like water. The form grew into a table, a large round table complete with chairs. One hundred all in all fit around the large flat stone.

Morgana rose, looking a bit fatigued, but quickly recovering, proud to display her work.

– This is our table of equality, Ted cried. – Our Excalibur, our Sherwood Forest. It's not a place, but a state of mind. Here we will all come and share our thoughts and dreams, our rage and passion.

– There is no head on this table, Liz stressed. – All among us have an equal share in it and right and duty to it. We will always be one hundred around it, but there won't be the same one hundred. That will change and shift with the tides and circumstances.

Exactly one hundred were present right now. They sat down, and the chairs, with its smooth surface fit them like a glove.

We sit here once again, they thought, like we have done so many times before, and will do so many times after.

– Everything is coalescing. Past, present and future becomes one. The future is now.

Delphi, Gabrielle Asteroth shared her visions with them. Her distinct crystal balls floated above the table, with the squeaking ravens and the mists of souls. The girl's skinny form glowed even through the ceremonial clothes she wore.

– It's ours, now, Stacy declared. – Northfield, the entire city, new and old is ours, ours to use as we will…

– And so is the world.

The hundred rose and rejoined the others on the floor. It remained an effortless process not a process. They sensed a shift, a gasp from of those present. Gabi turned and faced Ruth Warren. Ruth approached her with tears in her eyes. The tall and stocky girl knelt before the tall and skinny girl, and still seemed to tower above her. She choked and bowed her head. Gabi touched her cheek, granting her comforting touches. It was enough. Ruth rose on her feet, and the two girls embraced.

Most of those present understood, or at least strongly suspected what had just happened. A powerful charge of emotion filled the air.

Everyone walked outside, through the tunnel, walked to the city, to the Main Street of Oldtown. It was… pleasant taking their time, not having to rush things, enjoying the slow passing of time and movement.

Stacy Larkin, choking with emotion cried out to the massive crowd gathering on Main Street, embracing them with arms and mind. The music rose slowly in volume and intensity. The festivities began, savage, heathen revelry which the world had hardly ever witnessed.

The journalists and TV-stations present got their mouth full, and more material than they would ever know how to handle, most of it much too rowdy to show on primetime television. There was very little nudity and open sexuality just then, but what was inferred would be sufficient to make those watching the countless private reruns in the various studios soaked in sweat.

There were sounds of distant thunder, distant battle, but people still filled the streets, still celebrated as if their last day had come.

Stacy danced among them, as she did at Everett Moran's side. And it was clearly unnerving to most people, even among the freethinkers present here, because she beneath the shell, the varnish of skin, hardly looked like a human being at all, but like a wild beast in the wilderness. And that was no exaggeration, no silly description told through the eyes of a mundane person, but the obvious truth.

The torches burned high, the smoke oozed thick, as she stepped up on the low stage.

– What happens here have value far beyond this city, this land, she cried.

They greeted her words with applause and loud shouting.

It was a storm standing up there with its fist raised, one clothed in flesh, but nonetheless the Storm personified.

– The world is looking at us, she shouted. – Current human society looks at us with fear and loathing. Do you know why? Because we can't be ignored anymore. We can't be threatened anymore. We can no longer be swept under the rug or thrown into a dark dungeon without repercussions.

She invaded him, invaded his very being, and like a tall wave she swept him with her, swept him far at sea. Ted Warren remembered ancient times and times to come on equal footing.

The hundred and the many hundred braves following them walked up the rise to the Hill. Twilight had just fallen on Northfield. The night descended slowly on them all. Tall campfires burned on the shore of Fire Lake. No more cameras, no more envious, cruel eyes followed them. Ted caught a glimpse of McKenzie remaining outside his tent and surveillance center, saw him staring at Frazer Hill.

Stacy undressed in front of him, displaying herself to him, and any sort of distraction faded from the front of Ted's conscious mind. He undressed, too. They all did. She slipped close to him, caressing him with soft, enticing touches, kissing his lips. Someone beat a drum. He didn't know who. He imagined no one knew.

– I told you I would fuck you one day, she grinned. – But then again, I did already, didn't I? Even after I told you that I would.

He attempted to ponder, to logically consider the ramifications of her words, but failed completely, and he didn't care.

– We've been so many things to each other, she whispered, – and we will continue to be in the eons to come.

You talk too much, he thought, but didn't say it aloud.

He grabbed her, pulled her powerful body close, and they fell there in the dry grass, surrounded by the sea of writhing bodies.

The two-legged wolf growled, and hot females rushed to him, to his giant form. Hundreds of wolves howled at the moon. Hundreds of fires reached for its cold face. The wind raged through the forest, warm and loud, and practically unnoticeable, except in eager, astute souls. There was more dancing, mindless movement, more racing thoughts. Liz, soaked in sweat, rocked up and down in Phillip's lap. She froze and fell on him, completely spent, soaking up the rampant energies of the sea of flesh covering the shore and forest and castle. They rested for a while, relaxing briefly in each other's arms.

– So, you were actually «Guinevere»? He said incredulous.

– No, I was «Arthur», she corrected him. – We all do that occasionally, switch gender. It gives us a necessary different perspective. You know that.

He did and it still unnerved him.

She kissed him on the brow and left him, rising above all the bodies and seeking and finding instantly those she was looking for. Her beyond powerful form hovered above Ted and Stacy. They, too, were in-between engagement. She grabbed Stacy and pulled her into the air. Stacy let herself be pulled, the sweet smile in place.

Liz brought them across the lake and to the roof.

The two of them stood there, face to face, measuring each other.

– You're more like yourself than you ever were, Liz finally said.

– But then again, so are you, Stacy shrugged.

– So, what is your advice for me, Merlin? Any particular dark cloud on the horizon?

Her voice turned a darker hue.

– I'm afraid they are too many to count, My King, Stacy replied with an even voice, one not turning a darker hue. – You need to be more specific.

– I won't accept any trickery from you this time, Liz said. – Consider yourself warned.

– I would be wise to heed such a warning, wouldn't I, my Once and Future King…

Liz stepped close to her, looking up at her eyes for a moment, before grabbing her hair and pulling her head down, kissing her hard on the lips. Stacy gasped, several times, before relenting and giving in to the other's advances, returning her affection.

They both fell down on their knees, began caressing each other roughly and intimately.

– You've never switched, Liz spoke softly in her ear. – You're like Jahavalo…

She put the other woman down on her back, touching her below, making her spread her legs. The stench rose, rose from them both. Liz crawled on top of her, as the other's hands and power touched her, touched her all over. Both gasped aloud, and noticed how thought, how reason once more was slipping away, and they welcomed it.

– Sweet girl, Stacy hissed. – Sweet girl, sweet girl, sweet girl…

She kept repeating it until all voice turned to moans, and they, like everybody else writhed and heaved in others' arms, and wild abandon ruled them all, and all thought, all reflection was left behind.

A thousand sighs and gasps and wild cries resounded by and above Fire Lake.

The Round Table was full. They all sat there, holding hands, being connected in ways they never before had imagined or conceived. The mountain hall was full. The gathering's entire attention was locked on those sitting around the table, the glowing table, the glowing figures around it, cloaked in mist and shadow.

Carla Wolf and Stacy Larkin spoke more or less simultaneously, or alternately, to the point of it being difficult to distinguish their voices.

– Human society has become a Machine, civilization itself a destructive construct ruining Life on a massive scale speeding up its work second by second year by year, until nothing but the Machine remains. Feel it, feel the Wrongness wherever you go, wherever you cast your attention. It's everywhere, almost indistinguishable from humanity itself.

They felt it, in ways more powerful than ever before, for each new image and situation and display the ceremony brought them. Carla, Stacy, Gabi, Ted, Liz and the rest used their powers in tandem, to expose the world for what it had become, ridding themselves and everybody present of the illusions they had lived with for so long. They saw, felt Boston, experiencing how it rebuilt itself, how its tentacles reached out to its neighboring areas, corrupting everything and everyone it touched.

Oddly enough Stacy kept using both American and English phrases. Everybody noticed it, but they didn't really wonder about it. It seemed strangely appropriate.

Images, sensations, sounds and emotions assaulted the gathering, as they were given powerful reminders of why they were there.

They saw everything, everything wrong, but most of all they saw its root.

– Our challenges aren't over, to those believing they were, Stacy stated calmly. – It is now they truly begin. Jahavalo, powerful and sneaky as he was, was merely one man. What's awaiting us out there is an entire world gone wrong.

Civilization stretched out before them, covering most of the planet, increasingly more for each passing second. They saw, experienced how bulldozers and excavators and countless other tools relentlessly cleared, ruined more land.

Everybody noticed how well Stacy and Carla, and Martin, Lillian, Jason, Everett, and Ted and Liz, and the rest related to each other, how they finished each other's sentences and completed each other's movement.

It was a Magick night, there, around the Round Table, one many recalled, at least dimly having experienced before, long ago.

There was a lot of merry drinking, and those without a healing power got seriously drunk, and puked their guts out, but even then, the smile, the wide grin stayed on their face.

But chosen sentries among them stayed alert all the time. The gathering never let its guard down or down for long. Individuals monitored the situation down in the city, to scan for immediate threats. There was none. The media, the soldiers and the intelligence agents were kept successfully away from The Hill and were none the wiser.

Liz and Ted sensed easily McKenzie down there. He kept staring at The Hill, without really being aware of doing so.

Stacy walked through the forest at dawn, a shadow even in bright sunlight, now virtually invisible.

She stopped, turning her attention to her right in a small clearing and spotted Betty. Green eyes twinkled and burned.

– Long ago, Betty cried, – the twin sisters of Merlin and Nineve and Nineve and Arthur's son Mordred destroyed the free society of Camelot from within, making Jahavalo's conquest of it an easy task.

– But Mordred isn't here, won't be here this time, Stacy pointed out, – and neither are Merlin and Nineve, really, not anymore.

– Are you sure? Betty wondered, shaking her head.

– Will that be all, Kwaiala? The regal figure burned against the other, smaller, shaking form.

– That will be all… for now, My Lady.

The Kwaiala left her, left her alone. She waited, waited there for a while, before moving on.

He stood on the edge of the Hill surveying the city below. She knew that. She had pictured him in her mind for minutes, easily picked him out from the background noise. It wasn't like she was able to read his mind, but she could easily locate him.

Linsey Kendall turned around the moment she stepped out of the forest behind him.

– Hi, she greeted him with the sweetest of smiles.

– Hi, yourself, he returned the greeting.

Both gave the other their most dazzling smile. Mutual attraction pulled them together and they mated there at the edge of the forest, while the sun rose on the sky and burned the land and life there in equal measure.

3

Ted and Stacy walked with the children through the city. They had taken easily, instinctively to her and he relaxed. It was as if she and most of the others had always been one of them, and they had been, of course. The children recognized natural interaction when they saw it. It was the way they had been brought up and experienced life among their kin since birth.

«Kin» was the extended tribe.

And Stacy was far closer to many of them than that.

The city looked like and smelled of fresh green, and wherever Stacy walked that sense increased in potency. It wouldn't be just smell and sight either, but the very quality of the air, and the sound of birds and life in general reaching them from everywhere.

When the occasional army truck passed them, it certainly felt totally misplaced. The exhaust fumes made everybody cough, and the children, reacting to any threat or imposed discomfort in a possibly violent manner would have gotten very cross, if they hadn't been toilet trained, hadn't learned restraint long before they had ever gone to the toilet.

– They're such precious tykes, aren't they? Stacy mused and grinned.

There were dozens of them, all the children belonging to the Warren extended family, displayed deliberately. Phillip had called it «a great photo opportunity», and he had been correct, of course.

– What we're doing has never been done before, she added, and he knew she didn't mean just this walk. – It's bigger than we've ever attempted before.

– The time has come, Ted said.

– *Yes!* She breathed and looked at him with twinkling eyes, and briefly resembled the eighteen-year girl she was.

Northfield was really two, virtually separate cities, Oldtown, the tiny part and Newtown, ten times bigger, stretching across quite a bit of land to the south. But during the last few weeks Northfield, its very face had changed dramatically, and had practically ceased to exist as a modern city. Over half of what had been the regular citizens had so far moved out and people kept packing up and leaving. They saw several families load their things on trucks as they took their scenic tour.

– They're making their choice right now, Stacy said, when she noticed his glance. – Everybody still in Northfield does.

There were those choosing to stay, and everybody that had done their pilgrimage here since early September moved into the empty houses. An entire new community was forming, replacing what had been.

– The gods lived with their worshippers once, she said. – Now, they will do so again.

He looked at her, studying her. She turned and grabbed his hands.

– But this time there will be no gods, no worshippers, she stated firmly. – This time will be different.

She kissed him on the lips. Passion burned within her, within him, equally strong in them both.

– They will look to us for guidelines, he said slowly.

– That they will. She nodded.

– But the only way we'll guide them is by example, and by encouraging their own, inner star.

52

They passed the collapsed factory. People were moving in the ruins dressed in contamination suits, cleaning up the rubble and the poison. Some also worked in the river, and on a large garbage dump nearby.

– There is a lesson here, for all of us, children. She taught them with her intense demeanor. – This is the price for human hubris. No one can live close to this or in any of the nearby houses for decades. It's impossible to clean it up properly. The poison has infested the ground and groundwater deep down for miles down the river, and this… this horror is common all over the planet.

Rage and despair twisted her perceived demonic features further. She didn't hold herself back anymore, and it didn't scare them. They saw it as something completely natural and right.

The fairly small, strange entourage walked on. They reached the suburban areas with their dry, burned lawns. People stared at them. Some were outside, most inside. Ted waved to them, the children, too, and Stacy joined them with a sweet, sweet smile.

A few people returned the wave. Most did not.

– I used to walk around the city alone, she mused, – feeling sorry for myself. Things are different, now.

– You're the Triple Goddess, one of the children cried out, – and all the world will bow to you.

Lillith acknowledged the child with a slight smile and nod.

It was true. She was all the ancient legends made flesh.

The woman's long black hair seemed to move independently of the wind, as if it wasn't influenced by the here and now at all, but of winds long gone. She looked young and innocent, looked ancient.

– Jahavalo attempted desperately to recreate Atlantis, she said, looking softly at the older man by her side. – He never understood it properly, never understood its pitfalls, its horrors. We do and we, you and I, Ror Ken shall recreate it, recreate everything about it worth saving.

The familiar hammer ran down his spine, and he looked, deliberately, with open eyes, at the ancient witch by his side.

They walked on, wandered the entire city, taking their time, taking in the sights of their home. The green was everywhere, and where Stacy Larkin passed by it increased its growth. She didn't have to consciously will it anymore. Tall buildings, blocks of flats, they were all covered in growth. What would usually take decades had happened… over night.

Ted felt the others' presence. They checked in on them now and then just to be on the safe side. Particularly Gabi did. She could be there in an instant if serious trouble arose.

But the military presence wasn't really present, thanks to the numerous telepaths on the job. They took care of McKenzie and key figures in his command. McKenzie frowned a lot, knowing something was… amiss, but not being close to figuring out what. Every time his thoughts circled around it they were *diverted*. It was a wonder to behold. In his eyes they did a lot to interrogate and harass the locals. His frustration over the obvious lack of results was palatable, and in his mind, he had already reached the conclusion that this was a colossal waste of time. In just a few days they would leave, and the entire Black Dome event would become yet another unsolved «incident» in the White House files.

This time was different, though. People knew about this. The entire world knew. The world had changed, and it would continue changing.

– Can you feel it, Ror Ken? Lillith said. – The subtle changes, the gathering storm? One major player has been removed from the board, and everybody's rushing in to fill the void.

He could. He had become extremely sensitive lately.

And he had always sensed it, sensed the flow, the world's patterns weaving and reweaving themselves.

The pattern had been broken and was slowly resetting itself, but it was more like a jigsaw puzzle than anything resembling what had been, any orderly march. Excitement filled him.

They moved, flowed through the changed streets of Northfield. It was bright daylight, but Ted Warren imagined it was night, that they were bathing in shimmering moonlight. The moonlight superimposed itself on the day, and reduced it to nothing. The moon was more powerful than the sun.

Raven Moonstar looked pleased at him.

The ravens squeaked.

He grinned, meeting her stare unafraid and thrilled.

They passed the ruins of Scott Thompson's Pyramid, of the Gyrich estate, and a dozen others, ruins or downtrodden all, such pleasant sights, some useful, some not at all. Then they returned to Oldtown, passing the burned-out church, and further down Main Street the school. There were no more cars driving on Main Road, on its green pastures.

Ted and Stacy stared. Even the children stared, and they had grown up with it all as something completely natural.

Main Street was filled with spirits, with souls, with shadows, everyone not having left for other places on Earth. They stared, too, at the small group of living humans.

Stacy swayed. Ted grabbed her and held her, or she would have fallen, she would actually have fallen.

– Dizzy, she mumbled.

Ted scrutinized the spirits. He sensed no menace, no true menace from them, from any of them… only excitement.

He looked at her, at her sweaty, pale face.

– Sick…

She doubled over and threw up, all over herself and him and the gazing children. Grass and trees grew fast all around them, incited by her life-giving fluids.

A sense of relief and joy rose within him. He and the children began laughing.

– Very funny. She dried vomit from her jaw. – Why…

She froze, looking incredulous at them, at the street, where the spirits had faded

54

away.

The truth dawned slowly on her. A smile transformed her face.

The children ran off in different directions, while howling and shouting pretty much the same sentence:

– STACY IS KNOCKED UP. STACY IS KNOCKED UP!

<h2 style="text-align:center">4</h2>

He walked by the old buildings on his way to the Green Rose Tavern, what had been Haldoway's Inn. A line of girls stood with their backs to the wall, and with their hands on their backs, proudly displaying themselves, all smiling enticingly to him.

– Hello, Jason, one said.

– Hello, Jason, the next in line repeated.

And so it went, with all the five girls.

They were all Warrens, a sister and cousins, and other fairly close blood relatives, all young and desirable and filled with desire. He couldn't read their minds, not even the surface thoughts. They had all erected their shields, all being experienced in the use of their powers.

– Michelle? He wondered, looking at the first, biggest girl.

She felt like Michelle, looked, sounded and smelled and tasted like Michelle.

– It's so nice to see you again, Jason, she spoke softly and pleasant.

She had changed noticeably. The other girls giggled and hummed, both in his ears and his mind. Her confidence was quieter, now, was real, now, and not suffering from the low self-esteem he had learned to recognize in her.

But there was something, something chilling still about her he couldn't quite reach.

– Have I changed so much, My Lord? She teased him. – It's just been a few months.

– For me, he said. – For you it has been ten years.

– Silly me, I forgot...

He did recall them all, he believed, in flashes from last night, but only like more fevers in the darkness.

The underlying cruelty was still present within her, he sensed that, but it was muted, faint, but there was no weakness in her eyes, not anymore. She stood there proud and challenging before him.

– I'm Theresa, Jason. The second girl presented herself with her sensual smile and pose.

– Theresa? Little Theresa?

It slipped from his tongue before he could stop it. She was Mike and Linda's daughter. He heard her pleasant laughter. She had been eleven the last time he had seen her.

– I'm Lydia, Jason...

The way they said his name... was like music, and it entered him, and instantly made him twitch and burn below. There was no pretense here, no false modesty or prudence. These were women having grown up among people seeing sexual prowess and satisfaction as something perfectly natural and right, to be enjoyed whenever one felt like it. They were sexual beasts stalking him.

– These two cunts are Pearl and Ruth, Michelle chided. – They're too shy to open their gaps for anything but gasping in awe of being in the presence of the great Jason Gallagher.

Then, they all opened up to him, allowed him to truly see them, and their state of mind. He was swept away by the giant wave, its hot waters surrounding him on all sides.

They walked upstairs, to the upper floor of the tavern, to the giant bed. In many ways the giant room looked exactly the same as it had just a few days ago, but in the most important aspect it looked completely different.

The world and his perception of it had changed dramatically.

The five girls undressed slowly and relaxed, already wet and ready. They wriggled their butt as they headed for the bed, and he knew it was completely involuntary, instinctive.

Michelle hushed them on to the bed, made them kneel there with their head bowed. Then she knelt, too, in front of the other four.

– Greetings, Samhain, Lord of the Condemned, she said softly. – Welcome back to your court, your Place of Power. Please accept these sacrifices as a token of my undying devotion.

And there it was again, what he couldn't grasp. A brief thought quickly fading in the rush of passion.

He undressed slowly, savoring the sense of power. Dark, sparkling shadows danced around his body. He grew to full size while they watched. They saw him, as he slowly let go, and they grew absolutely frantic in their anxiety and need. He watched Michelle. She was right. This was his place, his new Domain.

They saw him, saw him swell and grow to fill the room, the entire building, except for the non-existing room number 13 below. Everything he had become blinded them, and their entire attention was focused on him.

He entered the bed, flowing towards the five kneeling females at its center, hovering above them for a moment or two while studying them, while studying himself. A hand touched Michelle's cheek, comforting her, comforting them all.

– Your very touch burns, Michelle gasped. – You're not holding yourself back anymore. You remember, don't you? Tell me you remember.

– Yes, he heard himself say. – I remember everything.

And by that admission alone, images and sensations of cruelty and bloodshed and horrors of unimaginable scope flooded his conscious mind.

– I knew it, she gasped, – knew the moment I saw you again.

– How is it… like? Theresa pulled herself closer to the two of them, momentarily falling out of the role-playing.

– You'll know, Michelle said, throwing herself at Jason.

Theresa and the others pulled close, too. Jason touched Michelle, embraced her, took her into his embrace. She yelped in ecstasy. He touched them all, without

56

touching them, and they moaned long and hard and fell to him like ripe fruits, and he couldn't help but feel the power, the pleasure stemming from the might he exercised over them. Then it mattered no longer. He gave in, like they gave in to every baser instinct possible.

He saw them, saw the girls wriggling their butts in Samhain's honor, as he put Michelle Warren down on her back, as he pushed deep within her physically and mentally, and it was so different from the last time he had done it, ten years ago, such a short time ago.

– YES, JASON, she shouted. – YES, MY LOVE.

He knew her, her immortal self, as he touched her Ti Bon Ange, the Shadow permeating space and time. What he had only glimpsed in fear during those days in London was now clear and present in his memory.

The others, the sacrifices sought him out when he had emptied himself in her, and she rested dead and still on her back. They offered themselves to him, to Samhain, to the lord of the realm, and yelped in joy when he accepted them. They were *new*, these four. Though powerful in their own right, they gasped in awe face to face with the old god.

The five touched each other, as they had learned to do, with both hands and mind. It brought them to a frenzy of desire in seconds, and Jason, Samhain touched the other four on a level even beyond that. His power, his special power was touch. His omnipresence was everywhere in the room, and he touched the sensual creatures surrounding him on all sides, invaded them through the air they breathed. Lydia, his aunt's daughter rubbed her butt at his groin. He pushed himself between her legs, missing her hole. A flash of irritation flared in him, and with that thought he froze the constantly moving females, trapped them in his amber. They still moved, but only to his moves. In a flash he glimpsed Michelle's speculative look, as she studied him, as she worshipped the ground he touched.

He placed Theresa on all fours and fucked her hard and ruthlessly. A moment later it was Lydia, and then Ruth and then Pearl, and then Theresa yet again. She came and he came, in a violent flow of pulls and pushes, in growls and moans. The sensations… they were so fine-tuned that he could sense every hair he touched on the girl's skin and in her hole.

It went on forever (and he knew quite a bit of forever).

– I know! Theresa howled. – I KNOW!

She fell and they fell and he fell, and he relaxed on his back in the midst of the lovely sirens. There was more touch, more kissing and fondling, affectionate and rough and beyond enticing. The four chuckled and gave him goodbye kisses, as they dressed, waved and giggled, and left, and left him alone with his treacherous queen.

– They're children, Michelle said. – Pay them no heed, My Lord.

He didn't really. He focused all his attention on her. She shivered visibly, but stubbornly met his eyes, eventually giving him her crocked grin. He watched her as she stretched in obvious pleasure, displaying herself to him, only to him.

– May your queen ask you a question, My Lord? She asked softly.

He nodded, hardly aware of doing so.

– Why didn't you just smash our shields when we approached you in stealth? You could do so without even trying.

– Perhaps because I, too, have learned something, he shrugged.

She sighed happily and gratefully in his arms.

He heard the sounds of the ruckus outside. It didn't seem to subside, but on the contrary increase, as the afternoon faded to twilight. He heard it beyond hearing, as he saw beyond seeing and sensed beyond sensing. Everybody participating in the battle against Jahavalo had had their powers increased significantly.

– It's a marvel beholding you, she whispered into his ear without being close to his ear. – You're more, far more powerful than you ever were… before.

He nodded, easily understanding her subtle hint.

– Your realm was destroyed in the glorious battle against Jahavalo, she declared. – You should remake it as soon as possible. It shouldn't present any problems with your present power level.

His realm… He remembered it, the way it had been, millennia ago, before he had left it in disarray.

– I feel no need to do that, he shrugged. – It existed and only had significance to me in another lifetime, in all meanings of the word. I used it because it proved to have a practical application, that's' all.

She smiled and the smile unsettled him.

– You're absolutely correct, of course, she nodded. – We won't need it to be great warriors in Father's war.

There was awe in her voice, a quality in it irritating him. She smiled, hiding nothing of herself, deliberately opening up like a flower in bloom.

He left the bed, and she did, too. They dressed, and didn't bother to shower. Like virtually everybody around here they enjoyed the stench of their sex just fine. They took their baths in Fire Lake, and didn't need hot water and soap.

They walked down the stairs to the bar. It was packed already. No one seemed to be noticing them, but continued the celebration, and he preferred it that way. The two of them walked into the street, the open field called Main Street. He felt the wind blow there, stronger than almost anywhere else.

And he sensed… more, the very moment he stepped outside, and he wondered why he hadn't sensed it before.

Bee stood with her back to them, with her arms crossed. She turned, and as she walked to him a smile broke on her face.

– Hello, Father, she greeted him, slipping into his arms, kissing him shyly on the cheek. – I'm so pleased to see you, see that you are well.

She had grown up, or at least looked like she had. He looked at a young woman with only a passing resemblance to the child he had briefly known. The characteristic necklace twinkled around her neck.

He sensed hardness in her, but nothing even approaching the image Ethel had shown him.

But she was clearly frail, in a way, clearly not enjoying the level of confidence and inner harmony the other young males and females in the family he had encountered here did. But then again, she wasn't exactly kin either. Ethel had practically made her, created her to be a singular, fearsome creature. He strived to mask his concern.

– It's nice to see you, too. I'm sorry for not coming to you when I woke up, but I…

– You had other concerns. I understand, Father. I'm a big girl, now.

He frowned. The way she spoke when she called him Father. It was the same tone of voice Michelle used, when she spoke of or to Ted.

She was big, not as tall as he or his blood-kin females, but tall and with a well-built body.

He saw the seething power within her, so much energy that it saturated her cells, that she seemed to his enhanced senses to be composed of energy. She displayed it to him proudly.

– I've been preparing, she said, – preparing hard every day and night during those ten years. I suffered my Trials not long ago, and know my name, and I've taken my place among my brothers and sisters in the struggle.

– That's good, he heard himself say, not pleased with his reluctant tone and repeated himself: – That's excellent.

She smiled happily to him, so brittle, so eager to impress him.

– With the addition of you old gods we're finally complete, ready and able to take the struggle to the next level. The Final Days are here, Father.

And Jason Gallagher was overwhelmed by both exhilaration and anxiety, by both heat and cold, standing on his spot on the windy street.

5

Liz and Ted did visit McKenzie in his tenth, subjecting themselves to the «debriefing», interrogation, in order to put his mind further at ease, further off track. They were put in separate rooms, a well-known technique used to verify people's story.

– It was quite the ruckus here, Ted told McKenzie and everybody behind the one-way mirror. – And I couldn't even begin to make sense of all of it, even if I had an entire lifetime.

– A pentacle burned in Main Street, Liz told them, - burned by itself. Whatever fuel they used, I have no idea what that was.

Stacy connected the two of them, making sure there were no slipups. It was easy. They conveyed a certain worry with their well-known confidence, pretty much like ordinary «ghost hunters» would have related their experience in a paranormal hot zone.

Cole Bruckner and the other survivors of the first investigative unit had vividly related their experiences, of course, but only succeeded to come off as complete lunatics, and they were all on their way to the nearest military hospital, or «containment unit» for the hopelessly insane.

Ted and Liz told half-truths and lies, weaving them into a somewhat non-consistent whole they knew were quite common between people having experienced smaller, similar events.

- We never found anyone or anything that might be behind it all, no reason or rhyme, Ted said. – As far as I am concerned, it stopped by itself.

- Could it happen again? Liz shrugged. – I would say yes…

And that was that.

The soldiers and intruders left. They packed their gear and their massive amounts of equipment and took off. It happened quietly, without any big words or the usual display of pride and conceit.

- Some people know, Carla said to the others gathered at the edge of the forest hill with her. – There are those out there able to put together a closer to the truth scenario. Some people always know.

It was inevitable. The many thousands of witnesses fleeing from the area would share everything they had seen, spread it on the Internet in explicit detail and passion, and those with knowledge looking for such things would know to separate facts from fiction.

But that was the future. The immediate present was saved from cruel and intrusive forces.

The new masters of Northfield moved into the houses used by the officials, only hours after they had moved out. There was no rush, as there was plenty of room for everybody. Smiles lingered on everybody's lips, along with the determination of facing all the upcoming trials they knew would come.

Ted and Liz, Stacy and Gabi, and a few of the others met in the catacombs. There was no one there right now. They met inside, far below the ground, under tons of rock, because they could never rule out satellite surveillance. Someone, somewhere could and would always be watching, and even meeting inside an ordinary house wouldn't hide them or even obscure them from infrared scanners and even more accurate emerging technology.

– Years of paranoia is finally paying off, Phillip chuckled darkly.

Gabi opened up a hole in the air, and they all walked through it, and the cave faded into an alley in another city entirely. They started walking and soon they were walking carefree and wild through the busy streets of San Francisco.

People noticed the group almost immediately, of course. The times when they could go anywhere unnoticed were long gone. People pointed and stared.

– It's no big deal, Liz shrugged. – We've always been noticed several impossible places simultaneously.

– It will only add to the legend of the Janus Clan, Stacy nodded.

Ted took in the scene, like he did everything these days, in a storm of emotion and excitement.

– We never went to California, he pondered. – We never set our feet here.

– It was *his* Domain, Stacy said. – You instinctively stayed away, stayed away from the place where he was at his strongest.

They were still hesitant to speak his name, as if he was still listening somewhere.

But his influence was lessening. They sensed it everywhere, both in themselves and others.

60

– Mark Stewart and David Gidman didn't, Phillip scowled. – And neither did my father.

No one made any further comment on that. It remained an unpleasant subject. They refrained from looking at each other.

– There are good times, too, the young woman with black eyes pointed out, insisted softly, just a little on edge. – And this is a good time, one long in waiting.

They felt it, how right she was. Like a poignant thought of spring, it settled within them and lifted their spirits from the inevitable melancholy.

She was all things simultaneously, and she inspired them, inevitably.

There was a tavern at The Wharf known for its radical guests and owners. They walked inside it, and instantly created yet another poignant stir.

The Children of the Midnight Fire visited the tavern by the sea, and created instant excitement, instant apprehension.

They got that a lot.

Some embraced them and others pulled away, but the Children of the Midnight Fire pulled them all towards their pale shadow. The tavern had been practically empty. During a span of fifteen minutes the word got around and the place filled up with excited and curious people.

It was a place of shadows this, like any tavern worth its name, a place where rebels and warriors met. The travelers felt instantly at home here and didn't really need to do anything to be heard. It was enough to speak, and just being there, and it felt like a valve on their shaken souls.

They sat at the center of a circle, yet another circle, and had a low-key conversation with the gathering, held a great, informal meeting, and even though they could never allow themselves to completely relax, they felt at home here, at ease here, too.

– This city is also civilization, of course, Gabi said, blushing a little, in the company of strangers, – but like some cities a kind of urban wilderness, in spite of the corruption, bursting with Life.

It no longer sounded strange that a thirteen-year-old girl spoke words of wisdom and truth. On the contrary, it felt right and potent.

– You've come far already, Ted stated, – on your way to true freedom. I salute you!

Between him and Liz the people of the circle glimpsed a shimmering sword, or imagined they did.

The Janus Clan walked the street some more afterwards, followed by a selection of their most recent recruits.

– He couldn't break their spirit, Gabi said brightly. – Not in a hundred years.

– But he broke most peoples in thousands, Stacy gently, harshly reminded her. – He settled here because he had everything worked out. This would've been one of the very first places that would've fallen totally in his thrall.

They headed, without conscious thought for a building in the business district. Lillith had been there before, as a spirit. The others sensed that behind her smile and cunning and everything. It was downright amazing how much they sensed, without trying.

The group walked straight inside, past security and sentries. No one attempted to stop them. They walked on their feet to the center of the building, before Gabi opened a portal to the top aerie, to the office, of what had been the center of operations in Brian Garrett's San Francisco.

Marianna Vogel rose abruptly from her chair.

She quickly knelt on the floor. They took one glance at her, at the wreck she had become and looked. She had been totally dependent on her master, and everything was quickly falling apart both within and without her.

Stacy hesitated momentarily, giving her a look of contempt, before kneeling with her and cautiously caressing her face, gently brushing her broken mind.

They didn't take over the place, the organization. There was nothing left except a lot of confused and suffering people. The travelers' features softened visibly.

– The Dollmaster leaves nothing but puppets in his wake, does he? Liz said.

They remained there for a long time, for not more than a few minutes, while cold, cold chills of infinite relief trickled down their spine.

6

William did two haunting paintings during his nights of frenzy. He seemed totally obsessed, even for him.

It was one of Stacy alone, and one with her and Ted, Liz and Jason. They were quite similar. A single figure or four behind a campfire in the forest, their faces and bodies bathing in both silver light from the moon and the golden glow from the fire. The images were «frozen» during twilight, but it was still dark around the fire, where the creatures of the mists and shadows stared at the world. On branches and shoulders sat the ravens. The style seemed, at first glance fairly mundane, but after just a few seconds of watching the beyond haunting quality reared its eerie head. The scene seemed to flow from the canvas to the shimmering air in front and become real.

The two paintings were called «Children of the Midnight Fire» and «Daughter of the Midnight Fire», and caused an instant sensation when they were put on display in a gallery in Boston. The numbers of visitors were doubled and redoubled several times, and in just a week it filled up every day. A day after that a queue formed outside early in the morning.

A journalist interviewed a fan outside the museum.

– It's unbelievable, he cried, – I get totally, joyously fucked up just by glancing at them.

– But reviewers have mostly given the paintings bad reviews, the reporter insisted.

– What do they know? The man farted, very loud, making the journalist squirm.
– Reviewers are the parasites of culture, in my opinion, and don't know shit about anything. They give their personal opinion, presenting that as the only viable view.

– But *why* do you like them so much?

– I can tell why I am practically *ecstatic* about them, the young man said. – I like all his paintings, men these two are amazing, just amazing. We see the *Human Being* there, a creature unfettered by civilization, by all the walls and chains surrounding us. We see the Night there, the deepest wells of existence itself. Perhaps I'm reading too much into it, you know, but in truth I feel I'm way too modest on behalf of the artist…

The journalist's network shelved it. The Phoenix Green Earth Network, however managed, by a fluke to record it and send it during prime time, of course.

A lot of discussion followed, doing so on many levels, both on and off the Internet, and even mainstream, establishment media. They had no choice but to follow suit. They didn't have monopoly or their previous power of censorship anymore.

Nothing was truly shelved anymore.

The four, the true creatures of fire and shadow once again reached out into the world, observing and changing what they observed. It was amazing what they could do together. They were more than the sum of their parts, far more.

A ghost, a spirit from Northfield revisited her husband. He lived in a dump in Kentish Town, North London. She appeared before him the way she had looked when she had been alive, had a body. He attempted to embrace her, but couldn't do that, of course. She soothed him and calmed him down, and they talked, had a low-keyed conversation. It didn't last long, really, just a few minutes or a few hours, but it felt like an eternity. She smiled and faded before his eyes. He picked himself up from that moment on, and decided to change his life.

Things went bump in the night (and day) all over the world, as the spirits moved into their former homes, sometimes without any noticeable effect and sometimes with spectacular, noisy and also violent results.

The entire Green Rose building and the open space at its center at Main Street in Northfield's Oldtown was glowing, pulsing in a ghostly light. People danced and celebrated between tall fires and the heavy raindrops. In the non-existing room number 13 Liz and Ted and Gabi studied her floating crystal balls for hours and hours.

It was intense, a lightshow to rival any they had previously experienced, but they didn't back away from it, but on the contrary dived deeper into it, pushing both themselves and the girl.

She could pretty much reveal the present to them, at least anywhere they told her to look.

The paranormal hotspots were easy to find. A school had burned down, and killed a majority of the students, and they had built another on the same spot. It was the paranormal equivalent of building on a nuclear site. It was now.

The *returning* students sometimes looked just as solid as the current batch, sometimes transparent. Teachers were made to pay, pay a lot. Pranks, also by the living children took off like a rocket.

They saw George W. Bush in his office, the furrow in his brow growing deeper and deeper day by day, as the protests outside his current residence grew to ever bigger proportions.

The past was not much of a problem. She filled in some of the spotty parts of their personal history, making everything clear to them.

The future was an incoherent and distorted jumble.

– It used to be somewhat clear, she said, – at least the more mundane events, but now everything is a cocktail of conflicting glimpses. I could see what the most probable events were at the time. Now, I no longer can.

They saw themselves, Ethel, Nick, Stacy, Jason, Bee, Michelle, Linsey, George W. Bush, McKenzie, Barack Obama, and a string of others, also a lot of people they didn't recognize, some of whom made them very uncomfortable and anxious. But it was impossible to grab one single image and hold on to it.

They watched Corinne Barbeau wake up from a nightmare, soaked in sweat. That image, for some reason lingered longer than the rest.

When Gabi began showing signs of fatigue they stopped, saw no reason to continue.

– We should try again, Gabi stated stubbornly. – I'm certain I can control it.

– We will try again, Liz said, – but later, with a lot of help. You're exhausted, child, and you must rest.

– That's an order, Ted told her sternly, with the look of mischief still infuriating Liz.

– Yes, Phoenix, Gabi acknowledged with hero worship in her eyes.

The sharp, clear air hit them outside. Colder weather had finally come to New England. It was still a fairly high temperature, but nothing even resembling what had dominated the area for so long. They followed the girl to the house further down the street that had once belonged to Laurie Isherwood.

– You *will* be very useful to us, Ted told her, – but only if you take care of yourself.

The girl brightened and ran up the stairs to the house. Not long after she waved excitedly to them from her room. They knew she would go to sleep, sensing her fatigue even at a distance. She was a bright, very bright girl.

They knew her, and by knowing her they knew what she knew, sensed what she sensed. The world transformed around them. No, not the world. Their perception changed. It happened suddenly, and so slowly that they could measure it, quantify it moment by moment as it happened. The street, everything about it, its composition, its smallest parts changed beyond measure in their eyes, their senses.

– Goddess, Ted breathed.

– It's another upgrade. Liz shook her head, in wonder and fear, and beyond fear, and awe, and beyond awe. – But so soon after the previous?

– I don't believe it is, Ted said. – It's just another result of that, another inevitable consequence.

Like one being they glanced at the Hill.

– You know, she mused, – I was going to mention it, mention the fact that its Shadow has seemingly grown since we came here, but I realize now that it is a hopelessly inadequate description.

The others present in the street, inside its houses, both those sensitive and not noticed it. The two Warrens sensed the change through them, saw the two creatures open like a flower, and its red, white and black petals spread through the air, until they began falling and faded, but lingered as they hit the ground.

Frazer Hill cast its long shadow on the totality of Oldtown, but there was a far greater Shadow cast far wider, two distinctive pieces of it mingling, blurring around the edges. Countless eyes looked stricken at it. It seemed to be everywhere and nowhere. Everybody stood perfectly still, frozen in its ember…

… until the illusion faded, and everything seemingly returned to normal.

Everybody approached them. Ethel, they noticed her first. She wasn't here physically, but they saw her as a transparent figure, with an unfathomable expression in her smile. Nick, Jason, Michelle, Everett, Gabi wide awake, Bee and everybody else, physically present and not. They sensed everybody within their inner and outer circle. Lillith sat on her throne at Ravenscourt and smiled affectionately to them.

Stacy stood there, right in front of them, frowning uncertain to them, as they were smiling uncertain to her.

Liz turned to Ted, taking his hands.

– We're becoming *attuned,* she said, – more and more each time. Can't you sense it?

– I can *feel* it, he nodded, – in the deepest bones of my being.

She smiled happily, beyond happy to him.

That night, as the current one hundred gathered around the Round Table the mood and excitement, if that was at all possible ran higher than ever.

– We've always had power, Liz Warren cried, intense even beyond her unusual intensity. – This is true both to those with and without an active, dangerous ability. Power to change both ourselves and the world. Every single human being has that ability to break out of confines, to find power unheard of. We have found it. It is at our fingertips, in the palm of our hand, and in our hearts and minds. At our core we know what it means to be Human. To those among us with doubt, know this: know that there is no longer any logical reason for doubt, not beyond the tiny piece that always will and should be in us all. To those who have despaired for not being in the right place at the right time: know that you have found it, found that moment both without and within yourself. This is it, my friends. These are the final days. This is the Twilight Storm, the end of the horrible unbalance that has so long plagued mankind and our many victims. Know that the best and the worst and everything else are ahead of us…

There was happiness, apprehension, and everything between and beyond surging through the gathering, a low rumble of voices and fevered thoughts and anticipation.

In every little shadow and corner of the great hall, they glimpsed themselves and the world.

7

The hard rain began the next day, an even, steady downpour heralding the late, very late New England fall. It felt weird in a way. The heat had been there so long.

They had been in it for so long. And they knew it would return soon. It was all in their bones.

No matter the heat outside, it could never compete with the boiling blood flowing through their veins.

It was a kind of bittersweet respite this, as they briefly, as much as they could, disregarded the rest of the world, even as they slowly began reaching out to it again in combined increasing efforts.

Stacy's true power was strategy, really, giving the movement an angle, a focus they had previously lacked. She remembered, faintly, clear as night directing *armies* across vast fields.

They remembered her doing it, too.

– Our problem, if it can be said there is one is basically twofold...

She stood before a computerized map of the world, a giant screen, as they had their first strategy meeting. Stewart and Ruth, more comfortable with the fairly new technology than most of them handled the controls.

– The number of warriors at our disposal increases too fast for us. It is, by definition, an uncontrollable situation. We have trouble deciding how to deploy them. There's a problem of logistics, and ultimately, means: What do we truly want and how do we go about achieving it? What will happen when we stop playing around and start doing in earnest?

There it was, out in the open, what had festered under the surface for so long. Ted and Liz glanced at each other without glancing at each other, as was their want, and the beyond powerful chill yet again passed down their spine.

– As you pointed out, my once and future king: we *have* power, also beyond our genetic gifts. For the first time in centuries, we have become a force to be reckoned with in this world. Our pure military power is still not up to par, but it *will be*. So far, we're only one force of many, but that may change, if we so desire...

This was no longer an eighteen-year old girl. Those who had known her in Northfield this fateful fall knew that beyond conviction, now. She had changed. So had they all, but she most of all.

– Thank you; Merlin. Liz clapped her hands in mockery. – An excellent presentation.

That would be the last time that name was mentioned.

– Thank you, my king, Stacy chided and curtseyed.

Lillith, the ancient goddess of the hunter's moon looked at them all, included them in her mighty embrace.

– «Give me a place to stand and I shall move the Earth», Archimedes said. It was firm logic then, and it is, now.

Everybody looked at the left side of the map. They understood. Understanding wasn't hard, wasn't hard at all. Stacy used her powerful mind as a sharp, precise instrument and pushed a few keys on the keyboard, and the landmass that was the United States grew to dominate the image on the screen.

8

Stacy and the rest started training in earnest, training martial arts and similar under the supervision of Linda and Mary and others. They were, like all recent recruits driven beyond exhaustion, mentally and physically.

Days and nights grew to weeks, as they and their powers turned even more into sharpened tools, as their memory and sense of self expanded further, something they would have deemed impossible before experiencing Linda's relentless taunting and teaching.

At the height of winter, Ravenscourt looked more imposing than ever. Looking at it from her position above, all kinds of thoughts crossed Lillith's mind. She levitated above the forest between the castle and the town below. There wasn't ice on Fire Lake, only a little snow here and there on land to mark the brief and practically non-existing winter. She felt the cold, but it didn't bother her anymore, no more than the heat of summer had done.

One casual thought and she descended, and landed on the roof below. She descended the stairs to the attic. The door opened itself to her, closed behind her. Such actions had become second nature to her by now.

She scanned Ravenscourt from its top to its depths and marveled at the variety of powers and people she found. It was like a beehive of activity and life, and it brought a huge smile to her lips.

– Come, she called. – *Come!*

Linsey gave very little outward notice when he heard her call laced with numerous subtexts and layers. That was what telepathy was. Speech was a barrier. With communication mind to mind very few fortifications remained.

She smiled as she entered the cozy room with the large bed and the fireplace, one of the places at Ravenscourt where people could go and have a modicum of privacy. He noticed her smile as he made his way up the stairs. She saw him and sighed in anticipation and impatience. He passed through the giant hall, with its mirrors and large windows. The windows, always open during the warmer parts of the year had now been closed. Then remained only the stretch up the stairs to the attic at the end of the hall.

He entered the room with the large bed and the fireplace. She sat on the bed, nude and seething with desire. His excited state changed to full-blown lust.

The first few signs of her pregnancy had begun revealing themselves, the no longer flat belly, the bigger breasts and wider hips. His mouth turned dry in an instant. She chuckled in his mind. He began undressing, hardly conscious of the act.

She met him at the center of the bed, calmly, but still with the energy of a hungry beast. His eyes flashed in fire. He actually felt it the moment it happened, in a way totally shocking and new to him. She purred in his ear and his mind, while rubbing herself at him, beyond eager. Her Name echoed in his mind like a mantra.

– Lillith, he mumbled. – Lillith, Lillith, Lil Lith…

– Kas Ken, she mumbled against his shoulder. – Kas Ken, Kas Ken, Kas Ken

He froze. Suddenly, he was Open, and stared horrified and beyond fascinated at the Universe, the Earth and existence itself at his feet.

– Yes, she said softly, – you finally remember who you are.

Her black eyes twinkled while meeting his.

They focused solely on each other. The world faded, memory faded, until nothing remained but the burning need. He pushed her forward, on all fours, grabbed her hips and pushed himself deep within her. Her moan rose and descended, and everybody within miles heard it and sensed it, and felt it physically, and if they hadn't been used to being in a state of heightened arousal all of them would have jumped each other instantly. Now, when some of them did so, they did so a bit more somberly, somewhat in «control» of themselves. The ravens squeaked and flapped their wings. Ravenscourt itself stretched its walls and twinkled in shadow.

Stacy rode Linsey, hard and ferocious. She dug her claws deep within him, but he could take it, and return in kind. They choired their growls and moans, wild and passionate, making the castle, and the ground beneath it tremble and shake. She shouted loud in her ecstasy when she came, and he did, too. The flames of the fireplace stretched and danced, and at one, finite point engulfed the room. She fell on him, as they both fell, into the far depths of past-climax.

– Goddess! He gasped, listening to his own voice from far away. – Goddess!

She grinned in mischief, as she slipped close to him, as she kissed him somewhat softly, as she cuddled in his arms. Her chuckle echoed through the caves and between the walls of Ravenscourt.

They rested there, relaxing, playing with each other's skin and hair and limbs.

– They heard us, didn't they? He said hoarsely. – Felt us, all of them?

– They sure did, she chuckled.

And her chuckle was like water hitting an underground sea, spreading like circles in a pond, but growing stronger as it spread, not weaker, an ongoing explosion in the waves of the world.

– It is comparable to what Beth does, when she's fucking, but her effect is mostly physical and mental. Yours are deeper, affecting everything we are, like the sea compared to the wave.

– Lillith is Magick, Stacy said somberly. – She will always be Magick incarnated.

He hesitated, and had halfway made up his mind not to say anything when he noticed that she looked at him with her penetrating eyes and knowing smile.

– How is it, to… be two people in one head, to integrate that into your personality?

– You forget several things here, my sweet and horrible Kas Ken…

He was overwhelmed by a flood of memories, all those he so far had failed to acknowledge, and fresh sweat covered his body in the course of a single moment.

– I'm not two people, but three, and I have hundreds of personalities integrated in one, something you will have, too, quite soon. And to answer your query: it feels good, feels like having devoured countless flavors of ice cream in one bite. I'm finally myself again. After countless lives where a part of me was missing, I'm now whole and hearty again.

She was warm, so very warm. He burned himself on her skin and her mind, her seething Shadow.

– The waiting is done, she declared. – All our failures, all the lost battles no longer matter because we're here, and we're alive, and one major obstacle has been removed from the board, and we have one final chance to get it right.

He shivered, as if there was a draft from behind, pulling at him.

And then he realized that there was truly a draft from behind, that the door was open, and he turned around, and saw Betty stand there with lowered eyes, waiting to be acknowledged.

Stacy waved to her, signing for her come, to join them.

And Betty did, closing the door. She removed her scant clothing during the first three steps of the ten she used to reach the bed. The marble skin glowed bathed in the fire, and its color was virtually indistinct from that of her hair. She crawled into the bed and snuggled against them both, kissing first Stacy on the lips and then him, uncharacteristically shy and reserved.

– Thank you, Beloved Infernal Mother.

Linsey realized that she was sincere, that she wasn't kidding in any way.

– Why are you behaving like that? He asked abruptly, irritated.

She looked bewildered at him, striving to explain the unexplainable.

– What do you expect? Stacy said. – She's in the presence of her Goddess, and she knows her place.

He wanted to comment on that, say something, anything, but his surroundings were overwhelming him. With awakening came even greater awareness. He found Betty smiling at him, more beautiful and sensual than he could remember seeing her.

The three bodies sought closer. Betty rubbed her butt at him, slowly, deliberately, as she began kissing and fondling Stacy. He turned hard in an instant and pushed forward, and hit between Betty's thighs, hitting the mark at first attempt and penetrated deep within her, and she gasped close to Stacy's lips, and Stacy gasped, too, and the big female looked like an eighteen-year-old girl again. Their minds mingled as their bodies did, and sounds of the house and its dungeons echoed in his head stronger and stronger and stronger, until all three of them crouched there, entangled, resting in its each other's arms, totally spent.

Ravenscourt itself rested, briefly, as its residents did, breathing with them, its breath shaking the treetops, as the snow melted as fast as it hit the ground, as the tall fires in the great cave hall hissed and danced, and the night turned to day, and more stirrings of mankind's true new age asserted themselves.

CHAPTER FOURTEEN
The Shining Ones

Cole Stephenson sat in the backseat of his luxurious six-door limousine. The car's movement was hardly noticeable to him. Whatever outside influence there might be didn't reach his spot in the moving vehicle.

The car had one-way mirror windows. He could see out. No one could look in, like some raffle enjoyed trying to do each time the car stopped for red light. The female driver handled the car like a pro. It pleased him how well trained she was.

She was dressed in her blue uniform, one he knew displayed her body well. The face he glimpsed in the mirror was painted and unmoving, like a mask.

On the right side of her neck, by the single plaid was tattooed a millipede. The sight sent a thrill of excitement through him. It always did and never got old in his mind.

People passed by outside. They glanced at the car on occasion, but even though some was angry, they made no attempt at doing anything to utilize their anger. Everybody… or almost everybody was well trained.

Another brief smile touched his lower face.

A cluster of tall buildings rose in front of him. The silent driver took off from the road. Stephenson hardly noticed the turn. The car dived under the street's surface. A door opened in the wall, and they drove inside the private garage complex.

Eleven other cars had been parked at the far wall. He took his designated place as twelve.

A woman, a drifter peeked in, just as the door closed comfortably behind him. Two bullets penetrated her, one through the head and another through the heart. He saw it on his watch monitor.

The snipers were in place. He noticed them, even as he ignored them. They didn't bother him, but comforted him. Two spotters moved in and removed the body, everything proceeding in a fast and efficient manner. No one saw anything or noticed anything, and if they did, they would be dealt with.

The driver opened the door for him, and he disembarked the car. She stood straight until he had stepped away from the car. Then she closed the door.

– Thank you, Alpha One, he said absentmindedly.

He knew he didn't imagine it when he saw love and devotion in her eyes.

His focus shifted quickly to the blank wall to his right.

He walked to the designated, unobtrusive spot so clear in his mind. There was nothing there, nothing an untrained mind would notice.

– Who are we? A voice spoke from the wall. – Who do we serve?

His response came easy, unconcerned and passionate.

– «Humanity is a garden, a city, the cold flame deprived of the true light».

A low click reached his ears. A low hum supplanted it, as the wall slid aside and revealed an elevator. He stepped inside, followed by Alpha One. There was no panel, no buttons anywhere. Everything was smooth in here. The wall slid back in place. There was a slight pull, as the small casket rose, and they were being transported to the designated floor.

Muted electrical lights met them in the hallway upstairs. As they walked further down the corridor, as they penetrated deeper into what revealed itself to be a Roman/Greek setting, all electrical lights faded away, and only natural lights remained. There were sentries here, pointing the way, but they were blind, their head covered from the neck up, gasping, as they strived to breathe through the fabric covering their open mouth.

The loud sound of their breathing made a grin break on Stephenson's face.

He was given the hood and robe at the final door. At the sentries' humble and respectful insistence, he allowed himself to be dressed.

In a circle-round room with no windows the Roman/Greek theme permeated everything. The few candles and torches illuminated the twelve chairs. Eleven chairs had been filled. Stephenson sat down in the twelfth. The thirteenth chair at the center was empty. The twelve all wore a hood and a robe. Behind each of them stood an unmovable figure.

No one said a word or even moved very much. One of them, Dusan Machajev glanced at his watch, then clearly catching himself and rejoining the others in their stoic appearance.

The thirteenth chair by the altar remained empty.

A bell began tolling. It was an actual bell, not a recording, a deep, potent sound, making the room and entire building shake. The torches and candles flickered. The bell tolled thirteen times.

Silence reigned in the room and within the circle.

The twelve people rose, practically simultaneously.

Stephenson took one half-step forward, a little hesitant. The others nodded, encouraging him. Stephenson nodded to them, to himself.

– Humanity is a garden, a city, the cold flame deprived of the true light, he began.
– We are the Abraxas Omega - The All and the End, humanity's true destiny.

He paused. He stood still, deliberately, looking at each and every one of those in the circle.

– We first met in this circle, this Hall of Power, eons ago. We are meeting still.

He and the circle repeated his words, shouting them, a catching noticeable in their combined voice.

– WE ARE MEETING STILL!

– We are the arm, the hand, the finger, the foot of the thousand, the thousand real people of the world. Our symbol is the Millipede, because that's what we are, a thousand feet marching united towards our manifest destiny.

– MANIFEST DESTINY

– We are those illuminating the shadows, those shining the light in the night. We shall persevere. We were present at King Arthur's table, when the church fathers met in Nicaea, at the last supper of Christ, in the golden halls of Egypt. Our ways are unchanging. We are eternal.

– ETERNAL

They returned to their chairs.

Silence returned to the Hall of Power, for one, two five seconds.

– Our fears have been realized, Stephenson said. – We have observed the customary time period, and can only reach the worst possible conclusion: Our Esteemed Leader has been taken off the board.

– I concur, the tall man on the left stated. – It's the only viable conclusion.

– There is great unrest in the flock, Machajev agreed.

The others noted a clear ironic twist in his voice, but chose to ignore it.

– That is usually the case when a major player is removed, the female on the right said, – and this event is comparable to a major earthquake. The state of affairs is usually normalizing itself within a given timeframe, as the quake is absorbed by the rest of the members of the Council, and the countermeasures in place.

– I will put it to you, though, Stephenson said, – that these are extraordinary circumstances.

– I will agree with that assessment, the woman said.

– And then there is the matter of who is behind it, the man sitting opposite Stephenson growled. – Behind the… disturbance.

– Because of the Leader's regrettable insistence on secrecy, a matter I raised with him in private a few times there's no way of knowing for sure, but there aren't that many candidates, are there?

They nodded to each other.

– In this man's opinion the time is now ripe for implementing the emergency protocols. Do I have the assembly's support in this?

– All of them? A woman to the left wondered.

– No. Stephenson shook his head. – Only those we are required to implement when a Leader is gone. I see no justification for further action at this point.

– At this point?

She needled him. That was pretty clear. He chose to ignore it.

– Yes, he replied. – We will be on high alert for years to come, preparing for possible aftershocks, of course.

– Of course, she acknowledged.

– It is such a gloriously efficient system, he shrugged. – It has worked well for centuries and has been constantly perfected, even as the Cabal's total control over the world has inevitably slipped, to a degree where we guide instead of rule.

– It was inevitable, the man on the left nodded. – The world has long since grown too big, too uncontrollable for the old ways to work properly.

– So, Cole Stephenson pushed on, – do I have your support?

– You have it, the man on the left said.

The others mumbled or nodded or in other ways voiced or showed their agreement.

The meeting was adjourned.

2

Early spring changed to early, full-blown summer.

Stacy had a big belly, like many other females in the transformed city of Northfield. Her breasts and throat felt sore, and just standing felt like an effort, the act of moving like an art. Watching herself in the mirror she saw how big she truly was, bigger than even Tamara and Beth, who were a lot taller than even she was. Malvin, the big black, still not quite adult cat rubbed himself at her legs, purring loud and intense, demanding attention. Bending down to scratch his ear was an effort, so she didn't and did the deed with her mind. It didn't spook him, like it would some animals. He had grown used to it since he had been a kitten.

She found herself in the living room, in the house on Main Street, Laurie's old home. It was well insulated. The sounds from the busy street didn't really reach her, but practically everything reached her mind. She watched Martin and Lydia through the window. They were making out to the enjoyment of everybody present, and several couples joined in on the fun.

It was all wonderfully bashful and carefree, and felt good to watch, to behold and experience, without the shame still so prevalent in society as a whole.

She faced the mirror, studying herself. The face had become slightly bloated, but kept its youthful, innocent form, even with the heavy makeup. A frown disrupted the harmony, like a rock hitting a still water. She turned abruptly and walked with quick steps to the bathroom. Hands found the tap and turned it. Water flooded the sink. She bent down and cleaned her face, rubbed it and washed it until she could spot not a single residual spot of the makeup. The face looked both more innocent and mature. Black, wicked eyes grinned with the mouth to haunt her. She grabbed a towel and began drying herself, both the hair and the skin. Hands brushed and combed the hair almost by themselves. She used both a comb and a brush. It took a while before she was somewhat pleased, but when she returned to the living room she was somewhat mellow, somewhat relaxed. She faced the mirror again, studying herself, the alien and yet so familiar features.

Sensitive fingertips touched the small statue of Janus on the shelf. Her skin still tingled when she touched it. They had thrown out a lot of Laurie's stuff when they… remade the house, but had kept things such as this. She looked at the dipole faces, seemingly opposites, identical twins in the mirror.

Lillith's two current «maids», Lydia and Ruth approached the door, Lydia's face and mind glowing from the recent fucking. She opened it to them, granting them access to Lillith Raven Moonstar's chambers. They entered the room. She saw her back through their eyes, experienced herself through their senses. When she turned, they appropriately curtsied. She nodded, even though she wanted to shake her head.

— May I touch it? Lydia asked, breathing a little faster in Lillith's presence, like most people did.

Stacy nodded. Lydia reached out a hand and touched her belly.

— There *are* two, she exclaimed brightly.

It wasn't strange that she, a powerful telepath could sense that. Stacy had for months sensed two distinctive thought-patterns in there.

– Yes, two, Stacy said. – One from each body, from different fathers. It's a «miracle» that they survived the transition, the strain, but they did.

They looked at her in awe. It wasn't often the theme of her unique origin came up.

She sensed her two daughters in there, saw through their eyes, as they floated through the darkness. They were half-sisters, and didn't resemble each other more than siblings usually did, but they would still be born as twins, and share a unique bond their entire lives.

You will never be separated, she told them, but live your life in fierce harmony and calm fire.

They understood her. Yet, they didn't. How could they, without the experience tinged with sadness and loss she could never truly share with them.

She noticed the very characteristic shimmer in the air, like she always did the moment before Gabi appeared, followed by Tamara, the giant towering above them all.

– It's time, Raven, the girl stated calmly, just after she had stepped down on the floor.

– Everything is ready?

– Everything is beyond ready.

The girl's face cracked in a smile. Stacy sensed how deep that smile was, and nodded pleased to herself. Only occasionally discontent and sullen thoughts flashed through Gabi's mind. She was loyal and dedicated. Stacy was pleased with her.

– Let's walk today, Stacy decided. – It's such a beautiful day.

The sense of disappointment and of being let down instantly flashed through Gabi, but Stacy had been prepared for that, and countered it with a soft touch of her hand and her mind. The girl knew what she was doing, and reacted with both gratitude and annoyance.

Her skin was almost as pale as Betty's, and not because it was her natural color.

You hardly go outside anymore, Stacy told her gently.

You don't have to worry about me, the oracle snorted. I can take care of myself.

Not if you're behaving like a little child, you can't, Lillith scolded her.

It couldn't be said to be a battle of wills. The young teenager bared her neck almost instantly. She shook a bit before relenting, before submitting to her superior.

I'm sorry, Raven, sorry, sorry, but it's so hard sometimes.

I know. C'mon, let's go.

Tamara hardly knew that anything had happened. Ruth and Lydia did, of course, but in this case, they didn't betray any outward emotion.

They stepped outside. The hot wind and the heat from the gathered crowd struck them like lukewarm waves on the beach. Stacy wasn't really worried, even if there were quite a few new arrivals present. There always were.

She and her protectors kept their guard up. They always did.

What had been left of the school and the church had been torn down and removed now. In the buildings' place were only more trees, plants and fresh, green grass.

She spotted Udo in the crowd. He was alone, or rather away from anyone else in

74

the tribe, in the extended clan. She felt a sting of worry as she walked to him, as she cautiously took him into her embrace.

– Why don't you come with us? She asked him gently.

He followed them, more out of it than she had ever sensed him. She felt helpless in his presence. He seemed to slip farther into disarray for each passing day. She had made an effort to help him, but in his madness, he had become one of those people close to inaccessible to her. His mind seemed able to change just as much or even more than his body.

The crowd followed them on their path through Northfield, like they always did. Raven Lillith Moonstar enjoyed their presence, their close proximity. The sideshow of the ravens joined them, landing and staying on people's shoulders. They squeaked and flapped their wings occasionally, but they mostly stayed quiet and calm, a fact that didn't fail to make an impression on people.

It was a spectacle, though, inevitably, of another world.

– Can you sense it? Gabi asked excitedly.

– I can, Stacy confirmed.

– I can sense it, Gabi kept talking, distracted scratching the raven on her shoulder, – sense the veil, the wide-open doors. I can feel spirits as they slip through, as they are headed for the pale shadow in there. An old woman is dying, taking her final breath right now. She leaves her husk behind and cross the boundaries to the Far Lands.

Stacy sensed it, not with Oracle's precision and accuracy, but her perception had been vastly extended since their return from the shadow world. Distance and measurement had, like her transformed into something new and different.

The distance to the end of the street wasn't exactly the five steps her body and mind measured. It seemed like more, much more, even though her feet didn't use more than five steps to reach it. Space folded in on itself many times around her. Logic stated that her perception had changed, not the reality, but she wasn't absolutely confident that this was the case.

She saw the city as a painting, but it wasn't really a city anymore, but a collection of houses and trees and fields in a strange, vibrant expression. The creatures in hood and robe, and also others nodded to her and danced and swayed in her vision. Happy chills flowed down her spine.

Red flower petals fell to the ground. They weren't «real», weren't part of others' perception, but they were there, speaking to her loud and clear. She shivered and couldn't hide it. The tall, skinny kid by her side rubbed her shoulder and comforted her somewhat.

– I visit them, Gabi said, – some of them.

– You're doing what? Stacy said.

– I visit them when they die. I point them to the pale shadow.

Lillith saw it in her thoughts. Gabi showed her, focused on her memories, making it easier to read her chaotic mind.

– You play the Angel of Death?

– No, the girl said shocked, then catching herself, frowning. – Or maybe I am, a little.

Stacy shook her head in amazement and released a pleased chuckle.

– I didn't think I could be surprised anymore, but you certainly surprised me.

The girl blushed in happiness.

– Is that good or bad.

The grown woman hesitated just a bit.

– I don't know.

Then she shrugged.

– Don't overdo it, okay?

– I won't, Gabi said. – Honest!

– Very good, little priestess.

She rubbed the Oracle's pale and blushing cheeks.

An image, unbidden returned to Lillith, of the sweet, young priestess before her turning into a demonic, sadistic creature.

Suddenly suspicion rode her, rode her hard, and she looked at Gabi, and made her blush even harder, and she sensed shame in her surface thoughts.

– I take from them, the girl whispered.

– You... *take* from them? Stacy said, unable to keep the anger, contempt, condemnation and shock from manifesting in her voice and presence.

Gabi shrunk in her tracks, quite removed from the demonic creature from Lillith's dream.

– Only a little, as they pass me on their Journey. It strengthens me. I need it to help Ted... Phoenix, help you and all of us. Opening and closing portals are... taxing.

Stacy relaxed, even though she was still breathing faster and the calm returned slowly.

– I'm only borrowing it, you know, the girl said, braver and even bold when she sensed acceptance. – Like I did with the praying from the church.

The two of them kept walking. Most of the people watching didn't notice anything different.

Lillith pulled the girl into her mindscape, casually. The girl faced the undiluted presence of Lillith - Mother of Demons, with no physical restraints keeping her from seeing the Shadow. Lillith stood there, watching her calmly, not scolding her, but allowing her to see and sense the concern fully.

– When you're tired you tell us. You are valuable to us all, a jewel, but you are not our slave, are not an object we can or will command at the expense of your... health.

– You were prepared to sacrifice me, *Moonstar*, Gabi said inflamed, – and I agreed. No sacrifice is too big, too much.

In here, there was no hiding. The girl's anger and more was notable, palatable, like a red glow, an eye stabbing Lillith all over her Shadow.

– Yes, it is, Lillith said softly. – I realized that, almost too late.

They were back in the warm sunshine.

– Don't overdo it, she told the girl lightly. – Don't cross the line.

There was no implied threat there, it hadn't come to that, only a calm warning, one born of concern. Gabi acknowledged the difference with a nod.

– I won't, Raven. Honest! You will be pleased with me, I promise.

Stacy sighed. The ravens did, too, expressing her emotion, as they always did. People took pictures.

– Perhaps we should charge a fee? Tamara said brightly.

The world reentered Stacy's surroundings. She realized startled that it had been gone for quite a while, and couldn't decide if she or Gabi had done that.

The heat reentered her body, warmed chilled bones.

They approached the bus station, a building, like all buildings in Northfield vastly different from how it had appeared six months earlier. Ahead was an almost closed-off alley of trees and growth inside a building, where they would have appeared, if Gabi had transported them, the waystation by the waystation. They walked through it. The plants shivered, when she, their maker passed through. From there it was only a short distance, a small plaza or field to cross to the actual station.

Betty waited for them, for her outside. She called attention to herself, as she always did, but now more than ever, with her deep-red and revealing clothes matching her hair, looking very much like the warrior witch Lillith remembered.

– Greetings, Beloved Infernal Mother.

She curtseyed deeply.

– Greetings, sister, Stacy replied softly.

The girl, the experienced woman rose to full height with a question in her eyes.

– The past is gone, Stacy stated, emphasized. – The future is now. Let it begin.

– Make it so, Betty whispered.

They kissed, lips to lips, burning flame, dancing shadow, hair and skin mingling and mixing. The two entered the way-station side by side, Betty shivering, waxing and waning at the other's right hand.

The small group stood by the bus, turning their heads before the new arrivals emerged.

– Mother of day, mother of night, Ted cried out for all to hear, greeting her.

Stacy acknowledged him with a nod and a playful smile.

Liz was there, too, a little more in the background right then, but soon reentering the center stage.

Gabi ran to them, her face glowing in adulation and hero-worship.

Linsey was there, and Everett, too. Stacy greeted them both in equal measure, giving them her attention and affection, before turning towards Liz and Ted.

– Lillith is ready, she declared, – to begin her Journey in the modern world.

The crowd gathered around them. People's excitement and enthusiasm filled her and strengthened her and empowered her in countless ways, but also unnerved her a little, and she looked exasperated at Ted.

– Okay, he said, speaking up, – who wants to join us on our little expedition?

Everybody raised their hands and cried out.

– I regret to inform you that the bus only has room for five more, he said. – Lillith will now choose between all her present worthy companions.

Thank you, Ror Ken, she acknowledged. You were always good at this.

She filled him and Liz in about the recent development concerning Gabi the Oracle, while she walked among her worshippers, her subjects, her fellow warriors and fiery human beings.

I did sense it, she told them, did sense something, but only at the edge of my consciousness. Gabi is very intelligent and mature, very cunning, almost cruel in her approach to everything she does. I think, I do believe she's telling me, telling us two things, one more fact in addition to the obvious: She's informing us that she could have hidden it from us if she wanted to, so eager to prove herself.

She stopped in front of a boy, choosing him among many, making him glow in love and dedication, forever hers, forever her knight. This was an excellent opportunity to scan all of them and she did. There were no fakes among them, no one even raising her suspicion. She picked three boys and two girls at random, sensing Ror Ken's approval.

There was none or little resentment in those not chosen. She scanned for that, too. They were all like open books to her. Good wishes were directed at those entering the bus.

They are innocent, Ror Ken, way too much so.

That will be taken care of shortly, he replied. They're new and haven't started on our training program yet.

I'm certain they will enjoy that, she snorted.

Just like you did?

His full laughter warmed her some more.

It was so crazy, so devil-may-care, so full of life.

She recalled the training, its brutality and hardship, its almost sadistic teaching.

They boarded the bus. It was fairly ordinary, but had some features they didn't broadcast, like electronic detection equipment. Lydia sat down in the control chair, and turned the satellite feed and all the other stuff on.

– I'm so happy that we leave as little as possible to coincidence's mercy, she told them all, imposing on those among them fairly unaware of the potential dangers the necessity of caution. – I approve.

She had learned that, both in this life and all the previous.

Paul, the driver started the engine. The doors closed and the vehicle rolled out of the building, the no longer so busy bus station. They met another bus on their way out, one of the few arriving today.

– All the buses are ours, right? Tamara asked.

– There are exceptions, Betty replied, – but they are few, and we have pretty good control of them, too. All of ours come from Boston. This way we can limit the flow a bit, or Northfield would be full in weeks. As it is now we manage to train and send off almost as many as we receive.

– To conquer the world, Gabi stated proudly.

The bus left the green and lush town and started on its Journey south.

3

Stacy and Betty sat in the backseat, clearly enjoying each other's company. Betty played the guitar, A hard rain's a-gonna fall by Bob Dylan and they both sang, a very cheerful version, Stacy with a woefully inadequate developed voice. The rest of the travelers studied them in awe for a while, before they joined in, and the song filled the bus and the minds and Shadow of everybody present.

At least some of those present dried tears of laughter and poignancy afterwards.

Linsey sought out Ted, waiting for what he deemed to be the right moment. Ted looked at him, waiting with infinite patience, making the other look flustered away.

– I can't choose between them.

Linsey shook his head in despair.

– Why choose at all? Ted shook his head in disgust. – Is that notion so far away in your mind? Haven't you learned anything yet?

There was a slight pause before Warren shrugged.

– Choose not to choose.

Boston was first stop on their Journey. They didn't drive to the bus station, but to the Phoenix Green Earth house by the wharf area. Construction crews were busy all along their route and they would guess all over the city. Almost six months after Anton's ravages there was still a lot of work left before reconstruction would be anywhere near complete.

– The ruins of a major modern city, Stacy mused. – Such an exciting, consoling sight, isn't it?

They agreed, voicing their agreement in loud shouts and cries.

– It's so comforting, Ted said, – knowing that the seemingly vast forces standing against us are nothing compared to what is aiding us.

Elmore and Celeste and their coven, and all the rest that had joined the Boston chapter of Phoenix Green Earth lately welcomed them, as they stepped off the bus and headed inside. Everybody stared at them with wet eyes, but did no more than that.

– No kneeling? Liz chided them. – Very good!

– We use your teaching to steel ourselves, Goddess, Elmore said, – to fight, faced with your Might against the overwhelming need to crawl at your feet, against the inevitable sense of inferiority.

– I like him, Liz grinned.

– They recognize you for what you are, Phoenix, Betty said, – like most of our kind the moment they meet you face to face. They know that the ancient prophecies aren't only true, but were modest compared to the reality. One of you would have been something in itself, but there's a score of you.

Yes, the meeting started, as they often did with reverence, but changed, quickly, like most gatherings they visited to a more informal setting, where a strange scenery of relative normality asserted itself.

But most went without saying in this assembly. Quite a few of those present understood, at least to a point. They were witches in fact, as well as name, like most of those visiting.

There was dinner, and performances and deep-felt conversation and conviction, in the anticipation of the evening and deep night.

– It always ends up with fucking, a girl whispered to the boy on her left.

She reddened when glancing in Stacy's direction. Stacy couldn't stop herself from grinning.

It turned dark quickly. The remaining of the day just flew away. They sat inside, in the living room, in the hall. Those living here gathered in a circle around the visitors, looking at them with the shiny eyes they recognized so easily.

– Thank you, Stacy said to Elmore, a bit ironic, – this actually reminds me a bit about ancient Egypt.

– We thought it might serve you, Your Highness, he bowed.

Stacy, the soon to be nineteen-year-old girl, felt both embarrassed and pleased, both like Stacy and Lillith, and it didn't really create any conflict in her.

– Surely this time we have the tools, both in terms of numbers and power and skill to make true our desires?

A girl stood up proudly, striking her chest, looking humbly at the visitors.

– We have become a force in our own right, Ted acknowledged, – have become the powerful wave we dreamed about becoming, but let's not forget that it isn't the first time. We've failed so many times, even beyond victory. More is needed, much more to push beyond any expectation, to a way of life that won't just last a few years, a thousand years, but *forever*.

They spoke it, breathed it with him, his words as familiar as breathing.

He sat still, seemingly fairly relaxed, but they imagined they saw him standing, his fist raised in front of him, his eyes burning, seething, like the dusk sun setting in the ocean in the far west.

– Forever is such a big word, the girl said weakly, – but I believe it, believe it when you say it.

She raised her glass to him, they all did. The red wine flowed down her throat, more than a little bit of it ending up outside her mouth, on her jaw and chest.

She's yours, Betty told him, yours to do with as you please. They all are. With just a few well-placed words, without your powers, you made them yours, erasing any doubt they might have entertained. I love you, My Lord.

He stood up. Everybody looked at him, beyond attentive and dedicated.

– The tyranny surrounding us will retaliate. It will have no choice, as our influence grows, as it will do, as it will explode in the coming years. We have, for so long been reluctant, afraid to do what's necessary, but as we now let go of our reluctance, our fears everything will explode in the cauldron human life truly is. The upcoming major confrontation is inevitable. And when it comes there's no way we will be able to protect you, if any of you have ever entertained such hopes. We have done our best to prepare you for what's coming, but know that it will never be sufficient. It is in that moment we will all be tested, beyond endurance and will and strength.

Everybody drank their glasses empty and put them back down. Betty walked around and put water in the glasses. A lot of those present stared incredulous at her.

80

Stacy walked in her tracks. She put up an index finger to them, evoking their attention. A wound opened up in her palm. One single drop hit the water in the glasses. The water began boiling, expanding, flooding the glasses and the table. They looked mesmerized at it, at her.

– Drink and be merry, she cried, as she released a drop of blood in the last glass.

They did, emptying their glasses to the last drop, and stared absolutely astonished at each other and her when it was done.

And then the fluid, the blood, the wine exploded within them, spread to every corner of their being. Those with powers began exhibiting them in totally uncontrollable ways, and those without felt a sense of being, of themselves they couldn't possibly compare to anything in their existence before this very moment.

Everyone was drawn into Lillith's mindscape, her sense of the room and the gathering, and when Ted and Liz and the others joined in, everything transformed yet again. Stacy, Liz and Ted stood there, shadowing everyone else, totally dominating everybody's perception, and gasps of horror and delight and marvel filled the room, and the infinity within each human being present.

Everyone was exposed as the creatures they were, unable to hide anything of themselves, and certainly not to the Shadow roaming and surveying their being.

The trio in their midst spoke to them without audible voice, even without thought

No matter where you go from now on, Children of the Midnight Fire, of the Sherwood Forest, no matter how lonely you will feel, we will be there with you, for all your upcoming days and nights.

Ted undressed, and he wasn't merely removing his clothes, but… unfolding himself to them, revealing what rested underneath. They might have believed that they had known what he and Lillith and the rest were, but that had just been a pale, very pale imitation of how they truly looked like.

Perhaps we should have held ourselves back, Liz said to them. Perhaps we should have hidden ourselves from your view, but we trust you to handle it, trust you not to shrink to whimpering worshippers in our presence, when you behold the Human Being's potential in all its magnificence.

Something happened then, something more, and she blinked, he blinked in surprise, but shrugged it off, as the events of the night proceeded to what had been described as a foregone conclusion every time the Janus Clan visited their supporters.

They fucked, fucked all night long, mated in an endless sea of bodies until dawn and beyond, until their state of extreme awareness faded into a pleasant haze of endless dreams.

4

WASHINGTON DC
APRIL 4, 2006

Liz blinked, Ted blinked, and their ongoing transformation took yet another dramatic turn.

– It was as if I could truly both hear and convey thoughts there, she said. – I know we were swept into Stacy's powerful mind, but that didn't feel like it was all there was to it at all.

– I know! Ted nodded. – I felt it, too.

– We *are* becoming synchronized, she whispered in his arms. – I despaired because I feared it would never happen. And what's more: the period of us being powerless, if it is there at all, is becoming increasingly short and insignificant. I felt a bit weak on the bus just before we arrived in Boston, or what in hindsight may be interpreted as such, but that was all.

She sighed in happiness, and he found himself responding in kind.

They left the bed and dressed. The house itself was fairly quiet, but there was quite the ruckus outside, where «journalists» and establishment media had gathered since early in the morning, and been basically ignored by those inside. Ted and Liz walked downstairs. The guys received them with smiles and various types of greetings.

– There you are, Stacy said. – We feared for a moment you wouldn't make it…

There were a few dozen people gathered in the building's entrance hall. This was a fairly mundane bunch, not a society of witches, like in Boston and some of the other branches of Phoenix Green Earth they had visited. They didn't have the actual ability to see the travelers for what they truly were.

But the taint of worship was still very much present in their eyes.

– Are we ready? Stacy asked those present and replied to her own question. – We are ready! Grant entrance to our guests of dishonor then.

Lydia and Ruth opened the big doors and the press rushed inside.

– Calm down people, Tamara told them. – There is more than enough room for everybody and no need to rush anything. Please be calm and follow the proceedings in silence and contemplation. Take your pictures and record your images and sound, but no flashlights or artificial lighting, please.

It was in the middle of the day, but in spite of this the torches seemed to illuminate the hall and its gathering in far more potent ways than the sunshine outside.

The giant elf facing them was enough to give them pause, to momentarily stop the newshounds in their zeal. The rest the room and its strange mood did.

And then there was the sight of Stacy Larkin, Linsey Kendall, Everett Moran and Betty Morgan on the low podium by the stairs.

Gabrielle Asteroth entered the podium with flowers in her hands and in her hair. The stage was set.

Almost the entire bunch from Northfield and London was here. Nick was the only one playing, playing his haunting tune.

Stacy was still dressed in a robe and hood, but one far more elaborate and expensive. It was heavier, for one thing, black, with deep red and green thin and thick strands, sewn into the fabric. Her big belly was totally exposed, and the breasts and hips were also prominently shown, though in a subtle way. Her face and all exposed skin had been painted in the Janus Clan's tribal colors and shapes. Ruth and Lydia had spent hours painting her this morning.

So, what do you think? Lydia asked her.

It's very elaborate and beautiful, Stacy replied. Thank you.

The others on the podium had also been painted, but not to the same degree.

– I am Thalama, the Gypsy Queen, she called to those that didn't belong. – I welcome you to our little soirée.

Stacy, the mimic had a great moment when she made a perfect imitation of Laura Bush…

Then she turned to her companions on the podium. The music changed, turning somber, even more haunting. She grabbed Linsey's hands, meeting his eyes with a steady, though intense look.

– We are human beings, she said, – such as it should be. Under the Moon's many faces, eyes stretching into darkness I take you as my current mate.

She picked one flower from the bouquet in Gabi's hands and handed it to him. He grabbed it just as she let go.

His eyes twinkled and burned her so pleasantly.

– Under the Moon, I accept, he said.

And what he added with his mind, without the barrier of speech was so much more.

She kissed him on the lips, standing there, enjoying the moment.

Then she turned to Betty. The redhead blushed, and the low hum from those that didn't belong turned loud and noisy.

– Under another face of the Moon I take you as well, Thalama, the Gypsy Queen stated sweetly.

– Under another of your faces, Queen of the Hunt, I accept, Betty said softly, a tear in her eye.

Accepting the flower the Moon handed her.

Then the Moon changed face again, facing Everett.

– And know that I renew my pledge to you, my love, she said, – if you still want me.

– I do, he said, with a voice perhaps even a tad hoarser than after their first mating. – You're different, but the same.

– And so, my King, are you.

The music faded slowly to nothing, and the low in the hall grew ascendant. The applause among her kin started slowly, and stayed muted, but happy. She loved it every time hands met and parted. That, too faded, faded from her ears, not from her mind and Shadow.

She turned and faced the spectators with cameras and microphones and all that.

– I will now answer a few questions, she said.

A barrage, a deluge assaulted her. She waited patiently until it turned quiet again.

– Yes, Morgan, she said, – what is it that you want to ask me?

He frowned because she knew his name, but quickly recovered his fairly professional stance.

– Given the fact that polygamy is illegal in this country, what kind of reaction do you expect from the authorities?

– As long as they don't acknowledge the legality of the ceremony and me as a priestess with power to marry people, I'm certainly not losing any sleep over it. I wouldn't anyway, but as things stand, I see even less reason to care.

– So, you don't see your… pledges as valid, as true, then?

– I see them as far more true than stupid church vows or ordinary civil pledges, she shrugged. – We don't need a signed paper to confirm our emotions. We know!

They got the distinction of the one word. A few were laughing. Morgan wasn't.

– Next question… Louise?

– I understand that the Larkin family fortune now is being administered by the Phoenix Green Earth foundation?

– That's old news.

There was more deliberate shrugging.

– It doesn't bother you, doing that with your inheritance?

This time there was no shrugging.

– It's being put to good use, to counteract the insane ventures other fortunes are spent on, among other things.

The young woman handled the sharks like a pro, and made them eat of her hand. Afterwards, they could never quite put their finger on what had happened, exactly what she had done.

– Luanne?

– Who's the father?

Luanne asked sheepishly.

– I don't know. It could be anyone in a pool of hundreds…

Luanne did not ask any follow-up question.

The «press conference», séance ended. Stacy pulled back with a sardonic smile playing on her lips.

The four walked up the stairs, fondling and caressing each other as they did. Thalama turned once and waved. The others didn't.

Not long after that screams of delight reached the gathering from the attic, heard by people all over the house and on the streets outside.

The night descended on the house not that far from Pennsylvania Avenue and the reddish light and shadows cast by the torches grew even longer. The four returned from the upper floor to the late dining, not having showered, stinking of body juices.

– The media has left again, I see, Stacy said lazily. – Very good. I can't stand the very presence of those vultures. There are only us again, and those seeking us out.

She was glowing, not in light, but in emotion, passion and far more, surrounding everybody present. Those uninitiated among them, feeling it, or something like it for the first time began gasping and suddenly had trouble breathing.

– G-goddess? A boy struggled to catch his breath.

– No, not a goddess, Peter, she said softly, – «only» a human being.

She noticed a few concerned glances and stray thoughts from Loeh and Travis, and others from Northfield, as they recognized the «Call of the Goddess».

I can control it, she told them subdued. I'm not Laurie. It's just an expression of liberated, unbound joy, that's all.

And by the thought alone it faded, and she fought against the taint of regret.

You're so powerful that you don't know your own strength, Ted thought, but that shouldn't keep you from utilizing it.

She realized he had picked her sending from the very air, even though it wasn't meant for him. A thrill shot through her.

He frowned. She noticed it, almost as an afterthought, and it was caused by something else entirely, something distracting him from the here and now.

What is it? She asked him, sensing his distress.

I don't know, something about the word «tool»…

She smiled, as she sat down, giving away nothing of the worry she suddenly felt.

Astra, the girl in Boston used that word. Do you remember her?

I do. He nodded, his mind working overtime.

Liz noticed their conversation, too, of course.

I scanned her, Stacy told them. She checked out. They all did, like everybody here, everybody we've encountered, both in Northfield and on our Journey. I've made it my business to be proactive, but perhaps I, we have still been lax when it comes to security.

She brought in Betty, Nick, Beth, Martin, Jason, Stewart Ruth, Gabi, Carla, Everett, Linsey and Lydia, too, brought them up to speed with a flash of thought.

Be ready, she cautioned Gabi.

The telepaths began roaming the minds of everybody present, known and unknown. It brought no result. Everyone was okay.

There was a draft, as the door to the street opened, and four people entered.

His name is Larry, Martin by the door said, and there's something wrong with him.

Something horribly wrong, the sentiment echoed within Stacy.

Do! She told Gabi, and the girl instantly surrounded everyone in the room, the dining room in a protective bubble.

Martin and the others, in the outer hall remained unprotected, even though they and Martin himself used their powers to erect their own, less effective defense.

I've encountered people like Larry before. Stacy shuddered. Someone or something done to him has cast a shroud on his mind, his very self. What we see is only a shell, a facade. He has been brainwashed. What most people see is only a program. He doesn't even know himself that he isn't the person he appears to be, a perfect spy, one believing he's a rebel seeking out others like himself. We wouldn't have known either, wouldn't have any change of knowing, if not for our rather unique ways of detecting them. Even a casual scan may not reveal the truth. I see… see a millipede. Others have it tattooed on their necks, but he doesn't. There's nothing in his thoughts that I can reach about where he comes from or who sent him or runs him or anything. I guess our old friends Kurt Meinz and Anton Berkowitz would have called him a remarkable piece of work.

A chill passed through everybody privy to her thoughts. A powerful ghost from the past finally reasserted itself.

The question is what he's doing here, Liz said. Is he an infiltrator, a saboteur… or an assassin?

He isn't carrying explosives, Martin said, at least not any I recognize.

I dare not go too deep in his mind before we know more, Stacy said.

There may be all kinds of danger doing that, Jason acknowledged.

Stall him, Ted told Martin. Let's see if anything happens.

It might be dangerous, Linsey said.

Martin knows the risks, Liz said abruptly. Do it!

– That's a great necklace you've got there, Martin said casually to the newcomer.

– Thank you, Larry grinned. – It was my mother's.

The four were received like any other guest. Two of the four, Allan and Tessa were long-standing members of the Washington office, and had known Larry for several months, and brought him in after a thorough, but mundane checkup.

Martin should have been here, now. He could have detected any bugs.

Martin Keller's province was the smallest of things.

Send him away, Ted said.

Martin Warren nudged him, just a bit.

– Oh, shit, Larry said with regret. – I have an… errand to run tonight. I forgot all about it.

– That's okay, Francesca by Martin's side said sweetly. – You can return another day, or if you want to meet the travelers do so in any other office you may visit.

The intruder left. The group within Lillith's mind slowly relaxed.

He could have brought anything with him, Betty said, undetectable explosives, poison gas or just himself, which is probably dangerous enough. He's certainly a highly skilled and deadly operator.

They relaxed slowly, while all kinds of possible scenarios rushed through their mind.

Follow him, Liz told Silverhair through Stacy. Do not take any risks or ever leave your protective bubble, do you understand.

Judith rose, smiling, seemingly relaxed. She left the room, heading for the bathroom, and during a moment no one could observe her she faded away, and floated through walls until she was outside, and behind «Larry», as he walked down the street.

Stay with her, Ted told Gabi and Lydia. Don't let her out of your «sight» for a moment.

Always expect the unexpected, Liz said. We've been too lax in that regard as well, lately.

– Something has come up, people, Stacy said. – We must all leave, now.

She nodded to Gabi. Gabi, without revealing that she was actually doing anything opened up a gate in the very air, right there on the wall. Everybody, even though they knew some of what the travelers were capable of, looked astonished at each other.

– Step through it, Ted said calmly. – Quickly.

86

– What about those out there?

– They won't be joining us right now. Don't worry, they'll know we are gone.

– I'm certain they will, a boy stated, both stunned and a little caustic.

Everybody rushed through the gate, and appeared on the other side, in a cold and empty apartment in New York City, the change, the certainty that the party was over visible on their faces.

There are such small things, Lydia sent, but a prelude to so much more.

They looked across Manhattan, at all the lights blinking like tears, burning like embers in their hearts.

5

Gabi opened another portal, to London. All of them appeared in the giant bedroom, with the giant bed. Jennifer Woodstone and several of the others there awoke, a bit startled, but ready in an instant for what the world might throw at them. The rest of the numerous nude people rubbed their eyes.

– Go! She commanded them.

Everybody that didn't belong rushed out of the room, not certain what was happening, what they had seen.

– Nice entourage, Liz remarked.

– Thank you, Phoenix, Jennifer said, fairly relaxed, – what may I do for you?

Information was downloaded into her mind, so fast that it brought on a headache. Their anxiety brought on hers.

Gabi opened another portal.

– This will bring you to our Richmond office. Stay there until further notice. Stay strong.

– Stay strong! Everybody repeated.

She closed that portal and opened another, taking them to Jennifer's underground laboratory, the closed off part. Then she opened yet another portal. Everybody disappeared through it, except Jennifer and her aides. Gabi closed that from the inside.

Jennifer and the rest dressed in protective suits. Martin and the others appeared not long after that. Blood samples were taken and examined.

Two days later she gave Ted her preliminary report.

– There is nothing so far, she told him, – and in my opinion, there won't be either.

Two weeks later, when she gave him her final report, she confirmed that.

Judith, Gabi and Lydia had followed Larry for days, without anything of importance to report, except that he was indeed a plant.

But there were no clues to whom had sent him, or what purpose he might have, besides spying.

That same night those among them joking about calling themselves The Inner Circle met in Gabi's sanctum in Northfield.

– I almost panicked, Liz said in anguish. – I felt it swell in me like a sponge.

Shadows hissed and danced around them.

– We… overreacted, Ted said. – By being way too cautious. There is no way we can protect ourselves completely. The attack, when it comes *will* result in numerous casualties, in fatalities. We must be ready for it, that's all.

Eyes shifted a bit, clearly uneasy, but no one filed any protest, either using their physical voice or their mind, and there were few secrets among these people.

– Agreed! Stacy said.

The others nodded.

– Where is Nick tonight, by the way? She asked innocently.

– He's *late!* Liz shrugged.

Gabi looked like she wanted to say something, suggest something, but she held her tongue.

And that was that.

The meeting of the incomplete Inner Circle was adjourned.

6

Cole Stephenson visited an old house, old money in Albany, New York. His pretty doll parked the car right outside the house's front entrance, among a row of other expensive, very expensive cars. She opened the door for him, and was, as always attentive and dedicated.

It was late in the evening, close to midnight. The two of them was received by a servant and taken deep within the walls of the old place. The walls in the entrance hall were covered by paintings of old men. A female servant took Stephenson's coat and the male led on through a heavily fortified door and down the stairs behind it.

The house was quiet, very clean and ordered. He nodded pleased to himself.

They walked the final stretch down a long corridor, one less decorated. Doors opened to yet another place without windows. The notion comforted Stephenson somehow, made his inner self settle somewhat.

Before him waited yet another circle of people gathered around a table. They greeted him in silence, in excited apprehension. He took his designated place at end of the table.

– Humanity is a garden, he began

– A city, the cold flame deprived of the true light, they choired.

He looked at them for a moment, imposing his will on them.

– It's time, ladies and gentlemen, he declared. – Time to recapture what the rise of the raffle of humanity stole from us.

– Why now? A man inquired. – What has changed?

They all looked at him, excited and apprehensive and cautious.

– Ladies and gentlemen, he declared. – There has been a breakthrough.

Everybody could hear everybody's breathing, suddenly, unexplainable.

– Several breakthroughs actually.

The woman standing behind him took one step forward.

– This is Alpha One, my Alpha One, one of many. She is trained as a personal bodyguard and is totally loyal, totally obedient. If I told her to kill herself or

88

any other pleasant and unpleasant task she would do so without hesitation. The bodyguard function is merely one of many we have integrated or could integrate into her personality, her pool of assets, if you will.

They stared at her, her empty, unflinching eyes, her relaxed but yet rigid pose.

– So, is she one of those trained from birth? A woman asked, making her curiosity known.

– No. Stephenson shook his head. – They will always, because of their lack of experience have a limited function and use, I'm afraid. The program is based on the pioneer works of Kurt Meinz and Anton Berkowitz. The candidates are taken when they are in their late teens and then tailored to our specifications.

– Does she… remember anything? One of the women asked.

– There's very little left, if anything of the original personality. They're stripped of everything not necessary for their function. There's very little original thought or independence left. What you're looking at is pretty much an organic machine.

– Very impressive, the woman said. – We can practically mass-produce them?

– Pretty much, staying on the safe side of detection, of course. Each unit takes a few months to produce, but by now we have a system in place that's pretty much self-sustainable. The alphas can be taught teaching chores as well. They're endurable, virtually to a point beyond death. There's no sense of self-preservation beyond the rudimentary. The mission is the only thing that matters.

– But she does hear us, talking about her?

– Does a pet care about what its owners talk about? Stephenson shrugged.

– But if we gave her orders…

– Do so.

The woman turned towards the woman in uniform.

– Stand on your hands! She said, a little louder than she would usually speak.

Alpha One obeyed instantly, easily achieving the feat. She remained in that position.

– Back on your feet, the woman said.

Obedience was swift, with no discernible change in expression.

– She would have remained in that position for as long as she was possibly able, Stephenson said, – if not the counter-order or another meaningful change in events had taken place, for instance me leaving. She's programmed to follow me, to care for all my needs, to anticipate and assess them.

A man turned towards her.

– Kill Cole Stephenson, he said sharply.

There was no reaction whatsoever.

– Obviously we have safety protocols in place. Stephenson smiled. – She would have obeyed if one she perceived to be of a higher rank gave the order, though. Even though she is programmed to be devoted to me that means nothing compared to the Mission.

– And what is the Mission?

– The Thousand Feet and its *associates*, Stephenson replied calmly. – To propagate its influence in whatever way we choose. But you would be mistaken to think there's any processing of data beyond the Program. There isn't. They serve the people behind The Thousand Feet, not its possible ideology. There's no change of the alphas rebelling and doing their own interpretation of the Mission. *We* define their reality.

– So, the organic robot doesn't have the three rules stipulated by Asimov? The man said. – Not in any form?

– Thankfully not, Stephenson smiled politely. – We all know how insane that would have been, don't we? I can assure you that these robots will not attempt to save us from ourselves.

Stephenson sensed the emotions of the people in the gathering. He had long training doing that, evaluating the mood of a circle. They were hooked. They had been so already before he began, and now they had been drawn in further. The sense of power lit their eyes.

– That was the first breakthrough I wanted to show you tonight, he said.

They awaited eagerly his further demonstration. If this had been a movie, they would have been unable to take their eyes off the canvas.

– Call down, Peter Kerkoff, your secretary, he told the woman, very casually and deliberately so.

She stared him down or tried to, before shrugging and pushing a button on the table.

– Yes? A male voice replied.

– Will you come down here, please?

– I'll be there right away, the gathering heard him reply.

– He'll be very excited, she mused. – He came highly recommended and has attempted to be… *promoted* the entire year he has been in my employ. His ambitions, a tad too strong, even to my taste have made me consider putting him down on occasions.

They heard him, actually heard his feet against the floor. He ran, obeying the executive order to the best of his ability. Sounds reverberated easily through the old house.

He knocked on the door. They could observe his flustered face through the video surveillance camera in the hallway. The woman, the lady of the manor pushed another button, and the door slid open.

Peter Kerkoff entered the room. He looked at them with a puzzled look on his face, one not hiding his unbridled excitement.

– You called for me? He said, wide-eyed, as he recognized the people in the room.

– Indeed, we did, the woman said.

She looked at Stephenson.

He raised his arm, calling Kerkoff's attention.

– Peter Kerkoff, he said casually. – Look at my ring.

The ring on his long finger, with the standard displaying the millipede.

Kerkoff obeyed and froze.

– Humanity is a garden, Stephenson began

– A city, the cold flame deprived of the true light, Kerkoff completed, his voice turning monotonous.

His features and his entire being… froze. It was a chilling sight that didn't fail to cause a reaction in those present.

– All this time? The woman said softly.

– Since well before we sent him to you, Stephenson confirmed. – He's one of our Infiltration Betas actually, an early prototype not without its drawbacks and quirks. We weren't ready to present them before further testing had improved the model.

– If there are infiltrators even better than him out there, I'm certainly impressed, the woman said, clearly shaken.

– Oh, there are, Stephenson grinned cruelly. – We have full control, now, and can create any desired type.

He lowered his arm. What had had a semblance of individuality didn't move, didn't blink or change expression.

– His birth name isn't Peter Kerkoff, of course. He was quite the obnoxious radical before we got our hands on him. Since then he has worked tirelessly to repair all the damage he has done to his betters and humanity at large.

The meeting was adjourned. They all looked at Cole Stephenson with a deep-rooted respect.

– This is certainly a reason for rejoicing, one of the men said. – We've clearly come one step closer to our ultimate goal. You have our heartfelt congratulations and support, of course.

– Thank you, Stephenson said. – I'll be sure to report that to the Council.

He turned towards what briefly had been called Peter Kerkoff. The puppet came to life, sort of, as his eyes turned attentive.

– I'm afraid I have to take him with me. He's useless to you, now, and needs to be reprogrammed before his use can be restored.

He nodded to the circle and turned towards the door.

– What about the other projects? The woman inquired. – Those more… esoteric?

– Still in place, even though most of our immediate hopes of success vanished with Anton Berkowitz' fall.

– Someone did something to him, the woman said angrily. – Changed him, and not with your scientific methods. It's even pretty obvious *who*.

– I agree. We're looking into it.

He made his way towards the door and the exit with his two puppets in tow. At the exit door the house's female servant returned his coat, and he and his two companions made their way out into the night.

They walked to the car. The servants sat down in front and he in the luxurious back. His Alpha One started the car and drove off.

He waited patiently, with a smile on his lips, until they were well out of sight.

– Display, he told the driver.

First nothing seemed to be happening, but then there was a draft, and then a breath of wind inside the car, ruffling his hair.

– Cease! He said casually.

The wind ceased, as if it had never been there in the first place.

Cole Stephenson leaned back in the seat, a brief smile of anticipation and triumph touching his lips.

7

Phoenix Green Earth spread their buses south and west in the United States, like they did throughout the world. The Janus Clan and all the other representatives of the new wave of radicalism dwarfing that of the Sixties swiped the American continent, Europe and the world at large with a very measured, deliberate and wild campaign.

They visited briefly the ghost town of Centralia in Pennsylvania, once a thriving community of thousand souls, now practically abandoned. Coal in a mine had caught fire in 1961 and still burned, creating all kinds of havoc and dangers all over the town. The authorities had declared it uninhabitable in the eighties and begun the evacuation. Now, there were only nine people left, insanely clinging to their old lives, being illegal squatters in their own homes.

There were other mining areas, victims of mountaintop removal, a technique used to easier gain access to the coal below, creating environmental disaster on a massive scale, scar upon scar in nature.

Everything was documented by video-cameras, buzzing machines flying through the ruined landscape. Ted and Liz, leading one group of travelers each operated them at first, but they found themselves increasingly unable to do so. Their power worked, worked better than ever, to the point that they ruined the machines, transforming them into junk in a matter of hours. No matter how hard they focused they couldn't keep that from happening.

Liz shook her head, studying a camera closely. It practically fell apart in her hand.

– Your power to disrupt advanced technology increases along with all your other gifts, Phoenix, Gabi said happily.

The girl's steady stare actually unnerved Liz a little. She caught herself in being unnerved and shook it off.

Martin had to take over as camera operator. There were no problems then. That part of her powers hadn't been passed on to him.

She and Ted hadn't passed it on to any of their children, as far as they knew, even after the exhaustive testing everybody was subjected to during adolescence.

There was one telepath on each bus, a deliberate choice Ted explained in some detail.

– It's time for us to take off the gloves as well, he told them. – Use your power, use it to make people see the truth, open them up wide.

The possible repercussions and pitfalls, very evident to them all, made more than one shiver trickle down their spine.

– Going south will be dangerous, he said, – but we need to do it, need to go to Texas and all the other soft bellies of the Machine, all over the world, where we'll find everything that's wrong with humanity and challenge it head on.

– In what is still referred to as «The Confederacy» the races are still pretty much heavily segregated, Carla said. – One of our objectives is certainly to break that mold, break it to bits… to dust. Humanity was once one tribe, and will be so again.

Stacy felt the excitement, felt pride swell within them all. They crossed a threshold, now, for better or for worse and they knew it, and it was good.

– We are aware of the processes ravaging us, Ted said, as if he had read her mind (a thought making her grin), – aware of where they might lead, if we're not careful. As we keep pointing out to you: the process of revolution is a double-edged sword. There have been times in the past, when the revolutionaries have won that they have become as bad as the people they fought. Nothing substantial has changed, yet another trust has been broken.

Stacy shivered in the heat from the many fires in their giant cave, their collective place of power.

This was the place, the focal point where they reached out to the world.

She sat on the bus, in a somewhat pleasant seat. Gabi was there by her side. In the bus were also Morgana, Udo, Pearl and Seymour, and other aides.

It was an overrepresentation of protectors, but Stacy could easily see Ted's point.

Besides, Udo needed her, not the other way around.

– Are you all right? Gabi mothered her.

– Of course, I'm all right, Stacy replied lightly. – The babies aren't due before in a two months' time. Both Beth and Nick confirm my own «diagnosis»: that I'm healthy as a horse.

She made sure the girl knew she appreciated her kindness.

– But are horses always healthy? Seymour wondered, being slightly ironic?

That made her smile.

Seymour and Pearl were Ruth's brother and sister, children of Patrick and Jean, grandchildren of Ethel. They didn't have the telepathic power of their younger sister, but had other major defensive and offensive capabilities.

The telepaths were spread on a dozen buses and journeys. A dozen telepaths! Stacy drew her breath. That sounded so impressive, like so many, but were so few.

This group drove further south, from Washington DC, on Interstate 95 into Virginia to Richmond. Their offices in Richmond and other southern cities had been preparing for their visit for quite some time. The mere rumor that they were on their way had created noise, and when their travel plans, very public became official the local Phoenix Green Earth members had become targets of a very public hate campaign. Stacy felt it easily from afar. Her power gave her a certain sense of distant places, even though it was harder to know the specifics.

– We could have taken the Amtrak, you know, Gabi said to her, as they sat alone for a while at the back of the bus. – It's faster, very expedient.

– You could just have teleported us all to various known locations, Stacy shrugged. – This is fairly pleasant and expedient and leaves us with more options.

On the computer screen she saw a man standing outside the Richmond office with a poster saying:

BURN THE WITCHES!

– Will they care that you are pregnant at all? The girl wondered with acid and fear and disgust in her voice.

— There are those that wouldn't, Stacy said. — We've seen that, in places with far less innate bigotry. But we'll deal harshly with them, and less harshly with the rest.

— We're through pussyfooting, Gabi nodded happily.

Stacy couldn't sit anymore. She sat firm footing on the floor and pushed herself on her feet. Her balance remained off, but she was able to compensate and handle it.

— I can 'port you off the bus for a while? Gabi offered.

— Thank you. Stacy smiled gently. — I appreciate it. But there can be no discrimination, not even the appearance of such, not for any of us, under any circumstances. Do you understand?

The girl nodded silently.

I understand, mother.

— I would like you to take me on a ride soon, though.

The girl instantly looked attentive at her.

— The next time you set out on the river Styx, when the time is right, I would like to be a passenger, to join you in your studies.

The girl curtseyed.

— Of course, Janus, she said formally, — you are, after all the goddess of the Crossroads.

Good, very good.

Stacy concentrated lightly and she rose into the air, levitating between the ceiling and the floor. Everything floated within her as well. It always felt pleasant and empowering.

Those on the bus that hadn't seen it before stared in awe.

Your gawking is inevitable, I guess, she sent to them, slightly patronizing, and made them gasp even more.

But also to make them feel shame, make them confront themselves, their thoughts about power, and occasional sense of inferiority.

Even you feel the need to kneel, she scolded them.

And finally, when there were no more distractions, she could let go, and enjoy the sensation of levitation. Keeping herself in the air was no effort. It just gave her more of the transcendent joy she felt every time she used her power in more than a casual way.

The road was fairly okay from DC, but the longer south they drove the worse it became. They were delayed by construction zones. The number of potholes, of uneven and patched up road increased by the feet.

They hit a large hole. Seymour at the wheel swore, and the air shivered under the onslaught of his annoyance.

— You win. Stacy told them all, levitating there, at the center of the vehicle, not really touched by the hitting of the humps and dumps. — We'll take the train next time…

It even took a turn for the worse as Interstate 95 joined with 64 and they approached Richmond.

– Does anyone know where we are? Seymour mused. – I have no idea.

They had entered a series of badly marked overpasses and spurs and flyovers.

– I think that is James River there, Pearl mused in an optimistic mood. – If it is, we're on the right track…

It was on the left, along with the old church with the broken clock tower. On the right was the Phillip Morris tobacco headquarters, with its old smokestack.

They drove through an area of warehouses, docks and industrial wasteland, a classic modern urban landscape.

It was still bright daylight when they reached the inner Richmond cityscape. The city's financial district was fairly similar to all others in all bigger American cities. The rest was pretty much akin to a civil war museum.

– I remember driving through southern Italy once, the woman with the black eyes said. – There were statues of Julius Cesar everywhere.

They shivered, realizing that this wasn't merely the young woman's memories, but someone's far older.

The local group, the many hundreds of them met the bus as it pulled in in front of the headquarters. Stacy took them all in, scanned them before the bus stopped. She sensed a range of emotion among them, everything from conviction to doubt, from excitement to curiosity.

And a few hostiles pretending to be eager participants.

Her travel companions had been alerted to those threats within a few seconds.

The man with the blue bandana, she sent. The girl with the striped shirt, and the one with the mole by her nose.

Quite a few people carried guns here. It was customary. Most of those on the bus did as well.

The hostiles are here as observers, Stacy informed her charges. They are spies.

The deluge met her, as she stepped off the bus. Gregory Leslie Stark met her, taking her hands. She sensed his power. He was the only one here aware of what he was. There were a few others that had suspicions about themselves, and a few more that didn't have a clue. Gregory had gathered them, sensing them, without revealing what he knew.

His power was Dust, its very nature, greater insight and command of it. She smiled to him.

– It pleases me to see so many recruits, she cried, – so many people unafraid and aware and empowered.

They cheered quietly. Her quickly gained reputation preceded her. They knew of her, knew enough to be impressed by her in advance, and now, when they met her, they sensed her power. She didn't hide herself, made no effort to do that, but let everything flow from her unencumbered, showing them who and what she was.

Gregory had to dry himself around the mouth. His eyes turned wet. She looked at him with fondness in her eyes, her black eyes.

He suffered dreams, frightening visual nightmares about a bird of fire and shadow rising from its own ashes. Lillith had recognized him immediately the first time Stacy had met him.

He grabbed her hands again. They all did eventually, all met the travelers with their heartfelt or pretend greeting.

– We are so happy to see you, Gregory said. – We can't properly express it in words.

– We are very happy to be here, Stacy said.

They exchanged more than words, more than a few warm meetings of eyes, so much more, all of them, whether they were born witches or not.

Stacy sensed it easily, how Gabi and the others appreciated beyond appreciation the warmth of the reception. These people knew life, Stacy sensed, knew its hardship, but still held on to its joy, both as a group and most of them also as individuals. It encouraged her to no end.

– You even survived the roads. It's a miracle.

– Yes, we did, Charlotte, Stacy said.

She revealed that she knew everybody's name, not holding herself back.

Charlotte glanced at her, before relenting, before accepting it, accepting that all the wild rumors she had heard was true, and it was as if she opened up inside, coming into her own. It was a process Stacy never got tired of observing and marveling at.

– I drive these roads every day, Charlotte grinned. – I know where a lot of the holes are, but I still hit them.

Stacy looked at the walls, at the slurs written and painted there. There was racial and just about any other type you could think of.

– We used to remove them at first, Gregory said, – but we don't anymore. We let them remain, to remind ourselves and everybody passing by what kind of people we're up against. We even take photos and record film and post them on the Internet.

– You did the right thing. Stacy nodded. – Prejudice needs to be confronted on all levels.

The air slowly turned a darker hue. It wasn't just that she instantly knew everybody's name. They also felt her presence in their mind or imagined they did. Most of them were elated by that fact, a few dreading it, an even deeper fear sneaking up on them.

– Let's go inside, she declared, – into our home away from home.

And everybody present was overwhelmed by a powerful trickle down the spine spreading throughout their body, embracing them. The sideshow of ravens was merely a tiny part of what made them all gasp and heave.

By the time they reached the living room of the old, worn office building she had formed a pretty complete picture of Ronny, Lise and Dusty, the spies, and began working on them without delay. She enforced whatever sense of happiness they might feel and dimmed their spiteful nature, modifying whatever beliefs they might have.

There were others there, people doubting the Phoenix Green Earth message or still sitting on the fence. She didn't do anything specific to them, confident she would win them over by her presence, fully aware of the impression she made on them all.

96

– It's really happening, now, isn't it? One in the crowd said incredulous.

The close to conviction in his voice warmed her.

– It finally is, Stacy confirmed.

Another boy stepped forward, having a lot on his mind.

– Yes, Ronny? She wondered, as she turned towards him.

And now the whispering began in earnest, both that of sound and of the mind. She heard them and felt them.

– You're just a young girl, he exclaimed. – How can Warren and the rest place so much trust in you?

– But that isn't truly what you're wondering about, is it?

She held her head slightly skewed, looking at him with her ebony windows of the soul. He felt himself slipping, she knew he did.

– How can you do what you do? He gasped.

– What am I doing, Ronny?

He had difficulties breathing. He couldn't meet those eyes of hers, and couldn't speak.

– I'm far older than you, she grinned.

– She's Lillith, the Mother of Demons, Charlotte declared, half between excitement and ecstasy.

That name had been spoken high and low the last six months, but hardly aloud. The low whispers turned to gasps and silent breaths.

– You aren't stupid, the lot of you, Gabi said. – You believe what your senses tell you. There's no need to use your reason here, even though you do wonder about how she can know the name of every single person she encounters. The narrow reason you're brought up with tells you that this isn't possible. Your true reason, on the other hand tells quite the different story.

Lillith moved, moved inwards in a circle. Some followed her, forming a wider circle around her and her sentries and aides. No one took their eyes off her. She stopped at the center. Everybody stopped that very moment. She sat down on her ass.

– It's both a good and bad thing that this came up, she said quietly, speaking far louder than words. – But in the end, it doesn't matter. Lillith and Stacy are the same. There's no telling where one ends and the other begins.

She chuckled, shaking her head, and in that moment, she hardly looked like a nineteen-year-old girl at all, and everybody knew that, knew it to the core of their being.

– There's so much I can tell you, so much I'll eventually tell you all...

When she looked at them, she looked at them all. It didn't matter that she sat with her back to half of them. Her black eyes were visible to those looking at her back as well.

– We'll start with the basics, what is one type of fuel, one poison of many driving the world of today. I'm going to tell you about prejudice, how it works. I'm going to tell you about the current society, through an angle not often heard, how we're all fucked up by it, how it's destroying everything making life worth living.

Her voice was spoken in their ears, both their ears, her presence right there, in front of them. They were sore afraid, unable to help themselves.

– My own history while growing up in what is seen as an ideal home is an excellent illustration, and before you say poor rich girl I want you to listen... listen good, and realize we're all victims, inevitably. You see, my parents were quite displeased with me...

Both of the pairs were, rich and poor, she thought, with thoughts she kept to herself.

– I didn't behave according to their specifications of what a good daughter should be. First, they closed off all my bank accounts. When that didn't work, when I told them to go to hell, when they realized they couldn't reach me through my wallet, by threatening to remove the expensive lifestyle I had grown accustomed to they sent a private operator to terrorize me and my friends, and then, as a final resort, they attempted to have me sent to a home for «difficult» rich children. All the arrangements had been made. I have all the papers ready for your study, for everybody's study. I have also the documented stories of quite a few other children of rich parents, how they were brainwashed and returned «home» as empty shells compared to the fairly free and independent human beings they had been or tried to be. Is it any strange that the current human society is so fucked up? Parents are so prejudiced that they can't even give their own children the benefit of the doubt. This is what *civilization* does to us. It's about time, now, that we go all the way, take any action possible to end a terror regime worse than the world has ever seen.

The relative dark interior of the old office building gave way to the packed parking lot the day after, where Stacy Larkin held her major Richmond speech.

There were no cars on that parking lot and thousands of people.

– Since time immemorial people, Seers and the common man alike have spoken about and feared a mythical, Kingdom of Death, something removed from us, a place we would end up after our bodies stopped breathing. But it was always right there, right *here*, right in front of us.

– The wave of her hand included the entire world, the reporter whispering into his microphone said, – not just her immediate surroundings.

– THIS is the Kingdom of Death, Stacy Larkin shouted. – Every piece of every city on Earth, all parts of *civilization* are the Nightmare, the Wrongness glimpsed by people throughout the millennia.

And the whisper of the crowd rose to a roar around her.

8

Remember my name, a voice whispered in the darkness. Remember your name, your Self lurking beneath the surface of your shell, your Mask.

Torches and tall fires cast its Shadow far around the derelict shed outside New Orleans, reaching into the streets, not merely Vieux Carrè, but the entire local urban sprawl.

The swamp, the trees, the very air and water whispered to them.

Lillith Raven Moonstar, the woman, the spirit with many names, many masks sat on a log in front of the shed, her late pregnancy not impeding on her movements in any visible way, not any the gathering could spot.

She waved her hand. A shadow seemed to grow from it, becoming a bigger hand touching everybody present.

– Death comes for me, she whispered in a strange, terrifying, ghoulish voice. – It *speaks* to me, and LIBERATES ME

They sought close together, helplessly frightened and fascinated by the display unfolding before them

– It speaks to me, she howled. – THE FIRE SPEAKS TO ME

Fire erupted from her waving hands, forming shapes of fire to go with those of Shadow. Screams rose from a thousand dry throats. Fire and Shadow touched them, making them whimper in pain and pleasure and a dozen less identifiable sensations. Drums hammered their ears, stabbed their skin.

It was April 30th, the night to May 1st, the Witchnight of Beltane, and the living and dead spirits were out in force in the wretched and deep night, visiting the warm bodies and seeking souls celebrating life in all its forms.

Stacy was nineteen and her time had come.

It had been only a week since the travelers had arrived in this city, but it felt much longer. The entire area stretched out to Stacy, just like time did. She focused on the people before her, but was also very aware of the vast land surrounding her.

The jar with the many spongy pieces was sent around. The people, the nascent witches sitting in the circle around the tall campfire grabbed one piece and put it in their mouth. As they began chewing they began sweating and their eyes turned hazy, and their muscles slackened. Gregory and Charlotte and all the others nascent witches they had gathered on their Journey south began their Vision Quest, joining those in other cities all over the world.

Stacy beheld her Shadow as a creature formed of the dancing flames before her, and it held no terror for her anymore. When It rose from the ground and spread across the City of the Dead that was New Orleans, she effortlessly joined with it. Lillith felt living and dead souls wherever she focused her attention.

She beheld the other telepaths, and then there was the Phoenix glowing darker than all of them combined. It trickled and burned so pleasantly within her.

Gabi came to her at some point, curtsying deeply, humble and eager. Stacy rose, glancing briefly at the dozen or so people writhing and sweating profusely on the ground, content that they were somewhat safe, before nodding in approval, taking the girl's hand.

The flames flickered, loosing, gaining coherence through their enhanced vision. The world turned inside out, as they entered the Shadowland, as they traveled its vast distances in moments.

There were drums and music, beyond music. They appeared at the Crossroads in a flash, but without the disorientation that had accompanied Stacy's travels there earlier in her life. There were many present tonight and power burned on every single spot, and they could still handle it. A thousand times thousand eyes of shadows beheld them and made room for them.

Gregory arrived, frazzled around the edges. He looked confused at them, looked in awe at the beyond powerful form of Janus, the Goddess of the Crossroads.

– Is it really you?

Gregory was no longer Gregory, but still fluid, unformed, not yet what he was destined to become.

– I used to wonder about that myself, Lillith grinned.

– I don't know who I am, he said, with despair evident in his «voice» and «face».

– You will!

He wanted to cling to her, she sensed that, a part of him did, but a far more powerful part of him pushed him further on his Quest. He faded in a flash, in an event she could easily note and observe.

Others filed past them, «speaking» in whispers. Some bowed. Even here they bowed.

Lillith and Gabi nodded to each other, deliberately patronizingly ignoring those lowering their heads. This had just been a distraction, a brief delay before their true purpose this night revealed itself.

They stood on a pier by a vast ocean. Gabi wore her black dress. Around her a few dark butterflies flapped their wings.

– This is as far as I can take us, she said. – I'm not Charon, not the Ferryman. He could go all the way to the other shore and back. That was his gift and his curse.

Even now the pier grew, stretching, reaching into the sea, the vast river. The two of them couldn't even glimpse the other shore. Somewhere out there was a dark tunnel, one formed by water and air and Shadow itself. When they turned and looked back at the shore they came from it was much farther away than the last time they had looked. They hurried back, feeling the constant pull of the vortex out there.

Surroundings in constant shift shifted again. Gabi maneuvered through it all in a way Lillith couldn't quite do. Images reformed out of Chaos yet again. They flowed through what Stacy instantly recognized as hospital corridors, physical reality not quite there, just out of reach, beyond the veil. But the stench of chemicals, of fear and rot was very much present.

– Wait for it, Oracle said calmly. – Any time, now…

– For Death? Stacy said.

– I can smell it, the girl said. – It's everywhere I go, no matter what I do.

Stacy wanted to comfort her, reaching out with her hand and mind, sensing before the girl pulled away that she didn't want to be comforted.

They stopped above a bed, hearing the faint sound of the alarm going off. A lot of people dressed in white rushed towards the still body of the pale woman. They grabbed the body and threw it on a portable stretcher, and rushed off with if. It gasped once and died. There was a lot of screaming and shouting instructions, of administering CPR and adrenaline and everything else modern medicine had invented to stave off, delay Death.

The running people didn't see it, but perhaps they glimpsed or sensed, somewhat the shadowy form rising from the decaying flesh. Stacy sensed the chill passing through a couple of them, but it didn't yield any tangible result, no change in action or even conscious thought. They denied what they knew deep down and kept rushing the shell to the operating table. The silver shadowy cord connecting the spirit with its former body withered by the second, even though it still held on.

The Shadow gathered strength, reforming, empowering itself, as the limitations it had known during its previous life broke down, caught between numbing fear and curiosity and the bombardment of the massive knowledge stored within its infinite formless form.

She noticed the two shapes beyond the veil.

– Are you, are any of you Death or Its harbingers?

– No, Christine, Lillith said. – He isn't here right now, and we're mere observers, or guides, if you wish us to be.

– But I *am* dead?

– Do you feel dead? Oracle wondered, curiosity flickering in her lupine eyes.

– No! Christine shook her head. – This feels more like a birth than anything else.

– It is, Stacy said. – Every piece of knowledge, everything you have experienced through hundreds of lives is returning to you undiluted.

Christine looked down at her body.

– I can still save it, Stacy said, – if that is your desire. I have that power.

A thousand thoughts passed between them. Speech was a barrier.

– I… know you, Christine said.

– I know you, too, Lillith said.

Christine looked down at her previous body one final time.

– It's old and frail, she said.

With that sentence, with that speed of thought, their surroundings shifted abruptly. They were still at the hospital, or something resembling the hospital, with the same walls and décor, framework, but there were no people. A moment later, and they were elsewhere, deep within the mists and shadows, and then they were back at the shore, slightly different, more aligned to Christine's perception than theirs. The cord broke, dissolved into a thousand pieces, before becoming one with the surroundings, Dust further expanding the Shadowland into infinity.

But the Shadow remained, pausing a little on Styx's shore.

– There is the boat, if you wish it, Oracle said. – There's no one to guide you through the currents these nights, but I think you'll do fine on your own.

– I will, thank you, Christine, or what had been Christine said. – But I think I'll fly this time. It's such a fine night.

One swift smile, and she was gone, pulled into the ether, where they couldn't follow her.

The two interlopers on these shores (there were many shores) were alone again, alone in the silence of the low, enormous buzz surrounding them.

– You didn't take from her, Stacy noted.

– She wouldn't have cared for me much if I had done that.

Oracle chuckled darkly.

The laughter stopped, abruptly. Opaque eyes stung the older teenager.

– Your turn, Oracle said.

Stacy looked at her with an inquiring mind.

– You pick one, Oracle said.

The temptation was almost irresistible, and Stacy had no desire to resist.

She was Lillith, the Mother of Demons. Her domain included the Shadow. It was easy. She just half closed her eyes, reaching out into the eternal sea.

A man floated towards them.

– Who are you? He asked briskly. – Where are…

– He isn't here anymore, Oracle shrugged. – We're here, now. All that was his are ours, or could have been if we had cared for it.

She gestured and froze him in the air, the moment before he would have charged them.

– You may speak if you want, but not move.

He stared harshly at them, the power of his hatred hardly containable, his eternal, growing form swelling as they watched.

– What are you going to do? He snarled.

His «voice» created a mighty ripple in their surroundings. Fear rose from the sea below, the sea that wasn't the river, but one of its tiny arms.

– Nothing. Gabi shrugged. – We just wanted to take a look at you, to study you, as you would an animal in a zoo, before we let you go, to rejoin the cycle without the perks your benefactor provided.

He knew, realized what that meant.

Suddenly he tore himself free, just before she let him go. It happened so fast and startled her, startled both women. He charged Stacy, heading straight for her womb, and she knew instantly what he was chasing.

She raised her left hand, creating her own ripple, her own mighty blow. He shook under its onslaught, in beyond violent pain, screaming loud enough for all spirits to hear.

– Do you think your hatred can match mine, my contempt for beings such as you? Do you dare oppose the will of the slayer of the slayer of gods?

He knew and as more information, more details were exchanged between his form and hers his paralyzing fear, held in check for a short while rose fully to the surface. Lillith held him in her grip, squeezing hard her claws of shadow and fire around his form, held him effortlessly while he screamed, reducing him to a sobbing child. He hung there for what felt like ages, at her mercy, begging her to be lenient, for any sort of compassion.

– You've had it easy the last few centuries, haven't you? She said softly. – He helped you pick and choose pretty much whatever shell you wanted.

He wanted to answer her, but she didn't allow it, not in any way, and bottomless despair overwhelmed him.

– I could make you my slave, you know. Worse, I could bind you. I could make you my shadow, reduce you in stature, until you were nothing but a shell, like you helped him do with so many for so long. It would be mandated. You wanted my children, wanted to steal their gold. What do you think? What punishment would you choose, if I asked you?

He wanted to answer her, to beg her favor, to spare him the worst of her wrath, but she had taken away all his abilities to communicate.

– But I'm not going to do that. I'm not him, not your Master. It is as my kind guide explained to you: You're a fish, and I'm going to throw you back into the water and you better hope you'll never take my bait again. Renewal, rebirth, second changes, all those things may not have meant anything to you in a very long time. Now, they'll do so once more.

She sucked him dry, almost empty, but she didn't take anything from him, of his self, not the smallest of parts. When she finally let him go he just drifted off, like a leaf in the wind.

– I know how you taste, now. I have your scent, have it forever.

He faded away, off their radar, into the multitude he had resented for so long.

Lillith's dark glow pulsed and burned. She leaked power everywhere.

– You've done this before, I take it, the girl said, filled with respect and reverence.

– Yes, before…

– You're like a battery, an enormous capacitor. Under the right circumstances there's hardly any limit to how much power you could soak up.

The lazy, content look in Stacy's hazy eyes turned a little bit more watchful.

She masked her thoughts, her fears from the child, from the all-seeing Oracle.

– I thought I could be your teacher, for once, the girl said, very sober. – How silly of me, mother.

Her words stung, like Stacy had known they would do.

Hands joined hands again, and they were on their way.

They walked through a city looking very much like New Orleans. It was night and the full moon lit up an abandoned Canal Street. This was Canal Street, an exact copy of the world outside, across the veil, the Abyss. In that street, warts and all, in that world outside there were lots of people. Here, there was no one, except them and the shaking girl crouched on the sidewalk.

– It's ugly out there, she moaned. – Ugly everywhere.

They knelt by her.

– This is no place for you, Gabi said, uncharacteristically gentle.

– So, I have to *move on*, is that it? The girl, the grown woman snarled.

– That's pretty much it, Stacy said. – For one thing, you're scaring the dipshit out of all the tourists.

– Heh heh, very funny.

The girl, the woman giggled darkly, in a way they could easily identify with.

– Don't think I don't know what you are, what you're doing.

She shouted and all the people on the real Canal Street heard it, heard the wail of the banshee and shuddered in their depths.

– I'm dead, the girl mumbled, drying giant tears.

– Do you feel dead? Stacy asked carefully.

– No, I don't, busybody, she choked.

She scratched long welts on her arms.

– I wish I did.

– There's neither death nor forgetting, Gabi callously informed her, – only the endless cycle and renewal. In a million years you will still remember everything. It will still hurt, at least if you don't *deal* with it.

The woman sniffed and dried her tears. Canal Street faded away. She stood up.

– I curse you, she said calmly. – Curse you both for all eternity.

And she was gone.

A man sat in his chair in front of the fireplace. He tried to make a fire, but no matter how many matches he used he couldn't. Nothing would burn. The matches writhed like snakes under Stacy and Gabi's feet.

– Who are you? He asked distraught. – How did you get in here? What's *happening?*

– You know that, Bernard, Stacy said.

– I'm dead, he choked. – I'm dead.

He looked at them with eyes dry like desert sand.

– Are you angels of Death coming to collect me?

– To you we are, Stacy nodded.

– I can't remember *anything* beyond this room, he whined, beyond distraught.

– You will! Gabi stated matter of fact, a threatening subtext clear in her voice.

– It's ugly out there, he whispered, – so very ugly.

The walls dissolved. He grew, to become his Shadow, and Power and Memory surged through him. Gabi touched him and a tiny speck of energy transferred from him to her.

– This is my toll, she stated in a hollow voice, – the coin of passage that is the Ferrymen's due.

He would have shivered if he had still been flesh.

– Is it wise to pay the Ferryman before the Journey is done? He wondered.

– That's the wrong question, she said with a cruel smile.

The tiny speck filled her form, making it swell.

– It isn't our job getting you all the way, Lillith said. – That's the easy part. We're broken mirrors making you face yourself, and without us you might have been stuck for ages.

He was so grateful. She knew he was, and he would thank them forever.

The three forms slipped into the raging stream. The male was quickly caught in its currents, but the two angels of death held their position. Several more shadows passed through them on their path downstream. The dark glow increased for each new form they touched. Stacy felt it, felt the transcendent joy, as it empowered her and the girl, and the now so very familiar twinge of dread and anticipation rose within her.

Is this it, mother? Have I learned my lesson? Have you?

The reply drowned in the buzz turned roar of the seething waters of life and death and knowledge and memory and transcendence and everything in-between.

CHAPTER FIFTEEN
The invisible Labyrinth

Stacy woke up in the large bed, soaked in sweat. She still felt it like she was floating in the stream of souls, soaking up its infinite power, the glorious pleasure of it still lingering all over her.

Most of the people had woken up long ago and left bed. Only Pearl and Seymour were still there in addition to her. Seymour was still inside his sister. Stacy smiled.

She rose and left the bed with some difficulties, the sounds and thoughts of the house slowly imposing themselves on her, supplanting those of her nightly dreams and Journeys. She stood by the window, not bothering to hide herself, looking out at the busy Bourbon Street. Her breasts and nipples pushed at the glass. It felt hot in the pervasive sunlight.

One thought and the impressions of the city of New Orleans were hers to enjoy. Almost one year after Katrina and Anton most of the city was still in disarray, not as much as the rest of the South-Eastern seaboard of the United States, but there were ruins, piecemeal houses everywhere. Katrina had made most of the poor population flee the city. Anton had made most of the remaining population move out.

The city and the surrounding area had become a kind of No Man's Land. There was law enforcement and soldiers and a kind of civil administration here, but still not fully in place.

The poor had returned from the more or less permanent tent camps in Texas when the news of the wealthy people's departure had reached them. After Katrina there had been a lot of talk, unofficially, of course among the wealthy and powerful to grab this change and finally make New Orleans theirs, but less than two months later nature had intervened again and thrown a large monkey wrench in their grand plans.

Stacy grinned.

In the dark corners and every ebony pocket of air around her she glimpsed the mouth, the giant face of her Shadow. It held no terror for her anymore, like she recalled that it in a distant past had once done. Her inverted mirror image might unnerve her now and then, but that was all.

The dip in the river of life and death, knowledge and power had strengthened her, empowered her further. Her awareness periodically soared to new and unknown heights. Sometimes it was as if she was still there, only by thinking of it.

You get unstuck. It happens sometimes.

She turned, fully aware that Delphi was there, right behind the veil, and had been for a while, and had been staring at her, studying her, measuring her.

Gabi slipped through, and stepped down on the floor. She wore a black dress, not the same, but one fairly similar to the one she had worn yesterday.

It will wear off in a couple of days.

I know.

So, was the experience to your liking?

It has increased both my awareness and power, thank you.

Delphi nodded self-consciously, as if dismissing an orderly in a merciful act.

– Boy, you're *big*, the girl grinned. – And I guess we haven't seen the end of it yet, have we?

– I image you haven't. There are two someones that still have a little bit of growing to do before they're ready to pop out.

They embraced and kissed each other.

– Charlotte sent me to fetch you all. Breakfast will be ready shortly.

Pearl and Seymour stretched and yawned on the bed, smiling, not really sleepy at all. They stepped out on the floor. The four of them stepped into the portal, the gateway, and they were on their way, appearing in the dining room after just a brief impression of the Shadowland.

Everybody gawked in awe, as they manifested out of the air itself.

Those gathering around the table embraced and caressed each other, stressing the warmth and companionship they felt. It was still fairly new and awkward to most of them, but they learned. They sat down and began feeding, and it felt good. Some of those present had dressed, others hadn't. It was a great chaotic lack of uniformity and formality, and Lillith was pleased.

Charlotte and Gregory and the others buzzed with excitement and enthusiasm. Breakfast and everything else were like a smorgasbord, an orgy of taste and smell to them. Their eyes lit up with life and death and everything between and beyond. She shared their abundant joy and empowerment, but also knew beyond knowing that there was a part of herself she could never properly share with them, whether she desired it or not. It wasn't something she kept contained, since that was something that could never be contained, never stay hidden, but she allowed it to be submerged into the multitude of emotion around the table.

Their Hell Week had ended, and they had initiated themselves into the secrets and life of a witch.

Gregory flooded with gratitude when he grabbed Stacy's hands.

– Thank you!

And the room and the minds in it were instantly filled with those two words and the enthusiasm and transcendent joy accompanying them.

Stacy's response was invariably the «Call of the Goddess», the sharing of joy among the minds present. She couldn't help it. It was the most powerful emotion, revelation of happiness in existence, and it was no wonder that it had led to the creation of religions in the past. They gasped and shook in further joy.

– You did it yourselves, she stated.

They sensed her concern, and understood it, at least to a point.

– That might be, Charlotte said, – and don't worry, we're all aware of the importance of self-reliance, but without your aid, your... push we might have wandered aimlessly for years and years. Some of us would never have discovered the joy of Being, of realization of Self.

106

Of Power.

[Troubled?]

The thought was faint, but easily detectable.

She focused on the two minds in her belly.

A bit, but mommy is all right, she told them.

– You're communicating with your children? Keira said incredulous.

She wasn't a telepath, but sensitive enough to pick up on what was happening.

– Yes, Stacy smiled. – Yes, I am.

– That's so cool.

And the bubble of thoughts erupted in the room once again.

– I saw you there at the Crossroads, Gregory said awestruck.

– That you did, she confirmed.

– Everybody stared at you, he said, – and couldn't take their «eyes» off you.

– They paid their respects, Gabi said. – At that moment of clarity everybody knew, beyond knowing who she is.

Stacy looked at her without looking at her, gave her the evil eye.

You're not helping.

Sorry, the girl replied humbly, not sorry at all.

Everybody turned towards Stacy. Those already looking at her began looking harder. She let it happen, allowed it to unfold, drawing them in.

Perhaps you are helping.

She looked into the eyes of each and every one of those present.

Then she pulled herself in, held herself in check, and hid herself to the world, for the first time in months. It was an effort, but she did it. When they now looked at her, they saw pretty much no more than a young girl, a pregnant young woman, one with very striking features, yes, but no more than that.

Charlotte opened her mouth to speak. Stacy held up a hand and a finger, silencing her. She waited. Ten, twenty seconds passed. Eventually no one made any effort to speak.

– What do you think Phoenix Green Earth is? She asked quietly.

They looked bewildered at her. Everybody did, except Gabi. The girl looked very smug.

– It's a radical environmental organization to bring every other calling themselves a radical environmental organization to shame, Keira said.

Stacy shrugged.

The gathering kept struggling, kept searching for answers.

– It's a revolutionary political organization formed to transform human society, Ronny said, – to bring true Change to the world.

– And how are we going to bring all our ambitious goals to fruition? Stacy asked patiently.

– You travel around the world, Gregory said. – You gather people, open their eyes to the problem, making them a part of the solution, forming truly alternative communities, training them as both warriors and thinkers.

– We certainly do, Stacy acknowledged. – But why do that, when we can just wave a magic wand and change everything?

A different kind of clarity brightened their awareness. It was easy to see for anybody, with or without a power to read minds.

– It's a group effort, Stacy said. – One made from the ground up. It has to be, since there's no other option. As Ted Warren has told us many times; even if all witches were of one mind and one desire, we would still only be a tiny group compared to humanity as a whole. We are Agents of Change, but we aren't gods, and we need the support of the multitude to succeed, also because we need them to be empowered, need for every single human being to think for himself or herself. We've spoken a lot about the pitfalls of revolutions, haven't we, about how they tend to fail, even as they succeed, about how they're absolutely useless if they supplant one hierarchy with another? The current society is a pyramid, with the few on top and the many at the bottom. We're going to tear down the pyramids of power. We're not going to chase off the current landlords and move into their house. And we ARE NOT going to build new pyramids or its equivalent. I would see it as an insult, quite frankly if anybody started worshiping me and so should all of you. You're just at the start of your path, your empowerment, and as your teaching, often harsh teaching continues and your talents grow in leaps and bounds, you'll come to know the world, existence and yourself in new and ever more exciting ways, and realize that the worst injustice you'll ever do to yourself, as that happens would be to yield to the temptation of misusing your gifts, to walk the Path of Power.

Her words and will echoed within them, lingering for nights and weeks and longer, like a slap in the face, a kind touch on the cheek.

They sat there gasping, only slowly returning to a fairly normal rate of respiration, as Stacy returned to being Lillith and Janus and the thousand names they knew her by in their nightmares and dreams.

The passion and the intensity of the nineteen-year-old girl got to them just as much as the age-old goddess did, and it pleased her, and the sense of nascent panic faded somewhat.

– This is your beginning, she said, – and a beginning is as delicate as the frailest china, and I'm responsible for you, for all that you might become.

– You have so much responsibility, Keira said softly.

She hesitated a bit, before touching the woman's cheek. Charlotte rushed forward and embraced her, and several of the others did as well.

You don't know the tenth of it, Stacy thought silently, not sharing that one with them.

They fed. Even after most of the meal was done, they were still hungry. A far greater hunger than that for food had been awakened in them. The process had begun in yet another place, in yet another group.

– To you, Stacy said, raising her glass – to this morning of joy.

They understood and she was content. As glasses clinked, they pondered her words.

The morning meal ended. They cleaned the table and did the dishes together, like

108

they did everything together. Excited minds and faces kept going, kept sharing.

– This is some house, Keira said in wonder. – I don't think I've ever seen one quite like it... except in movies. Vintage New Orleans, isn't it?

– It used to be a brothel, Charlotte said dryly.

– Yes, Keira nodded, acknowledged, seemingly unaffected at first, and then incredulous: – Really?

– It was, Stacy nodded, with a distant look in her eyes.

– Most houses on Bourbon Street were, actually, Gregory said.

– Gentlemen came from all over the South to be kind to generous girls, Charlotte said, jokingly, mockingly displaying herself.

– It's a nice house, though, Keira said, – filled with good and bad memories.

Stacy stepped away from the rest of them, deliberately, making her charges focusing on her yet again.

– We're on our own for a while, she told. – We'll learn and grow together, as we lay our claim on this ancient city of the dead and its surrounding area, one coven of many across the world, as you begin your first hesitant steps on the path that is the Invisible Labyrinth. These streets, these ruins are an excellent illustration of what's wrong with the world and inspiration both in our quest to remake, transform the world.

Her words and mind filled them, inevitably, as they began their daily chores.

Stacy showered and quite a few of them showered with her, in a room made for groups.

– I can't believe how natural this feels, Ronny said.

He had come around quite easily, as she picked off him the bigotry and repression brought on by his upbringing one piece at the time.

And then she had finally showed him what he was.

– It is natural, Charlotte said, not reproaching him, kissing him on the cheek.

It was both sensual and not, both a pleasure and a task. They didn't fuck this morning, content with enjoying each other's touch and presence.

There was no hot water, but the cold water wasn't that cold and very, very refreshing.

The electricity was still not working properly, and no one seemed able to fix it.

– This soap feels so great, Keira marveled. – It feels like... soap.

– Such a difference from the industrial shit, Charlotte agreed.

The air condition was working, at least partly, enough to make the inside a bit colder than the hot outside, enough to not make them sweat immediately after they stepped out on the bathroom floor, and began drying each other with the big towels in the same relaxed and pleasant manner.

Stacy dressed. The soft fabric felt good against the skin. She steeled herself against the treacherous sense of peace. With a slight increase in concentration, she began tracking her apprentices. Most of them were in the backyard garden, feeding the hens and geese and working hard on the soil, their skin and clothes quickly turning dirty. The backyard was really a ruin, a condemned property, one of many in the city. Gregory and Charlotte and bunch were out shopping, buying supplies. A wave of nostalgia briefly flooded the woman in black.

They grabbed their guns before leaving, preparing themselves for the hostile territory they would encounter outside their defined neighborhood. It was a ritual just as mandatory as breathing. Pearl and Seymour handled their weapons with practiced ease. Most of the others still handled theirs a little awkward.

The surroundings of the old house, so steeped in memories gave way to the giant ruin that the City of the Dead had become, as Lillith and her old and new charges made their way through streets littered with dust, bricks, and broken wood and glass.

Some of the large shards still had blood on them.

We need to get Ted down here sometime, Gabi thought brightly. There's a lot for him to photograph here.

There was. Stacy nodded to herself. He had an uncanny eye for catching the bizarre and horrific details through his lens, both the lenses of his eyes and his camera.

But he can't hold a camera anymore, can he? Gabi persisted. Not without ruining it.

No, he can't, Stacy thought. He needs someone to hold it for him, to actually push the button.

Advanced technology is anathema to the Phoenix, Gabi bristled.

The reminder alone made Stacy shiver and burn.

They left the French Quarter, crossing Canal Street and turned left.

It was a cloudy day, hot and humid. They were all sweating, the result of the cooling shower negated after just a few minutes outside.

Most of them had the natural ability to deal with extreme temperatures, and the rest was used to heat, but they still struggled.

– I think I'll cut my hair, Pearl decided. – That way it won't turn greasy so fast.

– At least it won't look as bad, Keira acknowledged.

New Orleans, the city had something, whatever it was, grabbing everybody visiting and living there by the tail, shaking dry and wet bones. It wasn't really diminished, even though the physical part of it had taken a beating, on the contrary. To Lillith New Orleans had grown the last year, and was still growing, expanding into the infinite.

She mumbled something.

– What was that? Gabi wondered. – I didn't quite get that.

– There is a City of the Dead in Cairo, Egypt, many centuries old, Lillith said, – where people live among their dead. They call it simply El'arafa - the Cemetery. It's still there, in the modern city. There are several other places like it, both presently and in antiquity. They spread and grow, unseen, beyond its physical borders.

– It's easy making Magick in such places, isn't it? Seymour said brightly.

– Yeah, easy, Stacy replied preoccupied, rattled around the edges.

She saw the old Egyptian woman in slow flashes, the early twentieth century witch wandering ceaselessly up and down El'arafa, weaving her spell. She saw her and Nancy Warren die at exactly the same moment, saw them reunite, becoming one,

110

fearsome entity. Stacy saw herself with absolute clarity in the mirror of the window to her right, and shook with excitement.

– The tombstones at the First Cemetery here, and also others across the city do look like houses, don't they?

That statement brought yet another set of impressions to their conscious mind.

Gabi nodded to herself.

They tensed, inevitably, as they approached their destination, the building at the end of the street that had been Harrahs' Casino. Johnson and his gang blocked their way.

– We don't want your kind here, he boasted.

– But we want to be here, Pearl said, – and if you want to stop us from entering, you better be prepared to back up your implied threat.

Johnson and his gang dominated their territory, their slice of the city, and constantly attempted to branch out and harass those allowing themselves to be harassed.

Canal Street and its buildings were seen as a kind of free zone, and that vexed people like Johnson.

– That's such a wise choice, Pearl grinned, when the other group kept their hands well away from their guns. – Do you know why it's such a wise choice?

Johnson stared sullenly at her. Stacy knew very well what he was thinking.

His nights are numbered, right? Gabi thought.

They are indeed, Stacy replied.

– Yes, you do, Pearl said to his face. – You know that I and most of the others in my tribe can draw the gun at the hip faster than your finger can twitch and kill you before you can blink.

And Johnson's thoughts turned even more to vengeance and cruelty, fantasizing about what he would do to them all and most of all to the females. Stacy didn't cringe, like a part of her might have done once.

– There's just no hope for improvement in there, is there? She spat at him.

None she could sense, no matter how deep she probed.

He scowled at her, but didn't make any move.

They walked past the sullen «guards» to the fairly packed hall inside, a place that had once been filled with roulette and Black Jack tables, and slot machines, but was now cleared of all that. Except for the remains of the carpets on the floor and a few remnants of what had been, it pretty much looked like a completely ordinary worn townhall.

Lillith let the mood and prevalent excitement of the place enter her and opened herself fully to the room and its people. It affected everybody, inevitably. No one could avoid sensing the change. Unfamiliar and familiar faces and minds turned their attention to her and her entourage.

– Goddess! A man greeted her.

It was very obvious what was at the forefront of his mind. Laughter rolled through the thick, humid air.

She grinned to him.

– Greetings, Raven, another man cried to her.

People of both sexes, of many tribes joined in, and greeted her as she passed them, touched her hands and some also her mind with a wide range of emotions, from devotion and respect to skepticism and cynicism to hypocrisy and duplicity.

All of it strengthened her.

Worshippers fell on their knees in their minds.

It strengthened her.

– I'm *so* pleased that you and your charges could come, a woman said, obviously insincere.

It strengthened her.

There was a provisionary stage at the end of the building, lit by a few badly working lamps, resting in darkness.

Go, Stacy told Gabi.

She did. Pearl and Seymour joined her. Stacy's roaming mind stayed with them as they rushed behind the corner towards the restrooms, at a spot they couldn't be seen and they faded away.

It happened almost immediately, an echo, a sigh in the wind. Stacy felt excitement and apprehension rise, pushed from her toes to the tip of her hair.

There was a shift in the air, a change in the quality of the pale darkness on the stage.

The mime stood there, dressed in black, her face covered by the characteristic white mask. Behind her, shadows and shapes moved and danced and flowed through the shifting reality experienced as real and true by the gathering.

She performed with spheres and sticks and knives, and it was an incredible sight, far superior to any circus performance they had ever seen.

A voice rose from the ground beneath their feet, or so it seemed. The gathering imagined that the speakers were on, and perhaps they were. The mime's lips didn't move, but then again, her lips were plastic and white paint. Something seemingly electric, but rather primal burned people's minds and bodies, their skin and bones.

There was music somewhere, or so they believed.

Two rivers, two wings

She read.

Like moths rising out of the fire

A shadow creature

As real, as sharp

As the air we breathe

The water we drink

She stood there, silent, unmovable. More mimes stepped forward from the shadows.

– There is something vaguely familiar with those words.

A journalist frowned.

– A man named Eric Carr quoted that verse of a poem from my diary, the mime said.

Now, her voice sounded completely normal. Her lips moved. There were more frowns.

The tall woman with the white hair removed her mask, and everybody beheld her face, and several of those present easily recognized it.

– You are *Linda Cousin*, the journalist cried astonished.

Linda smiled, a little ambiguous.

– Yes, I am.

The other mimes also removed their masks. Glory Burns, Shuen Parker, Judith Breen, and all the surviving members of Mike Warren's guerilla fighters revealed themselves.

The buzz rose through the ceiling. Several of the armed guards attempted to draw guns. They were dead and bloody before they had fired a single bullet.

– We won't tolerate any disturbance…

They stood there, silent. The present journalists finally got it.

– Where have you been the last fifteen years?

– Around, Linda shrugged. – Working in secret.

– But why come forward, *now?*

– It's time, Glory said.

Then her expression hardened, sporting a patronizing snarl.

– You just need to take a look around you at what has happened to this city and the entire south-eastern seaboard of the United States to realize what a beyond stupid question that is. And that's merely one reason on a *long* list.

– Current human existence is untenable, at best, Judith said angrily. – The only good news is that we remain fire, remain Human Beings in spite of that horror.

– I feel such a chill, Linda said, – such a profound sense of sadness and joy and it brings me on the verge of tears.

She paused a bit, before continuing, shrugging, not shrugging.

– I can feel the wind in my face.

That statement would be quoted quite a few times in the coming weeks, months and years and pondered endlessly.

– We are the Human Liberation Front, Glory cried, and we've become many.

That statement was also pondered at some length.

They pulled back, into the shadows and the strange, shimmering darkness.

It took quite a while before the guards that were still alive gathered sufficient wits and courage to draw their arms and rush towards the stage.

– Looks like the public meeting has been discontinued prematurely, Stacy shrugged, clearly not sorry.

People, allies, enemies and friends looked at her, and she granted them all her sweet blinding smile.

Gabi, Pearl and Seymour returned from the restroom area.

They walked outside, set course back down Canal Street.

A couple of police officers sent angry, ugly glances in Stacy's direction, but she quickly took care of them, dissuading their more than passing interest.

She hardly had to think about doing it. It had become second nature to her.

The eerie smile touched her face.

It frightens the others, Gabi told her, told her what she already knew. But not me. That smile, and what it represents is worth a thousand soldiers.

– The mind has finally become a weapon to be reckoned with, she said aloud.

The others nodded slowly, their view of caution changing, considering the girl's words and their implications.

– Yes, my mind is a powerful weapon, Lillith said to them. – But it's useless without a will to direct it, and warriors to back it up. We're all weapons, beyond deadly, beyond versatile, blades forged in the cold fire of the Earth.

And then an expression of clarity lit their shifting faces.

And you're so skilled at using those weapons at your disposal, Gabi thought, a legendary tactician, a queen of all trades, having grown more skilled than ever. I commend you.

The girl's taunts got to her, inevitably. Their sting burned in her heart. She ignored it and pushed forward.

They crossed the boundaries to the First Cemetery at dusk. Stacy saw, in another flash how it looked in that close Other World, how it pulsed and grew, reaching out to its surroundings.

The day had flown away and was only a faint memory. This was their time, and all the present faces lit up in expectation, including Stacy's, hers most of all.

Torches burned in the air, and in the Shadow realm their flames were vast bonfires touching many spots.

– Witches not Dreamweavers use these places to gain access to the Shadowworld, she taught them, – to the true world imitating the dream, the dream imitating the true world.

The other group approached them from the opposite side of the old graveyard, city of the dead. A pair of silver-haired heads flashed in the shards of the moon, the glow from those close and distant bonfires.

– Linda of the Shadow Blade, Stacy greeted the woman drawing most attention to herself.

Linda embraced her, in a rare show of affection. The others did, too, without reservations.

The cold draft, the hot blaze began blowing, descending from above and without, rising from below and within.

They gathered around her, around the Lillith, in a full circle, both the wanderers and the locals, around the moon, the blazing human forge.

– We must embrace our compassion with a burning heart, she called to them from the night and the fire, – must do so the same way we do our cruelty and determination to see our objectives met.

She walked among them with a closed fist, an open hand and what was beyond, showing them all what life was about.

One single raven stood on her left shoulder. The others had pulled back into the dark surroundings, just beyond the reach of the shimmering light cast by the torches.

– Humans have resisted and fought against the development of civilization from

114

the start, Stacy Larkin told them. – It was a sneaky thing at first, difficult to grasp and even comprehend, very much like a thief in the night…

They were with her, all of them, listening with open ears and open minds, noticing all the sensations she fed them, as she told her story.

– They fought in various ways, both instinctively and deliberately, Lillith told them. – resisting the existence that was death, what was slowly draining away the human spirit, killing all life on the planet, destroying everything making life worth living. Tall, unnatural spires, tombstones in appearance and fact, testaments to everything that was bad about humanity, clusters of dwellings fit for no creature rose towards the sky, devouring more and more land as they grew and multiplied like the cancer it was.

The listeners experienced it in a fast-forward motion and shuddered beyond shuddering. Stacy threw dry driftwood at the fire and the sensations grew even more powerful and intense.

– Official, accepted, forged history is truly, in amazing ways not actually revealing what really happened, except in a downright superficial manner. It is true what they say that the victorious write history, but it's worse than that. What children are taught, of history and life in general is a stunning and horrible avoidance of everything important to us all.

– During twelve thousand years of wars and strife there's only one single major conflict that really matters: that between humanity and the Machine we created from our own desolate hearts.

Hours, years, millennia passed by. Everybody leaned back with half closed eyes. The human beings gathered between the tall fires in the old, derelict cemetery sensed something more forging itself in the glowing insides of the storyteller before them.

– I remember, she told them, – and my heart fills with joy and anticipation.

And theirs did as well, tinged with ever so little apprehension.

She rocked back and forth on her ass, and they rocked with her.

– Humanity is the most powerful creative force in existence, she mused. – Being dragons spitting fire in the darkest and coldest of places, touching everything, we are not made weak with time. The steel of those with true resolve only grow stronger. The manifestations of power have been many and varied throughout time and space, but one such stands out beyond any other. There's a legend, one very persistent about a birdlike creature of fire and shadow rising from its own ashes…

– The Phoenix, Glory cried in terror and joy.

The gust of icy wind and hot fire grew that much more powerful, that much more present. Everybody began glancing around them, inevitably, staring at the Raven in their midst.

– I see a sword, Stacy said, – a sword of fire, shadowing the Earth, tempered in the hot furnaces of the desert.

Lillith's eyes opened wide and deep.

2

Phillip Caine's grin filled the screen.

– Good evening to all nice people watching us, watching the Phoenix Green Earth alternative news-feed broadcast to people all over the planet Earth.

Gayle Tadero's just as wide grin filled the screen.

– We've got a lot for you tonight, like we always have. There's no lack of lies and deception to be exposed, hidden truths and alternative possibilities to be explored.

Images first flashed across the screen behind them, then Phillip and Gayle faded out and the images filled the entire monitor window for the people watching it, either on the Internet or more traditional television.

There was a closeup of an UFO levitating above New York City, glimpses of others above other major population centers across the globe, images mostly taken almost twenty years ago, but also earlier.

The viewers saw photographs and film clips from the lands Israel colonized, occupied and terrorized in Palestine.

They saw images of bulldozers, excavators and other human tools breaking new ground and ongoing destruction of nature all over the Earth.

– One case in point among a list of thousands is the ongoing Israeli terror against a basically defenseless Palestinian population, Phillip said, no longer smiling. – Today we take yet another hard look at what establishment Western media love to call the Israel-Palestine conflict.

– We reveal more of the ongoing destruction of the wilderness and of life itself, Gayle said. – We attack the destroyers in a thorough and harsh manner.

– And we remind people of the days in 1987 when practically all mankind could watch the alien spaceships hover over our largest cities, events that practically no one in establishment media is talking much about. We're still ridiculed every time we do a feature on it, as if the aliens' presence hasn't long since been proven beyond doubt.

– This event exposes establishment media more than anything to me, Gayle said. – It also shows that some people's preference for denying the obvious is practically limitless.

– But here, as ever, Phillip grinned, – we will show you the truth and we will discuss it in an open and frank manner leaving no doubt that all sides and angles are represented, and every stone turned.

They were casually dressed, very casually… dressed in what couldn't be described as anything but rags. The room surrounding them looked like a studio of sorts, but not very tidy. The Phoenix Green Earth News Feed turned increasingly alternative in both form and content, not less.

The grin was never far away. Neither were the passion and the anger.

– We have a fairly traditional first main guest tonight, Gayle said. – Fairly traditional in our programs that is. Martin Keller has problems getting airtime with traditional media, but we welcome outspoken people here in our hall dedicated to true freedom of expression.

Keller appeared and sat down in one of the empty chairs.

116

– To offer a traditional view we have Professor in anthropology at Harvard University, John Corben, Phillip said.

Another man, clearly nervous or anxious sat down in the other available chair.

Simplicity ruled the room. There were no features beyond pure necessity distracting viewers from the four people.

Still… Keller seemed to draw attention to himself, to fill the screen, even when the camera wasn't totally focused on him.

Liz and Ted watched it all.

– He's… impressive, isn't he? Liz said uncertain.

– He is, Ted agreed. – We feel such… kinship with him, don't we?

Liz didn't voice her reply, but she still agreed.

Images, words and night and fire filled the screen, Stacy Larkin on tour with her entourage.

– During twelve thousand years of war and strife there's only one single major conflict that really matters: that between humanity and the Machine we created from our own desolate hearts.

She spoke in Houston, Texas, to yet another mixed crowd of a hateful mob and excited people. The two watching felt the surge from both groups, felt it when she pulled it inside herself, used it, catalyzed it and returned it to the crowd backed by her seething power. They watched the succubus strut her stuff and yet another small knob inside them was switched on.

The program returned to the studio. But even to those watching it on screens across the world, it seemed like the mood and words from Houston lingered and burned in their buzzing mind.

– Thoughts? Gayle prompted Corben.

The man was fidgeting, not really his usual confident self at all. He knew with a start, if he hadn't realized it before that he wasn't on his home turf, the easy lane other, establishment media outlets had provided him with.

– I don't know what to say. She is clearly… overreaching.

– In what way? Phillip asked good-humored.

– The problems are blown out of all proportions, the solutions *way* too far-reaching.

– The way I see it the problems can't be exaggerated, Keller said lightly, but still with his usual intensity, – and the solutions can hardly be drastic enough.

He picked a big object from his right side. It was the painting. The World Grinder by William Carter Lafayette.

– One certainty becomes increasingly clear today, beyond niceties and polite speech, one obviously overriding all other concerns: Life on Earth is dying. This is the inevitable result if civilization is allowed to continue to its horrible end.

The painting showed two earths with a giant meat grinder between them. The somewhat healthy was sucked into the grinder and appeared at the other side as a burned out, shrunken globe in Space.

– Then, there is a book… Gayle said.

– Then, there is the illustrated book, Keller nodded.

– You and Lafayette wrote it?

– He illustrated it and I wrote the final version of it, with contribution from quite a few great people, but Ted was really the first that fleshed out his thoughts about the ongoing nightmare we all suffer.

– Suffer? Corben yelped, totally out of character compared to his usual jovial and patronizing self. – Are you nuts?

They ignored him.

– We've created a data-animation based on the projection, Gayle said. – It's drawing a stark and inevitable picture. Hundreds of years of destruction will be shown in minutes.

The presentation began with a view of the Earth from Space placed on the left part of the screen.

– This is a photograph taken thirty years ago, the voice said. – Notice the bright colors, the strong saturation?

Another photograph, another image of Earth appeared on the right.

– This is recent. Notice the grayish taint? It's unmistakable, really. Comparing the two images you can practically see the added pollution. Industry-friendly agitators have claimed that the recent picture is taken during winter on the northern hemisphere, but that's just yet another bullshit attempt on their side to keep people from learning the truth.

The haunting film of ages to come began, remarkable in detail and horror. At first it showed existing, real-life footage, but then it began revealing the upcoming years, the inevitable future.

– These are artists' representations of London and surrounding areas in the seventeenth century. We can see that even though the city's development is extensive, it is nothing compared to today. Take a good look.

Superimposed were photographs from present time. The difference was beyond startling.

– Take any urban area on Earth and you will see the same.

One section of the film showed a totally pristine landscape. Slowly a village appeared, a growing village, becoming a city, slowly reaching out to the surrounding areas, until practically the entire screen was filled with industrial development, dark smoke, big buildings and there were hardly any green spots left anywhere.

The film moved beyond the past and the present.

The perspective was that of a bird or something like a fast-moving chopper flying across the land and the sea. New York, the streets of Manhattan Island was covered in water. The stark winds started blowing. Deserts began spreading in earnest. There was no more ice in the Arctic Sea during the summer. Heat boiled and killed people in the cities during the hottest parts of the year. Trees died at an alarming rate. Giant, frequent storms became common. The ice on Greenland and West Antarctica began to disappear. The truth became visible with the naked eye. Life in the sea, especially vertebras became practically extinct. The acidification completed what the pure poison started. Pockets of sulfuric gases rose from that much hotter ocean and poisoned all life coming near it. The winds made staying outdoors almost

118

impossible and then, not long after that all houses of wood crumbled around those hiding in them. Tall buildings were abandoned for security reasons. Mankind started burrowing into the ground, creating vast undergrounds compounds. Decades, centuries, millennia passed. The planet became a dry, dead husk, very much like the painter of the World Grinder had envisioned.

No one said anything the first few seconds.

– A great film, Corben said with a dull, dry but clearly ironic voice. – Great visuals, but in terms of accuracy…

– In terms of accuracy it is very much on the money, Keller stated. – It's the inevitable, logical end of civilization, of Earth as long as humanity refuses to live like human beings.

– I would agree that current human society has problems, almost anyone I know would, but you advocate a return to a time when humans lived a short, dismal existence in caves. That is both a way too drastic and unnecessary solution.

– Ah, you're forwarding the cliché, the myth of «Stone Age» life…

Corben open and closed his mouth, attempting to reply, failing miserably.

Keller continued in a fairly relaxed, but very patronizing manner:

– I've been asked by desperate people lately, people desperate for assurances: «Shouldn't at least civilization remain an option»? «No», I reply. «Civilization isn't an option. We've tried that for thousands of years and it doesn't work. It's a collective suicide in progress. Does a physician tell a patient who has slit his wrists and is about to slit his throat that this is an option»?

– But the transition, the return to a better life won't exactly be pleasant, right? Tadero asked him the inevitable follow-up question.

– I'm afraid not, the guest acknowledged. – We've ventured so far off course the last ten thousand years that the upheaval is bound to be dramatic. I only know that the alternative, continuing our insane tailspin suicide run is far worse. I know. Everybody knows, if they truly open themselves up to their surroundings and tainted inner life.

Keller/Gudmundson/Morningstar blinked, and in that blink, he could see, through the countless eyes of his tiny helpers, through thousand eyes people's reactions to his words and visual storytelling, in their homes, in front of their computer screens or their «smart» phones, and he smiled. The Lord of the Flies smiled, and felt sorrow and joy beyond imagining, and they did, too.

– Look at the city, he said with a chill in his voice. – Look at the City stretching on forever.

He turned to Corben, and pushed his eyes at him like hooks.

– That is what you're supporting, with your ignorance and your inability to see beyond your circumstances.

Corben gasped, visibly gasped.

– What are you…

He visibly pulled himself together, back from the brink of what he viewed as the abyss. Keller witnessed it from his point of view.

– This… what you have showed me is pure speculation, and it's no big deal at all.

– Spoken like a true slave of the Machine, Keller applauded. – You're just afraid of changes you don't understand, that's all.

Corben frowned some more, but then he suddenly looked relieved, as if a great burden had been lifted from his heart.

– Or, he spat, – you just want to change a well-working society in order to please your own ego.

– The world has changed irrevocably the last twenty years, with several major and countless minor events.

Keller did not lose his cool, even though his intensity progressed a notch or so further.

– You won't pretend that it hasn't, will you?

Corben glared at him, attempting to speak, unable to do so, glaring at him in something very similar to hatred.

Keller shared it all, with Lillith, with Phoenix, with many, even Corben. The connections to his distant past reconnected with his present in a way he had only rarely experienced.

– The inequality we see today, he said calmly, pointedly, – that we've seen for so long, between people and the sexes came into human life with civilization. Before that it was practically preposterous and rare. It's still preposterous, but no longer rare. Civil disobedience is not our problem. Our problem is civil obedience. The entire world must rebel against those in charge, eliminate the very foundation for their power. This is a given, but one that evidently must be repeated many more times before people get it: they can't rule without the support of their subjects. In other words: toppling a tyranny isn't really that hard. It just requires a slight shift in consciousness. You are guilty, John Corben in not rebelling against the tyranny. You are guilty of supporting it in all things that matter.

Corben practically jumped up on his feet.

– What have you done to me? He shouted, sweat pouring from his skin.

He turned towards Tadero and Caine, with eyes hissing like a snake.

– You are… biased, he shouted even louder.

– Nonsense! Gayle replied with passion. – We ask everybody the hard questions, you know that. It's just that the «experts» and proponents serving the establishment aren't used to that, to have anyone question their bullshit.

Corben turned red with rage.

– You allow these insane ideas to be broadcast. You should be… b-be arrested, be p-punished.

His words ended in an unintelligible babble. He stopped, and rushed out of the studio.

Tadero, Caine and Keller remained, not attempting to hide anything of their smug expression.

– It's amazing, isn't it? Tadero said, suddenly solemn. – They never seem to learn, to move beyond their rigid behavioral pattern.

– More and more do, Keller said.

Caine turned and grinned to the camera.

– And with those words of wisdom we will now take a slight break. Welcome back for more fun stuff soon…

3

Lillith returned to Northfield, to the green and pleasant land. It embraced her, as she embraced all its aspects, pulled it and its people into herself. The buildings and streets covered in growth spoke and whispered at her center. She noticed amazed, and a little startled that the difference between what had been Newtown and Oldtown, minor for quite some time, was practically erased.

The Hill glowed in Shadow, welcoming her back. She knew they had started calling it Raven's Mound.

The giant beast of a hairball called Malvin practically assaulted her, rubbed himself on her feet, appearing like a black panther in her eyes.

– You beast, she chuckled, – you roaring beast.

The two Chinis, Chini Richardson and Chini, the jungle priestess approached her.

– Greetings, Goddess, the priestess said. – We have the honor of being your servants and protectors today.

– What she said, the other grinned.

There was both a healthy disrespect and awe and worship in their eyes.

She walked and they followed her.

Her impressions imposed themselves on them. She did that without thinking now. It affected them, inevitably in profound ways.

– Lillith has waited so long for this moment, this age, hasn't she? The priestess said softly, gasping in delight.

She has.

For a brief moment she couldn't tell whether or not she spoke with her mind or vocalized her reply, and she didn't care.

The Phoenix was so close. She sensed them wherever they walked or flew.

– Let's do the scenic tour, she told them.

They looked even closer at her, at her beyond enigmatic presence, their curiosity getting the best of them.

– I feel a need to ponder, to pause and consider some more, she willingly informed them. – I know it will only strengthen my resolve.

– You don't need to explain yourself to us, Goddess, the priestess said.

Lillith looked closer at her. Chini, Glow could be quite enigmatic herself, at least to most people.

– Yes, I do.

Malvin joined them on her stroll, exactly like the giant panthers had done in Egypt so long ago.

The three reached an area of Newtown totally transformed. Buildings were hardly buildings anymore, but hills and hurdles. The entire block had been refitted to a training area. Mary held a self defense course for new initiates, driving them mercilessly through a labyrinth of both mind and body, far harder than she had done at her place in Denver.

Ellen supervised the children, teaching them about Magick and life.

– You need to master your abilities, she told them, – and you need to learn how to defend yourself, both with and without them, learn to fight hard in order to increase your changes of survival.

The children nodded solemnly.

Lillith and her two maids studied the various spectacles of Northfield in silence for a while, studied Mary and Ellen that had both learned the hard way what they taught.

– You haven't spoken much, young Chini, Lillith remarked softly. – Have you nothing to add to our circumstances?

The girl was taken a bit aback, but straightened herself, pulling herself together, giggling a bit before responding.

– I'm sorry, Stacy. All this still seems amazing to me, even after the years I've been a part of it. And as impressive, imposing Ted and Liz, Nick and the others might be, you're even more so. I can't help it, I feel like I'm a mote of dust in your presence. I must constantly remind myself that it isn't so.

– Your awareness serves you well, young Richardson, Stacy joked, shrugged. – You just have to make sure it continues to do so.

– How did you make my father join us? Chini blurted out. – How on Earth did you manage that?

– Your father was your authority figure, wasn't he, far more than most fathers? He continued to be also after you liberated yourself from him physically?

– Answer me, the older, younger girl choked. – *Please!*

– It's quite simple. I just gave him an offer he couldn't refuse…

– You snapped your fingers and made him yours, the girl cried aloud. – Why don't you do that to the world?

The birds rose from the branches of the new trees. The ravens squeaked and flapped their wings. Recruits running through the gauntlet were briefly rocked in their focus.

– You're not the first I've had this conversation with, Stacy, the young girl said softly. – You won't be the last.

They walked on. Mary and Ellen waved. Stacy returned the wave enthusiastically, giving the thumbs up. Dozens of thumbs echoed hers. Everyone they encountered greeted the trio one way or another.

The old Gyrich estate entered their view. Stacy saw it in her mind's eye long before that, through the vision and senses of everybody inside.

William played the piano, the grand piano. Its chords filled the building, reaching the wild-growing garden outside. Helen accompanied him on vocals, her voice soft as quiet rain. Stacy listened to the lyrics and swallowed hard.

– It isn't loud? Chini wondered. – Is it?

Both Chinis noted Stacy's change of mood, of course. Everyone in close proximity did. The priestess dried a tear from the Goddess' cheek.

– It's so funny, young Chini mused. – I don't understand the lyrics, but I understand them anyway.

She chuckled with stars, dark and warm stars in her eyes.

– I've learned to deal with apparent contradictions since I joined this outfit…

They entered the central building of the estate, what had been the Gyrich home, the neighbor house to where Jill Stafford had had her nightly performance.

Kyle was painting. Stacy led the two others up the marble stairs to a bright, large room.

The boy sat in front of a canvas. He had been immersed in his work and hadn't actually sensed her approach, but when he did, it was his presence that filled her mind. Their common mindscape grew to something far «larger» than the sum of their parts.

The painting was of her, was of Lillith. She stood on the shore of Fire Lake at night, with her hands above her head, reaching into the night. It was like she reached up with both hands and grabbed the moon. The lake burned in shadow and dark fire, both visible and not.

Do you get goose bumps? William Carter Lafayette asked her, like most non-telepaths in the inner circle of the movement forming thoughts in his mind she could easily pick up.

I do, she willingly admitted. The painting… makes sense, beyond evocative and startling. I am the Witch of the Fire Lake, but I could never express it quite like this. He's a rare talent, isn't he?

They spoke and Kyle listened, even if he seemed to ignore them.

He is. It is as if he possesses all the ability to paint most of his bloodline have lacked.

She saw the painting unfold on the canvas and in his mind. It grabbed her and held on. She beheld the future and spoke again, in whirl of water and air, time and Space. Wind and time were blowing through her.

– If you wish to find the secrets of the Universe think of the flesh and the infinite power it contains.

They heard her, all over Northfield and in pockets and crannies across the planet.

And it was good.

Timothy Carson sought her out, like she had known he eventually would. She walked alone then, to the chagrin of those who would serve her, no matter how gently she dismissed them. The two of them met by the old graveyard, faced each other at the spot where witches had once suffered and burned.

She closed and opened her eyes, still easily seeing his heated stare and generations past caught up with her.

– Why didn't I tell you anything? She spoke softly, like a mother would to a hurt and bewildered son. – I wanted to give you a change to come to me.

– You're not her, I know that. Why do I feel it like you are?

She turned towards him.

– That is easy to answer and explain. Your soul speaks words your mind doesn't necessarily understand. I'm everything she was and you know that, know it beyond knowing.

– Why do you talk about her in third person, then? He said angrily.

– Because I am so much more, she said quietly. – Her memories and personality, everything she was, is immersed into the multitude Lillith *is*. Just like Stacy's eventually will be.

He crumbled a bit and ran into her waiting arms, his eyes filled with tears. She smiled a little tender, as she comforted the older man.

They sat on the wall, two excited young people exchanging experiences and the deepest secrets. She sat there, staring into the Void, into the familiar well of his eyes.

– For a long time, a very long time I was afraid of my own Shadow. Our Shadow is always close by. I could just reach out and touch it, but I feared everything it was, everything I was. I saw it as a giant mouth intent on devouring me. It was only when I finally accepted it as a part of me the fear faded away like the trifle it is.

He knew what she was talking about. She saw it in his eyes, his eyes of mind and soul.

– My new surroundings in Northfield, the change in circumstances brought forth my power from obscurity, from Sleep.

– How can you stand it? He blurted out. – The mixing of all those identities?

– People keep asking me that, she replied. – It isn't hard at all. The Self doesn't weaken, doesn't fracture with awareness, but strengthens beyond anything you believe you can imagine. All you need to know yourself is to draw upon a fraction of the confidence resting within your boiling core. Each life is one voice, rising from the multitude of our unending Self.

– I know, he choked, – I've always known, but I still missed you... and Stella.

She knew, saw him as she had always seen him, as memory yet again assaulted her.

– We will always miss those that aren't with us, she said, shrugging deliberately.

They sat there, sharing everything that was to share. Pieces and fragments drawn forth in just minutes once more made Memory grow ascendant in their mind.

They parted.

– We will be apart for hours and perhaps nights and days, now, she said. – That isn't truly different from the years we spent longing for those who weren't there, is it?

– I guess so. He shook his head and a loud, brittle laughter rose from his larynx. – Not after I've pondered the subject for a few hundred years, anyway.

It was a good joke. She knew he would be alright, that he would weather the endless past and future.

– Speak to your... sister, Lillith said casually, fooling nobody. – You may be able to reach her in ways I can't.

– I will.

She saw him and Gabi chat, saw the girl's angry expression soften, not knowing whether or not it was real or imagined.

– You know him, don't you, know... Morningstar from long ago?

The young man turned for a spell and called to her from afar.

– Long ago, she nodded, a bit distant.

– No wonder that, he nodded, – the way you lived everything up.

There was no anger in his voice anymore, but there was spite. She grinned.

She continued her scenic tour. The two Chinis rejoined her. She nodded her approval to them, putting them in their place.

Even young Chini knew what she was, now, what she had been and might become.

– I regret to inform the Goddess that the Phoenix isn't here right now, the older Chini said, – but the Goddess knows that, of course.

And Chini knew that Lillith knew that Chini knew. She was a shrewd priestess.

– Yes, it suddenly dawned on me that I can feel It, no matter where on Earth It is.

And the imprint of awe didn't leave the faces of the two accompanying her.

She knew and felt so much, so much that she couldn't properly determine how much she in truth felt and knew. It was alright. She had lived with that, with that pleasure and horror forever, well-aware of the fact that she always would.

It didn't bother her anymore. The giant mouth no longer held any terror for her, except as a tiny twinge somewhere she couldn't scratch.

She saw without trying reality unfold, past, present and future, and it was just as useless as it had always been.

Behind her wide-open eyelids rose the fire and shadow of existence, the rush of wind and time, and she witnessed as it happened Nix Olympia on Mars have its eruption, experienced the unfathomable sight of a frozen river breaking in spring and more than anything…

The Dragon traveling through infinite space.

4

The «break» in the broadcast from the Phoenix Green Earth studio wasn't filled with advertising, but with protest demonstrations from various sites all over the world, against pollution, greed, governments, capitalism, civilization itself, corporations, the market, social injustice, the rich, the police, war, militarism and just about anything. Rage and passion filled the screen and the room where people watched.

Somewhere, anywhere streets filled up with protesters and police officers. Writing on several posters cried out:

JUSTICE FOR JUSTIN

And on another set of posters:

JUSTICE FOR ALL VICTIMS OF POLICE BRUTALITY
IF YOU WANT TO KILL SOMEONE AND GET AWAY WITH IT
BECOME A COP

And on yet another:

THE POLICE ARE THE EAGER BULLIES OF THOSE IN CHARGE
BLAME BOTH THE BULLIES AND THEIR HANDLERS

Martin Warren interviewed Desmond Lynx, one of the community leaders.

– Our movement isn't about protesting against singular acts made by the police, Lynx stated calm and measured. – We're protesting against the very existence of the police, anywhere.

– What do you say to those telling you that this is a preposterous demand? Martin asked casually.

– We keep telling them the obvious truth, Lynx replied. – Theirs are the preposterous and ill-informed opinion. We tell them that the police are a fairly new invention created around the start of the industrial revolution as yet one more way of the rich and powerful to control a given population.

– The biggest bullies and murderers in the LAPD have been PROMOTED! A girl standing close by shouted aloud.

She held up a sign:

STILL NO JUSTICE FOR RODNEY KING

The shouts and noise from the nearby streets picked up yet another notch. Lydia, carrying the camera was almost hit by a stone. It was on its way towards her, but to those watching, it seemed like it changed direction at the last possible moment.

– The Network for Exposure of Police Bullying and killings is a coalition of groups monitoring and opposing the always intimidating and violent policing, Lynx said. – The way we see it, the need for such a network has been grossly underestimated for a very long time.

Martin nodded to him, and Lynx nodded back. Lynx turned and walked off, returning to the boiling kettle close by. Martin turned towards the camera.

– We will stay here and record everything, of course, with no illusions of the police respecting the critical press. We will be right there, in the thick of the action… You will get the best footage you're likely to get from any protest. You will witness head on when the beyond brutal police officers start bashing in more skulls and break more bones, and all officers doing that will be put on the list, the long list we're compiling.

He would know who they were, know their names and innermost life. It would sicken him, but he would keep doing it.

Lydia joined him, and as they held hands and walked towards the center of the growing disturbance Ruth and Stewart joined them.

The image on the screen shifted from the streets of fire to the relative calm of the studio. Martin Keller sat there with Gayle Tadero and Phillip Caine.

– Welcome back to the Phoenix Green Earth studio. Phillip said. – We continue our extended interview with Martin Keller on a variety of subjects, as we keep monitoring the situation on the streets, the places where you will find our reporters.

– So, Martin, Gayle said, – what do you think of Desmond Lynx's new initiative?

– It's clearly a very good thing, Keller replied, – one that should have been initiated a long time ago, and what makes it even better is that this is only one among many, rising from many different angles of mankind.

– Like lots of other truths kept from the majority of humanity, Caine nodded.

He turned and a camera zoomed in on him.

– We will start the second part of today's program with startling cuts from a documentary made by radical filmmaker Carlton Magendie. It's called «The day a mirage visited Earth».

126

The cuts started with the introduction:

To those wondering: In our research to this film, we've followed rigidly the rules laid out by J. Allen Hynek concerning alien encounters, which is basically that it shouldn't count as an encounter if it isn't witnessed by several people independently of each other. To those wanting to know more, read Hynek's book the UFO Experience and everything else he has written on the subject.

Incredible images of giant disks hovering above cities filled the screen. The accompanying voice seemed more than a little lame in contrast.

– This is the sight that met people in all major cities on Earth when they looked up one crisp autumn morning in 1987. There are tons of photographs and films and recordings, even from CNN and other mainstream media, virtually unprecedented in the time before the Internet took off. There are countless witnesses seeing the same things independent of each other, not only of the disks, but of close encounters of the third kind all over the planet. Yes, this is a film about the alien visit in 1987. For the record, we don't question the fact that it happened. Our angle is quite different from that rather silly stipulation. We ask, simply put *why* it has hardly been discussed at all afterwards, except in the first few days and weeks since the event.

A man walks down a desolate road. He's clearly troubled, haunted, with far more than his years painted on his face.

– This is Morgan Whitfield. He's one of millions that had a particularly intense alien encounter during the dramatic events almost twenty years ago. He has put all his unedited material, films, audio recordings and writings at our disposal.

Carlton Magendie walked with Whitfield to a fairly secluded spot in Hackney in northern London. That footage was occasionally supplanted by Whitfield's own, from twenty years ago, a fact easily revealed because of the grainy film. Sometimes, when the camera is directed at the sky the giant hovering disk is very distinct and visible.

– There, he points. – I saw them right there.

They reach a turn, a green spot where a smaller flying saucer is parked. On the grainy film what looks very much like human beings stand ready to board the craft. They evidently spot Whitfield with his camera and seem posed to act, to charge him, but then they turn and rush up the shiny white boarding «stairs». The camera shakes in the human's hands, but he stands his ground the seconds it takes for the craft to rise from the ground and reach the open gates of the giant disk above.

– They looked human, at least before you took a closer look. Perhaps they had some sort of camouflage equipment, but that seemed to be failing. Their… shuttle didn't seem to function at peak efficiency either. Something was up, something clearly upsetting them. That part really struck me as funny. Here we had a technologically advanced species able to travel billion of miles through hostile space and something here, on Earth scared the shit out of them.

Several other testimonies and recordings were played, also about how the governments of Earth had kept the truth of the alien presence a secret from their population. More revealing interviews and footage showed that beyond reasonable doubt, and it was all part of the indisputable truth being revealed.

The broadcast returned to the studio, where Phillip, Gayle and Martin Keller were joined by Magendie and one other man.

– We welcome Carlton Magendie, the filmmaker to our program, Gayle said, – and also Nelson Peterson, professor in Astrophysics at Cornell University.

– Let's hear from the filmmaker first, Phillip said. – You worked with this film for five years, Carlton. What's your first and paramount impression after what must have been both a frustrating and exciting time for you?

Magendie waited a bit before replying, as if he was collecting his thoughts.

– I guess it is this: old lies and deceptions die hard.

– Old lies and deceptions die hard, Gayle nodded. – Please explain this to our audience, Carlton.

– It is quite simple, really, Magendie sighed, sighed with an edge in his voice. – During my conversations with public officials, scientists and others one is tempted to believe that those well-known, world-wide events never took place…

– So, what do you think happened with the memory of those astonishing events? Caine asked him.

– That one is easy to answer. Those in charge attempted and *attempt*, in their desperation to bury it, like they do with everything truly important threatening their hegemony, struggling with all their considerable might to turn it into yet another fairytale.

Gayle and Phillips held their tongue, allowing him to continue at his own pace.

– I mean, during and after the events themselves it wasn't just those that was proven beyond doubt, but virtually every single «conspiracy theory» connected to them as well: an alien craft crashed outside Roswell, several crafts flew above Washington DC in 1952, people were kidnapped and experimented on by the aliens, there was a place called Area 51 where the craft from Roswell was hidden and governments of the world, some of them in cahoots with the aliens created a massive covert operation to discredit and ridicule anyone that set out to prove their existence. The list is practically endless. Documents and documentation were disclosed that left no doubt about the involvement of governments and also private operators and mainstream media, an involvement and obfuscation continuing to this day. And the worst of it is this: it still works. Prior to 1987 humans discussed eagerly what would happen if we were indeed visited by extraterrestrials and it was proven beyond reasonable doubt. We now know the answer to that question: not much, at least in the short term. An obfuscated humanity is still reeling from the shock, attempting to deal with it all, in denial about it, as it is in denial about so many things.

– Any comments, Professor Peterson? Gayle interjected.

Peterson looked flustered. That was clear by a casual glance. He was hesitating beyond hesitation.

– The first question I ask myself, he haltingly began, – is this: where is the evidence?

The others started laughing, started cracking up immediately.

128

The loud sound filled the studio, filled a million living rooms world-wide.

Gayle dried her tears, fighting to keep the laughter contained and failing miserably. Phillip fell off his chair. He actually fell off his chair.

A semblance of order was eventually restored in the studio. Everybody looked attentive at Peterson.

He didn't look good, didn't look good at all.

Then, it was as if he pulled himself together. Determination lit up his eyes.

– I'll tell you where the evidence is, he stated, suddenly completely relaxed. – It is in this suitcase. Added to what you've already pointed to, that is out there, this should be sufficient in spades.

He opened the suitcase and threw a thick pile of documents and a laptop on the table.

– I won't claim that everything is here, he said, – but I would claim that very little is missing. The laptop is updated with the most recent events. I think you will find it very satisfying.

They stared stunned at him.

– Among other things, it covers my many years as a debunking agent. He continued speaking, clearly more apprehensive. – I've been fed up with my... role for some time. I hereby request whatever... *asylum* you're able to grant me. My former masters won't be pleased after this, I can tell you that for free...

The incredulity didn't quite leave the faces of the others for hours.

– Did you... get to him? Ted asked Betty.

– Don't look at me. She shook her head. – I didn't do anything to him and I can't find any evidence of tampering either. I put it to you, good sir that this man decided to come forward on his own. He's one brave bastard. And he's also one of many examples that our campaign is actually working. He was clearly encouraged to do so by the standard we set.

He stared pointedly at her.

– This calls for a celebration... My Lord, she said subdued, but then she grinned wider than he had ever seen her grin.

– EVACUATION, Martin Keller shouted.

Gabi stepped forward. She had been set to perform, to sing with a band and was dressed in her Goth costume and wore the white makeup.

– I'm afraid you are absolutely correct, my good man, Phillip said, turning to Peterson. – This is no longer a healthy place to stay.

He grabbed the thick pile of documents. Gayle grabbed the laptop.

There were about a dozen people in the small studio. Everybody rushed through the portal Gabi opened. Peterson hesitated some more for a moment or two, but they didn't need to shove him. They would guess that he had seen a lot of weird, even eerie events in his capacity as debunker and one of the establishment's most trusted advisors during the years.

The view of the empty studio was broadcast about a minute longer. Then it shifted to the outside. It was just in time. A rocket made its way through the air. Less than five seconds after it had been caught on camera, it hit the evacuated building and blew it to smithereens.

She returned to the exclusive fashion store near Bleeker Street, with lots of support, firepower at her side. Nick, Liz, Martin Keller and about a dozen others formed a protective bubble around her.

There was nothing there, except empty space and cobwebs.

– He called himself John, she said. – Only John. He was powerful enough to evade our… my most powerful probe. To my power it was as if he wasn't there or anywhere and as if he didn't have any abilities, any at all.

They knew that. She had told the story several times. The mere fact that she repeated it now showed how distraught she was.

Northfield Dome, the former football stadium was just as overgrown as many other previously important places in the now so green city. The cameras showing the arena from all sides easily picked up on that. There were also other distinct differences between here and elsewhere in the United States on this day, July fourth, 2006. While flags and marches and celebration were very much visible most other places of the nation, there was nothing even resembling anything like that here. Standing on a platform at the center of the pitch, Ted, Liz, Karine, Stacy, Linsey, Ivan and Carla held an impromptu press-conference. A horde of journalists and reporters covered it, their bodies hardly visible in the tall grass.

Before, during and after many protests on the day gained far more attendance than the «celebration» and unrest exploded.

– Today isn't Independence Day, but Enslavement Day in the United States, Ted shouted, – a celebration of warfare, rape, murder, genocide, conquest, oppression, injustice and nationalism.

They didn't use microphones. His voice carried far, even far outside the former sports arena. Gabi, Ivan and Linsey helped make it reach even farther than it otherwise would have done. The two men enhanced the sound. Gabi had opened portals to various spots within the city. Everyone in Northfield heard it. They heard it in the wind, when they tilted their heads and the various corners where they found themselves.

– We have an instrument called the Bullshit Factor, Liz said. – It starts chiming fairly quickly when I listen to most people, and on days like this it's chiming constantly. You hear more rubbish during just a few hours today than during many days throughout the year.

– Dangerous stuff, Linsey stated, – stuff designed to lull people to sleep. Most people still take refuge in nationalism and religion to avoid taking an independent stand on *anything*.

– Stuff about how great America is, Stacy spat, – what a great place it is to live, how superior it is to other countries. It is all pretty standard material, really, since boasting «national pride», hypocrisy and similar are common everywhere on present day Earth. I would say it is slightly worse in the empire that is the United

States, though. An empire continuing and refining its proud tradition of the before mentioned warfare, genocide, conquest, oppression, injustice and nationalism. What are people celebrating? Their own gullibility? Their knee-fall for the forces of tyranny? Well, I say to hell with you all. You can be certain of one thing: the reckoning is coming and then you will no longer be able to hide your head in the sand anymore and will actually have to wake up, to actually have a true opinion about something.

– As you know we, Phoenix Green Earth, have already quite a few candidates ready for the midterm congressional election, Linsey said. – We can now happily declare, in spite of the draconian difficulties for smaller political parties and movements that even more are accepted as candidates. I have decided to run in Colorado, for the Senate, and Lynn Fredericks will run here in the great state of Massachusetts, also for the Senate. Jane Morris will run for the house of representatives. We have also countless great local candidates in almost all states. Midterm elections will not be boring this year, folks.

– And on that happy note we're adjourned, Ted grinned.

The entire happening was broadcast on the various Phoenix Green Earth channels, of course, and it had its highest viewer rating in history. Many people even contacted the various establishment channels to tell them to «quit their usual bullshit», and even more stopped watching those channels altogether and stopped their subscriptions where that was necessary. Revenues fell across the established boards and a sour stench spread in the boardrooms.

The support for the wars, militarism in general and even «our soldiers» dropped to an all time low, even lower than during the end of the Vietnam War.

The number of protests and protesters swelled again.

Stacy and Tamara rested on the hammocks by the farm. They held, in spite of the strain put on them by the two almost full-term pregnant females.

There was peace, even as peace was denied them.

The life surrounding Stacy soothed her. Humans and animals and plants hummed in her outer and inner ears. Malvin bit her finger.

– Things are heating up, now, right? The giant was both apprehensive and excited.

– I would say so, yes, even beyond expectation. It's amazing how a few well-placed words can do more than the most violent act sometimes, even though there was violence that day as well. And our actions, violent and not the next months and years will only add to that. It is kind of strange when it is all finally happening.

Troy and Shadow had been told to keep their distance, but Stacy felt the relaxed tension in them, how they were ready to act at a moment's notice. Safety was an illusion even here, or anywhere.

– I wish I could be your sole bodyguard, like in the old nights, Tamara sighed.

– Sure, Stacy nodded pointedly, adding a large grin, – that added weight and little growth in your belly shouldn't be a problem at all…

The giant girl scowled at her.

They relaxed in the hammocks. The sun warmed their bodies. Even the sweat felt pleasant. Their bodies remained bloated and swollen everywhere. Stacy smiled as she touched her big, big belly. The two inside smiled in return. She could see them.

– Can you… connect him and me again? Tam asked a little awkward.

Of course.

And there he was as well. They were all connected. His thoughts, not having been so often stimulated not so coherent as her girls.

It won't be long now, she told them.

– It can happen anytime, I guess, Tam mused.

– It will probably be a few more days, Stacy acknowledged, – but yes.

– It feels so good, the big elf sighed.

She turned, or tried to twist her awkward body towards her friend and had to settle for turning only her head.

– Oh, Jill, I…

She stopped, stricken.

– Sorry, I…

– It's all right, Stacy assured her, shrugging, – perfectly all right.

– I'm really sorry, Tam persisted. – It was a slipup. I…

– *Please,* don't worry about it, Stacy emphasized.

Tam relaxed, turning limp again in the hammock, returning from her slightly anxious state.

– I was going to say how much I love this, she said subdued, – all this.

– I know. Stacy reached out with a hand and the other grabbed it. – I do, too.

Mutual warmth coursed through them both.

They rested in the hammocks, enjoying the day, and each other's company. Birdsong filled their ears. Stacy closed her eyes, allowing her thoughts to drift, to fly free.

The ravens squeaked. It didn't startle her. It no longer did. She had been aware of their elevated state for some time.

She noticed how Shadow made a slight step forward.

– Goddess…

Stacy knew. They were about to have company.

Thirty seconds more, less than a minute and a worn woman and boy in worn clothes approached her.

– Come… She bid them when they hesitated.

They stood close to her. The boy touched her belly.

– We were told the Goddess were with children, the other said, – and felt we needed to be here.

– We recognized you immediately, he said. – You told me to seek you out when I was ready. Well, I'm ready now.

– So young and so ready, she said softly.

It was good, felt good and it brought a smile to her face. She rose, with some trouble. Tam did as well. They stared wide-eyed at the elf-like woman towering above them.

– Well, you made it, Stacy said, – with not much time to spare.

Time flowed like mercury in the afternoon sun, in the hot night's moon.

132

The next day, at dusk the drums began beating from the hill, from Raven's Mound. People gathered on the shore, the circle around Ravenscourt, walking barefoot in the soft sand. The bonfires reached for the heavens, the depths of mankind.

Except for Gabi's notable exception, almost all the females of child-bearing age, witches and not that had lived there before the Janus Clan and Phoenix Green Earth had joined them had big bellies and were ready to give birth. All of them, Hazel, Kate, Tam, Doris, Vicky, Andrea, Morgana, Loeh, Lori, Melanie, Meta and all the rest gathered in a circle around Lillith. They were *fifty-three* all in all. It was as if some of them had been waiting for her, even holding out a little longer just to accommodate her schedule.

But most of them were pretty much synchronized and had been from the start. They were fairly certain all of it or at least most of it had happened right here, on these shores, on the wild night not long after they had escaped from the Asylum, where sensuality and desire had exploded into an orgy of emotion and passion.

There was a happy, but tense mood around Fire Lake. All healers and plenty of assistants, everybody that could possibly be of use were present.

Lots of other members of the movement waited not far away, out of the way, eagerly awaiting the news.

Establishment media had been denied access. Choppers circling in the air, far away couldn't really observe much, not even with extreme binoculars or telephoto lenses. A thick mist, a strange soup of fog and disturbances in the air had gathered around Northfield. Pilots attempting to fly closer were quickly lost, confused beyond their wits. Nothing or literally nothing showed up on otherwise sharp-as-a-whip satellite photos.

The drums beat and shook air, flesh and ground alike. Stacy sat there, sweating and breathing with the rest.

It felt so pleasant all of it. Eyes closed, eyes open seemed to catch everything. The hum rose from everybody's throat. Stacy smiled as the water broke and the ground below turned green and fertile. She walked into the lake. The others joined her as soon as their own water had broken. Submerged in Fire Lake they felt its heat, its lovely warmth. Everybody sensed and saw everything. It felt so good, was such a hum of joy.

She screamed and an echo of multitudes followed her sound of pain shaking the spheres.

Her vocal chords screamed, her mind screamed.

– I had forgotten, she mumbled, – forgotten what a drag this is…

The cautious laughter warmed her. It echoed within her, like everything she did echoed without. Pain shook her again, as she shook flesh and air and ground and water, the very fire dancing and chanting in the approaching night. She shared it, all the pain and joy with everyone close by. It went on and on and on, and there was no end to it. She felt it, how the tiny piece of flesh slipped down her hole, how it pushed itself out bit by bit, and it was such a beyond powerful and happy experience.

Relax. She soothed the minds distressed by her pain and the monumental events taking place. *Mommy told you about this, that it could be a little scary, but it's all just a part of life, my babies.*

Slipping into everybody's mind was like slipping into the water, effortless, sliding on warm, pleasant ice. Jill Larkin dumped herself into the Fire Lake covered in fur and hair. Fire Lake turned dark with blood. They looked amazed at the small creature, as the fur and the hair faded away and returned and faded away again, until smooth, human skin remained. Betty pulled her up of the water and cut her biblical cord. Hers was the first tiny loud scream filling everybody's ears. Stacy accepted her from Betty and smothered her in kisses.

It's funny, all this feels very much like a dream, Raven sent to Betty.

Isn't that how it often is with all powerful precognitives? Betty shrugged unconcerned. *It is difficult to distinguish between past, present and future, what's «real» and what's not.*

And then as the minutes, eternities passed by what seemed like a thousand powerful tiny wails filled the night. Samantha Larkin joined her sister in Lillith's fawn. Both of them stared at their mother with big eyes. Samantha had smooth skin and the boiling fireeyes of the Janus Clan.

Stacy called Jason and Everett to her, introducing them more closely than previously to their daughters. The two men held each of them up, joining them with the night above. Jason and Samantha's eyes flared in tandem.

Every mother devoured the placenta in what felt like more than a correct ritual. They felt how it energized them, returned their strength. Lillith was flooded with the memories of all the times before she had done it.

– There was a time when this was mandatory, was pure necessity, she told them all, – and one night it might be again.

Time flowed in Lillith's mind. Time was Now.

All the new mothers gathered dressed and groomed in front of an international press corps on the overgrown pitch of the derelict Northfield Dome. Some fed the children, others didn't. The photos were done quickly, before the interviewing began.

– You're just a goddamn, modern fertility cult, aren't you, with your mindless orgies and magical ceremonies?

– I would say that is one, obvious truth, yes, Vicky said unconcerned.

– One truth, the man said puzzled. – What do you mean?

– We are many things. We are the rainbow, not one single pale color. If you absolutely want to label us, you'll need a protracted, goddamn scorecard.

She was great. The others snickered.

The bundle in her lap suddenly grew fur. She panicked slightly and managed, somehow to keep her calm and make him change back.

– You're pro-choice, as I understand it?

– Yes, she replied. – To us the US-distinction is meaningless, however. We see those calling themselves pro-life as pro-death, as anti-choice.

– But you breed like *rabbits*.

– Was that a question?

He looked flustered at her.

134

– I guess we do. She shrugged again. – But we don't have the need or feel we have the right to decide for others. And we have women doing abortions. There's no pressure either way.

Her years as student liaison at Northfield College clearly paid off. Stacy and others were ready to step in, but there was no need.

– What do you have to say to your parents? I understand they have disinherited, disowned you…

– I have nothing to say to them.

The interviewing or «press conference», more or less touching base with all the fifty-three, back and forth went on for hours, as the Northfield branch of Phoenix Green Earth patiently and methodically replied to the silliest and nastiest of questions.

And everything was broadcast live on the Phoenix Green Earth channels, of course.

– So, Stacy, what's with the new, colorful and more practical costume?

– It isn't a costume, but my clothes…

– So, why the change in clothes?

– I just wanted a change, that's all. There's nothing more to it, except that, no further significance.

They looked far more common than her robe, cloak and hood, but the change felt good, and they were practical, very practical. She knew she would be able to move in them. They wouldn't slow her down.

– So, what's your secret?

She looked good-humored at the woman.

– Most of your «sisters», even though they're all healthy are nowhere close to getting rid of the excess fat, but you seem to be succeeding exceedingly well with that.

She had. In a few days there would be no signs of the pregnancy at all, no scars or anything and little extra fat, except what was needed for motherhood, for nursing her children.

– I guess I'm fucking special that way as well, she replied calmly, ignoring the female «health reporter's» nasty tone. – I'm pleased to say that even in a sisterhood and brotherhood of special people I stand out.

The smile seemed to be spreading from her face and filling everybody's vision.

– So, what about your children?

This time the reporter strived really hard to keep the nastiness out of his voice, but the implications of his «question» were clear enough.

– They will grow up knowing love, knowing the world in ways far better than other children. We won't destroy them, like current mainstream society destroys its children, but teach them and encourage them to teach themselves about life and existence in general.

He wanted to say more, but she held up a finger, and he froze completely.

– It's amazing, isn't it? No matter how bad current mainstream society treats its children, its defenders persist in the illusion of benevolence, doing their utmost to portray alternative ways of living and child rearing as wicked and wrong. As always, I weep for current mankind.

– You are a young and unwed single mother with what most people would say is a questionable background holding highly political speeches all over the world…

Another sleazy bastard tried, pausing deliberately, waiting for her to reply to his introductory comment. But she just looked good-humored at him as well, and he had to complete his «question».

– Do you foresee any special difficulties because of that?

– Yes.

She grinned, and everybody knew she had turned the tables on him.

– As long as society is as it is, with extensive prejudice against many types of people my brethren's path to the glorious Senate and House of Representatives will be harder than most, but as our current president is fond of saying: we will prevail.

– Will you say the midterm elections this year is a… preparation for those two years from now? Another asked.

– I will say that, yes. We need to start early because of the pesky rules and regulations designed to keep truly alternative political parties and movements away from public office, the obstructions both parties enthusiastically make and support, in order to keep their dominant position. The road then will inevitably be easier if we prepare the ground now, both in financial and political terms.

– Do you think and hope that this will create much anxiety in the halls of power?

– I both hope and believe that it will…

She could sense it, see it without trying.

– So, what happened in Northfield?

Corinne Barbeau asked softly.

Stacy exchanged glances with some of her sisters and Corinne saw it.

– I think you're asking the wrong people or entities or whatever was behind it, Stacy replied, and suddenly seemed very vulnerable.

– I asked Ted about it, Corinne said good-humored, – but he said he wasn't here for very long, no matter how it seemed, so he didn't know much.

– Well, Stacy said, also good-humored, – I was there, we were there all the time and we don't know what happened either. We've heard the rather fantastic descriptions, of course, but we can't *explain* them.

– There were deaths and disappearances, and a girl named Jill Stafford, actually one of your sister witches that disappeared without a trace.

– Yes, we will always wonder what happened to her.

Stacy said with a straight face. She was well aware of the fact that she was an accomplished liar, but was often astounded about how good.

– You kinda look alike, Corinne said.

Stacy knew that Corinne didn't *know,* but she was *good,* an investigative reporter of the old school, one that knew how to ask the right questions.

– Everybody says that, Stacy sniffed and dried a tear.

6

The Phoenix Green Earth news and debate studio continued with a recording of a protest at Beit Omar, the occupied and colonized West Bank, Palestine.

There was almost no break from the powerful visuals of the studio being blown to pieces and the ongoing transmission.

Tamara Farley stood with several others from the organization and quite a number of Beit Omar locals. They faced soldiers from the Israeli army and Zionist settlers.

– People with heart attacks and others in need of instant medical aid have died because you won't let them pass through your checkpoints, Tam shouted, – and you ask me why I am here. You sicken me!

– How did you get here? A man in a suit asked her enraged. – You're banned from Israel.

– I wasn't aware that I was, she snorted. – I am a Jew, right, and all Jews are automatically granted access to the «Holy Land», right?

She spat venom and sarcasm.

– Where is the camera? A soldier beat up a young teenage boy. – We know you have a camera.

– I can indeed promise you that everything happening here is being recorded, Tam confirmed for him. – From this moment on we will record all your crimes.

– We will identify you, Ted said, – keep a record of you all and what you do to unarmed and more or less defenseless people. We will be more zealous than even you are with the children and your other victims when doing so. You won't get away with the excuse that you're only following orders. Even though you can be certain we will go after the people at the top as well.

The situation had turned tense when a soldier from the Israeli Occupation Army had been captured in Gaza a few days earlier and the escalation of the «conflict» was almost certain. IOF had made repeated intrusions into Gaza and the Palestinians had answered with their usual homemade, far from effective rockets.

Ted looked straight into the camera, straight at Gabi that stood there and recorded everything happening at the protest from her invisible position in the Shadowland. Others stood inside other gates, filming the entire area within the circle formed by the gates.

It was beyond thorough. They didn't miss a single spot.

A small boy, he couldn't be more than ten confronted one of the soldiers, holding up a poster. It was a drawing of an Israeli soldier and a descriptive text:

NAZI THUG

– Disgusting bug, the soldier snarled and struck the boy with the handle of his rifle.

The boy fell. The soldier lifted his rifle again.

Then he stopped, then he… froze.

– Do you strike children?

The voice alone chilled the man to the bone.

– Do you strike children just because you don't like the truth they reveal? Ted Warren said.

The soldier met those bestial eyes briefly and couldn't look away.

– Are you human at all, Remy Rabowitz? Warren said softly. – Yes, you are human, and that's what makes this so horrible.

Shaking hands whitened around the weapon.

– Yes, I know, you want to shoot me, want to kill anyone rocking your narrow perception of the world. C'mon, you would probably get away with it, too, at least in Israeli courts.

Rabowitz, scowling slowly lowered his weapon.

There was a lot buzz in the soldiers' radios.

– «Don't make us look bad», Ted translated and related from Israeli (Modern) Hebrew. – «We will get these assholes soon enough».

His translation was fluent, as if he was born to the language. Both Israelis and Palestinians turned wide-eyed in wonder and anger respectively.

The protests continued. Cries in both Arabic and English echoed in the valley. NO SEPARATION WALL. TEAR DOWN THE WALL, NOT OUR HOMES And

STOP STEALING OUR LAND. END THE OCCUPATION AND COLONIZATION

Sometimes in the afternoon, as the protesters were actually about to end the protest the soldiers returned in force, bringing teargas and bullets coated in rubber. There was a viciousness to it all that also was very much visible on the film. Most of the protesters pulled away, but a few stayed, forming a protective circle around Ted and Tam, standing their ground. Tam and the others pushed a handkerchief at their mouths, but coughed and had tears flowing from their eyes. Ted didn't. His eyes watered, but he didn't cough, and he stared at the soldiers with burning eyes that seemed to completely negate the tears. A boy, about twelve had been hit by a rubber bullet in the face. He screamed, wailed in pain. A large swelling grew where the bullet had hit him. Blood trickled from the wound.

The soldiers «arrested» (abducted) a few of the domestic protesters, like always and that was that, yet another day in Beit Omar, Palestine.

People licked their wounds and returned home, those who could, even more determined to keep on fighting.

7

The program returned to Gayle Tadero and Phillip Caine in the studio. Both looked at the other, not the camera.

– Wow, he exclaimed, in what was clearly a spontaneous, not a planned statement, – that was powerful.

– And the «best» is yet to come, Gayle said excited and somber.

They turned towards the camera.

– Welcome to Phoenix Green Earth news studio, Phillip said. – We're back on air after what to say it the least has been strenuous days.

– Our previous location was bombed by the United States government and partners, Gayle said, – and we will return to you with unequivocal proof of that, but in the meantime: Don't believe their lies, not for a second. They claim it was a terrorist attack, of course. They always do that these days…

– This shows how important the alien presence is, Phillip said, – and how important the US government and partners think it is.

– Martin Keller is still here. Ted Warren and Tamara Farley have also joined us, to share their experiences in Beit Omar, in occupied and colonized Palestine.

She turned towards Keller.

– So, what are your thoughts on the latest developments?

– There isn't really that much to add, Keller replied both serious and humorous. – The US government's actions, as usual speak pretty much for themselves…

He straightened in the chair.

– I have to say, though, I feel a great sense of renewed purpose and joy when potential whistleblowers like the former Professor Peterson step up and come forward with their knowledge and enthusiasm. We are really ruled by clever illusionists and many people's total and beyond dangerous inability to see through those illusions, and it is so great when someone breaks through that ceiling of ignorance and denial.

Cornell had cancelled Peterson's tenure.

He was hunted by the authorities on unspecified charges and demonized in establishment media. The PGE underground network served him, like it had served Linda and the others for fifteen years.

The number of people watching the Phoenix Green Earth broadcast and other independent channels kept rising.

It had now more than tripled after the latest developments.

– You have obviously done a pretty thorough study of alien visitation yourself? Gayle said to Keller.

– I have, he nodded. – I have to emphasize that I don't have any special insight on the matter. The information is pretty much available for everybody able and willing to dig a bit, to part the facts from the bullshit.

– Please tell us briefly about your conclusions.

– Again: they aren't that unique. The aliens themselves aren't really that unfathomable either. There are basically three easily identified races or types of beings that have visited Earth the last few thousand years, even though some might be content with observing and not interacting with us. There is the Tachiti, «the Lords». They look pretty much like us, at least when they want to and are not put under a closer scrutiny. It was they that up to 1988 cooperated with the world's governments and conducted extensive experiments on people. Then there are the Grays. They, too conducted experiments, but their involvement or interest is clearly more aloof, more the equivalent of us studying an anthill. Then there are others we don't have any names for, pure observers or explorers that just might be passing through and probably don't care about us at all. The world «unfathomable» may apply here.

He chuckled.

The others looked good-humored at him.

– Yes, he said. I will be more than happy to share the joke with you.

He chuckled some more and shook his head.

– The entire SETI-program was an integrated part of the ongoing deceit, and they still keep it going. Their confidence in people's intellect can't be very high, can it? Is the joke on them or on us? It's all completely ridiculous and sobering simultaneously, isn't it? It certainly illustrates how far those in charge are willing to go to hold on to their positions.

– And the «terrorist-attack» against our previous broadcasting facilities stresses the point…

Phillip added cheerfully.

– Yes, they have the advanced, «salvaged» technology, more manpower than ever and a beyond effective propaganda machine to truly remake their tyranny into something even worse than before now, Keller said, – and as the stakes are rising, so is their zeal to implement all the tools at their disposal and to brook no interference from even imagined enemies. The final days are here. Either we stop them, now, or we don't.

The camera focused on Gayle.

– We thank Martin for coming to us. He, like many these days fight government and corporate power at a great threat to his well-being. As stated, all the documents and info about human cooperation with the aliens have been downloaded onto the Internet and also truly independent networks. Everybody can and should study the material in depth. Summaries are also easily available. Remember to be on guard concerning sights set up to deliberately confuse and distort our material.

– We will now move on with our interrupted program, Phillip said. – The upcoming coverage is also pretty much ignored and distorted by establishment media.

The two hosts had a low-keyed conversation with Ted and Tam.

– The two of you spent two weeks with a family in Beit Omar, Palestine?

– We did, Ted said, – and we filmed and experienced the impacts of the Zionist occupation and colonization closeup.

– We were part of a diverse international group staying in the area, Tam said. – We pretty much knew what we were getting into, but many of the others didn't. It's quite funny how everybody doubting the validity of the Palestinian freedom struggle stopped doing that after just a few days. That's all it takes to convince those sitting on the fence about which side to support.

The film showed holes in the wall in several houses. The interior walls had also been damaged. Several preteen boys and girls were displayed on large-scale photographs.

– The boy on the right is Yussef. He's twelve years old and has already been abducted several times and been imprisoned for a year since his tenth birthday. The soldiers broke into the house one night. They made us all stand in line and «searched» the house, smashing the interior to rubble. Yussef had participated in the protest earlier that day, «breaking the conditions for his release» and they grabbed him and kidnapped him again, imprisoned and tortured him. This is one of many methods of terror the Israel Occupation Army employ against the Palestinian population. Many children are imprisoned and beaten badly and even tortured and abused, returning to the outside world beaten and broken.

Her voice was even, seemingly calm, shaking at the seams.

They documented, thoroughly, methodically and unmistakably the Israeli terror against the Palestinians, took the viewers through lots and lots of filmed material and witness-accounts and atrocities.

– There is truly no doubt concerning who is the bad guy here, is there? Gayle said, unable to keep her anger from manifesting.

– In other, true conflicts between sides approaching equal strength, lines are often blurry, Ted nodded. – In this one, everything is pretty much black and white. The Zionists were the invaders, the colonists, occupants, were genocidal from the very start and have continued being so. It says a lot about the power of propaganda that they've managed to turn this around, to make many people see the victims as the aggressors. Humanity has allowed this horror to continue to this day. It's time to finally put the foot down.

On that, too, Ted thought, on everything.

He would later describe that very moment as a watershed, even though it was clearly one watershed of many.

And his power of displacement, farsight, stronger than ever before showed him the stir his words created around the world, not merely in Palestine.

They realized that he wasn't only speaking about that, but realized the further implications of his words.

The camera changed from Ted Warren's glowing eyes to Phillip Caine's wide (but pointed) grin.

– Well, people, Caine said, – we've finally reached the end of this program. Let's give thanks to you all and also many thanks to the United States' government and all their supporters for making it such a memorable event.

Gayle smiled, too, very sweet and very lovable.

– And we end the program today with the new song from Asteroth and the Ravens playing their song «When», asking the pertinent, beyond crucial question: at what point do we claim self defense?

The studio turned dark. The fourteen-year-old girl in the white makeup looked ancient, her ravens like the most terrifying of demons. Many watching would insist they saw bird characteristics there.

The drummer made the first strike. Heathen tones beyond heathen and all labels filled the studio, filled thousands of homes and young and old people's minds.

When

The girl sang.

When is enough enough?

How many must suffer and die

Before we strike back?

Before we truly strike back?

The music and its accompanying images filled the world with pale and dark shadows.

Corinne Barbeau woke up gasping and soaked in sweat, haunted by persistent past-sleep dreams. She ran, ran through a dusty, reddish landscape surrounded by fireeyes and dark hair. The shivers kept stamping down her spine.

She stumbled to the bathroom and filled a glass with water, drank it empty, filled the glass again, and devoured every single drop of water, unable to wet her parched throat. The cold water of the shower soaked her body. She drank from that, too. The Thames's water, cleaned seven times (at least that) before reaching the tap, was never fresh, never tasty, and she never enjoyed it, but now it didn't seem to matter. She had breakfast. The taste of the food and drink didn't seem to register on her buds. She looked at old recordings, an interview she had made fifteen years ago.

It felt like yesterday.

She watched herself shake hands with Ted Warren. It wasn't the first time she had rewatched these recordings. She had lost count of how many times she had done so. The frown kept crossing her brow. Words and phrases kept mixing with the feverish dream-images of the desert.

The phone kept ringing. She ignored it, even as she realized that she was supposed to go to work, that she should have done so hours ago.

– I agreed with what Mike said about society. I agreed with his observations. I just didn't agree with his conclusions.

There was something there, making her frown, something about his wording, but she had to shake her head, not getting it.

– And now you've turned a new leaf.

– Yeah, you could say he encouraged me to set out on a new path… in a backward sort of way.

That exchange had made her frown for fifteen years and increasingly so lately, with the intensity of her reoccurring dream.

– *I agreed with what Mike said about society. I agreed with his observations. I just didn't agree with his conclusions.*

It seemed like such an innocent statement…

The sound of the fridge from the kitchen distracted her, or seemed to distract her.

Then, she got it, she finally got it, and felt so silly because she hadn't done so immediately. Sweat soaked her, soaked every single piece of her clothes, and it felt like she hadn't showered at all.

– It's quite an epiphany, isn't it?

She turned startled and looked straight at Betty Morgan. The frown grew deeper.

– It was like a wall, wasn't it, one keeping you from probing deeper and remember things that truly matter.

Matter matter matter

– You have a decision to make, Betty stated calmly.

And then she turned and took one step towards the wall, and vanished, faded away in the blink of an eye.

Corinne sat there, staring at the wall for a long time. The phone rang again. She reached for the receiver and put it to her ear.

– Hello?

– What's the matter with you? Alan Zarko said, very cross. – You were supposed to be here five hours ago. Estelle had to do the interview.

– I'm sorry, Corinne whimpered. – I overslept.

She didn't really catch his words, his long monologue. Long repressed memories, *memories* mixed with the realization of how fucked up her life had become. She broke the connection and left the receiver off the hook. The motions went through her after that. She alternately choked and giggled, until she finally reached some kind of calm, of peace. Her body rose from the chair, standing straight. It didn't take that long to pack. She even removed a few items from the small suitcase in the end. She stood where Betty had stood.

– I'm ready, she said aloud.

There was some kind of shimmer in the air. She had glimpsed it when Betty had vanished and saw it even clearer now. She stepped through…

… and reappeared outside the castle on Fire Lake. She had seen photos of it, but they didn't do it justice compared to the overwhelming reality.

Far older images assaulted her like a flood, now, when she had acknowledged the truth that she had denied for so long.

There was no one there. She walked inside. Ted and Liz Warren and sixteen other people waited for her there. She choked and felt how her eyes were filled with tears.

– My Lord, My Lady, I've come to serve, to resume my long-neglected service. I would never betray our sacred trust. I'm ashamed that I, in my forgetfulness even considered it.

Her speech-pattern had changed notably. She noticed it with a happy shrug. It didn't really matter.

– We welcome you, good knight, Liz said softly. – Welcome home!

She who was now Corinne Barbeau choked in joy and heard it repeated time and time again in her mind.

Welcome home!

9

The sun settled on the right of the Hill. That still felt strange to Stacy. During those dramatic first two months of her life here she had believed that it would always settle behind it. But this was high summer, and the evenings were long and bright.

Lillith sat alone in her study at the farm, in front of her computer, tapping the keyboard. She participated in discussions and exchanges on the Internet. She welcomed the distraction.

She wrote fast, without using her hands at all. The keyboard, set at maximum writing speed seemed to be tapping itself. When she had started doing her telekinesis writing months ago, she had faced some initial difficulties, but had quickly mastered the technique and could now write much faster than anybody using their hands.

«You don't hold humanity in very high regard, do you»? A young man wrote.

«On the contrary», she responded, «I hold it in very high regard. Not the sheep-like, submissive humanity of today, of course, but what we once were, and we can be again».

«You're just one more single mother having it easy», another young man spat.

«Wow», she replied, «another misogynist on a warpath against women»

«You're a slut», a woman wrote.

«Do you enjoy being a mindless echo of patriarchy»? Stacy wondered.

Most of the servers on websites or discussion groups she entered broke down or experienced serious problems quickly, overloaded because of the war between her haters and supporters.

Conservative groups and media, including major parts of all establishment media made sure to report the criticism and vile hatred against her, of course, but that mostly created yet another backlash against them.

«It's quite funny», she wrote, commenting on it, «the eager voices of tyranny have a hard time reconciling the fact that they don't have monopoly on defining the truth anymore».

And in another comment:

«I'm not single by any stretch of the imagination, by the way. My daughters will have the advantage of having many fathers and mothers when growing up».

And the dark and vibrant laughter shook a million homes.

She turned off the computer, hardly tired or even frustrated, but still deliberate in her choice for a break. Blessed silence filled the room when the machine stopped making noise. She lingered a bit, enjoying that, before turning towards the shimmering hole in the air.

The dark-clad woman stepped through one of the permanent portals created by Gabi and ended up on one of the balconies at Ravenscourt, looking at the twilight landscape still illuminated by the setting sun. There was activity everywhere, but right now she felt like she was alone and that solitude felt right. She didn't turn off her extended awareness, but muted it just a bit, enough to relax more in her own mind.

She retreated to her bedroom, frowning a bit. Yes, it was her bedroom, even though others also used it. Here she and Linsey and she and Linsey and Betty had consummated their first union. This was a kind of private place to her, one she could retreat to if she so desired.

The door opened to the hall and to the long rows of children resting in the cribs and small beds. They enjoyed their afternoon nap, but would soon be very vital again, until twilight ended, and night settled. There were no maids there to watch over them right now. That made Stacy frown, but didn't really unsettle her. Toni and the other male and female maids could have a perfectly valid reason to not be

144

present.

Stacy was drawn to Stephanie and Jill. She made sure she didn't disturb their sleep and just stood there, watching them. It felt great seeing them with her eyes now and then. She looked forward to holding them, feeding them and fussing over them later that evening.

Something…

She turned abruptly, but there was no one there. There was a cold draft, but she sensed no one, and suddenly all of this felt so very, very familiar.

When she turned again, she saw the woman, saw another, different Stacy Larkin not more than five steps away. Startled, she realized that a chill passed down her spine.

– Greetings, the other Lillith said, her voice a deep rumble.

Stacy stared at herself, her mirror image and had to admit to herself that she felt intimidated.

– I take it you have no doubt that you're facing yourself, a future, improved version of yourself?

Stacy shook her head. She felt no thoughts from the dark figure, but there was little or no doubt concerning her identity. The sense of menace felt very familiar and all too obvious.

The Other walked to her, touched her, touched her skin. The hand felt warm and dry. There were still no thoughts leaking, no sensations whatsoever.

– Yes, this is I, the Other stated, – your other, older and wiser self, traveling in the flesh, not only in the mind.

She chuckled.

– Boy, I look so timid, so young. Memory can be such a funny, fickle thing, can't it?

Their faces looked exactly the same. The hairdo and clothes were different, different enough to separate the two of them.

Stacy still didn't say anything, attempting to match the Other's calm, unflinching stare, failing miserably.

– I have questions, I would imagine?

The patronizing flair appeared unmistakable.

The nineteen-year-old drew breath hard.

– Why do I hide myself?

Stacy asked angrily.

– That one is easy, the Other replied, another dark flash added to the rest in the deep abyss of her eyes. – I don't want myself to know anything.

– Why did I come here then?

The Other just looked at her, and in that look, was everything she needed to know.

– Because I have experienced this from the other side. I come because it has already happened.

– Very good.

The Other applauded, bringing her palms silently together.

– So, there's no other reason then, no important *message* I need to convey to myself?

The Other sniffed the air a bit, looking at the children, breathing with a smile on her face, enjoying herself with that very patronizing flair, making Stacy wonder if this was how she appeared to others.

– I just wanted to see myself, see everyone.

She reached out to her surroundings. Stacy sensed that, sensed the immense power behind the undetectable probe. She tried reading it, tried influencing the mind behind it, tried moving her body, in vain.

Her other self turned back towards her with a smile on her lips.

– I thought I couldn't possibly become more powerful, right? I believed the rather meager gifts I've gained for myself this early in the game were it?

Stacy knew she looked very timid right then.

– Yes, this is how I appear to others. And, yes, I can be intimidating, I can be cruel, I know this, know that I will go to any lengths to achieve my goals.

Stacy shivered. It wasn't unpleasant exactly, but countless emotions in one. More than anything she felt anxious, a warm, warm trickle extending all over her body.

– Well, this is it, you know. The visit was short but sweet. I will see myself again in the mirror sometime.

Stacy wanted to ask, ask countless questions without answers, but she held her tongue.

The Other returned to the specific spot at the center of the floor, where all the children surrounded her equally.

The smile turned into a grin.

– I will tell myself one thing: I'm doing everything right. Stay the course and I will see all my wildest dreams and yearnings be fulfilled. All my carefully orchestrated plans will come to fruition.

And then Stacy was alone with the children again, speechless beyond words.

As she heard the others, as she heard Toni and the rest, kept away by the Other, heard them return, she composed herself, hid herself and arranged her features and mental signature in carefully structured layers.

The dark summer twilight embraced her with approaching joy and apprehension. The night had come.

CHAPTER SIXTEEN
A land given them by God

PALESTINE/THE MIDDLE EAST
Summer/Fall 2006

It began, as if often does with the smallest things, hardly noticeable at first.

Ted and Liz were woken up in the middle of the night in the London Nothing Hill residence, not long after they had gone to sleep.

Israel had «voluntarily», in a move they called the «disengagement» pulled out of Gaza in 2005. Now, they returned, returned again, a move once again furiously condemned by a passionate Arafat, a man clearly renewed of purpose.

The pretext to their aggression this time seemed to be the «kidnapping» of an israeli soldier, one captured on a previous recent «incursion» into Gaza and the usual, not very dangerous rockets with a rather lousy target hitting rate sent by various radical Palestinian factions.

Mukataa المقاطعة, «something separated» was the name used to refer to the offices and administrative centers of the Palestinian National Authority.

Arafat had more or less been in Israeli house arrest at the one in Ramallah, in what was mostly ruins the last four years, and had never left it since his return from his miraculous recovery in November 2004. His popularity kept soaring among the Palestinian population and he and his party Fatah had won a resounding victory during the January elections.

Operation Cast Lead began. The small city, the tiny slice of land called Gaza drowned in blood. The IDF (Israeli Defense Force) or rather IOF (Israeli Occupant Force) or ICF (Israeli Colonization Force) bombed hospitals, schools, ambulances, hotels and everything in their sight, filling men, women and children with lead and shrapnel and blowing them apart and poisoning them with white phosphorous and several other poisonous bomb components.

Phoenix Green Earth broadcast everything in graphic detail. The soldiers searched for the reporters and photographers, but they could never locate them.

The IOF massive and bloody campaign kept going, kept building momentum throughout the night, the next day and even weeks to come.

They hammered Gaza and its helpless population relentlessly, leaving hardly more than ruins.

No established news channel covered it this close. They remained distant, like they always did in Palestine.

Liz and Ted and the extended Janus Clan watched the raw footage as it arrived. There was a lot of it, but they watched all of it. Almost all of them stared at all of it.

Ten telepaths put together was able to watch all of it, and broadcast everything to the rest. A jumble of images and sensations made a kind of horrible sense.

It was put on the Internet unedited as soon as possible.

The room and all of its loose objects began shaking. It was tangible in the very air, even as fireeyes began flashing.

– GABI! Liz shouted.

And Gabi was there in an instant.

She shook because they were shaking, because they were the wind shaking everything.

– LYDIA, Liz shouted.

– I'm here, Aunt Liz, the girl said.

– «Aunt Liz», someone giggled, practically hysterical, an example of the tense mood dominating the room.

A mighty blast pulled them away, and Liz and Lydia and Gabi flowed through the Shadowland, in what wasn't distance at all.

– Visual only, Liz snapped uncharacteristically to Gabi. – No openings yet.

They saw it all at close range, as it unfolded, the explosions, the flesh and blood and pieces of bones decorating walls and streets.

Liz blinked, and in that brief darkness was a thousand moments. She shook her head. She kept shaking it.

– I thought I had seen it all, she marveled, her voice shaking in vivid emotion.

It was later, perhaps many days later, she knew that, knew how her prescience played tricks on her. As was often the case she experienced it more than once before it actually happened.

A small boy, four or five crossed the street. He was caught in a hail of bullets and was shot to pieces. It happened so fast. She didn't react fast enough. The boy, or what was left of him, fell to the ground, hardly more than stain on the many cracked rocks.

A whoosh of noise drowned the sounds in her ears. She couldn't turn it off.

The Israeli soldiers that had fired the bullets and their wicked laughter froze in her vision. They had shot the boy deliberately. It was impossible to conclude otherwise. She zoomed in on them.

– There's no excuse, for this, she said aloud.

They heard her. There were no other people nearby. The voice thundered in the air around them.

– If we do anything they will just come down harder on the people here, she said, practically mumbling.

Her eyes started flashing. Gabi and Lydia's heart started beating harder in excitement and joy.

– They will do that anyway, Elizabeth Warren said. – They can't do much worse than what they're already doing.

She saw it in her mind and gasped, for the first time in a long time. Events and sensations rolled through her like quicksand, like lightning.

Lydia relayed her thoughts and words to the others, but it wasn't truly necessary. They heard and shared.

One soldier directed her rifle at her fellow soldiers. She frowned, and then, when

148

she pulled the trigger, she screamed in protest and shock. They fell like dominoes. They shot her. She stumbled to the ground. Another started firing at his comrades. They shot him, too. The remaining soldiers stared at each other in horror. Then they started running, fleeing from the scene as fast as they were able.

One soldier started laughing, a loud and insane laughter. He shot the soldier in front of him. Another shot him. Everybody fired at each other. During mere seconds open warfare had erupted between the members of the previously so homogeneous platoon.

Only a few reached the nearest command center. They were babbling incoherently and impossible to shut up.

No one watching them could mistake the stark fear dominating them.

But it didn't truly impress the command staff. The experienced officers laughed outright of the rookies and wrote it all off as a result of inexperience.

Rockets and bombs kept raining down on Gaza.

Planes, Liz snarled.

A moment later, Gabi had brought them high up. Gabi, without being ordered to speeded up time within her bubble. Time outside slowed down until the fast planes hardly seemed to move at all. Liz took control of the pilot's limbs, like she had done with the soldiers on the ground. The plane turned around and fired at the other planes. Several of them fell before they had the chance of avoiding the rockets. The scenery on the ground repeated itself. Sweaty and terrified pilots made their way back to base, but it didn't end there. One plane didn't land, but crashed and took out many planes and lots of personnel and equipment on the ground. Communication lines were red-hot. Liz smiled.

She still smiled when the three of them returned to the others.

– We did so much and so little, she sobered.

The slaughter on the ground continued unabated.

All eyes in the room that could started flashing in fire or shadow. The... pacing began. There was some sleep eventually, but not much.

Days, nights, years passed in the shadow, the mire of their troubled mind.

– How many children are dead so far? Ted asked Betty.

– Impossible to tell, she said, somewhat calm, – but all counts and predictions say at least hundred.

– The fourth largest army in the world, he said to them all, in the gathering in the cave later, – and we will take them on. We will punish them for their beyond inhuman acts. We thought we were prepared, convinced we knew what would be coming and when, but we weren't. The enemy surprised us again, found us practically unaware. We should focus on this for a while, focus almost exclusively on this.

His voice was deadly calm. Those hearing it experienced shakes of frost. They had believed they knew him, but realized abruptly that they hadn't, and that amazed them, amazed them beyond anything.

– The fourth largest army in the world, Stacy restated. – Only the United States, Russia and China have bigger armies. That means they surpass United Kingdom,

France, India, Argentine, Canada, Australia, Germany… among others. They have 175 000 active soldiers, a reserve personnel of 450 000 and almost 3 million men and women they can call on in a major crisis. They have enough planes, ships, equipment and ammunition to fight for years and their big daddy, United States keeps supplying them with more…

– We will take them on, Liz stated. – We will, at the very least make them leave all current Palestinian «territories», but necessity may make us reassess and expand upon that later. Let me emphasize one thing, though, before we begin: The Zionists aren't the final enemy, because there is none, except the Machine itself. They're just one more distraction, one more hurdle on our Path. We will be going easy on them at first, giving them only a faint idea of what is awaiting them at the expected escalation. We will be sticking our heads into a hornet's nest and shake loose everything there is to shake.

– They have mutants in their service, Stacy said. – Either those mutants are forced to serve the Zionist hierarchy, or they do so voluntarily, eagerly, as convinced Zionists. The Zionist leadership has clearly known about our kind for decades, at least that, and has wisely accepted them as at least a tolerable part of the Jewish people. No matter, even if they are few, it makes our task even harder. We're limited by logistics and our small number. We must make even our disadvantages work for us if we are to succeed.

– But when this part of the job is done, Martin Keller said, – we will have struck a giant blow at what stands against us. The Zionists, if you will, might be said to be one of the first lines of defense of the forces we oppose. When they fall, everything, the soft underbelly of tyranny in the world will be exposed. The professed masters will become desperate and sloppy.

The seriousness imposed on the gathering worked. They knew what was at stake, knew that the stakes had been raised significantly.

Betty looked at each and every one present.

– Now, she stated calmly, excitedly, – now, it begins.

Lillith turned to Ted and Liz.

– These are your final warriors, Phoenix. With these you will succeed, fail, and succeed again.

Seconds flowed like eternities.

– You know that? Ted asked her. – You know that for a fact?

And received only a grin in return.

The thunder and lightning followed them, like always, into the inhuman bombardment in Gaza and the Israeli terror in the rest of Palestine.

– Look at it! Ruth spat in distress. – The planes and bombs and bullets are p-practically everywhere. There's no pattern, no weak spot to exploit.

Liz and Ted and Stacy did pull back, studying the battlefield in front of them. They watched and ignored Gabi's watery eyes becoming like open wounds.

Their eyes stayed dry.

– I w-want to k-kill them, Gabi choked. – I w-want to k-k-kill them all.

Bodies, ripped asunder were thrown everywhere, men, woman and children. There was no dispute in the international community about what happened, what was happening, but very few raised their voice in protest and even fewer did anything worthwhile to end it.

A joint session of the United State congress voted unanimously «to support israeli self-defense».

Zionist Hasbara, propaganda used the few planes exploding and Israeli soldiers dying for everything it was worth.

– Fuck them! Liz swore. – Fuck, fuck, fuck them!

The Phoenix Green Earth assault force held back, allowed much of what was happening to continue.

– There's no way in hell we can stop it anyway, Martin Keller said. – We can only document everything and stay with our long-term plan.

Betty didn't state aloud the next day's children's fatalities. She just put the report quietly and in anguish on the desk at Ted's side.

– Remember, Ted told the others, during a briefing seething with emotion, – we will fight them, will make them pay, but we will *not* become them.

They nodded solemnly, passionately.

– I remember your speech that a given ethnic group shouldn't feel superior to another, Gayle said somberly. – I know you weren't speaking specifically about the Jews or even the Zionists, but right now it feels very much like you were.

It had begun long ago, with the smallest of things, with a butterfly, butterflies flapping their wings. The Phoenix had flapped its wings for the first time not that long ago…

The wings, though new and unproven still brought hard winds.

Its burning mind, taking flight across the world zoomed in on the land of Palestine, one drowning in blood and misery, thriving on rebellion and a lust for freedom hardly seen any other place on current Earth.

The large West Bank Palestinian city of al-Khalil - known to Israeli Jews and most foreigners by its biblical name of «Hebron» was under siege. Jewish «settlers», armed to their teeth and protected by the israeli army had invaded a fairly small part of it, but one more than big enough to make life a living hell for the Palestinian population living there.

IOF pulled out of Gaza again, after having left even more death and destruction in its wake.

Hospitals had become useless, practically non-existent. Water pipes and sewer pipes had cracked all over the land. Well over a thousand Palestinians, among them at least 300 children had been killed and only a negligible number of israelis. This was no war, no conflict, but a massacre.

There was condemnation by some western leaders, but slow and half-hearted, in spite of the massive documentation of IOF atrocities.

– This will not stand, Ted and Liz choired.

They stood at the center of a bombed-out street in Gaza City, shaking in rage.

THIS WILL NOT STAND!

And everybody heard them and didn't misunderstand, every single human being on this Earth. They knew they did and that at least pleased them.

The Janus Clan and Phoenix Green Earth as a whole threw themselves even more into the fray of public opinion, imposed their presence even on establishment media and all over the Internet. Those in charge, both of the media and those pulling its strings tried to keep them out as always, but this time they wouldn't stand for it. The twelve telepaths made certain that representatives of their movement became a part of broadcast discussions. They used this opportunity, used their own rage to more than ever before strongarm themselves into public consciousness, to even the odds just a little.

The various interviewers had a deep frown on their forehead. They knew something was «wrong», but couldn't pinpoint the actual reason for it. It turned into a series of unforgettable events.

– You're not sitting there defending child killers, are you? Ruth said with a voice filled with sarcasm.

– Uh, israeli officials have assured us that the allegations will be investigated.

A roar of wrath and scorn filled the studio from the audience.

– And we all know the value of those «assurances», Stewart chuckled darkly. – There's a long precedence for whitewashing after IOF-massacres. Besides, as we all know: the orders came from the very top.

– Allegations? Ruth said sweetly. – You will not claim that facts are in doubt here, will you?

Footage was shown from the massacre.

– This is antisemitism, the friend of Israel said.

– Showing unedited footage is antisemitism?

The sweaty and pale man in what was now a very hot seat turned even more so.

– You should just stop attempting to weaponize antisemitism, you know, Ruth told him gently. – It has worked for way too long, but just doesn't anymore.

Another studio, another scene just a few days later.

Elie Wiesel, the Zionist Nobel peace prize winner was, as he often was, called in to comment on some injustice or another in a different part of the world. This particular evening it happened to concern a massacre in Tibet. A squad from the Chinese army had killed five Tibetan adult civilians.

– There may be times when we are powerless to prevent injustice, but there must never be a time when we fail to protest.

Elie Wiesel said with just the right inflection in his voice.

– Very ironic statement there, from a hypocrite of the first kind. He supports Israel's horrible acts without batting an eye.

Tamara Farley said.

Everybody in the studio stared at her in shock. At this point, during ordinary circumstances this direct transmission would have been cut off and «technical difficulties» would have been identified as the culprit.

But this time crucial members of the crew made the show stay on the air.

– Oh, I agree very much with Wiesel's statement, Tamara shrugged. – I just wish he would have applied it to himself and his fellow Zionists as well. The fact that he has supported the ongoing Zionist genocide of the Palestinian people tells me everything I need to know about this particular Nobel laureate.

She got to him, she knew she did, sensed how he practically exploded within and she would have done so even without Everett's aid.

Wiesel was sweating hard, and the zealot no longer lurked just beneath the surface.

— You're no better than all those assholes you criticize, are you? She grinned.

— IMPUDENT GIRL! He cracked before everybody's eyes. — SELF-HATING JEW!

The moderator looked visibly concerned and attempted to smooth things, but he didn't even manage to open his mouth before Wiesel kept going.

— The land of Zion was given us by *God,* he spat, and saliva flowed from his mouth.

She knew he wanted to kill her then, to squeeze the very life out of her. She would have known even if Everett hadn't revealed to her the man's hatred in all its glory.

The room, its very people stared at him with shock, now, and not her. The smile stayed on her lips. For perhaps the very first time she knew what Stacy, how Lillith felt. Her lips curled in a snarl she knew well.

— Fortunately, I'm far from being the only Jew rejecting Zionism and its horrors. At the next opportunity you might repeat your *Hasbara,* your «explanation» that all Jews working against Israel are «self-hating Jews». And you might make fun of my ears. That will work with most dull-witted people.

He wanted to, wanted it so very much, but he was unable, unable to even speak.

— No, how can those criticizing Israel be anti-Semites? How can anyone? It's kinda hard when both Jews and Arabs are Semites... And we point constantly to Israel's *actions* and to those supporting those actions. «By their deeds you shall know them»...

She stopped for another moment, her stare turning even more pointed.

— The «accusation» is meaningless, is Hasbara, is Zionist propaganda and should be ridiculed every time it's uttered. Every time an Israeli Jew hurts his finger or stubs a toe it is covered extensively in Western media, while mass killings of Palestinian children are practically ignored. We will no longer *stand* for such a horrible state of affairs.

She stood out in the hall later, besieged by journalists, surrounded by Everett and the others in a protective embrace.

— No, she replied to a pointed question, — I don't find my words harsh at all. In my opinion they can't be harsh enough.

— He couldn't handle it, Everett commented, shaking his head in amazement and disgust. — A young girl and her commitment to justice and truth exposed him beyond doubt as the vile human being he is. His humanitarian mask came off like the deception it has always been.

— This isn't Jews against the world, she said quietly. — It is Jews and the world against Zionism, against a despicable, racist ideology destroying both life and the spirit.

The protesters gathered in the street outside the hall began applauding and stamping their feet on the ground, and yet another crack showed in the thick and tall wall of tyranny, the pervasive lies and deception dominating the world.

2

The garbage filled the streets of East Jerusalem, the Palestinian half of the city, the part basically ignored by the Jewish city council since the invasion and occupation in 1967.

The late night stayed quiet, except for a few loud and distant cries. Ted and Stacy appeared with their people. The stench immediately overwhelmed their olfactory sense.

– This is disgusting, Betty said, her voice filled with anger and emotion.

– Yes, but it's also perfect, Ted grinned.

She and all the rest had long since learned to recognize that grin.

They looked at him with expectation in their eyes.

He lifted a bundle of garbage cans with his power. It took some fine tuning, but he managed to raise it into the air without spilling too much. Gabi lit up in an enlightened smile. She opened another portal. Ted threw the bundle through it.

– I think we may have found our true calling... at last, Ted remarked casually.

The wicked grin grew on everybody standing in front of him, all the most powerful telekinetic warriors in his army.

They hauled garbage through various portals for hours, the twelve telepaths making sure no one came close to discover their labor.

Dawn grew slowly in West Jerusalem that morning, very slowly. People walked around in a daze, as if sleepwalking. The usually very efficient and well-equipped garbage haulers of the Jewish part of the city struggled the entire day and long into the night and the next day to get everything off the streets, and then they had to do almost as much work to drive it out of the city and to the very modern (but struggling) garbage disposal facilities.

National and international press rubbed their heads, but had a field day, and some of them even interviewed Palestinians that could enlighten the world about what had been the practically non-functional garbage disposal system of East Jerusalem.

– We've been waiting for years for this, one old man said, almost doubling over in wicked laughter.

It was pretty clear that there was a double meaning to his words.

Phoenix Green Earth broadcast it as well, of course, but no more than they otherwise would.

– Just this one time we're happy to report soft news, Gayle grinned.

Her grin couldn't possibly grow any wider.

Attention was also called to the massive effort of the occupation authority to remove Palestinians from East Jerusalem altogether. People that had been thrown out of their homes and lost their property through the deliberate long-term tactics of the zionists were interviewed extensively in the ever-growing Phoenix Green Earth news services.

– People here are forced to demolish their own homes, an old woman said distressed. – If we don't, we are fined up to 300 000 shekels.

Retaliation, when it came was neither unusual nor unexpected. It was less obvious, but no less noticeable to those knowing what to look for. The number of arrests and harassment cases rose significantly, in the eastern part of the city and on the West Bank in general.

– This is classic occupation tactics, Betty shrugged. – Nothing we didn't anticipate.

– People can take it, Sasha, one of the recruits from Ramallah said. – They've taken much worse.

She had also taken in stride the revelation about the nature of her new friends.

Look at her, Lillith told Ted. Behold potential attained. It will always be personal in some way to her, of course, but she has already grown beyond her limitation and upbringing. There's reason for pride here.

As always, he was not exactly certain what she was talking about. There were plain words, but also the ever-present subtext. He made no attempt at holding back the flaring inside and knew Lillith smiled. Images briefly flooded his mind.

Sasha joined the thousands of devoted faces parading before both their eyes, and then, at least he understood this subtext, this scenario. The irritation faded and he looked startled at Moonstar.

We can never properly know all our warriors, Lillith stated softly. They will never be more than brief candles flickering before our eyes.

– You're quite correct, Sasha, Stacy acknowledged. – Your people are prepared for the inevitable backlash and so are we.

– We are, Ted nodded. – We're through pussyfooting.

The separation wall towered above Ni'lin and cast its long shadow across the town. The group appearing out of nowhere chose the most remote part of the wall. They looked transparent as they walked the final steps to their designated spot. It would have been easy for them to stay completely hidden, but they wanted to breathe the air, the scent of the land.

Stacy and Nick put their hands on Gabi's shoulders. The others present put their hands on Nick and Stacy. Gabi touched the wall with both hands.

The guards in the watchtower didn't see them. They were distracted by troubling images of dead Palestinian children. And that did trouble them. The Janus Clan made sure it did.

Gabi mumbled something.

– I can feel it, she said. – It wants to decay, to crumble. It's practically crying out to me.

Nothing visible happened at first. Slowly, so slowly that it wouldn't have been noticed by anyone, Gabi started glowing. A rumble shook the wall. Sweat broke on Gabi's forehead. A shimmer resembling dust rose from the structure in both directions, both far to the left and to the right. There was a loud crack.

Now! Gabi hissed in her mind. NOW!

They poured even more power into her. She shook, but held out against the onslaught.

The wall started falling apart, crumbling before their eyes, their enhanced senses. Large chunks of it turned to dust. The rest fell apart at the seams, fell apart as large blocks for miles in every direction. The men in the towers fell. Some died instantly. Others were smashed so hard that blood flowed from their skin and others sat up unharmed, confused and scared beyond their wits.

Fences where the wall had yet to be raised were pulled apart and spread for the winds.

Everything stopping people from crossing the line where the wall had stood was gone.

Stacy gave Gabi a little added boost of healing just to make sure. Gabi smiled to her in calm gratitude.

– I feel fine, she marveled. – In fact, I feel great. This was fun!

Power sparked and flowed within and without the slender body.

Dust and rust rose in and above al-Khalil at dawn. Its Old City and almost its entire H2 area, as defined by the Oslo Accord resembled a ghost town. The Shuhada Main Street was practically deserted. Five hundred Zionist «settlers» and thirty thousand Palestinians existed within H2, but it was the heavily armed settlers, eagerly supported by the israeli army that were in control. Another massive set of checkpoints made the mere act of moving around a nightmare for the Palestinians.

The settlers were allowed to have weapons, the Palestinians were not. If the Palestinians complained to the israeli soldiers when the settlers treated them badly and with violence, the soldiers just grinned and basically ignored the situation, if they didn't abduct the Palestinians making the complaints. There were tons of footage and documentation about this, and, as usual it was all ignored by western establishment media. Phoenix Green Earth showed their documentation through its channels, but it didn't make any difference with western governments.

But it made more Zionist Hasbara, propaganda fall flat on its ears and that slowly created yet another channel for change, made more and more people all over the world joining in the support of the Palestinians.

Josef Goldstein fired a round of bullets into one of the nearby buildings from the roof of the building he and his family had occupied. He heard loud screams.

– I love the stench of terrified cockroaches in the morning, he shouted in glee.

He walked back inside, to the breakfast table and his wife and children.

– Did you get any of them, father? His oldest son, ten-year-old Josef jr. asked excited.

– I think I did, son, he chuckled. – I think I did.

Josef and his fellows in the community, among many other israelis and its supporters had been in a foul mood for weeks, now. They felt the tide of change, no matter how hard they attempted to deny it.

He studied himself in the mirror later, a little dismayed. His face looked puffy, the skin around his eyes swollen. He remained there, reluctant to move on, hardly noticing that Josef jr. moved past him and stopped before the toilet bowl. The boy crouched and threw up, the vomit decorating the bowl and much of the surrounding area.

The sight made the older Josef hurry to the bowl as well, and he contributed to the decoration in hard and painful moves. The stench turned sour and foul.

– The neighbors have it as well, his wife said. – The entire street has it, even some of the *aravi*.

She spat the last word.

– But not all of them?

She nodded in affirmation.

– Not even many of them.

She nodded again.

His frown turned deep and set.

Carla sat on the ground not far away, focusing hard on her task.

– Even though there are distinctions, it's hard to distinguish between most of the members of the two population groups. She shook her head. – They're practically the same people. It would be funny, if it wasn't so tragic.

She had started using her power to contaminate the ground and water supply for the small Jewish population of the city. The first results had begun showing after a little more than two days. She felt it, how the poison grew and festered, how it moved through the ground, into the very environment of the fortified houses.

It had been a while, a long while since she had done this, or something similar, but it returned to her quickly, without effort.

The Earth moved her, and she moved the Earth. Ted felt her do it, felt her and the Earth. Drinking water and food and everything became tainted, dangerous, bent to her will. Her rage moved that part of her. He knew that well.

– I can do it on a much larger scale, she said. – Differentiating, like I'm doing now is much harder. The Ashkenazi is very easy to identify and single out, though.

She still sounded uncertain, as if she hesitated every time she took a step, once again slowly being filled with the confidence of the others. He frowned, Liz (and Nick) frowned and watched the tiny organic… entity grow and spread, to encompass more, far more than the human body. A deep chill and deep wonder trickled down his (their) spine.

Ted noticed how Lillith studied him, smiled to him and evaluated him.

Moving on, moving on, moving, one step, two, ten, ten thousand in one, beloved bird!

He realized, Liz realized startled that he/she/they picked up her thoughts.

Josef vomited his entire stomach in one bout, or so it felt.

His son walked towards him… and vanished in thin air.

Hundreds of children appeared in the streets of Tel Aviv in less than ten minutes, thousands more the next hour. They left alleys where no one had seen them appear out of thin air. Many of them were screaming in distress.

– You're not welcome here, a voice told Josef from behind.

He turned abruptly and there was no one there. When he rushed through the apartment he found his near panicked wife, but none of the children. The cry of distress rose from all the settler homes in and around al-Khalil.

The voice… Cold sweat broke on his brow. It had been the snarl of a young girl.

– Your time is up!

He rushed to the table and grabbed his machinegun. His finger pushed the trigger at the voice. His wife screamed in pain. He saw how blood flowed from her many wounds.

She writhed on the floor, blood spreading from her broken body.

– You shot me, she screamed in anger. – You asshole, you damn asshole!

And she swore curses in Hebrew.

We're through pussyfooting, a voice hissed in his ears (both his ears).

His wife died cursing his name.

He sat down on a chair, clutching his gun. There was much commotion outside. He heard the soldiers run through the streets and heard commands be shouted.

A woman stood by the door, one he had never seen before. She had red hair and eyes filled with green dancing flames.

– Hello, Josef, do you have anything to say for yourself the last few seconds on your time on Earth?

He stared at her with total incomprehension in his wet and dirty eyes.

– Well, have you?

He blinked and kept blinking.

– You hit a child in the arm with your «reckless» shooting, but you don't care about that, do you? You've done that and worse many times before and will do it again, do worse, and you will keep teaching your children your vile doctrine until someone puts a stop to your inhuman actions against the people native to this land.

– They're vermin and should not be in the holy land at all, he said puzzled. – They deserve whatever they get.

– It makes me warm around the heart to hear you say that…

He screamed short and sharp. Pain shot through his arm and it hung right down, useless. The pain clouded his vision, made tears jump from his eyes.

– Yes, that is what being hit by a bullet feels like.

Pain clouded his eyes, while he desperately attempted to make his useless arm work.

– There's no such thing as a «good settler» on stolen Palestinian land. «I'm a nice racist, a nice torturer, a nice thief». And you're worse than most. You are only one among many, and you will all pay, will all suffer. To you the Law of Three will be real and true.

She looked at him with her demon eyes.

Or perhaps a Law of Ten will be in order in your case…

She spoke to many people simultaneously. It suddenly dawned on him, as her voice made a choir.

He finally made his arm work and fired at her. The bullets went right through her and hit the soldiers on their way in. They returned the fire and shot him to pieces with a hail of bullets.

– Your own actions brought your downfall.

He heard her voice from far away, fading in a landscape of mist and shadow.

And then Lillith was there, to fetch him, and he recognized her, and he turned sore afraid.

Total pandemonium ruled in the beyond brutal invaders' settlements in al-Khalil. Some of the soldiers or the settlers ventured too close to the Palestinian houses and areas or attempted to shoot them on sight. They vanished into thin air.

Soldiers leaving their barracks vanished the moment they ran through the doors. Planes in the air disappeared from the radar and from Palestine altogether. Calls of distress and disbelief kept pouring into the IOF central command, practically collapsing the network. The planes appeared in space, thrust away from Earth with the same speed as they had entered the portals.

– They will move out there forever, Gabi said without regret.

Every single Israeli plane in the air that day faded from the Earth's atmosphere, never to be seen again.

All members of the Janus Clan once again remembered vividly Ted's words to them: *We're through pussyfooting!*

A platoon of IOF-soldiers and armed settlers reappeared inside the main police station in Phoenix, Arizona. A wild firefight commenced seconds afterwards. The scenario repeated itself on many other police stations and military barracks in the United States. Lots of the battles and their bloodbaths spread to cities and streets. Lots of footage were recorded, events so monumental that they could not be ignored by establishment media outlets.

– That should take care of some of the inflated goodwill Zionism enjoys in the United States, Lee chuckled darkly. – Even the attack on the USS Liberty is nothing compared to this.

The world changed that day - again.

It changed the next day and all the days after that.

The IOF-soldiers, going apeshit and berserk did not surrender, even to overwhelming forces. They kept fighting until death. Very few of them were captured alive, and those that were had very little sensible things to say, especially in the madness taking hold of them,

– HELL, one woman shouted. – I'M IN HELL, GOD HELP ME.

– How did you enter the country, a very peeved CIA-agent asked her. – What was your objective? Have you and your superiors taken leave of your senses?

– We were there, then we were here, the soldier whined, with big tears flooding her face.

He received no reply, none making sense.

– She clearly belongs in an… an *institution*, the psychiatrist whispered nervously to the agent.

– When we're done with her, the agent stated firmly. – If we're ever done with her…

– The fact is that none of them is making any sense, another man with nervous twitches at the corner of his mouth said.

– They're mere arrows sent to the target, the chief interrogator mused. – The question is who is the bow and who is holding it, and what the fucking objective is.

He was cursing. A man that never cursed did. The others glanced at each other.

The interrogation and survey ended like it had to, inconclusive.

The strange and frustrating events didn't end, but grew in numbers and scope. The world kept changing.

No guards outside the room where the israeli government cabinet meeting was held were the wiser for some time. Agitated voices, unusually so, cried out in there, several doing so simultaneously. The guards stood there, a considerable detail glancing uneasily at each other. Then the room turned silent. The soldiers glanced at each other some more. Time passed and some of them began looking hard at their watches. It took at least a minute after that before one of them, the Captain knocked on the door.

She pushed down the handle. It wasn't locked. She gave the signal, and everybody readied their guns. They rushed inside, into the empty room.

All the soldiers froze. They remained frozen, even as they kept moving, kept searching the floor, the entire building and the surrounding area, even as a growing panic filled their every thought.

It eventually became undoubtedly clear. Prime Minister Ehud Olmert, his deputy Tzipi Livni, the entire cabinet and major army and public officials and various individuals both attending the meeting and not had vanished all across the country.

Olmert, Livni and the rest looked around them with confused and wet eyes. They found themselves in a dark room filled with shadows. Snarling armed men and women surrounded them, manhandling them, quickly dealing with those among them attempting physical resistance.

– MOVE!

– What *is* this? Olmert squeaked.

– SHUT UP!

A strike to the head made him dizzy and he almost fell. He stumbled on.

They were pushed and dragged through a dark hallway to a bright lit room they still imagined were filled with shadows. They recognized a courtroom when they saw it, and yet another deep chill was added to their growing panic.

Everybody in the room was masked and carried guns. The beyond uneasy prisoners were herded down on benches and chained there, ankles, wrists and neck. They attempted to speak up, but were quickly beaten into silence.

– You haven't gained the right to speak, a man hissed at them, – but believe me, you will be given ample opportunity to defend yourself and your actions. You can speak for days for all we care. We have time.

The woman sitting on the judge's bench hammered her club at the wood. Silence finally descended on the hall. Only the whimpers of the prisoners were heard.

– This is not a court of law, the judge began, – but a people's tribunal gathered in order to determine guilt and its degree.

Linda pulled off her mask.

– And I'm certainly not a «legal judge», she shrugged. – I'm merely one of several representatives for humanity, finally fed up with a murderous racist tyranny almost without precedence in human history.

The prisoners recognized her. Their eyes turned wide and huge.

160

The «proceedings» began. Witnesses, both willing and unwilling were called to the witness stand. The formalities of court proceedings were followed to a painful degree. There was no jury, no peers of the accused judging them, but this, as had been pointed out was no court of law either.

A man was led inside and to the witness bench. He shook visibly and stared hard at the people sitting behind the desk, at the accused. Olmert stared shocked at him.

The man sat down.

The persecutor removed her mask as well. It was Glory Burns.

– Do you swear on your honor to tell the truth? She asked him.

– I do, the man coughed and repeated it nervously, but determined. – I do!

– What is your name, sir?

– My name is Absalom Goldstein. I am, or was a colonel in the Israel Defense Army, also called Israel Occupation Army in occupied Palestine.

– What were your duties?

– The simple and horrible answer would be extermination, he said, very matter of fact, with an even voice. – I was in charge of operations during the Gaza massacre. My orders that day, given directly to me by Mr. Olmert himself, were in short «to eradicate an entire generation of Palestinian mothers».

Olmert wanted to speak, to snarl, to protest and make an angry retort, in vain.

– That was his direct words?

– It was, and everything he added to them was equally explicit, making no room for interpretation. Others will confirm the truth of my statement.

– So, why come forward, now? Glory asked him.

– Because I'm sick and tired of it. I know I can never make up for my part in it, but at least I can give a detailed account of what has happened and is happening and will keep happening as long as Zionism exists. I've been part of an ever more vicious system for decades and want all of it exposed to the world.

The recorded, unedited footage of the proceedings appearing on the Phoenix Green Earth website and television broadcast, and also at other independent news services days later with only limited comments showed his face close up, his intent, determination, and shame. Later archive footage showed him in full uniform. People watching were not in doubt that it was him, and about his honesty. Many more witnesses, both reluctant and willing came forward later.

– I witnessed many atrocities. Ariel Sharon, the previous prime minister hated Yasser Arafat with a vengeance and his cabinet, including Olmert supported it. The cabinet eagerly participated in the poisoning of Arafat. Sharon and Olmert were livid and incredulous when Arafat survived and even made a total recovery. The bombing and isolation of the Palestinian Authority were stepped up further.

– What about the killing of all the children? Glory asked.

– They don't care about that at all. On the contrary. Killing and imprisoning and terrorizing and torturing and abusing children is seen as «useful» in destroying the Palestinian morale, in terrifying them into submission. They've also stepped up the terrorizing of Palestinians on the West Bank. I thought it couldn't become worse, but it has.

He sat in the witness booth most of the day and even returned for more the next.

– Yes, he nodded empathically. – Tzipi Livni pretty much presided and presides over it all. She's a right hand «man» even more eager than the boss.

In a special, stormy and panicked session of the Knesset, the Israeli parliament appointed Benjamin Netanyahu from Likud acting prime minister. He had quit the Sharon government in 2005 because of his disagreement about the disengagement in Gaza. Now, he returned, clearly triumphant.

The «inner circle» of the Phoenix Green Earth watched him from their spot in the Shadowland. They didn't need their powers to discern his motives and plans.

– He was the logical, illogical choice as replacement, Keller sighed.

They didn't need any kind of psychic power to predict what would happen next either, what the new government set in motion all over Palestine. The new administration, in open rooms and halls packed with guards armed to their teeth shouted in loud voices and their aggression filled the streets with even more blood.

All military «reserves», basically consisting of the entire population of Jews in Israel and Palestine of conscription age and upwards were called in.

Jews marched in New York and other major cities, crying out «not in my name», protesting against Israel and Zionism in general.

Ted and Stacy and the others noticed Gabi's fatigue well before it became apparent, her small slipups and mistakes.

They put their foot down the day she strived to open a portal.

– You will take a prolonged break, now, before you're exhausted, Liz ordered her with an unusually kind, but yet stern voice, – both because of your own wellbeing and if we should face an unparalleled emergency, one where we will be forced to use all our resources to exhaustion.

The girl nodded pale and drawn. Ruth and Lydia took her to bed, to a silent and distant room, where they would guard her and never leave her sight.

A hundred-kilo concrete roadblock outside Bi'lin keeping people from driving out of the city was moved by people with a single rope. It was an eminent technique that the local resistance had used several times before. They had two pregnant women in the car. The nearest functioning hospital was in Ramallah, not that far away, but the road there was filled with roadblocks.

A voice through speakers reminded people of the curfew.

– EVERYONE MOVING OUTSIDE AFTER DARK WILL BE SHOT ON SIGHT.

The speaker amplified it so much that it hurt everyone's ears within many miles of the tower, one filled with soldiers.

They had started the process of replacing the fallen wall with fences, but had yet to do so in this area. It was pretty much a free pass through the darkness. The small group stopped the car and left it there, leaving the bright lights of the village behind.

In a house nearby soldiers broke into two houses close to each other. The doors and most of the walls in front of the already damaged buildings broke down in piles of dust. Stacy had no trouble registering it as it happened. She saw children

162

crouch in corners, while parents and other adults were struck to the ground. Similar «operations» were in full force all over the West Bank.

She hardened herself, closing both hands into fists, and she relished the pain of her nails digging into her palms.

– This is your legacy, Jahavalo, she snarled, – one of thousands.

She stood still for a long time in her bedroom in Ravenscourt, letting go, allowing her rage to flow freely. It spread across sea and land and air, and it was as if everyone in existence was hers to read and everything was hers to tell.

3

The informal court «proceedings» against the former government and officers and soldiers continued unabated.

It dragged on for weeks, feeling like months.

– We have the right to defend ourselves, Olmert said on the stand. – Israel is surrounded by enemies.

– You claim the right to defend yourself against those you are constantly attacking, colonizing, occupying, brutalizing and killing, against children and what are almost exclusively defenseless people? Glory asked, sounding very puzzled.

Olmert turned even more pale and ashen. He could no longer hide behind the Hasbara, the Zionist «explanation», propaganda.

They walked through the countless testimonies with him, confronting him and the others again with the many details.

Many more were dragged kicking and screaming to the court and charged, from top to low officials and foot soldiers.

– We're mere servicemen, a soldier whimpered. – We have no choice but to obey the commands given to us.

– In other words, you were just following orders? Glory said, seemingly impressed.

The soldier couldn't speak, couldn't make his voice work. He got it. Everyone watching did.

A woman of the court stepped forward. She still wore her hood. A strange… shimmer surrounded her form. She seemed to come from far away, as if she wasn't really present in the room at all. Her eyes, her livid eyes burned them all.

– You can't do anything to us, one of the many accused crouching there in chains and bracelets yelped. – You have no authority. You…

– We don't need any authority, except what we grant ourselves, she said, her voice like an icy river in spring, – and our right and duty as human beings to correct the gross injustice people like you commit.

She pulled back again, to the place by the wall those accused imagining she had occupied during the proceedings.

All attention was directed at the judge, at Linda Cousin.

– For weeks we've been sitting here, in this hall, listing to testimonies given independently of each other. Those testifying rarely knew each other in advance and had little or no knowledge of the testimony of others and certainly not its details, but pretty much confirmed each other's statements. I'm ready to pronounce the sentence, now, one just as meaningless as when all humans judge each other, but none the less fills a burning need in us all. There must be a reckoning. The earth itself screams for one.

She looked them over. Her ice blue eyes made ashes of them all.

– You're not prisoners of war, but war criminals and worse waging terror against children and what's basically a helpless population. It cannot even be said that you've waged war, but committed countless untold massacres, massacres that now will be related for all to know.

The hooded woman stepped forward again, suddenly standing right in front of the soldiers on the far left.

– You're not Moshed, but five-year-old Yussef, which you filled with bullets from a short range.

Her voice echoed through the room, as she stopped in front of each and every one and pronounced their deeds.

– You're the worst of the worst, she told one man, – and in this sordid gathering that says a lot.

She pulled back. Linda spoke again, spoke to them all.

– You've preached might makes right for a century. We're quite simply returning a small measure of it to you. You'll feel a bit, just a bit compared to what you've put others through. It pleases me to see the fear in your eyes mirroring that of your victims.

The sentencing continued through the day and week, an endless procession subjected to spite and contempt.

– HANG THEM! The choir of the mob shouted. – CHOKE THEM SLOWLY. RIP THEIR LIMBS FROM THEIR BODIES!

And this was just a small selection of everything.

In their cells, in their sleep, the prisoners heard the shouts as a constant flow. It never let up for a moment.

Ted and Liz, through their proxies Martin and Lydia snapped countless photos. The sound of the SLR-cameras also haunted those crouching in their cells.

The hooded woman left the court. She closed the door behind her. Silence blessed her sore ears. She walked down the hallway to the restroom. She stopped or seemed to stop before the door, but kept moving forward. A shimmer filled the air in front of her and she slipped through it, and appeared in the restroom without ever touching the door. She stopped, drawing breath, taking the measure of the room and herself.

It was even quieter, an island of silence she appreciated beyond belief.

She removed her hood. Judith Breen looked at her face in the mirror.

Another hooded creature appeared behind her, materializing out of the very air itself.

– You've become quite skilled, Gabrielle Asteroth told her, – taken quite a few steps forward in the mastery of your power.

The teenager was just as obnoxious and full of herself, as she usually was. Judith

164

shrugged, even as she was hardly able to keep her gathering joy contained.

– Give me your hand, the girl told her eagerly.

Judith did. Gabi grabbed it and pulled her close with surprising strength.

One single step each forward and they were off into a realm of mist and shadow that were unlike anything Judith had experienced alone.

Impression, sensations and a multitude of voices cried at them from every possible and impossible angle. It bothered Judith. She couldn't claim otherwise.

– Are you good? The teenager asked.

Even the girl's voice sounded like a choir, a multitude.

– I've been preparing for a long time, Judith replied. – I can handle it.

Clouds gathered and split a thousand times in a second. Without Gabi as an anchor Judith knew she would be lost in here, endless driftwood with no destination or direction.

– This is amazing, the woman mused. – This is absolutely…

She held her tongue and focused on taking in as much as possible.

They stopped, just like that. Asteroth made them stay «still» and «hover» in the Void, a vantage point giving them a nice, limited view of the vast maelstrom surrounding them. There was a flash, one of Shadow, one of thousand in two hearts beating like one. They stood on a beach, the beach. Grains of sand rose and landed in an endless stream.

– It's *so* interesting how your perception of it is different from both mine and Lillith's.

The sea, the endless sea reaching out from the tiny beach became a stream, and the stream, the stream became the river.

The River of Souls.

Of consciousness, seething emotions and everything between and beyond. Judith Breen gasped, and her gasp echoed in the landscape of mist and shadow revealing itself to her.

They stepped into the river, the flow. One moment they were outside of it, the next bathing in its searing energies, howls cutting them like a thousand black blades.

Gabi let go of her, and just for a vast, horrible moment Judith feared she would be pulled apart and become driftwood in an ocean without end.

Power soaked every tiny piece of her being, and just like that… control was achieved. Fleeting lives touched her, but didn't sway her.

She woke up in her bed the next morning, forever more even stronger attached to what she had always been a part of.

But now she was more, forevermore.

An unmarked road stretched out in an unnamed desert.

– We will take action, President Bush said in a televised address. – God charged me to lead this country against our enemies and be confident that I shall.

He looked beyond weary and downtrodden. The bags under his eyes were visibly growing during the address.

He faltered and hesitated visibly before speaking words clearly not in the script.

– We will take action against somebody.

He said to the open air, not even attempting to speak into the microphone.

– Who was the President talking about? A journalist asked Dana Perino, the White House Press Secretary in the pressroom later in a rare delivery of a somewhat intelligent question. – Who is this «somebody»?

– We're discussing and investigating a number of candidates and options, Perino said, sucking his thumb. – Everything will be made very clear eventually.

A choir of incessant questions flooded him.

No more than five hours after the end of the address the number of protesters outside the White House had tripled.

– There will be no Palestinian state, Benjamin Netanyahu said curtly from his pulpit in the Israeli national assembly. – We will no longer accept any liberties from our enemies. That includes our neighboring nations. We've been patient for way too long, and will take what is ours in order to ensure the safety of our people.

Phillip Caine slapped his hands together during the ongoing Phoenix Green Earth news coverage and broadcast.

– He didn't mention «Greater Israel», he chuckled darkly and shook his head in disgust.

– He didn't have to; Gayle nodded.

And in a million homes across the Earth, even in the previously ignorant western societies people understood what they meant. They had been profoundly educated lately and had also read up on issues on their own, both on the Middle East and the world at large, and began waking up in earnest from their long slumber.

Waves of applause thundered in the hall of the assembly and played on Netanyahu's sweaty, hateful face. Those watching in the shadows and mist felt his contempt for everyone different from himself like a fist deep in the gut, the most stinging slap on the cheek.

The recruitment to the Phoenix Green Earth picked up significantly, picked up even more than it had done the last year. In some cities, like New York and London there were actually lines of people forming outside the offices.

Sally Regehr, sitting behind one of the counters inside sent Andrea and Gregory to do the registration from the back of the queue as well, making everything go smother.

– It's so ironic, she told those behind the nine other counters. – I actually learned that while working at a burger joint…

– Customer services at its best, Sasha joked.

– We could've had more offices in each major city, and online registration, Nathan mused without actually considering the issue.

He was the «manager», residing in a small room at the back of the building.

– Ted and bunch prefer keeping it a close and personal process, Sally told the clever man what he already knew. – They wish to take a good initial look at as many of the recruits as possible, as effortlessly as possible. Gathering lots of them in one place accomplishes that.

– I certainly agree. Nathan nodded. – It also makes the initial step harder, forcing said recruits to make an effort before joining up, helping us to pick the toughest

166

and most independent among them, those better suited to serve our long-term interest.

Sally looked impressed at him. He was a shrewd old goat.

Andrea and Gregory worked fast with the queue, handling out registration forms and small tablets to write better on. The others knew that she moved slightly faster than most people would do, but not fast enough to cause suspicion or much suspicion.

– Thank you, Gregory said. – Please walk inside and sit down in the hall after you've completed writing down your information.

A woman received a form.

– Thank you, she said. – I'm looking forward to hand it to the Jews. Their global rule has been allowed to continue for far too long.

– We don't accept racists in our organization, I'm afraid, Gregory told her. – And for your information: many Jews are actually strongly opposed to Zionism and Israel. Many Jews are members and can easily be counted as our most valuable members, also for their ability to see beyond the Palestinian issue, as we all strive to do even now, confirming to ourselves that it is only a small piece of the puzzle.

The woman looked aghast at him, before reddening with anger.

– So, you're part of the New World Order as well, she grinned triumphant. – Figures.

She carried a gun. Gregory could practically smell it on her. She was about to draw it when she gasped and staggered. Gregory made her, reaching out aggressively with his empathic power.

– Are you alright? He asked, reaching out a hand, masking his elation in worry.

His power was a song within him, and he relished the sound of its voice.

– I'm fine, she snarled. – Don't touch me!

She rushed off the fastest she was able, in a cloud of angry, hateful thoughts he could do nothing to mend.

– Some of you may be smarter than her, Andrea said quietly, – attempting to conceal your racism, your disgusting bias, but know that we will weed you out. We have no patience for racists, for such low-life scum.

A couple of others hesitated before they pulled back and left.

Those that remained pulled inside, both hesitant and not, as if drawn to a center point.

– You doubt, Sally told them. – That's good… as long as it doesn't put out the fire you all carry within.

– You suspect correctly, Nathan added his dry voice. – The wind blows everywhere, in every possible direction. It's up to each and every one of us to choose our own path.

– If every human being did that, Sally continued, – humanity would be in far less trouble.

– That's not some half dead and withered slogan, Sasha stated, – but a truth we all, deep down share. You will feel all that, all those thousand directions hammer you with each step you make on the new and exciting and dangerous road ahead.

The doors closed. It sounded to the recruits as if they slammed shut.

– Yes, the door closed you off from your former existence, Gregory stated curtly. – From now on, forward is the only possible direction.

Forward… the word seemed to linger and echo in their mind.

The final applicants of that batch reached a hall, where quite a few others sat and waited impatiently for the stragglers.

– It's time to leave, Sally declared. – Your future awaits you!

They recognized her, she saw that with half a glance. They were up before she had finished speaking. When she left the hall, they rushed after her.

Gregory and Sasha opened the double doors in a hallway leading into a darker corridor. Andrea guarded the rear. She saw no signs of enemy activity in the street outside, where a new queue was already forming. The recruits followed Sally down the dark corridor. The double doors closed. Some of the recruits turned their heads and glanced behind them. Gregory and Sasha had not followed.

– I'm your sole guide, Sally told them. – Follow me and I'll lead you to your new life.

The air began shimmering. It was very distinct for a moment or two before the effect faded. The corridor looked exactly the same.

There was a growing light ahead, coming through an open door. Sally walked through it and they followed her.

They stepped out into the light. A city street appeared to them, one with fairly low, no more than two-story buildings.

– Is this New York City? A woman asked incredulous.

Sally kept walking in front on light feet, as if she was taking a stroll through a nice, peaceful neighborhood.

– There are no people, a man said.

Everyone looked, but they saw no one.

– Where are we? He asked anxiously.

Sally turned and grinned.

– I can tell you one thing: We're not in Kansas anymore.

The wickedness in her eyes both scared and excited them.

– But then again, we never were. You said goodbye to all that shit the moment you signed up.

She crossed the street. There was another open door in the nearest building. She walked past it. One of her charges bent down and touched the ground. It felt solid enough.

– This is… amazing, a woman said, – such an amazing setup. It seems so real.

– It isn't real? Another swallowed hard.

– My five senses tell me it is. My sixth is telling me in no uncertain terms that it isn't, at least the solid bricks and ground we experience.

– Your… sixth?

– Yes, she said brightly. – I've always had the ability to perceive what's hidden, what most people don't see. Several well-known members of Phoenix Green Earth have written articles and blog posts about it. I came here in order to learn more

168

about it, myself and the world.

– And you shall! Sally assured her. – You'll learn more than you could ever imagine.

Ominous thunder sounded not that far off. They approached another door or gateway, one that seemed to expand as they walked closer.

– Is that a giant face in the sky? A boy whimpered.

– We all see shapes in the clouds, another male shrugged it off. – It is our vivid imagination hard at work.

– Yes! Sally said.

And they exchanged uncertain glances, unable to tell what she had actually replied to.

They walked through the gateway, into the dark, into the shimmering brief, prolonged twilight, and emerged into a world of light, shadow and darkness, of powerful smells and sensations, of tears, blood and joy.

Groups of people on their way to Ramallah with sick children and pregnant women in the deep night broke through the weakened wall at several points. One of the pregnant women, having yet another contraction bit her lip and walked on. The others supported her the best they could.

A chopper flew over them, bathing them in its powerful lights.

It flew away and those on the ground breathed sighs of relief.

They saw the lights of the city and imagined it was just over the hill, knowing there was still quite a distance to go.

A small woodland of Olive trees surrounded them. Lots of trees had recently been removed. The ground had suffered the attack of bulldozers and excavators, making most of what had once been a considerable «forest» seem like a wasteland.

– That is Sasha, a small boy brightened, – and Jenia and…

He named five trees before his father signed for him to be quiet.

They froze a little, as a sound from the right they could not quite identify reached them. All of them stood still for moments. There was no other sound. They resumed their cautious walk.

A dry branch broke to their left. Voices reached them, and they glanced at each other with a resigned look on their faces.

A group of soldiers emerged from the darkness.

The soldiers quickly closed in on them. The pregnant woman gasped and couldn't move very fast, could hardly move at all. Those supporting her held on to her that much harder.

– Look what we have here…

They stood there, those that would be able to make a run for it, hesitating, glancing at the woman that couldn't.

The soldiers started firing, and now everyone ran. None of them got very far. A massive number of bullets hit all those fleeing in their backs.

No bullets were fired at the pregnant woman at first. Then the leader fired a low salvo hitting her feet. She fell. They surrounded her with infinite patience.

– This is always great, a female soldier grinned. – We kill two with one salvo.

They filled her belly with lead. She bled out there on the ground. They stood there watching. Her body shook one final time and laid still.

4

– We cannot save everyone, little one, Lillith said softly. – In fact, we can only save a handful.

– I know! Gabi choked. – I know it perfectly well.

The United States, as always, kept resupplying the Israeli army with lost and used ammunition and equipment. It was mostly from a stockpile already in place in israel, but also more from various nearby sources.

IOF, for various reasons needed lots of supplies.

Factories in the United Kingdom and elsewhere produced parts vigorously. Israel had an entire network of production facilities around the world serving them, doing so practically exclusively.

– I'm shaking with rage, Phoenix, Gabi said with clenched teeth.

– Very good, Liz said. – Keep that rage burning! We will all need it, in the days and years to come.

They materialized partly into a hall where deadly weapons were built on numerous assembly lines. The dismal sight made them even more enraged.

The humans present in the hall didn't realize that anything was happening at first. The machinery seemed to… blur, and then fade away, and no more than empty air remained.

It was just Liz and Gabi. The girl didn't need help from a power source like Stacy or Lydia anymore.

– This is easy, she said. – I don't have to strain myself at all.

They were gone, just like that. The people left stared at each other in bewilderment and distress.

The two of them moved on to other factories and production facilities, removing the equipment completely.

There were guards in some of them. They waved their guns, but there was nothing to fire at.

When Gabi began showing the first signs of fatigue and Liz put a stop to that night's incursions, the number of viable factories had dwindled significantly.

– We should do this at all military production facilities, Gabi stated curtly.

– That is an excellent idea, honey, Liz joked. – Why haven't we thought about that before…

Later she conferred with Ted and the others in the leadership.

– We have thought about it, she said, – but we haven't really *considered* it, have we?

They did, and more subversive thoughts stirred and awoke in their already fertile subversive minds.

– This… Keller said, – our brush with Zionism has forced us to grow.

– And we continue to do so, Lillith said pleased.

– It's a good idea to not touch the US stockpile within israeli borders, Jason said, –

170

risky but good.

Everyone smiled solemnly and exchanged glances.

– It's a honey trap for the ages, Stewart said. – I can't believe they will fall for that so easily.

– Insane, power-hungry people have done far worse mistakes than that, Lillith said. – They have yet to realize the might we have at our disposal, mostly because they lack the necessary imagination.

– They're still convinced that their failing equipment is due to some hacking genius, Everett shook his head. – They're familiar with our kind, with the concept, but they still fail to realize the implications of our existence.

– We must act as if they will realize their mistake at any time, of course, Ted cautioned them.

– Of course! Linda snorted.

There were more grim smiles.

– Give people like the zionists enough rope, and they will, with a little help, hang themselves, Keller said. – Their zeal, their naked aggression and bias will prove their undoing. They've hardly encountered any serious opposition for decades and have almost forgotten what it's like. They've been allowed to do anything, whatever they please, without retribution or fear of retribution.

He spoke strangely, his accent always noticeable to those listening. It was as if he almost spoke from personal experience. Everyone in the room knew why.

The room faded away before their eyes, becoming the world and its stage again, time resuming its flow.

The conflict level on the various Israeli borders picked up. They watched, filmed it as it happened, on the battlefield and in every single room plans of conquest were discussed, and it was all on the Israeli side.

– Benjamin «Bibi» Netanyahu appeared in all his pompous and fake wrath on Israeli television.

– They fired at us without provocation, he shouted from his dais. – We've every right to defend ourselves and rest assured that we will do so.

The entire hall stood up and applauded him. The ceiling of Knesset, the Israeli national assembly practically rose several meters.

– Does he truly believe his own propaganda? A voice said close to Rick Harding's ear.

He turned around. A man, a young boy with dark fireeyes stood two steps away.

– Do you, brother?

Was there... was there sadness in the man's eyes?

– You can't get to me, Rick snarled. – I'm protected!

– Are you?

Harding struck out. His fist went straight through the other man.

– You're not stupid, brother. You don't ask how I can be here.

– I know what you are, Harding gasped.

– And you know what you are, Martin Warren stated. – You've had dreams, nightmares your entire life. That was certainly one reason why you joined other

171

American Jews in this distant land. You wanted to know, and they told you and trained you and successfully brainwashed you to follow their tenet of domination and superiority.

Several other people came running, doing so from all over the building. The moment they all had stepped inside the room, the hallway, everything surrounding them dissolved in Shadow.

– That was almost too easy, Ruth Warren said.

Everyone looked around, stricken and angry.

– She's not here, Martin told Abe Galbraith. – This is her domain, but she isn't the domain. You can't reach her. Nor would you have been allowed to.

– You can't hold us here, Galbraith gasped.

– We can, actually, Stewart Warren said. – We're far more powerful than you, especially when we cover all angles and control the setting, like now. But we have no wish to keep you here against your will, at least not for long. We wish only to educate you, and keep you out of the way while we crush the monstrosity that is «Israel» to pieces.

– We're the Janus Clan, Lydia Warren said. – Welcome to our Kingdom. It used to belong to your Lord and Master, but now it belongs to *us*.

Her triumphant voice echoed through the void, the landscape of mist and Shadow.

– Nothing is… working. Harding clearly struggled, a deep frown growing on his brow.

– We took you long ago, Ruth grinned wickedly. – You're already asleep.

– You dream nothing but our dreams, Lydia chuckled. – You're nothing but dust in our wind.

They fell, the ten that had been whisked away from everything they had known fell, and there was no end to their fall.

– You will pay for your acts in the service of Zionism, pay dearly. There will be no end to your suffering.

Laughter echoed endlessly in their ears, and there was no real difference between that and the deep, deep darkness they descended.

An aide approached Netanyahu. He turned and looked irritated at her. She whispered something in his ear. The Janus Clan saw how he turned pale, literally saw it, and many others did as well.

They watched as insanity, always there took hold, irrevocably and forever.

– The Palestine issue is certainly a litmus test for any politician, Linsey said. – If he or she supports Israel they're unfit for office.

He stood on a dais in a seething hall filled with people in Denver, Colorado flanked with his wife and daughter, holding hands with both, feeling the power flare between them.

– Blaming Palestinians for firing rockets at Israel is like blaming a woman for punching her rapist. Blaming others, previous spectators for acting like human beings instead of signaling quiet acceptance is equally horrible. I say to you all out there: any Zionist firing weapons at defenseless people will from now on find retribution. A man or a woman firing a weapon at unarmed people will shoot himself or herself.

Chaos ruled in the hall. Even the sharpest, straining fireeyes had trouble spotting everything going on and the brow above those eyes was covered in sweat. Noses imagined they smelled the oil and powder from loaded weapons and ears feared they heard the sound of firing pins being cocked. Chaos spread from the hall, from many halls and hallways and big and small arenas across the world, as newfound awareness lit many a dull pair of eyes.

Almost the entire israeli military might lined up at the Lebanon, Syrian and Jordanian borders. Not long after that troops and tanks rolled into all three countries, massacring everything, men, women and children in their wake.

The extended Phoenix Green Earth Media and news service covered it all in graphic detail. The staff had been considerably expanded lately. Phillip and Gayle were only two of many, now.

– We have footage, indisputable evidence recorded by an israeli soldier showing that the IOF has raided the US stockpile within israeli borders.

They watched Netanyahu closeup as he received the news about the footage, sensed it the moment he cracked, irrevocably. He rushed to the nearest communication device and issued new, even harsher orders to his troops, spitting saliva left and right, looking very much like a parody of a banana republic dictator. That film clip, with accompanying photos trended on social media for weeks.

Dust turned red as the zionist army kept marching into the three neighboring countries.

Planes, one of the most advanced war machine models available to man flew ahead and dropped their bombs, further softening whatever feeble resistance there was.

The invading army seemed unstoppable.

The commander smiled ever broader as the tanks wrecked ever more villages and denser populated areas on their path.

But a frown stayed on his brow. It grew deeper and deeper as the invading army progressed further into Lebanon, Jordan and Syria, and as it appeared more and more like a Sunday walk in the park.

– There's practically no resistance, he mused. – I would have thought there would be some…

His aide looked at him as if he wasn't right in the head. There was a pervasive, uplifted mood at the command center, one that certainly would turn into loud cheers at any time.

The planes… The commander looked at the monitor. They had held a steady course forward. The first firing of rockets had gone just as planned.

The planes turned in the air. He practically saw it, watched it, as if he had suddenly become able to see far ahead… or if someone showed it to him. The planes started firing at the advancing Israeli forces. Now, it was people in uniforms being blown up, instead of defenseless men, women and children.

The flying war machines unloaded all their remaining munitions on the army it was supposed to support. Metal and flesh were torn apart on an even more massive scale.

Then the planes started crashing to the ground like kamikazes. The once so mighty Zionist forces shrunk to nothing in minutes. The Lebanese, Jordanian and Syrian army waiting at a safe distance stared at it all with open mouths.

A shimmering creature appeared before the three commanders for the defending countries. They looked at a completely ordinary woman with completely ordinary features. The face moved like flesh, looked like flesh, but she knew they suspected it was only a mask.

– Time to get going, she offered casually. – Time to get your ass in gear, don't you think?

She turned, as if to leave, even as she was fading.

– What are you? One of the men asked. – What's happening?

She turned back briefly, even as she kept fading.

– The gods have returned to this world, in order to finally set it right.

The three men stood there frozen, in their common command center, unable to act for several seconds.

Slowly, hesitantly, with increasing confidence and eagerness they started giving their orders.

The three armies attacked what was left of the majority of the israeli forces. There was some disorganized resistance, but not much. It was over in just a few hours. They were boxed in, most of them unable to return to the israeli border. They were fired at from every direction and killed in droves, until the few that were left surrendered.

– Look at them, a Jordanian commander, cried out. – The fourth largest army in the world and one of the most advanced has been reduced to insignificance. It is as if someone just snapped their fingers and *made* it happen.

The deep chill mixed with the excitement and stayed with them.

Long rows of chained men and women were taken away, brought deep into Syria and Jordan.

The woman with the mask resembling flesh appeared to them, to them as individuals and groups.

– You will never be free, she told them. – You will spend the rest of your lives atoning for your horrible crimes against children and basically defenseless people. No one will find you, rescue you. Your brethren will be too busy to even look for you. I would start wising up fast, if I were you.

Syria regained the Golan Heights. It happened without significant resistance.

The Jordanian army crossed the Jordan Valley towards Jerusalem. There were skirmishes, but no effective countermeasure.

In the United Nations general assembly United States and British representatives called «for the hostilities to cease». They were met with mocking laughter from huge parts of the other representatives. Even at the Security Council there were smiles hidden behind hands covering faces.

– We need to act fast on this, the United States ambassador shouted with saliva

174

flowing from his mouth.

– Russia will not support any action in Palestine by outside forces, the Russian ambassador stressed.

– Neither will China, the Chinese representative said.

– The aggressor has been defeated, the Russian added. – I would say that the situation has resolved itself in a very satisfying manner. We should continue to monitor it of course.

And that was that, really.

The situation had deteriorated so fast, so unexpected. The United States Navy had no aircraft carriers in the area. The closest was the one stationed in Iraq.

The nearest airbase was Incirlik in Turkey, but it had no permanent foreign aircrafts assigned to it. Response was not, could not be immediate.

«Diplomats» were leaning on Abdullah the Second, since he was seen as the weak link, but he had suddenly grown a backbone and refused to back down, stating that «he was sick and tired of watching Zionist aggression».

The US Senate and House of Representatives acted swiftly enough, voting «to give Israel all kinds of military and logistic support».

But the actual United States support of the israeli state was mostly monetary, a staggering three billion dollars annually in military support alone, and based on israel having a functional army.

They and also the UK parliament and other European national assemblies, in spite of critical voices pointing out the obvious fact that israel was the aggressor, voted to bomb Syria and Jordan.

Again: if the operations had been planned in advance, they would have been implemented in a matter of hours,

But they hadn't been.

The US stockpile was empty, its content either destroyed or taken by hostile forces.

– The nuclear option is a GO! Netanyahu shouted to his advisers and aides. – We will receive immediate support, or we will create Hell on Earth.

They looked at him, at least some of them clearly hesitant.

– Do it, he snarled. – Bomb the advancing troops in the Jordan Valley, bomb the Golan Heights, Beirut, Damascus and Amman. Activate the bombs in the European embassies. Make sure that trustworthy, essential personnel is present and can assure that the orders are carried out. We will blame it on terrorists. That always works.

«Trustworthy, essential personnel» translated: the Zionist fanatics able and willing to give their lives to the cause.

Everything was reported live from the Phoenix Green Earth broadcast center.

– Take out Oslo and Stockholm first, Netanyahu spat. – Sweden and Norway have been a thorn in our side for years. They think we're too far away to really hurt them. They will discover how wrong they are.

The aide walked to the phone at the other side of the room. He picked up the receiver and started giving clear, concise orders.

Netanyahu frowned. He believed he heard someone running in the hallways. The aide put the receiver down. Another phone started ringing. Netanyahu looked at it. A thicker film of sweat was suddenly covering his forehead. The aide picked up the other phone. He replied and then listened.

– It's the President, sir.

Everyone watching the Phoenix Green Earth webcast and broadcast saw how the prime minister stumbled across the floor and grabbed the phone. They saw him put the receiver to the ear, and heard President Bush's voice clear as day.

– *I can't help you anymore!*

The connection was broken a moment after that. Bush had broken it.

Another aide, sweaty and deeply shaken jumped into the room and stopped there, froze there. She was still almost shot by zealous guards.

– The television, sir, she gasped. – The…

Someone switched it on. Netanyahu couldn't tell who. His eyes, his entire attention stayed glued to it.

It showed splitting images from the Phoenix Green Earth newscast. The right showed the room with Netanyahu, the left devastated Stockholm streets, with roasted bodies and parts of bodies everywhere. At uneven intervals a recorded repetition was shown: the conversation Netanyahu had had with his aide not that long ago.

– There's no way they can spin this, Gayle Tadero said into an open microphone, shaking her head in distress. – They've gotten away with numerous atrocities in the past, but there's no way they can ever get away with this… is there?

She didn't appear very confident on behalf of her own statement.

– They will probably claim they were only defending themselves…

Phillip Caine spat.

The broadcast's attention shifted to Oslo, where equal devastation was displayed. Insane screams echoed between the ruins and spread across the Earth.

Several other phones started ringing. They appeared very loud and penetrating. A downright pained expression grew on Netanyahu's face.

A man, an officer walked into the room, red-faced, very agitated.

– You clumsy shithead! He shouted. – We had a good thing going, sticking to the long-term plan, moving forward in a slow, deliberate manner. You've ruined *everything!*

He shot the prime minister twice in the chest. Others in the room drew their weapons. A full and completely confusing firefight where everyone seemed to fire at everyone broke out.

When it ended somewhat, most of the people in the room were dead or mortally wounded. The firefight continued outside and spread from there, to include major parts of Tel Aviv. Various factions kept firing at perceived enemies and the struggle showed no sign of slowing down. In the end, the zionist nation showed itself to be no better than the typical clichéd image of a South American banana republic.

The deluge had started and couldn't be stopped. The israeli army and the large part of the adult population serving in the army had been decimated, its vast arsenal of weapons lost on the battlefield and confiscated by rival armies. One of the most brutal regimes in existence had finally met with worthy resistance. The zionist nation colonizing and occupying Palestine had suddenly lost its advantage, and become the underdog.

The Jordanian representative spoke in the UN to livid protests from the israeli ambassador.

– For decades the major nations of the world have allowed the rogue state of israel to proceed with its mad and beyond violent scheme of dominance in the Middle East. You guys have not helped us. Western nations, with the United States in front have instead bombed some of us back to the Stone Age and even financed extreme religious forces in our countries in order to destabilize our region, making it ripe for the taking for your zionist friends. You threaten to attack us again if we do not comply with your insane demands and stop defending us against israeli aggression. I will tell you this straight up: Do it, come and bomb us, terrorize us even more than you already have. We will not retreat, not stop advancing towards Jerusalem and Tel Aviv. We will use this change to do what we should have done long ago: liberate the Palestinian people and put a stop to zionist colonization of Palestine, and thereby also ending a clear and present danger to all countries and people in the Middle East.

Thunderous applause had already started before he ended his speech. It grew to incredible proportions shortly afterwards, and totally overwhelmed the israeli representative insane shouting.

The Norwegian and Swedish ambassadors asked for sanctions and for war crime charges to be brought against israel in international courts, and they got massive support. Only United States, United Kingdom, France and a few others voted against it, and only a few others abstained.

Norway, Sweden and Denmark broke with the «defense alliance» NATO only minutes afterwards. Germany and almost all others followed in the next few hours. The organization, one of the most aggressive military alliances in existence ceased to exist.

The Jordanian, Syrian and Lebanese armies countering israeli aggression met with surprisingly little resistance. There was little organized defense in place, and the zionists fought more among themselves than against the enemy. Almost all important cities and military installations were taken in a week. The rest fell fairly quickly after that.

– Push the buttons, the acting woman in charge of crucial installations told her underlings.

– Which one? One of them asked her with weary eyes and several guns directed at him.

– All of them! She shouted, spittle flowing from her mouth.

He obeyed the orders reluctantly, but with the panicked haste brought on by the firearms directed at him. A huge electronic map showed the world. Cities on it blinked green, except Oslo and Stockholm, still flashing in red.

He frowned. It was a very deep and worried frown.

– What is it? The woman snapped.

– Nothing is happening, he said, a thick layer of sweat covering his face. – The equipment must be… faulty.

– Shoot him! The woman screamed.

This time there was no hesitation or *disagreement*. The man pushing buttons died in a hail of bullets.

– Find out what's wrong, she snarled to the remaining technicians, – and do so *fast*.

Shooting, quickly growing in intensity started up outside.

Another woman rushed into the room. Those with drawn weapons, already high-strung filled her with bullets.

She crouched there on the floor, laughing her heart out.

– We're on TV again, she gasped.

And died.

There was an explosion downstairs. A heavy fortified door was blown off its hinges.

– Shoot them, the woman in charge shrugged. – Shoot them all!

Her people did. People fell to the floor in pools of blood.

She walked to the board and pushed the big red button herself. A blinding white light filled the room, and then the camera showed mostly open air and ruins.

A few settlers in al-Khalil fought against the Arab army. They were killed quickly. The others surrounded and were removed from the occupied and fortified houses, their arms confiscated.

– That's a zionist for you, a soldier spat. – They don't fight when they don't have major odds in their favor.

French, British and American fighter jets were on route to the Syrian and Lebanese borders from the base in Turkey. Their objective, given through sealed orders was «heavy bombardment of all major cities».

Then president Bush's meeting with his cabinet was shown on all major independent networks around the world. The words spoken were more than clear enough, not to be misunderstood.

The planes were quietly recalled through more sealed orders and coded messages.

– The United States was holding a joint exercise with our loyal allies, Dana Perino, White House Press Secretary said. – That was what the US cabinet meeting was about.

Loud, mocking laughter greeted his words. Even the most loyal establishment media shills couldn't hold it back, only pulling themselves together with an effort. They attempted to focus on the sweating man behind all the microphones. Perino went on with what was basically a monologue, explaining «the exercise» in more detail.

King Abdullah held a speech broadcast to an entire speechless world.

– Free and fair elections will be held, the moment we determine that all refugees that want to return have returned, no less than two years from now. Age old claims will be respected. Stolen properties all the way back to 1948 will be returned to the rightful owners or their descendants or relatives. When we say free and fair elections we mean it. International election controllers will be allowed full access everywhere. It will be held in the spirit of what western democracies claim to be, but never have done, at least not in a very long time.

The remains of the occupation wall were demolished, reduced to dust in full daylight. The sound of explosives sounded all over the West Bank. Loud cheers accompanied every salvo.

Palestinians, refugees on and off their own land for almost sixty years started returning to Palestine, also to what until recently had been within Israeli borders, bringing their keys, the symbol of their exile and eternal hope of return. It was a trickle at first, a trickle becoming a flood.

The remains of the insane venture that was israel ended, both with a bang and a whimper.

5

Earlier that year, in May ten-year-old Mahmud woke up in his bed in a house outside Ramallah. The military police came as they often did, in the middle of the night.

He remembered seeing the bulldozers make large holes in neighboring houses. This night they paid his family a visit. The front wall to the house was pushed down. Loud, painful noise filled the air. A blinding light made Mahmud shield his eyes. The sound of heavy boots against the ground made his eyes bleed.

Someone grabbed him. A brutal jerk pulled him out of his bed. The soldiers gathered the family in what was left of the living room.

– THIS IS MAHMUD? A soldier spat at the mother. IS THIS MAHMUD???

– Yes, yes, mother sobbed.

– He has thrown stones, the unit commander stated. – He will be imprisoned until the trial.

Protests were met with brutal beatings of both adults and children in the household.

Mahmud started crying when he was dragged out. The soldier slapped him on the cheek.

There were six military vehicles outside, everything from tanks to a jeep. The streets were filled with soldiers armed to the teeth.

Mahmud and several other children were blindfolded, and their hands cuffed behind their back. There was more slapping. Mahmud received them, and he heard other contacts between cheeks and palms. They were taken to the local police station, basically situated in the closest zionist settlement. There was no one there.

– The police officers will arrive in the morning, the unit commander informed them. – We will lock you up until then.

They were all thrown into their cells alone, still cuffed and blindfolded. The boy sat there on the bed, shaking, beyond scared and horrified. The sobbing continued for a long time, until nature took its course and it slowly stopped.

He sat there, his eyes slipping shut under the blindfold.

Then, suddenly someone, someone that had been there the entire time slapped his cheek. He shouted in stark distress and began crying again.

Sometimes later, much later, when he started turning sleepy again, there was another slap, and another.

– There will be no sleep for you, you little *rat!*

It was much, much later. They grabbed his arm and pulled him on his feet and dragged him out of there. The brutal walk seemed to last forever. He couldn't see anything, could hardly hear anything, except the constant ugly voices speaking brutal insults and curses in his ears.

– You better cooperate, rat boy, one of the voices hissed, – or you will *pay!*

He screamed, totally out of it, but then they started beating him, beating the air out of his lungs, making all sounds stick in his sore throat.

The choking and sobbing became a constant in his new and horrible existence.

He sat on a stool. They pulled the blindfold off. He sat in a bright room with lots of lights in his face, hardly able to see anything but shadows, and the occasional brutal face appearing close to his sore eyes.

– You've thrown rocks, the interrogator snarled. – You will confess having done so.

– But I haven't, he sniveled. – I never have.

They slapped him again. A female soldier squeezed his genitals. His scream turned to a wail.

There was hardly any sleep. They kept him awake, until he slipped into something that might be described as waken dormancy. He didn't really dream. A constant nightmare kept him in a state of horror he couldn't wake up from.

They placed a paper and a pen in front of him, a document written in Hebrew he couldn't read. He signed it. His hand shook so much that the signature became virtually unreadable. They had to give him three more chances until they were somewhat pleased with his performance.

He was allowed to sleep. The harassment stepped down a peg, even though it didn't cease. He couldn't quite get rid of the shakes.

They started force-feeding him. He didn't really want food and vomited most of it, even though some got through his system.

There was a lawyer there in his cold cell at some point. He couldn't recall much of the conversation afterwards.

– You will be put before a judge soon, the lawyer impressed upon him, – and it's imperative, if you wish to get out of here faster that you declare yourself guilty.

Mahmud stared at him, staring at nothing.

– If you don't do that, you will stay imprisoned until the trial, one that might not be on for years. If you're smart, your parents will pay a small fine, and you're out of here after a few months.

Mahmud was alone again, with the sounds and silence.

He realized he was in a courtroom, recognized his parents, even as he ran to his mother. His mother spoke gently, but firmly to him, told him he needed to be strong, and that he soon would be home. He nodded and put up a brave front.

The court negotiations were a mere formality. There were no surprises there.

He returned to a cell later that day, and stayed there, stayed there, stayed... forever.

He returned home one day. His mother and father and siblings welcomed him. Everyone hugged him, hugged him hard. He walked to his room. It resembled his cell. In his mind he saw little or no difference between that and this. He stayed there all day, all night.

Breakfast, dinner and evening meal was pretty much the same in the ruin that was left of the house. Repairs had been negligible and pretty much reflected his state of mind.

He heard his mother speak to her sister in the kitchen. They were whispering, but he had no trouble hearing what they were saying.

— Sometimes, in my darkest moments, I fear he's still in prison, and only his body and not Mahmud himself was released and returned to us. What did they *do* to him there?

They got it in bits and pieces, as others repeated what they had told them before and they listened harder, and their hearts turned cold with fear and anguish and hot with rage.

A woman visited them one day. She knocked on the door, they knew she did, but she still seemed to flow, to move effortlessly through walls and air.

— I can show you, if you let me, she said with quiet sorrow and rage. — At least some sort of understanding will be yours.

The fireeyes burned them. They knew who and what she was. A shiver caught them, as they sensed the tangible change in the air, without and within. One, two, thirty seconds later, they knew everything they didn't want to know about Mahmud's experiences in the israeli «penal» system.

Ruth and Stewart walked around in the West Bank, hardly more than shadows to the occupying forces, but a very tangible presence to the oppressed and occupied.

The IOF noticed a qualitative change as time passed. The parents and even the children seemed less and less afraid with each new brutal raid, but met them with a quiet confidence of resistance that could no longer be denied.

— We're arresting him, the officer said with arrogance painted on every feature, as he brutally squeezed the arm of the boy he held on to.

— You're not arresting him, the mother in the household said. — You have no legal right to arrest anyone. You're kidnapping him, like you have so many others.

And right out of the blue the officer started shivering, shivering so hard that it almost turned visible. It was as if he experienced everything waiting for him in the coming months, as if his bleak future painted itself on his insides with every new event.

— The Palestinians are acting up again, a liberal US Senator stated in an interview with the Zionist supporter New York Times. — Everyone, they included would be better off if they chose peace.

— Privileged white men, living in the greatest military power in history, lecturing a people living under a brutal occupation to be peaceful, really stink, Tamara stated with contempt in her voice during a demonstration outside the newspaper headquarters just a few hours later.

A few nights before everything changed The Janus Clan freed every Palestinian and political activist incarcerated in israeli military and civilian prisons. They focused on the many children first, helped imprisoned, terrorized and tortured children escape.

– This wouldn't be of much use to you earlier, since they would just kidnap you again, but it may be different this time.

The scared and brutalized children slowly filled with hope looked at the shadows in their midst with wide eyes.

The new, gloriously failed israeli invasion of neighboring countries began. The Arab incursion into Israel and Palestine as a whole began not long afterwards.

The world had changed irrevocably, and continued to do so.

– It's quite ironic, of course, Phillip Caine said on air. – They've killed numerous Palestinians, including thousands of children for decades, but the moment they were exposed doing something unequivocally bad to white Europeans, they were done.

– Israel was this close at igniting its own private Ragnarok on the world, Gayle said. – They were stopped in the nick of time. I'm so relieved, so damn relieved that humanity seems to have survived Zionism. This should be a valuable lesson to everyone supporting it. It should also be a lesson to voters supporting warmongers and racists in their respective country.

Phillip faced the camera, staring right into it.

– I did it. I, with a little help from people seeing it as I did destroyed Zionism. It had gone too far. Zionism and its insane proponents had to be stopped cold.

Gayle faced the camera, staring right into it.

She repeated Phillip's words. The recording was put up on the Phoenix Green Earth webpage and their personal blogs. Many others followed their example in the minutes, hours and many days to follow.

A shaking man standing somewhere in the rags remaining of his IOF uniform spoke with a bowed head and shaking limbs.

– Something reached for us, and destroyed us, something straight from the *Abyss*.

– The Golani brigade, israel's «elite brigade» is more used to beating up farmers and kids, a Jordanian soldier standing before the Tel Aviv government building spat. – They're not that great when they face real resistance.

Abe Galbraith and Rick Harding and the others sat in a courtroom surrounded by other prisoners, the same courtroom used to charge and convict so many other Zionists.

Rick hardly followed the proceedings. They didn't seem to have anything to do with him at all. Completely different sets of thoughts roamed his increasingly active mind.

He waited in his cell later, in a world filled with mist and shadow. He noticed the shift immediately, spotting the shape before it manifested in his vision.

– You really screwed up this life, Rick, but take comfort in the fact that you will make amends.

He knew who this was, knew the dark eyes and black hair almost as well as his own.

– You used Gaza as a weapon testing ground. We used you for similar purposes. Your usefulness to us is at an end.

Fear haunted him more than shook him. He felt shame, not guilt, not really. It was far beyond that.

Ted Warren spoke to a gathering in Ramallah, in jubilant Ramallah, the day before the Palestinian Authorities moved their headquarters to Jerusalem.

– Jerusalem isn't important, he said quietly, – and you should stop seeing it as such. It's not a prize, but a mirage, a false call in the night easily led people see as something completely different from what it is.

– We should heed this man, Yasser Arafat, standing by his side later, during the first seconds of his speech stated firmly. – He speaks wisdom. We should never let our own pride ruin what we've won. We should always guard ourselves against the fault in ourselves, what led to the fall of our enemies.

The Al-Aqsa compound was reopened for all religions, and kept open, in spite of ongoing unrest.

The desert stretched on for miles in all directions. The small group of people could see no end to it.

– We're setting you free, Linda Cousin said to the former israeli high officials. – You no longer matter. Whether or not you eventually once again become a part of what remains of the Israeli society and the future Palestinian democracy is practically inconsequential.

– You should be able to reach safety in a fairly brief amount of time and easily enough, Glory shrugged. – If a few of you don't make it, however, we will not shed any tears.

– My guess is that you will probably settle outside Palestine, when you no longer have the upper hand.

The first new maps where the name «Israel» was supplanted with Palestine had already been printed and gone into circulation. Most online maps had changed it weeks ago.

Olmert and Livni, and the rest exchanged glances, as they watched as their jailers faded away and joined with the vast sand dunes surrounding them.

Linda sat in a non-descript room, at yet another undisclosed location a few days later.

– Anyone using religion as an excuse to commit atrocities will ensue our wrath, she said. – We'll not exclude any small or big dictator or would-be dictator, but we have a special place in our warm, warm hearts for those playing the religion card.

Glory sat by her side, the smile seemingly spreading to the entire room and to everyone watching the broadcast.

– Militarism will no longer be tolerated in any shape or form.

The message was scrawled on walls all over the world:

THE PERPETUAL WAR IS ENDING

CHAPTER SEVENTEEN
The happy winter of discontent

Jason Gallagher woke beside the big, shaking shape and realized startled that Michelle had managed to hide a piece of herself from him, after all.

He put a hand on her shoulder. She shook it off.

– Please, don't touch me! She sniffed.

But she didn't resist when he grabbed her again and turned her around, forcing her to face him, and that worried him most of all.

She made no effort at blocking him, to fend off his invasive probe. His eyed widened ever more the more he discovered of her beyond deep despair, the reason for her ebon mood.

– You shouldn't b-bother with me, My Lord, she choked. – I'm not worthy of your attention.

An unexplainable sense of dread made cold sweat cover him from head to toe. He forced himself to touch, caress her, knowing it didn't fool her the slightest.

– Explain yourself! He heard himself say, unable to keep the steel from his voice, the cruelty from the subtext of his thoughts.

She shrugged at him with the wet, ashen eyes.

– What is there to explain? I'm wide open, now. You can see me better than I can see myself. Our aunt, our dear aunt Betty tamed me, making me useless. I have resigned to my fate. It's just as well!

– Stop that. He shook her. – Stop that right, now.

She looked at him with pity. She looked at him. The so very familiar snarl of a smile he loved so much turned to ashes before his eyes.

– Everything I am tells me that at some point in the near future I will lose everything making my life worth living, and I will commit a deliberate, methodical suicide, and it will be a relief. I don't know why, only that it *is*.

He heard her speak.

– I froze and couldn't move, couldn't do anything. I'm worthless! I don't blame you for blaming me. I blame myself far more.

He looked at the broken creature in that nondescript room and undisclosed location. That image, that sensation superimposed itself on the beautiful form in front of him.

– What could it possibly be that will… There must be something we can do. Others should be able to…

– I went to Ethel, she snarled.

That stunned him, stunned him even more.

– She was unable to discern the details. She told me that I, like you, like Ted and Liz and Jeremy and Gabi and Nick am one of her blind spots, an agent of time and chaos and change, a mist she can't penetrate.

She grabbed his outstretched hand and kissed it, drowning it in spittle.

– It must be you, she said. – That must be it. I cause your death, somehow. I know I couldn't bear that! But why can't I *see* it? It doesn't make *sense!*

He saw her stand in that nondescript room with the rope in her hand.

– All the light has left my life, she stated with a voice and spirit dead and gone.

She giggled darkly.

– It's funny! I never saw myself as a person in need of light.

The dark, bleak room faded, and he returned to the bedroom and its pale lights, and the still, somewhat spirited girl.

– I must stay with you all the time, she insisted, begging him. – I must never leave your side, and you must accept it and never stop c-caring about me, no matter how clingy and insane I become.

He kissed her, forcing himself to kiss her hard on the lips. She sighed content and responded instantly. He kissed her again.

– You're not a child, he stated. – Your existence isn't dependent on another being.

– I thought so, too, before meeting you.

She stretched, displaying herself to him, mind and body and shaking spirit.

– Don't worry, my love, I will not be a burden to you. I know I can pull my own weight. I'm not some weak creature in need of protection and cuddling.

She put up a brave front, but inside she was shaking and an open book to him.

– Hard times, truly hard times are coming, she stated. – I know that. I've prepared for it my entire life. I'm ready.

She clung to him, her nails breaking the skin on his shoulder, drawing blood. He hardly noticed, her big, beautiful fireeyes close to his, appearing to him like true windows to the soul. Sultry lips met his, stealing the air from his mouth.

Cooling lips pulled back, sensing his detachment. She shrugged. He shook his head, imagining that the bright morning light couldn't quite reach him.

He realized startled… that her nightmare… also had become his.

2

Stacy and traveling companions returned to Texas, to its hatred and intolerance and suddenly raging passions.

Their previous visits had created massive support and opposition. The hall seethed with rage and a wide range of emotions. It strengthened her, making her power sing.

She received a warm welcome from the local Phoenix Green Earth representatives.

– We've gained so many more supporters and potential voters since the last time you were here, Elsa Redmond told her enthusiastically. – We've become so crazy that we think the impossible is actually possible.

«The impossible» was seats in both local and national Senate and House of Representatives.

Stacy Larkin stepped forward to the dais and the microphone. She was dressed in her robe and hood of violet and black. No one present was able to take their eyes off her. Her pervasive voice and presence burrowed into feverish minds.

– The Democratic Party has practically been eradicated in Texas, she cried to the packed hall. – The Republicans, the Good Old Party is shaking in its foundation. They saw Texas as a sure bet, but we've made all such old and quaint convictions void, and have become a force to be reckoned with... in Texas, in the United States... and the world at large. We've proven that it is possible to overcome a system rigged in favor of the establishment. We've shown people hungry for true change that another world is indeed possible.

The cheers shook the walls and the ceiling and the very ground beneath their feet.

– Forces of ignorance and intolerance have dominated this land for way too long. It's about time people rise up and tell them that this quite simple isn't an acceptable state of affairs. Do you Texans enjoy being screwed? It's very tempting to believe that when you see how easily you're being fooled by the simplest propaganda. Fast talking politicians who can make convincing arguments for citizens to vote against their own interests are a skill corporations and the wealthy pay lavishly for. Voters should stop rewarding them for it, of course.

There was a kind of press conference, or rather questions and answers afterwards, where all people in the hall were allowed to ask questions.

Contrary to similar events it kept going for a while, once more a far cry from the smooth, professional shows ran by both the Democratic and Republican parties, collectively baptized the «War Party» and called that by an increasingly bigger part of the electorate, and the population as a whole.

– HEY, Stacy, a bold voice shouted from the crowd gathered in the hall, – why don't you run yourself as a candidate anywhere?

– I probably would, Stacy shrugged, – if not the founding fathers, in their infinite and infallible wisdom, and everyone following them, hadn't decided that I'm too young to run.

Her many supporters had no problem picking up on her biting sarcasm, and laughed heartily.

– It's no big deal, she stated. – I mean that! We have more than enough great candidates to pick from, in all elections, at local, state and national level. I have no desire to run only for the sake of running.

– Do you really believe it is possible for you, your... movement to get anywhere? A mainstream journalist asked, very presumptuous and condescending. – There hasn't been a successful third party in the United States for hundred and fifty years.

– It's about time then, she said and shrugged again, very deliberately. – Many things work against us. Ballot restrictions are merely one of many making it an uphill battle, but we fight on and do so with obvious success. As stated, we have pushed out the former second biggest political party in Texas. Many things the War Party has designed in order to keep itself in power don't work anymore. We have no trouble getting the necessary number of signatures in each state. The demographics previously aiding it don't anymore. Gerrymandering doesn't work anymore. We make huge swaths into traditional voters fed up and not willing to take it anymore. Similar processes are afoot all over the world. We're ready to take on those in charge

186

everywhere, on all levels, both the visible power and those behind the throne.

– So, you're not liberals then?

– No, not liberals, not *progressive*, not conservative, not Democrat or Republican, left or right. We refuse to play that game. We pick a few pieces of our politics from both sides of the War Party, but most of it is brand new or at least brand new in public mainstream «consciousness». My guess is that mainstream establishment everywhere will keep using all the usual derogatory words when they talk about us and refer to us, though…

– You're not even a traditional green party, are you?

– No, all previous green parties anywhere have been hopelessly lacking in boldness and necessary drive to truly change human society. We are not! Even if the old «green parties» had won elections and done everything they wanted to do, it wouldn't have been even close to sufficient in order to save the world and all life here. We see such simple truths easily and are willing to take any action necessary.

– You're not even going to do anything to restore Israel's rightful place in Palestine, are you, an angry voice came from the back.

– We're not, Stacy shrugged again. – We're very pleased with the recent developments. The zionists and the zionist Jews don't belong in Palestine, and have committed every horrible act possible in order to displace the indigenous population there,

She paused deliberately. It was very silent in the hall.

– Israel's Jews persisted in their claims that God had given them the land of Palestine. Americans use the same insane rhetoric about the land they stole from this continent's indigenous population. It hasn't, shouldn't have any validity in the real world. No one has been given anything by God. There is no God, only humans exploiting people's belief in one.

The loud chatter and shouts picked up further. Second by second the angry noise filled the place to its edge and beyond, to the streets outside in the packed locale.

– What is your take on people dumping garbage outside the White House? The mediator spoke fast and asked in a desperate attempt at mediating.

– I support it, she grinned. – I wouldn't bother with it myself, but we all choose our unique way of protest.

All hell broke loose inside and outside the hall.

3

The busy small town surrounded the two of them, welcomed them with running and playing and laughing children. They walked down the street to a house between two trees where several women worked in the garden. Everyone looked up and most stared as they entered through the gate.

– Hello, Abby, Liz said softly.

A woman approximately fifty years old smiled to them.

– Look at the two of you, she said with one taint wonder and one taint bitterness.

– You look like you haven't aged a day.

She looked strange, at least upon taking a second look at her, her form indistinct, as if she was just as much smoke as flesh and bone.

Most of her companions and the children gathered in the garden kept staring at them.

– My apologies, she sighed. – Many people, even some here tended to view my stories from my time with you as… exaggerated. Even knowing what they know, they couldn't quite fathom it.

– Very soon, now, there will be no more doubt, Ted stated.

A young girl stared at him with wet eyes. She blushed hard when he turned his full attention to her.

– This is Alex, my youngest daughter, Abby said.

She was about fifteen, well trained and well aware.

– Hello, Alex, Ted greeted her casually.

– H'llo, she mumbled shyly.

– She has a crush on you, a boy said in contempt, very inconsiderate.

Liz looked at him, and he started blushing as well.

– This is Gareth, Alex said wickedly, – and he has a crush on Liz. He will kneel before her and lick her feet.

Everyone gathered in front of the two visitors, looking attentive and excited at them.

– I've trained them, trained them all, Abby said, – more than suspecting this day would come.

She had done an excellent job. They saw that at one glance.

– Well done! Liz acknowledged.

– Come inside, Abby offered, – we're about to have supper.

The inside smelled even more of herbs tearing at their nostrils. They stepped into a pleasant abode with soft light, a mix between the daylight and big candles. It encouraged a peace of mind they couldn't help but pick up on.

Everyone studied the two extensively, eagerly, with a curiosity that couldn't be denied. The two made no attempt at putting a stop to it, at countering it, but allowed it to happen, even encouraging it. They drew everyone's attention, and no one could look away.

– What you did in Palestine was just awesome! Alex blurted out.

Liz and Ted glanced at a shrugging Abby.

– Even if there's no definite proof, it's a badly concealed secret that you orchestrated or at least took part in the latest development there.

The two of them knew that, and it wasn't unexpected.

– Zionists and fundamentalist Christians have called you the epitome of evil long ago, Gareth said eagerly. – Their vitriol has merely picked up lately.

Ted and Liz didn't voice a comment, but a big smile broke on their faces.

Everyone sat down by the large, round table, a setting the two guests were quite familiar with. Dinner was served. Conversation and interaction began in earnest.

Time… slowed down to the two of them, a sensation not unfamiliar, at least not lately when they wanted to take their time with something, something important and precious.

Candles burned at a relaxed pace, just like the hearts of those gathered around the table. It felt… pleasant, and they savored that, for as long as they could.

The dinner began. It was courses of both sea and land animals, and both meat and vegetables, pieces and fillings of it they basically handled with their hands. Liz grabbed a large shell filled with meat, spices and a bit of everything, devouring it with a more than content expression drawing her features.

– It is remarkably easy changing things on a small scale, she said between the bites and swallows. – It's also remarkably difficult to do it on a bigger scale, and to make it last, to wake up people to such a degree that they will never wish to fall asleep again. It is that awakening, that prevailing awareness we more than anything wishes to accomplish. Those in charge, those wishing to be in charge can never rule without eager pawns and soldiers doing their bidding. Most people aren't used to having their convictions challenged. They've gotten away with that for way too long.

– They have, Gareth said eagerly. – But once you've taken them on, they will wake up and never return to their old and trite ways.

– Thank you, Gareth, what a sweet thing to say.

She gave him the sweetest of smiles, and he turned red as the sunset.

The big fireeyes studied him, appraising him in a deliberately condescending manner.

– Here is the deal, Gareth, and this is true for Alex and other young people here as well: While we will probably have sex with you a lot in the future, it won't be any time soon. We in the Phoenix Green Earth firmly believe that sex should be voluntary and that it shouldn't be enforced, either directly or indirectly and your hero worship makes it impossible for you to make an informed decision in that regard, in that regard as well. It's no joking matter, I'm afraid. We, Ted and I decided long ago that we wouldn't own servants or slaves, and we will hold ourselves to that standard to our dying day and beyond. The truth is that I could just wave my little finger and make you mine, and even though a tiny part of me will always find such a thought appealing, the dominating part of me detests the idea, the very notion of that. We started out on the Path of Power long ago, but there are still things we won't do.

– I heard you speak about that, the boy choked. – I understand! I do!

He jumped to his feet and rushed out of there.

– I understand it, Alex said embittered. – In fact, I have no trouble understanding it at all.

She stayed, sullen and resentful.

Ted raised his glass with his huge, infamous smile in place.

– Now that we've gotten that out of the way: cheers!

Everyone but Alex raised their glasses with doubt in their eyes. Glasses met and parted.

– Your tranquil life is done, Ted stated. – Your life from now on will be far more agitated and dangerous.

The drinking and eating and celebration picked up again, a bit slow, but true.

– Was that why… was that why you… Alex wondered, clearly agitated.

– It was one reason, Liz shrugged, – was a part of your education, but not the most important, not by far. I was being honest, direct. You will see a lot of that…

– «Life is too short to mince words», Alex quoted from the PGE handbook. – «Everyone should learn to speak up, speak their mind, no matter the cost. That alone will improve the world in dramatic ways».

– Very good, apprentice, Liz said, very condescending.

Alex kept staring stubbornly at her, at them both.

Gareth also did that, when he returned.

– I'm so glad you came, Abby stated empathically. – I knew there were things I couldn't teach my children, unpleasant things that you could.

– Some things can't be avoided, Ted said lightly. – There will always be hurdles to challenge us. It's good!

– You taught us all a lesson, Gareth stated startled, – Not just me.

Liz smiled to him with those big eyes of hers, with half an eye. It was more than sufficient to make him red and excited, a state of mind only growing when his cock started pushing at his pants just a few seconds later.

Alex and several other young girls and boys around the room began breathing faster.

– You're just candy, in more than one meaning of the word to any cruel and hungry predator out there, Ted said. – Job number one is to remove that, that dangerous naiveté, but also teach you to hold on to some of it and to never let it go.

He and Liz grabbed their bags and pulled up something looking very much like a lamp. Abby's eyes grew wide.

– This is for your benefit, not ours, Liz said lightly. – We can sense those with powers, and have no need for artificial means in order to spot mutants.

The words created a stir among them.

– Don't feel bad if it flares. Don't feel bad if it doesn't. You will all be great warriors fighting for Earth, humanity and all life on the planet and beyond.

The snarl of the smile couldn't be denied or rejected. Everyone had their attention on them.

They put the two lamps on opposite sides of the table. The blue light flared up the moment they switched them on. Both of them had to withdraw several steps in order to make it flare down.

– Here's how it works: one and one will step close to the lamps. One moment is sufficient. If nothing happens by then, it won't! It works on everyone, including children and infants, so one and one at the time, please.

It all seemed fairly business-like, but with an underlying intensity those meeting Liz and Ted Warren for the first time could not help but notice.

Abby, braving the way stepped forward to one of the lamps. It flared up. Her children were next. It flared up anew. Alex lit up like the lamp. Gareth did as well. The bright smiles returned to both their faces. Others came forward, lining up

190

eagerly. One froze startled when the light flared.

– But…

He stepped back, at a loss of words.

Another kept standing there for long seconds. The lamp didn't light up the slightest. He looked aghast at it, and kept doing so as he stepped back.

– It must be faulty, he said.

– It isn't, Liz said lightly.

She turned towards them all.

– Some of you have been disappointed, she said. – Others have been dealt the biggest shock of your life. It has been revealed to you that you aren't quite what you believed you are. This is good, an excellent start of your new life. You, most of you will be brought to boot camp and taught survival and hardship and rebellion several vast levels above what you imagined were possible, and then you will truly be changed.

– What if we… flunk? Alex choked.

– That is highly unlikely. Almost no one has so far. We are very good at what we do, and we have drill sergeants at our disposal that would have made the army green with envy…

– You said almost? Some recruits have flunked?

Liz grinned in acknowledgment to the girl, at her ability to see and cut through inconsistencies in speech.

– Less than one in hundred, she shrugged. – And they don't really flunk either. It just means they're assigned to different tasks that don't involve physical hardship and intense mental stress. We have quite a few members with physical and/or mental «handicaps» doing an excellent job for us. One in thousand flunk, truly flunk, to the point of being a danger to us and to themselves. We try to handle them as best we're able, one individual at the time.

Alex's lower lip shivered just a little.

– Does that answer your question to your satisfaction, young Draper?

– It does, My Lady, Alex replied stubbornly.

Nothing overt happened making them do it, but some of them started turning towards Ted, and not many seconds later, they had all done so. They straightened and looked attentive at him.

– It's a good thing we finished the first part of today's tasks early… since our plate for the rest of the evening is quite full…

– Your life in the Phoenix Green Earth has started already, Liz said. – It's a modest, but not unimportant beginning of your education. Watch and learn!

Two groups led by Liz and Ted respectively left the house some time later. The two walked up and down the street in manner visibly possessive and confident. The others noticed and more or less copied their manner.

– This is truly something, Alex bristled. – The street seems startlingly different, somehow.

– I've spent my entire life here, Gareth said subdued, – but I've never experienced it quite like this before.

The two of them looked at their surroundings with new and excited eyes.

– This is merely the beginning of your life's journey, young Gareth and young Alex, Liz told them.

There was no response when they knocked on the first door. Ted knocked several times, quite hard.

– They have probably gone on an impromptu holiday, Alex said, very helpful. – We announced the festival well ahead, making no secret of our intentions.

She kept blushing when he looked at her, clearly hopelessly smitten. He refrained good humored from shaking his head.

They walked to the next door. He knocked that door a little more impatient, unable to help himself. He heard them in there, heard them scurry and whisper.

– They are home! He declared with a wide grin.

Alex and the others kept staring at him, still not certain of what to expect.

The door opened. A man and a woman stood there stunned.

– Good evening, Ted said amiable, very amiable. – I and some others have traveled quite the distance to visit old friends on their feast tonight, and we wonder if you would like to join us. Trust me when I say it will be an evening to remember.

The two in the door stared open-mouthed at him, echoing a few in his entourage.

The very amiable, charming man with his huge grin (and huge fangs) walked on one side of the street, while the equally amiable, charming woman handled the other side. Some people refused to even open the door. Others slammed it shut after having briefly opened it.

– I've heard of you, a man smoking a stinking cigar snorted. – You're a great joker.

And slammed the door in Ted's face.

He could hear those refusing to open the door, hear them whisper among themselves in the misunderstood conviction that he couldn't hear them.

But a slow trickle of the curious and the slowly awakened followed the two and their entourage down to the house between the two trees at the end of the street.

– The neighborhood will never recover, Liz chuckled.

An uneasy laughter followed her carefree words.

4

Small and big events brought the rolling snowball further down the long slope. It picked up vast amounts of snow with each new turn.

Liz and Ted visualized it, experienced the sensation of it all in increasingly powerful ways. Sometimes they couldn't quite connect to their surroundings and experiences. The next moment they connected better than ever.

Betty sat in a circle with a group of people, in a warm, warm room where the one fireplace seemed to be immersed in all the four walls.

– I'm going to read from you five crucial verses of the first chapter in our ancient book Tales of the Thousand Fires, she said, – read aloud a truth you know by heart.

She sat with a large and dusty old book in her hand. When she opened it, everyone present could easily see that all the writing was by hand.

– The moment doesn't catch us. Pray that it does. We don't catch the moment. Pray that we don't. We are the Janus Clan. We brought ourselves into the world thousands of years ago.

Each time we touch the Earth we make it shake in joy and everybody shiver in terror. We bring transformation and Change beyond recall or regret. There is no return to the life that was.

Right from the start we burned with the prophecies of the Prime, the one that in a far, far future would come and liberate us all from the confines of the horrible Machine poisoning humanity's spirit, the Machine destroying everything making life worth living. It will crumble the nuts and bolts to dust with a single wave of Its mighty hand. The twenty-one bells herald Its coming, Its first and second double decades, Its thousand years.

Our visions burn at our core with expectation and terror. Past, present and future, it's all the same and it's all now.

When the Prime, the Phoenix, the fire and shadow of existence touches the Earth, when it catches the moment, nothing will remain of the old world. Flesh and blood will turn water and land red.

I dream of Its coming, of the spark igniting the world. I can dream of nothing else.

Distant butterfly wings are flapping in the air, creating the first stirrings of the coming Storm. From perceived modest beginnings can come the most powerful of expressions.

The fire stopped burning and the room turned dark, and those gathered there could see better than ever.

Ted and Liz walked with Betty on the streets of Las Vegas eighteen years ago, once more hearing her speak her cryptic words.

– We are of the desert, she told him. – It's whispering to us, even far at sea. You know that, now, know what you've always known.

The long trail from there to here, with all its detours and turns ran through their mind like a slow-moving train. Ted and Liz saw the river teeming with life and vitality, flooding the riverside and everything in its way.

Then, at some critical juncture they saw it turn lifeless and devoid of vitality, as if every sign of fire had been sucked out of it in an instant.

A shudder beyond shudder passed through them both.

– Something was left unspoken that day, Liz said. – Even though we suspected something, we failed to pinpoint it properly.

Her analytic mind, like his kept analyzing. It didn't really surprise him that she knew what was on his mind, or that their thoughts circled on similar subjects, even though that, too, had picked up lately.

They found themselves in the library in the house at Frazer Hill. The Janus Statue stood in the window. They walked there. One of the books on the table began flapping its pages. They touched the statue, reaching out with one hand from each side. A thousand images and sensations, at countless angles made themselves known to them. Some of them were familiar, while others had a kind of skewed familiarity they still recognized and acknowledged.

The pages kept flapping in the wind, making them unreadable.

They were at a gathering, entertaining a group of journalists again, Ted and Liz, Betty and Nick and a bunch of other members of the movement walked ahead of the leash of so-called newshounds. Corinne was there, giving her former colleagues the runaround. All of it felt very familiar to Liz and Ted, as if they remembered it, had experienced it many times before.

– Christians have labeled my books satanic, of course. Karine said good-humored to the journalists. – It's so obvious that it's hardly worth mentioning...

She walked among them, too, with her wry, very wry smile in place.

– We're witnessing something completely new with Phoenix Green Earth, Corinne explained, – something vastly different from every other major alternative movement. Truly autonomous societies are growing up all over the world, societies not exactly ignoring what is, but clearly disregarding it and its importance.

Some of the mainstream journalists even took notes. They exchanged flickering, restless glances.

The Janus statue stood there, twinkling in the shimmering window light. In a sudden burst of inspiration, they walked to it and touched it.

– You know what you are, Betty told them, standing before them immersed in mist and shadow. – You don't require me or anyone else to tell you.

They once again saw her kneel before them, in reverence and worship.

– You *are* the Dragon, the cleansing fire prophesized by countless Seers throughout history.

They saw that as well, the marching of history, the story behind her story, and it did bring awareness, bring knowledge, though not necessarily wisdom.

Liz made one of her occasional visits to Jennifer and the London clinic. Jennifer did the usual, complete checkup on her. Liz held out the long, grueling process throughout the afternoon. The sun had started turning red when Jennifer returned to her in her office.

– Nothing has changed. Your biological clock just isn't ticking, in any way. Your ovaries are pretty much like mine. They keep producing eggs way beyond the limit of most women.

Liz nodded, not really surprised or anything anymore.

– Nothing at all has changed? She asked casually.

Jennifer reddened slightly, as if she was caught in a lie or at least an omission.

– It's hard to say for certain, but if I should guess or speculate, I would say that your energy level, already elevated considerably above average, even average for mutants and your family members... has grown further. I have to do all my measurements indirectly, since your very presence, like Ted's is, to an increasingly higher degree disrupting the instruments.

– Have you ever seen anything like it? Liz asked quietly.

194

– I've never even heard of anything similar, Jennifer replied.

She elaborated when the two of them had a night out in town later.

– You needed to actually touch the instruments the last time I tested you, Jennifer mused. – Now, you don't even have to be in close proximity in order to disrupt or at least affect electronic devices.

They sat at a whiskey bar in the intersection of Shaftesbury Avenue and Charing Cross Road. People and cars passed by constantly, in all directions outside.

They spent a few extra seconds convincing the bartender that they needed far bigger whiskey glasses, and that they needed two bottles at the table, giving people one more reason to stare at them.

– We should consult a physicist or something, Jennifer said. – Perhaps such a beast can do what a biologist can't.

– Cheers! Liz said and raised her glass.

Jennifer did that, too. Glasses met and parted, and the special tuning fork sound echoed in their fine-tuned ears.

Then Liz did frown, and she clearly pondered the issue.

– What is it? Jennifer wondered, beside herself with curiosity.

– There is something, Liz said and shook her head, – something I can't quite grasp or pinpoint, that I feel like I should.

She shook her head some more.

– I get a lot of that.

She looked out on the street again. The entire wall was of glass. Everyone could see everything happening outside, could watch everyone passing by. She saw more, of course, sensed far more than most people.

– It's good thing that you retain some… uncertainties, Jennifer said, – some doubt about who you are.

That made Liz look closer at her.

– You're daunting enough as it is, Jennifer said. – Sitting with you here, going out with you feels so great.

Liz just looked at her without speaking. Jennifer reddened.

– Father treated me as a teenage daughter for quite some time, and it wasn't until we hooked up with you guys that he started loosening up his… his grip on me.

– That *is* difficult to believe, Liz remarked. – How old are you… your current body?

– I can't say for certain… something in the range of two-hundred years or so.

– And he put you on a leash all that time? He didn't abuse you, did he?

The rage was suddenly there, in her voice, in her entire appearance, like a living thing.

– No, nothing like that. I was a wicked girl, my mother's daughter, my mother being a cruel, power hungry Voodoun priestess keeping him prisoner for decades before he freed himself. He clearly saw her in me, and wished to make sure I didn't take after her.

Jennifer was clearly distressed, but calm.

– But you have children?

– Oh, yes, he allowed my big and small… indiscretions. He wasn't that kind of father.

– My father was a mundane, Liz said, – and he wasn't very pleasant. He didn't deal well with what his children were at all. He exposed himself, revealing his bias, his intolerance for everything different.

The rage was still there, after all those years.

She couldn't help it. The tables and the glasses on them began shaking. People looked perplexed around them.

– I guess I was lucky then, Jennifer shrugged.

– Perhaps I was lucky as well, Liz mused. – Perhaps he unwittingly showed me how not to act, how to not treat my children.

They grabbed each other's hands in mutual agreement. The shaking stopped.

– Now, I'm twice glad that we decided to make it a night out, Jennifer said.

– I am, too, Liz joked. – I can't properly convey how great it feels to be advised by a far more experienced woman…

Jennifer's smile turned soft and tender.

They had another drink. It did burn in their throat and their stomach.

– It is ironic that you're far more used to public appearances than I am, Jennifer said.

– You have quite a bit of catching up to do then, Liz responded lightly.

Jennifer poured another drink to them both. They drank.

The alcohol did work on them, when they fed it to themselves in such an even, constant flow.

Liz felt Linda out there, somewhere, unable, as always to pinpoint her whereabouts. Lee was actually easier to spot. The other three in the stealth group as well.

– It's good we have these salty nuts, Jennifer mused, – or the balance in our bodies would have been way off fast and been quite painful. There have been times when I've overestimated my own constitution.

Liz nodded to her, to herself.

– It feels ridiculous for us to worry about such mundane shit, doesn't it?

Liz nodded again, not speaking this time either.

They had more salty nuts, a mouthful of them, requiring an excessive amount of that, too, in order to balance the intake of alcohol. Their digestion system worked overtime. It made the body shiver in a more or less pleasant hum.

This room, the streets outside remained just as alive in their buzzing mind. Liz finally spotted Linda in the shadows down the street. She spotted Yvonne on a rooftop nearby. Morten was on the roof with the French woman. Liz saw Yvonne in a strange light that she couldn't quite get a grasp on, and she had never seen before anywhere.

A few moments passed by, as she pondered it. Then Jennifer raised her glass again and they had yet another toast, and it slipped her mind.

She frowned, as it dawned on her that she had been both distracted and distant lately. The liquor burned in her throat and her stomach, and created countless

196

variations and sensations within. This place and the streets outside were safe, as safe as it would ever be, and nothing distracted her from her troubled thoughts.

They walked outside, in a street, a crossroad filled with people. Judith stood on the corner, not really there, very much there to those with the ability to see the invisible. She hid in a bubble of her own making, but still very much present and ready to take action, if the need should arise.

Then, with one slight stray thought Liz reached out further to her surroundings, making it all a part of her. Jennifer gasped and stared at her with awe in her pretty eyes.

One single glance seemed like a thousand, a thousand angles and flickering moths of flesh and bone and mind within her extended reach. She practically became the entire intersection and started filling out the adjacent streets.

Everyone felt it, especially the sensitives, but also every single mundane individual present in the extended vicinity.

Then Ted appeared as well, his shimmering flesh not exactly present, but his consciousness certainly had a very pronounced presence. A circle, a circle burning in ghostly fire formed around them. All lights in a wide circumference blinked. Engines and all electricity stopped working all over central London. Cars pulled to a halt in the streets and planes stopped functioning in the air above. The flash of missing light seemed to last well beyond the moment of a common blink. Everything seemed blanketed in Shadow. Others also saw him or glimpsed him in the few moments before he faded away, and electricity returned.

Liz feared she couldn't breathe, until it dawned on her that her respiratory system had been vastly improved from one moment to the next, and that was merely one of countless improvements both she and Ted experienced from vastly different parts of the globe. She kept experiencing new aspects of it as she and Jennifer Woodstone, and their cohorts made their way down Charing Cross Road.

Jennifer attempted to keep her excitement, her wonder in check, but failed miserably. Liz looked at her, studied her, one of her casual glances so much more effective than the other woman's feeble attempts at illumination.

Liz could read her, could send to her and could pick up thoughts in the well-guarded mind with a casual effort. Her telepathy, present for years had become full blown.

I'm used to my father, Jennifer thought unprompted. I always feel… small, feelsmall inhispresence. I can't help it, but you…youyouyou

She who had been Val Musante, but had long since become so much more sat on her throne surrounded by her closest subjects. She blinked and started breathing faster and had no control over it.

Martin Keller faced Ted at the loft in Ravenscourt, surrounded by the many infants. A hum rose from their throats and minds. A smile broke on Lillith's shadowy face, as she paused in her speech at a town hall meeting in Boston.

You recognize it, don't you? Ted stated.

I do, Keller acknowledged, in one way, but in another… I don't.

Thisisnewnewnew

They felt it, how the outward manifestation of abilities was just a pale reflection of what was boiling and thriving and growing below the surface.

– I can feel it, Michelle brightened. – Can't you?

Jason didn't voice a reply. There was no need.

– The Phoenix did a *sweep*, she added, beyond excited. – In one single act of reaching out, it made contact with us all. It's yet another watershed in its growth.

The effect of the added power faded, returning gradually to a level slightly higher than what had used to be normal. Michelle ran up the stairs to the loft, to the nursery.

She stopped in front of Ted, standing there with lowered eyes and blushing cheeks.

– This one is ready, father, she stated humbly and eager and arrogant, all of that simultaneously, – ready for whatever is coming, ready to serve the Dragon in all things.

Jason stayed below. He didn't have to join the others upstairs in order to see what was happening. Open eyes, closed eyes saw it all in a crystal-clear vision.

Betty arrived at the loft, too. Her eyes glowed in green as never before. She didn't speak, but joined Michelle standing in front of Ted.

Linda placed herself in front of Liz, almost to the point of standing still and becoming visible to bystanders. Lee got a strange look in his normal eyes. Even Carla and her attention seemed to be drawn to Liz.

Gabi appeared before Ted. To his enhanced vision the air around her had become a shimmering circle more distinct than he had ever seen it. The girl's doe eyes looked at him with unquestionable devotion and love.

– Chrysalis, butterfly, chrysalis, butterfly, dragon, she said hoarsely. – Chrysalis, butterfly, dragon, Phoenix.

Ted and Liz felt the powerful tingling down the spine, and even that was broadcast through minds and ether across the planet.

– Chrysalis, butterfly, chrysalis, butterfly, dragon, Gabi droned on. – Chrysalis, butterfly, dragon, Phoenix.

She choked, stopping herself with an effort, but the words echoed seemingly forever in her mind, and in the shadowland, she walked and breathed.

5

Time marched on, and no one could catch its steps.

Jennifer left her work to an assistant and joined Liz and also Ted on their travels.

– My existence has been way too tranquil for far too long, she stated, a little subdued. – I've wanted to live it up for quite some time.

Both excitement and apprehension boiled within her, pushing in the same direction. She looked like a little girl given a new, unproven toy.

They arrived at Ravenscourt through the portal. She took in all of it with big, twinkling eyes.

Her senses sought and sought, but didn't succeed in finding what they sought.

– No, your father isn't here, Liz said. – My guess is that he finally decided to let you go, to let you set out on your own.

Heat and chills, anxiety and joy surged through the seemingly young woman.

– It's just a guess, Liz shrugged.

Jennifer hid a smile behind a hand covering her mouth, knowing she didn't fool the other woman for a moment.

– I'll let you settle in at your own pace, Liz said. – Michelle, for purely practical purposes will be on hand to assist you in doing that. I'll leave you in her very capable hands.

Michelle, considerably bigger and taller than them both was suddenly standing right there. Jennifer had felt her well before she appeared, but was still startled.

– Hi, Michelle greeted her brightly and reached out a hand, – it's so nice to meet you.

They shook hands.

Jennifer took a closer look, beneath the bright smile. Michelle kept smiling.

– It's great to meet you, too, Jennifer said. – I appreciate you helping out.

– Don't think twice about it. We're one big, happy family here.

Liz waved to them from the door. They both returned the wave.

Michelle turned towards the newcomer.

– I have duties, but since they're quite extensive I can still take you on a tour while doing them. You can even watch me during the execution of my performance, if you should so desire.

– That sounds like a plan, Jennifer said.

– Very good. My first task today is a class in critical thinking and analysis for the older children.

The young woman's tone and demeanor was light, casual, but Jennifer sensed a deeper context to the words, to her. She recalled startled that the suave, sophisticated woman had father issues.

They left the house and set out on their walk across the vast wilderness the town had become.

– We're teachers, Michelle stated eagerly, – and any group of teachers can, at ideal conditions change the world in one or two generations by changing the perception of the students. It will probably take a little longer than that, but we should never doubt that it's doable. The main problem today is that those in charge are very pleased with current human society. It serves them. They don't want to change anything, except by amassing even more power and control.

She floated them easily across the water to the other shore. Their feet stayed well above the surface. Jennifer felt the tug as she was pulled along Michelle's powerful frame and mind. They landed on their feet in the soft sand and headed into the dark forest.

The shadows revealed themselves to them after just a few steps. The voices whispered in their ears.

Jennifer glanced around at the eerie surroundings, the enchanted forest. They imposed themselves on her. She giggled happily.

It was filled with spirits. They whispered to her vast threats and happy dreams.

The two of them reached the edge of the forest and stopped for a moment, looking down at the now totally overgrown city.

– It looks like it has been abandoned for decades, Jennifer said amazed and subsequently frowning. – But… not completely.

There were pockets of open spaces and of less growth.

– Such is the power of Lillith, Michelle chuckled. – This is her current primary playground… if you don't count the entire planet, of course.

There was something akin to awe and even worship in her voice and expression. Jennifer couldn't help but pick up on it.

– She's our mother, Michelle stated abruptly, – the Mother of Demons.

Michelle changed in subtle ways. Her voice turned deeper, her appearance… darker. It was a startling effect not unknown to Jennifer. She had observed it often enough in her long life.

– She gathered us at the far end of the world to fight her nemesis, and now the nemesis is gone, and we're all free to do as we please.

She grabbed Jennifer, held her in her grip, her iron-hard grip, and Jennifer froze on her spot.

– He was so small, thinking such small thoughts, and anyone thinking like him is just as b-bad as he was.

Jennifer nodded, a glimpse of understanding darkening her eyes.

They made their way down the slope, to the field, the burgeoning forest. Four people, two females and two males met them just as the terrain started evening out. Jennifer recognized the nervous energy raging through them.

– Hi, everyone, Michelle said pleasantly. – You all know Jennifer, I presume? She has decided to take a more active part in our venture, and Liz charged me with showing her the ropes.

– Hi, Jennifer, they choired.

– Hi, she replied, – it's so nice to see you all again.

Everyone grabbed her hands and hugged her and kissed her and made her feel very welcome, but the nervous energy persisted, and they hardly even pretended that it was a casual move when they turned towards Michelle.

– Are you well, powerful daughter of my father? Shadow asked lightly, very lightly, uncharacteristically obscure, holding the other's hands. – It's October this month, unless this one's is very much mistaken, and she is not.

– I'm okay, Michelle replied, clearly evasive. – Nothing has changed. I want to live, more than ever. I still don't understand. The mystery continues to befuddle me.

Troy, Timothy and Beth all gathered around her. She allowed it, fighting to suppress a choke Jennifer had no trouble catching. The five of them had some kind of bond, and Jennifer wondered what it was about.

She watched as Michelle straightened and picked herself up from the mire of her despair again.

– My duty is to Jennifer and to my charges today, she said. – You're all welcome to join us.

– That's the most insincere invitation I've heard in a while, Timothy chuckled.
They all chuckled.

Michelle seemed to become more upbeat by the second, as she led on across the emerging wilderness.

Jennifer sensed something then, something familiar, but still unnerving. Jason Gallagher approached them. She sensed him, saw him well before he emerged from the fast-growing forest. Michelle started smiling and ran to him long before they met face to face. She embraced him and kissed him.

– I missed you, she practically whimpered, smothering him in kisses, – missed you so bad.

She stepped back, but still held on to him, clinging to him like nothing else mattered. The big smile stayed on her face. She couldn't or wouldn't take her eyes off him.

She danced on. Everyone followed her. The terrain changed around them, in both visible and invisible ways. They reached a hollow in the wild garden, feeling it, how it had been made, grown, its power making everyone shiver in delight.

A group of children, facing the rise and the approaching adults sat in a half moon at the deep of the hollow.

– Good morning, thinking, feeling beings, Michelle greeted them.

– GOOD MORNING, MICHELLE, the children choired.

She walked down and sat down on her ass and with crossed legs at the center of the opposite halfmoon, right in front of them.

– Many want to change the world, she began, – but most people, both those that want to and those that don't keep claiming it's a hard, almost impossible process.

They looked at her with curious eyes. She knew she had them in the palm of her hand, knew they were listening to her, to what she had to say and that felt good. A warm, warm feeling broke within.

– What those behind those voices fail to understand or mention, of course is that the world changes all the time. The question is who's doing the changes and in what direction those people take them. Today, as we all are very much aware of, the changes in question take us in the completely wrong direction. Those in charge don't really want to make fundamental changes at all, but just want more of the same. They're fine with how things are and want them to continue that way.

The children and also the adults attending the lecture studied her with attentive and astute minds, listened to the nuances of her voice and watched as her features shifted and changed.

– The truth of the matter is that the world can be changed in one or two generations. What's lacking for doing that isn't opportunity but *will*. Teach children true independence, true critical thinking wherever they go. Teach it in school. Make it a major part of a child's day and week and year. Start teaching adults as well. Hold lots of small meetings and also big, creating a world-wide classroom of truly open conversation where nothing is kept off the table. Two generations, forty years, tops. That's all it takes, with dedication and relative benevolence and true freedom of information. A tyranny wishes to oppress a given population, wishes to keep its people in invisible mental chains surpassing all the physical ever used. It's that simple, that hard.

They filmed her. She didn't notice until the end of her speech and smiled with a happiness threatening to choke her.

Her voice rose in strength, even as it turned deeper.

– Those in charge rule and stay in power because we, their servants allow it. We just need to stop doing that, on all levels, and we, and the world will transform. We are the agents of change we have been waiting for.

She imagined the applause, practically its silence as it rose from the shaky ground and hit shivering flesh.

She stepped «down» from her stage. They rushed forward, walked eagerly to her and surrounded her with open, trusting faces. It was alright. It wasn't her task or burden to break their trust, to ruin their innocence. That fact gave her comfort, somewhat.

He met her halfway. She sought his embrace. It comforted her, calming her raging depths.

Jennifer watched them interact. It looked and felt amazing, nothing short of that. She had trouble catching where one ended and the other began. Each of their Shadow, very visible, almost tangible to her mingled and mixed, constantly pushing and pulling at the other in an unending, endless dance.

They both turned and looked at her with their fireeyes. She felt it, felt herself burn, surrounded by fireeyes, by fire.

The children ran off with loud shouts and cries. The group made its way off the Hollow, feeling lighter, heavier, different as they did.

– It's so great, watching the kids grow older, Beth said, – observing how well they relate to each other. I never had that. I'm so happy that I've had it with the People for so long and still have it.

The others felt her happiness, unable to keep the smile from manifesting on their lips and within.

The People... that word, name, term resonated within them, and created yet another warm, warm feeling in their depths of depths they couldn't deny.

– I heard about the People, Jennifer said, – heard about them the first time when I was very young.

She felt like she had come home as well. The feeling, sensation was so pronounced that she could hardly contain it.

– I need... need to measure Phoenix, she stated, more than a little awkward.

– You need to measure something that can't be measured? Shadow wondered puzzled.

– I do! She stated calmly.

They looked at her again, but didn't really study her, didn't look at her with suspicion. They trusted her.

The group crossed back and forth in the overgrown city. Jennifer placed her instruments. A plate with her equipment hovered in the air behind them. In most other places people would have found that an eerie sight, but here no one reacted to it, not in any way she could discern.

The instruments started broadcasting almost immediately. She studied the monitor in her hands. The screen lit up slowly and began showing her information.

– Liz is present, she explained. – Ted isn't.

– How can you tell? Troy wondered.

– Her energy readings are slightly different, more and less volatile both, changing during the period of the moon. It pretty much corresponds with her menstrual cycle.

She got a good look at the entire area in the process. Each new part looked different from each other, prompting a different emotional response. It was hard focusing on her work when she approached everything she saw and experienced with the wide eyes of a child. She cast anxious eyes behind her, as if someone followed her or she suspected someone did.

– It's like Liz told you, Jason said to her. – Your father isn't here. He has moved on. You should do the same.

He sounded notably ambiguous when he spoke. She nodded to herself, and he did, too.

They walked to what had been the Isherwood ranch-house. She studied Jason some more, his reaction to what had to be familiar surroundings.

– When I walked this way the first time, it looked completely different, he explained, fairly unnecessary. – Its dramatic change corresponds well with everything else we've experienced.

They knew what he meant, knew every word and intonation intimately.

– You may call this our resident high-tech center, Michelle explained to the newcomer. – It's certainly one of several across the world. We use such centers to collect data and information, and to a certain point analyzing the flow. It's also our main gateway to social media in Northfield. We have long since become an integrated part of the organic technological web.

– It's so strange hearing it be called organic, Jennifer mused.

– It certainly fits with one meaning of the word, Michelle shrugged.

Jennifer looked amused at her, at the sophisticated modern woman looking more like an ancient mythological creature to those probing deeper, those penetrating the surface.

– We're certainly not discouraging individual visits to the web and social media, Michelle kept going, – but this is where it gets organized.

Jennifer realized startled that the two of them had more in common than she had initially believed.

Their keen senses heard the tapping of keyboards well before they entered the house. When they stepped inside it turned into a crescendo. Jennifer frowned, noticing immediately that something was... off.

– You hear our resident superfast typist, Michelle grinned.

It dawned on Jennifer that the loudest typing sounds originated from one specific part of the living room made hall they entered. She cast her attention there, to a girl which hands moved so fast over the keyboard that they were hardly visible. Her right hand moved just as fast to and away from the mouse.

– This is Andrea Natchios. She's many times faster than the average typist, so fast that it is in fact the machine setting the limit for how fast she can type.

[The Climate Change is a hoax], one antagonist wrote.

[The true hoax is those decrying Climate Change], appeared below almost before the above sentence had been completed. Then a long row of additional information followed.

Needless to say, no one could keep up with the girl. She crumbled any opponent to dust in a few seconds.

Jennifer studied the girl. Her eyes moved as fast, even faster than the hands, her attention so focused on the screen that she probably didn't know they were there. Jennifer looked startled at Michelle.

– She's totally immersed…

– … in what's happening on the screen? Michelle acknowledged. – I would say she is. We must practically drag her away when we decide it's time for her to take a break. She probably wouldn't, if it was her decision to make. We've considered making a system feeding her automatically. She's so fucking effective. It's a shame interrupting that kind of dedication.

Wicked Michelle reared its ugly head. Jennifer nodded slowly.

– Can you imagine how it is to be her? Michelle kept pushing, smiling at the other's response. – She can see the countless moments between the moments. To her one second is an eternity.

Jennifer shook, caught in a deep, deep chill.

– It's a thing of beauty, Michelle marveled.

Jennifer blinked.

– You… pushed her into this!

– I helped her develop her talent, yes, Michelle shrugged. – You should have seen her at first, how awkward and practically helpless she was in spite of her potentially impressive power. She could hardly run through the forest at elevated speed without stumbling in roots before I got my hands on her. Now, she can kill a crowd of ordinary people before they can blink.

– You have a talent for that, haven't you? Jennifer heard herself say.

– I sure have. I do that with all those in my direct care. I'm their cruel drill sergeant taking them to new heights.

She fixed her stare at Jennifer.

– But I don't need to do that with you, Daughter of the Horned God. You know what life is about.

Almost everyone looked up from their keyboards and stared. Even Andrea cast a fast fleeting look before resuming her typing. The shy glances of awe and respect Jennifer saw in their eyes were not unfamiliar to her.

– Don't mind them. They are beneath you.

– Yes, they are, she shrugged.

Getting off on the shame she exposed in their cast down eyes.

– Have no fear, Troy told them. – We can build a throne she can sit on, so you can kneel in her elevated presence. Come to think of it, there are more than enough entities in our holy city you can kneel before if you so wish.

– I have always found Troy... funny, Shadow frowned. – Do you all find him funny?

One boy stood up, stubbornly keeping his eyes up.

– Ted and Liz and... and Lillith keep saying the same to us...

– But you never listen, Jason said softly, making everyone stare at him.

– We never listen.

– Why is that?

The boy looked bewildered at him.

– Because they're not very convincing, right? Michelle said. – Because you can feel their might more than you feel it in anyone else, because their very nature contradicts their teaching.

A long, long silence descended on the gathering, the room, the very air they breathed.

And everyone looked awestruck at her.

6

They had returned to the Hollow, as the shadows had started growing long.

– It has been very... educational, Jennifer told Michelle sometime later. – Thank you!

– It was my pleasure, Michelle said.

They hugged and kissed each other's cheek.

Jennifer waved as she joined the others and only Jason and Michelle remained.

She glanced at him, taking his hand.

– I'll come with you tonight, of course.

The silence, lasting seconds was tangible. He studied and probed her. She allowed it with a shrug. There was no will to resist, not even the slightest tiny slice of refusal.

– You've never shown that much interest in participating before.

– It's different, now. I need something to take my mind off things, and I told you I will go anywhere with you.

She paused and pondered a bit more.

– And Mother will need me, will benefit from my presence.

The word «mother», the distinct way she pronounced it, sounded very much like that of a child, a progeny speaking of her mother. It startled him, but didn't surprise him.

– And I'm drawn to Phoenix. The attraction grows stronger, not weaker every day.

He had noticed, how she and several others were drawn to Liz and Ted, how they gathered around them to an even greater degree than others, almost as if it was an involuntary, subconscious process.

– I need to do this, need to do as much as possible before... before...

He couldn't find the strength within himself to reply and stayed silent. Even his mind felt numb, like a heap of wool totally lacking in sensitivity. She reached out her left hand. He grabbed it, and they walked off the Hollow, even as it stayed with them, even as it kept clinging to them like wet paper, with a grip they couldn't break.

The night dawned and stayed with them. Stacy, Jason, Michelle, Yvonne, Lee, Carla, Linda, Judith, Trudy and Morten, and a slew of other warriors walked through the living dark, to the designated portal ahead. It fizzled and burned in their mind.

– You shouldn't join us, Mother, Michelle implored her, – shouldn't risk it.

– I need to feel it, Stacy replied, – feel it on all levels.

She shrugged.

– We're all at risk, wherever we go.

Sentries guarded it far and near. No one would be able to go through it undetected, and even if those standing close were taken out, others would notice that, and sound the alarm. Lillith nodded pleased.

– You're practically a delegation going out tonight, Martine said, not hiding the concern, more than implying that someone felt that there was more than a strong reason to *be* concerned.

She had come far since her days as a nun. There was hardly anything left of that person. The way she dressed and behaved made the others more than suspect she was overcompensating for her pious days.

– Some of us just need a change of scenery, Trudy said lightly.

– May I come as well, Mother, Martine implored, clearly addressing Stacy.

– You may, Lillith permitted.

Martine took five steps forward and joined the group, becoming a part of it, its organic, constantly moving flow. It didn't take long, measured in seconds until another had emerged from the shadows and had taken her place as sentry.

– Ready, good people? Lee called their attention.

Everyone responded, one way or another.

They turned and walked the few steps into the shimmering hole in the air.

The world changed around them, turning inside out, downside up. They floated on air not matter, in a realm never quite solid.

– I'll never be quite used to this, Martine breathed with shiny eyes. – We were one place, Now, we're somewhere completely different.

Even her voice sounded different, not quite sound, not quite anything like that.

Michelle sent her a condescending stare, but couldn't quite make a production of it. She remained preoccupied, distracted, as if she was somewhere completely different.

They emerged on the other side. Buildings, streets, nature faded in once more. They took it all in, constantly moving their eyes, getting attuned to the flow of their surroundings.

Their minds and bodies prepared for whatever would come at them. Everyone with the proper knowledge and training would easily notice how they related to each other with each and every move.

206

They, as individuals and a collective entity noticed it immediately, the strange vibrations in the air, in the ground, in their flesh and bone and deepest recesses of the mind. Stacy felt a deep pain in her gut, as if someone had stuck a hot poker through it. It came upon her so sudden that she couldn't contain it, keep the others, all the others, including the non-sensitives from noticing. They also caught the cold sweat on her brow, and attentive eyes and senses grew even more attentive.

Michelle felt like she was caught in a vice. The image of herself standing on the chair imposed itself on her vision.

Everyone stopped and looked at her.

– I feel it, she whispered, – feel the noose tighten around my neck. This is the night. This is the time.

Those that didn't understand, that hadn't heard the story still understood. Images, sensations assaulted them like knives, like, sharp, dull blades.

– You must go back, she told Jason, – must return through the portal right now.

– I don't need to fear death, he said calmly. – You know that. The man meeting me in Samara is myself.

She stared at him with abject confusion, nodding once, twice.

– I don't understand, she whimpered. – I just don't understand.

They looked around them, at the picturesque, small town, catching nothing from the people, the curious eyes passing them. Everything looked normal… except for the ants crawling through their veins with sharp, sharp claws and fangs. They turned their heads and studied the portal. It looked calm, not agitated in any way.

– We need to close it, Trudy said. – We might be seriously compromised.

Stacy nodded, and she prepared to send the prepared message to Gabi. She frowned when it didn't work. Linking with the others in order to boost the signal proved equally ineffective.

– Something is blocking, interfering with the portal, Judith said.

When she told them, all those so inclined noticed.

– There is something, she said, – a shimmering energy preventing me, probably all of us from accessing the Shadowland in any way.

– But I should still be able to contact Gabi anywhere on the planet, Stacy said, visibly shaken. – It is like something… someone has blanketed the entire town, keeping us from reaching out.

– If someone can do that, we're in serious trouble, Jason said. – The fact that our precognition didn't reveal the threat, at least not directly or specifically tells us more of the might of our unseen foe.

– What we should do, the only thing we can do is to follow our initial objective and use that to investigate the matter, Linda said.

They nodded. It made sense. Linda, as usual cut through everything like that sharp blade.

Michelle took the front, Lee the rear, Linda the left and Judith the right side, and they moved down the street. The tension made their limbs crack and their minds boil.

– Is it me? Michelle wondered. – I know Jason has been caught in my nightmare.

Perhaps I've caught all of you now?

She looked more and more like a frightened young girl, and they couldn't help but picking up on it.

– No, Lillith said, – we're caught in the reason for your nightmare, like we should be.

A warm, warm feeling surged through Michelle.

– Thank you, Mother, she gushed at the younger woman. – Thank you so much.

– Even she, a powerful goddess in her own right worships you, Mother.

Martine rushed forward, presenting herself to Lillith, bowing her head in her presence and her honor.

– I worshipped the One God, she continued, – leaving him behind when he was revealed as the quintessential snake-oil salesman, but even though that made me wiser, I can't help worshiping you. Is that wrong, Mother?

She pulled back, unable to keep that wide smile from manifesting itself.

– Yes! Stacy stated calmly.

Martine sniffed and nodded, and nodded again.

The scenery at the diner, at the cafeteria with the very old-fashioned design looked almost insanely mundane. They took a good look at it before stepping inside, both with their five and extraordinary senses. Five people sat on various spots in the rather large room. Low-keyed music sounded through hidden speakers. One man sat alone in the left corner.

Jason and Michelle stepped inside, and walked straight to the man in the blue jacket. The others were with them, with every step, every breath they made. Jason shared Linda's hawkeyed vision, watched how she kept an eye on the entire street through everyone's rapid-moving eyes.

Some of us should stay out of the loop, Trudy cautioned them, in case they attack us through that.

Everyone nodded in agreement, knowing beyond knowing they stepped on shaky ground. There was no way to be certain or safe, not of anything.

– Calvin Martin? Michelle said aloud.

He nodded, looking at her with wet eyes.

– You contacted us. We're here, with a powerful contingent, like you instructed.

Like they had felt compelled to do in their shivering apprehension.

They saw nothing incriminating, nothing threatening in his mind, no matter how deep they probed. That didn't exactly put their mind at ease. Stacy realized startled, like she should have realized immediately that she couldn't read him, couldn't read him beyond totally casual surface thoughts at all.

– That's my… my power, he said with a weak smile. – I'm pretty much neutralizing any attempt at intrusion.

Stacy felt… shitty, felt the non-physical vibration somewhere within. The frown on her brow grew deeper and deeper.

– I got caught up in it, Martin said with a deep frown. – I was brought in for testing and didn't realize until later that they didn't test me for meningitis or anything like that. I had a headache, a splitting headache. I thought I was sick. They

208

told me they gathered people like me, told me they were assembling… an army.

– Did you at some point or another before they made contact remember anything about a blue light or lamp? Jason asked.

– I do, the man said. – It was the strangest thing. I passed a strange-looking lamp in a store-window, and it flared the moment I got close, and faded as I walked on.

It is a trap, Linda thought.

We knew it would be, didn't we? Yvonne thought.

It's a very elaborate trap, Linda insisted. They know what they are doing.

Michelle felt something nip her. Stacy heard wind whisper, not in her ear, but in her mind. Jason saw death and decay all around him, in everyone he looked at.

– I met the other people, Martin continued unabated. – I trained with them, and bid my time until I could escape. I've been on the run ever since.

I can hardly feel her anymore, Stacy thought, hardly feel *Lillith*.

It was like the connection had broken or at least been partly disrupted, a scary, horrible feeling she couldn't recall experiencing before, one sending her into something akin to full panic-mode.

She rushed into the cafeteria, reaching Martin in what felt like only three or four steps, but also ten times that. Her hand, formed like claws grabbed Martin's exposed skin. Pain surged through her. She registered astonished that blood flowed from her nostrils.

– He's a decoy, only a…

She penetrated deep within him, and found nothing, nothing but a program pretending to be a person. He had been brainwashed, rinsed and programmed to fit his makers' scheme. It was nothing there but an organic machine.

He was the trap, at least the first part of it.

His power spread outward. He could indeed keep people from reaching him, but The Thousand Feet had still gotten to him with their mundane and cruel methods. His power didn't exactly paralyze those standing close, but they suddenly felt weak and disoriented. He didn't start this, Stacy thought. Someone else did and…

It dawned on her that no one could hear her.

A one-two, one-two, she heard him shriek, shriek, shriek in his empty self.

Jason struck him down. One strike and he was dead.

His power didn't immediately fade with the death of his body, but seemed to be amplifying itself into one single, prolonged final burst.

The air sizzled and burned, bathing them all in the horrible energies. She sucked whatever life, energy was left out of him, his husk. She grabbed one of the other guests. Life filled her, filled the air, countering what weakened them. How did they test this? She heard Trudy wonder. Stacy knew. They had killed him and brought him back numerous times, had explored his power, his glorious power in detail. People doing something like that, and even worse things saw other people like nothing but tools to be utilized, and would do anything in order to implement their objectives. Such people were the masters of the world. I knew that, Stacy thought. I've always known.

She stumbled outside, knowing without knowing that her two demons were behind her. They joined her other children outside. Lillith remained fuzzy in her consciousness, like a distorted broadcast. She felt a presence, an overwhelming presence she dimly recognized. The sound, the sense of something moving through the air reached them. Rockets approached them from all directions. They grabbed hands and made them Go Away with one burst of power. It remained a struggle, but they managed.

– Company is coming, Martine said, her fear mixed with joy and expectation.

She, like the rest of them had trained and prepared for this forever.

The air thickened. They could see it with their normal eyes, and in an extremely pervasive manner with their deeper senses, a palpable presence impossible to miss.

Several signatures made themselves known to them. They still didn't see anything, couldn't pinpoint the danger properly. Stacy focused just a little, and a loud scream, vocal and not added itself to the shimmering air.

Calm stayed with them all. They had long since learned to handle external pressure. Everyone knew that this was a test that would push them to the wall. A proud smile crossed Lillith's faces, hidden and not, even as all their features twisted and burned in inhuman focus.

Know that I am proud of you, beyond life, beyond death. Even if we die, we live.

The voice made Martine and Michelle and several of the others shake with emotion, even as they kept focusing on what was ahead, as they kept preparing themselves with an iron-hard will.

Mind is a slippery, slippery floor, she told them.

She couldn't get a lock on any of the minds around them. The interference remained strong and potent. Her heartbeat picked up and affected the others as well.

– Are we already there? Michelle whimpered. – Have they already c-captured us, and started working on us, brainwashing us?

Everything did seem strange (stranger than usual). Either the simmering air made them lightheaded, or something else did.

– They're already here, Jason said, noticing, realizing it a fraction of a second before Lillith did.

The... discord attacked them with everything it had at its disposal.

The wind picked up in less than a second. It struck them like knives. The telekinetics grounded themselves and everyone on the spot. Dozens of large, heavy spears with hooks rushed at them. A bright, stroboscopic light and loud sound exploded, disrupting their concentration, making those unable to protect themselves fall.

Jason and Michelle held hands, standing their ground, counterattacking those that they could hardly even sense. Shouts of pain and horror added to the horror assaulting them all.

Spears began hitting them. One hit Stacy in the belly and pushed her backwards, nailing her to the wall. The searing pain broke her concentration. Her power flared, affecting friend and foe alike. She spotted the young woman levitating in the air. The wind originated with her. She commanded it with ease, with an ecstatic grin painted on her twisted features.

Stacy snarled, making two of the flying spears penetrate the woman. The wind stopped blowing. Lee grabbed the spear in Stacy's gut, breaking it in two. He grabbed her and pulled her off it. She screamed in more pain. Memory assaulted her of the previous times she, the warrior witch, had felt such pain.

Yvonne hung nailed to the wall by one of the other harpoons. Blood flowed from her mouth. Both Stacy and Lee jumped towards her. Something else hit Stacy. She stared astounded at her missing hand. A cleaver had cut it off. People began dying around them. Yvonne drew her last breath. Stacy watched as her spirit fled the body. The deaths fed her and Jason and the rest. The seething energy in the air strengthened them beyond belief.

Stacy's hand grew back in moments. Her gut healed. Smaller arrows filled with poison hit her. It worked. Waves of dizziness hit her, once again disrupting her power. Trudy cut off the head of an enemy fading in and out of her vision, and suddenly all the attackers turned visible and notable. Stacy heard Martine gasp in fear. Dozens of people charged them simultaneously.

So many, many, many, Martine gasped.

Stacy felt an even stronger chill. She saw the horrible faces beneath the masks, the images of dull, ruined human spirits. Machines charged them, organic, yes, but no less machines. Savagery artificial and frighteningly effective attacked them. Linda used her swords and cut those close to her to pieces.

Trudy was practically gutted from head to toe with two cleavers dancing in the air. She kept fighting far beyond death's door, even after her spirit had fled her body.

Stacy took control of the cleavers and started cutting the attackers. There was resistance, but the other controlling them was no match for her. He let go of the control and attacked her directly instead. Stars clouded her vision. She finally identified the telekinetic through the haze her mind had become. Bliss attacked her. Everything suddenly felt so very, very pleasant. She couldn't focus. Fear dull and horrible and distant grabbed her. She lost control of the cleavers again. The multiple attack made her knees bend, and suddenly she realized what was happening: the attackers focused on her. Startling thought, action and fear were one, singular move.

LEAVE, she told Michelle and Judith. TAKE AS MANY AS YOU CAN WITH YOU

They looked stunned at her, but command and action and realization were one with them as well. Judith struggled. Michelle didn't. Both managed. They faded and many of those standing close to them did as well.

Stacy finally managed to identify the cleaver. The man died with a loud rattle. The others either rushed her or attacked her from a distance. Another realization struck her. They didn't want to kill her, but capture her. They knew she was deadly, even more deadly when being mortally wounded and obviously had put safeguards in place in order to keep that from happening. Everything had been focused on her from the start. The others were expandable. She wasn't. Thoughts unpleasant and frightening kept churning through her head. They wanted her. She wondered why, briefly, before ignoring it and giving the fight her all. Hypodermic needles floated in the air. She caught a flash of that, just before they penetrated her skin. A horrible dullness spread through her body, paralyzing her mind. She dropped to her knees. Lassoes fell over her head and tightened around her body. Loops tightened around her neck. They kept their distance. Five of them struck her with long bamboo sticks. Details lost meaning to her. All voluntary motoric function ceased. She glimpsed the ground just before she hit it with the face first. Everything faded into a horrible, dull darkness, and she couldn't act anymore.

7

She felt like she was floating, drifting away like nothing. Sometimes there was the sting of needless. They kept her in that somewhat steady, so clever horrible state of semi-consciousness. There was the occasional flare of awareness, but never strong enough for her to act.

Everyone even remotely close to her was mutants. She felt them like distorted lights in her haze, hazy mind. She couldn't drain them, at least not from a distance or as easily as she might have been able to drain others, and her captors, her true captors knew that. Bastards. *Bastards.*

It had felt like a long time since the last time she had been violated, since she had been helpless, but now it revisited her like a spiked boxing glove in the face. She fell into a prolonged state of shame and despair and couldn't tell whether or not it was prompted by the drugs.

The distorted roar of an engine shook her dulled mind. She realized dimly that she was loaded on a truck. Something… cold grabbed her. Metal arms and hands squeezed her arms. A contraption tied around her head covered her eyes, forcing her to keep them open. A mask, a breathing mask was put on her face. The sick stench of poisoned oxygen reached her mouth and lungs and veins. Her hands were forced behind her back. Bracelets connected with chains were locked around her wrists and ankles. More needles injected a continuous stream of poison into her veins. Metal hands let go of her, dropping her into water. She sank to the bottom of a container. There was a bright light coming from several sources blinding her. She heard the sound of a winch and glimpsed a large, heavy metal plate be lowered over her prison. It was put on top of the pool. Everything was silent. She was cut off from the world.

— She's *suffering,* Michelle shouted, shaking her domain, her pocket realm and those enclosed there with her. — They're taking her away. If we don't start chasing them, now, we may never find her, and they can take their time breaking her.

They had watched as she had become more and more agitated and nodded curtly. She brought them back out. Judith returned with her people only seconds later. Morten shook when he stared at Yvonne's broken body. The others focused everything on what lay ahead.

— Whatever is blanketing the area and closing the portal to us is still there, Judith reported with audible anguish in her voice.

They rushed to the closest cars, Morten hesitated only momentarily before joining them.

– WHAT HAPPENED? A man shouted to no one in particular.

He stared at those rushing him covered in blood. Michelle grabbed him and drained him. Jason and the others able to do that did the same to others. They started glowing. The doors of two cars were ripped off. Everyone jumped in and started the engines without keys. Jason drove one car, Linda the other. They drove off on whining tires.

– I can feel her, Michelle whimpered. – She's totally out of it, totally unable to resist whatever they're planning.

Jason tried using his cell phone and was met with a very telling message.

NO COVER

– The energy is keeping all signals from penetrating it. Damn!

He looked shitty, unusually agitated, though not as bad off as the companion by his side. Everyone was eager, dedicated, but there was a desperation, an uncanny apprehension to them both, one they were hardly able to contain and surpassed that of the others by a mile.

Linda stayed calm, driven. Only the tight-stretched lips exposed her anxiety.

They took no chances and just brushed all cars off the road before the given driver had any chance of doing anything, of becoming a danger, all the cars they met or that followed them. There was no restraint anymore. People died in droves. It was a wild, incredible and sinister display of violence, fire and blood.

– Death sustains us, Michelle shouted. – DEATH SUSTAINS US!

She and Jason didn't need touch or close proximity. They caught what to them was seething energy from dozens of meters off.

Boogey nine o'clock, Martine thought.

They got it, diverted it, but it exploded. A stroboscopic light went off. It affected most of those in the cars, but Jason and Michelle it didn't affect at all. Linda lost control. Jason swept both cars into the air.

It had been so long. The drugs stretched out the moments, making her feel like she had been there in the tank forever. She caught glimpses, flares of what happened outside her cage. There was no driver, at least not in the driver's seat or anywhere in the vehicle. The mechanical arms had at some point fitted headphones on her. Words whispered endlessly in her ears. Images began dancing on the screens covering her eyes. She knew what this was and shouted in an attempt at overwhelming the voices at least. She was unable to close her eyes. A muffled scream rose from her throat, in no way successful in its task.

The communal screaming began. Everyone nearby heard her silent scream. Those in the cars certainly heard, and felt both joy and terror, and it wasn't new to them.

Two men stood in front of a monitor and watched her. They also watched how the large truck entered a warehouse, how it drove down a ramp, several ramps closing as their value ended, several floors down, until it was deep below the ground. It reached a sort-of garage down there, a place where it was a very tight fit. The giant door slammed close behind it.

– It's a thing of beauty, isn't it? One of the men shook his head in wonder. – She's trapped. Everything is fully automated. Even if we wanted to free her or she could work her magic on us, we would be unable to help her.

Henry Gyrich couldn't take his eyes off the squirming, desperate creature floating in the tank.

– This must be a very satisfying turn of events for you, the other man remarked. – You knew her back then, before she rose to infamy, no more than a fucking year ago.

– It is quite satisfying, Henry nodded.

He had been recruited by the organization shortly after his untimely departure from Northfield and had grabbed the chance, the chance at revenge, vengeance with both hands. He had always suspected that the people showing him the ropes knew more than they led him to believe, and he had been correct.

Jasper Carlton put a disc in a player. A young girl with empty eyes stood there.

– I am a girl, she hummed. – I am a pretty, pretty girl.

– Soon, Carlton said pleased, – the High and Mighty Stacy Larkin will be just like this little sweetie, nothing but a puppet we direct, and what a great tool she will be.

Stacy heard her, somewhat, a thin voice humming a song sounding like a children's lullaby. Her agitation reached another unheard-of level. The water began boiling around her. Bubbles surrounded her shaking form.

– The system is unable to compensate. They should take steps to increase her dosage. My God, what a specimen she is!

She heard the man's voice as well, but she couldn't act on it. Everything had become involuntary, her muscles and mind only reacting to outside input.

Other people not present in the building or even in the area pushed buttons, and the boiling stopped. The captive hung suspended in the water once more, doing nothing but the weak movement of a drugged creature.

– It is working, she heard, heard a voice filled with twisted joy.

He had a hardon. She couldn't help but picking up on his arousal. She knew well that her boiling sensuality could help her, as it had before, but this time was different. There was no one close enough for her to drain. The choke worked itself up her throat, never truly reaching the microphones.

– She will despair, Gyrich stated. – She is human, and she will eventually submit to the programming, and then she will be ours, and that will turn the tide of everything in our favor.

His voice was thick with triumph, with righteous anger.

She frowned, or imagined she was frowning, and couldn't imagine why.

A prolonged dark flash blanketed her vision, keeping her from seeing the constantly shimmering images imposing on her consciousness.

– Her support group, what remains of it is approaching. Carlton noted. – We knew they would, of course. We are ready for them, if our countermeasures aren't working.

– They won't work, Gyrich stated. – The contact between her and the others are just too strong.

214

He frowned and couldn't fathom why.

– But that is something we can use to our advantage after she's tamed, of course, use against them.

He had patiently waited for his chance, for this very moment, like a salmon swimming upriver to spawn.

A deeper frown touched Stacy's brow. She sensed another, another… presence, one so malevolent that it made the two men in the observation room resemble kindergarten bullies. A violent shiver passed through her.

She could glimpse his face, his form not a form somehow. It lingered in the ether, like a sword, or an iron shaft heated by a forge. The iron, cold as ice burned her skin, and she whimpered in fear. She knew, knew what this was, even though her dull mind couldn't articulate it.

Jason had returned the cars to the road. The urgency haunting him had only grown, grown far beyond anything he had ever felt (and that said a lot). Sick fear made a sour stench rise from his throat.

– The remains of the attack force and a squad of numerous mundane soldiers await us ahead, he said aloud.

Then, suddenly Stacy appeared in the air on front of them. They hardly recognized her. She looked like any timid, cowed young girl.

– I am a pretty girl, she hummed. – I am a pretty, pretty girl.

The image faded.

– No! Michelle practically screamed. – NO!

She turned to Jason, a study in wrath and boundless desperation and horrible terror.

– Death sustains us, she hissed. – Death is our friend, our ally, our eternal companion.

He nodded, nothing more. Her face and eyes lit up in boundless expectation.

The tank became her world. She had spent such a long time there that it felt like a womb. Emerging from it felt like being born. She had become compliant, empty. All her fangs and claws had been pulled. They filled her. Her programming, training began in earnest.

Stacy stood at the center of a circle of twelve men. The thirteenth man stood behind her, holding her shoulders. She felt such love for this man, a dedication and worship always there, always present like a warm, warm glow in whatever remained of her self. A constant, pretty smile brightened her pale face.

– I act on your will, she said with her weak, hollow voice. – I am an extension of you. I am at your bid and call, and that is my only function, my only joy.

There was no need for them to speak. She caught their every thought and had learned to anticipate and act when their thoughts became desire, when they grew beyond a certain point. She was their hand, their devoted servant in all things, their foremost tool in their holy crusade to reshape the world in their image, to make the crucial, long-awaited final adjustments.

Their faces flickered on the screen covering her eyes, their voices sounded in her ears, teaching her their gospel. She asked herself how many hours had passed, how many centuries, how long she had to stay here, suffer here, asked herself why her brothers and sisters didn't come here and rescued her. The start of resentment burned in her sore throat.

She began twisting and turning, welcoming the growing panic and rage making her lose control, all control. The water didn't boil. She wanted it to do that, wanted it more than anything. She

Machineguns played up. She heard them, but feared it was only her imagination again. The clashes began between the mindless slaves and her children, her mighty demons. A smile formed on her drawn, drawn features.

– She's close, Jason said embittered. – I swear I can almost smell her.

But there was nothing anywhere they could pinpoint, nothing showing them what they needed to see.

He stopped the car. Linda stopped the other exactly the same moment. They stepped outside.

The enemy approached them, hidden by the terrain, but not in other ways. Whatever or whoever had been able to hide them earlier was gone, probably reduced to one of the countless cold bodies in the town they had left behind.

Jason and Michelle nodded to each other. Everyone nodded.

– We will do this! Carla agreed.

They looked startled beyond startled at her.

She changed, practically transformed into someone or something they hardly recognized, something wild and feral and wicked.

The dying began.

– Frank? Stacy whispered. – Is that you?

She stood in front of Henry Gyrich, levitated in front of them, as real as flesh and blood.

Jasper Carlton froze in fear and incredulity.

Henry blinked, and in that blink was an eternity times infinity squared.

The world turned itself inside out, at least to him.

Henry shook and couldn't stop shaking. He stood in a room, a completely different room with two women. They were smiling, smiling to him. It was high summer, a bright day making its mark on the room with many windows.

– Sandy? He said stunned. – Iris?

– Long time, no see, they choired. – It's so nice to see you again, Frank.

Frank Forester stared at Iris Carson and Sandy Pendleton across a gulf of lives.

– Time is of the essence, Frank, Stacy told him. – I could have fought against this horrible contraption for weeks, but if I'm not rescued now, I never will be. The King of the World is coming for me, Frank, and he won't be deterred.

– Why didn't you say something? He asked, accusing her.

– I didn't remember either then, she said with regret, – at least not enough to recognize you.

– What are you doing, Henry? Carlton said incredulous. – She's doing something to you, isn't she? She shouldn't be able to do that. We need to…

Henry grabbed a chair and struck Carlton with it. Carlton went down.

216

– Don't kill him, she cautioned him.

– I know! He choked, almost sobbing.

He grabbed Carlton and lifted him up, putting him on his shoulder. The big man felt like a feather. Frank Forester felt strong, confident and dedicated. He walked at a quick pace out of the room. The draft in the air pulled him down the dark hallway. He opened the door to the maintenance shaft. Its darkness didn't bother him when he stared into it, when he climbed down its long tunnel with Carlton on his shoulder.

Carla made the trees grow and attack the mountain's defense force. The branches choked and cut them. Only a few made it out of the forest. They were killed easily. Jason and Michelle soaked up the lifeforce. Carla felt how the ground drank the blood. Jason stopped the bullets without thinking about it. Instinct, rage ruled him, the deep horrible drive within he had only occasionally tapped into.

One more line of attack came at them from all sides. Michelle jumped at one flank with a beastly snarl. It didn't affect the brainwashed mutants, but the ordinary elite soldier grunts were scared shitless. The bubble of reality surrounding her protected her, at least to a point. She had to leave it in order to fight, but she jumped in and out with an effectiveness she couldn't believe. Linda fought with a cruelty and effectiveness even a notch improved from what she was usually capable of. Morten fired weapons with both hands without considering his own safety. He was screaming with s wrath tearing him up within and without. Lee tore the enemy combatants apart with both his mind and limbs. Martine moved between them, not doing one wrong step. Some of them were hit by bullets or by deadly bursts of power. They kept fighting. Each new death sustained the death gods, making them burn with power, with power almost unheard of.

Frank Forester emerged into the hall where the truck and tank were hidden. He put down Carlton and walked straight to it, pulled by the siren call from the captive within.

The water began boiling again, and this time it didn't stop. Stacy removed the mask, removed the covering for the eyes and the headphones with her mind power. She opened her mouth. Water flowed into her mouth, down the throat, filling her lungs. She couldn't breathe, and the body shook even harder. The white light burned behind her eyelids. Her clothes burned off. The collar and bracelets melted around her neck, wrists and ankles. She coughed, doing so ever harder, her body attempting to get rid of the water in her lungs, in vain. Eyes turned its attention outside, to the life, the salvation she sensed there. Frank pushed himself at the wall outside. One moment later Stacy's body left the center of the tank and pushed itself at the wall closest to the living being at the other side of the wall. Contact was immediate. The body seeking survival beyond all else began glowing in an even stronger light.

Flashes of thought, of communication flared and died between them.

How could I do it? How could I be someone like Henry?

You were angry. You wanted to get back at us, at us all.

I'm so sorry, sorry, sorry

Henry Gyrich's body ended, dissolving in a fiery ball of fire and dust. Lillith burned through the thick metal wall as if it was paper. She rose into the air. Jasper Carlton turned to dust, and left only his clothes. Lillith burrowed through layers of building material, feeling the fatigue quickly, fearing she didn't have the power to reach the outside.

She appeared into open air like a bullet, with little or no control, coughing hard, still feeling like she didn't get air to her burning, burning lungs. It hurt so much. The pain penetrated every single piece of her body, her screaming mind. She managed a somewhat controlled landing, but collapsed there, on the steaming ground, surrounded by misty air, coughing up an ocean of water.

Two shadows approached her, rushed towards her. She recognized her death demons. Three faces lit up in relief and joy.

Something resembling a bolt of lightning descended on them. Most of the force hit Jason and Michelle and pushed them backwards. She hit the ground hard. He was gutted by a dead branch nearby.

The remaining force stunned Stacy, paralyzing her further.

A man stood there.

– John, she breathed through gritted teeth.

She had no trouble recognizing him, even through the blinding power he emanated, no trouble recognizing him for what he truly was.

– I steal destinies. I will take yours and slip into your spot in the scheme of things, and I will use it, not squander it like you have.

Towering over her like that, he felt beyond powerful, invincible.

He had patiently waited for his chance, for this very moment, exactly like a salmon swimming upriver to spawn.

He reached out, grabbing hold of her with an invisible hand. It was like being grabbed by icy anesthesia. She released a loud and long whimper and collapsed on the ground.

– That was almost too easy. She heard his voice through a haze she desperately attempted to breach. – You made it easy for me by allowing yourself to be weakened by lesser beings. Everything is set, now. I will take everything important from you, adding your might to my own, and then I will be master of the world.

She saw it unfold, saw it happening, experiencing it as real.

Michelle looked at her in nameless horror and dread. Michelle saw her reduced to an empty shell, one that still breathed and moved, but that for all intents and purposes had lost everything making her an active, empowered human being. Michelle saw how her horror, her fundamental despair spread to them all, practically infecting them on a fundamental level, and Michelle knew her nightmare was becoming real.

She glanced back at Jason, Jason gutted by the branch. Blood flowed from his wound and he was pale and weak. She glanced back and forth, and choked in distress, unable to commit herself.

Don't worry about me, he shouted at her. Go!

Something clicked inside. Conviction suddenly grabbed her. She rushed forward, placing herself between the man and the crouching, shrinking creature on the ground.

– Take me! She offered. – Take me instead!

She blocked his contact with Stacy, disrupting it.

– Your fight with her may take days, and if it is an even match like it still probably is, it will leave you weak and defenseless. I offer myself. I will not resist

He frowned.

– You will sacrifice yourself for her?

– I am her servant in all things. When you have conquered me, I will become yours.

She bowed her head, casting her eyes to the ground, baring her neck to him. He chuckled in contempt and triumph.

– This is an unexpected bonus, almost too good to be true. I will have you both, of course.

She sensed him grab her, taking her in his possession with a thousand claws puncturing her hide. The pain grew quickly beyond bearable. It hurt so much that she couldn't scream, couldn't utter more than a few weak yelps.

– Your destiny is certainly powerful…

He frowned.

Then he screamed, in terrified revulsion. He tried to stop the process, but it had been put in motion beyond a critical point and couldn't be stopped.

He let go of her and collapsed on the ground. She watched him with a beyond pleased grin. He shook in horror and a despair he could never shake. She saw him walk to that dark room with a noose around his neck, saw him jump from the chair and hang from the rope, until he hung dead and still.

– I'm free! She cried elated. – FREE!

Jason had freed himself. He was still bleeding hard, but healing fast, even faster than he otherwise would have done, bloated with all the extra power he had absorbed. She rushed to him, looking softly at him.

– She has a profound effect on us all. What befalls her, befalls us all. He would have devoured her soul, her very reason for being.

He nodded, more than sensing the truth of her words.

– Life is a feast! She declared.

He stood a little unsteady on his feet. She took his hand and dragged him eagerly with her.

– C'mon, my love, let's *prove* that! Let's turn the world upside down.

Stacy fought herself up, too, her joy mixed with the inevitable weariness her ordeal had imposed on her.

– Everything is okay now, Mother, Michelle gloated. – We have survived the worst they can ever throw at us, and we are thriving.

She stared down at John Mathers with her predator eyes, no longer having trouble reading him. He had become an open book. She saw the same as Michelle. His destiny was fixed, his fate certain. He glanced fearfully at her, his eyes like that of a child fearing the darkness.

– The blanketing is gone, she stated, shrugging.

– Another mighty power languishing in a nameless grave.

Jason shrugged, too.

He and Michelle hugged each other fiercely, kissing each other so much that they hardly came up for air.

The three moved away from there, meeting up with Linda and the other survivors further down the valley, hardly even acknowledging the wreck of a human being they left behind.

8

Gabi rushed into her arms. The close contact with the smaller body warmed Stacy in amazing ways. Lillith's power leaked all over the place. Everyone nearby caught some of it. She was calm, restless, agitated, cut open, focusing on not draining those easily drained, fearing she would fail. Her power, stable for months had become uncontrollable once more.

She shared her memories with them, focusing on that part of her power, hoping it would suffice in containing the ravenous beast awakened within. Flashes hit her, as she relived the horror and also the visit of her future self, and her wicked, enigmatic smile.

They had gathered their dead as they returned to the portal. Sliced bodies, body parts floated in the air as they practically carried the broken flesh without consciously willing it. Judith lived, badly, mortally wounded. Stacy healed her with a casual thought. Michelle and Jason stayed close together, relentlessly pursuing their physical and mental contact.

The entire urban area had become a ghost town. People had fled and kept fleeing like rabbits. The members of the Janus Clan, reduced in number, but not in power, not at all in power stepped through the portal and returned home, home to Northfield, to the glowing castle on The Hill, on Raven's Mound.

Hectic, panicked activity slowed down and halted, and everyone, everyone in Northfield met them. They stood in a circle, a full moon receiving the weary, ecstatic travelers returning home from the war.

She caressed Gabi's cheek. Gabi accepted it, visibly shaken and down.

– I'm alright, little one. We all are.

Morten rushed to her, completely beside himself. He looked like he had lost Yvonne a thousand times, and not just one.

– Bring her back, he pleaded, demanded. – Please!

– I can't, Lillith said. – She's out of reach, is beyond me.

He accepted her words with a choke, a snarl.

Liz and Ted faced her. They had been there all the time since her return.

– They knew about us, she related, – about our powers and limitations. It was an amazing display, really.

She revealed her fangs with her own choke and snarl and enigmatic grin.

– And now… we know everything about them.

220

Her senses had expanded yet another level, at least one. She took in everyone present with one glance, one direction of attention.

– Our final enemies reveal themselves, pointing to themselves, Ted said, – like we knew they would, and we have to crush them like we would bugs, without losing sight of our ultimate goal.

Everyone nodded empathically, with rage and grief and every shade of emotion under the moon present.

He signed to Gabi, and she closed the gate. They could easily see how it shrunk to nothing.

The procession formed and began its long walk around the mountain, the dead carried on stretchers, their pale skin painted in blood glowing in the light of the setting sun.

They walked half the way around Raven's Mound until they reached the concealed broad tunnel leading into the rock. They walked through its darkness, its fire and shadow. Light shifted and burned constantly on walls and on people's faces. Lillith tracked the denizens of Northfield as they walked through the tunnel and descended the passageways from above. Everyone, also those that hadn't joined the procession, gathered for the ceremony in the hall deep below the castle, gathered by the round table and pentacles made of rock.

The hall gave off the same eerie quality as it always did, the pervasive shimmer in the air, the haze on the ground. They could only glimpse the ceiling high above.

Those with the fireeyes burning the strongest, and also some others, stepped up on the largest pentacle. Dry branches flying in from every direction made the yet cold bonfire. The cold carcasses of flesh and blood were put on the top.

Trudy was the one exception. Her still body was put on one of the slabs.

Ted took one step forward, distinguishing himself, somehow from those standing with him. The people in the hall fell silent. All chatter ceased.

– We knew this moment would come, he cried. – We also know that more such moments will come.

The powerful voice choired with the echo, matching it, filling every part of the air and the rock itself, lingering in ears and flesh alike.

– We bid our kin and fellow warriors a good journey tonight, Ted Warren said quietly. – We say not goodbye, but «until we meet again». The loss or prolonged absence will always be felt. We remember those missing from our campfire.

Liz stepped forward. The scalpel jumped from a table and into her hand. She started determined and without hesitation the process of cutting the fire from Trudy's eyes. She held the body frozen on the slab. It didn't move the slightest. Those watching the saving of the eyes for the first time watched it wide-eyed and with both a chill and wonder filling their being.

– She was the closest thing to a mother I had, you know, Michelle told Jason. – She told me about my birth mother and what had happened to her well before others did. She also told me that Liz had killed, butchered her, executed her and why.

Nick found two rings with transparent glass. He opened them. Liz put the ruby organic tissue into the hollow metal casing.

– Her eyes and fire will stay with us forever, she declared.

– FOREVER, the gathering choired.

Nick closed the casing and fused it… forever.

Michelle threw up, making a big splash all over the ground and those surrounding her.

People came to her and touched her and comforted her.

She shook her head and gave them a pale smile.

– Thank you, good people, she said, – but you misunderstand.

They did understand when she turned to Jason with a radiant smile.

– Two death gods beget life, she said solemnly.

She took his hand.

The body, the empty shell of Trudy Warren rose into the air and joined the other cold carcasses on top of the heap of dry wood. Ted and Liz rose into the air.

– Even if we die, we still live, they choired.

– EVEN IF WE DIE, WE STILL LIVE, everyone choired.

– The drums are calling, calling us home, Liz said. – Listen to them, and you can hear the heartbeat of the dead. Some people light candles for their dear departed, but we don't do that.

She paused a bit, one heartbeat, two.

– No, let's not light candles for them. Let's light roaring fires, because that's what they were... what they are.

– They died fighting, Ted shouted, – as warriors. The battle is won.

Fire burned the names on the wall. Red, white and black flower petals fell from the distant air and hit softly the floor.

– Until we meet again, he said.

– UNTIL WE MEET AGAIN!

The gathering roared.

Flames rose from and embraced the giant heap of dry wood and roared, matching that of a thousand parched throats. The dancing fire reached for the ceiling, for the sky. Everyone within the mountain could hear its song. Many outside could as well.

9

The room was silent, absolutely silent. Its sparse light remained still, dead. John Mathers stood on the chair, making a hangman's noose. He discovered to his surprise that it was an easy, somewhat satisfying process.

The task was done. He put the noose around his neck and tightened it.

Michelle Warren appeared right in front of him, her triumphant grin making her face even more demonic. He looked at her with dull eyes. Her presence didn't change anything, didn't matter one way or another.

He took one step forward. The noose tightened. He began kicking and struggling. The body's agitation waxed for a few seconds, but then waned. He hung there, dead and still.

222

Energy flowed from that dead and still body and into her. She shook in wild laughter. Her fireeyes lit up like stars.

10

The Phoenix Green Earth media news was on 24/7 with mostly new material, now, and then some. Several studios operated simultaneously and also independently of each other. It also broadcast in Spanish, French, Russian, Urdu, Hindi and Mandarin, to mention a few. Several hundred people gathered in a studio for an announced ten-hours low-keyed conversation.

Jane, Lynn, Jason, Michelle and a panel of ten sat at the center of the room, close to the «audience», surrounded by the many breathing entities, the sound of their beating hearts in their ears. Michelle heard it, heard all of it. It wasn't exaggerated to claim that she was glowing, that the glow of her fireeyes had spread all over her body.

– Good evening, Jane greeted everyone. – We're gathered here tonight to talk, to talk about anything striking our fancy, or rather what is burning in our gut. We will not make haste, not hurry in any way, not cut any corners, in order to go where we are going.

Lynn Fredericks and Jane Morris had aged well. No one would take a look at them and say with confidence that they were approximately fifty years old. They still burned with the spirit of their youth, the way Ted and Liz remembered them.

– We will begin with tonight's first thought, Michelle said, – one burning in your gut, one that come what may need to be expressed.

She looked around, turning her chair 360 degrees. No one spoke up, even though it was clear that many wanted to do so.

– Let me start then, Lynn said. – I have one thought that should be repeated many times, and everyone should hear.

It burned within like fire. Everyone even remotely sensitive watching her could see that.

– We want to end modern slavery, to stop it cold, she stated solemnly. – We've wanted to do so for quite some time, but now its end is overdue, like so many other horrible things.

There was a new quality added to her voice and her features compared to her previous public appearances. They were all more or less like that, visibly more driven, determined.

– But isn't slavery long since ended? A boy wondered.

– Not even close, Lynn replied passionately. – A recent UN-report puts the number of slaves on Earth in the millions.

– And that should really be seen as a conservative number, Jane interjected. – People are forced to work more or less for free in many places. Many, especially members of minority groups are convicted on trumped-up charges just to fill the judges' quotas. Prisons are a thriving business earning enterprises billions.

– That's so true, a girl cried. – I see little difference between wage-slavery and actual slavery anyway. We're working ourselves to death, and the already wealthy become even wealthier. It's insane!

It took only a few minutes for the Internet to be buzzing. That buzz only grew from there.

– No living being belongs in jail, Lynn declared.

– But where do we put the criminals?

– We need to find another solution to do that as well, Jason said, – like we should with everything.

– And let's not forget that the word «criminal» is complete bogus, Jane pointed out. – If that word has any, any validity at all, it is the criminals who are in charge.

– Hear, hear, the assembly choired.

– We should open all cages!

– And let all creatures roam free.

– Those in charge wage war, the perpetual war spoken of by Orwell, Jane spat. – They should definitely be locked up, if anyone should.

– One more insane thing, Lynn cried, – is the fact that when you don't want to bomb a country, and kill millions of people, the establishment and the establishment media paint you as the radical.

She shrugged deliberately.

– It's so very important, even crucial to see through the lies and deception and propaganda spoken by the establishment and the establishment media, and when you do take steps to break out, you shouldn't do it halfway, shouldn't play the establishment's game. If you want to join the resistance, you must join the resistance, not the establishment masquerading as the resistance. Too many people do the latter.

The recruitment to the Phoenix Green Earth started picking up even more already hours after the program had started. The Green Earth Party's election campaign did as well.

Lynn was its candidate for the Senate from Massachusetts, Ted Kennedy's seat. He looked old and frail. She steeled herself, as she traveled the state numerous times in the weeks before election day. She and other Green Earth candidates gained in the pre-election polls every day.

This was a so-called midterm election, in the middle of George W. Bush's second term, but there were still many senators being elected, many seats both on state-level and nationally up for grabs.

All the seats in the House of Representatives were on the line.

– Don't be fooled into believing the Democratic Party is the answer, she cried at a meeting in Boston. – It's time for you to stop fooling yourselves and vote for true alternatives.

Boston was a Green Earth Party stronghold. She received a truly enthusiastic reception there. Her voice grew louder, notably more powerful.

– We, those of us gathered here today and everyone like us are the future. We have waited for so very long to become the people we've been waiting for. We're fed up with waiting.

224

So-called third-party candidates had traditionally no chance at being elected, at least nationally. They were usually not even close to be a contender in what had been a race between the two establishment parties.

All that had changed the last few months.

Polls weren't just promising. They were unambiguous, impossible to interpret any other way.

Jane fought against Nancy Pelosi in California, in one of the Democratic Party strongholds. She was gaining on the old, shrewd politician every day.

– Don't be fooled, Jane cried at a packed football stadium. – Nancy Pelosi and the Democratic Part have no true merits, nothing but decades of oppressive establishment politics. It's time to end her destructive reign once and for all.

People in the streets outside, unable to enter the packed meeting shouted with those inside.

Linsey fought for a Senate seat in Colorado.

– We have reason to be hopeful, he said at a packed meeting in Denver, – but let's not get ahead of ourselves, or take anything for granted. Let's treat this for what it is: an even bigger incentive to work harder than ever, to fight on all the way to election day.

The applause hit him like a wave. He felt the power.

– The United States needs change, true change beyond niceties, beyond the incremental, he shouted. – The world needs it. We've been lenient for too long, and we won't be anymore.

Two puzzled commentators spoke on CNN.

– Kendall's victory in Colorado seems like a foregone conclusion, one of them said, looking like he had bit into something unpleasant.

– I will have to agree with you here, the other said, – even though there are still two weeks to election day, and he would be the first to point that out. The thing is, everything about his past that could have stopped him is already out there. He has never been secretive about it, but has instead practically been bragging about it, and he remains popular. His popularity has even helped other Green Earth Party candidates elsewhere, not just in his home state, but across the nation and the world.

– Both he and Stacy Larkin have made a sweep in the Southern States, haven't they?

– They have, and there is no doubt she would have been elected, if she had been eligible. The candidates she has endorsed are doing great as well. Every time she shares a stage with someone, their support swells. And to top it all off: we see that the Green Earth Party has become the main opposition to the dominant party in both red and blue states across the board. The value of the Cook Partisan Voting Index is clearly diminished this amazing year. The establishment poll survey companies tried for a while keeping them out, but that tactic failed as well, when the more accurate polls got all the attention on the Internet. We're looking at remarkable events, remarkable!

– What about the election in two years if this should be this year's result?

– That is another interesting question. I have no doubt that both the establishment parties will try doing some kind of gerrymandering and similar attempts of control in the states they still control, but how will they do it to be effective? Their old power bases are crumbling both nationally and on state level. California is no longer the safe haven for democrats. Texas is not for republicans. There are major structural, downright unpredictable changes within the electorate in virtually every state. And so on.

He clearly forgot himself in his excitement, using phrases and expressions and angles not exactly appreciated by those owning the network or its advertisers, but didn't seem to care.

Liz and Ted were asked questions after leaving one of the Phoenix Green Earth Media buildings by journalists camping outside.

– Why don't the two of you and other older Warrens run?

– Well, as you know, Burt, some of them *are* running, Ted said, – but Linsey is the main politician in the family at this time. We, the two of us and others, as you know are working in other areas to support him and all the other *excellent* candidates.

His smile lip up the entire sunny plaza.

Linsey and Betty held a press-conference after his speech, an even louder ruckus than their past performances.

– So, you are against wolf hunting?

– I most certainly are. The wolf shouldn't be hunted. Its inherent value aside, it is very useful to nature's balance, keeping the hyena in check, for one thing. It's a major tragedy how this great beast has been decimated in numbers and demonized throughout history, and it must stop.

– Do the two of you consider each other married to each other?

– We certainly do, Betty said, looking at him with love in her eyes.

– Do you consider yourselves married to Stacy Larkin?

– We do! Betty replied. – She's a lovely young woman.

– What about Everett Moran? Do you consider yourselves married to him as well?

– We most certainly do! Linsey shrugged.

They had answered these questions often.

– But you aren't legally married to them, are you?

– No, Betty replied with a radiant smile, – we've chosen to adhere to current US law in the matter...

The journalist drowned in her sarcasm.

– As long as it is truly voluntary people should be allowed to marry whoever they want, and as many as they want of both sexes, Linsey pointed out. – This shouldn't be hard to implement, to make into law, really.

The noise picked up in the hall.

– What about child marriages? One passionate soul spat.

– I said truly voluntary, Linsey said sharply. – That child marriages are still legal in most states, and are certainly one more horrible state of affairs we will change - contrary to the two establishment parties.

The «journalist» paled and had trouble articulating himself. He was a well-known employee in liberal media.

— We share, Betty said, — both between ourselves and others. And that doesn't take anything away from us, but gives us more than we can possibly describe. The one-woman, one-man ratio standard dominating today's family structure is what's unnatural, not other constellations.

— Then why are there so many couples?

The liberal said angrily, acidly.

— The reason is cultural, of course…

Linsey smiled sarcastically.

— The most natural is an orgy, really.

The man sat there gasping. He couldn't quite get sufficient air.

— So, you're basically what anthropologists have deemed you to be, a fertility cult?

— That's just as good an explanation as thousands of others. We're many things. Labels don't fit us at all. We embrace joy in a basically joyless world.

— The two-party system's view on morality is just as whacked as everything else, Betty stated. — Only the brainwashed and the whacked believe any of the two parties, any part of the War Party has any true solution to humanity's dire problems. On the contrary, both parts are happy to make them increasingly worse. Everything goes from bad to worse to horrible in their capable hands. They don't want to change anything. They're perfectly fine with how it is.

— Isn't that a rather crude and rude way of describing your political opponents?

— It's way too polite, Betty shrugged. — They deserve far worse.

— We will go for the jugular, Linsey stated, — and change everything from the ground up. Humanity will save itself from the horror it has created.

He pushed a button. A record of Keith Alexander, head of NSA appeared on the large screen.

— Why can't we collect all the material all the time? Alexander said, very grumpy. — There's an ever-stronger need for collecting information today.

— This is an example of the quality in the men in charge today, Betty shouted, shaking them to their core.

— There is no need for surveillance, Linsey said, — not unless you're a tyrant or servant of tyranny needing it to further your oppression. Surveillance should be illegal, of course. We will make it illegal, everywhere.

— And do you really think the voters will accept such preposterous policies, the «journalist» from the establishment media spat.

— You know they will, Linsey Kendal said quietly.

The «journalist» sat there with his mouth open, unable to articulate the smoldering rage filling him. He was not used to having his opinions challenged, in any way.

— We don't accept large donations, Betty said. — We take only money from the ninety-nine percent of humanity, those suffering under the yoke of the world-wide corporations and oligarchs and those supporting them. We reject the aid of Big Oil, of Big Pharma, of AIPAC, of NRA, of Wall Street and their like.

— The Democratic Party loves those, Linsey said, — loves any power center, where they can draw support and funds.

– How long will idiots participate in the charade that is the Democratic Party??? Betty shouted.

The roar pushed the lids off the ceiling.

It ended like their public performances usually ended: in loud ruckus and disarray.

Ellen and her students watched it all on one of the training grounds in Northfield. They watched it as they moved. It didn't really prove difficult.

The broadcast ended, and the exercise picked up in earnest.

They sat down afterwards, soaked in sweat, exhausted beyond all boundaries.

– My entire body hurts, a girl said happily. – Even my bruises have bruises.

Laughter from her fellow recruits echoed her joyous statement.

– It was so violent, a boy said. – I can't help feeling a little bad about that.

The others looked awkward at him.

Ellen raised a hand, stopping the others from voicing their displeasure.

– That's alright, she said. – It's a good thing that we speak out about our concerns, that we have reservations, have doubt about our chosen path.

She turned towards the boy.

– I used to be like you, she said softly. – I used to preach non-violence. Liz showed me how wrong I was. She opened my eyes with a few well-placed moves. I realized that it was like she told me: that we can't give ourselves yet another disadvantage by giving up on violent responses to a violent, beyond brutal and oppressive society.

– I feel so aware and so good about this, all this, the boy said sullenly, – and I'm not certain I should.

– That's good! Ellen said.

The boy nodded, and so did his fellow recruits, and she knew that they had all taken one more step on the path they had chosen, and the warm, warm feeling within grew further.

She joined Beth and Eloise in the library. They walked up the stairs, to the Hall of Mirrors. Bee had already started her training. Ellen saw, practically felt how the sword cut through the air, how the blade sizzled and burned as the young girl moved with deadly accuracy, and her energies reached far beyond her flesh.

Bee stopped, not the moment she noticed them or the moment they entered the hall, but later, at a point only she could name.

– Teachers…

She bowed her head, bowed her head just a little.

– We feel we can't teach you that much more, Beth said. – You're far ahead of your classmates. We've decided to move you up a level, to teachers that can better handle the special challenges you represent.

The girl's face cracked in a smile, before she caught herself.

– Thank you, teachers.

They hadn't needed to say anything, didn't need to say anything. She knew where to go. Her body moved, even as her mind was already there. She walked further up the stairs, to the roof. The two waiting for her there greeted her in a thousand different ways.

228

– Greetings, Beelzebub, the man said.

– Greetings, Samhain, greetings, Halja, honored father, honored mother, the girl said.

Michelle looked good humored at her.

– At least they taught you humility and good manners.

Both pair of fireeyes burned at her, and once again she felt that irrational jealousy and sadness because she didn't have them.

She approached the two, and stopped right in front of them, standing face to face with two of the most powerful beings on Earth. Jason had always been beyond powerful. She had always sensed his greatness, sensed it from she was a little girl, when she first met him. Michelle had made a quantum leap lately. She hardly looked like the same person in Bee's beyond sensitive eyes anymore.

– You are unique, Jason said. – We will help you make yourself even more so. We will cultivate even more everything making you special.

A warm, warm feeling rose within and filled her up, filled her to the brim.

– But how, father? I'm pretty powerful already. Ellen and Beth have made me hone my abilities for months, now, without considerable progress.

– She told you they couldn't teach you more, Michelle said. – We can!

– Of course, mother, Bee mumbled. – I stand corrected!

The three of them laughed together. It came off totally spontaneous and free, and they shared the good feeling among themselves.

– Your father and I went through some totally life-changing moments lately, Michelle said. – It opened us up further to the world, and to you, and everything.

Bee imagined she could see actual flames in her eyes.

They seemed to spread to the entire space surrounding them, and beyond. Bee saw it, saw them as they danced and twisted and shook at the precipice reality.

– You can feel us, right? Jason said. – I mean, sense all of us?

– I can, she replied and frowned. – Many of us can to a varying degree sense each other, but Beth and I found that I could do it better than even omega telepaths like Stacy… like Lillith.

Even the way she voiced the name was different. It sounded distinctly different on her tongue.

She sensed it before she spotted it, spotted the powerful blue light overwhelming the output from the dying sun. She recognized the blue lamp, the mutant tracker system developed by their enemies.

– Harmonize yourself with it, Samhain commanded.

She looked startled and a little hurt at him. His will was like pikes of ice and fire penetrating her.

– Yes, Halja said softly, uncommonly so. – You will be one of our hounds, tracking your own kind.

Bee fought to focus her thoughts, directing her will, attempting to ignore Halja's patronizing snarl, focusing her attention on the blue light in front of her.

It… spoke to her. All energy did, to some degree or another, but this spoke to her.

And beneath, beyond that, something deeper roared at her.

Her eyes flared in the same blue light. Then, the presence of Jason and Michelle hit her like a velvet glove in the belly. The blue light turned dark. It spread from Beelzebub to the entire house, immersing everyone within it, spread across Fire Lake and the forest beyond, and Northfield as a whole.

– Break contact, a female voice told her, after what felt like an eternity.

She blinked and couldn't quite identify the voice.

– I've helped you, surrounded you in my reality, isolating you even from me. The rest, you must do on your own.

– You've learned to control your powers, Jason told her. – You know how.

Bee stood there, frozen on the spot, breathing rapidly. She looked around her. There was no one there. She was all alone in the vast space of Michelle's realm.

It took only a slight change of focus, and she was there. The beyond powerful stars that had gathered inside of her faded slowly to embers.

Michelle let go of her, and she once more faced the two of them in the large world.

– You just need to focus even better and handle the overload, Michelle shrugged, – and learn to divide one star from the rest, all the rest.

– There are so many, Bee whispered.

– We will locate them all, Michelle stated.

– I felt like I was drowning, the girl said, – drowning in them, like I was losing myself.

Michelle touched her cheek, comforting her.

They trained the entire day, using many different scenarios. Bee stood there gasping, while striving to contain and at least in part control the energies surging through her. Her hands glowed in the blue flame, matching her eyes.

– These flames are the sign of your mastery over your power, Jason told her. – You control them. They do not control you.

She bit her lower lip until she bled. The pain aided her, helped her focus.

– Yes, our close proximity hurts you, Michelle said. – Endure!

The two stars standing in front of her obscured everyone else farther away, but as she focused on the small dots, they slowly gained a bigger spot in her surroundings. She picked them one by one and pulled them close, able to tell both direction and content.

The energies touched her, as she touched them. They invigorated and tired and hurt her simultaneously.

– I feel the Storm, she gasped. – I never thought I would.

She felt it, at the point of exhaustion as the relentless training continued.

After what felt like hours, ages and endless repetitions, she dropped exhausted to her knees.

– Get up, Michelle snapped. – Begin again.

The girl stood there swaying on weak legs, unable to recall the interim between her kneeling and her standing.

Michelle and Jason pushed her and kept pushing her. She became enraged occasionally and attacked them, but they handled her easily. They made her bare her neck to them, but they made no effort at breaking her, at taming her. She understood the difference in a dim part of her mind.

The world and its flesh, its burning flesh opened up to her. She walked through the halls and hallways of Ravenscourt after the ages of training had finally ended for the day. The girl fell like a feather down the stairs and trails. She walked in a daze. Someone spoke to her, sounding very far away. When she turned her head and spotted Ellen, she could only glimpse her, almost as if she wasn't there. It dawned on Bee that she registered only mutants, that everyone else had become like ghosts, as far as her power was concerned.

She joined a party, one where they celebrated their successful initiation into adulthood. A few of them burned in her vision. Most hardly appeared at all. She participated in the celebration, the dance, the excited talk, somewhat, unable to hide her detachment.

The others looked at her with understanding in their eyes, giving her her space, the perceived need for privacy. They admired the necklace and its jewel, and she allowed it. She treated them with patronizing disdain. They were still like children, and she wasn't anymore.

She returned to the sleeping hall, to her mattress. Her power kept overwhelming her other senses. Some of the mattresses seemed empty, even though her mundane vision told her differently. She undressed, both aware and not of her nudity, and in this, she was pretty much like everyone else here. The mattress and the blanket and the pillow welcomed her. She fell asleep, very aware of it happening. She experienced it like removing a veil. One tiny brush of the hand, and the dreaming began.

The people gathering in the valley in the center of the forest came from all over the country, and the world. They filled the spaces between the trees and even climbed the trees in order to be closer to each other. Loud, angry cries filled the air.

– Long live the wolf, a woman directing the gathering like a conductor shouted. – Death to its hunters!

– LONG LIVE THE WOLF. DEATH TO ITS FAKE HUNTERS!

The woman standing on a branch in the tallest and biggest tree was tall, with illustrious blonde hair and Asian features, an obvious, but in her case a strange, even eerie dichotomy.

She began changing. The people of the gathering mumbled among themselves. They watched her, unable to take their eyes off her changing form.

The creature stood on two legs, not a wolf, not a human being or both. No one staring at her, at it could decide. The werewolf stepped from myth into full-blown reality before their eyes. It stood still, almost frozen, making no threatening move. Fear still shook them. It took a long time before their hearts, and they calmed down.

– You are here to kill the wolf hunters, too? One finally asked.

– I'm here to slaughter them and feast on their putrid flesh.

Her voice was not exactly a voice, not exactly a somewhat decipherable growl, but something in-between.

She took one step forward, balancing perfectly on the not so thick branch, gaining their complete attention.

– Anyone succeeding in killing a wolf will die the moment it does, in horrible pain, she cried. – The wolf will live! I am not alone, neither here nor elsewhere. Many will collaborate on the task of defending the wolf, both aware of each other and not. Savage nature will rise again, and humanity will be diminished, once more only one unremarkable species roaming the world. Humanity will rise, will improve, will remember, becoming the great beast it has always been.

– How do you know? One curious soul wondered.

– You could just as well ask me if I'm breathing, she said, her features contracting in a very human smile.

My dreams, my endless pervasive dreams.

She returned to human form. It happened practically by itself, and she didn't fight it.

– We will go after the wolf-killers. We would need help, mostly logistic help locating them, but after that we would take care of it. I swear to you: within a month no one will hunt wolf anymore.

The excited and anxious hum of the gathering filled the forest. Bee shared the dreams with the wolf. She could not stop them from manifesting, and she was unable to tell whether or not she was sleeping. Her feet becoming paws raced on forest ground. She felt it as the two-legged wolf stopped on a rise and tilted its head backwards, and howled at the distant, suddenly so close moon. Other two-legged wolves appeared and approached her, approached their mother.

A number of men and women in various uniforms were dragged into a courtroom or a reasonable facsimile of one. They were seated, not very pleasant. Linda Cousin preceded over the gathering. She looked at the defendants with unkind eyes.

One man was made to stand. He stared at nothing, didn't really see the woman sitting right in front of him.

– You're charged with killing unharmed people, the judge stated, – with using your position as a policeman to shoot people that were no threat to you. How do you plead?

– I was freed of all charges, he protested.

– You were deemed not guilty in a beyond biased court of law, she corrected him. – You will find it quite different here. We will examine the evidence, not obey social impediments, but rather do our best to correct them.

Bee shared Linda's dreams, too. They were similar to those of the wolf, but also different, clearly more personal in nature. Linda smiled to those running by her side. Bee sensed her joy, her anticipation, her dark hunger.

They showed the film of the police officer shooting the man from behind only standing three steps away. The brown-skinned man fell on his belly still alive. The officer walked closer and shot him three more times. The brown-skinned man didn't move.

– Your case is one of the most decisive, obvious, Linda remarked. – I don't think we really need to see more. We've already heard your defense and find it utterly

232

lacking.

He jumped to his feet and attempted to run, but fell after the first few tryouts. He crawled across the floor, while she walked calmly behind him.

– We don't really believe in crimes and punishment here, she remarked, – but in your case we will make an exception.

She shot him in the leg. The man screamed. She shot him in the other leg. More screams filled the hall.

– This is way too nice, she told him offhand, – not in any way sufficient to match your crime. A thousand years of hellish torture wouldn't be enough. You're a racist bully, one of the very worst type of human being in existence. You will never show any remorse or attempt to better yourself, at least not in this life. I hope for your sake that you will improve in the next, or in the thousand after that, because we will be watching you. We will never forget you!

He crawled all the way to the wall, and turned there, watching the devil approach. Shaking with terror, tears flooded his cheeks. He attempted to speak, to articulate himself, in vain.

She shot him in the belly.

He jumped with his body, crumbling on the spot. A loud whine rose from his throat.

– We could've let you live, but we've chosen you, chosen you and others as an example. You will serve a purpose, serve as a warning to everyone else like you. Everyone waiting in their cells are already shaking and pissing themselves. I can practically smell the stench. Those still out there will wake up every night soaked in sweat, waiting for us to come for them, and the next wanting to copy your brave act will keep his finger off the trigger, and will at least pretend to behave like a human being. Thus, innocent lives will be saved. They will be able to live their life without fear and your reign of terror will end.

She shot him in the right upper arm, and then the left. She directed the barrel at his head. A soundless scream rose from his open mouth, his wide-open hurting eyes. Then, she pulled the trigger again. There was only a click.

– Oops…

She turned to Glory.

– I told you to load my gun, didn't I?

– You did, Your Grace, Glory said humbly. – My most sincere apologies…

She couldn't keep up the pretense and laughed out aloud.

Linda turned back towards the man and shrugged.

– Oh, well, we wanted you to suffer. No one promised you an easy death.

She left the courtroom. Everyone else followed her. The wounded police officer remained. The camera zoomed in on him.

He attempted to move, but was unable to do so, so he sat there and bled out slowly. His stomach wound started hurting horribly eventually, and the pain made him scream, and he never really stopped.

Not until he shook one final time, and all sound left him, and the bloody carcass slowly turned cold.

– We will take care of all the police officers that have killed defenseless people, take care of all of you, Glory shouted into the microphone and at the camera in front of her. Expect us!

A hunter had a wolf in his sight. He pulled the trigger. The bullet flowed forward against the four-legged creature across the divide. But at some point, it disappeared into a hole in the air. The hunter frowned, as it dawned on him that the bullet had somehow missed the target. He shrugged and prepared himself to fire another shot. The wolf hadn't moved. It wasn't going anywhere.

Something struck the hunter, struck him hard from behind. A horrible pain surged through him. He gasped. The rifle slipped from his hands. Blood flowed from his body. He realized stunned that he had been shot.

– That is your bullet, a voice told him. – It is in fact the bullet fired from your rifle just now. Ballistics will confirm that. The investigation will probably conclude that you shot yourself, no matter how unlikely that is.

She sounded like a girl, a teenager. He managed to twist his head, to look behind him. He saw no one.

– Each bullet a wolf hunter fires will hit the person firing it. You will repeat that truth in your fever vision many times before you die. So will many of your fellow hunters. The truth will spread, until wolf hunting has ended.

The scene was filmed and spread on the web. Several similar scenes were filmed. Wolf-hunting ceased completely in a matter of days.

Armored police vehicles that had been used to beat up protesters exploded, sometimes with officers inside, sometimes not. Judith stood in front of one burning van.

– I don't accept police brutality, she cried. – I don't accept being brutalized every time I express my opinion in public.

Military units and planes exploded. Drones exploded. People directing the drones were blown up.

The message went out all over the web. No hand holding a club will fall. No drones will fly! The world has been such a shitty place for so very long. Enough!

Animals were freed from zoos and «animal parks» and any incarceration.

– You support TERRORISTS! Linsey's opponent shouted at him.

– On the contrary, Linsey responded quite relaxed. – You and people like you are the ones supporting the true terrorists, that have supported military aggression against innocent civilians both domestically and abroad for such a long time. Thankfully, people are finally fed up with it, fed up with monstrous military spending and failure to spend those funds on truly worthy pursuits like people's health and on building a society where everyone is included.

The man kept opening and closing his mouth, struck mute.

– You will not tamper with the votes, voices whispered to people with dodgy intentions in what was suddenly very dark rooms, – but deliver them exactly as you find them.

The voice cut into their very bones. The people got the message.

Linsey was elected with a landslide. Most of the others were as well. Many others gained lots of support and some of them were elected to local, to state-level and national positions. The Green Earth Party was confirmed as a force to be reckoned with in US-politics.

Betty and Linsey stood there waving, accepting the accolades of the large crowd. Each breath felt like the sweetest elixir.

The blue lamps were put up in all major cities, in as many places that were practically possible. Follow up teams were organized. They sat up surveillance cameras recording everyone passing by. The obvious irony of that act made them pause and consider briefly, before moving on.

Bee took part in it, more than sensing her contact with the tool, its mighty pull. She kept dreaming even as she walked, even as she interacted with her brethren.

The ice was boiling everywhere, but especially in Antarctica. Massive amounts equal to small countries of it vanished in the rising heat, more and more every year.

The wolf sought high ground. It ran on all fours, but not as an ordinary wolf would do, but between. It could stand on two legs, was actually made for it, but it could run even faster on all fours with the right technique. It was obviously well versed in doing so, had learned how long ago.

She made the kill close to the highway. The two-legged prey believing himself to be a hunter with the AR-15 rifle hardly had time to cry out. No one saw anything, even as cars drove by below. The kill was easy, more like a shrug than an effort.

Her cubs waited eagerly for her in their den. She threw the meat at their feet. They started dissecting it, the need like a hunger within.

She joined them after a while, when they started yawning and had fed well. She didn't stop until she no longer had room for more. The cubs pulled close to their mother, happy and content and without a care in the world.

She hid a part of herself from them, doing so somewhat successful. They didn't, couldn't know what resided deep within her heart, at her deepest core.

Content, with her stomach full and her cubs rubbing themselves pelt to pelt, she still dreamt about the giant bird of fire and shadow. It filled her consciousness more than anything else. She whimpered in joy in her restless sleep.

CHAPTER EIGHTEEN
Blue light flaring

The next shift of moderators hired by the Internet firm the International Movie Data Base gathered in the large hall filled with screens, as they did three times every day. Rows upon rows of monitors attracted one operator each. A low electronic hum filled everyone's ears as they sat down and logged in.

– So, how long have you been doing this? Klara whispered to Ben.

– Just a couple of months, he replied, pondering the issue. – It's long enough, really. We hear more and more talk about reducing the staff even more than the latest layoffs. In ten years, all of it will be governed by algorithms and shit, and the owners can make even more money than they're already doing.

The others nearby couldn't help but overhear and glance uneasily at each other. The loud klaxon horn interrupted their unpleasant line of thoughts. Their workday began.

Their eyes glued to the screens, they began typing and pushing buttons. It was a straightforward, intuitive system, easy to learn and use. They didn't really have to think, just sit there and do what they were hired to do.

A boy in front by the window chuckled.

– This guy just wrote fuck again. He's doing it all the time, but spelling it f*u*c*k, so it won't be caught by the automatic controls. He's really great at avoiding the fucking censorship.

The boy related it all like a sports commentator to the rest of the hall and seemed to thoroughly enjoy himself...

Klara attempted to focus on the screen in front of her, to ignore the banter and ruckus around her. There was a discussion going on in one of the groups, a very heated discussion.

The United States is the biggest danger to peace by far, a boy wrote.

She pushed the delete button without consideration.

– You did the right thing, Ben said. – That socialist fuck had it coming.

She blushed and gave him a happy smile.

Klara grew distracted with Ben for a moment. They achieved eye-contact and didn't look away, drowning in each other's eyes, and she felt the exhilaration deep within.

Then, the markers began flashing on the screen, and she was drawn back to it. There was something that needed to be dealt with all the time, at least at the most popular discussion groups. It was very busy for a while. Her eyes stayed glued to the screen. She was being pulled into it, drowning in it, forgetting everything else.

Klara grew... excited.

– There is something to be said about this job, guys, she mused. – We have real power here.

They looked astonished at her.

– It's true! She insisted, feeling the dawning rush, an unknown, very powerful excitement. – We were insignificant gnats, but now we affect lives.

– Yes, you understand!

The raspy voice from a direction they could not place froze them on their spot. They could not move or bat an eye.

The room turned cold, ice cold. They imagined they could see their own breath in the air, only dimly realizing that part was only in their mind.

Everyone turned slowly, facing the woman standing there, everyone knowing she was there before they had actually spotted her with their eyes.

A dark and sinister woman towered above them. They couldn't take their eyes off her. Waves of fear struck them. They were unable to move.

– I've come here to fetch you to my service, she told them, the coarse voice making their ears bleed.

The words didn't really register in their minds, their suddenly so aware self.

– You will do exactly as I command, or you will be punished, will suffer the consequences. I could have made you mine by snapping my fingers, but I've decided to take it slower this time. It's more enjoyable, and it serves my purpose better. Count yourself «lucky».

How can she imagine that we aren't hers already? Klara wondered.

– This outlet will, from now on promote my thoughts and vision. You, my dedicated servants will make it into something truly memorable.

Her words and indominable will hammered them. They sniffed in despair, even as they eagerly did her bidding.

– I want to go home, a boy sniffed.

A whiplash hit his butt. He screamed in terror.

– You will never go home again, but serve your Goddess as long as you breathe and beyond.

She walked among them, taking their measure, finding them wanting. No one dared oppose her.

– You should only blame yourself for this. Your eager service to tyranny was bound to create some kind of backlash eventually. It was a sure bet that you would piss off the wrong person sooner or later… and now… you have!

– It isn't our fault.

One voice rose through the boiling waters.

– So, you were just following orders?

– This is just an Internet discussion site and service.

Many more excuses followed. They all fell on deaf ears and felt beyond silly and lame the very moment they were uttered. Everyone and everything fell silent. The nightmare in their midst grinned.

– You served tyranny and order. From now on you will serve freedom and chaos. Your old lives are at an end.

Everyone fell on their knees and bowed their head.

– Yes, you fall in line without resistance, because you've already submitted to those you believed to be powerful. You're already well trained in servitude. You will require no extra work.

She pictured it in her mind. In her eyes they were already there. She had already moved on to other matters.

There were other Internet discussion sites and services. They did them wholesale, devouring them like a hungry predator. It was a boring, but also strangely satisfying task. She who had been Valerie Musante flashed her fangs in a cold, dry grin.

It... began. Something changed on the Internet and the world at large during the next few weeks. A world already changing in drastic ways took an even stranger turn. People scratched their heads at first, when quite a few mainstream discussion sites and groups made dramatic turns towards the unpalatable and rough, without anything even smacking of censorship or internal jurisdiction.

Doma started laughing her cold, raspy laughter on the second day, and didn't stop for a while. The entire vast estate shook with it. Everyone's flesh and bone shook.

«God does not exist», a man wrote. «People believing there is a god or gods don't believe in themselves, and thus we have the fucked-up world we see around us every day».

«You fucked-up slimeball», a Christian wrote. «You should be crucified slowly. Your death should be one long suffering».

«All good God-fearing folks should roast all atheists over open fire», another Christian shouted.

«We should hang all misogynists», a woman said. «That would show them. They've tortured us for centuries».

Heightened tensions on several levels brought major unrest to many former calm white neighborhoods. It exploded on New Year's Eve into open riots and slaughter. The slightest disagreement led to major grievance and violence. Formerly ordered suburbs looked like war zones.

Klara looked at Doma with unqualified worship in her eyes. Her entire being worshiped Doma.

– Civilization is only a veneer, Doma shrugged. – This has been building for a long time. It just needed the right catalyst.

She felt her fangs and claws, the shards beneath the skin and in the deepest recesses of her magnificent mind.

She knew, now, like she had done since that fateful night in the military bootcamp so long ago that they had always been there, waiting patiently for the catalyst, the proper circumstances... to set her off. If it hadn't happened that night, it would have happened at another point, as inevitable as night followed day.

The catacombs reeked of blood and rotting human flesh and piss and shit. She walked with a casual stride, making all her soldiers bow their head and pay allegiance to her. They were like children, but they were her children, her beyond dedicated and cruel warriors. She couldn't keep the smile from playing on her lips, and she didn't want to. It was all so very, very enjoyable.

A man, a young boy with skin covered by welts crouched in a corner of the cell. He jumped on his feet and stood at attention the moment she entered his space. His hard cock was only the most obvious sign of his excitement. She experienced

238

all the rest without effort.

She circled him, doing so exactly like a bird of prey. There was no effort involved. She knew what she was, what she was capable of. It was all so very, very enjoyable.

– You are so unlucky, she hissed softly in his ear. – I could have made you more or less mindless like many of my other worshipers, but I won't. You would have been obedient, but dumb and ineffective. I want you and others to be aware of yourselves, of your potential as a god in a form of a man. It makes everything so much interesting. The Goddess loves her strident worshipers, and even more her holy warriors of power. It makes her life so much more… stimulating. You honor your Goddess with your strength.

She walked on, with him trailing her without her making any visible move to make him do it. He was just yet another moth in her surroundings.

Sounds from the training hall reached her. She hardly had to focus on it to hear it from far away. Sam was doing her thing, what she did best, unfettered by misunderstood notions of morality.

The brutal instructor had become so skilled. She could beat them to dust without damaging them. The Goddess smiled. The Goddess was pleased.

– Are you okay, Val? Charlotte asked softly at some later point.

She was the only one still calling her Val, that dared calling her Val.

– Do not show your disrespect in too obvious ways, servant, the wraith snarled.

– Forgive this silly servant, Doma, Charlotte whispered, and bowed her head in submission. – She's merely concerned with Doma's well-being, and with the execution of her will.

Doma allowed her closest adviser her indiscretions. She always did.

She had picked her, at the moment of her ascension to be an independent voice at her court, one that would always speak up when others wouldn't dare. Charlotte had performed that role adequately.

Doma could sense everyone within her eminent domain. A slight shift of focus, and she could zone in on each and every one of them. She knew their simple yearnings, whatever remained of independent thought. It was a very satisfying moment, as she once more could confirm to herself that she was the master of all she surveyed.

She frowned. There was… a disturbance. At first, it felt so light that she could hardly sense it, as if there was nothing there. Then, she did feel it, feel it like a hammer, and there was no doubt that it was there.

Ted Warren crossed an invisible line and entered her domain, and suddenly, he was everywhere within it, just like she was. An ecstatic smile darkened her face.

He did not speak. He hardly acknowledged those in his path, the few attempting to block it, except by brushing them aside like others would have done with flies.

The siblings Rupert and Priscilla attempted to sway him with their pheromones. He pulled them close and grabbed them, burying his claws deep within them, and gained their power. Doma felt how he grew even more powerful. She knew he could use that to enslave everyone he encountered. He did not. He left the half siblings in a ditch by his road, his path and walked on.

She watched with glee as everyone avoided him after that, pulling away from him as if he was poisonous, as if he was the most poisonous snake in existence.

He reached the house, the royal castle. She felt the moment he stepped inside like a slap in the face. Her cheek sizzled and burned. Each new step increased her pain. She bit her lip to shreds. The blood strengthened her, made her feel high and powerful.

He felt the surge of his power, and timed it just right. It happened the moment he stepped into the great throne hall. The wave shook everyone there. Doma gasped, unable to keep it contained.

There was an echo, equally powerful in the greater Los Angeles area. Doma watched beyond fascinated as Liz Warren glowed like a sun, a shadow embracing the entire enormous urban spread.

Ted Warren stopped in front of the throne, in front of her, below the throne, but she had no sense of him being smaller. She imagined he towered above her.

– You're exactly like I pictured you, she said out of breath.

– You didn't always. There was a time in your youth you had loftier goals.

– I learned my lesson.

Her snarl did not rock him, but he did feel it.

– I could break you, he shrugged, – but then you would be useless to me.

She tried striking at him with her powers, tried influencing him, overwhelm him like she had done easily with all the others. It failed to such a point that it didn't rock him in any noticeable way. She knew her heart wasn't in it. Her heart. She curled her lips in self-contempt.

She stood up and knelt, very deliberately at his feet, submitting to him with lowered eyes. He knew she could hardly imagine another way of joining him and his cause.

Everyone in the hall, on the estate and beyond joined her there.

That bothered him a bit. He didn't allow it to stop him or even slow him down, but pushed on.

– I stand at your disposal, father. We all do. I pledge myself and my soldiers to you and your cause without hesitation or doubt.

It was like he couldn't sense her power, but it hardly affected him. He didn't brush it aside. It just wasn't there, not to him.

– You will all need extensive retraining, of course, he said curtly, – but that is merely another welcomed challenge to us.

He signed for her to rise. She did. Everyone did. She blushed subjected to his ruthless scrutiny.

You should leave a few behind for practical purposes. This place will remain useful to us.

Yes, father of day, father of night, she brightened.

She belonged to him, and his purpose. There was no deception in her wide-open mind.

A portal opened up in front of them. They stepped through it. So did almost all the soldiers. Only a few caretakers remained.

240

They appeared in the great hall in the mountain below Fire Lake, below Ravenscourt. A wide circle of people welcomed them. Val felt them, their passion, the totality of their being.

A place like this should have been my home, she thought, haunted by regret, snarling at herself.

The rage sustained her, like it did him, them. Brief happiness and a sense of belonging brightened the fire in her eyes.

– Don't attempt to extinguish the fire within, he instructed her. – Embrace it!

Yes, father.

The wide circle welcomed the new arrivals, embraced them in flesh, in mind, in Shadow. She did take part in that, briefly. It did move her. She glanced at her father. One glance sufficed.

She moved on.

2

The blue lights flared. It was like the entire world turned light blue.

The digital map lit up, showing every single place the blue lights had flared.

– There are so many.

The polluted cloud hung low over Beijing. There wasn't really any space between it and the ground. The air had become one single dark mass. A massive number of cars made its way in both directions on the highway, in all four directions at the intersection.

A small bike made its way past the slow-moving vehicles. The bike took off from the main road and reached a calm, settled area, a small island within the stormy sea. Man Chi sighed in relief. She reached a parking lot filled with cars. There was a small gathering of bikes at the far end. She rolled hers there. The muted sound of the tires overwhelmed all other sounds. She left it there and walked into the building. It consisted of one giant hall. A circle of people sat on the floor at its center. There was one empty slot. She joined the circle, filled that empty space.

Hands held hands held hands held hands.

– The Goddess of the Moon, one man cried.

– THE GODDESS OF THE MOON, everyone choired.

They threw photographs of Stacy Larkin at the center of the circle. Some landed face up. Others landed face down. They saw first the photo at the forefront of their mind. Then, other faces they knew to be the same woman began appearing in their memory, their total recall.

– The Goddess of the Earth, a woman spoke up, and the choir echoed.

– THE GODDESS OF THE EARTH

More photos were thrown into the circle.

– GODS OF DEATH

Photos of Jason Gallagher, Michelle Warren and others joined the growing heap.

– The God of Time.

Nick Warren's face flashed before everyone's eyes.

– THE GOD OF THE SUN

Travis Nichols present and past joined the heap of memory.

The heap grew large.

It turned quiet eventually, quiet enough for whispers to be heard.

– The Dragon, Man Chi whispered.

A choir of whispers echoed in the Void.

– THE DRAGON

It turned quiet for a moment.

– The old gods, the survivors of the one god's rampage have returned. The new god is rising. The Phoenix burns in the sky and on Earth.

– IT TOUCHES THE EARTH!

They shared a modest meal, a feast of food and drink. She watched them, their body language and mannerism. They spoke to her with their silence, more than their verbal voice. She shifted her attention between them, and between them and others.

– Behold, Beelzebub, Lady of the high and low places, Theresa chided the girl surrounded by blue flame.

Bee heard the screams, the wails. Everything gathered in her like a sponge, a goblet of blood, a trumpet blowing its horn. It returned the sound to the world with a mighty shout. It shook her, rattling her bones.

Man Chi rode her bike through the poisoned air, on the dirty ground. She traveled home alone, the deep fire within concealed in her shell and hammering skull. The motorized vehicle appeared. The lights from the approaching car blinded her, even though it reached her from behind.

The car pushed her off the road before she had a chance of preventing it. She landed in the ditch several steps from her bike. The spinning wheel and its vibration distorted her sight and hearing.

She rose. Several men and women climbed out of the car.

– Greetings, Man Chi, the woman in front said, – please, come with us. You made a good effort at concealing yourself from us, but now your old life is over, and the new begins.

Man Chi bowed her head in acquiescence and took one, two steps forward.

The sudden blossoming of the blue light between her and the men and women startled the girl. That did, more than the appearance of the armed government officials.

A female form fast as lightning wielded something resembling a sword, but that clearly was some sort of directed energy, the blue light turned sharp as a blade. She cut down the front woman and man before any of them managed to fire their weapons. The man behind them, however did, but the bullet went haywire. Two men and two women that had been breathing just a few seconds ago had been reduced to mutilated bodies on the ground.

The blue and dark blade was put away. The creature wielding it turned towards the startled girl, the startled girl seeing another young girl in front of her.

– They were up to no good, Bee told the girl in Chinese. – They had nothing good in mind for you.

– How did you know? I've never…

– You've never revealed your true desires and nature to the world? Perhaps some of us see clearer than others.

One of the bodies burped, but didn't truly move. It was just the ruptured lungs making one final effort at breathing.

– I'm Bee, I can sense your energies. I'm the perfect hound. I can sniff out our kind from miles away without aid. Man Chi of the River Valley, you're one of The People, and need to come with me. The Chinese government will not look kindly at the dead goons they sent to fetch you.

Man Chi could not get rid of her startled expression the first few moments of rapid breath.

Rage flooded her. It was practically visible, even to a mundane eye, moments before harmful energies flowed from her hands and hit the other, hit her hard.

Bee shook a bit, but never lost her smile.

– Thank you, I needed that, needed the recharge. We will be a great team. The Oracle has foreseen it. You will love her.

The shimmering creature looking like a young woman tilted her head slightly and looked at the other girl that glanced at her bike.

– Yes, there is a choice.

Bee told her with a ghostly voice.

She reached out her hand. Man Chi hesitated a bit, just a bit before reaching out hers. Bee took it and pulled her with her into the hole in the air where she had appeared only a minute ago.

3

The two beyond tall and athletic women fought hands and feet, and with the seething power erupting from their feverish mind.

They seemed evenly matched. Val Musante and Michelle Warren went at each other with everything they had of their considerable might and made ground and walls and trees shake and break. The very air sizzled and burned around and between them. Fists and feet and the mighty powers of their mind hit sturdy flesh. Blood flowed all over the hall.

Val gained the upper hand. Michelle shook her head as the dizziness overwhelmed her. Val could have ended it then, but she kept punishing her sister in beyond wicked and brutal ways.

Michelle dropped to her knees. Val grabbed her hair and held her up, keeping her from collapsing on the floor. She struck her face again. Michelle hung in her ruthless grip.

– Do you yield?

– It's the fucking rage, Michelle mumbled through her mashed mouth. – I can't match that.

Val's iron fist struck her again.

– Do you yield?

– Yes, yes, damn you.

Val let her go, leaving her as slaughter on the floor, and straightened with a triumphant expression in her eyes.

– You're one of the sacrificial lambs. It's just as well. You're not fit to be anything else.

Val kicked her one final time on the head. Michelle didn't move. Val left with a wicked laughter.

Michelle regained consciousness in a world of hurt and fought herself back on her feet. She felt bad and looked the part, her face beaten to a pulp.

Val stepped into the next room. There was a portal there. She stepped through it, not hesitating for a moment. There was a forest at the other side. All the sounds and sensations filled her. She heard human activity in the distance and made her way there. There were guards on heights and in hideouts. She ignored them, but acknowledged their ability to conceal themselves in the terrain with a brisk smile, knowing that others lacking her superior senses would probably not have spotted them.

She reached the Hollow. The sight and experience of it, no matter how much she resisted it, created a pleasant and excited thrill within the forge of her being. Her kin, both of blood and inclination, had made this, made all of this, everywhere.

Beelzebub, glowing in blue stood at the center of the Hollow, surrounded by her charges, all of them blazing with power.

– I gathered you, she shouted. – I will train you, like others have trained me.

She noticed Val, no matter how much the older woman attempted to hide herself. Val knew the moment she did, the slight tilting of the neck well before the girl sent the involuntary glance in her direction.

Val stood up on the rise, revealing herself to them all. They mumbled to themselves and sent her anxious stares.

– ATTEND ME, CHARGES, Bee shouted and struck the ground with the wand. They did, standing on attention before her, pleasing Val to no end.

– You will fight two and two, Bee instructed them. – You've had a modest crash course before this, but know that you've now reached another level of skill and danger. You will fight for real, or you will answer to me. You will fight until you or your opponent are bested.

They went at each other, with the wand as their only weapon. Beth Alver sat at another of the four rises, looking very inconspicuous, almost invisible. She studied the fighting, pretty much like Val did, but contrary to Val very focused and astute. Val knew she measured the injuries, ready to intervene if they became too extensive, when there was a danger to life and health.

– You practice an impossible combination of brutality and compassion here, she said agitated to Ted and Liz, her father and mother, hating the catching in her throat.

– It isn't strange that you believe that, Liz told her curtly. – Almost all your important experience screams it at you.

244

The moment, the exchange with them seemed to stretch on forever. She attempted to shake it off, failing like she would ongoing rain.

– It is raining all the time, another dark presence told her.

The tall Chinese girl made mincemeat of her opponent. She had the moves and the brutality necessary to prevail. Her opponent was beaten. She struck him one more time, just to be certain he was down. The familiar heat surged through Val.

Man Chi turned to Bee and raised her wand above her head.

– This warrior salutes Beelzebub, the Lady of High and Low Places, she cried.

She turned towards one of the raises.

– This warrior salutes Aphrodite, the Goddess of unbridled passion, she cried.

She turned towards the second populated rise.

– This warrior salutes Ares, the Goddess of War, she shouted.

Val shook, suddenly assaulted by memories of countless lives.

She heard the sound of a thousand swords being drawn, the gasps of a thousand shells of flesh and bone giving up their spirit, and she could not fathom how ignorant she had been only seconds earlier. A louder mumble rose from the Hollow. The cruel and triumphant smile spread to her entire face.

The beyond exhaustive from dawn to dusk exercise finally ceased. Tall fires were lit in the Hollow when the twilight turned dark. Val joined the nascent warriors and their instructors. Beth walked among them and tended their wounds. The young recruits looked at them both with awe in shiny eyes.

They were believers, and why shouldn't they be? They had felt Val's poignant presence the moment she approached, and the fighting had become far harder and more brutal than it would have been. They felt Beth, now, like they had felt her then, and all the time.

– Water, My Goddess? Man Chi offered her in a cup.

Val accepted the cup and drank the chilled water.

She rose and turned away from the fire.

– Won't you stay, My Lady? Aphrodite offered her sweetly, making no effort at hiding her intentions.

Val remembered them in fiery embraces around another campfire long ago.

She walked off without acknowledging the other woman's sweet promise.

Bee followed her into the darkness. Val stopped and turned. Bee stopped as well.

– You're too kind with your charges, Val remarked. – The presence of the healer more than suggests that. They have no rights to life until they have emerged victorious from the dark tunnel. They're worthless lowlife until they do.

– A wicked woman once predicted that I would be wicked, too, Bee said passionately, – or either wicked or nice, but I say I've become neither, and that is also how I prefer it.

– If you had been trained by me, you would have been that magnificent creature of power.

– I am! Bee snarled with a distinct challenge in her voice and appearance.

Val chuckled pleased. She turned and walked away, inviting Bee to attack her from behind.

Nothing happened, and irritation surged through Val. Mere weeks ago, she would have made the young warrior pay for her indulgence.

She returned to the portal, to the building in Northfield Main Street. She walked down the stairs and stepped outside, onto the busy street. People acknowledged her in big and small ways. Most of them didn't recognize her, not completely, like Man Chi and others had done, but they sensed, knew enough to show her proper respect.

The sounds from the tavern reached her. They drew her there. Her steps brought her there, before her conscious mind did. She stepped inside, into the moist and noisy room. It pleased her to spot Michelle. Her face had still not healed completely. Signs of Val's treatment remained. Val chuckled, just loud enough.

Everyone glanced at her with flickering eyes. Val's laughter grew louder. She walked to the bar and ordered a beer. Morgana set out to do it, but Jason handed her one first. Val smiled to him. It pleased her when he returned the smile, when he studied her with the beautiful fireeyes. She felt the attraction between them like an electrical charge, and could not hold back a tiny gasp.

She sensed her people, her soldiers. They were spread across the city forest. They were still hers, still served her. That pleased her, too.

Someone turned up the music and people began dancing. It just happened, from one moment to the next, like a spontaneous, uninterrupted flow. She could not help being impressed by the sight, the sensation of it. The pattern entered her consciousness through all the senses. She

She sensed a presence, familiar but unidentifiable. It brushed against her and rose her... her fear. She could not stop the startled expression from appearing. Sweat covered her brow in an instant. She shook her head in incredulity. It didn't put a stop to the bad feeling.

The passion in the room grew more potent by the second. A male moved in on her with obvious intentions. She discarded him without effort, without any outward display. A few moments later the same scenario repeated itself with a female.

Val stepped outside, into the chilly air. It affected her. She could not fight it off, could not stop the violent shaking. A loud chant filled her ears, imposed itself on her mind, her self. She realized dimly that she was under attack, but she was unable to fight it. There was nothing solid, nothing to focus on. Then, it felt like a thousand needles stabbed her. She screamed, or attempted screaming, but no sound escaped her lips. Her eyes turned dull. She floated away on that dullness, into that nothingness, until nothing but that lack of awareness remained.

She had a sense of being carried, a sense of strong, brutal hands squeezing sore limbs, but nothing beyond that manifested. She kept drifting on a cloud of dull pain, unable to affect her reality.

– Wakey, wakey, sleepyhead, a nagging voice and slaps on the cheeks woke her up. Michelle slapped her on her cheek, and Val opened her eyes wide.

– There you are. I thought you would sleep forever.

Michelle sat on her heels close to her. One moment later she stood several steps away.

Val jumped on her feet and at the other woman.

She stopped in midair, frozen like her face, shock engraved on her twisted features.

– You're in my domain, now. I decide what goes here.

The words registered in Val's dull mind, but didn't really catch on. Their meaning only dawned slowly on her. Michelle walked to her and grabbed her jaw.

– You'll be a nice, housebroken pet.

– Never!

Val mumbled.

Something akin to an electrical shock surged through her. Val screamed, screamed her heart out. She hung in the ruthless grip of the master of the realm.

– Oh, don't worry, Michelle shrugged, – this is merely the opening gambit. I suspect pain won't really get to you. You can handle pain. We will just work a bit with it in order to make you receptive to our teaching.

Val's cunt burned. It certainly felt like it did. The scream grew desperate.

– Or perhaps pain will work. You will discover that I can be very inventive.

She pulled both arms out of their sockets. They hung down, completely useless. The scream rose to a high pitch.

The captive's breathing grew beyond labored. She hung there in the cruel grip of the goddess of the realm.

– You will probably be able to pull your arms back into the right position, but rest assured that I will keep dislocating them until they stay put where I put them.

She moved her prisoner upside down. It took only a casual thought.

– You will never be free. Never, ever. If you expect father to rescue you, to intervene in our private discourse, you're a bigger fool than I ever was.

She struck Val in the abdomen, pushing air from her lungs.

– You're such a grateful task, such a sturdy play-doll. I can practically do anything to you without really harming you… much.

She grabbed the jaw with one hand and a tooth with the fingers of the other… and pulled the tooth straight out. Val's mouth stayed open. The scream seemed endless. Michelle began drilling deep with her mind into another tooth, straight into the place where it hurt the most.

Val lost her voice at some point. By that time, she hardly knew forward from backward anymore. It had all turned into one, prolonged eternity of torture, misery and terror.

– I WILL KILL YOU, she screamed at some point. – I WILL…

Her shout was cut off. Michelle tore her arm off. Blood flowed from the wound and splashed Michelle's face. She laughed beyond darkly, far beyond. Val shook hard beyond hard. The scream died in her throat.

– You will stay here, with me for all eternity, Michelle shouted at her. – It will be a fucking MERCY if I should ever decide to put you out of your misery. You are nothing more than a fly. I will enjoy ripping off your wings no matter how many times I do so.

Hours passed, or so it felt. The regeneration process began.

– Look at that, the arm is actually growing back. Who would have thought.

Val gasped and whimpered. A constant wail rose from her beyond sore throat. Michelle began rubbing her cheek, comforting her.

– It hurts, does it not? Everything hurts horribly. It would have served you to be unconscious during the regeneration process, but rest assured that I will keep you awake during every moment of it.

Val nodded, nodded, nodded. She collapsed in heartbreaking sobs. Tears flooded and kept flooding her face.

– All the floodgates are open.

Michelle tore off the other arm. Val began shaking in cramps and didn't stop. The arm shriveled and died. All the blood and flesh removed from the main body turned dark.

– I could just disable you completely. I'm confident we could remove all four limbs and make them stay off. My guess is that you are like most of us, that you can survive anything. I will just keep you in my dungeon, and come and play with you at uneven intervals. I'm confident that you will make a cute and obedient doll, an excellent slave of my desires, my every whim. I can't even imagine how much fun that will be.

Time passed, stretching out to eternity, to nowhere.

Val hung there, having lost all sense of time and herself, shaking in fright and horror beyond horror. Michelle put her on her knees. The prisoners knelt before the giant bowed and broken.

– Yes, Michelle said softly. – You're ready, now.

She slapped her on the cheek. Val hardly noticed the kind caress.

– Listen up!

She stared attentive at the wrathful face above.

– We will have us a little heart to heart, now, my pretty doll. You will be eager to answer all my questions. We will play questions and answer until I am done with you.

– YES, MICHELLE, PLEASE MICHELLE! QUESTIONS, QUESTIONS…

Another slap on the cheek.

Val nodded and choked and nodded again.

– I trust you will be absolutely honest.

– Yes, Michelle, honest!

She hardly understood the words. They just reached her ears and flowed garbled from her mouth. It held no significant meaning for her.

– We will return to the moment of your ascension. Do you remember, lovely bird?

– Yes, Val nodded, – remember. Val remembers well, so well, well, well.

Another slap. The giant filled her consciousness completely. She stayed there.

– You are naked, now, Michelle chuckled. – It's all so very, very, very pleasing.

Val didn't react, one way or another. Her mind stayed numb and empty, even as a roar of sensation kept charging through it. She had no defense against it. It hurt, hurt so much.

– You were naked then, feeling absolutely helpless and fearful and timid. You saw yourself and your friends, yes, your friends in the grip of a brutal, dominant male without mercy or compassion. The rage aided you, but it also doomed you. You embraced power, embraced the very Path of Power. You became that so very attractive condition and lost yourself forever.

Val nodded to herself. That sounded so very, very right.

– You could have used your power to resolve, defuse the situation, but that wasn't enough for you, was it? You were no longer weak, innocent Val, but a god walking among mortals, one without concern for those who didn't deserve any.

She chained her sister's head and feet. The collar hurt, and Val was totally unable to resist its sinister influence. Val had no strength left. The empty space within her left no room for that.

– You really fucked up this time, Ares, not even recognizing a death goddess when you met her and fought her head on. You hardly remember yourself, are hardly more than Val, and now you're not even that tiny glow.

The giant pulled the smaller, broken form and soul on her feet. Val noticed that she pulled her realm back into herself, sending both of them back to the larger reality.

Val stumbled in her chains at Michelle's side. She didn't see where they were going. Everything in her surroundings remained a blur.

They reached a spot where a significant number of Val's old underlings had gathered. Michelle threw her on the ground.

– Behold your goddess!

The crouching woman imagined she heard cruel, condescending laughter. Val's head kept hanging in shame. She sniffed again. The big, black hole just grew bigger and bigger and bigger around her.

Michelle turned to Val again. Val felt like her beyond cruel, older sister was stealing all her breath.

– I guess you have learned your lesson…

– Yes, Michelle, Val choked and choked and choked.

It felt once again like forever passed her and passed her again and again and again there on her ongoing, horrible descent.

– You're just a broken thing.

Val nodded or imagined herself to be nodding. She looked at the dark cloud of a face hovering above her and shook subdued.

She watched as Michelle frowned, and that made her frown as well. Michelle reached out a hand.

– Take my hand, sister!

– There is no need for this, Val choked, – no need for more deception. You've proven your superiority. I will serve you and worship you and slave for you for the rest of my days.

– Life is a feast.

Michelle stated.

That made Val look at her. She realized astounded that tears had filled her eyes, and that they didn't burn, but rinsed sore, sore skin.

Val rose on unsteady feet, astounded that she could stand at all. She felt strong arms embrace her. She collapsed in those arms and started sobbing, hard, wrecking sobs and laughter of pain, relief and joy.

4

Michelle removed the chains and the collar. They stood there facing each other.
— You may do with me as you please, now. I foresee many centuries with the cruelest, most inventive torture.
She fell to her knees, submitting herself to the other's mercy.
Val struck her down. She started kicking her and kept kicking her, making certain she stayed conscious the entire time.
Then, she stopped, just stopped. Her hands hurt, as if she still felt each strike.
— Thank you, she whispered. — I really appreciated that.
Michelle fought herself back up. They began making out on the spot, ignoring the stunned, wicked laughter of their surroundings.
They touched in gentle ways, laughing euphorically.
— My popcorn therapy worked, Michelle breathed. — I don't fucking believe it.
Val frowned.
— That's not the expression. It's...
She stopped and shook her head.
— You're yanking my chain again.
— Yes, Michelle admitted. — Yanking!
She led Val away. Val felt very peaceful, a well of contradictory emotions of rage and gratefulness, and hundreds of less identifiable feelings.
— It did work, she stated. — You're a genius!
— There was nothing to it, Michelle snorted. — I had a great time. I will be happy to repeat it at a later occasion.
Val didn't know where they were going. She didn't care. She knew where they were heading.
— Race you!
But they didn't really race each other, on their way up the hill, through the forest and all the long, deep path to Fire Lake. They ran side by side at a pleasant pace. There was no hurry anymore. Ground became water surface. Air became water. They swam in the lake, touching each other more than not. They treaded the water lips to lips.
— I remember how you felt now. You were always a pleasant piece of flesh. I can't believe I forgot. I forgot so much. I'm sorry.
Michelle kept pushing lips and front at her. The lake began boiling around them. Loud and happy and free laughter kept erupting from their throat. They returned to land and made their way back through the forest. Small branches and leaves attached themselves to their body. It covered their surface completely. Except for the fireeyes and the mouth. They knew they resembled specters, wood spirits. They did cause a stir when they descended the hill on their way back to town. They didn't

speak, but still communicated on a far deeper level. They weren't one, but they covered each other like two parts of a Venn diagram. They excelled in it.

– We are pain and death and strife, Val stated, – but that is far from everything we are. I forgot that, too.

– You won't forget again, Michelle stressed, – at least not for the next hundreds of years.

They kept touching skin against skin. Their core brushed against each other like the prime fire burning within.

Some took their photo. Several others rushed closer to catch them as well. Reality turned inside out around them. They heard the sound of loud screams, both of lust and pain… and there was no difference. Val nodded to herself, waking up further by the second. She wondered briefly if she would ever stop. Then, she stopped. Excitement grabbed her, grabbed them both and moved them down the green street,

They reached the tavern. Jason waited for them inside. Everyone within its fluid walls noticed their arrival. Everyone gasped in beyond savage anticipation.

– Greetings, Samhain, I submit another sister for your approval.

He looked ageless. They both saw him as he truly was. More words of silly jest were exchanged. They hardly heard them, and forgot them the moment they were spoken. Val and Jason reached out with their hands the very same moment. They touched and shook equally hard. She was not intimidated by him. She knew she would love him, that the two of them , the three of them would fill a hole in each other. It felt just then like they had wasted eons.

Skin touched skin against skin, but the casual brush beneath that touched them far harder.

Wind and time blew through them.

5

– They were supported across the board, the presenter said. – It's a wave of changing convictions. They even beat Pelosi in California, in *California*.

– It's a fucking awakening, one from the audience shouted. – It's finally here.

The ruckus erupted in the hall. Praise and scorn rained down on the most recent speaker. Only the heavy presence of guards kept it from escalating.

A fairly well-known man was one of the participants in the subsequent debate. Everyone watching him, both recent new friends and foes agreed there was a changed man sitting there. Their agreement ended there.

– I have only recently realized that I've lived a lie most of my life. I've been a racist and misogynist and religious zealot, and I am deeply ashamed of myself.

Liz and Ted paid little or no attention to the audio and video on the screen in a distant room of Ravenscourt.

Brief excitement touched them, but that was like nothing compared to what the event in this room made them feel.

Establishment media didn't deny themselves the usual pleasure of distributing their propaganda.

ECOTERRORISM WON THE ELECTION

GREAT PROGRESS FOR ANTIFA

But it didn't have the bite of old. Almost no one watched the old channels anymore, and those below fifty certainly didn't.

People opened up in droves, pondering things they had never truly pondered before.

– The true line in the sand is drawn between those defending today's inhuman society and those fighting for true change with every fiber of their being, Lee told a reporter.

The reporters from Phoenix Green Earth filmed it as well and filmed themselves doing it, and everyone knew the direct transmission would be rerun many times.

– We should stop attempting to understand right wing and centrist fanatics, he stated with a happy snarl. – We've tried that for way too long, and it hasn't really worked for us. Now is the time to show those oppressive dirtbags the contempt they deserve.

The hammering of drums imposed on the broadcast a bit, but not excessively so.

Ted and Liz and Jennifer and another man, Rollo Mason had redecorated the hall completely. Machines filled most of the space. The machinery had lots of added protection they knew had been added in an attempt to protect it from their more than erratic power.

There was a constant low hum occasionally sounding like a roar in their ears. It kept shifting, rising and falling like a fast rollercoaster, without a discernible pattern. Jennifer failed gloriously in concealing the excitement in her voice and expression.

– I have, with generous aid from several sources without and within our organization gathered extensive material from earlier and early in your life, x-rays, dental records, the works, even Kurt Meinz's «work». If you look at those data-enhanced images and recordings, you can practically see the energy, all the way back to your early childhood.

They did. They would gather that they saw it with far better clarity than she and Rollo did, also spotting what wasn't there.

– You will see that it, at a certain point passed a threshold. The graph is a close approximation to a hyperbola, a slowly rising line suddenly rising abruptly, revealing a force suddenly becoming many times more powerful than it once was. And beneath that…

They heard the terrible and joyous song always there.

She looked at Rollo, leaving the continuation of the presentation to him. He hesitated a bit before taking the plunge.

– This is truly extraordinary, he began. – I can safely say that I've never encountered anything similar in my research or life… or so I believed.

He hesitated again, and this time it was quite notable. They waited patiently.

– It is smaller, of course, but… you have an electromagnetic field similar to that… of a star.

That did startle, did stun them.

252

– That sounds completely impossible, Liz said, clearly skeptical.

– I believed so as well, but the readings are… conclusive. The signature is distinct. It can't be misunderstood or at least I can't see how it can be.

– We have experienced lots of strange shit, Ted said, – but this is something else.

– It is something else, Jennifer stated. – That's the point, of course. I didn't know what to expect when I contacted Rollo. I certainly didn't expect this, not in my wildest dreams.

– In fact, you have the same or at least similar electromagnetic… frequency like that of a distant star I measured through background radiation recently, Rollo added. – It's truly amazing!

– Which constellation? Liz heard herself ask.

– That of the *Phoenix,* in the Southern Hemisphere near Tucana and Sculptor.

That didn't surprise them. It resonated within them in very familiar ways, a scent, a taste, a sound, a touch, an image that had always been there, beneath the eyelids.

Rollo walked closer to the screen, as if that would somehow bring clarity.

– This is some weird shit. The light is blue shift, not red. And there's more. If I'm right, though I can't see how I can be, this light has bombarded Earth for millions of years… and it's growing stronger, not weaker with the passing of years.

– The light… it comes from a supernova explosion, isn't it?

Liz heard herself say.

– Yes, but how did you…

– What if the explosion wasn't in the distant past but in a far future?

A light lit up his eyes.

– Yes, that might explain…

He shook his head.

– On the other hand, it might not. This is infuriating.

They did sense fear, even though his scientific curiosity currently overwhelmed that. The two of them and Jennifer exchanged glances. They knew more than he did.

– So, any idea, if you are asked to speculate what it all means.

The bewildered scientist thought well and long about that one.

– It has something to do with your elevated energy levels, of course. It I should make a preliminary conclusion or at least the beginning of one, that would at the very least be the start of a foundation for a theory or rather a hypothesis.

He hesitated for the third time.

– Jennifer has been kind enough to share her research with me the last few months, both on you and other… mutants. That was certainly an eyeopener of gigantic proportions in itself. But as stated; the two of you are something else, even compared to that.

He cackled. It sounded completely off.

– She swore me to secrecy, but that is pretty much redundant, at least as long as you guys don't want to go public. I could present as much overwhelming scientific evidence as I possibly could, which is already considerable, and it would be completely useless, would make me the laughingstock of the entire «scientific» community.

– Keeping it a secret from general humanity is something both we and our enemies agree on, Ted shrugged. – That is very funny.

– If they told the truth, or even something approaching the truth about us, they would also reveal so much other clandestine stuff, Jennifer said. – The massive secret history of humanity would be exposed for all to see.

– It will be, Liz said, – but at a time of our choosing.

Rollo packed his bag. It was done quickly. He traveled light.

– I'll be in touch, of course, and I guess you will, too.

He shook their hand and was off. They got a deep sense of him again, and there was nothing there they hadn't sensed before, both from a distance and closeup.

Ted and Liz stayed with Jennifer. They could pretty much read her mind. They still waited patiently for her to speak up.

– I wanted him out of the way before I spoke of this, she stated.

They sensed the full range of her emotions, from terror to awe and back again.

– Something out there is transcending time and space, and you are... connected to that.

They let her speak in her own way and pace.

– You remember the instruments I set up in and around Northfield?

They smiled at her. She was funny sometimes.

– You are here and there, at several of them simultaneously. None of the other psychics I've checked do that. Your physiology is also different. Their aura, in spite of slight occasional differences looks pretty much like other humans.

– We're all human, still human, Liz pointed out. – We can breed with other humans and our offspring can breed with them and give birth to viable offspring.

– Yes!

Jennifer acknowledged, but clearly not done.

– You are the Prime, she stated, – the one we've been waiting for, the one that will set us free from all shackles. Betty's mysticism and my science agree.

She fell on her knees before them, in something very close to religious fervor.

The room turned absolutely silent. There was no noise from the machinery anymore. They heard the sound of the lake, the rustle of wind in the treetops, the growl from the depth of the forest.

6

They started dismantling Cole Stephenson's kingdom, his very life. They started doing that to the other twelve as well, doing everything simultaneously. They mobilized on all levels, at an unprecedented scale. The undeclared war that had raged for centuries, millennia escalated in notable ways.

The growing army, moving in stealth and not, violent and not encroached on «Illuminati» territory. Cole Stephenson and the others suffered uneasy dreams, while all secrets were plucked from their minds. One telepath was assigned to each one of them. Lillith coordinated them. She and Gabi sat in the Oracle's sanctum and

254

moved the troops around wherever they needed to go. Lilith sat there with a raven on her shoulder. Stephenson and the other twelve had an army of loyal, hardened men and women surrounding them in a protective shield, and many other unwitting helpers and foot soldiers. The Phoenix Green Earth started chipping away on all of it, doing in earnest what they had done and prepared for for quite a while.

Twenty-one formed the circle in the mountain hall. Lillith sat at its center.

– Merely removing the headsss will do usss no good, the Dark Goddess hissed. – They will quite simply grow more. We will work us from top to down, from down to up, attacking Hydra on all partsss of its body, keep chopping off the centipede's feet, until there are no more left.

The outer circle hissed and burned, its oozing flames stretching and dancing. There were shifting lights and shadows everywhere. Lillith was glowing in an eldritch glare. She drew her power from within and without in ways she had never done simultaneously before. Those in the circle felt her power like a beyond tangible force. Everyone in Northfield noticed. Many across the world did as well.

She saw herself, reexperienced yet again herself as the centipede's humble tool, their eager slave. Rage surged through her. She soaked up energy from the twenty and one around her, and her power grew, peaking on uncharted charts. Everything turned a dark red. In the red glare, she saw everyone and everything in the sharpest textures of shadow. These were not hers, not *its* twenty and one, but still powerful. They would suffice.

With the added boost, she touched everyone in Northfield, and grew even more powerful.

– This is my task, she cried. – These are my nights.

She swiped the nursery, touching all the power there, growing further in understanding and scope. The buildup burned within her. She felt its potency long before, many endless moments before it happened. Her heartrate picked up. Everyone's did. The thing within lingered as the pressure grew. There was a hurdle, a dam, a threshold keeping the power from expressing itself. She felt it just before it happened, felt the dam breaking, felt herself and the others crossing the threshold.

What wasn't tangible, wasn't matter rose from the flesh it inhabited. The astral form of the twenty and two roamed free outside its shell. There was initial euphoria as they left inhibition behind. A chill far colder than absolute zero entered them from within. Thought was action, action was instantaneous here in the space between worlds. She had learned so much, gained so much power since the first time she (Jill) had done this, and she (Stacy) had found her exhausted on the dusty loft.

But this was different. That had been random, a hesitant tryout. This was well-prepared burning, directed purpose.

Twenty and two split up, and spread across the planet, staying together, burning as one. She (Jill) blinked, she (Stacy) opened her eyes wide, and she (Lillith) opened her true eyes, and the Goddess saw the world and everything and everyone in it.

She saw the one and twelve, saw them as a group and as individuals, how they watched the world with greedy eyes, how that was almost all they did. They were destroyers with a one-track wicked, cruel and calculating mind.

A giant warehouse burst into flames. Those working inside scurried outside and ran like rabbits when the flames seemed to reach for them, to lick their backs.

Everything was brief flashes, out here in the shadowland. They persevered hanging on with their teeth, with the greatest ease. The Centipede headquarters were surrounded by snipers. Those guarding the entrance realized that something was afoot when they spotted several groups moving in on the building from several directions. They prepared themselves and their weapons with steady hands and calm minds. They had experience with this or events similar to this. It had happened several times the past decades.

The veteran on the closest roof fired the first shot at the man walking in front of the insurrection. Nothing happened. He frowned. Something hit him in the back. A sharp pain made him cry out. He realized that he had been shot. He attempted to turn around, to confront the invisible enemy, but he had been paralyzed. The bullet had hit his spine. He crouched there and heard muffled cries of pain from many spots around him. One of his men fell with a loud scream, and hit the streets far below. He watched the insurrectionists gather below, watched them enter, invade the building unopposed.

Lillith watched them with a pleased smile, as they roamed the building, as they searched through it, as they fetched any kind of information gathered there. There were both hardcopies and digital files available. The information would soon be broadcast on all true independent channels, verified through countless sources independent of each other.

People witnessed wide-eyed a spectacle developing in their street. Linda Cousin and her warriors fetched well-dressed people from their offices and dragged and pushed them to the middle of the road. Some of them fought. They were beaten in hard and brutal ways, and quickly being reduced to wet rags.

– They're establishment shills, The White Rose cried, – eager tools of the wealthy and powerful.

Barrels were rolled out to the middle of the street. They were opened. The stench of tar ripped into everyone's nostrils. The men and women in suits resisted a bit more when being dragged there. They were beaten hard, and resisted no more.

– This is not punishment, Glory shouted. – This is marking them for future punishment. Their names and faces will be household all over the world. They will be pariahs. Remember them.

The captives were lowered into the barrels, into the tar. They were being pushed beneath the surface. They spit and coughed when they were being dragged back up.

Feathers were sowed on the ground. It covered it from the barrels to both sidewalks. The unfortunate suits were pulled from the tar and rolled in feathers. Massive applause echoed between the buildings.

It lasted for quite some time. To them, it seemed that much longer. They were finally released. Linda and her warriors retreated back into the shadows and the mist.

– These are the one plus twelve, Linda stated in a communique released simultaneously on the Internet. – The names of their many supporters currently being exposed and tarred and feathered will follow later. They are important names. The Thousand Feet has indeed had a crucial impact on human society for centuries, and its Cabal even more so. Let's not forget that and also note the names of their predecessors. But let's also remember vividly that this is merely one power center among many, remember that the system is our enemy, not primarily its most eager servants.

It flashed across the screen as she spoke the names aloud.

CHARGED AND CONVICTED FOR

CRIMES AGAINST HUMANITY
AGAINST ALL LIFE ON EARTH

Cole Stephenson
Dusan Machajev
Bass Perlman
Clayton Powers
Taylor Lowell
Eleanor Rothridge
Grant Stevens
Rudy Paul Jones
Cole Slater
Yah Wi Lin
Allison Stone
Sherman Roberts
Calvin Levine

She descended on his private island like a hawk, very casual, very calm. Cole Stephenson frowned, noticing the moment before she manifested in front of him. Her spirit form appeared to him in all its glory. Chill and heat flowed through him.

– You cut your hair, you, the hippy billionaire. That is funny!

He glanced around with cold sweat on his brow.

– The power dampeners are in place, she shrugged. – They are working, but not on me.

She looked good humored at him.

– I used to work for you once. You let us go eight weeks without pay during the pandemonium closedown. One of my friends died.

He was an open book to her. She peeled off each thought like an onion.

It's amazing. I understand you, all of you so well, now. It is as if I never struggled with it.

She undressed him thought by thought.

– We will dismantle your kingdom, dismantle you, everything you are, until you're nothing but a squirt on a hot rock.

Yes, the launch codes for the nuclear ballistic missiles were sent out, but nothing happened. How strange…

We will not allow you to implement your burned earth tactics. We will do everything to fight civilization, except full exchange of nuclear ballistic missiles. Such weapons will never again become a threat to humanity.

The fact that the Cabal had made an effort into lounging nuclear missiles was also shared extensively with everyone.

They moved in on to the Thousand Feet subsidiaries. She shared it with him, like her fellow traveling spirits shared it with the others.

– We will meet again, of course, she said softly, – but by then, robbed of your privileges, your entire support network will be gone. If you choose to continue your horrible war against the rest of us, you will merely be one single fart in our tasty soup, hardly even a nuisance anymore.

Other people on the island, his servants and sycophants had started noticing that something was happening. She raised a hand. All electricity, all the computers, all the electronic equipment started failing. Cries of distress began filling the heated air. A mighty wave hurled Stephenson and his closest associates at the nearby white wall. Screams of terror roared in many sore ears. The scenario repeated itself at thirteen spots across the planet.

A spear hurled itself from what seemed like nowhere, and penetrated Stephenson's arm, nailing him to the wall. More screams echoed from those around him.

Lillith stopped the relentless barrage a bit, smiling to him, to them all.

– Do you know how satisfying it is to finally put a stop to you and your horrors, and make you suffer terribly in the bargain?

He and the others looked at her through a thick haze of pain, and they began to remember, and she grinned when she spotted the dawning awareness in their eyes.

Another spear hurled itself through the air from nowhere, and hit his other arm, all the others' arms. They were all nailed to the wall. The pain was engraved in features, in their screams and wails.

– This is merely a tiny retribution for the massive pain you and people like you have caused and are causing.

Humanity saw it, experienced it through the broadcast of powerful minds. They saw, experienced poverty, starvation, hunger, wars, assassinations, torture and oppression.

The thunder rolled, the bells tolled each time another spear penetrated soft flesh, beating hearts hammering flesh from within. Cole Stephenson and the other twelve faded away, until they drew their final breath and eyes turned vacant and dead. Raven Moonstar, ancient and new chuckled in wicked triumph.

– I know the futility of it, know it isn't futile as long as we acknowledge that. We open the door wide. All we have to do is step through.

Thirteen events repeated themselves across the world. Many smaller accompanied them.

The power approached its limits, burning itself out. They kept pushing beyond those inevitable limits, until everything dissolved into nothing, and only the white pain noise remained.

Twenty and two crouched on the floor, burned out, exhausted, feeling more dead than alive, slowly regaining their vitality and strength.

Current human society remained, basically untouched. The all-too common frustration returned to them with a vengeance.

Others moved in to fill the void. The Phoenix Green Earth handled them as they appeared. They kept up the pressure, the high level of vigilance and awareness. Until there were no more obvious candidates.

And when the attack ended, everything had changed, nothing had truly changed.

The current inhuman local, domestic and global society took a beating, but absorbed the damage. Its defenses shook, but held.

– The system is both astonishingly resilient and brittle, Martin Keller said, – with countless redundancies in place. As long as it is there, it is almost impossible to affect. A theory I read once stated that one had to kill off millions of opportunists to keep positions of power and oppression from being filled.

His words created unpleasant chains of thoughts in them all.

– We expected this to happen, Stacy shrugged, still having trouble speaking properly. – This was just one more opening gambit on our all-out assault on the system, the Machine. Our long-term plans remain active.

All media, including the much-battered establishment news outlets were filled with material about the world-wide, very public executions, and even hinted about their mysterious, chilling aspects.

Many people didn't forget about the strange visions and sensations of that day. The world had changed, and kept changing.

All the vile deeds of the Cabal and the Thousand Feet were exposed, and thoroughly documented. Tales of brainwashing, torture and assassinations and manipulation of national and global elections were relayed to humanity at large. The big picture was thoroughly explored. The documentation was put on repeat. It was impossible not to catch it, to have it burned into the cerebral cortex.

There was a notable and growing unrest of an increasingly restless population. An even higher number of people joined those already protesting in the streets. Establishment media attempted to spin the information already out there, the added exposure of an already straining society, but the many waves kept growing to a deluge.

Another field office of Phoenix Green Earth Media was bombed, and this time with people still inside. It had become like a battlefield. Bodies dead and alive littered the ground and the remains of the floor everywhere in the vicinity of the destroyed building.

– The president condemns this cowardly attack on the free press, Dana Perino, the White House Press Secretary declared on his next briefing. – We have been given reliable intel, clear indications that this was indeed an al Qaeda attack.

– Any idea of their possible… motivation? A fairly aware establishment reporter asked, surprising both himself and others.

– I think we have pretty much established that these… people don't need a reason, Perino snorted. – They just want to blow things up, and in their dark jealousy do all they can to destroy our freedom.

– We've seen no evidence that this was a foreign operation, Phillip Caine said at another press briefing later that day.

– Who do you believe did it, then? An establishment reporter asked him.

– That remains to be seen, Phillip said calmly. – Rest assured that we will expose those behind it.

A change, one more watershed moment had manifested in human life.

The establishment stooges on primetime television and cable looked downright shitty. They hesitated before they spoke in low voices. A commentator suggested that they looked like they feared their own shadows. It spread from there and to human society as a whole. The stock market took a dive. They watched it on a computer screen with grim satisfaction.

– The stock market is a good indicator of otherwise hardly visible changes, Lillian mused.

– It is certainly encouraging, Jason acknowledged.

– We did the impossible, Lillian said, – and it still wasn't enough.

They felt down, but the fire kept burning within. They kept putting one foot in front of the other.

– We made one giant leap forward today, Ted stated.

As usual, he had put everything in perspective for them.

His determination, and their own kept them going like that troubled river.

He noticed later that they were studying him even more than usual, as if something new had dawned on them, and he realized that it had, and that small moment had done that.

– Jason is different from the rest, too, Liz said softly to him when they were alone, – and so are Nick, Carla, Stacy, Gabi and several others. We're a virtual plethora of variety.

– You sound so proud, he said.

– So do you! She stated.

The Dark River kept flowing down from the mountain towards the sea.

Identifying those behind the bombing proved relatively easy. Exposing them as government agents proved even easier. They resigned the day after the exposure.

– This was a military exercise going wrong, nothing more, another government official stated with a straight face. – It's very regrettable, but shit happens, you know.

The man chuckled, and the gathered establishment journalists actually chuckled with him.

One more scandal of many added itself to the Bush-administration's rapsheet.

The agents were just charged with a misdemeanor, in the tradition of brutal and murderous police officers.

– They're just patsies, Phillip Caine shrugged at another press conference. – Even if it, by some miracle should be true that they acted without actual approval, the true culprits are far higher up, at the very top. We will keep pushing for them to be charged with terrorism, of course. The established tradition giving government officials exemption from being charged to the full extent of the law is just as insane as any other similar practice.

The number of protesters outside the White House grew to unprecedented levels. Washington DC became a besieged city. Similar events took place in other capitals and cities across the globe.

A society on the breaking point broke further.

Ted streamed a videorecording, one going viral immediately.

– The movement and its members are under siege. I'm not telling you anything you don't know here. We're constantly attacked by public and private government and its representatives. They bomb us. The police and law-enforcement in general are hassling us, beating us up and killing us, but as we keep stating; we won't stand for it. We will defend ourselves with all tools at our disposal. To those very representatives, I have this to say: Expect a response every time you assault us and persist in your intimidation tactics. Previous social movements have been destroyed by deceitful and meticulous establishment forces. We're stronger than they were, better prepared to deal with everything you throw at us. We won't stand for it. We will match you action by action, respond in kind to whatever you may dish out. Be aware that we do not acknowledge your power to arrest, detain and kill us. No one should!

The spontaneous protests began not many minutes afterwards. Even more people flooded the streets.

Liz and Ted gathered with a support group at Times Square in New York City.

– We have ongoing, potent dreams, visions, Liz shouted, – about a world free of exploitation and inequality and oppression. The wealthy and the powerful currently ruling this world will not decide our future. *We* will!

There was thunderous applause, loud shouts and a noise of another world. They still heard her voice loud and clear. Then, they heard the music, the beat and the chords, the strange and beautiful discord. Some imagined they saw dark flames dance and expand around the two Warrens' modest human form.

– Picture this in your mind and dreams and self and core, Ted Warren shouted quietly. – You're running through a vast forest, one without end, and there's no destruction, no oppression to suffer anywhere. We're so close, now, closer than we've ever been for thousands of years.

And those listening to his words did picture it, did imagine it with their wide-open eyes.

They heard the terrible and joyous song always there. It repeated itself in constant variations, always the same, never quite the same.

Phoenix didn't turn up its power. There was no need for that. They quite simply… let go.

Everyone on the square and quite a few beyond experienced the powerful sensations and impressions. They ran through the forest. Their five senses accompanied that experience. The kind wind touched their skin. The scent of the air and plants and animals rubbed their nostrils and their buds. They heard and saw everything in a kind of elevated manner. The Phoenix walked among them, even as they remained on the low stage. It was almost too much.

Ted and Liz reined themselves in, their presence turning less imposing. Some choked in relief, others in disappointment.

Gayle Tadero smiled to the camera, to the world. She sat in her studio at an undisclosed location and read from a script.

– This is our list of brutal murder cops exposing themselves. We will present their actions in detail, and their full name and home address. Let's see if their colleagues, their partners in crime stand guard around all those houses. This will continue for quite a while. The list is long and sordid, and more names will be added as we go.

She began the reading and showing. Each face flashing on the screen was accompanied by extensive background information. She began showing signs of fatigue when Phillip Caine replaced her later, as he in turn did, when the next replaced him. They kept it going for days.

Linsey, Lynn, Jane and the other Green Earth Party senators and representatives gathered with Stacy for a press briefing in a Phoenix Green Earth building on Pennsylvania Avenue.

They stepped up on the low platform. Lynn, Linsey and Jane placed themselves behind the microphones.

– We have put forward a proposal in the House to defund and disband the police on the federal level, Lynn declared. – We have no illusions that it will gain a majority, but we see this as only the first tryout. There will be many more later. We will also work on state and local level to implement it and also to dissolve all police departments, and to rebuild from scratch a community-based patrol working with its neighborhood, not against it. All of these people will live in the given neighborhood they're patrolling. They will be invested in it and not work as an invasive force.

– All killings of unarmed people by police officers will be reexamined, Jane said, – and charges will be made, and it is more than likely that there will be a massive number of convictions, all of them long overdue.

The flow of questions began a few minutes later, if possible, even more agitated than most Phoenix Green Earth's meeting the establishment media.

– But police officers are our protectors? One establishment journalist stated puzzled.

A loud buzz from all the other «journalists» followed his rhetorical «question».

– They are our bullies, our terrorists and murderers, Stacy said. – As stated, they have escaped the consequences of their actions for far too long, but no longer. They will no longer be safe from prosecution.

– Police organizations have stated that they will no longer provide security at your rallies…

– I've got a newsflash for you and them, Linsey grinned. – They never have. We don't need them. No one needs them, except those bloated with wealth and power.

The briefing ended like most of such briefings ended these days; with mute end dissatisfied «journalists», and with the recordings living their own lives on truly alternative media and social media across the world.

262

Ted listened to the tapes again. He didn't need to do so, as he knew every word by heart. He kept listening, in the hope of gaining illumination, understanding. It had become a habit, an empty repetition giving him ever less peace.

Stacy and Michelle's bellies grew big. They both began growing occasionally distant as they communicated with their children. Both needed to be cared for during their most distracted moments.

Time worked different for him and Liz compared to the others. By the time a given notable event happened, they had experienced a variation of it, a set of probabilities narrowing to one many times.

– Is this how Ethel experiences it as well? Liz wondered. – Or is her ability more precise, more like... Mike's?

They shared each other's visions, doing so on a regular basis, now. It didn't offer further illumination.

– Stacy's is more imprecise, random, he mused, – is coming to her in dreams or similar.

– While Gabi is practically experiencing hers, but mostly through manual use of her orbs.

– It's becoming muddled again, as the future becomes increasingly unpredictable, he said, – as if everything is coalescing into a future crux, one where all possibilities are colliding into an explosive climax.

– We've experienced that before, she said.

Their thoughts returned to Padstow and what they could never truly leave behind.

– But we know more this time, he said, – from Nick and the others and the diaries collaborating our visions.

Hands grabbed hands grabbed hands. They and the rooms turned quiet.

Stacy and Michelle gathered with the others with bursting bellies at the shore of Fire Lake when the time was nigh. Everyone sat there, waiting for their water to break. Liz and Ted watched them and shared their experience of it with them in their way, as Stacy did in hers.

– I'm nervous, Michelle admitted, as if she had swallowed something vile.

Everyone laughed. Jason and Val caressed and comforted her. Val had begun to show herself. She looked with deep affection at her paternal sister and brother.

– It is amazing isn't it, Liz said, – how well Michelle handled her.

– Amazing, Ted acknowledged. – They're like two negatives cancelling each other.

– It was the most probable outcome, Liz said. – I just didn't understand how it could be... until now.

Michelle and Stacy's water broke simultaneously. The smile broke on their face, and they walked into the lake together. Stacy gasped a bit as the surface caught fire, as her control slipped. Michelle, soaked in sweat, gasped for breath. Stacy rubbed her cheek.

– Your tyke, with both his parents being a Warren, is a bit of a bother, but you should be able to handle him.

– Praise the wise Mother of Demons, Michelle growled in an ancient tongue, kissing the other's hand. – Hallowed be her name. We would all be lost without her.

Stacy's features softened. She kissed the other on the brow. They began making out at a slow, pleasant mode. The labor pains came in waves. Others surrounded them and comforted them further. The making out turned into slow sex. Pain became pleasure.

– Those not doing this miss out on something infinitely precious, Andrea gasped.

Stacy experienced it all through her for a while, how she experienced everything in slow motion, how she could savor it all, the entire experience.

Then, the flow of the Dark River resumed its common speed.

Relax, she told her anxious daughter, it isn't much longer to wait, now, just a bit longer, down the rabbit hole.

Michelle screamed, as another, more powerful flare of pain surged through her. She crouched. The others held her, comforted her with thousands of tiny touches. Stacy screamed. She could not help but share that as well. Her midwives handled it. They had grown used to handle powerful telepaths giving birth.

I never get tired of watching this, Liz sniffed.

She grew a bit eager, and the others noticed that she and Ted were there, with them.

Beth dried Michelle's brow.

Feel pain, woman, feel joy, she soothed the suffering giant.

They split two pairs of legs, widening further what was already widening. The contractions began in earnest.

– You may start doing the actual work, now, Val told Michelle.

Michelle sent her the pointed stare. Then, she screamed again. Stacy screamed again. They became synchronized, moving and breathing as one.

– Yes, Goddess, Michelle gasped.

Small heads appeared between wet thighs. Tiny bodies plopped into the warm water. Beth cut two umbilical cords. Loud infant screams pierced everyone's ears. Stacy and Michelle devoured the placenta as they were brought to shore. They joined all the other new mothers resting at the edge of the dark forest.

They rested comfortably later. Their newborn sucked greedily on their nipples. Ears were filled with the sound of sucking. Their eyes stayed closed, but they still saw everything around them. They sensed even more. Michelle and Stacy sighed content.

– I love this, Michelle said startled. – I just love this!

Val kissed her. Jason kissed her. And everything was right with the world.

8

The unrest picked up further. It spiked in both the likely and the most unlikely of places. Establishment media presented it as riots as usual, while the many independent outlets, among them Phoenix Green Earth showed the police breaking the skulls and bones and shooting of unarmed protesters.

264

– This shouldn't be hard to report correctly, Gayle said. – We see time and time again how aggressive cops attack and kill peaceful protesters.

– Calls to defund and abolish the police are rising across the nation, across the world, Phillip said. – And this time, there's a definite sense of it not being a passing notion, but something lasting. The old institutions are breaking down. People's trust in them isn't merely waning, but dissolving completely.

– We have gathered a number of people in the studio tonight to discuss that and similar issues, Gayle said. – We ask «what good are they»? What good are the Senate, the House of Representatives, the judiciary, the police and military? First of all, we welcome Senator Lynn Fredericks. Great to have you here, Lynn. Hope you didn't have too much trouble finding our studio.

– Glad to be here, Gayle, Lynn said sheepishly, – and no, I didn't have too much trouble…

– You're a newly elected US Senator for Massachusetts, Phillip said. – Perhaps you have a fairly positive view of current United States institutions compared to many other US citizens?

– I can safely say I do not, Lynn stated calmly. – We in the Green Earth Party favor working for a true alternative both outside and inside the electoral process. We're not locked to outdated modes of political work.

– If I understand you correctly, you don't have much respect for your fellow senators?

– How can I? They're totally out of tune with reality, as usual, and have only harsh words for all the people with justifiably strong concerns in this country and the world. Even those very few in the two main parties showing limited support for the protesters offer hardly more than platitudes. They don't change their voting, their undying support for the bloated military and police budgets and the ongoing rewards they grant the wealthy and powerful. This country and the world are in desperate need for a reboot if humanity shall have any change of a life, and they offer nothing but their outdated solutions and more massive corruption.

The roar of the large crowd hit Ted Warren like a soft wave, and he returned it to the gathering stronger than he had received it, and the crowd went wild. Betty and Jennifer and the others standing there with him smiled in something resembling ecstasy.

He raised his hand, and it turned quiet, as if he had waved a magick wand. The fireeyes looked at them, at them all with its beyond penetrating stare. They heard the music, the discord.

– The riders come at dawn, he began, – come when the sentries and a weary populace are dog-tired and unable to keep their eyes open anymore.

Soldiers screamed and howled outside Eboracum, outside Jórvík, outside Old York, fighting and dying by the blood-soaked wall.

– The riders came long ago, and they stayed, he spat. – They work constantly on our resolve and our will, making us docile and unwilling to lift our head in pride, to raise our sword to defend ourselves. We have allowed them to do so for so long that we've almost forgotten what it means to be truly free, to enjoy true freedom as easy as we breathe. We feared we had lost our aggression, that it was bred out of us, that we had lost the ability to fight against the true oppressors, and they felt confident that we were correct. I'm happy to report to you that we were both wrong.

The loud cheer filled the square and the many adjacent streets and alleys.

– Our fight isn't against a foreign power or the various outcasts in this country, in any country. Of course, it isn't. Our true fight is against those who would be lords, kings and queens, who would even entertain the thought of ruling and/or dominating others.

The cheers and applause and the stamping of the feet took off. It never seemed to fade. When it finally did, Jennifer stepped forward.

– We will march to City Hall, she shouted, – and nothing and no one will stop us.

She was wearing a Che Guevara cap and a variation of the original Black Panther Party uniform, carrying herself with audacious pride and the incarnation of wrath.

They stepped down from the low platform. The march began. Ted, Betty, Jennifer and the others marched in front. The police flanked them on both sides, every step of the route. The singing and the beating of drums and subsequent moves began in earnest. The march turned into a dance.

– Look at the boys and girls in blue, Betty shouted, – how ridiculous they look.

Everyone heard her. Loud laughter followed her patronizing statement. The boys and girls remained enraged and smug.

– They're really looking forward to something, Jennifer said to Ted.

Yes, the officers dressed in combat gear had their orders, and they had been given well in advance, and were not in doubt. The fuse had been lit, and the slow explosion had already begun.

All this, the entire setup strengthened Ted further. Power surged through him.

Betty and Jennifer had no trouble picking that up. Their smugness beat that of the officers by a mile.

Ted saw it from the air as they approached a given point on the route. The police prepared its well-prepared action. Sometimes, they would attack outright, or they would start firing unprovoked, indiscriminately into the crowd, but today they prepared the «kettle-maneuver», a way of surrounding and squeezing the protesters between the massive numbers of police officers. The Phoenix Green Earth had previously sought to avoid such a scenario, but now they deliberately allowed it. «this long, but no further», the police shouted silently at them. Ted smiled. He felt such a rush, and had to pull himself together to not go overboard.

He blocked the cops, snapping his fingers and breaking the kettle. They hit a barrier and could advance no further. They hammered empty air and looked completely ridiculous. He watched as their features twisted themselves into puzzlement and growing frustration and abject fear. The protesters just walked past them, while they were forced to stand there and watch. There were condescending laughter and comments.

Ted sensed the buildup as a tangible force. It kept strengthening him, but also made it more difficult to control his power.

– I've had ENOUGH of this, a policeman shouted.

266

He drew his gun and shot the policeman closest to him.

It didn't turn quiet. Perhaps it would have if it had happened ten years ago, but now people had become so accustomed to brutal and insane actions by police officers during protests that they hardly reacted.

The officer shot another colleague. Another rushed him. He shot him as well. Someone shot him. He was felled by several bullets from all sides. Some missed and hit other officers.

– YOU ASSHOLES, another shouted, and began firing indiscriminately at his colleagues.

It descended into total chaos from that point.

And now, there was unrest, the first signs of panic.

– Stay calm, and keep walking, Ted shouted. – Let's leave them to their insanity.

Total chaos erupted around the protesters. Ted managed to deflect most of the bullets, but not all. Some participants in the march were hit.

– Carry the injured, Ted shouted.

Beth made her way to those with the most serious injuries. She slipped through the crowd with a sweet smile, and they let her pass. A man gasped for breath, close to death. She grabbed him and used her healing power to the max. She shook in pain. The bullet erupted from the wound, and the wound closed. Those closest to her grew wide-eyed and stunned. The man she saved even more so.

The participants in the march removed themselves ever so slowly, or so it seemed from the calamity in the street they had left. There were no more police officers guarding them.

Jennifer jumped on Ted's shoulders and stood there, balancing easily.

– We will march to City Hall, she shouted. – Pass it on.

Her message was repeated down the line with anxious and excited cries.

Everyone kept looking around them, kept stretching their necks to the point of it becoming painful, kept looking for cops, and didn't spot any. They kept hearing the sound of guns being fired, but only as distant, unimportant thunder.

Beth kept healing the injured. Her power soared as well. She hardly needed to strain herself. It got away from her, too. She noticed that everyone standing close to her became visibly excited, as the boundaries between her various powers were breaking down, and Aphrodite grew ascendant. More and more people grew aroused.

– The Goddess of unbridled passion, someone hailed her.

The call was echoed through the crowd. One of those she had healed, a woman began caressing her. Beth freed herself easily enough, with a skill born of long experience.

They reached City Hall Square. Ted and the others jumped up on the base of a monument. Beth joined them there, red-faced and aroused.

Ted raised a hand and the assembly turned quiet.

– We're not responsible for this carnage, he shouted. – Countless recordings spread on the Internet as we speak will show that. We did nothing except utilizing our constitutional right to protest. We came here to protest against grave injustice.

Now, through the total insanity exhibited by the local forces of law and order, one more of hundreds of reasons has been added to that.

– We were invited here, Betty shouted. – The city council did that by its irresponsible and thoroughly immoral actions. They have, in fact sent us countless invitations, and we will take them up on it. We like it here, and we will stay, stay as long as we choose.

All of them stepped down from the very temporary platform, and joined the people gathered on the square. The people in the crowd smothered them, touched them briefly. Only a few of them exhibited anything even resembling old-fashioned hero-worship or worship at all.

– I'm styling, My Lord, Betty assured him. – I've grown powerful, too. I can take the pressure from the massive crowd easily.

She had caught his concerned glance of course.

It made him smile.

She and Jennifer, on the other hand, could not stop worshiping him. That made his concern return. Betty looked good humored at him.

They set up camp, several camps across the square. Everyone started devouring the food and drink they had brought, everyone so very hungry and enjoying it so much. The police stayed away. There wasn't a single police officer or similar in sight.

Betty and Beth returned from a tour of the square.

– Not a single provocateur in sight, Beth reported.

She looked flustered, and he easily understood why. People had already started the golden copulations in the streets. They were fucking unrestrained, both nude and not.

– Many people call me by name, she stated.

– They do that with most of us these days and nights, honey, Jennifer said. – People either remember or they learn. It's good!

Summer twilight descended on the City Hall Plaza. Ted sensed Liz and those accompanying her during similar circumstances at another public space, the two shifting and blurring in his mind. Outsiders brought more food and drink to the occupiers. Most of them stayed. Song, dance and music filled the plaza, the square, the occupied house or territory.

«Advanced» establishment enforcements are on its way, Nick informed him.

Ted had already sensed the disturbance in the pattern, the ether. He didn't need to close his eyes halfway anymore. All the old tricks aiding them had become redundant. He watched as out of town SWAT teams and federal special forces arrived in non-commercial planes. Stewart and Ruth were on hand at the airport. Ted saw through their eyes as they held hands and prepared the warm welcome with excited smiles on their lips.

The men and women found and checked their weapons as they proceeded to the vehicles that would take them to town.

– They're coming, he informed the others. – Some of them are, at least.

Betty's ecstatic laughter echoed pleasantly in his ears.

One member of the special forces seemed to freeze momentarily. He yelped in shock and terror. Stewart and Ruth had taken total control of his body. When he directed his machinegun at his colleagues, the two young Warrens were controlling him. They made him pull the trigger and shoot his fellow team members. Stewart and Ruth aimed for the head. Some of the bullets hit the armor protecting their body, but lots of them hit the mark.

The others finally managed to react and return the fire. He went down in a hail of bullets. Stewart and Ruth picked a woman to take his place. The carnage continued. Most of the federal «aid» to the occupied cities were decimated in similar ways.

People watched it on their phones and on television sets in store windows.

– This has happened before, an overexcited reporter practically screamed into his microphone, – among other places in New York City in 1979, events leading to police forces practically evacuating the entire Manhattan Island. The reason for this collective... madness remains unclear. Independent researchers have speculated that the generally violent mindset of the officers and agents has led to them tipping over into mental instability and overwhelming rage.

They were coming, the few special forces members left that had managed to slip through the net the Phoenix Green Earth leadership had cast. Their vehicles stopped a few blocks away and made the final preparations to begin the massacre.

– They haven't been told, Betty said. – They're unluckily unaware of the fate of their colleagues.

Their nightmare began the moment they stepped out of the vehicle. One of them started firing at the others. When that person had been stopped, another picked up the slack. The mighty assault force was reduced to Swiss Cheese in minutes. The stench of flesh and blood dominated the scene completely.

All government forces in the area, stricken with terror, pulled back, returning in a state of beyond shock and terror to the dark hole they had emerged from. Wild cheers erupted among the protesters when the news reached them. It went on for minutes, fading only slowly. In Ted's ears and mind, it did continue far longer.

– They believe they have control, he cried. – They don't realize what we have realized long ago; that control is an illusion.

There were more cheering, a bit more muted.

Large bonfires were constructed from dry wood. The Dance began. It turned wild in just a few minutes.

– APHRODITE, the crowd chanted, – COME DANCE WITH US AND MAKE IT GOOD FOR US, AND WE WILL MAKE IT GOOD FOR YOU.

Beth Alver walked to them, walked into their midst and raised their fervor to a downright savage level.

Jennifer and Betty Danced before Ted. They undressed and displayed themselves to him.

– Phoenix has no reason to worry, they choired. – Our worship will not ruin our service. It will only make us better at it. Our passion will not diminish our reason.

They approached him from two sides, pushing themselves at him, giving him sultry kisses on all possible spots of his skin. He undressed. They helped him with low chuckles of anticipation and thick, thick desire. Other females joined them.

The low chuckle of desire rose to a roar in his mind.

The roar of the square and beyond bloated his mind.

Everything was filmed, and the blatant lack of concern by the participants because of that fact made it even sweeter, an even better experience for him. He lost count of how many people that touched him. Everyone left a tiny piece of themselves in him, in his boiling cauldron.

A young woman squeezed his cock with her large lips, making certain he emptied himself in her. She laughed in profound happiness.

– I will carry your child, she whispered in his ears, – a child of God.

That did bother him a bit, but he didn't allow it to rock him.

There were countless others loving him without worshiping him.

His power seethed and burned in waves afterwards from him being bloated with energy. It felt... pleasant. The higher level did no longer make him lose control. He sat at the center of the circle with the others of the Janus Clan present. He sat more or less still, with his face frozen in one direction, even though those in the circle imagined he turned often, and faced all people around him.

– The cities, all human life must be transformed, he began. – We will coat the buildings in growth, bringing the wilderness to the city instead of the city to the wilderness. It's long overdue. We must rewild, reverse the horrible destruction of civilization if humanity and life on Earth shall survive. It's so easy to do. The horrible forces of the establishment don't fight the destruction, because they are its proponents, because they will lose their power if it ends. If all food and energy and crucial services can be attained within walking distance, everyone will become self-sustained, and that is a big no, no to those in charge.

– It is so great, such great simplicity, a girl spoke up. – And such a great way to reject and ignore the current society, and still fight it. If we all manage to become self-sustained, with food and electricity and the works, all important things, the establishment would have no hold on us anymore.

It dawned on more and more of those present, and those watching it across the world what was actually being discussed. Excitement grew by the second, and even more by the minute, and by the hour many had already started discussing and planning and acting on it.

– Modern technology makes it easier to implement by those not trained to be self-sustained, Jennifer said, – but ultimately it isn't necessary. This can be implemented anywhere, in societies with any technological level. Those in charge want to keep the awareness of such beautiful simplicity from the majority of people. Let's stop them from doing that, from doing that, too.

– Money will become obsolete, Betty said. – Trade will become unnecessary. I'm not saying it will not exist, but at a lower level, no longer needed for survival or even to thrive.

– The establishment will not accept this development, of course, Ted said. – They will become even more desperate and violent the more they lose their hold on people. We witness that every day, no matter the alternative society we're attempting to make. Even private gardens are illegal some places. We must become even better

270

at countermeasures. We must work even harder in our day-to-day life to implement the thousand dreams.

One more message of change and transformation spread more or less uncensored across the modern world. The establishment media kept serving its propaganda against it, but previous conclusions held: It had lost a significant chunk of its bite.

In some cities, the police changed tactics. They didn't use guns, but fell back to their old tactics of shields and clubs. The protesters met them with scutum shields, with wall shields and spears, with more than two-thousand-year-old warfare. The cops just didn't reach them. And each time they got close, they were stabbed. The teargas grenades were thrown into canisters filled with water by people wearing protective gloves. A gloved hand covered the opening while the cannister was shaken. The gas didn't get out and lost its potency. The police, deprived of their final tool of terror, were forced to withdraw. The huge crowd of protesters remained.

A bunch of militarized cops invaded an occupied building. The moment they stepped through the door, they were transported to Timbuktu. Almost all of them had stepped through before it dawned on those left that something was wrong, that people vanished before their eyes.

Those vanishing through the portal appeared in Timbuktu in the middle of the day, subjected to the hot, searing sun. They looked bewildered, beyond bewildered at each other. Many of them took a permanent leave of their senses at that very moment. The rest of them never quite recovered from their ordeal. Most of them would never wear a uniform again.

Several cities defunded and abolished the police and organized inclusive community watches in its place.

– The new neighborhood watches initiative has been a resounding success, Gayle reported. – Even though there have been initial birth pains, the number of deaths and injuries have fallen dramatically. Most of the unrest has been due to the aggressive and violent actions of former police officers.

People stood in line to be interviewed.

– We've waited for so long for this to happen, and now it finally has, a black woman said brightly. – It's such a wonderful development. We have or will soon have everything we need right here. We will continue cooperating with other communes in order to build a network of free communities.

The headlines in establishment media screamed its poison at people.

COMMUNISTS OVERTAKING AMERICA

There were talks and joint proposals in the Senate and House of Representatives from the Democratic Party and the Republican Party to outlaw inclusive community watches and defunding and abolishing police departments. It met with massive opposition.

– We will certainly do everything in our power to make certain those proposals are not made into law, Senator Linsey Kendall from Colorado stated in front of the Lincoln statue.

The Green Earth Party mayor in Denver was just as adamant.

– We will not accept federal interference in this matter. The joint defunding and abolishing of the police and implementing inclusive community watch initiatives are the right action for our city, and we will defend it with everything we are.

Other voices across the nation joined her.

The black Green Earth Party mayor of St Louis and many others joined the protesters and the watch in their neighborhood in their vigil.

Right wing militia attempted to patrol the streets, but was pushed back to their own, isolated neighborhoods.

There were a few altercations and gunfights, but the militia pulled back quickly.

– These guys are cowards at heart, a neighborhood community defender stated. – They are eager to shoot down unarmed people, but run when they're met with true resistance.

Ted and Liz met new recruits in the forest. They stood at the bottom of the Hollow and the recruits sat in a half moon. The Phoenix seethed and burned in everyone's awakened senses.

A boy asked a question filled with hope.

– With the new awakening and all, haven't we won already?

– No, current human society is dominated by centrist fanaticism, Ted replied. – That doesn't go away overnight. The current final confrontation is still coming, and the conflict, the fight for true freedom is unending. The threat of oppression is very much present even after thousand years without it.

The Phoenix overwhelmed everyone present. Everyone fought to handle it, gasping in anxiety and awe.

– Life will always be a struggle, Liz said with a fist raised to her face, – but we *can* make the challenges stimulating instead of oppressive, creative instead of stupefying. The fire within is worth any sacrifice to keep burning.

Everyone, including those with limited senses watched how the two of them shared a shape of fire and shadow, how it danced and seethed between them.

– You will do your best, Ted stated calmly, – your very best. You will never bend for the forces set on destroying your spirit. You will swear on that, to us, to yourselves.

– I SWEAR!

The mighty roar echoed through the forest and the concrete jungle with equal strength.

9

A video trended on the Internet. It showed several human heads displayed on a wall.

– These are all people that have been hunting many animals to extinction and close to it, the voice said.

Footage was shown of the people on the wall while they fired at wild animals from a distance, and had photographs taken of themselves and the dead prey.

– We have entered the Sixth Great Mass Extinction Event, one similar to the meteor extinguishing the dinosaurs. Humanity is doing this. We have become like a cosmic disaster. Humanity as a species is doing it, but I have chosen to highlight these bastards. I'm happy to report that others are focusing on other areas.

The woman paused a bit, before ending the video.

– As you can see, there is room for more, far more heads on this wall. They will be placed there in the coming months. I'm just one of many. There are many people hunting the false hunters. Expect us.

Ted and Liz were dreaming the old dream of buildings rising in pristine wilderness. Their foremost night terror made them squirm in horror. They watched as the relentless machine destroyed ever more land, ever more of Earth's remaining wild nature.

– The vibrant raven cries loud enough to be heard in the loudest noise, the blackbird in their dream cried happily.

They frowned. Ravens were their friends. The beautiful black bird should not be in such a good mood.

Then, the nature of their dream changed. They noticed it, a watershed moment, from one tick to one tock.

The old, exciting dream of crumbling buildings returned, and they gasped in joy. The fast march of buildings, a fast-moving jaw gobbling wild nature wholesale crumbled to dust before their burning eyes. The violent, destructive process they had witnessed with such despair during many lives turned around and began reversing itself. The gray faded and in its place returned forests and moors and mountains and moist jungle. A loud shout of happiness rose from millions of throats.

The endless mist and dust cleared, and they watched the core of corruption and destruction appear in its midst. The giant, shiny Machine towering tall enough to pierce the sky began decaying, began fading away like dew before the morning sun.

They woke up with a huge, content grin on their lips.

Karine practically glowed with visible excitement when she looked at the people gathered in the large hall from her low platform.

– We will try something new tonight, she began. – Thank you so much for coming all of you. You show up in unprecedented numbers these days. I can safely claim that it will be worth your while.

She was met with loud applause. Some of those present frowned, as if there was something happening, something they couldn't quite catch or fathom.

– This is a great moment to me, she grinned. – I can finally, with this tiny device, do some of the stuff many of my friends and fellow warriors can do naturally.

– What is it? A girl braving her own insecurity asked.

– It is a communication box, but also far more. We got it, confiscated it from the aliens visiting us, or rather leaving us twenty years ago. They used this and similar technology to simulate paranormal powers. They never developed such powers themselves, and that was why they were so dedicated, so desperate to examining humanity, why they spent thousands of years here.

A man frowned.

– Didn't they look pretty much like us? How can that be?

The woman on the stage nodded.

– It's a fair question, she acknowledged.

She waited a bit, allowing them to wonder, to wonder a bit longer.

– One basic code of life wrote itself billions of years ago, on a long dead world, seeding the Universe with meteors and meteorites, blasted through eternity and infinity by an exploding star. My guess would be that its «descendants» seeded countless planets with life as well. It isn't unlikely that it has produced similar results on countless worlds.

When she spoke, it was as if they caught far more than mere speech, even far more than mere thoughts. They experienced the story she related, as if they told it, as if they were present, had been present when it happened.

– No matter, she mused, the stated. – The Tachiti froze long ago at an evolutionary dead end. It is hard to tell why. Perhaps they experimented on themselves, blocked their emerging mutant powers by exterminating all mutants of their species. Humanity will not do that. The mutants will at some point become humanity, and will continue to grow into eternity.

They saw that, too, through her fertile imagination, and many pondered the issue for the first time, and there were both despair, horror and excitement. Some of them left the hall seething with hatred. Most stayed with wonder in their eyes.

– That was a nice introduction, she grinned, eliciting laughter. – It is time to begin.

Then she changed, her entire appearance changed. The grin faded, even as they still imagined it to be there. The sky turned dark, and the sun turned red.

– The sun is going down on the human species, and on all life on Earth.

She stared at them, and her eyes seemed to burn straight through them.

– Researchers from the Queens University, Ontario, measured 22 degrees Celsius at Melville Island in the Arctic in July. The average is 5.

She kept the steady stare at them.

– You know that this is merely one of thousands of similar developments. You know that the birds, the bees and many other species are going extinct, know that human society has killed half of all animals on the planet the last fifty years, know that humanity has become the Sixth Great Mass Extinction Event, has become like a cosmic disaster like the one that wiped out the dinosaurs. The pressure from modern human society has become so massive that there is no longer room for the animals. We kill off all life, and thereby the foundation of our own existence. We commit collective suicide. That is what we're up against, boys and girls.

They experienced more than heard everything she spoke about. Sensations and impressions accompanied her words.

– We must scale back human society, scale it back to a point where it no longer threatens all life on the planet, including ourselves. We must stop our collective suicide. That is the way to proceed, the only way to proceed. We will rewild the entire Earth. We will move the wilderness into the city, stop moving the city into the wilderness. We will no longer shit in our own nest, and by making that choice, we will also create a truly just and equal society without tyranny and oppression. It

274

is that simple, my brothers and sisters.

There was laughter, and cheering and loud declaration of agreement spreading far beyond that hall, beyond that building, and it was merely one of thousands of buildings across the world where the same event took place.

Linsey Kendall, Betty Morgan and other members of the Green Earth Party gathered at Wounded Knee in the Pine Ridge reservation. Linsey and Betty stood on a low platform and held a short press conference.

– Good afternoon, Linsey shouted, not using a microphone or speakers to enhance his powerful voice. – Barack Obama, one of my potential opponents chose to declare his candidacy at a place important to the United State of America. My choice is important to remember the giant stain the brutal European settlers and invaders have made on this land. I will thank the reservation council for allowing us to meet here today, especially since neither I nor most of those joining me here live in the reservation have any connection to it, and since we don't necessarily agree on all political issues.

Establishment journalists had traveled there in force. They knew what would happen. They still retained basic journalist skills.

– I have an announcement for you today, on the fortieth anniversary for the death of Che Guevara, October 9, 2007. I come a little late to the party, but there is more than enough time. Today, right now, I announce my candidacy for the presidency of the United States. I hope to become the Green Earth Party candidate, but I am confident that no matter who our candidate is, he or she will make an excellent effort at winning.

Moat of the natives applauded, though certainly not everyone. The hum rose from the gathered newshounds.

– Previous administrations have tried to ignore our problems, just passing them on. They don't care. They are happy. Their masters are happy. They don't want any significant changes. They have wrapped themselves in the flag, embraced the illusion, the unnatural state of nationality, of nationalism. The time is overdue for someone to change that, and that someone is I, and my fellow members of the Phoenix Green Earth and the Green Earth Party...

The word spread like wildfire across the land, and continued to do so. One more wildfire of many. It did take root, and burned with an intense flame.

Lillith was touring again, accompanied by a small group of aides and guards. They traveled by train or used their private buses. Gabi traveled with her most of the time, except a few detours here and there, when she was called to perform her task as the Keeper of the Gates.

Tamara returned to her old friend Stacy. The two of them embraced each other and might no longer be strangers.

Gabi, though still skinny, had grown tall and also filled out during her fifteenth summer. Lillith looked at her with amusement and poignancy in the black eyes.

– This time I will see you grow up, she stated.

– Yes, Mother, I believe you are correct, the girl acknowledged. – That makes me very happy!

There was the same underlying tension between them. It remained, no matter the situation and mood they found themselves, no matter how many times they touched each other with affection, how many happy and compassionate smiles they exchanged.

Stacy hung suspended in the air in the middle of the bus. She didn't move from that spot no matter what moves the bus made. It was a great relaxation exercise. It sent her consciousness constantly in new and startling directions. New ideas came to her in an uneven flow. Some, she discarded outright. Others, she kept pondering.

She didn't need to strain herself during levitation, even prolonged levitation anymore. The entire exercise felt casual, like walking. She imagined that she did walk, and enjoyed the movement. She felt the desire from all the males and some of the females. It strengthened her. She was practically bathing in powerful emotions. They empowered her like the very lifeforce surging through their flesh.

Jane stepped into her sphere, waiting to be acknowledged. Stacy opened her eyes, and lowered herself to the floor, and gave her her undivided attention.

Jane looked dizzy, but calm up at the tall and big woman. Stacy knew she remembered her, that she knew who she had been before. Lillith remembered her as well. The memory appeared strong and distinct in her total recall.

– It's so strange looking at you, she said, – and at Ted and Liz and the others, and see other people.

– We're the same, Stacy stated. – So are you.

Jane knew that, knew it well.

– There are twenty-one of us, she said abruptly, – and we've followed you, the three of you through many centuries. It still feels strange to say that, but it's true.

Lillith was cast back, in obscure memory. It usually wasn't as strong as Stacy and Jill's memories, but sometimes it was.

THERE ARE THOSE WHO KNOW

She heard herself speak, cry out in a room filled with candles.

– There are those who know, she repeated with a remote look in her eyes.

Everett, sitting by the driver looked up with startled eyes. Tony Farlani, the driver turned his head, and almost drove the bus off the road. Stacy smiled a bit, a sore smile she couldn't quite lose.

Gabi rubbed her cheek affectionately, like a daughter would do to a distressed mother. Tamara did the same, like a sister returning after a long absence.

They reached Detroit. It hadn't improved since their previous visit, was still a prime example of an urban wasteland, with abandoned houses with missing windows occasionally covered with cardboard. She sensed the excited mood almost immediately. People pointed at the bus. Some of them waved. Those in the bus waved back.

– There are hostiles, Stacy reported to her fellow warriors, – but they're staying in the background… for now.

Tony grew a bit agitated. He still had trouble with bursts of anxiety. His life as a drug addict and homeless before The Janus Clan had found him kept haunting him. Everett rubbed his back. Tony looked at him with grateful eyes.

276

– I keep having the dreams, he said.

– You all have them, Lillith said, – but you shouldn't apologize, or feel the need to explain anything to us.

They reached a distinct area, one where the Phoenix Green Earth dominance was even more pervasive, with decorations on walls and windows and sidewalks.

– We come to our own here, Everett stated pleased.

People of all colors stood lined up together with assault rifles in their hands, ready for anything.

Tony stopped outside a large community house. A huge crowd met them. A few departed from that and stepped close as the travelers departed from the bus. A tall woman grabbed Stacy's hands.

– Greetings, Moon Shadow, she said with a loud voice and stubbornly raised eyes, and distinct irony in her voice. – Mara and the People of the Urban Wasteland welcome you.

– Thank you, Mara, Stacy responded. – We're very happy to be here.

The two women kissed lips to lips. Stacy felt her, and knew that the other woman felt her, too, that she could not avoid feeling her. Mara's eyes widened, and even though she fought against the rising awe, she could not quite contain it.

– Goddess, she whispered, and bowed her head, unable to stop the movement.

Stacy sensed her shame. She wanted to rub her cheek, but knew that would only make it worse.

All the travelers exchanged hugs and kisses with the group gathered around Mara. An aloof Gabi treated everyone with visible contempt. Stacy sensed the envy of those standing farther away.

They walked inside, to a large hall with a low stage. Mara noticed her brief glance, very perceptive.

– We know you prefer low stages, Mara said. – That, too, sits well with us.

They entered a room with a large round table covering most of the room. Lillith and her Guard brightened further. They nodded to themselves. Yes, they had come to their own.

A small fountain flowed at the back of the room. It distracted Lillith. She imagined it to be considerably taller and bigger.

The travelers were seated around the table and all the remaining seats were taken by the locals. They were exactly the right number. No one was left out. It made Stacy smile, made everyone smile.

Food and drink were served. Glasses were raised. Cheers were exchanged. The meal began.

Will you be a problem? Stacy asked Mara.

The young woman looked up startled, catching herself with an effort.

No, Goddess, she assured the younger woman with a garbled, noticeably untrained mental voice. Mara will make the Goddess, make herself proud, and she won't allow her insecurities to ruin anything.

A commendable attitude, Stacy nodded, but striving too hard is not without its potential pitfalls. Never forget that!

Mara won't, My Goddess.

You're a cute girl, Lillith said, clearly patronizing. You will be an excellent temple priestess at my Court.

Mara's blush was accompanied by a wide range of emotions.

Yes, My Goddess.

– It's so great that you are here, a young man cried. – We've looked so much forward to your arrival.

– That is nice to hear, Finlay, Stacy said sweetly. – We've got lots of ground to cover, but it is our intention to cover it all.

The travelers enjoyed the casual hospitality. They found it so refreshing compared to the more formal gathering they attended in establishment settings. They didn't really have to explain their words and actions. The Detroit branch of Phoenix Green Earth was well prepared for their arrival.

Stacy frowned at some point. She identified the cause of that almost immediately and without effort. It still startled her.

The thin outer layer of the wall seemed to… deteriorate, to slide off that further in, to dissolve into dust. Stacy studied the others, all the others, and no one noticed, not even Gabi, it seemed.

She pushed into the girl's mind, and that made Gabi notice that something was up.

Do you do that?

Do what?

Stacy showed her.

The girl looked fascinated at the display revealed to her by Stacy's powerful mind. She was more than a bit jaded, but Stacy did see unmistaken interest in her eyes.

I'm not. Either you're doing it without being consciously aware of it, or you're seeing something yet to happen. Is not that self-evident to you?

It should have been, Stacy willingly conceded.

It's probably just one more upgrade, Gabi shrugged. Your future self told you that you would have them, that you would become something dwarfing your previous self.

Gabi grinned wickedly.

Time was flying. An imaginary clock on the wall ticked slowly down to night. The hall filled up with people. The adjacent rooms and hallways were filled up as well. The entire building filled up. There was no room for more, not for a single body more. Quite a few had to stay outside.

Stacy and Mara climbed the few steps to the stage. Mara walked to its edge.

– Yes, she shouted loud enough for everyone to hear her, – this is Stacy Larkin. Please listen, listen hard to what she has to say.

She pulled back, fading into the background. Stacy took center stage.

– Greetings everyone. My name is Stacy. You will use that name when you address me, not any of the more esoteric names you may have heard.

They heard her, within and without. She made certain they did.

– HI, STACY, everyone choired.

The many people, many minds present strengthened her. It didn't weaken her in any way, as it once might have done.

– There are those who know the world is not how it's supposed to be, she shouted. – A growing number of people does. I'm willing to bet most people gathered here tonight do.

Tony repeated those words soundlessly in her ears.

– Up to this true new age, the Democratic Party and Republican Party mostly shared states between them. Only voting in a few, crucial states has mattered on the upper ballot…

She smiled. Everyone was pulled into that smile

– Well, there are no safe states anymore…

A loud cheer followed her triumphant declaration.

– Things will fundamentally change with President Kendall or any other Green Earth Party candidate as US president. He and his administration will need your continued support, though. The potential presidency will be only one of many approaches we will take to truly change the world. We debated at length among ourselves whether or not to take such an establishment approach, but we decided to give it a try, careful not to sacrifice any of the before mentioned alternative approaches in the bargain. It's so very important to guard against the danger of being sucked into the system, to not become a part of it.

She spoke at length, and they listened. There were both frowns and exalted moments of understanding, and everything in-between. She knew she had them, that they would eat of her hand. Those thoughts came to her, no matter how much she fought against their rise.

It turned even quieter, even as the building seethed with expectation.

– We need to scale down human society, she stated. – All other actions against climate heating, the mass extinction, general destruction of nature and threats to all life become meaningless without that crucial move. We also need to remove the inhuman machine from our lives, and create a truly just and equal society with microscopic levels of prejudice and bias. Drastic, beyond drastic measures are needed to protect ourselves against ourselves, against the horrible Machine we have created, that keep recreating us in its image.

She ended her speech, but they knew it wasn't the end, that there was more to come. A hand with fingers formed like claws seemed to rise by itself, as if it was independent of her body. It caught fire. There were loud gasps. The fire turned into a large ball of flames rising in the air. It hung suspended there, above the gathering.

– It's true! A lone voice cried out. – All the stories are true.

The woman rose into the air as well, levitating above them for a prolonged time they imagined stretched into minutes. The ravens rose with her, forming the large shape of wings. Those gathered under this roof tonight knew it wasn't a trick.

She put the tip of the index finger to her lips. It turned absolutely quiet.

– There is one more thing I will do for you tonight. It will be a shock to your system, your most precious beliefs. I wouldn't do this if I didn't think you could handle it without becoming mindless worshipers. Experience the world as it might become, if we are bold enough and skilled enough, fight well enough. You will remember this. You will never forget it. You will remember it forever, and know we need to be at our very best and fiercest to live and thrive.

She bathed them in her energies. It penetrated deep within them, deep within deep and stayed there. They felt her on all possible levels, felt the Embrace of the Goddess. Everyone shook hard. Load moans and cries rose to the ceiling.

– THALAMA, GODDESS OF DESTINY, they choired.

She took a bow.

– The werewolf of Locus Bradle is rising, she cried. – It keeps flapping its wings like an infant, slowly getting the hang of it.

She ended her performance, lowering herself to the floor, landing in their midst, surrounded by their sweat and body juices and heated thoughts.

The rage remained. That did please her.

– You will all be powerful warriors in your own right. You will not let yourself be stopped by anything.

– YES, STACY, they shouted.

She walked among them. They touched her, and she touched them far harder. It took time to reach them all, but neither she nor they felt the passing of time. They made room for her, even in the barrel of fish the place had become. She slipped effortlessly between them. Everett was there by her side. Baron Samedi beat his drum.

– Everything seems so very bright and promising, now, doesn't it? A girl wondered with desperate hope in her voice.

– We've lived through moments of hope before, Raven Lillith Moonstar responded, – and it has ended in heaps of ashes. Do not be deceived. Keep fighting hard until the war is truly won, and stay in shape after that.

She continued her uninterrupted walk. The small touches and minor gifts she received from each and every one of them felt as great as it always did. She confirmed to herself that this was the way it was supposed to be. It happened. She heard the music loud and clear, heard the sound of the flowing Dark River. A burst of emotion overwhelmed her, and tears dropped from her eyes.

– The Goddess is crying, one said nearby.

– It's tears of joy, Everett explained to the boy.

The touch turned more invasive, kinder, rougher, some females and males really into *comforting* her. She granted them her sweet smile, but kept her distance.

She had touched, tasted them all.

– Let's brave the streets, she said softly, – present ourselves to the city in an ongoing manner its citizens will never forget.

They frowned at that, more than anxious in her sensitive mindscape, but that didn't overcome the still rising exhilaration. When she stepped outside and walked down the street, everyone that had experienced her speech and performance followed her with beyond eager smiles.

Smiles, plural.

She began scouting almost immediately, scouring the surroundings for hostile thoughts. There were some, but none she identified as dangerous. She kept her alertness high, having no trouble feeding herself the necessary energy to do so. It was more a matter of not overdoing it, of not feeding herself too much.

The ravens rose from rooftops. She felt it, felt every flap of the wings. They were her eyes and ears, her everything. The age-old connection grew more powerful than ever.

They spread out across the city, across the land, the country, the world, doing so time and time again. She wondered when her relationship with them had started. There was no definite moment she could recall, no matter how far back she reached. She knew she had accepted it, embraced it at some point. It felt so right. That, too, did.

The dance began at some point. She made sure they heard the music, felt the beat and started moving. Fenris, Anubis, Baron Samedi, one of Earth's age-old death-gods joined her. Everett's face, like hers changed slightly or not at all. Everyone imagined they did. The two of them danced together in a sea of flesh. The rhythm stuck in her legs, matching the beat of her heart, exactly like the flapping of the ravens' wings.

She saw it, with half closed eyes, accompanied by the sound of a million feet hammering the ground, saw the sky turn red, to the point of it seemingly bleeding in her wide-open eyes.

The large square filled with people coming from far and near. No one was speaking, but there was a hum, was a chant rising above the buildings, falling below the ground. Fenris growled, and she matched its growing happiness with her own. The proud howl of the wolf and the happy squeaks of the ravens shook every single building within its reach.

They danced into the night, into the blood-red dawn, feeling not the slightest bit of remorse or fatigue.

CHAPTER NINETEEN
Destiny's hand

«You were wild once. Don›t let them tame you» - Isadora Duncan

Mara said goodbye to her old friends and associates, practically embracing everyone there, and joined her new on the bus, as it moved on.

Stacy sat by the window in the bus and stared at the indistinct landscape passing by outside. She sat there, glimpsing images, receiving sensations both alarming and hopeful. They came to her one by one. Everett rubbed her cheek. She felt his lips against her. Tony squeezed her hand. Gabi granted her her happy grin. The big elf embraced her with her strong arms. Mara handed her a glass of orange juice.

She remained there, apprehensive, curious, hungry. Stacy acknowledged her.

Why did My Goddess choose this woman?

She learned to form coherent thoughts.

Because you needed it, Stacy thought, not sharing that.

– I've learned to trust my instincts, Raven Lillith Moonstar replied lightly, – and there's always some random element involved.

She paused a bit, making the other woman attend her, catching her complete attention.

– It's such a joy.

Mara's face cracked in a happy smile.

Stacy watched the landscape outside pass by. Some time had passed. She didn't quite know how much. Sometimes, she lost track of time, of the place, of herself, just drifting off.

Something made her aware. An irritation at the back of her mind suddenly jumped to the front.

The vision overwhelmed her in seconds in a way that had hardly happened before. The details cut into her like razorblades. The earth had become a million scars, one single scar covering the entire planet. She first shared it with them involuntarily, then deliberately, with her hands rolled into fists.

All untouched nature had vanished. The ocean had disappeared. Everything had become an infertile, dead globe.

She stared at nothing. Everyone stared at her.

– I think I fell asleep, she said with a very hoarse voice.

She gathered everyone around her. They sought to her, for comfort, for relief from the horrible sense of loss and despair grabbing them. It felt like they stood for hours like that, while their hands rolled into fists, and the hard, passionate determination slowly reawakened within them.

The gritty, urban land they traveled through affected them. It would have affected them before as well, but now it made them despair and rage even more. A curtain

282

caught fire. Stacy realized that she had rolled her left hand into a fist so hard that her nails had drawn blood.

Gabi studied her, both anxious and with anticipation.

– The Raven should fly, she stated. – We're all ravens, but none more than you. You were made for this. You made yourself for this.

I did, Raven Lillith Moonstar thought. I bathed in the forge, and tempered my steel, so I, in turn could temper others.

Tony played iconic Bob Dylan on guitar and harmonica. It was something about the way he sang and played, both desperate and filled with yearning that made it something special, made it echo within them all.

They sat there around the fire, by the highway and hummed with him.

Lillith sat alone in the shadow later and reached out with her power. When she feared she had reached her limit, she kept reaching out farther. It didn't even prove that hard. The process had long since become intimately familiar to her. Only the power behind it had grown into something strange approaching alien.

She sensed Phoenix without effort, and she knew it sensed her. They brushed against each other's wings. She could easily focus on almost all the mutants under her wings, and increasingly to those not in her vast circle. The process proved increasingly easy. Some noticed her. Most didn't. They all noticed her presence and shivered in their skin.

They reached Chicago, a sort of end station on this particular journey, and so fitting. She had not been here forty years ago, but Ted and Linda had been, two young teenagers thrown into the cauldron of the world. They reached the more unsavory part of town. It was not notable at first, but then they entered an area with derelict buildings.

At first, it looked like typical derelict buildings with large holes in the walls, but as they drove further into the area, they saw how more and more of the walls were covered by plants. Lillith immediately saw the design, as something different from random growth.

Gabi studied her again.

– It reminds me of Babylon, Lillith breathed, clearly lost in memories.

One slow blink, and she found herself there, in ancient Babylon. She stood on a balcony flanked by Liz and Ted, waving to the crowd gathered below.

They stepped off the bus. It had stopped in front of the building a few seconds earlier. A large door stood ajar. People flowed through the narrow opening with exalted joy painted on their faces. Stacy saw only the vast, dark opening. It didn't scare her anymore. She recognized immediately her own face, herself smiling at herself.

There were lots and lots of the usual hugging and touching. She bathed in their devotion, the pleasant heat of their bodies and minds. She saw two sets of events unfold before her, and while that wasn't unusual, she hardly saw as clear as tonight. Now and the past mixed in her vision and her mind and shadow. Her eyes flickered constantly. Her impressions changed with each slow flicker.

Black eyes staring at them brought shadow, brought night. She knew it did. It didn't bother her anymore. She knew it had bothered Iris, and, to a certain extent Nancy, but neither Jill nor Stacy.

Gabi studied her with excitement in her deep, deep eyes. The girl breathed a name in homage and worship.

Stacy focused on those closest to her. The flickering ceased. Her eyes grew steady, her stare pointed. Elliot Androvi noticed her attention beyond the casual. The first deeper stirrings of remembrance surged through his being.

– Welcome! He greeted her. – It's so great to have you guys here.

He grabbed her hands, excited like a boy. She reminded herself that he still was a boy at this stage of his current life.

I have been dreaming about you, about them.

She caught his faint echoes of thought. He studied her with the so very familiar frown on his brow. She kissed him on the lips, and felt his initial surprise and reluctance give rise to the beginning of understanding.

– It's so great to be here, she said softly. – We've heard many good things about you and your project.

He reddened. She ignored that, and rewarded him with her sweetest smile.

She didn't play favorite, not in any way most of them noticed. Everyone embraced and kissed everyone. They disengaged with reluctant chuckles.

– Please, join us inside, Elliot said eagerly.

Everyone filed inside, into the large entrance hall, into the warm, sizzling air. Steam turned to vapor, and vapor to dots of mist, as they made their way deeper into the building.

– We're already self-sustained, he burst out with pride.

He had intended to wait with the great news, but was unable to contain his excitement any longer.

– We did a bit of self-study, he said, – but most of it have we picked up from your programs. It works! It feels so amazing, so beyond amazing.

They entered the deeper parts of the building, and it turned even hotter. The heat smothered them. Hydroponics, plants growing in water covered most of the hall and the walls.

– We grow all our food, he continued. – We get all the heat we need. It's below zero outside, and we enjoy pleasant temperatures over most of our territory. We still have a few kinks to work out, but we're *getting* there, and the best part is perhaps that we cooperate with other communes all over the world to sustain and improve everything. It's happening everywhere.

She heard the word «amazing» in his mind again. It echoed from his depths to the forefront of his consciousness. She granted him another smile of approval, knowing that she had to tell him at some point that was not now that this was not his destiny, that it might be something even more… startling. She squashed the brief burst of shame and regret within.

– The survival crash course taught me so much. It continues to do so. Everything here, and what you taught us in the forest. You try to cover all eventualities, don't you?

– We try, she said, clearly distracted.

They reached a small, intimate hall. The sense of familiarity struck Lillith to the point of her feeling it like a physical blow. She approached the low platform a thousand times before finally stepping onto it. In a peaceful moment, in a slow flash, she saw the destinies of many of those gathered here.

All speech, all sound faded to zero. The ancient goddess of the hunt faced her congregation.

– I am, Stacy. I am Jill. I am Nancy. I am Karama. I am Iris. I am Penelope. And many others. I am Thalama. I will guide you to your destiny. It's so close, now. You just have to reach for it, and grab it by the tail.

The surge rose from the crowd and hit her softly. She drew breath slowly, pleasantly.

– The other side, the shadow world is different. It is a mirror, but skewed, sometimes twisted. You have access to it. The access never goes away. There are people, the servants of the Machine that want to fool you into believing that you don't have that access, or even that there is no such world at all. They only have power over us if we let them, but we don't. We don't acknowledge their power over us. We reject it, reject them!

The low roar turned loud and filled her mind, her consciousness. She fell half asleep standing on the platform, reaching ASC without trying and was dreaming, dreaming them. A slight shift of focus, and she stood in front of them, each and every one of them. Unrest and excitement both grew in the hall. She looked at one young man with her head slightly tilted, and with a pointed stare, well aware how her black eyes worked on him, on most people.

But he was not like most people. She noticed that well before he spoke. He returned her pointed stare with both calm and excitement.

– You named your most recent incarnations… and then, you named one of your oldest. You picked her deliberately from the boiling sea.

Yes, she had. There were both Lillith and Thalama, and they were, in this night and age pretty much the same. The realization, the added realization brought further excitement and commitment.

She sat at the center of a circle made of flesh, of mind, of Shadow, bathing in it, like they were bathing in her. She slipped into her altered state of consciousness. A soft and excited smile broke on her face. Further determination grabbed her and pushed her forward.

Let yourself go, she told them. I will aid you, push you beyond your perceived limits, your perceived truth.

– I remember you, another male cried. – I remember you with razor-sharp accuracy.

She kept giving everyone her stare. It didn't matter that she sat with her back to some of them. They still saw her eyes, her black, black eyes.

– You will identify your core, find your cauldron, she stated, – and then I will help pushing you far beyond that, all that, until you hardly recognize yourself, until you finally do. Thalama will catch you in her lap, and throw you out at deep, deep waters, and everything will make sense.

She restated herself, but it didn't seem like she did. She added a little emotional and actual context with each new statement. They grabbed the candy she waved in front of them, making them do their own will.

You have your tasks. They are not unimportant. They weave the web of life we return to humanity and to the Earth. I grant you your destiny, the one you choose with every fiber of your being.

She led them through the streets. Their number grew with every step she made. The small hall grew to the great stadium where she embraced those cheering her by the thousands.

Caution reminded her of her failures, of her losses, helping her to stay grounded… to a point. The raven flew through the night, and she knew where she was headed.

She branched out, beyond preaching to the choir, like she always did. Her feet turned wet. She swam through deep waters and strong currents… and enjoyed herself immensely. It was very much visible when she met up with yet another group of reluctant radicals too close to being liberals/centrists.

– We're happy with the success you've had, but we also have some concerns, a man said with a very familiar wrinkle on his brow. – Isn't it better to take a safer, slower route to the implementation of our goals?

His «arguments» were dry as withered leaves and just as interesting. Her smile widened. She sensed the anticipation of those following her.

– Are you aware of where your childish, irresponsible attitude will lead us? She snarled.

She did hold back, but to a far lesser degree than she used to do. He shook as if she had sent thousand painful low-grade electrical currents through him.

– Incrementalism is dead, she declared. – The slow and cautious path is dead. Centrism is dead. Liberals have fortunately been reduced to a tiny group without true influence and reasons for existence. No one in their right mind would listen to them or their feeble suggestions anymore.

They shrunk before her, lost in their mire, striving to fight themselves out of the quicksand pulling them down.

– Your destiny is quite different, she stated, knowing that at least some of them would get it.

They were moths burning in her fire. She didn't hold back. Some of them bent their neck. Some of them even knelt in their mindscape. She rejected them with a shrug of contempt. Some of them met her with a new, fierce determination. She accepted them with a snarl, welcomed them with the Charge of the Goddess, and they could not stop gasping.

The walk through the Chicago streets continued in a seemingly endless flow of motion. The number of followers picked up with every new block, every new step within the giant circle. The celebration stretched into days and nights. She stopped counting after a while, and so did her brood. They enjoyed food and drink in the rain, in the hard rain. There was no lack of either.

286

People performed for her. She performed for them. And there was no difference.

They reached a corner, with a dark alley. Very few noticed the creature lurking there.

A woman charged forward with a loud shout and stabbed Stacy in the chest. The blade penetrated her body to the hilt. Shouts of shock and horror echoed between the brick buildings. Everything turned deadly quiet. The woman attempted to pull the knife back out, but it was stuck. She pulled back and froze when Stacy directed her attention at her. Some of those present wanted to charge the woman, but Stacy held up a hand and stopped them from doing so. She kept her attention on the woman.

– You missed my heart…

You didn't, she thought.

She pulled the knife out. Blood flowed like a river, two, five, ten seconds. She ripped her clothes in front, exposing the wound. The would-be assassin stared as the wound closed and healed. She ran off, howling like a banshee.

Stacy's people flowed to her and touched her. The healing sped up further. Gasps of relief and astonishment and worship sounded through the crowd.

The walk continued, with even more elation bloating the street and Thalama's heart.

I will make my queendom on Earth, she thought. I will not repeat the endless mistakes of the past.

Their energies filled her, bloated her. Her power grew to an explosive and so very seductive level. She rose into the air, descended deep below the ground, spreading horizontally and vertically, touching all things, all beings.

The scene shifted to the pressroom in the White House.

– To suggest that we, the United States, are killing innocent people is just absurd and very offensive, Dana Perino, White House Press Secretary said, seemingly genuinely baffled, on November 30, 2007.

That was clearly supposed to impress the journalists gathered there, but it didn't, just didn't, not anymore.

Martin Warren remained standing. He looked bored. There was a mood of unheard anticipation in the room.

– I'm not «suggesting» it, but saying it… he stated. – It's the obvious truth, of course. My question to you Mr. Press Secretary is if anyone in particular will ever be held accountable or if you will just continue killing children and non-combatants with impunity.

Perino shook. He couldn't stop shaking.

– We've given you, given everybody undeniable proof that you *are* killing totally innocent people, and that you are well aware of it, exposing your statements on this and every other matter as the ridiculous and dangerous horseshit it is. US government is sociopathic and sick at the highest levels, showing a pervasive pattern of disregard for, and violation of the rights of others. Well, you won't be able to hide that anymore. No one buys your horseshit anymore… sir.

– GET THAT MAN OUT OF HERE! PERINO SHRIEKED.

The guards, already on the move speeded up. They stumbled in their own legs and fell, fell hard. They couldn't get past a certain point, as if there was a barrier there. Perino turned pale. He rushed from the stage. A patronizing laughter chased him off.

– Mr. Perino clearly refuses to respond to the allegations against the administration.

Martin spoke to all cameras, not just the one operated by a chuckling Lydia.

One more disastrous White House performance ended.

The growth spread from the city and from the forest, across Ravenscourt, until it covered all of it.

Stacy returned to Northfield. Malvin practically jumped her, purring loud enough to wake the dead. He had become so big, the biggest housecat she had ever seen. There was no fat there, only hard muscles and good-humored menace and passion. She pushed him down on the side and rubbed his belly. He allowed it with a patronizing snarl and purr. It dawned on her that he was imitating her.

Her bedroom waited for her, welcomed her, like a pleasant old coat. Betty welcomed her. She knelt on the bed.

– Goddess, she breathed.

Linsey sat in the big chair. The three of them nodded to each other. They needed no words, no communication of the mind even.

The extended Janus Clan gathered at Ravenscourt for the winter solstice celebration. Everyone gathering in close quarters like that made everyone's power surge. They all felt it. They couldn't avoid feeling it. Their numbers had grown to such a degree that they could hardly deal with it anymore. The random hundred sitting around the round table represented only a fraction of those present. People sought the higher levels on the walls in order to retain the somewhat intimate close proximity. One circle became many.

Liz and Ted drew the power into themselves and released it in powerful bursts that couldn't be denied. Those nearest them crouched and gasped. Those farther away seemed just as affected. Lillith chuckled in an uneven, ongoing flow. Her powers also soared this night.

Soon…

The three of them stood in a triangle, a seething cauldron of power. Lillith didn't hide anymore. She couldn't either, not to them, not completely, but she made no attempt to do so.

They zoned in on Ethel, just like that. To call her reaction euphoric did in no way give it justice. They zoned in on Nick, seeing him in a new light, shadow, light, shadow.

He's not really here, is he?

Gabi seemed like an adult to their sixth or sixty-sixth sense. So did Kyle. They burned with the darkest shadow. Their burn burned in Ted and Liz's gut, or what they imagined were their gut.

Words are… inadequate.

We knew that long ago.

288

The present became the future. The next few months appeared clear and present in everyone's mind. It changed as they saw it, into strains of probability.

Guidelines, Liz swore. Nothing more.

– NO quarter for any establishment shill.

Ted shouted at a crowd.

Probability turned into certainty, uncertainty.

These are your instructions, Phoenix told its army of warriors. Heed them.

They would spread across the Earth, one small piece of the giant whole. Ted felt like that whole sometimes. Then, he didn't, Then, he did.

Nick and female and male youngsters toured China and India, meeting up with fellow mutants, with other parts of the People, finding more allies and enemies alike. Ted experienced their travels as if he was there, or almost like he was there.

He returned to the present with a start, still not quite certain that he had.

– I love that there are only natural fires here, a voice sighed. – It feels so pleasant, so right.

– Look at her, Ethel told Ted. – She's a work of art, isn't she?

A slew of seemingly unrelated statements sounded in his head. He could sort of distinguish them from «real» voices.

– That's why, Liz cried. – That's why she made Ruth and Bee. It was no whim at all.

He studied her. Her mouth didn't move. Her mind didn't speak. She returned the curious glance, knowing that something was happening.

He saw the future her as a sort-of isolated image. There were no details surrounding her, only an indistinct shimmer.

She reached out a hand. Then, he was there, taking her hand. They joined in a spot coated in white, in gray, in mist clearly not mist. A circle of people held hands around them. They recognized each and every one of them.

Liz blinked and stared at him, even as they shared the vision. Both shook imperceptibly.

They still did as people began leaving the cave and spreading out in the town and the terrain. Everyone surrounding them in a vast uneven circle shook as well, without being able to tell why.

The wind whistled in leaves, leaves that weren't there. It whispered in everyone's ears. They saw naked branches wherever they looked.

– I know trees are supposed to be naked this time of the year, Phillip mumbled, – but they still give me the chills.

Liz cast him the usual good-humored look, faking it a bit, just a bit.

She couldn't keep the flow of her power to reach him, but it didn't matter. He was basically clueless, like he had been his entire life. She regretted her condescending thoughts briefly. Then, she didn't.

He could hardly avoid noticing her contempt, could he? She imagined he couldn't.

She found herself walking with Ted and Ethel through the whispering forest later, without being quite aware of how the walk had begun. It had just happened, like soft, almost unnoticeable rain.

– Are the visions of the leaves on the trees the vision, Ethel wondered, – or are they masking the true vision?

It dawned on Liz and Ted that Ethel was talking shop. She had a genuine interest in their opinion.

– I don't know, Ted replied before Liz could stop him.

– Mike did know, didn't he, Ethel mused and nodded. – He was certain. There was no doubt in his mind. He saw far beyond his own lifetime, and was willing to do anything to make it happen.

– You have a very valid point there, Liz said generously.

They took a slow, pleasant stroll through Northfield and the surrounding area. The People greeted them wherever they walked.

– They know who their masters are, Ethel remarked.

The other two made no vocal response to that. She clearly sensed their disapproval.

– You must see yourself for what you are, she insisted. – That is the only thing missing, now. There is only one year left, now.

Only one year left.

She knew!

It echoed within them, stronger each time.

A slight shift in attention, and they were distracted. Northfield, Northfield's swarm of mutants were being born, and they felt it, felt every bit of it. Ethel began breathing faster. He looked astounded at her. She pushed herself at him, and kissed him with burning lips.

– I know who my masters are, she whispered.

Liz grabbed her jaw and assessed her with predatory eyes. Ethel's breathing picked up further. Liz let go of her. They walked on. The sound of fighting reached them. They were pulled there.

– Look at her, Ethel whispered to Ted. – She's a work of art, isn't she?

They watched Bee as she trained a group of recruits.

– But she isn't the way you envisioned her, he pointed out.

– Isn't she? Ethel teased him.

Bee and Man Chi demonstrated their prowess to the recruits, making them gasp in awe, and then, when the two moved even faster and showed even greater marksmanship, they just stood there, frozen, out of breath.

Ethel pushed her back at a tree in moves impossible to misinterpret. She began unbuttoning her blouse. Her radiant fireeyes turned misty. She began rubbing her exposed breasts. The female moved, and one move seemed like many. Her sensual performance grew even more enticing. The two birds of prey moved in on her from two sides. Liz suddenly looked very different from how she used to. They kissed Ethel on the neck. Pain cut through her. Power flared between them. Ethel turned soaking wet below. She gasped and kept gasping. They ripped away all fabric covering their bodies. It didn't require any noticeable conscious thought. Ted and Liz's power grew, as they devoured hers. They didn't take much. They could have taken so much more. The big woman floated between them like a sheet in the wind, putty in their hands.

They heard Stacy speak, not far away, far away, as close as the space between two fingers.

– The Locus Bradle isn't done with us, of course. It never will be!

A loud moan flowed from Ethel's wide-open mouth.

Liz grinned wickedly. Ethel whimpered in fright, moaned in horrible need. Their frontal lobe burned so hard that it hurt, even though they hardly felt it. They knew it showed through the skin, through the skull. Ethel whispered soundless words. She levitated before them. They turned her round and round. Liz slapped her butt. Ethel's scream echoed in ears miles away.

They roamed her sex with flesh and power. She couldn't move. Her hands were locked behind her back. Her legs spread wide.

A band began playing somewhere in town. The three of them glimpsed the people and the instruments, but could not quite catch the background.

– Sweet girl, Liz hissed in her ears. – Sweet, sweet puppet.

She still looked young, like they did. Her body, like Liz's was clearly that of a more mature woman, though.

Ted put her down on all fours. Liz slapped her on the butt. She kept slapping her. Ethel screamed. Jason easily heard her on Main Street. Everyone did!

– I LOVE YOU, VIRGIL, Ethel shouted. – I LOVE YOU!

Tears jumped from her eyes. Ted grabbed her hips, part of her sore butt. She sniffed in sudden, breathless anticipation. He pushed himself into her. Her scream made all the birds in all the trees fly up from the branches.

The band played only acoustic instruments. The music still reached long and far. Gabrielle Asteroth danced somewhere. A thin layer of sweat covered her brow. Her hair reached her hips and flowed around her body like whisps of wind. The members of the band gasped as one person. Both the females and males had trouble standing. Some of them dropped to their knees. They couldn't keep the occasional discord from manifesting, but they kept playing, playing, playing.

Jason Gallagher froze on his spot on Main Street. Everything seemed suddenly to open up to him, to reach him undiluted. The members of the band, both those standing and kneeling, began swaying, leaves in the breeze. Ethel's features cracked in ecstasy. One loud moan turned to one long wail. Her voice mixed with Ted's dark growl.

Jason stood still, distracted, hardly noticing anything around him. Then, he did. He turned his head. Janet Caldwell stood only two steps away from him, but it wasn't the Janet he had learned to know. Feature by feature, she looked very much like her, but there was something about her making deep chills pass down his spine.

She smiled to him, a dark, dark smile.

– You are not him, at least not yet, she said. – You might not be or might become him eventually. I'll keep searching and waiting.

The deep shadow in her face seemed to lighten. She stumbled. He had to catch her to keep her from falling.

– What happened? She asked startled. – How did I get here? I can't remember.

She returned to the young woman he had learned to know. He held on to her.

– You looked a little out of it, he said casually, – but you seem okay now.

– Okay? She said distressed.

– Okay, he stressed. – It isn't exactly rare that people have an episode or two around here, you know…

He studied her, watching her calm down. She giggled a bit.

– That's true, she nodded empathically. – Thank you.

She kissed him on the cheek.

– I'll see you around.

She giggled a bit more and ran off.

He turned and headed for the tavern.

The musicians, completely spent, stretched out on the ground.

Ethel crouched in Liz's arms. Liz held around her and hummed a lullaby to her and rubbed her head.

He walked through the packed bar. Some greeted him with loud cries. Others with silent cheers.

She sat nude on the bed when he entered the upper floor.

She was making a noose, clearly an expert, doing the job in a fast and efficient manner. He almost felt it as she did, as she made the final tightening, and the noose was ready for use.

– I'm a dark god of death, just like you, my love, but my symbol isn't the skull. Our new sister will certainly feel that if she keeps being disrespectful.

He knew that, and she knew he knew that. He didn't voice a reply. She caught easily his silent negative response. She grinned and stretched out on the bed, displaying herself to him. The stench of her sex ripped into his nostrils.

– That was some show. Mommy and daddy know how to throw a party.

Val rushed into the room with blushing cheeks.

– Did you guys feel that?

It was a rhetorical question. She knew they couldn't avoid feeling it.

She rushed into his arms. She was soaking wet and warm below as well. Demand and desire dominated her entire being. She pulled down his pants. His cock rose big and hard. The two horny females sighed in anticipation.

Michelle joined the other two by the bed. She held up the noose. Val bent her neck. Michelle put the noose around that sweet, sweet neck and tightened it. Val gasped, striving to breathe properly.

– Ares is ours to command, beloved. She's an easy mark.

She pulled the rope, pulled her sister close and kissed her on the lips. Moans rose from both throats. Jason and Val removed their clothes as well. It was a more or less effortless, automatic motion.

– I feel Thalama's hand, Michelle whimpered. – She moves us around like puppets.

Val kissed her hard on the lips. The big girl crumbled in her grip. They turned towards Jason. Val kissed him first, then Michelle. Val's big belly was a bit troublesome, but not more than they easily handled it.

– Strong big brother, she whispered into his ear.

292

They rubbed themselves lazily at him, playing with him, enticing him in countless playful ways. He grabbed the rope and pulled. Val turned limp in his grip. He placed her on all fours on the bed. Michelle turned even more eager. He grabbed her around the jaw and squeezed. She turned limp as well. He placed her by her sister's side.

– Please, My Lord, she begged him.

– Please, My Lord, Val begged him.

He played with their cunt a bit, making them even more frantic. He slapped their butt, making them cry out, repeating it until they turned compliant. They sniffed in burning need. He had no trouble feeling the scale of their need and grinned wolfishly.

He slipped into Val. She cried out in happiness.

– Yes, I'm yours, yours, yours.

She repeated the last word each time she exhaled, until a series of moans supplanted it. He shifted back and forth between them a bit, devilishly patient, fingering the one he didn't fuck. He came into one, but Val and Michelle came simultaneously. Every single move and sound made it seem like they had both received Jason's seed. The musicians began fondling each other. Others were pulled into their circle. People joined in heaps in ever wider heaps of warm bodies. More explosive joy echoed across Northfield. More and more took up the mantle. A massive orgy spread across town until everyone participated. The ocean of sweaty bodies reached far outside the town's boundaries.

Stacy moved among the heaps of sweaty bodies and excited minds. They reached out to her with hands and minds. The rock-hard determination, the iron will, made her move on, made her reject them all. She sought the lesser populated area around the hill. She rushed up there on light steps, ignoring the cautious voice from within, rejecting centuries of caution. She stopped at the top, at the edge of the whispering forest. She turned and looked at the town below. One town turned many in her powerful mind growing even more powerful.

Thalama stood at the edge of Frazer's Hill. The sexual frenzy below reached a crescendo of lust and energy. It made her burn with anticipation. She watched as the glowing mist rose into the air and reached for it. It entered her in a slow, steady flow. Her giant Shadow manifested. Its mouth opened wide, and revealed the mighty darkness within. Its mighty hand reached out and touched every single living being in a wide, wide circle.

2

Michelle moved with urgency through the terrain. She rushed up to Raven's mound and knelt before the giant shadow. The shadow acknowledged her.

– I seek… counsel, My Goddess.

– You don't need it, Thalama shrugged, speaking with her hollow, ghostly voice, discarding the shaking flesh at her feet.

– YES, MY GODDESS, Michelle cried and ran down the hill. She attempted to float, but couldn't quite make it.

So, she moved like most people would by putting one foot in front of the other.

She found the four together, like she usually did. Troy, Beth, Shadow and Timothy. She didn't waste any time and directed her complete attention on Troy.

– You haven't had the dream in a long time, have you?

He looked stunned at her.

– No, I haven't. How did you…

– I have! I started having it shortly after our rather unpleasant experience where I liberated myself from my fate. A new one formed almost instantly.

Something passed between them.

– I have taken your place among the twenty-one, she informed him gently. That is my true Fate. It was never yours.

He stood there frozen in front of her.

She kissed him softly on the cheek.

Beth stepped forward and kissed her. The others did, too.

– I will be seeing you, sister.

Then, Michelle Warren was off like the wind.

The three of them walked into the theater, their venue for the night. The sisters flanked their brother. Val, in her maternity dress displayed proudly her big belly. The countless flashes didn't bother them. They imagined they weren't there.

– Who's the father?

Val didn't deem them worthy of a response.

They walked out on a pitch on a football stadium. Large shadows flickered on the grass, in spite of the powerful lights bathing the ground. The place was packed with people. The three of them sensed easily the anxious excitement, the excited anxiety. None of the thousands of people present could avoid sensing it to some degree or another.

– We share! Val cried.

Suddenly weak-kneed she had trouble staying on her feet, and the other two had to grab her and support her.

– The young goddess is excited, My Lord, Michelle chuckled.

Vali kissed her, kissed him, with beyond passionate zeal.

There was a wide platform at the center of the pitch. The audience cheered as one when the three walked up the stairs and entered the slightly elevated circle. The three joined those already there, facing them as they looked inward, as they looked outward at the audience with just a minor twist of the head.

It turned quiet, as the anticipation grew.

– Welcome. Gayle greeted everyone, – to this evening's Honest Conversation, this great inquiry into modern human life and fuckups.

She got the required laughter and attention from the audience, the quiet acknowledgement from Jason, Michelle and her brethren.

– Racist pundits keep telling us that there are lots of *undocumented immigrants* at our meetings. I've been shown no proper verification of that, but in case it's true, let's welcome each and every one of them, shall we…

The laughter changed to loud cheers.

I've become great at this, she thought with uncontained pride.

– We will discuss any controversial subject, and we will encourage complete openness in both questions and answers. Life is too short to mince words, right?

She was rewarded with a loud roar from everywhere around her.

It turned quiet. The anticipation didn't dissipate, but grew.

– So, Jason, how has the Christmas preparations been for you? Phillip asked.

– We don't celebrate Christmas, Jason replied. – We did our celebration at the Winter Solstice two days ago, a night humanity has celebrated for many thousands of years, long before Christianity fucked us up.

More laughter and happy sighs echoed among the audience, their anticipation rewarded already, even as they knew more, far more was to come.

– To me, Christmas is an excellent illustration of the total insanity ruling today's society. I most certainly wish everyone a horrible Christmas.

The shadows grew deeper. Everyone noticed. They couldn't avoid doing so.

– I understand you guys don't hold Christians in very high regard…

Jason smiled. He referred to Michelle.

– «I follow the teaching of Jesus Christ», she imitated to perfection. – How stupid is that… worshiping a man that never existed, either as a god or a man. There is no true evidence that he ever existed. The few historical «sources» seemingly bringing evidence of his existence are Christian forgeries.

– The people behind Christianity basically wanted to domesticate the population, Val said, – making them sheep instead of wolves. The strategy has been an astounding success.

– You don't say. Michelle feigned surprise.

– I do say, Val feigned a lack of ability to catch irony. – I believe humanity needs to become true warriors again before it's too late.

– This is also, among many things a meeting highlighting the Green Earth Party's participation in the presidential and general election next year. You're all heavily invested in that, are you not?

– We are, Michelle said, – I certainly support our participation. We should not put our eggs in just one basket, but many. We will fight the establishment, the ongoing tyranny in every way we can think of, including elections.

She felt easily the hum, the roar rising from the crowd surrounding them, felt it so much better than she had before. The smile broke on her face.

– We have an expert with us tonight, Phillip said. – Lynn has attended the US Congress for a year, now. What are your impressions, Lynn?

– One of the first things that struck me was how chummy the democrats and republicans were when the cameras and microphones were turned off, Lynn Fredericks said. – I noticed the us versus them mood from day one. «Us» being the representatives, «them» the American people. Their appearance of enmity is just that, a theater, a masquerade designed to deceive people. It just grew more pronounced the longer I spent in their company. They attempted to isolate and intimidate us when it became clear to them that we wouldn't play ball, but that didn't impress us like it would a neophyte democrat, like we've seen a thousand times. We were wise to their ways, and have done everything in our power to disrupt the proceedings, to keep them from screwing us all even more than they have done. With our number of representatives and senators set to increase significantly, we will make it even harder for them. They will do everything in their power to stop that. We must rise to the occasion.

Lots of the people in the movement knew what she was actually saying. They raised closed fists above the head.

She's one more of mother and father's strays, Michelle sent to her two siblings. They have drawn to them thousands like her and made her into a lethal weapon, into tempered steel.

– There is an army of them, Val stated.

Lynn ended her impassionate statement with a fist raised above her head. A roar rose from those standing on the grass.

– Everything has become so clear to me lately, Michelle said.

She grabbed one hand of each of her companions and gave them a radiant smile, as if to dissuade the worried frown on their brow.

– The desert is growing at an unprecedented rate, she cried with her penetrating voice, – growing both in nature and in human hearts. It reaches places where it has never been.

Those sitting close to her easily caught the images of a barren landscape she projected. Everyone at the stage and at the pitch did to a smaller or bigger degree. There was something extremely poignant about it that no one could avoid catching.

Life is a gift, she stated, she beamed, she snarled, and humanity is throwing it away.

Everyone heard that loud and clear, far clearer than any sound. Those sitting closest to her bled from the nose. Jason and Val healed fast, but the others had to put cotton in their nostrils in order to contain the bleeding.

– I believed I knew what power was, Val said startled. – I was wrong, so very wrong.

She smiled to them both, smiled with her entire self. It was quite the remarkable, enticing experience.

– I try to recall the time, the person I was before… before, but I cannot do so. It's all gone into a black hole.

– It doesn't matter, Michelle stated. – All that matters is who you are now. *Now!*

Val nodded eagerly.

Jason rubbed her cheek. She rubbed her cheek against his hand. The three of them registered everything, all the passionate and great words being spoken around them, and their excitement grew further.

– I hear that the recruitment to the various police-departments is falling drastically, which is such a fucking great development, one of the panelists said. – I guess the bullies are not so brave when the odds are no longer in their favor.

– They call our criticism irresponsible, another eager voice cried. – Few things are quite as ironic as when representatives of the establishment claiming that others are acting irresponsible.

The subsequent laughter made the establishment shills on the pitch very uneasy.

– Those eager servants object to being called «sheep» or «mindless puppets», Michelle chuckled. – What do you call people that are willingly and eagerly fooled time and time again? Is calling them mindless puppets fair or not?

– But that is fundamentally unfair, the representative of the progressive part of the Democratic Party shouted. – We live in a democracy with aware and informed citizens.

– What you say is just yet another mindless defense of mainstream society. I must ask you if you are proud to be a robot. Your entire line of argument is pure establishment propaganda and I reject it.

I *reject* it!

Fire surged through her, and she could hardly contain it, contain herself.

– All current public and private governments, aided by their supporters and bullies, are waging war against their own people and against nature, Jason added. – Anyone denying that obvious truth is both unaware and uninformed.

The crowd went wild.

3

Linda, Glory, Judith and the rest of their urban guerilla group faced the camera. Linda read from a prepared statement.

– We will now read the names of all CIA-operatives and executives across the world. – Yes, it may lead to their death. Good riddance to murderers and establishment shills. We will also read the names of all police officers that have killed unarmed people. A bit of repetition doesn't hurt.

– NO quarter for any establishment shill, and certainly not for its assassins, Glory added.

– This will take some time, Judith said, – but if you miss something, rest assured that we will return to all of it numerous times. And it is and will remain available anywhere, anyway.

They alternated with the reading, and the documentation and the conclusion. This, too, went on for days. They slept quite a few times during it all.

The very familiar courtroom appeared on people's monitor across the world. Linda the judge sat in her chair behind the desk. Five chained people were dragged into the room and placed on the front benches. They had been beaten and didn't look good. Fear and incredulity and anger shifted in their sweaty and bruised faces.

– Good evening, Glory spoke directly into the camera. – Welcome to tonight's proceedings. The first charged on this late day are the police officer Joshua Fenwick, charged with shooting and killing an unarmed woman in a wheelchair, his colleague Egbert Roberts that lied for Fenwick's benefit, his boss Burt Reinhold that ordered the victim's family to be severely harassed, the attorney general Ellen Horn that failed to prosecute Fenwick and last but not least; Oswald Merrick,

Fenwick's union representative that also leaned hard on the victim's family to make them drop the civil suit against the city of Chicago.

– As stated, Linda stated, – this is not a court of law. We will determine guilt, and will act swiftly to achieve a semblance of justice. There is no way Odetta Williams will ever have anything even resembling true justice. Hopefully, her family will feel some small consolation after we're done. I should point out that the cases we try here are very obvious. There is no doubt about the guilt of those tried. We will eventually get to those killing in secret as well. May they all sweat gallons fearing our vengeance.

She pushed a button, and a recording was shown on a monitor. A black woman rolled her wheelchair through a park. The first thought striking those watching was the extreme quality of the film, the razor-sharp images, the great sound, the happy song of birds.

She crossed a street, a road cutting the green area in two smaller pieces.

– It works like a charm, she cried to the person doing the recording. – How are you doing?

– Everything works great at this end as well, a man said. – Everything is uploaded directly to the recording studio. It saves us from lots of work.

Odetta gave him thumbs up. The filming continued. Sometimes, he would stop and choose another angle. They both had a good time. Odetta certainly had. It was notable on the film. Those watching could see how she struggled with her chair, with the manual turning of the wheels on the fairly primitive chair, but also that she had lots of practice, that the handling had become second nature to her. She crossed hurdles and fought herself up fairly steep slopes without experiencing major difficulties.

The police-car approached them from a distance. Those inside turned the sirens on and off in what the two making the recording experienced as sinister. They knew what this was. They had suffered from similar events from an early age.

– Be calm, Zane, Odetta cautioned him.

Those watching with their heart jumping up their throat imagined they could actually see how the camera shook, how he couldn't quite operate it properly in his shaking hands.

The patrol-car stopped closeup, almost close enough to actually bump into the wheelchair. The two officers stepped out.

– Good afternoon, Joshua Fenwick greeted the two making a movie.

Odetta and Zane mumbled something unintelligible.

– Do you have any business here? Do you have a permit to film in the park?

– Ah am exactly where ah am supposed to be, Odetta Williams stated calmly. – And, as it turns out, we do have a permit.

– May I see it, please?

She squinted her eyes slightly, as if to protect herself from the bright light. Her hand reached into her pocket and brought out a piece of paper. She handed it to him.

He looked at it, practically stared at it, clearly not caring at all. The twisted grin grew on his face. He tore the paper to pieces.

– No, no permit.

– That was a copy, she shrugged.

His grin faded out as her faded in.

– You're something of a pain in the butt, Odetta, he remarked, – and we're sick and tired of it. You won't be for much longer.

He took a step closer to her. She didn't move, but stayed her ground.

– You crossed the road outside the zebra stripes.

She didn't reply, didn't respond in any way.

– Do you have a driver license for that wreck of a two-wheeler of yours?

– A driver's... license?

She looked at him as if he was a bug on a windshield. He began breathing faster, began sweating. He drew his gun.

– You stay still, now.

– We have kept up with your racist crap for way too long by now, she said quietly.
– We're leaving.

She turned the chair around and wheeled away.

He pulled the trigger. The camera shook. Odetta shook. Fenwick fired again. The wheelchair turned over and Odetta hit the ground. She stared straight forward with frozen eyes. The man operating the camera took one step back, then, one step, two steps forward. He filmed Fenwick. Fenwick turned his gun on him, and fired. The camera showed the sky briefly before hitting the ground. The next bullet hit it. It was pushed across the ground, still recording. Fenwick fired again. The image turned black.

Linda turned off the recording. Fenwick stared at her with insane eyes.

– You're guilty as hell, she shrugged. – Your execution will be long, hard and painful. You will serve as a warning to all your peers. Congratulations!

Judith shot him in the left leg. He screamed and fell off the chair. Glory shot him in the right. His scream turned into a whine.

– You're just a dog, Glory remarked, – but for now... you'll do.

Egbert Roberts jumped to his feet, attempting to make a run for it. Judith and Glory repeated the process on him. Two whining wrecks writhed on the floor, slowly bleeding out.

– We're moving on, Linda said, – calling the first witness for tonight's proceedings.

A nervous, but determined woman entered the courtroom. She sat down at the left of Linda.

– Just state your name and tell your story, Linda instructed her.

– My name is Lyssa Thompson, the woman said. – I work at attorney general Ellen Horn's office. She and police chief Burt Reinhold didn't think I would hear them, but I stood at the other side of the door and listened closely. I didn't have any trouble hearing them. The conversation was mostly about how they would «make this go away». They went into detail about it, also about the extensive harassment of Odetta's family, and their lawyers.

Then, she went into extreme detail about it. She played recordings of later meetings, both at the office, and when they gave instructions to various underlings, thugs for hire, both cops and not.

Her testimony ended. The room turned completely silent. She left with her head held high.

A man entered the room. He looked both haunted and determined. He sat down in the witness chair, and began talking before Linda could speak.

– My name is Stanton Donaldson. I worked at Oswald Merrick's office. I used to do work for him, lots of work…

He, too, went into extreme detail. The haunted expression never truly left his face.

– It was wrong, okay, he cried eventually. – I finally realized that and got fed up. I will work for the rest of my life atoning for the suffering I've caused.

He left the room with bowed head.

There were more witnesses, many more. There didn't seem to be an end to them. The deluge finally ended. The deadly silence reentered the air.

– THEY'RE LYING, Horn shouted.

Then, she whimpered.

– They're all lying.

Glory shot her in the belly. Judith shot Reinhold the same place.

They both shot Oswald Merrick. He screamed. He crouched on the floor with tears flowing down his cheeks.

Linda nailed Fenwick's arms to the floor with two knives. He hardly screamed at that point, even as the horrible pain kept rising, rising, rising.

The room resembled a slaughterhouse. Merrick died first, for some reason, without really being that much more wounded compared to the others.

– You lucky bastard, Linda snarled at him.

Time stretched out to infinity once again. There didn't seem to be an end to it. Fenwick begged for mercy. He did so several times. Linda grabbed his tongue and ripped it out of his mouth.

Much more time had passed. The camera zoomed in on his face. His breathing turned shallow, his skin even grayer.

– I want you to remember this the next time we meet, she told him. – I want you to never forget it.

There was a glimpse of understanding in his eyes, before reason, all reason finally left him. He drew his breath for the last time. His eyes grew empty and dead.

The image faded to black.

There was another shift in scenery. A young black man stood in a clearing by the edge of a forest. He held up a sign with clear, distinct writing.

FIGHTING
WHITE
SUPREMACY

He and a group carrying rifles walked through the woods. They stopped at the edge of the other side.

They watched a group of white males with a black prisoner.

– I haven't done nothing, the scared young man whimpered.

300

– Listen to the monkey. It can't even speak right.

Two men held him. A third struck him in the belly, striking him several times.

– You exist, monkey. That is reason enough. The fact that you dared ask a decent white girl for a dance is almost incidental.

They put a noose around his neck, and dragged him to the nearest tree, beating him some more when he made feeble protests. One of the men threw the rope over a thick branch. Two others received it at the other side. They pulled it until it was tight as a piano-string.

– Any last words, monkey?

The boy attempted to speak, but couldn't do it. His mouth moved, but there was no sound. They dragged him several steps further, until he stood beneath the branch by the old hangman's tree.

There was a loud crack. One of the men was hit. Blood flowed from his chest. There were several more cracks. Several more men were hit. Some of them fell. The rest attempted to flee. They were shot down fast and efficient.

One of the wounded crawled on the ground. He didn't get very far before a foot stepped on his back.

– We were only kidding, he sobbed.

They shot him through the back of his head.

The young boy hadn't moved. He looked at his rescuers without truly seeing them.

– Do you want to join us, young black man? A black man said curtly.

The young man nodded, still unable to speak.

– Then, join us, now, a white woman said. – Join in on the execution.

She handed him a rifle. He accepted it with shaking hands.

A man writhed on the ground, unable to move.

– Kill him off, the black man bid the shaking young man.

The young man fired his first shot… and missed from half a step away. He and his hands stopped shaking. He fired again. This bullet hit the wounded man in the back to head.

The cracks kept echoing through the forest for a few more minutes. Before everything turned quiet.

An Asian man wearing gloves put the statement

FIGHTING

WHITE

SUPREMACY

on the tree. The white paper, the black writing both seemed to glow in the dark.

4

NORTHFIELD, MASSACHUSETTS
FEBRUARY 29, 2008

Lillith Raven Moonstar stood on a low rise on the field north of Northfield.

– Gabrielle Asteroth, our Oracle has reached Sweet Sixteen, the tender age of four… and her time has come.

A wild roar rose at the heavens. A blushing Gabi rushed to do Raven's bid, and joined her on the rise. Another wild roar shook the ground.

– THANK YOU, ALL OF YOU, she cried.

«All of you» was a seemingly endless blanket of people standing around the low rise.

She had grown the last year, filled out in all the right places. People had begun watching her in new and exciting ways, ways making her blush in discomfort. Daniel and Stacy and the others walked with her back to town, guarding her from the worst of the attention from those cheering at both sides of the trail.

– You could just skip this, you know, Stacy said casually to her, as if telling her something she didn't know.

– No, the girl said and shook her head in determination. – I wanted this. I want this. Thank you, Raven! Thank you for this, all this.

She embraced the young woman by her side.

– You don't need to do anything resembling an initiation, Daniel attempted again to convince her. – You've long since done that many times over.

She gave him a sweet smile, making him blush.

– Thank you, but I want this, all this.

She seethed with power after several recent visits to the Dark River, and knew Stacy sensed that. She smiled, and knew Stacy sensed that, too. The smile widened.

The Dark River stayed with her, stayed with her all the time. The pieces of the departing spirits she had caught burned so pleasantly within her. Her power could flare up any time, and when that happened, she had a hard time controlling it. She glanced at her left hand. It turned transparent. The shadowland called to her, called to her all the time. The hand turned back to normal. She sighed in relief.

She turned to Daniel and began kissing him, making the onlookers roar good humored, distracting herself.

Stacy touched her jaw, appraising her, taking back control. Gabi looked defiant at her.

– It will be a birthday party echoing in eternity, she assured her temple priestess.

– Thank you, mother, Gabi breathed.

They reached the town, and from there, there was only a short walk to Main Street, to a main street that had become a stretch of forest, where the ground and all buildings were covered in green, in wild plants. The trees had branches making them easy to climb. Most of those serving as spectators did that, making another circle. The birthday girl gathered at the center with those she viewed as her closest family. Martin and Lydia, in a casual, effortless move carried the sacrificial stone from the great hall in the Hill with their telekinesis.

Gabi frowned. She reached out and touched the rock, and sensed its energies.

– Yes, it still contains the remaining energies from the ceremony, Stacy confirmed. The energies from the sacrifice, and what followed. Happy birthday, pumpkin!

The girl looked at Stacy, unable to contain her anticipation.

– Never say I don't do anything for you, Stacy shrugged.

302

The deep drum began beating. The Hollow, or what looked like a Hollow to everyone there welcomed the Child of the Abyss. Gabi felt very welcomed. The adult «elders» gathered in a halfmoon circle behind the large flat stone.

– You may climb the rock and stand on it, now, sacrificial lamb, Betty suggested.

Gabi hurried to obey the prompting, suddenly as eager as a horse pulling its reigns. She sensed, felt the energies far stronger than she had done twenty-eight moons ago.

Nick, ancient Nick pointed to himself. She devoted her entire attention on him.

– Welcome, child of the Midnight Fire. Welcome initiate, to a life already yours.

Heat surged through her. The words burned her within and without. She knew everyone in the halfmoon circle, both as people and gods.

Lydia and Martin rose into the air, and started painting her face. Gabi watched the colors as they burned, as they changed, as they turned alive on her skin.

– You have already suffered a harder path than most initiates, Betty said softly, – but an essential part of yourself is still missing. You need to claim it, or you will never be whole.

Ruth rose into the air, until she levitated in front of the child. She held out the cup with the smoking brew and the spongy piece. Gabi accepted it, hesitating a bit, just a bit before drinking it all and chewing the spongy piece. Her mouth turned slack, and dizziness overwhelmed her, but she kept chewing. She stood there swaying. The cup fell from her weak grip. She dropped down on the stone. It turned into a giant gap, swallowing her whole.

The world shifted and changed around her. The both familiar and suddenly unfamiliar surroundings of the shadow world appeared to her. She had little or none control this time, being hardly more than that dry leaf in the wind. She knew what this was, had read about it, heard about it in exhaustive detail. It still stunned her in its terror and wonder.

She walked the streets of Northfield, but they didn't look like she remembered them, didn't look like that at all. They stretched out endlessly before her. She walked through the same street repeatedly, but it wasn't the same street. It changed with each new walk-through. Buildings changed. The clothes people wore changed. Everything looked new and shiny one moment, worn and destitute and decayed the next. People wore modern clothes one moment, the next they didn't. She recognized fashion from earlier decades and centuries. There were no Northfield, only the untouched wilderness. She reached the big, open marketplace. It had once been dusty and gray. Now, it was green and wet and beautiful. She spotted the witches, the mutants, the People, her people, so many, numbers beyond numbers.

This is the Crossroads, she mumbled to herself. All paths, all time lead here. All paths are wrong. and all are right.

– Humans desire or may desire willing tools for their ambitions, Stacy said gleefully. – You must guard yourself against others, as well as yourself.

She sounded different, sounded the same.

Gabi the witch stood in front of a mirror. She saw Stacy, saw herself, saw the girl, the adult, the Oracle, the Asteroth.

Her father had never acknowledged, did not acknowledge that part of himself, but she had, once Jill/Stacy had set her on the right track. Gabrielle Asteroth had embraced her path.

Information hammered her, way too much to process. There was no chance in hell of doing that. The girl, the adult grinned at herself. Move Beyond, beyond the process, and look towards what isn't, what is. The trek revealed itself to her. The green road turned into a trail on the forest bed of eternity. She knew eternity, infinity or believed she had, but she had been so wrong, so woefully wrong. The lake of fire burned beneath her, above her, around her. This wasn't that horribly wrong, fake, pale version in the christian bible and teaching, but something far more, something beyond immense.

The fire was first, and we are its Shadow.

It was what had frightened the religious zealots out of their wits, and the knowledge they had sought to contain, to hide for so long... in vain. Asteroth the Demon smiled.

She was pulled into the air, the ether. There was no direction. All directions were One. She hovered above the Temple of Shadows. One glimpse, and she left it behind. She was Traveling. She knew that, even as she forgot. Her feet moved. She put one foot in front of the other, feeling like she had walked forever. Her feet splashed into mud. There seemed to be no end to it.

Sometimes, it's nothing but mud.

The loud, wicked laughter hurt her ears.

She sniffed and dried her tears. There seemed to be no end to them. It wasn't supposed to be like this, this suffering without end. She stumbled and almost fell. She walked on.

She stumbled through a city she didn't know, through unfamiliar streets. Ruins covered in plants surrounded her on all sides. Decayed spires filled her vision wherever she directed her attention. She no longer fought herself through mud, but tall, swaying grass covering the street from structure to structure, ruin to ruin. This was not a garden, but a pure, unadulterated wilderness. Civilization was long gone from this place. Her worn features cracked in a happy smile.

A crowd emerged from nowhere and started to relentlessly assaulting the traveler. She kept them from reaching her easily enough. It took only a slight change of focus. She grinned in relief and triumph.

The traveler reached an open square. A lone figure waited for her there. Waited for her.

The woman was dressed in leather. She had a bow and a keg of arrows on her back. Gabrielle Asteroth had grown up, had become an adult in all ways, had become a warrior witch of her own merit. The features of the grown, confident woman were familiar to young Gabi, but not the striking confidence, the patronizing grin.

Gabi stopped in front of her, and stared at her with envy and could not take her eyes off her.

– Will you look at that...

304

The voice sounded different, too, and not just because Gabi heard it from outside herself.

– You resemble Stacy, she heard herself, her young self say.

– She was ever our progenitor, the creature shrugged.

The enticing adult woman directed her full attention on the girl.

– Goddess, was I ever this… small?

Gabi felt flustered, wronged, furious, awestruck. The woman looked good humored at her and grabbed her jaw, assessing her, as if she was something strange, unknown. She let go. Gabi felt weak, drained.

– Your task is small, easy. Even you can't screw it up.

Gabi strove to speak, but failed miserably.

– Yes, I remember this. I was you, was this frail creature crouching before me, now.

Gabi straightened in defiance and further frustration.

The older, confidant Gabrielle grabbed her and pulled her away. One blink of an eye, and they found themselves hovering in space, looking down on the blue, changed planet.

– The Earth as it will become. The home, the playground of the People.

The continents had shrunk. All coastland and much of the inland had been consumed by the rising ocean. It was an amazing sight, and Gabi gasped in awe.

– You love that, don't you?

Gabi nodded eagerly, practically forgetting about the older version of herself hovering by her side. Then, it did dawn on her, and she looked at herself with luring eyes.

– Why do I not explain myself to myself?

– Because there is no need. You will do what you need to do, will play the part you need to play, and when you many years from now meet your young and incomplete self, you will treat her with the disdain she deserves.

She faded away, and Gabi was once more alone. Gabi moved on, pulling the reins again, yet again, yet again. She wanted this, had always wanted this, whatever it was, whoever she was. The pained frown appeared on the young face. She climbed the hill, yet another hill, no different from the one, the many she had climbed before or all she would climb. It looked different every time. The loop haunted her. The ongoing onslaught of the path hammered her like cold, hard rain. Hard rain fell.

The long walk continued. The sore feet kept putting one in front of the other.

They gathered around the fire. She was only one of many. They huddled in the heat, in the burning shielding them from the chill and the rain, the endless rain. In the others' empty eyes, she spotted the same bewilderment, the vast incomprehension.

Why do we do this? A girl howled in terror and despair. Why put ourselves through it?

Why? One of the countless travelers asked. She had no answer for herself.

Who am I? She asked. The others had no answer for her, for themselves. They asked her the same question, and she looked at them with abject confusion. She, covered in sweat and dirt, glimpsed the same unrecognizable face in the mirrors around her, in the dancing flames, the fierce, shifting shadows. Embarrassment and shame and rain kept hammering the young, suffering female on her road to Nowhere.

You are self-contained, a boy she didn't know told her. You are enough.

She laughed, a shrill laughter rocking her. He faded away with a sad face.

The moving, shifting tattoo on her face of a bird, a creature of shadow and pale, beyond powerful fire *meant* something, she knew it did, but she could not recall what. She didn't understand.

She was looking for something, an essential piece of herself. She had searched so long.

– This place is empty, a man cried, – as empty as a bloodless heart. You will find no answers or anything resembling a life here.

The cruel laughter echoed forever in her befuddled mind.

She knew this man, knew him intimately, all his angles, all his tales, but she could not remember.

Flickering rays of light surrounded her. Everything flickered in the piecemeal her existence had become. She arrived at one place. The next moment, it was gone, vanished, eviscerated forever. It stayed a part of her. Everything did.

Leave sadness behind, a voice told her.

Yes, she nodded empathically.

Leave happiness behind, the voice beckoned her.

No, no, she whimpered.

Gabi whimpered, as she hung in a dark place, in chains hard as rock.

Then, in the end, there was the Ghoul.

«Is this what you want»? It taunted her. «Is this the life you envision for yourself»?

She awoke on a plain, in the same position she had fallen asleep. To say it was enormous didn't do it justice. Sunshine traced it in all directions. She knew what this was. It had no end. Infinity was just that.

Stacy, *Lillith* stood in a relaxed, self-confident pose just a few steps away with her arms on her back.

– There you are, she said cheerfully. – You took your sweet time.

Gabi rose, brushing dust from her coat.

– I remember, she whimpered. – I still don't remember!

– You will!

Lillith looked different, looked the same, enigmatic creature, in a thousand different ways.

A glance, and the endless forest beckoned. Knowledge brought knowledge, but not understanding. Lillith faded away, always there, with her.

She jumped and danced during the crossing of the endless plain, in joyous sadness, but most of all Hunger. A rush of wind, of rain not seen blasted her. Anticipation surged through her, as familiar as that half-forgotten dream. A part of her, deeper than any thought, any reason, any passion had always known about this place.

306

The plain ended in the huge forest, like it always did, a gathering of trees and stench and beauty and horror more massive than she could remember. The path repeated itself endlessly. She paused on her trail through the forest. As a matter of habit, she tilted her head a little to listen. She heard the echo in the wind, in the whistling between the trees and from the treetops. Goosebumps grew on her exposed skin. She moaned in delight.

A witch faces danger, the voiceless voice whispered in both her ears. It is the bread and milk of her/his life, and brings untold pleasures and long-sought understanding. We swim like fish in the Dark River. We excel in its bounty.

The laughter rose from her throat. It reached her from all angles around her. Then, she froze, imagining that the entire forest turned quiet. All the sounds, all the birds' singing… ended. She shivered in fear, in excitement. She observed with a single glance the forest from above. She had believed the field to be vast, but the forest actually was, was infinite, and that concept, that reality suddenly made sense to her.

She was running, sort-of. Hunters were chasing her, but that hunt, that danger felt remote, unimportant. She walked on the dry forest bed on the trail through a swamp-like forest, breathing its moist, warm air. She drank from a pond, studying herself in its mirror. The dark hair, the pale skin, the ghostly, but healthy complexion. The deep, deep eyes. She spotted stars, galaxies, universes in those deep pools of human, inhuman consciousness.

The wind was blowing once more. The runner, the tired, exhausted runner was slowing down. She felt dog-tired, but on another level, she hardly felt tired at all. Excitement kept fueling her flesh and bone engine. She could taste the blood in her slack mouth. It invigorated her to no end.

She stopped by another pond, one mirroring the forest, turning it upside down. She turned upside down, too, revealing her Other, her horns and twisted features. It didn't shock her. She had glimpsed her before, halfway into, out of mirrors.

Asteroth.

She breathed silent and aloud.

She was indeed Asteroth within and without. The name echoed in the open glen with the pond, whistling between the trees. With that name spoken aloud, so much turned crystal clear in her mind.

A… being appeared between two trees, a human form with wings coated in shadow and pale fire. She recognized it in an instant. It was here, there and everywhere, the same in and out of the mirror. They looked at each other for ages. Her world, her universe expanded further. The flames spread from it, and to the fire at large, ghostly flames licking all things. The trees didn't actually burn. Nothing did. If anything, the fire made the trees grow, not burn.

It filled her being, every single piece of it, and she could hardly breathe.

She woke up on the sacrificial stone, gasping for breath, feeling like she was saturated with air. Eyes opened wide. She couldn't believe how wide. The quiet roar of the crowd hit her. She rose to her full height. The roar rose a bit higher. She floated down to the ground without effort. Daniel met her when she landed. They kissed passionately.

– It feels so great, she cried, – so unexpected and beyond great. I believed I knew everything, but that was mere bluster.

She glanced to the side at Lillith, at Janus, at Ted and Liz, at Phoenix, seeing them briefly again how they truly were. She bowed her head.

Daniel looked closer at her. She straightened again, smiled sweetly at him, and rubbed his cheek.

– I feel so strong, so powerful, she said, excited beyond excited. – I knew it would be something, but not like this.

The dance, the celebration began in earnest. The cave had long since become too small. The entire town had become their canvas of fire and shadow. Gabi repeated those two words, those impressions, sensations in her mind, in her very self. She danced with Daniel. The smile spread easily on her flushed skin.

In a whirl of dancing couples, they passed Stacy and Everett on the floor, the forest bed.

– You were concerned of me getting too much power, and then you give me even more power. What gives? What… changed?

Stacy didn't respond, not vocally or otherwise. The black eyes stayed fixed on the girl. This was the cold, distant creature Gabi couldn't quite fathom.

– It is your birthright, Daniel stated. – No one can take that away from you.

She focused on him and only him. Everyone else faded away.

– Time to blow this sad party, don't you think? She said seductively.

– Yes, he agreed, – we've spent enough time lingering here at this dreadful place.

Her laughter echoed so loud that it bounced off the sky. She made a gesture and a portal opened. The others noticed and directed their attention at the two. The two waved, and stepped into the mist and shadows. They appeared at the top of a mountain with a small cabin.

– My parents brought me here when I was an infant. I think they wanted to hide me, from the world, from all of you. But it made her stir crazy, and they left, and then they ended up in Northfield, of all places, the very center of things. Fate is certainly a mean bastard. Mine was preordained long before I was born.

She laughed some more. He grabbed her arm. She turned towards him with that sweet smile in place.

– I am Asteroth. I am yours!

She kissed him softly.

– I'm going to Phoenix, submitting to It, to Its very purpose. But I want the offspring to be yours.

The cold, clinical being briefly, only briefly overwhelmed the jubilant girl.

She led him through the open door, into the cabin, to the large bed and the warm, warm fireplace. They stood front to front, so close that air couldn't fit between them. She undressed in front of him, seductively, enticingly. Him undressing happened faster, rougher, impatient. Her nipples hardened when he played with them. She touched his cock in playful, very playful ways, as if she had long experience doing it. They moved on the bed, pushing themselves at each other so hard that it hurt. He moved on top of her. Both lost more reason with each new thrust. Moans and growls mixed and interchanged. One single scream rose from her throat, from his. Everything turned dark around them.

5

A strange event occurred on April 6. The Olympic torch was put out in London, thrown into the fountain at Trafalgar Square.

A symbolic act, and nothing more than that, but not without merit, and strangely reminiscent of current headlines.

They watched the further rise of Barack Obama, watched as establishment media attempted to once again making the Democratic Party and Republican Party primaries the alpha and omega in people's lives and not quite succeeding the way they used to.

– My friends, alternative media is no longer lacking fangs and claws, Gayle Tadero boasted, – and everyone knows it, feels it in their bones. The one-sided establishment propaganda of the past is a thing of the past. If you have just arrived, welcome to our 24/7 news-broadcast. You will get real news here. Yes, we are a part of the Phoenix Green Earth movement, and you should keep that in mind, but our claim is that our great record as a truth-seeking channel speaks for itself. No one lies and deceive here without being challenged about it. Try us out and find out for yourself.

Lynn Fredericks held something that could go for a standup comedy session at a dark, sweaty hall, a far cry from the townhall meetings of the establishment parties.

– Senator Obama seems to become the Democratic Party's candidate for the presidency, she began. – And while that carries some elements of surprise, it doesn't truly matter. The fact that he's a black man attempting to become president doesn't truly matter. What matters is his policies or lack of them, and his failure to truly stand up for black people, for minorities, for everyone impoverished under capitalism.

A sense of excitement, anticipation surged through the crowd, one quite notable, impossible to avoid noticing.

– His speeches «a more perfect union» and the one on race and politics are, like all the others filled with generalities and bluster. They are, to be blunt pure bullshit...

Laugher and incredulity surged through the crowd.

– He keeps yapping about American exceptionalism like it was something real, instead of the sinister and ridiculous deception it is. It is a ruse played by every single establishment candidate, revealing them as just one more snake-oil salesman.

She kept talking, talking, talking. It was obvious that she had a lot to say. It erupted from her throat in what seemed like an endless flow, as people by the tables forgot about their drinks and stared and listened.

– I count several slaves among my ancestors. So does Linsey Kendall and many of our candidates. Can candidate Obama say the same? As stated, don't be tempted to vote for or support candidate Obama because he's an African American. Look

309

at his policies, his policies beneath the surface of polished deception and lies of an establishment candidate. He speaks of change, but to me it's obvious that he doesn't truly means it. He has even admitted on several occasions that he's an early nineties republican. I guess there will be some change compared to George W. Bush's policies, but nothing significant, nothing true…

She ended her monologue with one more fierce statement.

– We've heard the empty promises of the establishment parties so many times before. Why should we believe them, now, when we have true agents of change on the stage?

She drowned in the warm, tall wave hitting her from the sea.

Both the democrats and republicans were strongly divided within the respective parties. Disagreements festering for decades finally erupted into the open for all to witness. They had always managed to present a more or less united front, but no longer. With the added pressure and demands of true accountability, the cracks were showing for everyone to witness.

– So many niggers have registered to vote, a Wisconsin official sighed. – It's such a drag.

It was recorded, and became public knowledge not long afterwards.

Far more black people registered to vote after that.

Many people were banned from voting because of a criminal record. Various Green Earth Party representatives across the country did their best to counter that, succeeding in some places, failing in others.

The ruthless, relentless establishment propaganda were rolled out in full against the Green Earth Party and its representatives.

– Today, we will examine Linsey Kendall's Russian connections, 60 Minutes anchor Lesley Stahl said, and stared straight into the camera.

– His great grandmother was Russian, the man she interviewed pointed out, – and the Warren-family has certainly maintained contact with their Russian relatives.

– That's a great piece of journalism right there, Linsey said, chuckling a bit.

– One more example of what focus the establishment and its media will have in the coming months, Betty remarked.

She shrugged deliberately.

– If only they knew the truth, she giggled.

A few days later, CNN, in a manipulated image had Linsey wearing a classic Bolshevik cap.

– This is classic establishment propaganda, Phillip said on the Phoenix Green Earth channel. – There's little or no hold in its reporting, but people will, in general believe even the silliest claim if it's repeated enough times.

The establishment channels kept declining, in both quality and viewer attendance, and alternative media kept growing in importance. The old establishment methods just didn't work that well anymore. Facebook started a policy of removing all links from alternative media. Facebook shrunk to nothing in weeks after that.

– I will bring necessary change. Obama stated. – There is no need to support untested candidates or parties.

310

– We have already succeeded, Stacy Larkin grinned. – Barack Obama has already started defending the establishment and redelegated his empty rhetoric of change to lesser importance.

The strain was visible on Obama's face by then. The cracks were showing.

– Nothing will fundamentally change, Senator Joe Biden, the man more and more pundits deemed most likely to be Obama's Vice President candidate told a group of private investors. The recording of that went wild on the Internet.

– One of several aims is to put a stop to any chance establishment media might have to profit from their propaganda, Linsey said at a press conference a few days later.

– Why do you attack Obama more than John McCain? An establishment media reporter asked.

– Obama fools more people than McCain, Stacy said. – Obama is just one more snake oil salesman, but there are still people not seeing through that. It's criminally dumb to be fooled by such people and such groups of people, but we still have a job to do when it comes to exposing them.

– It's totally inconceivable to me how people can be so easily deceived, but some still are, Lynn replied. – Current human society is still dominated by centrist fanaticism. That is, more than anything, what we must expose.

– Centrist… fanaticism? The journalist gasped incredulous.

– Precisely, Lynn said solemnly. – Centrists, liberals have long since avoided having that term slapped on them, but their fanaticism has done far more damage than any other. Giving them a relentless scrutiny is long overdue.

John McCain had long since won the Republican nomination, and Obama was winning the Democratic. Everyone could see that, except Hillary Clinton and her clique of sycophants.

Linsey won the Green Earth Party nomination with a comfortable margin. He and Lynn stood side by side with their hands raised above their head.

– I expect you to tell me, give it to me straight up if my speech contains even the slightest bullshit so prevalent at the other conventions, he said. – We, the two of us, in conjunction with all of you will do our best to truly transform human society from the nightmare it has become. We will fight hard for our dreams to become reality. That's it. That's the speech. Thank you for everything you've done, and everything you will do.

He saw the sea of solemn agreement before him and rejoiced.

It was still more, far more, true debate there than at the Republican and Democratic primaries, and people saw that. People participated in droves, and became even more involved with the rebellion.

Gabi walked on her feet. Her nude feet touched the grass-covered ground. Daniel walked by her side, but she hardly saw him. She had her attention directed forward.

– I could have just opened a portal with a casual thought, she said, – but I kind of enjoy this, this slow walk.

He knew she was aware of him, then, that he still occupied at least a tiny part of her consciousness.

She turned to him. They stopped. She grabbed his hand and put it on her slowly growing belly. She kissed him on the cheek and turned and walked away.

She climbed the trail, walked up the hill on light feet, not looking back, not a single time. The dark forest beckoned her. She walked a little faster. The dark forest surrounded her. Its deep chill invaded her being. The excitement never left the doll-like face. Animals and spirits and malevolent spirits called her name, threatening and cajoling the human being that had dared entering their domain.

The pervasive heat hit her the moment she stepped out of the forest and onto the shore. It burned her on all sides, but most of all in front where she faced the burning Fire Lake. She had never seen it quite like this before. Everyone, even the dullest mind could observe its ethereal dancing flames, now. The flames turned even more intense with her arrival. Raven's Court didn't look diminished through the flames, but more powerful than ever.

People, temple priests of both genders paid their respects, called her name in similar ways to that of the Dark Forest. She ignored them, hardly aware of their presence.

She walked into the lake without delay, at a slow, languished pace. The water splashed her legs. The flames licked her frame. The warm water reached her chest, but didn't shrink her nipples in any way. They itched even more, so much that she could hardly bear it. She fell forward and started swimming. The water turned to fire, the fire to water, to the Dark River. She swam the calm sea, the rough currents. Fire Lake was both, neither. It shook and caressed her flesh, her buzzing mind. She heard a loud scream from the Dark Forest.

The shore rushed towards her like a mighty wave. Her feet touched the bottom of the lake near the islet. She walked out of the water. The shimmering heat hit her from all sides. It seemed to dry her and her clothes in an instant. She heard the scream again, the scream of mighty release that couldn't be denied or ignored.

Lillith, coated in shadow welcomed her with a soft, dark smile.

– You are Sweet Sixteen, and your time has come.

She kissed her on the cheek, and stepped aside, sending her on her way. Gabi entered the castle through the wide and tall door, the wind chimes singing in her ears. Liz and Ted and the nineteenth in their circle awaited her inside. She stopped before the two fireeyes.

– You have set up shop, now, have become gods, now. I am Asteroth. I am yours to command, Phoenix.

– Are you? Michelle asked. – Are you beyond doubt and reluctance?

She and Linda and the rest of the nineteen scrutinized Gabi far more than the Phoenix did. Ted and Liz seemed unconcerned, almost relaxed, casual about it.

– I am! Asteroth replied with a proud stance.

She reached out her hands. Phoenix grabbed them. Pain surged through her. Her scream echoed through the ether. Raven's Court, The Hill, Northfield transformed further. One wave spread from that single point and touched everyone within a wide circle. They had brought Northfield into the shadow world and the shadow world version of it into the material world, doing so with an ease that she had never

312

been able to do. The three of them voiced spells, dark calls in the night, in the shimmering afternoon heat. Everyone felt the change, felt the whisper in the wind, everyone coming from far away to this place of antiquity and mystery.

There was an instant shift, far different from what the two Warrens usually felt when they borrowed powers, far more primal. The girl whimpered in their cruel grip, but she handled it. Her power sang within them. Everything opened up, like a slow, pervasive explosion. They took her might and… tripled it. Only their many years of experience kept them from losing control.

The three of them slipped into the shadowland. They stood on the shore of the wide river Styx, observing as countless shadows crossed the deep divide. The raging stream surrounded them. The glowing spirits passed through, on their way to the Divide. The Divide, Styx, *The Dark River*. They visited hospital rooms, where dying flesh gave up its spirit.

They caught a faint echo, a faint echo even to them, as they wielded their mighty hand. The three of them slipped easily up a level, sideways a level, where a spirit waited for them.

– Ah, the Phoenix and its Oracle. What a magnificent sight you are, and still so far from what you will become.

The spirit bowed its head with a leering grin. They knew it, knew it intimately, as ever more secrets were revealed and ever more veils were brushed aside.

It faded away, pulled by the tides to resume its Journey. They resumed theirs, maneuvering the most powerful tides with only minor difficulties.

Liz woke up in silence, in the quiet, quiet night surrounded by warm flesh, and she sighed content. Asteroth, wide awake studied her with her poised stare.

Come here, honey, Liz bid her and reached out a hand.

Gabi moaned in happiness and pushed herself at the bigger frame. The young woman shook a bit, just a bit, before calming down in the strong embrace.

The three of them stood by a window, bathing in the warm glow of the low moon. Ted spoke in a whirl of water and wind.

– We humans see only the waves of the ocean, not the ocean itself. *Now, we do!*

The whirl returned the scrutiny, the engagement.

– The sky, Space looks black, but if we could see it all, see the dark or hidden matter, it would look shiny and blinding bright.

Dark matter was truly white matter. The three of them shook hard in fervor.

Gabi, wearing her temple priestess dress carried a tray with food and drink up the dark marble stairs. She walked through the Hall of Mirrors and passed by the windows with flickering curtains. Her sandals hardly released a sound as they touched the floor. The house spoke to her louder than ever. She opened the door to the combined study and bedroom and stepped inside. Ted and Liz had just dressed and sat in two deep chairs by the low table. The mere sight of them made the heart jump in her chest. The young woman swallowed hard and rushed forward. She knelt in front of them, an equal distance from both.

– Your breakfast, My Lord, My Lady, she breathed.

Liz signed for her to put the tray on the table, and she did so in an instant.

– You have eaten well, I trust? Liz said. – You need lots of nourishment these days, you know.

– Yes, My Lady, Gabi replied.

Liz grabbed her jaw and assessed her. Gabi didn't resist. Her body turned limp, malleable. Liz let go with a content snort.

– You may take your leave, now, Ted bid her.

– Yes, My Lord, Gabi cried. – Yes, Ted.

Liz's wicked laughter chased her out of the room and down the hall.

She met Stacy by the dark marble stairs.

– They decide when they require your presence, she told her. – You will always be available.

– Yes, Mother, Gabi choked.

Stacy brushed aside a lock of hair.

– They need to be strict with you, godling. You're young and bashful and inexperienced.

Asteroth looked sullenly at her, but stayed quiet.

Walk with me.

Gabi did. They flowed down the stairs, and walked into the wild-growing garden in the backyard. The plants danced in Lillith's honor. It made the young woman giggle.

– Now, tell me what's on your mind.

Asteroth didn't ask her why she just didn't read her mind. She sort-of understood why she didn't.

– Phoenix is anxious, Asteroth said with a frown. – It has always been to a certain point, but it has grown notably more so lately.

Stacy looked like she pondered the issue, but in truth she didn't.

– They're counting the days, she stated. – Today is June 21. In six months on the day, they're both fated to die.

Gabi gasped so loud that it hurt. The frown grew deeper.

– There are records, Stacy related, – tales from another reality giving us fairly accurate accounts of what is going to happen. Some of it is written by another Nick, some by another you. Your school projects were already written down before you did them.

She didn't have to say anything more. Asteroth opened a portal transporting them to the library, to the wall of books and ancient texts and scrolls.

– This is our version of the library in Alexandria, Lillith said. – It contains our experiences, past present and future, what has been, what is, what will be, what might be and what might have been.

She pulled out one book.

– In one reality, you and I and Everett and several others were born eight years earlier, and post-Jahavalo events happened between 1997 and 2008, not just from 2005 to 2008. Everything is more rushed, anxious, now. The pressure, I surmise is greater.

Gabi opened the book. She recognized her own handwriting.

314

Fourth part (excerpt and summary) of:
«Observations on evolution and development of Life in The Universe».
The further observations of Gabrielle Asteroth, born 1984-02-29

A somewhat pleasant chill trickled down her spine as she noticed the date. She flipped some pages, instantly immersed in the writing. Stacy pulled out another book. It floated into Gabi's hands. It was basically the same story, with variations, with her birth date set eight years later.

She put away both books a long time later. The sun had moved on the sky. The shadows had grown longer. There was still hunger in her eyes when she looked at the older woman. Stacy pulled out a third book and handed to her. Gabi recognized Nick's writing. She flipped more pages, her eyes growing wider with each one.

Edward Warren
Born: May 1st 1955
Dead: December 22nd 2008

Linsey was on the right. There was no death date on him.
Liz was on the next page.

Elizabeth Warren
Born: May 1st 1959
Dead: December 22nd 2008

Gabi choked distressed and amazed.
– You're an adult, now, Stacy stated. – You can handle it.
The patronizing bite didn't really touch Asteroth. It merely added to her anxiety and excitement. Stacy took her hand. The young woman looked startled at the older.
– Today, we will yet again celebrate life.
– We will! Gabi nodded empathically.
Liz and Ted descended the stairs, followed by the nineteen. Gabi rushed to Ted's side. The extended group walked outside, crossing the lake while getting their feet wet, while the flames licked their bodies and burned their mind. They reached the shore and were greeted by eager, happy and open smiles and the loud banshee wail from the forest. The wail didn't really worry them anyone. They had all long since grown accustomed to it.
The three saw what everyone at the shore saw and more. Everyone felt the power. The three saw the energy, the lattice between the nineteen and the two, still incomplete. Gabi looked at the two, then looked at the nineteen, then returned her gaze at the two. She nodded to herself.
– All the black is gone, she said with her spooky voice, and the remote look in her eyes, – but not the shadow, and not the fire.

Everyone studied her, but she hardly saw them.

– Two of you are missing from our company, our company of strangers, but don't worry. They will be here.

The remote expression in her eyes faded, and she regained her faculties.

– Our Oracle is so precious, Linda said.

Gabi suffered an instant blush.

There was a shared chuckle when they stepped into the forest, but it faded in the wind, in the loud banshee wail welcoming them.

– What is that? Sally wondered.

– Something growing louder every day, Lee said. – It's a choir, really, if you listen between the moments.

– You mean, there's a progression?

– There's a progression in all things, Lee said.

– There's something I keep wondering about, Sally said.

They looked at her.

– Why am I here? I've got no powers.

– You do, Carla said, – like all of you, but they're latent, currently unavailable in some of you. They might not and will probably not stay that way.

Sally and William and Glory and Giovanni and Morten and Diana looked astonished at each other.

– Sometimes, it is like that, Tony said. – You go your entire life without being able to actualize what's stirring within.

– You belong, Carla said. – You've always been here.

The last words echoed in the forest, in the ether. Ted and Liz felt what the others felt; an immense sense of belonging. It stayed with them with every step, through the pale shadow forest they knew so well, and when they reached the other side and looked down on the town, on Northfield, and when they descended the hill and reached the streets and were surrounded with the excited talk so pervasive everywhere.

– We will stay down here from now on, he stated, – We will not reside on Mount Olympus.

– Yes, Ted, Gabi eagerly responded.

The celebration had begun. It picked up further when they reached flat ground. People greeted them and honored them in all possible ways. Ted and Liz could easily gauge how they strove to contain themselves, to fight their immense sense of awe, in vain.

The night, the summer twilight descended on the town. It was hardly discernible from the shadow always muting the daylight. Tall fires lit up everywhere. They set fire to one house. Its immense dancing flames cast shadows everywhere. It felt like a sacrifice and strengthened them further. Countless spirits rose from its pyre. Glasses without number met and parted, and their content wet parched throats.

– It is so fun to do this without fearing government intervention, Giovanni said. – Such a thrill.

– A thrill of thrills, Michelle chuckled.

316

They had a toast.

Morten didn't speak. He just stared into the fire. He hardly spoke anymore.

His banshee wail sounded loud and clear in Liz and Ted's minds.

His joined with that from others in the village, with that of the world, growing louder by the minute.

Udo, in his solitude screamed louder than anyone.

Gabi looked at Ted and Liz. The others did, too. She sniffed in compassion. The two and one and nineteen sat around the large fire, the one there didn't seem to be an end to.

– Changing human society is hard, Ted said. – It has become more and more an unmovable, unyielding object, a Machine. We made it, constructed it slowly across the centuries, until there is hardly anything but *it* left, until it started forming, constructing us in its image, and we became machines ourselves.

There was a brief pause, almost unnoticeable.

– The final enemy is us, our submission to the Machine.

He felt the deep chill passing down everyone's spine.

– Conformity is a powerful force, Carla said softly. – It can overcome, crush even the strongest spirit.

Lillith sat close to them, even though not around the giant bonfire. She sat there with half-closed eyes, surrounded by warm flesh and fiery minds, and she was smiling.

– We lived among our worshipers once, Stacy had once told Jill. – We can do so again.

They did. If there was a line between them and the mortals anymore, it was blurry to the point of being indistinguishable. She watched them as they mixed and joined. She watched herself as she walked to the Phoenix, and sat down between them.

– You made the final step, she whispered in their ears. – You stepped down from Mount Olympus. You did good!

They made a closer study of her, as were their want.

– Too bad Tilla isn't here, she shrugged.

– She is here, Liz insisted. – We sense her. We've sensed her for years.

Stacy saw how they pondered her words, without really wanting to do so.

– We have everything we've ever wanted, now, Stacy whispered in their ears.

They knew it wasn't true. She received all kinds of shades of emotions from them. They caught her casual reading easily. She shook in delight.

– We've fought so long. This is our final chance at getting it right, and we will.

They were used to her speaking like that, in a kind of formal, boastful manner, but the wording still made a frown grow on Ted's brow, and she could just about keep herself from smiling.

A group of youths full of life and life's fire came and dragged them away. They allowed it to happen, joining in on the playful mood. She scouted her surroundings as they danced through the eternal township, so similar and so different compared to ancient Atlantis. Fifty thousand years. She marveled at the thought.

Ethel and her entourage crossed their path at some moment. They exchanged good-humored hails and greetings. Ethel, even Ethel seemed to be in an upbeat mood. Lillith looked at her with pity, and Ethel returned a puzzled look.

You will catch nothing from me, poor girl. I'm as enigmatic as a sphinx.

And the frown on Ethel's brow grew deep.

I remember you, poor girl. I've wanted to renew our acquaintance for a long, short time. It was only yesterday to me.

The forest town in its fairly enclosed space almost felt like the inside of a structure. The warm heat of the summer twilight hardly felt like outside at all. When they picked an abode at random, with the many open windows and doors, it felt no different, like the best of two worlds.

The two and one and nineteen, and several others undressed in a beyond casual way. Gabi rubbed her growing belly more than a bit distracted, with all her attention on Ted and Liz. She melted into their embrace. Every move felt so natural, so right. She sighed content. The pleasant, simmering heat from each and every person in the room caressed her. She began screaming in her heat soon, and kept doing so until she joined the others in sleep and dream much, much later.

The smile stayed on her lips during the night, the morning and the day. She hummed a melody without name. The house had several empty rooms. She chose one at random, and began making it hers, her new place of power. She did so without noticeable effort. The night spent with Phoenix had not really drained her, or drained her enough for her to notice. Surrounded by the two dozen bodies had been like floating in warm water. She recharged what little energy she had lost easily. It took only a slight dip in the stream. She reached out a hand, and that was basically it.

The three of them gathered in the room. She grew the spheres, the «crystal balls» from her palm. Each of them revealed a scene, an event of interest to them.

– This has become so easy, now, she breathed. – I can't believe how easy it has become.

The room changed in subtle way the more she worked it, the longer they stayed. Phoenix participated, too. She shared the room with the fireeyes, instead of dominating it, like she had with room 13 at the tavern.

She made one ball grow bigger. It showed a protest in a typical town. A police officer drew his gun and aimed it at the crowd. One of the protesters turned to him and said calmly:

– The moment you fire that gun, you're dead, do you understand me?

The officer backed off with insane eyes, and ran from the place. The scornful laughter chased him all the way through many a narrow alley closing in on him.

– It is working, Asteroth breathed. – We are gaining headway! People grow fierce and bold confronting authority. They just needed a strong push... a really strong push.

She shrunk the orb, and grew another. A group of teenagers wandered into the woods during the first day of their exploration of magick.

– Look at them, Asteroth snarled, – at their innocent eyes.

She was drawn to them, and her eyes were once again filled with wonder.

318

– Don't fear for them, Liz said softly. – They will learn, learn what the world is, what life is about, and fight fiercely anyone attempting to keep that from them.

– Yes, Phoenix, Asteroth acknowledged happily.

One more ball shrunk. One more grew. They experienced it like one, continuous process.

– The Democratic Party and Republican Party make any effort at creating hurdles for the registering of our candidates, Linsey told a crowd of thousands. – Know that we're fighting them every step of the way.

– It would have been better if Kerry had won in 04, a man shouted. – You can't deny that.

– What if Kerry had won? Linsey asked rhetorically. – It wouldn't have made much of a difference. Kerry was spouting the same insane war rhetoric as good ol' George. Democratic presidents have followed republicans in the past, and nothing, *nothing* has changed. Are you really this stupid, this without a sense of history, to forget so easily?

The man pulled back, literally fleeing the assembly.

The Oracle and her muses followed Linsey around for a few days, probing for enlightenment, hoping to spot something they had yet to spot or glimpse.

– Do you wish to hear Obama's true slogan? Linsey quipped at another assembly. – MORE OF THE SAME.

It was a good joke, and the reward reached him in the shape of hearty laughter and powerful passions, strengthening him, strengthening the three in the unremarkable, old, big, no longer empty and dusty house.

– Everything or almost everything is proceeding according to plan… isn't it?

Gabi wondered, suddenly uncertain, the frown deepening on her brow again.

– The general pattern seems to follow the plan, Liz mused.

– No, of course we don't ruin our children by setting boundaries for them, Linsey responded to a question the watchers for some reason or another didn't catch. – We set wide standards by giving them informal guidelines. We encourage them to grow and become truly independent human beings, but at their own pace and by their own desire, while we smother them in rough affection, preparing them for the hard, cruel world. We teach them truly critical thinking, teach them to think, not what to think. A child of the Janus Clan will become an adult in the true meaning of the word.

– Most other human beings today never become adults, Betty added, – but remain dependent children, never truly pulling themselves away from the guardians.

That made Ted frown again, but the potentially revealing thought or line of thought slipped his mind.

Linsey and Betty and Stacy and Everett attended a meeting arranged by an organization claiming to be independent, which usually meant the Democratic Party and Republican Party wowing voters and lobbyists for their support. But that, too had changed this year. Republican and Democratic officials looked with despair at the huge crowd gathering around the quartet.

– So, you guys are married? A young girl said with excited eyes.

– We are handfasted, yes, Stacy replied lightly. – It's a more informal bond.

– But also far more intense as long as it lasts, Everett said, exposing his beautiful rows of teeth.

And ours have lasted millennia, he thought.

– You will actually implement true pro-choice? A boy said incredulous.

– We will implement free abortion, both on state and federal level, fully paid for and left to the woman's discretion, Linsey said. - It is long overdue, like so many other issues in our current inhuman society. We will make any obstruction punishable by law. Anyone attempting to remove women's freedom will pay for it.

That did cause quite the stir and quite a few angry shouts, but all of that drowned in the thundering applause.

Gravity and joy kept warring in the hall.

– The insects... Martin Keller, Morningstar said. – They are dying. All the animals are dying. The plants are dying. Humanity is dying.

They saw it, right in front of their eyes.

– This is the true state of the world.

Everyone, the entire inner circle of hundreds in the Janus Clan rubbed their head, attempting to soothe a heartache that couldn't be soothed.

– Democrats have moved so far to the left that they now see the Constitution as a rightwing document, an obviously conservative man said angrily, with saliva flowing from his mouth, riled up beyond words from the excited conversation.

– People with common sense, however, Linsey replied calmly, – easily see that the Democrats have moved so far to the right that there is little significant difference between them and GOP.

– We must take back America, the man persisted in his delusions.

Betty almost doubled over in insane laughter.

He glared at her.

– You can't take back something that was never yours in the first place, she grinned and shook her head. – And «patriotism is the last refuge of a scoundrel». *Every* sane person knows that.

She shrugged. A move she knew irritated him immensely.

– Everybody should betray their country. We don't owe it any allegiance and there are countless reasons to oppose it, oppose the very idea of a country, of borders drawn on a map, of nationalism in all its forms. Like so many other things it's an insane construct of civilization.

– And the United States of America is at the very top of the heap, Stacy stated.

– Then, why are you bothering with the elections? A woman wondered.

– We try to follow a somewhat non-dogmatic approach to our approach, Stacy said, – choosing a multitude of simultaneous responses. The most important is the community building, though.

The Republican Party held its national convention in Saint Paul, Minnesota in early September. John McCain and Sarah Palin were nominated as president and vice president.

– What a bunch of sickoes! Gabi cried incensed.

All of it looked more completely insane to them, a long row of speakers sounding worse than the previous.

The three experienced the democratic convention in Denver in late August last. This one was, if possible, even more a theater than the GOP convention, with the insanity more muted, beneath the surface. Barack Obama and Joe Biden were nominated as president and vice president. They put on a good show, but the badly attended assembly didn't really invite enthusiasm. Obama looked drawn, like he hadn't had enough sleep. He almost sounded like a sleepwalker during his speech. All the usual pieces of the puzzle were present, but skewed, twisted.

Phillip and Gayle had a great time, an even greater time than usual when they analyzed the various components.

– They didn't exactly look their best, did they? Gayle giggled.

– They most certainly did not, Phillip agreed.

– You can practically observe the despair and desperation in their eyes, Gayle said, – and we have proof that their actions reflect that, and it isn't funny at all.

She turned serious. He turned serious. And they both looked directly into the camera.

– We have emails sent from the DNC-leadership to party-officials the same night, Phillip said. – We have witnesses and affidavits proving their authenticity. They say the following:

It appeared on the screen. Phillip read them, read all aloud.

– Ladies and gents; we must step up our efforts to keep Green Earth Party candidates from getting on ballots. Our friends in the judiciary will certainly be a big help.

He kept speaking for some length. It turned worse, not better as the reading progressed.

– We must take extreme measures to protect our way of life, one passage read.

It ended a long time later. Both seemed ragged, but with the inner fire intact and visible in their eyes.

– It's signed Nancy Pelosi, Gayle added. – You should know that this, shocking as it is, is only a small part of the documents in question. We have made everything available, at our websites, and those of countless others.

– We welcome Stacy Larkin to our program, eager to hear her comment. She will join us through video-link. As you know, it is no longer safe to physically join us in the studio, as the US government and its affiliates have attempted to blow us up and kill us for years. We will have a long line of brave guests later, including many unaffiliated with the Green Earth Party.

Stacy appeared on the screen opposite the two of them.

– Good evening, Miss Larkin, Gayle greeted her. – I assume you have a comment to this.

– I have indeed, Stacy said. – This move is certainly not unexpected, and just one more act added to a long list through the years of the two establishment parties doing their utmost to stop truly independent individuals from becoming candidates. We have prepared for it. We are prepared, and rest assured that we're ready to fight this, on all levels. We've already delivered documents charging the Democratic Party and its leaders with unlawful conduct to the Denver Police Department. We will seek more injunctions on both local, state and federal level. We're fed up with establishment's antics to prevent people from deciding what kind of society we desire. Enough!

The scene shifted to Linsey and Lynn leaving the main headquarters of the DPD. They were surrounded by armed guards. Those in the group with telekinetic powers and ability to form shields in the air focused on their surroundings, scouted for threats.

Linsey and Lynn held another impromptu press-conference right there on the spot.

– DNC-officials have, true to form already claimed that the emails have been «illegally obtained», Linsey cried with a loud, penetrating voice honed by genetics and years of singing. – The fact that those emails expose illegal activity doesn't seem to concern them at all. I guess they're used to getting away with everything. This time, they won't. We will pursue the matter, and we will make certain that they're judged by the full extent of the law, and we have just been assured by the Chief of the DPD that they will look into it. We told him that we will keep an eye on him, and his colleagues, to make sure they do their duty.

They took questions, answering the silliest and most loaded question with calm and patience.

– What do you say to those claiming you are Russian agents?

– That that is merely one more piece of establishment propaganda, Lynn shrugged. – You don't need a crystal ball to see the obvious.

– What is it with the heavy armament? Do you fear for your lives?

– Of course, we fear for our lives, Beth replied. – We would be stupid if we didn't. Violence is the tactic the establishment eagerly resorts to when the softer response has failed.

Her power flared, and even the most insensitive individual in her extended presence noticed as the Goddess of unbridled passions inadvertently asserted herself. In one tiny slice of time, they all felt it. The next moment it was gone like a puff of smoke, and they could not quite be certain of what they had experienced. She reined herself in, having learned to control, to contain herself in her later years.

She kept asserting herself, manifesting her power, her *might* at a lower, growing level, and she was far from alone in doing that. Ted and Liz felt it, like a storm within, without, from far away. They had felt it before their first meeting with her, with Beth Alver, but now, even though it was deliberately muted, it still felt stronger, felt far more powerful. She, like they, and others in the inner circle gained even more than usual energy from large crowds.

The reporters writhed in discomfort, sweating and breathing hard, most of them without knowing why, only a few feeling the embarrassing pressure below.

– What about the violent riots?

– You mean the peaceful protesters subjected to the brutal police brutality, of course, Lynn corrected him.

– But many of the… demonstrations didn't have permission to gather at the given space, another reporter interjected.

– We live in a society in which people must ask permission from authority to protest authority, Linsey chuckled. – What's wrong with this picture?

The establishment media, as usual didn't get anywhere with the Green Earth Party. They had a great story, if they would print it, but usually they didn't. It still got out, through alternative media, now, far bigger and reaching far more people than establishment media.

New York Times had a photo plastered all over the front page.

WHAT'S WRONG WITH THIS PICTURE?

It was accompanied with the usual twisted version of events. It hardly mattered anymore. The liberal lighthouse, and its employees became even more the nation's laughingstock. The paper's circulation and revenue fell to half of what it had been mere days before.

The footage returned to Gayle and Phillip and fellow news-anchors in the studio. They traced the events, the fallout, one more fallout from there, with guests and commentators.

– The establishment and its people become increasingly… frustrated, one said. – It's an amazing sight, really…

They ended one part of the program with showing footage from the Green Earth Party national convention in Houston, comparing it with footage from the two main parties. It was a completely different mood there, with true excitement and enthusiasm, and lacking the bluster and prevailing sense of superiority of the other two. The possible upcoming president and vice president, Linsey Kendall and Lynn Fredricks were presented with somber enthusiasm.

– We have chosen them as our foremost representatives this year, Stacy cried. – Give them a hearty applause.

The applause and the feet hammering the floor shook the building.

The image flickered and faded out. Gabi gasped and dropped to the floor. Everything turned black.

She woke up in bed later, still woozy, still weak. Stacy towered above her. She had trouble seeing her properly.

– You need to take care of yourself, not overextend yourself, you know that.

Gabi failed to speak, once, twice, before giving up, looking sullenly at the dark creature.

Stacy put her hands on her, and an immense energy surged through the skinny body, and Asteroth felt strength fill her anew.

She sat up. Her power had returned. Triumphant joy filled her features.

– Thank you, Lillith.

The lesser goddess bowed her head in gratitude.

– Your health is very important to me, to us all, Lillith said softly.

She rubbed the girl's cheek. Gabi didn't object.

– You may join us for dinner. You need lots of food as well, of course.

Gabi suddenly looked stricken.

– I must shower, and…

– You run along, dear. You have lots of time to make yourself presentable.

Joking, not joking. Asteroth looked sullenly at her.

The girl ran to the shower. She stopped before the bathroom mirror, studying her belly. It looked distinctively smaller than she had expected it to be.

– You are unstuck, Stacy told her. – It happens, you know.

I know! Asteroth wanted to respond, to snarl, but she held her tongue.

Her breasts, her hips, her body had grown bigger, fuller. She liked that, loved that.

Yes, Ted loves bigger females, Stacy kindly reminded her.

Gabi stepped into the shower and turned on the water. She cleaned herself thoroughly, spending far more time subjected to the water flow than was strictly necessary.

Stacy dried her with the large towel and combed her hair, preparing the temple priestess for the day. She found a dress. It fit the teenager perfectly. Gabi reddened by the full sight of herself, of her painted face in the mirror.

– Yes, you will find mercy in his eyes, Stacy shrugged. – Don't doubt that you are a worthy sacrifice. Don't doubt that for a moment.

– No, mother, the girl whispered.

Stacy had changed. She had become crueler, more distant. Gabi pondered that for a moment, until the two of them stepped into the dining room. Ted and Liz and Everett and Betty and Jason and Michelle and Val and Linsey sat around the smaller round table. A deep blush assaulted Gabi. Each of them greeted her in their own way. She gave them her best smile and sat down on her designated spot by Stacy's side.

A sudden hunger grabbed her, and she started feeding. Mother looked pleased at her.

I know, I need my nourishment…

She made certain that the other picked it up. Raven's features didn't change in any noticeable way.

– It's a good thing that you have offspring, Val remarked, – They will probably not be Dreamweavers, since that it is an extremely rare occurrence, but it increases the chances of more of them being born to the Janus Clan down the line.

– I think so, too, Gabi replied brightly, fearing they would see straight through her.

She did have a nice time in their company. These were the people she had most in common with in all existence.

– Nick sends his regrets, Betty said. – He wanted to be here, but was otherwise engaged.

– He usually is, Michelle said dryly.

Val rubbed Gabi on the cheek.

– You like Nick, don't you Cherie?

– I do, Gabi said.

– Don't worry. You will meet him again soon enough.

– I don't, Asteroth insisted. – It isn't like we don't meet on a regular basis.

All the adults laughed, easily catching the steel in the young demon's voice.

They all heard the music. It was on all the time, now, impossible to not catch, like a beautiful shriek in their outer and inner ears. It turned louder and louder and louder, in all the many states of their being.

– You keep... notes, don't you? Linsey asked no one in particular.

– We do, Ted said. – The events scrolled in the crystal balls and the visions match remarkably well the actual reality.

– There are minor variations, unexpected events, though, Liz pointed out. – It might be something important or something totally silly. We're always surprised.

– No one can control the Dark River, Lillith stressed. – We might be able to predict certain events, but never achieving anything even approaching control. Control is an illusion.

Everyone looked at her, noticing her wording and the quality of her voice.

– We must keep doing what we usually do, Ted stressed, – focusing on making things right on all levels.

They nodded solemnly, getting his clear warning. Asteroth nodded harder than all the others. The eager smile kept brightening her face.

– We can cling to the tail of the Midgard serpent, Everett said, – but we can't stop its ride.

Stacy squeezed his hand. He drowned in her black eyes.

– What we've been waiting for so long is happening, now, she said softly.

He nodded without knowing why, without being aware of himself nodding. A mighty joy filled him, filled him to the brim.

– You didn't meet up with us for the first time in New York City in 1931, she stated. – It was merely one more encounter among many, a chain of pearls flashing in eternity.

A trickle not cold, but hot as glowing iron flowed down his spine. She kissed him on the lips, her lips practically locked on to his. Two set of fangs rubbed against each other. He imagined her to be a wolf, a wolf bitch rubbing herself at him, her pervasive stench of body juices ripping into his nostrils.

They and Betty and Linsey withdrew from the company. Jason, Val and Michelle did so as well not long afterwards. Asteroth, Ted and Liz remained. Asteroth reddened under their steady stare. A modesty making her kick herself made her bow her head.

Life continued between the sessions, between the growing and shrinking of crystal balls.

When the Olympic torch was put out in London, they felt reasonably certain that it really happened, and wasn't happening only in their visions. Events proceeded more or less as it had in those visions. Linsey was elected as the Green Earth party representative. Barack Obama and John McCain as their parties. There were deviations, and the three in their study in Ravenscourt studied each and every one.

A group of protesters threw oil-based neon paint mixed with sand at the armored cops, obscuring their visors and thereby their visions. When they attempted to rub it off, it scraped their visors, ruining their visibility for good.

– That is certainly new, Gabi said, her face glowing with excitement.

– Where does that come from? Liz wondered.

– I don't think it's too far-fetched to suspect that we inspired them and bolster their creativity, Ted grinned, – growing hope.

Liz kissed him. Gabi kissed him.

There were other events, positive and negative and in-between. A group of police officers used grenades against protesters, executing dozens of unarmed people. Blood and guts decorated walls and pavement for several blocks.

– We can't be everywhere, see everything, Ted said glumly.

– But people are stepping up, Liz insisted. – They take their rebellion to the next level. We see it everywhere.

They returned to their desperate task. Gabi's hands hurt. She had a killer headache. Her entire body hurt. She fell again. Stacy attempted to bolster a bed-ridden Gabi, but... failed.

– It won't work anymore, she said softly. – It won't for quite a while. You need to rest, truly rest, the old-fashioned way. You won't even get near Phoenix the next few weeks, not if I can help it.

Gabi didn't object. She didn't have the strength.

– The music grows louder the closer we get to December 21, she whimpered. – It's like there is a wall there. We can't see anything notably related to it. We see only glimpses of the weeks before, and... nothing beyond it.

Stacy nodded solemnly.

She saw awestruck and fearful, through half-closed eyes the dragon soaring through space and time.

Election day, November 4, 2008 approached. Ted and Liz and Stacy saw it on their own, through their feverish vision. Some establishment polls had McCain ahead, others Obama. Independent surveys had Kendall.

Stacy saw herself go to Virginia and speak, so she did.

– What happens with humanity in the next few weeks and months will dominate the next thousands of years. We're committing collective suicide as a species. We've finally started waking up to that fact.

Her speech passed half-an-hour. She kept going, visibly driven beyond ordinary passion.

– The future belongs to us, she cried, – not the fat cats in their ivory tower. Pigs rule the world. FUCK THE PIGS!

The establishment media paid quite a bit of attention to that in the coming weeks. It didn't truly benefit them much, didn't have the bite of old. If anything, it served to stoke the flame. People began repeating it in greater and greater numbers. It became a slogan, a phrase of choice for millions of eager supporters across the globe.

Two establishment commentators, propagandists sat in a studio, bewildered and confused.

– What impact has it that Florida and Georgia are... no longer in play?

– It would have meant more if it had been an ordinary two-way race, the other replied. Kendall will most certainly win Colorado, Massachusetts and the entire rust belt. He may win Texas, California and New York, and if that happens, he has more or less clinched it.

– Let's not forget that a candidate only needs 246 electoral votes this time around, since Florida and Georgia don't count anymore.

The ravages of the hurricane Anton once more rolled over screens in millions of homes, showing how the two states had been practically obliterated and no restoration had been possible.

– That was really the beginning of the end of the old order, the other said, unable to conceal the misery in his voice and features.

In spite of the massive campaign from the establishment parties, the Green Earth Party ended up on the ballot in forty-eight states, an unprecedented number for a third party. There were countless flashpoints, big and small skirmishes and unrest, and cases of establishment retaliation. The struggle grew even hotter. The Janus Clan's forces were stretched thinner than ever. No matter how many new recruits joined them, it never seemed to be enough. Asteroth felt the fatigue coming on again, and this time her guardians forced her to pull away before she collapsed. She shed her bitter tears, in vain.

– You're a woman, now, Stacy scolded her. – Don't be a girl!

Asteroth gritted her teeth, and attempted to stare Lillith down, but failed before she had properly begun. The young mother to be lowered her eyes in submission and offered her neck.

– That's my girl, my good, little demon…

Gabi crouched on the bed, her eyes sliding shut, returning to her troubled dreams.

A man approached a table at an outdoors restaurant sometimes during the warm, warm afternoon. He seemed to be very particular in his choice, sitting close to the wall, with a nice view of the street and the rest of the restaurant. He looked quite relaxed, even serene. After ten minutes, he had yet to call for a waiter, like most others impatiently did. One of the waiters finally took pity on him, and he could order his meal. He didn't look at his watch when his order hadn't arrived fifteen minutes later. He didn't do so when it hadn't arrived half an hour later. His serene expression didn't change.

He sat there, slowly devouring his food and drink, clearly having all the time in the world. People left, but he stayed. All the people that had been there when he arrived had left. The day turned to twilight and even to early evening, and he made no signs of leaving. He had emptied his plate. The waiter came and removed it. The guest ordered desert.

It had just arrived when the phone finally rang. The waiter faded from his attention. He focused on the phone. He remained calm, not making haste in any way. Steady hands fit the setup of earplugs and microphone. He pushed the green phone on the display.

– Hello?

– You rejected the motion to keep the Green Earth Party off the ballot, an unknown voice hissed. – What's gotten into you, judge? What's fucking wrong with you?

– Nothing in particular, the man enjoying his desert replied. – One can even argue that everything is finally right with me. I certainly think so.

– There have to be repercussions, the other man kept hissing.

– I should point out that I've made a record of all my dealings with you people through the decades, the judge remarked. – It is quite detailed and explicit.

The other man cackled, an insane, eerie laughter.

– That would probably have worked years ago. It doesn't anymore.

He broke the connection.

The man sitting by the table by the wall at the sidewalk restaurant kept enjoying his desert, a selection of exquisite chocolate, vanilla and strawberry ice-cream.

He heard the whining of tires, as a van made its way around the corner at the end of the street. None of the other guests took notice, but he certainly did. It charged him like an ambulance or a hearse. It certainly looked like the latter in his calm, calm vision.

The side-door of the van slid open. Three men with machineguns opened fire. People on the sidewalk was hit before the hail of bullets reached the dinner guests at the restaurant. Every single person was hit. The man enjoying his desert was filled with led. Bullets kept hitting people at the other side of him. Blood and guts decorated the wall and the floor and flesh and fabric, making holes in all of it.

6

CNN called it a few minutes past midnight on the election night, declaring Linsey Kendall the winner in the presidential election 2008, half an hour after Kendall had done so himself, after he had won the state of Texas with the resounding support of fifty-three percent of the voters. He had reached 250 electoral votes, well over the required number.

Everett made its way to those on the stage, to Linsey, Stacy and Betty, and Martin and Lydia and the children and Lynn and her partner and children. Everett and his three partners began kissing and fondling, making out instantly, making a good-humored low hum rise in the hall.

A few commentators gathered in a studio at an establishment media network.

– The president elect has in truth done anything, admitted to any perceived immoral social deed already, one of them stated incredulous. – It certainly didn't diminish his popularity in any notable manner. None of the old soundbites works on him.

Democratic and republican pundits screamed insults and worse at him from all over the country. Phoenix Green Earth members celebrated. Phoenix Green Earth voters joined the party, joined in on the celebration.

– We did it, Kendall said in his speech. – All of us did. The victory does indeed belong to all of us. It's a great start of the process that will transform human society, transform humanity to something truly worthy of pride and joy.

He did pause, allowing, encouraging the beyond loud and wild cheers.

– We have far to go, and we should stay vigilant faced with the major forces of tyranny still very much there, but let us enjoy this night, the coming days, the coming nights for all they are worth, before the truly hard work begins.

The final count showed the win to be 288 delegates. The Republican Party got 113 and the Democratic Party 90, both practically eradicated in most states. The win in the House of Representatives pretty much reflected that. The Green Earth Party also won most of the senators elected. The old parties combined retained the majority in the Senate since only one third of the senators had been up for election.

– It isn't over yet, a gleeful commentator stated. – First, the delegates have to actually vote for Kendall. Then, Congress has to approve of the result.

– The vote is in early December and the Congress deliberations in early January, a very helpful, officious news-anchor explained.

A persistent dream repeated itself in his sleep and even as he grew wide awake.

The four woke up in bed together. The revels of last night still reached them as loud, frivolous screams from all over town. They embraced and chuckled endlessly just during the first few moments of awakening, disengaging after what felt like forever.

– It isn't over, Everett said.

– It never is, Stacy said lightly, fiery love brightening the black eyes.

He rose from the bed with some urgency.

– What is it? Linsey wondered.

– I must check on something. I'll be right back.

– We'll be waiting, Betty said seductively.

He nodded curtly as he dressed, as he pulled on pants and a jacket, revealing how distracted he was.

The three of them watched him leave the room. They spent more endless moments reveling in their intimacy. A long time passed before they finally pulled a bit back from each other.

– I think… Linsey said, – in order to save the world, we must rule it.

– Yes, Betty said. – Yes.

Stacy considered his words for a moment before nodding.

Everett enjoyed the fresh evening breeze as it played with his exposed chest. He moved with a distinct goal in mind. The persistent dream kept looping through his buzzing consciousness. Two wolves paced in front of a cave entrance. Smoke rose from both their gaps and the cave entrance. He reached Main Street, the street turned forest overnight. He had been there when it happened and still could not quite believe it. Stacy would tell him good humored that he was still stuck in his old existence, before the world had changed.

Her enigmatic features appeared in the air in front of him. She smiled sweetly to him.

The tavern was open. It was open all the time. People kept celebrating in bright daylight. That hardly mattered anymore. That didn't either. Loud shouts and the sound of broken glasses reached his sensitive ears from the bar. He stepped inside. The revels hit him like a fist in the face.

Circe sat by a table surrounded by worshipers. They entertained her with passionate dedication.

– Greetings, Anubis, she said hoarsely, clearly aroused. – Won't you join us?

He nodded to her without stopping, not voicing any reply. He climbed the stairs with light steps. The revels upstairs matched easily those below. The scene imposed hard on his mindscape well before he opened the door. People fucked on the bed and on the floor, everywhere on the floor. The sea of flesh rolled back and forth in his vision, like on a ship rocking subjected to tall waves.

Michelle moved for him as she approached him. The inviting, sensual smile mesmerized all his senses. Hardened and wet semen covered her thighs and most of her body. The fireeyes looked at him with a layer of thick, thick haze.

– Greetings, brother, she said huskily. – Welcome to the house of the rising moon.

She kissed him with her wet, sultry lips. Her playful tongue roamed his mouth. The visions assaulted him again, stronger than ever. The wolf roamed the land. Rivers of blood and carcasses and bones surrounded it on all sides.

Michelle's smile turned ecstatic. The she-wolf joined the male at his roaming. They sat on a throne of bones, surrounded by worshipers. Words, phrases, statements rose to the surface in Everett's mind. One slight move, and she had surrounded them in her field, her realm. One more moment, and Jason was there as well.

– You're Halja, goddess damn *Hel*, Everett cried at her.

He turned towards Jason.

– Did you know about this?

Michelle stepped closer, the chilling half smile filling the dark and bright halves of her face.

– Of course, he knew, Fenris, Vánagandr, Lord of the Dark River, she snarled happily, her dialect and speech changing in distinct ways. – Of course, he knew, *brother*.

Vánagandr, Everett thought his clinical thought, (Old Norse: "the monster of the river Ván").

Then, he couldn't keep himself from shaking, as ancient memories could no longer be contained. Seemingly small events from his life, from Everett Moran's life grew ascendent and all-important.

He changed, doing so without making a conscious decision about it, tearing his clothes to pieces. The two-legged wolf towered above them. Michelle, Halja, Michelle undid her sphere. Everyone in the room could see him. It wasn't the first time, but it felt different, considerably different this time. They came to the three of them, offering themselves. Val's smile copied Michelle's.

– Can you see yourself through their eyes? She asked her rhetorical question.

He sat on the edge of the Hill. Days and nights had passed. He couldn't say how many.

She came to him on the edge of dusk.

– My wolf, she breathed, – my beautiful, fiery wolf.

Stacy, Lillith, Thalama nudged his neck with her lips, breathing his scent.

The bus made its way north, on broad and narrow roads, on the edge of dusk.

Marcus Ranford and Kimberly Russel arrived with the same late bus from Boston.

They grew aware of each other slowly and explicitly, first through glances and then open study and slowly gathering smiles.

She brought her small children. He traveled alone. It felt a little weird at first. Then, they recognized almost everything, as if they had lived there their entire life. The trees, the streets covered by grass, the happy children playing there. Everything, every little nudge felt familiar in their so very aware and astute mind.

CHAPTER TWENTY
NIGHTS OF FUTURE PAST

THE PLANET MONTAN
120TH NIGHT 12061 AV (after Venus)

Montan filled their view, as they left the Space liner and the smaller ship took them down to the surface. It was a young world, bright with colors and promise. They landed right there at the Space Port, creating a stir of another world. They felt it. The buzz and shock among the travelers pounded them, hit them like a lukewarm wave, totally harmless.

But they sensed the massive reaction to their Arrival. It hit them like their presence hit everyone.

– Yes, they know, Analin stated proudly. – Your Power is flowing outwards in waves. Even though most of them don't know exactly what they know, they know, deep down, undeniably that the Phoenix has come.

In ever more potent waves. First the port. Then the surrounding area, and then, in the third or fourth heartbeat, the entire planet. Telepaths relaying the startling information. The most sensitive of Montan's people sensed more and relayed that, as well.

The floaters in the air shook. They spotted that easily. Pilots almost lost control of their crafts. Analin and the others breathed faster, in heaves and gasps.

The group walked towards one of the resident floaters, no doubt a taxi of some kind.

– People can't fly? Ted wondered.

– Quite a few, actually, Analin frowned. – But it's seen as… unfashionable these days, and is generally speaking not done.

– Are you serious? He said, directing his entire attention at her, and she immediately turned dizzy.

– Serious? She frowned some more, before lightening up. – Oh, you mean to ask if I mean what I am saying?

– For some unfathomable reason a lot of you aren't using your powers, Ted said. – I find that exceedingly strange.

She didn't respond in words, didn't know what to say, and she tried, tried desperately.

– Let's walk then. Ted sniffed the air, breathing in prolonged, enjoyable cycles. – It's a nice day for a walk.

– You can say that again, Liz seconded. – I feel like I haven't breathed fresh air for millennia…

Phoebe giggled. A few of the others did, as well. Analin smiled in awe.

The flavor of the unexpected had been gone from human life for so long, but now it had returned with a vengeance.

– Let's walk, she grinned. – It isn't far, not far at all.

And the grin expanded to engulf them all. They felt it, like a soft physical blow in the face. She opened up. They all felt it. There was no hiding in this society, not something like this, and many in close proximity caught themselves wishing they could hide.

Ted and Liz Warren, and Analin War'n and her tribe of wanderers walked in front, and the assembly of the curious and stunned followed them. And more people joined in quickly. They came in their ships or they came running.

But no one flew.

They walked through a landscape of green. But Ted noticed, easily, the gray spots, the artificial, tamed tone to the green. The sudden anger surprised him, and shocked those close to him and in the assembly. He recalled dimly that he had been used to handle his rage, but that felt like ancient history now.

People shook in their shock. They stared at him in a way totally uncommon to them. To people who had hardly felt even the slightest anger, rage felt like a storm, and what was emanating from the stranger in their midst was far more than that.

He and Liz jumped simultaneously out on the lawn, over the tall wall fence separating them from it. It seemed like such a casual, easy act. Analin and the tribe followed first, then the others. They all followed. Their mind followed their bodies without thought, filled with fiery thoughts.

– Take off your shoes, Liz commanded, in a way not to be denied, or disobeyed.

Her rage was not quite like that of her mate, but it was there, just as potent, just as indomitable.

– Feel the soil, she shouted, making their ears ring, – taste the wrongness, the total and utter horror.

Phoebe cried, tears flowing down her cheeks. Liz walked to her.

– You've never done this before? The Dark One said softly. – Not even you.

– No, Phoenix, the girl sobbed. – We weren't allowed, not even in my earliest memory.

– Of course, you weren't, Liz nodded. – Your parents have kept you on a tight leash all your life, like they, themselves were.

Liz and Ted didn't look at each other. They looked at each other through their minds' eye, so much more powerful than they remembered. It had even passed beyond telepathy already, what they saw in the others. They nodded, without nodding. Thought, decision and action were one.

One moment, they were on the ground, the next they flew, and pulled the entire assembly with them.

Loud cries of fear empowered them further, and they let their charges know that.

They took them high up in the air, high above the city, above the far mountains. Suddenly those pulled with them had trouble breathing, and they couldn't tell if it was because of the high altitude or the close proximity of the two creatures in their midst. Phoenix brought them high before It stopped. There was no sense of slowing down. One moment they speeded towards the far ceiling of the atmosphere, the next they had… stopped.

A human circle formed in the air. Loud gasps of anxiety and excitement rose from them all. A fire began burning. Just like that, in front of the two figures at the center of their awareness.

Darkness descended, grew from the very air itself. Day practically turned to night around them, also in their minds.

– Don't tell me… Liz said, – this is Forbidden as well.

There was no noticeable reply, no takers. There was no need for that. Their shame and regret washed over her. She closed her eyes briefly as she shook it off like dirt.

– The Circle hasn't been formed for centuries, Analin moaned in despair, at the beginning of Joy.

It is long overdue then, the Phoenix shrugged.

And its speech was far more potent than anything they had experienced before. It invaded them, on all levels. Countless overwhelming sensations accompanied it.

Another dramatic change followed the first. They hardly had time to breathe.

A forest grew around them, a true one, so different from the controlled environment they had experienced since birth. Alien, scary scents assaulted their nostrils and their souls.

It sounded, looked, smelled and tasted and felt like a forest, also extrasensory. No matter how everyone approached it, it was a forest, one most of them had never experienced.

– This is the Sherwood Forest, Ted told them. – It's not a place, but a state of mind. We've grabbed your attention, now. Consider that your first lesson, the first step on your path to Freedom.

– That word. Analin mumbled with her eyes closed. – The way you say it, with such… passion.

A passion shaking them all, beyond skin, beyond thought.

Mist and Shadow grew around the two at the Center, in one heartbeat, two, to surround them all. The man and the woman didn't move, made no overt gesture, dramatic or otherwise, but something moved within them, Analin sensed it, something… something gloriously deadly and unfathomable. It pulsed and grew for every new breath, every new blinking of an eye, and many eyes blinked, and hearts beyond number fluttered and struck a giant drum.

Another single beat, another breath, and the shadow and mist were gone. The forest faded, but remained, lingered in their consciousness, and the eyes still burned, a burning rivaling the daystar above.

– And now for your second lesson, Ted grinned.

He and Liz let go of them all. They fell immediately. Loud cries accompanied the return of gravity.

Analin stood there, looking at them. She hadn't fallen. Most the tribe had, but they caught themselves and rose back up.

– Will you let them fall? Kerron wondered.

– Of course, Liz said. – We're not playing games. We're through playing.

Some of those falling began floating, began levitating, and began flying. Their shout of fear changed into exhilaration, into joy.

334

A considerable number of them kept dropping like flies.

– Oh, well, Ted shrugged. – I guess some of you are unable to fly.

All those falling stopped, the length of their body above the ground. They hovered there for a few seconds, before they were dropped on the soft ground.

The tribe, the Cult of Samhain flew to the low building somewhere ahead. The flight was practically instantaneous. They landed on the plaza before the large door. It opened for them, in their honor, welcoming them.

– That door hasn't opened for centuries. Analin nodded to herself, a bit surprised, but not stunned.

The tribe, led by the two specters from the ancient past walked into the cool shadows. Analin sensed, felt how the Phoenix pulled thoughts and memories from her mind, and she didn't object. This was quite common and quite accepted. The Phoenix mastered their ways at an amazing speed, and the process was accelerating, and for the first time Analin wondered where it might end.

– The precise control you have over your powers, she whispered. – I have never seen its like.

– «The Phoenix shrugs and the ocean heaves», Kerron recited.

– You've awaited our arrival for twelve thousand years, Liz said, – and you won't be disappointed.

– I would have thought such legends were exaggerated, Ted said in wonder, – but they're not. This one isn't.

The Seer sat on a low rise in the second room. He looked old, but he wasn't. He looked distracted, but he wasn't.

– Welcome, It said, – to the Final Days.

And everybody hearing those words trembled, and when Liz and Ted War'n trembled the walls shook.

The room was filled with Dust, with Mist and Shadow.

«Move the Dust», the failed teacher told his apprentice, the young witch, Long Ago.

Move the Dust, and you hold the world in your hand.

– The Phoenix is the raw, untamed, savage fury of the Universe incarnated, the man on the rise intoned. – Nothing is beyond its reach. I tremble, because in Its fiery eyes I see Tomorrow, yesterday and everything in-between.

– It is me, Harrod, the girl with the ring of fire on her finger cried. – It is Analin. There was no reply.

She turned towards the two.

– I know him, she said, – or used to know him. It is said that he lives within his mind, that he is unable to sense the outside world at all. He senses only what *is*.

So fast. Everything happened so fast.

Images began forming in the dust, Analin and the others stared at it as if transfixed.

– That has never happened before, one of the men, Levy cried.

– Another first, Analin trembled in excitement and awe and expectation, and only a little bit of fear.

Phoenix had said they wouldn't be disappointed, and she knew that to be true. The Phoenix grew more aware of itself by the minute, and everything changed, faster than the wind.

The images, so life-like, so immediate transformed with the Phoenix's casual thought.

It was a recount of Memory, what they had recently done on their Journey, but also more. They saw Lillith give birth to the boy and the girl. Everybody trembled as they saw Jahavalo cross the Salisbury Plain and with a wave of the hand, the suffering of the thousands of people he made his workers, his slaves, create the Stonehenge Temple in honor to himself, to Destruction incarnate. A flash later was Egypt, the pyramids, and both Jahavalo and Lillith. The Shadow Women of the sands bowing to their masters. Later in Egypt, the Queen and her children, and her royal court. The blood-red stairs of Rome. The deceit at Nicaea. The culling of the followers of the old faith made by the christian emperors. The countless genocides of the various indigenous people. And in almost all of these scenarios were the man with a ponytail, the woman with the black eyes, several people with fireeyes, and the woman wandering the Earth. Twentieth century Earth briefly. Venus. The second rise of Lillith. The big migration. The encounter with Samhain. Now!

But the swirling mists didn't stop swirling. Liz and Ted stepped forward, becoming immersed in imagery with a potency briefly rivaling Phoenix. There were strange, unknown images, events depicted they didn't remember. She raised a hand. The image froze. It was of herself and Linda, in the Australian desert long ago, but different, changed from how she recalled it, and she recalled everything with extreme detail, now.

The man on the rise stirred. They noticed immediately, because the very air changed around them. He opened his eyes for the first time in several hundred years. The live visions faded, each and every one of them, except that of Liz and Linda. Liz spotted Ted there, of course, burning in her mind. The others, the twenty others were more indistinct.

The man on the rise attempted to speak, but was unable to.

Is that you, Ani?

– Yes, it's me, Harrod, Analin confirmed.

Even his eyes didn't work right at first, as various parts of reality kept shifting in his perception. Then, finally his eyes settled on the two creatures of fire standing before him. Ted and Liz saw themselves through his eyes, how their bigger shadow and fire form seemed to intermingle, becoming one, single entity.

– It's gone, he gasped hoarsely, hardly audible, even though they had no problem hearing him, and the strange dichotomy of that thought didn't seem strange at all. – It's all gone. It took it all.

– No, it's not gone, Liz told him, – just displaced. It will return to you.

She felt it all mingle and burn within her, within Ted, within them both, like everything, or close to everything did.

They were changing, and feeling the changes from second to second. They were changing, and changing yet again. And again and again and again. So far removed from what and who they had been only moments ago.

But the core remained. The core did this, propelling everything forward, and they were the core, finally, were the Shadow casting an ever-bigger frame in its wake.

Harrod stumbled to his feet, his legs not really that weak, even after centuries of non-use. He was of The People, after all. Ted nodded to himself, knowing that their muscles didn't really atrophy like the muscles of the humans he recalled would have.

The Storm raged inside him, and he welcomed it.

Humanity had grown, been empowered beyond belief, and so had the Phoenix. The time had come.

– It all went wrong, didn't it? The Tachiti is *ascending*.

Analin felt his eyes, his burning eyes on her, from far away, and knew exactly what he meant.

– Yes, she said. – The People are slowly, inextricably being sucked into Tachiti culture and society. The Lords understand the significance of economics and slow integration, the value of regimentation very well. And there are also other, clear signs that the experiments they did on us long ago are finally taking effect. That and/or the invasive nanotechnology many of us allow into our hearth and bodies. I tell The People this on and on again, but most of them don't listen. We are being domesticated, our savageness is bred out of us, like pets, and most don't care.

– We weren't ready, Ted mused. – We weren't well within ourselves when setting off into Space. Everything became unraveled.

He felt the presence of the Tachiti above and beyond, felt their growing dominance.

– That's true, too, Analin spat. – We're roasting in our own pot. Perhaps we deserve to be slaves.

There was silence, as Analin stood on one side of the room, and Ted and Liz on the other.

– But the Phoenix has come, now, Liz said softly.

Suddenly they were at her side. She froze.

– You shouldn't be able to do that, she whispered. – Not without me noticing it.

– The Phoenix is the raw, untamed, savage fury of the Universe incarnated, Liz intoned. – Nothing is beyond its reach.

She repeated The Seers' words, but in her tongue, it got a new, sinister quality. Analin started shaking. She smiled in something akin to bliss, but she couldn't keep herself from shaking.

– You're a sun made flesh, she mumbled. – A sun made flesh. A sun made flesh.

The sun invaded her very being, and left only smoldering ashes of what had been.

Let's walk outside. It was just a stray thought, but oh, so powerful. It hit the others like an irresistible compulsion.

They were outside already, in a blink of an eye, under the bright sun, not really that bright anymore, compared to the mighty forge in their midst.

Ted blinked and realization hit him.

I understand now. I understand everything.

And so did the others, even though they still only glimpsed it through conscious thought or even what went for conscious thought these days, so much more conscious than the time before this he remembered.

Harrod's eyes watered and burn. He blinked at the indistinct crowd gathering before the House of Delphi. They recognized him. They glanced incredulous and fearful at each other. The world was changing, changing beyond recognition and recapture and recollection.

Even Memory itself changed before their very eyes.

The two moved among them, among them all, and they were not just two, but many.

– A NEW age has begun, Ted Warren cried, in their ears, in their minds, in their very souls. – An age of FREEDOM, undiminished and WILD, even more so than it once was.

He stood before them, before them all, and so did Liz, right there, only a step away. They saw the two creatures mingle and become one, even though still apart.

– Look around you, he cried, – at your work. Yet another planet is being consumed by human folly.

They shook.

– You strangle the planet and all life with it, Liz shouted, and the shout rattled them more than the sun itself would. – How many planets have there been? How much like locusts have you become?

– But Jahavalo… a voice spoke up.

– Jahavalo was a shithead, with no thought of people other than himself, and his twisted scheme to make slaves of us all.

Liz walked among them, with her luring stare.

– And he succeeded, didn't he, even beyond his expectations? His greatest «success» wasn't his conquests, but that he made humans enslave themselves. His legacy lives among you, now. You were ripe, for the Tachiti's machinations. You accept their progress, their trinkets, like the various natives on Earth fell for the ruse of the technologically superior invaders. Behold your legacy, what you have chosen to become.

Your legacy!

There were shouts of anger and fear, mingling into one, single entity of emotion. A mob was forming, or it would, normally, but the two before them were beyond reproach, beyond vulnerability and weakness, and the possibility of surrendering to the mob's rage.

Their rage was so pale, compared to the glowing suns in their midst.

Ted spoke, and he, himself could hardly fathom the power of his voice, even his voice.

– The nanotechnology, nanites you have allowed entrance to your body are changing you slowly, inevitably.

They looked incredulous at each other.

He took one sample body from the angry crowd and pulled him forward for all to see. And suddenly they all saw, saw a transparent figure filled with blackness.

338

– This is the future, he cried, he showed them all.

A human in chains. Not physical, but mental, hooks buried deep inside them, making any type of rebellion impossible. The creature they saw was a function, nothing more, an extension of its masters. Very useful to the masters, but hardly even capable of independent thought.

– This is your harvest, your bitter end.

The powerful frame struggled in his grip, in vain.

And then they saw themselves walking around with a stupefied grin on their faces, grinning and bowing to the Tachiti, a life of happy servitude, a life where they used their powers, every time a Master commanded it.

Ted freed the man he held from the chains and hooks in his body. He did so with a stray thought. They stared stunned at him and the man standing up with tears of gratitude filling his eyes.

– Thank you, Phoenix. He gave praise in a loud voice. – THANK YOU!

A black, sickly mass floated above Ted Warren's open hand, what he had pulled from the man's body.

– This is blackness and disease, technology incarnated, he told them, he showed them. – This is what entered humanity's life so long ago, and we never fought it, never even considered its ultimate implications.

They saw Old Earth, a black, dead mass falling in Space. He and Liz showed them, showed it down their throats.

– Behold your legacy. She shouted. – You had a choice before, a choice to end it on your own, but now The Phoenix has come, and the only thing left for you is to pick up the pieces.

Ted sensed it, in his hand, the Disease. It revolted him. Before it would have staggered him. Now, it merely fueled his rage. He knew, startled, what to do. There was yet another glow of mist and shadow. The blackness changed in his hand. There was no hesitation anymore, no holding back. The blackness changed into Shadow, and then, with a cruel grin, he returned it to the crowd. They pulled back, in total, useless vain. It invaded them, purified them. It spread among them, exactly like a disease, but it was antibodies ridding them all of the sickness. They gasped in fear and joy, and fear again.

– Leave, he bade them. – Spread like the wind, and spread, give Life.

They obeyed, without thinking the voice that was like the wind.

But a few remained, like the Phoenix had known they would, like It had ordained.

He saw a giant Shadow hovering in Space at the end of time, and he knew what and who it was.

Analin moved by his side, and he turned towards her, knowing she was there.

Horror and Joy equally dominated her as she saw them, truly saw them, beyond appearances for what they were.

Even the horrible image of the wax dolls stuck in her mind for so long faded before the terrible, the beyond terrible fire of the creature before her, and she fell on her knees, baring her neck, giving herself to It, submitting to It in all things.

– The Tachiti will come, Phoebe stated, her features unusually solemn. – Their instruments will register the demise of their tools, and they will come.

– They will come, forced to finish the job so much sooner than planned, so far ahead of schedule, Harrod mused. – And…

He lit up.

– And the People will know them for what they are, and they will fight. I *see* it. It's glorious beyond belief. I see everything I didn't see before. It's not. It's…

Expanded. Ted didn't close his eyes. He saw the infinite and eternal Tapestry unfold, saw Yggdrasil, the Tree of Life, and its countless branches grow, not into the Void, but growing *from* it. The Void was the tree's soil.

Analin rose, drying her tears, both of sadness and joy.

– And what more do you see, Harrod? She wondered.

She saw him reach into the Nothing, into the domain he was privy to, into days yet to come.

He turned pale, and fell silent, unable to speak or even think, or in any way communicate the horror riding him.

– The Phoenix has come, she said, – and War has come. The Final Days are here, the Prophecy yet unfulfilled.

The truth of her words dawned on them all.

– «All enemies of the People shall fall before the Phoenix», she quoted the Prophecy, the immortal words of Betty Morgan surviving, unbelievably through the millennia. And she had quoted far older Seers and sources.

Thoughts raced like quicksilver. Ideas and plans rose like salmons up river. In a matter of seconds suns were lit and died.

– They will come here first, she said. – This is the ground zero of the infestation, as they see it. They will do anything, *anything,* to contain it.

– They are already here, Liz said with a coarse, ghostly and lazy voice.

The gathering looked up in the sky, the calm sky, where not a single wave was a froth top on the ocean surface.

Ted and Liz's hands clasped, and there was a flash of Shadow, and another flash, and yet another, and each was even more powerful than the previous. A million ships appeared in the sky above Montan. The emergency Klaxon horn sounded on all Tachiti worlds. The Great Game put in motion so long ago was near its completion. The mobilization started and continued with calm efficiency. There was surprise, and a certain amount of startled inward expression, but everything proceeded smoothly. Analin saw it, impossibly, light years away.

– They have no clue, she gasped. – They have absolutely no idea what is happening.

– They are carpenters, Ted said. – The architects among them, even though the effect of their work lingers, are long gone.

A hole opened, in existence itself, to a misty and shadowy world, to the Shadowland. They were all pulled in, without moving.

– This is still humanity's domain, Ted said, – humanity's place of power, but that won't last, as more and more humans fall under the carpenters' spell.

It had started already, the corruption, echoes of nanites in the mist. The Tachiti did everything artificially, copying, mimicking natural powers. They studied, indefinitely patient, taking dead and living things apart, discovering what made them tick. When they died, they died, and so it had been up till now, and it bothered them, bothered them terribly.

But now, true immortality was within their grasp.

A million ships filled Space above Montan in the first minute. Another million arrived the next.

They watched stunned, and with an unfamiliar, unknown, cold fear filling them, how hundreds, thousands and thousands of people faded from their view, and worse, from their instruments' view.

The People were pulled, without ships, far away, through the Shadowland, by a Might they had never experienced and hardly even imagined.

But the realization hit Analin, creating a sick feeling in her belly: They were fleeing. Even the Phoenix was no match for the Tachiti fleet, for their amassing technology, mass-produced through countless millennia. They were, after all only two, very small forms.

– We must…

She began the chain of thought, her eyes meeting the living suns before her, and slowly, slowly she nodded, eagerly, approvingly. A cold dread of excitement filled her.

– But there is no way we can reach Tachiti Inner Space from here, she stated. – There is no Path. There is no ship we can use.

We don't need any ship. She heard the voice, not a voice, and realization dawned on her slowly, and then she was afraid.

She beheld the fundamental forces of the Universe at work, and had trouble breathing.

The Path led them to one planet after another, in a string of disorganized jumps. She had witnessed the Dreamweavers' power countless times. But this was far above that. The Phoenix left a few of the People on each planet, with one single word of fierce encouragement: *Live!*

They infected the people there with their health, their freedom from the nanotechnology, the freedom from the chains that had bound them for so long, and Analin knew, beyond knowing that it had already become an irreversible, unstoppable process.

– The Tachiti has suffered a major setback today, a man shouted exalted. – Major!

– But it's not enough, Analin told him calmly, told them all. – They still got time on their side. It's not enough!

They stared at her, because they didn't dare stare at the two forms at her side. But it was useless, of course. The Phoenix was in their minds and blood and soul, and would always be, now, and beyond the end of time.

Hours passed, seconds more, as time crawled to a halt. The number of people around them dwindled, until it was close to nothing, to all, and what remained, in addition to the two at the center, was, was exactly twenty and one, and Analin understood, as she had for some time, as all the others remaining also did.

341

She remembered what she had forgotten. They all did. Tears formed in her eyes. She remembered an alley in a large city on Earth long ago. She couldn't recall the name of the city, but everything else was immaculately clear to her.

– I hated you, she said. – I loved you.

Harrod reached out a hand. There were tears in his eyes as well.

Ted nodded. Liz nodded. They all did.

– It is happening, she said with a huge, alien grin on her face. – It really is.

She turned to Ted.

– Do we know the way?

– We don't *need* to, he said, and his voice turned to a growl, turned to a roar.

They speeded up. Even the Journey through the Shadowland turned strenuous and painful. A vast hole opened up before them, and this time in the very reality itself.

And then they were in Hyperspace, and it rocked their existence beyond belief. They were there for eons, for a single, prolonged moment, and there was no time, no time at all. Analin and the others stared at The Phoenix in mute paralysis, saw how strands, how Night and Fire erupted from their being, as they, during that brief moment filled the Rocky Road with their presence, and Analin and the others gained strength as well, not losing it in droves, like they had always done before.

They erupted on the other «side» in a blazing bonfire of boundless energy, inside the atmosphere of the Tachiti home world.

TACHITI PRIME
121st NIGHT 12061 AV (after Venus)
IN THE FIRST YEAR IN THE TIME OF THE PHOENIX

The vision of the wax dolls flooded their minds, the minds of the twenty and one accompanying the Phoenix on Its Flight, the urgency of their mission growing beyond urgency.

They stared at each other in wonder, one almost erasing the qualms, the fear they still entertained.

– The Rocky Road, she gasped. – Every theory we have ever entertained about it is wrong.

– It's not another dimension at all, Harrod said.

The others, except the Phoenix stared at them both.

– It is the vast Unknown Matter of the Universe. Analin glowed with joy. – The Unknown Matter *is* the Universe, *is* its hyper-reality… its *Shadow*.

Everybody stared astonished at each other. In the midst of Death, they had not lost their ability to feel wonder. On the contrary. It filled them, beyond their brim.

The planet glowed in a strange light, strange Shadow, and it was recent. It had appeared only moments before they did, a precursor, an alarum of what was coming, of what was already there.

They rocketed through the oily, half dead atmosphere with unimaginable speed, towards the surface of woven metal below. Ships fired at them, attempted to freeze them in place with tractor beams, totally in vain. Their bubble resisted all attempts at even influencing it.

The sun cast gossamer strings from its center, cast cold, instead of heat, ghostly waves of night and fire. All nightmares of the Tachiti was realized. The entire population of billions tried screaming, but they could only stare, as the stark fear they could only recall through their deepest nightmares returned in an instant.

The Phoenix and its host, its circle of twenty and one landed hard, landed softly at the center of a vast urban area. The flesh and blood of thousands of lifeforms splashed everywhere in their wake.

Smoke rose as the bubble dissolved, as those inside opened themselves to their surroundings, as they pulled in the stale, more than dead environment, the dead world.

Something stirred in the ruins. A figure rose, stumbled a few steps towards them, before stopping. It was an alien, a Tachiti.

– You... I know you...

The already dead being whispered.

Ted turned towards him, smiling wolfishly, with a face filled with serenity, with peace, with savage joy.

– Yes, Achim Doll, we have met. And these are the last words you will hear, this proclamation that *humanity has returned* and we, as the aggressive beasts we are will remain a force in the Universe, until... until the end, the beyond of time.

The savage roar was broadcast far and wide.

Everybody heard Its words, on the planet, and off it.

Achim Doll glowed for a moment, before turning to dust before their eyes, as his life energy fed the twenty-three invading human beings.

The twenty and one heard the roar of the river, of the mighty waterfall washing everything away. What the other two heard couldn't possibly be imagined.

Ripples, ripples filed the air, filled existence, the very reality around them. They felt it, sensed it beyond any sensory input. Something had happened, was happening, would happen... would happen soon.

Something that couldn't be stopped.

Analin began feeling faint. The vast vampire power of the two at the center grew beyond control, like they wanted it to, like they craved. Analin saw Phoebe and Levy and even Harrod dissolve into nothing, but amazingly, she still held on, for one heartbeat, two longer, before she, too turned to dust. Her spirit rose in the air, lingering there, for a moment, before fading, more powerful than ever. Ted blinked, and in that blink was Forever. He remembered, like splinters in the mind's eye, flashes of fire in the gut. He was able to pull Memory forward at will, now, had become Memory, its potent force. The desert sand flowed at his feet. He smelled it. His feet remembered, and so did he. He remembered it all. As if it had just happened. And it had. As if it was still happening.

And it was.

The Tachiti Empire had been unchanged for tens of thousands of years, ever growing in power and influence. In one stroke it was all ashes.

The two forms, alone now, in air filled with dust, Dust began growing, expanding, mixing, becoming one giant Being. The explosion was silent. All sound, all sight and everything of the senses were blocked across a large area. Death was instantaneous. There was no blood, no flesh or even bones falling to the ground, only ever more dust filling the air. No one heard the Tachiti death scream.

The entire planet, covered by woven metal disintegrated, imploded upon itself. The system's sun began fluctuating wildly, visibly on all scanners, creating fear on all the observation posts throughout the star system. The explosion, a beyond intense sizzle of fire and shadow never before seen, spread into Space like feathered wings of a beating heart, covering vast areas of empty space in an instant, burrowing deep into all dimensions, all levels of reality. Spacetime shook in violent cramps. All nanotechnology in the known universe stopped working, until nothing but dust remained of machines everywhere. Spaceships dissolved in their flight. Billions of entities died instantly, many more in the seconds and years to come. The Phoenix absorbed, digested, feeding off the entire solar system, all the planets, all the rocks, even the mighty sun itself, and ripples in the water of Space spread outward, ever outward through all space, all time.

CHAPTER TWENTY-ONE
The roaring desert

«You fear whaƀs inside you. You fear your own power. You fear your anger, the drive to do great and terrible things».

Ras Al Ghul - Batman Begins

The Phoenix breathed the scent of the desert, like it had its entire existence. The desert was growing, expanding, conquering new land all over the planet. The scent grew stronger, becoming a stench.

By the sheerest coincidence they all gathered in the large hall, with no one else present.

The two and two and twenty-one had begun their walk long ago. This moment, now, it began in earnest.

Liz and Ted turned away from the window, the window with a view of everything. They walked to the center of the hall. The twenty-one formed an unbroken circle around them. Stacy and Everett stood outside it, looking in. Hands grabbed hands. Energy surged between the twenty-one forming a circle. Contact surged between them and the Phoenix. Ted and Liz, and the twenty-one, forming a half moon turned towards the wolf and the raven.

– They're the last, Everett heard himself say, – the final additions of the twenty-one, making the circle complete.

The twenty-one frowned, Kimberly and Marcus a bit more than the rest.

– You look at me that way because you know, Stacy said.

Everyone glanced at each other, and in every face, they found the familiar, the sweetness of Memory.

– There are those who know that the world is not how it is supposed to be, she said.

– THERE ARE THOSE WHO KNOW!

Everyone choired. And it hardly felt strange or awkward at all.

– We know, she stated solemnly. – We count among those few who still remember the world as it was when humanity was young, and not the tired, bowed creature of today.

They remembered, and a catching formed in their throat.

– Our fate is linked, Everett stated. – What happens to one happens to all.

– WHAT HAPPENS TO ONE HAPPENS TO ALL.

Each and every one of them joined in on the choir, and it felt perfectly natural.

– We know, Michelle said, – know what's at stake. We're ready!

– It's funny, Glory mused. – Now, when there's only six weeks left, everything seems almost anticlimactic.

– Speak for yourself, Gregory said with passion.

– The last three years have been amazing, Sally said. – I regret nothing, except that I didn't hook up with you guys sooner.

They looked good humored at her.

– I could have come earlier, Kimberly mused.

– I could have, too, Marcus said.

– But it didn't feel right, they choired.

Everyone looked good humored at them.

– It is happening, Carla said. – Everything is in the right place. All major events of the puzzle have come true.

Anxiety and anticipation coursed through them all.

– It is a major event, she added, – one more obstacle to overcome or lose. Nick knows what it is, but he won't go into detail about it, not in all the time I've known him.

– Why? Lee asked. – He would want us to succeed, won't he? The more knowledge we possess, the better our chances to prevail.

– He clearly doesn't see it that way, Jane mused. – He knows more than us, and if he withholds crucial information, there must be a valid reason for it.

– He has pushed us towards it our entire life, Linda stated, – and he hasn't exactly been kind about it. His objective clearly differs from ours.

She grinned a bit, more than a bit.

– He does want us to succeed, Liz said. – Everything he's done, no matter how brutal and uncaring more than suggests that.

– The question is how he measures success, Ted shrugged. – It goes beyond mere survival, far beyond.

– Mike knew, Linda said. – He knew everything. At least he claimed he did, and he demonstrated his skills as an oracle several times to me. He saw far beyond his own death, and it didn't bother him the slightest. The word «obsessed» is totally insufficient in describing him.

– He saw this moment, Ted said. – He might even have known what Nick doesn't know. The knowledge changed him, from a fairly kind, average boy to a monster. He chose to become one in one moment of utmost clarity. Nothing else mattered. Every step he took, every decision he ever made was done in order to achieve that objective, to serve that purpose.

Everyone drew breath hard.

– He was even crazier than I suspected, Glory snarled.

– He recorded tapes for me, Ted said with a remote look in the fireeyes. – I listened to them for years without getting it, but recently… I feel like they finally make some twisted sense.

Liz rubbed his arm. She comforted him with soft kisses on his cheek.

– My sister followed him blindly into death, Sally said, – and she didn't question that decision at all.

– I knew this was my destiny, Diana said. – I resisted it for years, until I finally embraced it, and I'm glad.

346

– What she said, Tony said with even greater passion.

A sore smile crossed everyone's lips.

Ted and Liz gave him a casual glance and knew he had come a long way from the person they had known many years ago.

He felt their heat, their warmth, and they watched the catching grow in his throat.

– It does feel great to share this with all of you, he stated.

Everyone nodded, the sense of shared experience all too real.

It began as a stirring in the fingertips. It grew up their arms to eventually engulf their body. They looked excited at each other. The pale shadow fire appeared above their head, hovering above each of the twenty-one like a Damocles sword, creating a strange excitement adding to what was already there. They and the two and two rose into the air, through the roof of the house like it wasn't there, and levitated in the air above it.

There was another buildup. Sparks flowed from Diana's fingers. She laughed giddily. Sally was coated in darkness, a living shadow clearly a part of her. Corrinne looked astonished at her ghostly hands. Everyone that hadn't manifested powers before did. Those that had enjoyed their powers for years felt far stronger. Michelle's dark laughter echoed in the Void. Stacy burned so hard that the others feared she would burn, that the fire would devour her. It didn't. It didn't seem like a concern at all.

The energy surged and kept surging between them. Michelle's field, realm engulfed them, isolated them from the outside world. Then, in one single burst, it spread to the entire town, making it slightly out of tune with the rest of the world. Everyone below noticed and saw the twenty and five, and pointed anxiously, excitedly at them.

The energy… faded, even as it lingered. They descended, hitting the ground with a soft thud. The circle dissolved, even as it lingered and always would.

They seemed to stand there like unmovable statues forever, even as the world reentered them stronger than it had ever done.

Phoenix - the 21:

Linda Cousin

Carla Wolf

Beth Alver

Lee Warren

Glory Burns

William Carter Lafayette

Giovanni Rossi

Morten Falck

Sally Regehr

Michelle Warren

Andrea Natchios

Tony Farlani

Martine Rabelais

Kimberly Russel

Elliott Marsten
Diana McKenzie
Corinne Barbeau
Gregory Leslie Stark
Rick Harding
Jane Morris
Marcus Ranford

2

Morten walked through the thickest forest in town. Vines danced to his tune, his will. A sense of wonder touched his face.

– Phoenix borrowed my power, Michelle said excited to Val and Jason, – and amplified it, just like that, by snapping its fingers.

They didn't really need her to tell them. They had felt it. Everyone had. A palpable, pervasive event off the scales.

– It amplified how all the twenty-one might use our powers.

She didn't have to stress that either. Diana, Corinne, Morten and Sally and the rest had eagerly demonstrated their newfound abilities to everyone in town for hours already.

– I believed it would be something, she breathed, – but I had no idea, no idea. It's so far beyond my expectations that I can't tell how far beyond it is. And I know that what it did is nothing compared to its true power.

Her excitement just bubbled over, crossing over into the incoherent worship they had sensed before.Her excitement just bubbled overH

She frowned, a deep frown she couldn't hide.

– It faded fast, she pondered. – Phoenix couldn't sustain that kind of power more than a few moments. Something is missing. Something is still missing.

Despair mixed with the excitement and neither won. They held her and comforted her. The shaking slowly ceased.

Betty delivered the daily report to Ted and Liz in their sanctum. She put it on the desk before the two of them.

– Have you missed one single day? Liz inquired.

– I don't believe I have, My Lady, Betty said brightly, – at least not in thirteen years and two-hundred-plus days…

They looked at her with their predator eyes. She straightened, standing at attention.

– There is enemy activity, she reported. – But it is muted, confused. One of our field operatives described it as ants wandering aimlessly through the hill without direction or meaning. We probably caught them by surprise. They're used to getting it their way. We should assume they will eventually regroup, of course.

She had major difficulties handling their close proximity. All her experience was for naught.

Liz browsed through the heap of papers. She flipped them with one hand, glancing briefly at each page, before moving on. It didn't take long. She shared her impression with both of them. Betty couldn't hold back a gasp of awe.

– It is happening, she breathed. – We're close to the finish line. Everything is in place. Only one, final, crucial ingredients is missing. Do you know what it is?

They didn't. She had no need for them to voice a response, either with their vocal chords or their mind.

– There is a wall, Ted said.

– A wall of time, Liz said.

A deep chill trickled down Betty's spine. She didn't want it to do so and felt that she shamed herself, but there it was.

– Mike, presumably saw through it, Ted said. – He saw us «rise».

– Nick might do so as well, Liz said, – but he's a wall, too. We can't read him, and he doesn't volunteer any true illumination.

– I've never been able to read him either, Betty mused. – With most people, and that includes telepaths, you get something, but with him, it's like there is no thought there at all, and that's clearly not the right impression.

They exchanged information pertaining to Nick in particular for a while. It did bring illumination, but nothing decisive. The two fireeyes picked her brain, while she only received from them. To say she was overwhelmed was way too pale a description.

She bathed in their waves, in their beyond pervasive flow.

– You're glorious, she mumbled. – Glorious…

She just drifted off, unable to offer any resistance. She didn't even try.

He woke up, even as the dream of him running through an infinite forest lingered in his buzzing mind.

Nick sat up on the bed, waking up to an empty room. He stood by the window on the upper floor, in the modest house on the small rise, looking out at his garden from his high vantage point. It felt higher than it actually was. Time flowed by itself. He didn't need to make it, and he didn't. He felt the immense being, the beyond powerful force making its way through time, on a collision course with some near future point. It was close, now. He could sense its breath on his cheek. He had never experienced it quite like this before, not this pervasive, this…

The tall and big and lean man took a stroll through the Northfield streets. People waved to him, struck up a conversation with him. Women offered themselves to him with sweet and enticing smiles. He rejected them without being obvious about it. They had no trouble getting the subtle message, and made no overt effort.

He did reach the house only a bit late. The slightly ironic smile lit up his face. He stepped inside. It felt different there, very different. The walls bulged. They whispered his name. He stepped into the large living room, the space appearing far larger than its purely physical measures. Everyone in the extended close circle, the family, the Janus Clan, the Shadowwalkers gathered there, the stragglers arriving just before or after he did.

He heard the music, the discord. He had no trouble whatsoever hearing it. They entered his sphere. He imagined they did that, instead of him entering theirs. He walked through a long dark tunnel without end.

– You are here already? Liz frowned. – You are not late?

She was sarcastic, spirited and angry as always. The ensuing laughter didn't mellow that.

He watched them both. She was perfect. So was he.

Everything directed their attention on them. It was impossible not to do so. Something had changed, and he wondered what. Each shadow held power. Each burst of energy penetrated them all.

– Something has changed, Ted stated. – We don't know what. A key element remains… missing.

Nick felt his frustration, the rage constantly breaching the surface, how it kept empowering him. It was a wonder to behold. Nick couldn't help staring in a somewhat relaxed awe. He had witnessed it many times before, but it never got old.

– Everything is proceeding well, Betty insisted. – There have been a few minor incidents, a few miscalculations where we've been infiltrated and exposed, but that was expected. It will just drown in the general noise generated by our activities. The winds of change *are* running wild.

The blush created by her excitement grew a tad more pronounced.

– Everything I've been taught since early childhood, is coming to pass, and far, far more confirming it a thousand times.

She cast an involuntary glance at Nick.

Ted turned towards Nick, giving him his complete attention.

– We need to know, he stated, – need to know everything.

Ted imagined he looked at a wall when he looked at his great grandfather, at the unfathomable sphinx.

– You want answers, Nick acknowledged. – Of course, you do.

He hesitated a bit too long.

– I'm fed up with you and your condescending antics.

The snarl laced Ted Warren's every word, every syllable.

Everyone felt the surge, the massive buildup. Several of those standing closest to it started bleeding from the nostrils. The result of Ted's sudden rage hit Nick mid-center and threw him across the room. He hit the wall like a ragdoll. They all heard the sick sound of bones breaking.

Ted stopped, stunned enough for his rage to pause.

The entire room had been reduced to rubble.

– I haven't lost control of my abilities in years. What is this?

– *Power!* Jason stated.

He dried blood from his jaw. He hardly seemed to notice.

Nick fought himself back on his feet. They heard the sound of his bones resetting themselves. He had all the eyes in the room on him, eyes split between him and the Phoenix.

Liz stepped forward, just one small step.

– You've stood in this room, at this moment many times before, haven't you?

Nick nodded imperceptibly.

– So, what's gonna happen?

– I can't tell you that.

– What can you tell us?

She snarled.

– I needed the two of you to re-bond early to make that bond strong and lasting and growing.

Something dawned on Ted, then.

– You killed her, he said curtly, almost calm. – You killed Tilla, killed her just as certain as if you had pulled the trigger.

Strangely enough, he didn't recall her death just then, but the car accident.

– You kept us from reaching Martin and Lillian, an event that would have quickly turned Tilla more powerful.

His initial rage made sense, then. He had known the truth deep down. He reached out a hand deliberately. It remained far from Nick's throat, but it still squeezed it. Nick hung in his cruel grip, gasping for air that wasn't there. Ted kept up the pressure. He sucked the power out of Nick without physically touching him, draining him like he would squeeze a sponge. Clarity lit two sets of fireeyes.

Ted let go, like he let go of something vile, as if his hand was covered in wet soil.

– You see yourself, rightly or wrongly as Proteus of Greek mythology, Liz said softly, – a being existing outside time and space, one not really touching the lives of those living within it.

– Yes, Nick nodded. – That's why I couldn't, can't lead myself. I tried several times at first, but failed miserably every time. But you, the two of you do touch, do see yourself as part of the world. Your empathy hasn't been ruined, in spite of decades of living through hardship and the world treating you badly. Even through your relative ruthlessness, your ability to make hard, even harsh decisions the soft spot remains at the heart of your being.

– It isn't quite the same as last time, right? Ted heard himself say.

– No, it has progressed… further, with heightened pressure, both in society as a whole and on a personal level. Israel's fall didn't happen or happened so soon in that other previous reality, nor did several other things, like Trudy's death. There are always unforeseen consequences.

He faced them, met their eyes in a somewhat calm, but intense manner.

– The stress level is noticeably higher. Something *has* changed. I don't know what. I know it's significant.

And desirable, so very desirable.

How could he tell them, relate to them how desperate he had become, with what zeal he had done his research and executing his plan.

– The Phoenix has existed at least one time before, Lillian choked. – It destroyed an entire city.

– Two twin cities and all the people not able to escape in time, Martin Keller said. – It felt like the entire world.

They held hands hard. Nick didn't respond.

– The Phoenix is an evolutionary trait, Carla stated, – a ultimate manifestation of humanity, of the People, perhaps even of the Earth itself. Burning Ice, Biting Flame...that is how life began, and that's how it will renew itself.

Ted turned towards Nick and froze him yet again.

– You may take your leave, now, he bid him. – You are hereby exiled, banned from the People in all things. The pain will stay with you forever. Even after a thousand generations, you will feel its sting.

Nick stumbled out of the room, staying with them, not fading like a nightmare after waking up.

– How can you do that? Ethel cried in disbelief and shock. – You treated him like dirt on the ground, doing so with a casual thought. You shouldn't be able to do that.

Everything directed their attention at her, then. Ted and Liz did, too. She felt it, just as unable as Nick to resist the ruthless probe.

– Why did you make Ruth and Bee? Liz wondered. – Did you do it on a whim, or is there a deeper purpose behind your actions we fail to discern? What else have you been doing behind our backs?

She probed the tall and big powerful woman just as casually as Ted had done Nick, leaving Ethel Warren beyond shaken, a shivering leaf hardly able to stand or speak.

– Everything up to this point seemed so c-clear and clear c-cut to me, she said, unable to stop her lips from shaking, clearly distressed beyond distressed, – but now, it's nothing but m-m-mud.

They watched her, as she rushed out of the room, as she rushed to catch up with Nick.

Liz stood a bit to the side. Ted didn't see her with his eyes. He had no trouble seeing her.

– Locus Bradle is the world, she whispered, hardly audible, but he heard it quite well.

Hand grabbed hand.

Ethel caught up with Nick.

– You shouldn't be here, he said, – should not fraternize with the Exile.

– I don't care, she choked. – There's nowhere else I would rather be.

Gabi hardly left Ted's side after that. He cast her one single worried glance he couldn't hide and sent her away, but she quickly found her way back.

Or she sought out Liz, with pretty much the same result.

– I will serve you forever, she stated with numb lips. – I know what you are.

She looked stubbornly at Liz.

– It isn't a stupid girl crush, she said. – The fact that I'm also here, with you should more than suggest that. The moth needs to be close to the flame, needs to burn.

As always, her chilling rationality worried them just as much as her puppy love.

Even as they sometimes felt beyond worry, beyond concern.

The stench of the desert stayed in their nostrils, or what seemed like their nostrils, stronger than ever, an enduring presence in their consciousness.

Stewart and Ruth walked hand in hand later.

– That was awesome, she cried, – just awesome.

– It sure was, he chuckled, – like witnessing a hurricane closeup.

He turned rowdy, began to fondle and kiss her.

She resisted his advances.

– Not now, she protested. – We should talk more about what happened. Don't you think it's important, too?

– I do, he grinned with his lips on her neck, – but not so important that we can't postpone it a few hours… or a night.

He continued his advances, pushing her back at a three, quickly wearing down her feeble protests.

She relented. He always managed to convince her of whatever he wanted to convince her of. She sighed and kissed him, responding eagerly to his growing ardor.

Then, abruptly, she stepped back and held him, looking at him, holding him with her stare.

– I enjoy seeing the fear in your eyes, she said.

She chuckled and left him, left him to rot. It felt so good, quite simply indescribably great. She stopped at a distance, where he could no longer see her, and looked down at her glowing hands. The sight and the subsequent emotion attached to it frightened her, excited her.

Ethel… appeared. Ruth didn't spot her before she stood right in front of her. The older woman applauded her slowly and silently.

– That is the way to treat arrogant young males, she said appreciative. – Congratulations!

– How is Nick? Ruth wondered, attempting in vain to mask her sudden anxiety, bewilderment. – Is he alright?

– He will be, Ethel shrugged. – He no longer matters. His work, his contribution is done. It's up to us, now.

Ruth frowned, feeling smaller when she looked down on the smaller big woman.

– Yes, I wished you into existence. You became my creation, my intended. You are here to serve the People. Rest assured that your contribution will not be insignificant.

– That's why, Liz mused. – That's why she made Ruth and Bee. It was no whim at all. Bee is a hound, able to find and identify all those we could just find and identify with the blue light, the machine. She has made our numbers reach critical mass. Ruth is also an energy-manipulator of sorts. They complete each other, and Ethel can draw energy from them both.

Ethel sought out Udo. She had no trouble locating him. He sat on a stub in the forest outside town.

– Stacy believes you're okay, but you aren't. You fooled her there.

– What are you talking about? He asked her with a sore voice.

– With me, you will find redemption, find the satisfaction and joy you deserve.

He joined her. She saw that before he realized it himself.

Gabi was breathing, breathing hard. Carla wet her brow. Stacy whispered comforting words in her ear.

– It will soon be over, and joy will be yours.

She stood with the other would-be mothers at the shore of Fire Lake.

– Breathe! Carla urged her. – *Breathe*!

– It hurts, Asteroth whimpered, snarled, mumbled. – It fucking *hurts*!

– I know, Stacy whispered, – but it will be alright, will be worth it. Just get on with it, little one.

Gabi turned her head and looked at her with tear-wet cheeks.

– Are you certain? P-promise?

– I promise! Stacy assured her.

The young woman heard the choir of voices around her. She knew that Stacy and Carla spoke to them all, but she still felt special, as if they spoke only to her, like all the gasping females did.

Gabi gasped. She froze. Then, she screamed, screamed loud enough to shake mountains.

The upper part of the head appeared between her thighs. Gabi pushed and screamed and pushed and screamed. The tiny body dropped down in the warm water. The rest of the content followed quickly. Carla cut the umbilical cord and gave the infant a dump on the back. His scream filled ears all over the shore and the gathering. Asteroth dumped down on her knees and began devouring the placenta. There was no hesitation, no delay, only the hunger.

She rested on a blanket hours later with all the other exhausted females. Rocky Asteroth sucked greedily on a nipple. Members of the People filed across the shore, congratulating the new mothers. She granted them her sweet smile and gratitude, even as she focused on the tiny bundle in her arms.

The pervasive autumn heat smothered her, and countered somewhat the prevailing chill within. She smothered the small head in kisses, suddenly overcome with anxiety. Stacy rubbed her cheek, comforting her. Asteroth grabbed the hand and kissed that, too.

She slept and was dreaming. She knew she was, even though it felt much more like a vision. No, not a vision… a memory. She realized that she had a reincarnation dream. The entity that would one day become Gabrielle Asteroth walked through what she recognized as an ancient middle eastern city.

The creature walked through the ancient city. Flames of fire and shadow danced around its body. Wings were flapping ineffectively, unable to lift it into the air.

Asteroth watched it through the eyes of the young girl, the body she once had inhabited. People close to the creature caught fire and burned. Their screams rose to the heavens. People ran, to no avail. Everyone within the boundary of the two cities was consumed.

The body, the shell, the ancient version of Gabrielle Asteroth caught fire and burned, tying her destiny forever to that of the winged creature, to that of the Phoenix.

354

She had no mouth, no throat anymore, but she was screaming, a banshee wail casting its echo across the Earth, across the centuries, across time and space, time/space.

It finally took flight, even as its flames set the two cities below on fire, leaving only ashes.

Lillian and Martin woke up soaked in cold sweat.

3

Linsey Kendall was confirmed as president-elect by the electoral college in early December. Five members charged to vote for him by the voters didn't do it, but voted for Barack Obama instead. But that was far from enough to stop the confirmation. Wild celebration erupted in the streets. More criticism of Kendall and accusations of «Russian connections» appeared in establishment media. It didn't mute the celebrations the slightest.

The seething human-shaped form of energy, the blue-shifted fire and shadow made its way back through the timestream from a distant future. It had devoured a star and used its vast energies to return to a present it had left a long time ago.

They walked through the Australian desert with the twenty-one surrounding them, like they all had dreamed their entire life. An extremely blue-shifted Southern Cross burned above them.

Liz and Ted awoke with a start, wide awake, without a shred of sleep-fatigue. Asteroth knelt on the bed in front of them, holding out a tray covered with food and drink. She didn't speak, making herself as inconspicuous as possible, hardly even there at all. Ted and Liz began feeding, devouring the delicious sandwiches and lemonade.

– Everything feels so much stronger, Liz mused.

It seemed like a completely redundant statement, as if she had spoken it long before she actually did.

Northfield Town, never really at sleep, woke up further around them. Thousands opened their eyes and saw the world with new eyes, and the Phoenix saw it with them. The two of them found themselves in the library. Asteroth remained by their side. She rushed to the toilet occasionally, unable to hold on to her piss anymore, but returned so fast that they hardly noticed that she had been gone.

– How is Rocky? Liz asked casually.

– Rocky is taken good care of at the nursery, My Lady. He's much loved. My duty to him will not interfere with my duty to you.

Her blushing cheeks kept warming them.

Betty and Jennifer entered the room. They behaved pretty much like Gabi did, with the same humble approach.

– My Lord, My Lady, Betty greeted them. – A… puzzling opportunity might have presented itself.

– Puzzling? He teased her.

She turned deep red.

– Yes, My Lord. A group of establishment shills pretending to be journalists/
reporters wishes to accompany the two of you on your world tour, on what they
believe is a plane across the world, stay with you 24/7. They claim they want a deep
interview.

– So, what are your thoughts about it? Liz asked her.

– I think it might be worth considering, My Lady. It will benefit us no matter
how they spin it. We will also have our own people onboard, of course. It will be
a triumphant celebration of our victory, and it will end on the fifteenth, more than
enough time to get back here, to our fortress before… before…

She choked the last word, sore afraid.

Jennifer stepped forward, drawing their attention.

– I've studied the old texts extensively, she stated. – I think I might have found
an inkling about what happened thousands of years ago. The danger remains, even
if Jahavalo is no longer a factor. My father and his mate are also concerned. They
know what might happen, even if they still don't remember exactly what that is. But
they know they failed thousands of years ago, and that failure keeps haunting them,
and that we've all paid for it since.

– We can't be afraid, he said with conviction. – We've prepared ourselves, taken
every possible and impossible precaution. Let's do it. Let's keep celebrating our
glorious victory.

– Yes, Ted, all three choired.

All three left, so very attuned to their wishes.

– They are so cute, Liz chuckled.

She turned somber, and reached out a hand. He grabbed it in a firm grip, and she
looked grateful at him.

– I can feel the force of your breath, sense the texture of your skin, sense it now,
and I'm not even standing close.

She took two steps towards him. He didn't move.

– Now, it's like a hurricane, she whispered like thunder.

They heard sirens from police cars, which was insane, since there were no police
cars anywhere near Northfield. It took them a moment or two to assure themselves
that the sound wasn't «real», that it was their power acting up.

She stood there, looking out at the yard and playing children with a distant
expression in the flaring fireeyes.

– I see a fire outside the window, but when I step outside, there's nothing there.
But there is something there. Perhaps in the very glass itself, perhaps beyond it,
beyond our reach.

– Presently beyond us, he nodded.

And the ember in her eyes intensified as she leaned against him.

– Go on, he insisted, – open the window.

She did, and saw only pitch black night outside.

– You helped me open my eyes to life, to fire. Now it is my turn to do it to you.
Both our turns, to do it together.

She looked astonished at him, as understanding dawned in her eyes.

356

– There is no fire in the window, of course.

Did he say that? Did she? Did it matter anymore?

– I'm afraid, she whispered.

She realized that she was afraid, that it wasn't just a whim. He kissed her, touched her and comforted her, and she whimpered happily in his arms.

– What the hell…

The sound of sirens suddenly intensified to the point of being ear shattering.

– Is this it? Are they coming for us now, Teddy? She said softly.

– They are coming for us, he responded curtly.

She nodded, dark in eyes.

The song of sirens faded in their ears as the imaginary police cars passed them in the streets outside and drove away from them.

Silence blessed them for a moment or two.

– I stare into the darkness and see the fire…

Fire shot from her hands. She yelped in joy. It proved no trouble sustaining it. She had complete control, and could play with it, juggle it like Linda did her tools. Fire shot from his hands as well. They were in tune, completely harmonized.

– This isn't fire. It's something more. It is *Fire!* What was present at the beginning of the Universe and is still with us… Forever.

– Fire was first, and we are its Shadow, he mused.

– And that feels so right, she cried. – It's certainly not one more empty statement.

A sort of peace descended with the relative silence. They had no trouble picking up a given sound within the confines of the town, but they chose not to do so. The town had become a kind of safe microcosmos, but even as they thought that, they knew it to be an illusion.

– We've been so caught up in everything that we've lost sight, at least to a point of the world, he said angrily. – We haven't thought about how truly horrible modern society is, not in a while.

– We were too caught up in the rigged game, the rules set by the gamemasters, she said, equally angry. – It's a good thing that we're shaken out of it.

What was both a deep chill and smoldering heat surged through them anew.

– Betty's suggestion is a good one, he said. – We, being kind and merciful allow the establishment fake newshounds, with their constant and deliberate misdirection to fly with us in our plane.

She chuckled brightly, but the unrest remained in her eyes. He wanted to comfort her, and to put her fears to rest.

– The plane won't even come near the southern hemisphere and far less Australia, and if something should happen, we have the twenty-one at our side, and be immensely powerful, both as a group and as individuals.

– All scrap of info we've gathered tells us that that is where… it will happen, she nodded. – Perhaps we didn't know that the previous time, but we know it now, no matter how tight-lipped Nick the bastard is, and we can choose to stay away.

She hesitated. He looked at her.

– He has walked over bodies to get us where we are now, she said angrily, – hardly caring about anything, except achieving his objective. Our lives would have been distinctly different without his «contribution». He won't give up.

Ted nodded, too, in poignant acknowledgement.

– He doesn't serve us, doesn't necessarily serve the cause, only whatever feverish objective ruling him since the day he entered the cave in the valley of kings.

Hands grabbed hands. They felt the intimate connection even stronger, if that was possible (and it was).

The observer *does* change what he's observing.

They heard his voice crystal clear in their head, felt his desperate need to communicate just that.

We're living on the edge between the possible and the actual, she thought gleefully, sending without making a conscious decision about doing it, her face cracking in a grin.

– Most people think life is an ever more narrowing path towards a single pinprick point, but it isn't. It's ever expanding, ever broadening, and never ending.

– In my teens I was angst, uncertainty and rage, Ted marveled. – The first two are gone, but fortunately the rage remains.

Both sensed Nick, at the edge of their consciousness.

– Let him, she snarled with contempt. – Let him watch!

They walked outside enclosed in ethereal flames, flames not burning their clothes, but still experienced as hot as the nuclear fire of the sun.

– «The only way to fix it is to flush it all away», they sang.

Laughter rose to the ceiling of the town and filled their minds and the hollow places of their selves.

They danced the night away.

4

The small airport looked exactly like the derelict, unused place it was; like it hadn't been used for years. The establishment reporters looked with dismay at the spectacle.

– We don't really fly much, Liz responded with a shrug to the incredulous stares.

– But you do have a plane? One reporter asked.

– It's a rental, she replied sweetly. – Your offer was quite simply too generous to resist. We searched an old scrapyard. It was a lucky find.

– Is she kidding? One whispered to a colleague. – I can never tell.

Ted and Liz stood in front of fifteen establishment reporters and journalists. The twenty-one stood in a half moon circle behind them. Linda and Glory wore their masks, but it didn't look like they did. They just looked like two more inconspicuous members of the crew.

– Welcome, Ted greeted them, – to this jump across the North Atlantic Ocean. I hope it will be memorable experience for us all.

The same establishment reporter looked bewildered at his colleague. The colleague shrugged.

Corinne Barbeau stood there with a portable camera in her hands, recording the event.

— You were an independent journalist? One of her colleagues or former colleagues asked.

— And now, I'm more independent than ever, she replied gleefully.

Everyone embarked the plane. It was fairly large, with a spacy interior.

— It resembles an Airforce One.

— That was one of the reasons we chose it, Michelle said good humored. — The temptation was impossible to resist.

— Did you pay for it?

— I could have, she shrugged, — but we have so many volunteers and small-time contributors by now that we hardly know what to do with all the money.

She looked at the man. He froze.

— Do you understand what that means? She asked, agitated at first, then smiling. — Of course, you do.

— People give us their hard-earned cash, Martine said, — keep giving even when they hardly have any, because they're *sick and tired* of existing in this hellish society. They're finally fed up with the sick game your wealthy bosses are playing. They love us. They hate you with a vengeance. Consider that the next time you're about to write yet another addition to your constant and deceitful and deliberate misdirection.

And he and the others suspected it wouldn't exactly be a pleasant journey.

— You used to be a nun, right?

Her story had been broadcast far and wide.

— I did, until I Fell, and found unlimited freedom.

She sounded completely casual about it, as if she was discussing the weather. He was clearly a catholic, and it did bother him. She smiled.

— You will stay in the back, Lee informed them. — It's a bit campy, but we will let you join us in front at our convenience if you behave.

The honored members of the press all looked like whipped dogs when they retreated to the dank space at the back of the plane.

— This is a good idea. Linda approached Liz and Ted in the front. — We brave the troubled waters in yet another attempt to bring enlightenment to the unaware.

She displayed herself to them.

— Do you like my uniform? I kind of favor it myself. It's a nice touch, don't you think?

— You look cute enough to devour, sweetie, Liz remarked, — like a flight attendant outshining all flight attendants.

Giovanni and Diana sat down in the cockpit and started up the plane. They did the checkup on their own. There was no tower to report to. The plane began taxing towards the fairly long runway.

The liftoff was smooth, even as the old plane shook, as if in fear. It started its flight across the North Atlantic Ocean and the globe. Ted and Liz sat by the front window and sipped wine.

– This is both pleasant and agonizingly slow, she moaned. – We are so used to the Asteroth express that we can hardly even imagine anything different anymore.

She frowned, and the frown seemed to have weight

– It seems both so mundane and so threatening.

And the moment she voiced her concern, it turned real, palatable, and just as obscure and unapproachable. She jumped on her feet and rushed, walked at a leisurable pace to the back of the plane. There was no need for her to do that. She could just as well have accessed the entire plane and everyone in it from her position in the pleasant chair, but she was itchy, anxious, longing to use her feet and mundane senses.

– Can I offer you a drink, sir? Glory asked a fat man in a huge chair, almost bursting into laughter in the process.

Is everything alright? Liz asked her.

The black woman did catch the urgency in her mental voice, but kept her face folded in the pleasant, impassive expression.

I have noticed nothing out of the ordinary, she responded.

There was really no need for her to consciously form the response. The question had set in motion several lines of thought Liz could easily catch and read, but they kept clinging to the old ways, or a semblance of such.

The outside of the metal bird seemed to be surrounded in an eerie glow. It faded the moment she focused on it, but lingered in her consciousness.

Liz read the minds of everyone onboard with a casual thought. She sensed nothing threatening or worthy of concern, nothing beyond a few spiteful bursts of racism, xenophobia. The itch remained.

The plane flew on autopilot. The twenty-three faced the establishment press like a half moon. Twenty-three pairs of eyes made the men and women across the room very uncomfortable.

– We're not in a hurry, Ted opened. – We have lots of time to cover all things. Ask away. But expect extensive answers, and you better not interrupt while we speak. Take notes and do the follow-up question when we're done.

He lectured them like they were children. Liz and Michelle and several of the others giggled darkly.

It… began, began in earnest. The members of the press asked the same, stupid «questions» and Ted and Liz knew those questions were completely immaterial. A stirring started in their belly and spread from there, burning as it made its way through their veins.

– Why are you so opposed to nuclear power plants? Isn't that a great solution to the dangers of climate change?

Liz chuckled in contempt.

– Nuclear power plants are even more dangerous than the climate change, she replied. – On an Earth soaked in poison, manmade radioactive materials are clearly the worst of the worst.

The answers were not merely answers, but answers, deep thought in a quiet room, between trees in a silent forest. Some of the men and women of the establishment

360

press had experienced it to a degree before, in the company of the two Warrens and believed themselves to be prepared, not realizing until this moment how much more powerful the invasive sensation had become.

– Yes, removing the borders, removing the countries themselves is a good move, Ted said, – but only if we also remove the corporations. Those mastodons should go anyway. They've never done anything good for anyone, except those in charge.

– Of course, the government and corporations don't want people to know the truth, Liz said, – so they torture and kill and suppress the few people expressing it.

– Corporations like Monsanto is a typical example, Michelle noted. – It produces poison and is poison. That is basically everything it is and have ever been. To list Monsanto's entire long list of crimes becomes a ridiculous exercise in futility. It's all available on the web anyway, no matter how much effort Google put into hiding the information.

– Letting animals and humans out of their cages is long overdue, Glory cried.

Victor Russel watched television with his fellow inmates in his prison. He looked up, as if sensing something in the air.

The answers began almost before the questions had ended. The layer of sweat on the interviewers' brow grew thicker and thicker.

– Wherever you go, in almost any casual conversation you hear some kind of racist slur, Jane snarled. – We're a world of racists, and it will stop.

That, too, will stop, someone unknown expressed themselves.

Three women walked on a road.

– People should be judged not by their ability to fit in in a horrible society, one of them breathed, – but by their desire and ability to leave it.

– That's so true! One of the others agreed.

– So very true, the third echoed.

And those present on the plane seemed somehow privy to that conversation.

Liz and Ted had the dream of them standing in the forest in front of the ruin of Tropicana Hotel in Las Vegas again.

– How can this be? The global heating will make the deserts grow, not shrink and certainly not disappear.

The clock was ticking. It felt almost funny. They could mark each tick, each tock, each tack. The seance of questions and answers had ended. The people asking low-quality questions had returned to the back of the plane.

Carla frowned. She noticed the shifting of the metal body as well, long moments before they all heard the screeching sound.

Ted and Liz realized abruptly that they had no time, no time at all.

Ruth and Bee appeared at the central axis of the plane. They were clearly phantoms, not really there…

They were there!

– What are you doing? He asked puzzled.

– A very good and necessary thing, Uncle Ted, Ruth said brightly, only slightly concerned. – You'll see! You will understand everything.

There was a major shift. Space, or at least the higher end of the atmosphere seemed to impose on the plane. They all felt the strong, beyond strong pull. It was like the plane's speed doubled or tripled or more, as if someone had put a rocket on the tail of the flying body. All of them lost their balance.

The plane slowed down, deaccelerating to what almost felt like a complete stop, but that was because the current speed was so much slower compared to the sudden, unexplainable acceleration.

The two girls faded. A man stepped through the door from the back-section. He looked like one of the journalists, was one of journalists that had participated in the Q and A. His face shifted and changed. Udo stood before them, a study in confusion and horror and rage.

– I'm sorry, he choked. – Sorry, sorry, sorry!

Liz and Ted surrounded them all in a protective bubble. Udo exploded, disintegrated in a major destructive force. The plane was split in two. Ted and Liz held on to the twenty-one and what was left of the plane. Blood flowed from their nostrils. The front of the plane, with its large wings still intact began its descent. Liz and Ted, with others joining in fought constantly to keep it under a semblance of control. It floated a bit, fell again, started spinning, steadying itself again, going down, down, down. Wind blew from every angle. Some of those around the two started floating, and hit the wall of air and mind surrounding them. Every time the two and those aiding them believed they had control, something else happened countering that. A piece of the wall was torn off. They glimpsed the sky, the eerie bluish sky.

The hull kept shedding metal pieces. Liz and Ted sensed the ground far below. Time seemed to rush at them, just as that ever-closer ground. Everything happened so fast, no matter how much it slowed down in their feverish mind. They had experienced something similar many years ago, but this was different. This plane was already a wreck. But they had also become more powerful and more in control of their abilities. So, it was an even match. They let go of even more shrapnel with each passing moment. As they handled tons of dead weight tumbling towards the earth.

Images, sensations filled all the twenty-one and two, as the two lost control of their other abilities, as they with an iron-hard will focused on retaining a strenuous control of the wreck. They burned, even as they knew the fire from the plane didn't reach them, that it was all in their mind. Five point six meters above the ground the dead metal bird seemed to freeze in the air, but they knew it was an illusion.

The dead weight hit the soft sand with a loud thud making their ears bleed.

5

A metal bird crashed in the dust, in the soft sand.

A mighty dragon moved through reality, swatting it aside like pebbles. Its wings were not flesh, but seething bursts of shadow. What it moved through wasn't air or even empty Space, but pulsing concentrations of Dust and Void and hyperspace and dark matter and energy.

– I can see it, Gabi whispered to Stacy. – A glowing pentacle in the sand, a nest of sticks and bones.

She saw it and through Stacy, they could all see it. They saw the burning plane.

– Death… is coming, Samhain said.

His body wasn't there, but his spirit was among them, hardly ever transparent at all.

The two in his company froze.

The flames spread in the dark cabin. Ted and Liz took stock. There were a few wounds, some bleeding, but everyone was alive and well. The two let go. The silence in the bubble broke as the world rushed back in. The two and twenty-three made their way out of the burning plane. Ted and Liz made sure everyone jumped down in the soft sand before they did. Everyone made their way off and away from the broken bird. All the supplies left in the hull floated out of there and joined the creatures of flesh and blood escaping its deathtrap.

What was that? Giovanni asked. What happened?

We were sabotaged and attacked by Udo and Ruth and Bee, and possibly others, Linda stated.

The heat from the burning wreck faded, as they made their way from the seething inferno, from the tall dancing flames and thick, dark smoke.

– Oh, no, Lee said distressed.

Everyone looked at him.

– We're in the Australian desert, west of Canberra, in our prevalent, life-long waken dream.

Everyone looked around and nodded in agreement. The so very familiar chill and heat and scent surged through them.

– Look, Andrea said, looking up.

They all looked up in the sky, at the Phoenix, at the strongly blue-shifted Southern Cross constellation of celestial objects. It was flashing and shimmering and seemingly growing in their eyes.

– This is crazy, Liz mused, Liz grinned, – at least compared to all common rational standards. A random scientist calls a random star constellation Phoenix, and it happens to be flaring up exactly when we expect it to do so.

She turned somber mere moments later.

– The future has caught up with us, Ted stated.

6

THE AUSTRALIAN DESERT
NORTH AND WEST OF CANBERRA
DECEMBER 21, 2008
(western, Christian timeframe)

– It is December 21, Glory stated, unable to keep the shivering from her voice. She displayed the changed date and time on her phone.

– Bee and Ruth and Udo did that? Beth said incredulous.

– Ethel did it, Liz stated calm as ice. – Somehow, she convinced the other three that it was the right thing to do, that it was a beneficial act.

– They combined their powers and actually sent us through a hole in time and space, Michelle mused, – delivering us exactly at this moment, at the moment destiny has ordained.

Something about her wording made Ted frown, but he couldn't catch the fleeting thought.

Liz and Ted held hands and reached out with their power, but nothing happened. They sensed nothing out there, nothing beyond the immediate surroundings. The frown turned deep.

– We can't sense anything beyond the immediate vicinity, Ted said. – It is as if something is… blocking us.

The others with far-reaching powers made the attempt, too. Everyone shook their head.

– I can't fetch them, Gabi told Stacy. – Something, a force beyond anything I've ever sensed is preventing me. I can see them, but I can't touch them.

She looked desperately, painfully at Stacy.

– Is it time itself preventing us from doing anything to prevent anything?

– I don't… know, Stacy replied with equal anguish. – I can't sense them either, and I usually can.

They looked at Jason's spirit. It shook its head.

Glory displayed her phone again. The display had changed in notable ways.

NO COVERAGE

Every single phone display showed those two words. The time and date still showed, but important functions no longer worked.

– We must gather our forces, Stacy said, – and make a concerted effort, but until we can do that…

– They are on their own, Jason said.

– We must move, Ted stated, – get as far away from here as possible.

He didn't bother hiding the anxiety, the concern in his voice. They would have caught it, no matter how hard he had attempted to conceal it.

– We should head for Canberra, Lee suggested. – Whatever danger is waiting for us out here must surely be less there.

The twenty-three nodded as one. They got going. It was a small matter to navigate under the summer twilight night sky. Several of them had lived with detailed views of that sky for decades. They moved as one.

– It's just another language, Ted said slowly, with the distinct frown on his brow.

The stars did speak to him, to them, to the Adversary, to the Phoenix with growing clarity.

The desert night embraced them more and more for each new step. Several of them walked with half closed eyes.

– I feel so at home here, Linda said.

The others glanced at her, but didn't contradict the statement. They were sweating,

364

sweating hard. Some of them had their first sips of water.

– The chill is soaking my bones, Tony said. – I can't make it stop.

Each step forward felt like a leap into the large unknown. They scouted long and far with their powers, sensing nothing significant.

– We are in grave danger, Tony said, – we must be. Everything tells us that we are.

The truth of his statement screamed at them.

The pressure within and without kept building. They kept charging forwards, towards what they imagined was the light-polluted horizon ahead.

– We should be good, Michelle stressed. – Between us all, those setting a trap will need to be pretty darn impressive in order to overcome us or even threaten us.

– But everything tells us that this is a well-prepared trap, Marcus pointed out. – We're supposed to be right here, at this very moment. The trap is well made. It stands to reason it will be well-executed.

They kept moving at a steady pace. Being constantly on guard and using their powers were tiring, and they had to portion it out, using it sparingly, focusing on using their passive and ordinary senses. The dessert sounds imposed themselves on them.

– There is life everywhere, Beth marveled.

Growls and screams hit them from every angle, and kept doing so. The stench of blood reached their nostrils. They stayed on guard. Carla turned her head. Kimberly sniffed the air. She undressed, starting the change before she had removed all fabric. Jane picked up the clothes as she threw them away. The large werewolf walked among them.

– There are people here, she growled. – People with guns. The scent is faint, but it's there. They stay away, stay just out of range, close enough to catch the scent, but not more than that.

Her olfactory sense painted an image of the terrain in the Phoenix's mind. It was an amazing addition to their own multitude of senses.

– They're professionals, Giovanni stated. – They've been told to stand back and they're also doing that. It would have worked against all ordinary opponents.

– They're waiting in the shadows, patient as vultures, Linda remarked.

Kimberly had trouble handling the heat with her thick pelt. She returned to human form, and redressed in the fabric Jane handed her.

– I'm sorry, Phoenix, she sniffed.

They walked, and walked on, as the burning sun rose above the horizon. Amazingly, the bright sunshine didn't quite remove the bluish light from the star constellation. It lingered, and if anything, it grew stronger as the long minutes passed. They found shelter, found shadow from the searing sun, but the bluish light kept caressing them.

– I remember the first time I met myself, Tony mused. – It was a terrifying experience. It was only several years later, thanks to Ted and Liz that I learned to appreciate it.

Everyone looked softly and good humored at him. Most of them had had similar experiences.

– Meeting your Shadow face to face is both a wonderful and terrifying experience, Carla said. – So, it stands to reason that in a world filled with intolerance and ignorance, where people have to suppress their true selves, as a matter of survival, people cry God or Satan or are institutionalized or something…

Hands grabbed hands, until the circle had formed yet again, making them choke in joy. It lingered, like it always did long after they let go.

Ted heard the flaps of a chopper. He didn't see it with his eyes, but the sound stayed distinct in his mind. Liz looked at him. They held hands again. They both heard the same sound, but not more than that.

The two and twenty-one did enjoy their brief time of relative peace. There was a bit of rest at the short recess, but when they moved on, it quickly felt like they had been walking uninterrupted a long time. The water in their bottles just faded away, shrinking to nothing, whether they drank it or not. So, they drank it, drank more than they would have and should have. They put it back in their bags fast, in an effort to keep it from evaporating.

The immediate surroundings drew itself effortlessly in Ted and Liz's mind, and were thereby shared by all walking with them. They started running at some point, and moments later, it felt like they had always done so. The twenty-three mutants didn't really strain themselves in the pervasive heat. The fire burned inside, and overwhelmed the hot forge outside. They realized quickly that their senses, their powers worked better when they did. Years of exercise, of rigorous training had paid off.

The Southern Cross glowed stronger above them. Ted saw that without looking at it.

Carla slowed down a bit, as if listening again, but she looked different this time. Then, she stopped with a few final steps, and the others did, too. She reached out her hands. Sand began rising from one spot and land in a growing heap ten steps away. She made a hole in the ground. Water began rising in the hole. She bent town and touched it.

– It's clean, she stated.

They drank. It was dirty, not exactly clean, as they would usually understand it, but still tasted fresh and great. They filled their almost empty bottles.

Liz and Ted had trouble listening to the surroundings above the happy buzz and stepped a bit to the side. It was sufficient. Relative calm entered their consciousness. Then, they heard it, a different kind of buzz. The first bullets reached them from three sides. Ted, acting on instinct put up his shield in front of Liz and the others half a second before he shielded himself. A couple of bullets hit him. He was pushed back. Liz jumped after him and grabbed his hand. The power flared between them. They swept the terrain, sensing no people nearby. The bullets had been fired from a vast distance, out of their range.

– It's amazing how she has determined our limitations, Liz said and shook her head in reluctant wonder.

They waited, and they kept extending their sweep. There were no more bullets fired. They glimpsed a few people in uniforms running from their hideouts.

Ted removed the bullets from his body. It was an automatic process, perfected through many years. The bullets rested in his hand, bathing in boiling blood.

– It does look rather pointless…

He frowned. Carla stepped forward. She grabbed the bullets. They watched her as she turned pale and anxious. He screamed and doubled over, suddenly overwhelmed with weakness.

7

There was running and there was pain, like a distinct, distant thud in his bones. He smelled the raw blood pushing the poison out of his system. The desert sun was burning above their heads, roasting the tiny group of humans making their way east, towards the sea. Linda was at his side. She had always been there, he realized now. He remembered her face clearly, all the lines there without ever looking at it. Liz was at his other side, her face even more radiant than he could remember. His consciousness soared and spiked up and down, like a rollercoaster, but always resting, as time went by on a higher level than it had previously. The desert invaded them, on all levels, but he and Liz also invaded the desert, the sand, the dust, the arid air. They weren't merely a part of it anymore. They didn't become a part of the desert. They became the desert.

– I can feel it, Liz mumbled, – the desolation, the power, the Life. It's wonderful.

The sun and the wind roasted them step-by-step. They kept running. His wounds had closed now, but his body seemed to be on fire. The poison still clashed with his immune defense system, one of the most wicked, virulent poisons he had ever encountered. Only a few bullets had hit him, but it had almost finished him, and it still could. It interfered with the use of his power, interfered with everything. Liz tried again to keep them all afloat, and managed for a few seconds, before they once more crashed into the desert sand.

Everybody looked at each other.

– Fuck! Liz cried out in helpless frustration. – I feel what you feel. Fuck those bastards!

Carla rose first. She stood still, listening. She was always listening.

– The poison is inorganic, alien, she said. – I can't remove it.

She sniffed in the air a bit. They knew it was mostly for show. Whatever she smelled with wasn't the nose. Whatever she listened with wasn't the ears.

– They are coming at us, she said.

– From where? Ted asked her, jumping up, sensing how every cell in his body screamed in pain.

His power spiked. His pain spiked. And Liz felt it, too.

– From everywhere. Carla shook her head. – I can sense the ground move all around us. Heavy artillery, soldiers numerous as ants, choppers and planes, just out of ranges. They're all over the desert, ready to welcome us, no matter where we're going. This is an even better prepared trap than we feared.

– And they knew we were *coming*, Liz snarled, – Which meant they had *help*.

– Who? Ted said.

She just looked at him and he paled. They could actually see his skin grow paler under the hot Sun.

– But why should she…

– I don't know why. I don't know why she has done a lot of what she has done. All I know is that it *is*.

She turned to them all.

– Come, let's keep going.

Ted rose. His every move was pain, but they kept running.

– How long to Canberra? He asked Carla.

– Not long. She shook her head. – Not for us.

They ran. Ted, Liz, Andrea, Kimberly and Carla in point. Every time somebody stumbled, they were there and pulled them back up. Bella, too, with her healing power. She kept doing Ted, but she just couldn't do it too often. She couldn't take from him, only give, and it weakened her.

– If Raven had been here, she would have fixed this in an instant, she complained, full of regret.

– You're right, he said kindly enough. – But she isn't here, and you're doing fine.

His words strengthened her. They could virtually see how she pulled herself together, rebuilt herself.

And every time somebody got too tired, she opened a vein and let them drink of her, and all fatigue, all signs of exhaustion vanished from their eyes.

– Are you okay? She asked Jane.

– I'm more than okay, Jane assured her, assured them all.

And she proved them right, by not falling behind. No one did. They were all driven, as if by demons.

The sun set on the Australian wilderness. The red cliff formations turned even redder, strange hues of fire and shadow.

– Wings, Ted mumbled. – I can see wings.

He looked at the setting Sun, and Liz did, too. There were light clouds there, seemingly spreading out from one focal point, brushing the sky, brushing the Earth. Carla looked, too, looked at them. Linda turned and stared. There was a strange light of fear and excitement in her eyes.

– They're coming, Carla warned.

And they were. The sounds of engines, so distant and low increased in strength and detail.

Ted grabbed Liz' hand. She grabbed his. There was a flash of blinding light, very much like that of the dying Sun, and suddenly they were all airborne. Lee released a triumphant call, raising a fist against the approaching planes, tanks and soldiers. There were incoming missiles. The two Warrens' eyes flared like the Sun, and the missiles turned abruptly in the air. Five, six, seven deadly flying machines blowing up planes, tanks and advancing soldiers. There were no more missiles, but the attackers kept advancing. Then a cone of fire erupted from the two figures in front of the levitating group, melting planes, soldiers and tanks. Hundreds of men and women screamed and roasted in their own fat.

And they ran, ran like rabbits before the pack of foxes with dripping, dripping fangs.

Yeah, run back to your holes in the ground. Stay away from us. If you return, if you come anyway near us again, we will kill you all.

And Ted and Liz Warren sent their first loud and pervasive, beyond powerful telepathic message.

– It's happening again, Liz shouted. – WE ARE GROWING!

Every death empowered them.

I can feel the fire, she sent. *It feels so good, so very, very good.*

Another quantum leap had been added to their growth, to the Power. They could sense it. They didn't need to. It shifted and flowed within them as a living thing.

The poison had vanished from his body, as if it had never been there in the first place. There were vapors around him, around her, not being affected by their travel through the air. And they realized it wasn't vapors at all, but two shadowy figures materializing themselves.

And they left the vast ground-based army behind.

Everybody was able to see the shadow creatures dancing around the two, now, and see them easily. The faces turned slowly into a smoky version of Ted and Liz' features. And the eyes, the eyes burned in dark fire.

Carla touched her temple with a strained look on her face.

– Are you okay? Ted asked her.

– Yes, Carla replied. – I can feel the Earth. For the first time I can feel it while not touching it. The winds are enough. Through the air I breathe I can hear the planet whisper. And I can feel you, feel you burn the Earth.

Two Teds looked at her, two pairs of firespitting eyes. Ted and the Shadow, mixing, separating, intermingling. Ted *looked* at her. For the very first time he looked at her. She gasped and collapsed there, suspended in the air by the shadows' power.

Lee touched her gently on the cheek, looking anxiously at her.

– I'm okay, it's just the damn fatigue, that's all. I'll be okay.

Ted and Liz looked around. Around them were twenty and one, exactly as they had seen in their vision, exactly as the Seers had prophesized for millennia.

«The two who are one are walking through the desert, surrounded by their twenty and one».

They heard the voice, the voice in the wilderness.

They looked at each other.

«Tired»? Their eyes asked each other.

– Are you tired? She asked him.

– I don't feel any actual fatigue, but the Power is waning.

It did, eventually after intense use. It fed on itself for a while, its strength growing by use... until a certain point, where it reached a limit, and turned itself off.

They landed, by cliffs lit by sunset and shadows, before they were forced to.

The moment Carla touched the ground the pained look in her face disappeared, but she shook her head in despair.

– I'm a liability to you.

The land surrounding them, surrounding her suddenly started to move. Geysers of sand erupted from the ground. The ground shook, as if there was an earthquake (and there was). Even the mountains seemed to bend and twist.

– You must be kidding. Ted grinned at her. They all grinned.

It was growing. Her Power. They were all growing. Bella's usually pale complexion seemed to glow in a deep, full color. The others, too, looked somehow… larger than before, larger than life.

Everybody, Carla, too, gathered in a ring around the two at the center.

– Yes, Ted said, Liz said. – This is the time, the final hour spoken about for thousands of years. Everything is happening simultaneously, everything is piling up. The future is now.

The vision overwhelmed Carla again. The knight in black approaching her, the knight in black lying dead and bloody among heaps of bodies, of fallen.

– The desert is whispering, she whispered. – Whispering to me.

– To us all, Ted said. – To…

He stopped. Looking at them, he saw their faces change, becoming pale and sickly. Just for a second, then it was gone.

Words, phrases, moments shifted, changed, becoming different from how he recalled them. The piecemeal words in the sky almost made sense.

Linda looked at him. Everybody else looked haggard, at least a bit worn, but she looked as healthy as she had done the first few seconds after the crash. He looked at Liz, reading the same expression of confusion and horror in her eyes, as he, himself felt.

– Canberra is close, Carla said.

There was another rise, another set of mountains towards the sunrise, bathing in the sunset's colors, of rusted iron. She didn't have to point for them to know the right direction to go.

– Death is close, Bella said frosty. – I can feel it embrace me like mist.

She was a healer. She would know. All healers had a kind of prescience. And they all sensed it, the shadowy figure walking over their grave.

– But Delphi said Death was the whirlwind, the firestorm, Sally said.

– Yes, Bella said.

Darkness descended on the desert as they started running, and even though they knew well that there could be tons of infrared devices hidden in the terrain recording their movement, the darkness felt, as always, as their friend.

– This area was green once, Bella said. – At least a lot of the area we're approaching was green. Major parts of New South Wales were a garden in the desert that is Australia.

She had lived most of her childhood, or what should have been her childhood here. Her accent remained. She spoke as she ran, and she hardly sounded breathless.

The mountains looked so close, but they ran hard for quite a while, and the mountains looked no closer. They stopped, resting. Ted levitated straight up, almost as high as he could come, surveying the terrain. His radar sense had made

370

him able to see in total darkness since early adulthood. This darkness was far from total, though, with stars, and the Southern Cross above, and the summer twilight dominating the night, but he saw the deepest dark easily, saw animals move in it. He spotted no humans. There were no signs of them anywhere. He lowered himself back down.

– No hostiles, he said.

– Any message from Raven or anybody else? Carla asked.

– Nothing. Ted shook her head. – Either something has happened or something… or someone is keeping her or Delphi from reaching us.

His and Liz' eyes met again, and sunset was still there among them.

They still didn't find water. Bella gave blood to those who needed it. One drop to each was sufficient. It expanded into their mouth, turning into a waterfall, strengthening them beyond what any water, any other nourishment would have done. It expanded to the point of them having trouble swallowing it all. Their eyes lit up in gratitude and clarity.

– The first population «centers» are just beyond the mountains, Carla said, – but they're hardly noticeable in these vast, open plains, and Canberra is still far away.

They ran, like dogs with their tongues hanging out. They were chasing something, but they were also running from countless manifestations of the Enemy, from other things they couldn't name. They were running towards it, to something beyond water, beyond blood.

There was a loud beep somewhere. They slowed down. Lee stopped first, then all the others.

– It's the cell phone, he said puzzled. – I programmed it to… to *scream* when we entered a covered area.

He pulled it from his pocket, halting the sound with a quick push. He handed it to Ted. Ted pushed one single button, and the monitor started flashing. He pushed the volume to the max, and everybody could hear the electronic calling, hear the anxious voice replying at the other end, from the other side of the Earth.

– *What happened?* They heard Linsey's voice and his relief and joy. – *You vanished from the face of the earth. We couldn't find you. Stacey and Gabi told us they had a sense of you being alive and well, but they are still absolutely frantic.*

– Our plane went down in Australia just hours ago, Ted said flatly. – Deep into the desert.

– In Australia? That's far off course. Did you say just *hours* ago?

– It was a well-prepared spell sending us through time and space, Ted said, just as flatly. – Ethel did it. She had help, but she did it.

– ETHEL??? But…

Linsey's shock was echoed between them all.

There was some commotion. Ted knew someone ripped the phone from Linsey's hand, knew who it was.

– Ted, Stacy said forcefully, – It is declared *open season.*

Ted closed his eyes briefly, before opening them again, opening them wide.

– The forces are concentrated in the Australian desert, around you, but they are really everywhere, UN Security Forces. We're fairly safe here, in DC, being in a public place, but they're going after all of us, everywhere. Listen… we knew where you were…

– How?

– Nick is here. He came to us after days of our ongoing failure to locate you and suggested we tried not merely detection, but also looked for places that might be… be closed to us. And the affected area is *moving*, moving as you're moving. She wants you and Liz *gone*. She has always wanted you gone, dead and gone. I didn't say anything, but I always agreed with you in your assessment of her. I've waited for her to make her move, but I sorely underestimated her, didn't expect something this… spectacular. We will do anything we can to counteract what she is doing… whatever she is doing.

Ted kept his eyes open. He understood: Don't keep your hopes up.

And they were cut off, like a blade cutting a thin rope. The phone went dead, completely dead. He threw it away.

Everything happened simultaneously, like they had always known it would.

– She wanted us to know, he stated, in a razor-sharp voice.

Rage coursed through them, welcome as rain. But for the first time in a very long time, it didn't comfort them any.

Liz rose in the air, scouting. Ted saw what she saw, clearer than he had ever done. He saw the Outback, sensed the dark air surrounding her on all levels, saw creatures move, move silently through the sand, too few for Carla to focus on. He wanted to scream, but when he screamed, he screamed in pain the moment Liz did, the moment a rain of tiny arrows hit Elizabeth Warren from everywhere. She couldn't deflect more than a few of them.

She fell. Ted fell. He wanted desperately to catch her, but was unable to do so. He writhed on the ground, in cramps and pain, recognizing what happened to Liz instantly. The poison, the same poison they had used on him, but she had been hit far worse. It overloaded her system completely.

Carla caught her gently. A geyser of sand met her on the way down, and she landed softly, as if there had been no fall at all.

– I should have sensed them, Carla cried out, wailing.

Linda grabbed her by the collar, enraged, cold as ice.

– Listen, you're not a god, fuck you. You're not omnipotent. You didn't, couldn't know they were there. Now, you *do*, and I need you to find them find them all.

Carla put a hand to her temple, concentrating.

– I can… sense them, she said slowly. – They're hard to get a hold on. They move silently, lightly, like shadows, but they're not. Seven, they're seven, surrounding us, like in a circle. They're moving in on us. I can take care of them, but I don't know if I can do it fast enough.

– I can, Linda said, drawing the black blade. – You take care of as many as you can to the east. I'll go west and work myself around the circle from there. Andrea, you come with me. The rest of you know what to do.

The two women slipped away like invisible lightning in the darkness. Andrea clearly faster, Linda clearly deadlier.

Five knelt down by Liz, touching her skin. They started shaking instantly and fell to the ground. The other pulled them away. Liz moaned. Ted rose, still in pain, but his eyes cleared. Bella bathed the five in her healing energies. It took time, but they recovered, once more demonstrating that this wasn't something they could do often. And especially not here, in the desert, where every step was a strain, even under ideal circumstances.

– Good work, Ted said. – Be alert, ready for anything.

Carla sensed the ground, the sand, the bushes. She first saw Andrea move like a panther. Not at top speed, sacrificing some speed for silence. Carla could hardly sense Linda at all, other than a change in the terrain, a footprint, where it hadn't been any before. Then concentrating, she sensed the air, the change in pressure when someone moved, and she sensed the seven antagonists. A geyser rose just behind one. Carla swore. Too slow. The man stopped, hesitated a fateful moment, and she got him. The sand flayed the skin from his bones. He died instantly. The rage, she felt the rage stronger than ever before, the rage of the Earth itself.

– One prisoner, Ted instructed. – I don't trust Linda and Andrea to bring back one.

The next, the one closest to them, she lifted up, on the wings of dust. He fell in their midst like garbage. Ted caught him instantly, lifted him up in his claws of Night and held him steady. His mouth was open. He looked at Ted Warren in terror.

– You're not afraid, Ted told him. – Not yet. You're frustrated because I'm keeping you from closing your mouth, to bite down on the poison capsule operated in a tooth. Don't be afraid, I'll not permit you to hurt yourself.

The personified rage standing there brought the doll in his grip close. Ted brought a hand inside the wide-open mouth, and pulled out the fake tooth. The man screamed, as blood flowed from the torn gum.

– You're going to tell me everything, moving your lips, moving them good., Ted Warren told him. – We will dig it out of you with the sharpest knives, using everyone at our disposal.

The helpless prisoner wanted to shout, to spit a curse, but he wasn't given a chance. A long, bloody rift appeared in his dark, tight clothing, a wound from his shoulder to his calf. He screamed. Ted repeated it, from the other shoulder, the other calf, making an x. The scream turned louder.

– I know you're trained to resist torture, even telepathy, but I can tell you I'm very good at this. I've always been, when I want to be. You will talk. You will sing, and you will never stop singing. No punishment is too much for you, such a willing tool of the tyrants.

Carla focused on one attacker, a woman. This time she got it... got it right the first time. Ted's rage echoed in her, amplified in her, like it amplified in him. Bushes attacked the attacker, cutting her to shreds. Carla imagined herself swinging the sword on the battlefield, finally, and she smiled.

– I will keep you awake, the Beast told the captive. – Bella, sweet Bella will keep you alive. There is no way out, no matter what you do, but it is my will that you tell us everything, *everything*. The choice you made, you made a long time ago, and I sense no repentance in you. You will repent in the end, but it won't matter. The vengeful god will be there when you fall, but he won't catch you. I am the one crying in the wilderness, and I will make you fall forever. When we meet again, many lives from now you better have wised up, or I will make this look like a Sunday school excursion, *do you understand?*

The man couldn't move, couldn't speak, couldn't move his head, couldn't even move his eyes, couldn't close his eyes. The giant mist-breathing Demon holding him... his eyes flared like fire.

Ted enjoyed the sensations, the impressions and sense of horror he got from the man's mind. It felt amazing.

– Yes, everything you were told in the briefings is true, Ted said softly. – That and much, much more.

He twisted one of the man's arms in its socket. The soldier screamed completely beside himself. He was about to slip into unconsciousness, blessed unconsciousness...

When Bella Alver Warren touched his forehead, and he returned to full consciousness and there was no escape from the pain.

– Yes, she stated, – healers are fully capable of dishing out pain. That's the other side of our double-edged sword. We just generally choose not to exhibit that part of our gift. But you are scum, Sergeant John Waynant, the eager servant of the destroyers of Life on Earth. *Life,* John, do you know what that means? Yes, all healers have a slight, telepathic ability. It's necessary, to achieve full contact with the sick... or our victim, and I can tell what you're thinking. It isn't hard, isn't hard at all.

Touching his jaw she rearranged it, and his scream turned to a thin, hoarse wail.

– We are skin molders, she told him proudly. – At least to a point. That's another, less known aspect of our power.

– GOD, HELP MEEEEEE

– God is dead, Warren grinned. – And he wouldn't have helped you anyway, even though you were his obedient soldier. He was quite a mean son of a bitch.

– Liz has stabilized, Carla reported, seemingly from far away. – I can't make her wake up, but she is okay, for now.

– Good, Ted breathed. – Good...

He broke Waynant's other arm several places simultaneously.

– Ordinarily this wouldn't have started to hurt for a while, but Bella is keeping your body's natural anesthesia from being released into your bloodstream.

There were tears, now, and hardly more than small, pitiful sounds of pain.

Linda returned with a sack of potatoes on her shoulder. Her black hair shone in the bluish light of the Southern Cross. The pale face, her dark clothes were soaked in blood. She dumped the bound and gagged woman on the ground.

– In case you need another one.

He tightened his grip around the sensitive spot on the man's hand, an act hurting

374

far more than most people without the necessary knowledge would guess, without having actually experienced it personally. Waynant's mouth moved, but there was no sound.

Ted looked at Liz, at her face. Her body, in full defense mode had shut down, shut off consciousness in order to fight off the poison. That was both good and bad. She didn't suffer, but like him, and all mutants able to heal themselves she could speed up, enhance the healing when conscious, with her will.

Waynant started talking. For a long time, there was only his mouth moving, and then, finally the sounds, the words started flowing.

I know many things, he said, with his mouth, with every nuance of movement in his body. Please allow me to serve you, to be the servant of the gods. Let me be lower than the worm in the ground.

His entire front, his shell of independence collapsed, and he revealed himself to be the sycophant he, in truth had been his entire life. He died there, in the desert as Bella let go of him, of massive shock to his system and in horrible pain, and there wasn't the slightest touch of remorse in Ted or in Bella.

Ted didn't have to nod to Linda. She pushed the woman's skin to Liz' cheek. She paled quickly. Liz opened her eyes, screaming. Linda pulled the woman away, slitting her throat. More blood nourished the desert sand.

Liz' dark half rushed to her, in one incredibly fluid movement.

– Pain, she howled. – It's all over me.

– Embrace it, fuck you! He swore, Ted swore. – Take it deep inside you and light the fire.

Suddenly, incredibly she stood on her feet. Everybody gasped and pulled back, inevitably.

– I will live, do you understand me? She grabbed his collar and tore it to pieces. – I will live.

She let go, as she collapsed slowly, towards the ground. Her right hand remained a fist.

– Yes, you will, he stated. – You will…

He grabbed her just before her body hit the ground. He lifted her and carried her, over the sand burning like fire, the glowing rocks. He was unable to fly, but he ran, ran like the wind.

They followed him, followed them, with awe and fear in their hearts.

Except Linda. She remained by their side, always by their side.

Andrea returned, rejoined them, a human figure clothed in speed and dust.

– There is no one out there, she reported. – Not for miles and miles.

They kept going, like ants, a small dust devil in the vast desert. They rested, in the shade of the morning Sun glowing behind the low mountains. They sat in a circle, with Ted and a comatose Liz inside. She was sweating and twisting, and suffering on the ground. Ted spoke and they listened.

– Ethel is a Multi, but she's most of all a precognitive, a precognitive to end all other precognitive. Like I and Liz, Mike, Nick, Stacy and even Gabi combined. She has seen this, planned it for a long time, perhaps since before many of us were even born. She has found the mundane forces, or they have found her, or they're just taking advantage of each other or whatever. She couldn't have done this without them. They couldn't have done this much without her. She *knows* us, perhaps even better than we do ourselves. The poison, the neurotoxin comes from her. No other would know how to affect me and Liz this way. She, like Jahavalo did, has always avoided direct confrontation with us.

– Why is she more afraid of you than the rest of us? Andrea wondered. – Nick, Martin, Kyle, Stacy, Lydia… they're all more powerful than you.

She faltered, her doubt concerning her own statement reaching her eyes before she had completed the sentence.

– You saw what Ted did to Nick, right? Linda said. – He shook him like a ragdoll. Nick was unable to even defend himself. Ted and Liz have long since surpassed all others.

Ted looked at her. Carla looked at her. Andrea nodded to herself.

Ted looked at them all, saw them through Liz' misty eyes, and once again he saw their faces pale and this time even change to skulls, to pale, withered bones. Not Liz and himself, but everybody else. Linda looked at him, and he saw acceptance, approval in her eyes.

He heard Kurt Meinz voice from long ago:

– You know, Meinz had said quietly, with a strange glare in his eyes, somehow echoing that in Ted's own. – I don't think anything is able to stop you, not even death. Delay you, perhaps, but nothing can really actually stop you, stop your flight.

– Shouldn't we get reinforcements soon? Lee asked. – Gabi could «land» them outside the area covered by Ethel's powers. Many of the People could come, and we could fight it out here. The time has come, hasn't it?

– There won't be any reinforcements, Linda told them.

Shocked and bewildered they stared at each other.

– The time has come. Ted nodded. – But no, all of us gathering here, in one place may be exactly what Ethel wants. We can't take that chance.

He nodded towards the southeast, towards the population centers.

– The dice is cast, he stated. – They want us gone, no matter the price.

He looked up a bit, sniffing the wind.

– They're waiting for us there. And if many «civilians» should die, and they will, they will only blame us. They have done so before, with major success.

He rose, standing straight.

– It's about Truth, he said. – It has always been about Truth. We have seen it twisted, and turned around so many times and now, finally, it turns back on itself.

– NO! Linda shouted.

She threw herself at Liz and held on, held her hands, pushed her face at hers.

– You won't sacrifice yourself, she cried. – You're too important.

They looked stunned at her. Ted attempted to pull them apart with his power, but she held on. The bluish glow surged between them. Both women screamed. They dropped to the ground and split apart. Both looked up with wide eyes.

– I'm okay, Linda said stunned. – I didn't think I would be…

376

She rose on somewhat steady feet.

– I am, too, Liz said. – I feel strong and powerful. The poison is still there, but lessened in scope and strength. My system is handling it effectively, now.

She rose on steady, strong feet. Liz glowed. She touched Ted and the glow spread to him. Something awoke within him, and when it did, it didn't puzzle him at all.

They heard silent thunder, and the sound of rain, and thousand other overwhelming sensations hardly rocking them at all.

– Everything has changed, she said with dark joy. – One small act, many small and big acts did it. Can't you *feel* it?

Everyone could. One more deep joy and deep chill passed down their spine.

– You're too important, Liz told Linda. – Your aid will be required one final time.

Linda nodded and her features transformed into an ecstatic smile.

The two and twenty-one gathered in a circle, exchanging sensations, impressions, thoughts.

– I can feel the fire, Ted said with his ghostly voice. – I can touch it and feel its power.

He looked up at the stars.

It's just another language.

The UN army was closing in on them again. It felt almost like an interlude. The two turned and held hands. The soldiers began firing at each other. Loud screams of desperation rose from already sore throats. Red soil turned soaking wet with blood.

Some of the soldiers managed to throw away their guns and drop to their knees. Some of them were hit by the indiscriminating fire. The rest remained on their knees or crouched on the ground, begging for mercy.

It turned quiet. They looked up with tear-wet faces.

GO AND FIGHT TOGETHER. KILL AND DON'T STOP KILLING ANYONE IN UNIFORM, NOT UNTIL THEY'RE ALL DEAD.

The voice thundered in their mind. They shook like leaves, exactly like leaves.

The remaining soldiers picked up their guns and turned, turned outward, returned to where they had come. They rushed forward at the advancing soldiers, spreading in a circle, killing everyone on their path.

– They will buy us time, Linda said. – We better use it well.

Everyone looked at her, and at the two.

– The Phoenix is limited, as long as it clings to its human origin, she stated. – It cannot sustain the necessary power… unless it kills, unless it kills… us, kills all the twenty-one and devour our lifeforce. Then, it might reign forever, or at least for a thousand years.

Calling what surged through them either heat or cold was hopelessly inadequate. Morten was the first to take that step forward.

– We're made for this, he cried. – This is the sole reason we exist.

Carla stepped forward. They all did.

– I'm Wolf, Carla said. – I'm Earth. I am at your disposal… Phoenix.

She looked at them both, the way she had always seen them, as one person.

Ted and Liz faced them all, looking them in the eye.

Ted looked exclusively at Jane. She was in no doubt about that.

– You were Elaine in the previous reality, he told her. – You, as Jane died in New York City, but you were reborn and still made your way to us.

– But the fact that you did survive brought one more piece of the necessary change, contributed to *this*, Liz said. – Time is a glorious lattice of coincidence and fate.

Jane looked at them with tears in her eyes. Everyone had that catching in the throat.

– I want you all to understand, he impressed upon all of them. – And I want you to agree, with all your heart.

– You are the Phoenix, Kimberly Russel recited. – You are the Power that will cleanse the Earth, and free humanity from all shackles. May you do your job well! All my life I've seen a fire in the dark, and you're it. I can see your heat in the blackest night. We are your twenty and one embers, your black, bright, black ravens, and we are ready.

Everyone nodded, some of them empathically, all of them determined. One by one they all stepped forward and recited the litany. The Litany of Fire. The choir rose from their throat like one potent voice. They made a tighter circle around the two, and then they stopped.

– No more running, Ted said. – One fundamental fact remains. When all discussions are done, there is just this, one, sufficient truth: Civilization destroys everything making life worth living. That's all we need to know.

– Yes, Linda said, both her hands rolled into fists. – And I will rather die than exist one more second in this machine, this... horrible death. Take your Power, Phoenix. Use it to the fullest.

Carla placed herself a bit between the circle and the two at the center, raising her hands, humming her song.

– This will take time, she said. – Do we have enough of it?

They saw the planes, saw them approach, heard the whisper as thousands of feet rushed across the desert towards them.

– We will make time, Ted growled. – Take whatever we need.

One casual thought and the planes crashed into each other and fell to the earth in an inferno of flames and dark smoke.

– It's happening, Martin Keller - Morningstar and Lillian Muller choired.

Val and Jason sat on the bed in the bedroom of the small Washington DC apartment.

– Phoenix needs her powers, Val told him softly.

– Now, you know why we didn't visit you, Liz told Michelle.

And Michelle's eyes grew wide and sore.

– This is a bubble of the Earth, Wolf howled the litany of fire.

Mist created of the air itself, rising from the sand, surrounded them.

– This is the fire of the fire of the Earth.

The circle caught fire first, then all the lines making the pentacle. Ghostly flames, not really burning those who sat near them.

The White Rose approached the two figures at the center. Ted looked away. Liz stared at her, regret in her fireeyes.

– Don't be sad, she said, Linda said to him, to them. – This is what I've always wanted. This way I'll be a part of you forever.

Wolf began chanting in some ancient language, if language it was at all. Liz and Ted began picking up on it, and began chanting, too, and then the Change began in earnest. The entire area seemed to… to transform, into something alien and strange, not strange at all.

They saw a village, a hut at its center. They saw a castle at the center of a lake, a fire lake. Images and sounds and smell and sensations beyond senses flickered on and off, faded in and out of their surroundings.

They all recognized this place, this place not a place.

Before what remained was only the vast and terrible desert, and the Hollow at its center.

– Give in to your rage. Let it sweep everything clean.

Linda handed Liz her knife, her black blade. Liz saw the blood on it, as a river, as a waterfall challenging Niagara.

– I know he won't do it, Linda said. – But you will.

Liz accepted the blade. Linda stood there, waiting.

– I choose this, Elizabeth Warren cried. – I choose to be Fire, to be Power, power without guilt.

She looked at Ted.

– I choose this, Edward Warren shouted. – I choose to be Fire, to be Power, power without guilt.

They all repeated, mumbled, cried their words. She spotted reluctant acceptance in Ted's eyes. It was enough.

She turned to him, one more time, one brief time.

– The soft spot…

– Yes? He said hoarsely.

– It's still there.

And she witnessed his eyes widen like open wounds.

Liz cut the air in a bow, a half moon, as the blade touched Linda Cousin's flesh for a brief moment, as it slit her throat. Blood flowed in the air, mixing with the smoke and the Shadow. Linda fell to the ground, dying with each breath. Liz let go of the blade. It fell into the sand.

Ted and Liz grabbed each other's hands.

The blood kept floating in the air, lingering impossibly, defying, seemingly defying gravity, while moments transformed into seconds and eons, until the silent wind started blowing, a traction sucking it into the two bodies at the center of the circle. Linda Cousin stopped breathing. Linda Cousin died, the ecstatic, joyous grin never leaving her face. There was a crack of thunder, and lightning in the blue sky. Reality seemed to shift, to change even further that very moment, when what wasn't matter rose from the lifeless body, and one moment was clearly visible to all, a Shadow, so much more than what she had been. Her body turned to fire, to ashes, and that fire was pulled into the two bodies at the center of the circle. Liz screamed. Ted screamed. And the scream made the ground shake, made the *Earth* shake, made it pause on its journey through the Universe.

Every creature on Earth sensed it, sensed it deep in their Shadow.

Stacy Larkin froze, staring blindly out on Pennsylvania Avenue. She blinked, and for every blink the world changed around her, as she staggered and had to support herself on the wall. Gabi blinked as well. Suddenly her entire body was covered in sweat, and she ran to Stacy.

Stacy saw it, she saw It, saw the creature bask in the fire of dying human beings, sensed its pain as it felt and was nourished by every single death on the planet.

– I feel it, she gasped, Lillith gasped, as Gabi attempted to comfort her. – It is happening, it's finally happening.

– Yes, God above and below, Betty cried with the massive joy filling her entire being.

Stacy straightened and turned to Linsey.

– It's time to go, she told him.

– Leave… He looked at the White House across the street, as if in pain.

– Yes, leave these wretched ruins, where so much pain has been inflicted upon the world.

She grabbed him, her claws digging into his arm.

– Can you sense it, she asked him, looking around in wonder, – the Book of Shadows burning? I know you can.

– Yes, Martin told Philip. – Your fear is well founded. These are the final days.

Lillith saw It become one with the raging Storm, The Earth's primal force, Life's infinite power so long neglected, suffering in chains. It hovered in the air, an enormous entity levitating under Its own power, in front of the wind, wind followed by destruction incarnate. She hardly recognized what It had become. A giant shadow, whose eyes burned in the flames of the Abyss, the incarnation of force. She saw, exalted and terrified civilization die under Its ruthless, irresistible Onslaught, a power with no equal released in her cauldron of a womb.

Jason crashed through the door, as he fell to the floor, and remained there, unable to rise. His eyes burned. His entire body burned in St. Elmo's Fire. They stared at each other, fully aware of what was happening, desperately attempting to catch their breath.

They looked up at the southern sky above Australia, at the Phoenix constellation among the stars, near Tucana and Sculptor. It was glowing and hissing, and they saw it display its wings. Everybody saw it, no matter where on Earth they happened to find themselves, indoors, outdoors, northern or southern hemisphere.

The flames, fire, not fire began rising. Not from the ground, but from the two figures at the center of the circle, the pentacle. They were ghostlike, visible, but no more so than the thick wind blowing around them all. Everybody in the outer ring sat tight together, holding hands, humming sounds arising from their throats. Shadows… grew from the flames, becoming the flames, as the flames became the shadows.

They saw the final enemy reveal itself, saw civilization, saw the Machine, almost sentient, very close to becoming that, saw its lattices and pattern at the cusp of birth.

One by one the people holding hands and humming began gasping, gasping for life as life left them. A sword of fire stuck out from Sally's chest, and then from the rest as well. Their bodies sagged and stopped breathing, and crumbled there on the sandy ground.

The Phoenix screamed in savage relief, as the enemy of civilization, of anti-life was born, as it was released from its gestation, its womb.

Everybody within the nest died, except for the two glowing figures at its center. Shadows rose and the shells they had inhabited burst into flames. One more scream rose from the two shaking figures at the center, and this time the Earth shook like a leaf. During the following second all the soldiers, every single individual lifeform outside the circle, from the smallest microbes to the biggest animals, for miles and miles away also drew their last breath. They all turned to desert dust in an instant.

In that instant a god, or to put it in more modern terms, a superbeing was born.

The Phoenix glowed in the sky and on the Earth.

Joined, they set themselves free, to live as power itself.

And all the electrical, artificial lights were turned off… forever.

All modern tools and weaponry practically melted slowly to slag in people's hands.

The Machine died with a loud wail of protest and whimper, its lattices, its web turning to dust in an instant.

Somewhere in a dark, dank place Ethel Warren lifted her head, and instantly knew. She rose from her chair, raising her fists above her head.

– no, No, NO!

In her cave she screamed at the heavens, at the depths, at infinite, unending existence, but got nothing but her own scream reflected back at her.

She fell to the floor, moaning in unspeakable anguish.

CHAPTER TWENTY-TWO
PHOENIX GREEN EARTH
DECEMBER 22nd 2008
The first night in the first year in the age of The Phoenix

The sky above turned white in the dark burning eyes.

The Rising… began. It began with the smallest of things, with the very building blocks of life itself, with strains of virus and bacteria and amoeba and insects and everything. Slowly the bird, the human bird of shadow and fire rose from the desert bed, leaving only ashes. One single frame, a combination of the two preceding it. From the desert night The Phoenix came. To the desert it would one day return.

The scream spread across the Earth, the scream of release, of rage, pain and joy.

It is a human being with wings, alternately male and female, human head, a bird's head. The feet are there, not there, as the entire figure seems to slip in and out of reality, a shadowy creature consisting of dark, fluid smoke, pale shadows, dark flames. The smoke, the flames and nothing but, and everything but.

It ascended, and as it did so, the landscape below seemed to slip away, the desert below seemed to shift, to become a city, to become a mountain, a forest, a landscape of ice, of eternal ice. Antarctica stretched on infinite below them, below It.

And there were a thousand deaths every time The Phoenix drew breath, every time It breathed fire. It sensed that this was different from the other times where they had burned out in seconds. There was no loadout, no discharge of energy… no significant draining of… fuel, not even the threat of such. It had become a self-sustaining process similar to that of a star.

Was she sad, was he sad, did It feel joy, did it matter anymore, they/he/she/It mused.

The Southern Cross seemed to explode in the sky, rocking even the Phoenix. Another almost identical being appeared from nowhere above the Australian desert, one still coated in blue, even as blue faded. The two faced each other… and merged. Twelve-thousand years of memories, of future history were downloaded into the recently risen creature during a single moment of powerful realization. The four, the two and two remained One. The purpose burning within remained. Everything became even clearer. The scream grew even louder. The wall of time dissolved, crumbling to dust, as if it had never existed at all. All limitations and the sense of any disappeared.

The Earth welcomed the Phoenix, and It embraced the planet, embraced Its womb, as It ascended Its birthplace, as they became One. It reached out with its Power, its limitless Might, to every corner of the globe… and beyond. It looked at the Sun, at the planet circling it. It reached out, beyond time and space.

Achim Doll, and his crew and ships on way back to the Tachiti system were blown to bits. Even crucial transmissions were stopped from reaching the intended destination. In fact, every scrap of information they had collected during their stay of thousands of years was destroyed. Phoenix captured the radio waves in their flight. A shrug and it was done. Time and space bent to Its will.

Antarctica melted. The process was already well under way, had been for some time, but so slow, way too slow… and the Phoenix gave it a… push. Weather patterns, the very air blanketing the Earth's surface, they sensed it, sensed its power. They sensed the energy concealed in the mighty waves, in the depths of the very sea, the ocean comprising two thirds, no, (soon to be) three fourths of the round ball they held in their hand. The sun, they felt its power, felt it in their hand.

Phoenix *touched* them. They all felt it. Jason Gallagher feared he would drown in it, in all the death, a million knives cutting through his heart. Samhain, the Death god, the transition god, laughed short and sharp.

Smoke rose from the now hidden land of Antarctica. On Greenland and on the Siberian Taiga heat and vapor rose from the land, the ever-warmer land. In India, outside Calcutta, *Kolkata* a butterfly flapped its wings, and the Phoenix flapped Its wings with it.

Two children, a brother and a sister played on a beach, before slowly stopping, running to their parents.

– Mommy, MOMMY, look at the waves, look at them dance.

The mother looked at the waves, watched them, watched them dance. There was nothing, nothing different about them. She looked at her arm. Gooseflesh broke out all over her arm, all over her body.

– I can swear… swear… The father attempted to speak. – Swear they are taller.

One wild wave swept up on the shore, rushing towards them, covering almost the entire stretch of dry sand, to their feet. Several other people got their feet wet, looking frozen and astounded at the suddenly raging sea.

The family grabbed their belongings, and hurried like rabbits off the beach. They were the first, the point, of everybody leaving the suddenly so very hostile beach.

In the Iraqi desert a platoon of United States soldiers stopped in their task, their task of beating up on a family, a father, mother and children. They looked up, suddenly very shitty and alarmed. One of the children, beaten and bloody started laughing.

- What is happening, Sarge? A soldier cried. – What the FUCK is *happening?*

The Sergeant stared at the sand, at the sand by his feet, stared hard.

A construction worker looked at a piece of concrete, looked at the green field behind it, the vast forest. Didn't it look… closer. The worker shook his head and kept working.

– The Mets are winning again, his colleague two steps away said, shaking his head in amazement.

– Yeah, it sure looks that way, the construction worker nodded.

There was a break, a short, five minutes break. The workers sat down, eating their lunch, their dry and wet sandwiches, eating fast to complete their meal in time.

Something kept nagging the man. It wasn't anything he could put his finger on, but he was distracted, constantly distracted. He looked at his watch. It would soon be time to go back to work. He sniffed, suddenly, shockingly, in sudden anger.

He rose and walked to the edge of the concrete, carefully studying the naked soil between the concrete and the field. The field was yellow, dry grass, but… but just by its edge… there was a line of green, fresh, juicy green. Unmistakable, eerie.

– Hey, Bob, his buddy cried to him, – time to get back to work.

He stood there, frozen on the spot, watching.

The other men and women joined him, staring ahead.

It wasn't evident, wasn't fast, but while studying the place for minutes, they saw the grass grow. They could actually watch it spreading across the soil.

- Okay, guys, the foreman cried. – Time to get back to work.

And they did, stumbling and subbing, filled with an unusual sense of foreboding.

Fire rose from the City. Flames stretched higher than the tallest building.

The Sergeant in the Iraqi desert lifted his left foot. There was smudge on it, nothing resembling the desert bed.

- That is soil, Sarge! The soldier shook his head. – That is goddamn soil.

And as they stared ahead and looked around them, with an ever-growing sense of panic, as they discovered the first shades of green on the ground, the family left, and they did nothing to stop them. Unable or unwilling to lift a finger they stared at the small group of people leave them in the desert sand.

Phoenix gasped, and images, events flooded Its mind, Its memory. It watched Time, watched Time unfold, and only a tiny bit confusion remained. Thousand years ahead, thousand years hence, it was all just a blink of an eye. Its mind expanded, as Its influence kept growing, as Its power slowly, during eternal seconds permeated the Earth, bathed its Life in Its Shadow.

In Washington DC Linsey Kendall took one step forward, crying out to the heavens.

– NO, this is wrong. You don't need to do this. It isn't necessary. We have won.

Mist and Shadow appeared before him, before them all, touching them in ways they had never before experienced.

See then, experience firsthand what would have happened, what we have won.

And Phoenix's voice was like thunder in their toes, in their hair, in the most distant part of their being.

And he did, they all did. Images, events, memories flooded his mind, and he experienced what had been, what would never be, and what remained was the overwhelming sense of untold suffering and a blackened, ashen Earth. And he staggered backwards, a shadow of a man, he and his beliefs shaken to its foundations, shattered beyond repair.

The voice, the presence appeared to every human being on Earth, as they were made to experience what had been, what would never be.

This is Elizabeth Warren, Ted Warren speaking to you, Human Beings, finally Human once more. We want to share everything with you. I am Phoenix. I am fire and life made flesh. We all are. Yes, you are, too. I am going to show you, *show* you what has happened, what is happening, and what would have happened if it hadn't been *stopped*. I am going to make you understand, and if you don't, after all is said and done, you can go to hell. And you will. You've asked yourself all your life if there is a God, and now there *is*.

Civilization began with a few scattered cities and agricultural communities thousands and thousands of years ago. A scar, physical, on both the Earth itself and Life on it. There were those encouraging this, actively seeking to exploit for their own gain this blight on the world, on the Universe itself.

And the pervasive movie, so much more than any movie they had ever seen, showed them, showed them everything they would never forget. They saw Jahavalo and his like, they saw the users, they saw their brutality and their cunning, experienced with dread how their ways became everybody's ways, how the cancer spread to all corners of the world.

Yes, civilization began, consolidated and flourished, and multiplied. Until it became a self-perpetuating process, until it gained a kind of life, even a sort of sentience, until its insane reign started dominating human life, human perception, corrupting it on every level.

As perception changed, so did crucial priorities.

Religion entered and came to dominate human society, to reduce us in stature, in power. Insanity became kings and kings became gods. Before a hierarchy was the exception, not the norm. Now it turned mandatory.

They saw Lillith, tricked and broken and remade kneel before Jahavalo, saw her become his vassal, his creature. They observed the events on the Salisbury plains thousands of years later, saw thousands of slaves pull the big stones, in the living god's honor, saw the pyramids rise in Egypt and in the Americas, giving glory to the masters, to the very concept of inequality. They saw Jahavalo, saw him make one small tribe into his prophets, his chosen people, his sacrificial lambs, as the monstrosity that would become Israel began. They saw creatures of night and shadow rise from the pyramids, making all humans fear the night and the shadow. They experienced Egypt's humble beginnings, the onset of Rome and China, of the first major kingdoms, the first dominating entire continents.

The word «civilization» means «city-dweller». That's all there is to it. It has come to mean everything good, everything worth striving for in this world, and it is a deceit, a horrible nightmare of our own making, one we have been unable to wake up from, one that would have dominated our lives to the very *end*.

People all over the world saw. They saw the coming of the Others, people born with fire in their eyes and others besides, heard them be called many names, many four-letter words. They felt the coming of the witch, the mutant, and saw it change nothing. They experienced everything they had never dared acknowledge, both about life in general and their own fear and neurosis, knew how the witches had lived their lives in secret on present day Earth, how the world was totally different from what people had been fooled to believe and fooled themselves into believing.

Yes, experience ghosts, revenants, aliens, psychics and witches, everything you never dared believing existed. Feel what would have happened with humanity if your twisted beliefs had been allowed to flourish further.

The UFO crashing outside Roswell in 1947 was hidden by the military. All subsequent sightings the next forty years, even though various governments and private enterprises sat on piles and piles of evidence, were denied and ridiculed. Until the Tachiti sat their plans in motion in 1987, changing everything, cutting loose their human contacts, the people enjoying the fruits of their cooperation.

The Kennedy assassination took place, executed by units within CIA, FBI and various other governmental and private enterprises. Shots were fired from the grassy knoll. The very bullets became ghosts, as humans themselves had become ghosts.

They lived with the Janus Clan, participated in the ongoing debate in their midst, about goals and means. In a glimpse there was Janus, Lillith, becoming, in truth, an angel of vengeance, taking her life, all life back, wresting it from Jahavalo's grip, opening up everything, giving back to humanity the gift of destiny. They saw the fateful day, one month from now, when Linsey Kendal had been sworn in as president of the United States. Lived the years as they passed by, as they rushed by, saw how even the Janus Clan, with all their power, all their power of will, had failed to stop the forces of civilization, how they hardly had managed even a preliminary stalemate.

The migration into Space began. It was more like an escape than anything else, to escape from increasingly horrible conditions on the home planet, escaping from one nightmare into another. The corporations dominated space exploration. People died and suffered by the millions during the excavation of the asteroid belt. They lived through the final persecution of the new humanity, its ascension to the throne, how it had changed nothing.

And then, thousands of years into the future, they saw how humanity became the creatures, the vassals, the mindless drones of the Tachiti, the alien race who had developed the civilized way of existence to a perfection far superior to anything humanity had cocktailed.

There were lines and lines of wax dolls, and nothing seemed real, nothing seemed true… except the mental chains and collar gnawing at their ankles and wrists and around their neck, the human being stumbling around with a stupefied grin painted on the unmoving face.

Linsey Kendall stumbled back, as he gasped in horror, as he desperately attempted to escape the lucid memories now dominating his perception.

Ted stood before him. Liz stood before him. They were smiling. One brief smile, and they were gone, vanished into the ghost and shadow land they come from.

– Unites States of America will not lead human migration into Space. Capitalism won't do so. Greed won't do so. Religion won't do so. Science won't do it. Civilization certainly won't.

A man fell from a high tower, and hit the ground far below. His working buddies on the ground rushed to his side. He was dead, but incredibly enough, he still lived. His face was an amazing split between boundless joy and fear.

– I can see it, he gasped. – I can sense its power.

Something rose from his body, something not matter, something not even energy, at least not a type human machines could detect. For the first time in their lives they

386

saw the Shadow, one human's eternal Self, in all its glory.

– LOOK! One of them cried out.

And as one they turned their attention to the green field, to the forest, and this time there was no mistake, definitely no trick of their imagination: The grass spread, but more than that. Trees were growing as they watched, small trees spreading from the sinister forest. The trees snarled at them and they were sore afraid.

– Yes, be sore afraid. There is reason to be scared, to fear the future, the future you have created. Rejoice, for payback is at hand.

Phoenix stood at the top of Mount Everest, the world's tallest mountain, shouting at the world, burning every little hair, every piece of skin.

One man in the crowded Oxford Street in London stepped forward, shouting at the heavens.

– But who decides what's right, what's wrong?

And the Phoenix was there before him, as It was everywhere.

– I do, I decide nothing is right, nothing is wrong. That is my creed. That is my war.

It turned Its head, and It was gone.

Floyd McKenzie stood frozen on the spot, in the oval office, in the White House. There was a whisper, and he turned. Liz grinned at him.

- Yes, this is your lesson as well as all others', she said. – In the millennia to come, you're gonna do something you never thought you would do; you're gonna learn, learn to be human, to be a man, not a robot.

Somewhere in the Shadowland Ethel Warren was running, and she would run for ages.

And the Phoenix was with her, every step of the way.

- Yeah, that's right, baby. Run, run, but know that you can never hide. You rank up there with Jahavalo when it comes to corrupting humanity. At the very least you're on the top ten list, and such lists are very popular these days... or at least they used to be.

Tears of horror flowed from Ethel's, from April Powell's eyes, and she couldn't see where she was heading, couldn't see the road ahead of her, and the scream of horror rising from her depths would last an eternity.

Somewhere on Earth a three-year-old boy blinked. He remembered. He remembered everything, as Phoenix was there to remind him.

It was everywhere, not only close to every human and every individual lifeform, but every piece of dust, as it was born into the smallest of things, the smallest of particles, the illusion of scale.

– There will be lessons, before the end, and everybody will listen.

Days later. The Janus Clan had returned to their home, their brief-home of Northfield. They had packed their few, necessary belongings, ready to move west, with the rest of the huddled masses.

The ravens squeaked, as they all rose in the air, forming a giant raven, blocking the sun. Stacy rose with the ravens. She was up there with them as they descended on the Janus Clan, the Janus tribe.

- It's a raven, Delphi cried in a ghostly voice. - Its wings are black and its feathers are blood.

Phoenix shimmered in the air, hovering above them all, but most of all above Nick and Stacy.

— Are you the Nick of now, or are you the Nick Warren returning countless times from the future lands?

Nick Smiled.

— I can't tell anymore. Even you can't tell.

Nick screamed, as Its energies engulfed it. He collapsed on the ground, close to completely drained.

— You will still live, even as you die, but you will not, never again return to your cave in the valley of the kings.

It addressed the others, and they knew it, even as It didn't turn.

— Take care of him. He will not be able to do that himself for a while.

— It will be done, Morningstar said.

And the Phoenix turned, turning Its entire attention to the tall, dark-haired ghost.

— Well done, Mother.

— Thank you, my son, my daughter, Lillith said, a tear forming in her left eye.

— Mike didn't do it, Nick didn't do it, Ethel didn't do it. You did, you Thalama, Goddess of Destiny. They were all your pawns, mother.

The wind shifted slightly. It was hardly noticeable to them, but It felt it in profound ways.

— I can feel them, you know, everyone dying. I'm strengthened by each and every death, and I can feel it all.

— I'm sorry, Lillith whispered.

— I can feel it, feel every toe, on every insect moving across the heavens and the Earth, feel the solar winds brush against my hair.

This was everything, everything Ted and Liz Warren was... *what endured.*

- It's strange. You would think this would cause us to grow into an aloof, detached being, but we feel now, more, stronger than ever. We are more human, now, than we ever were.

And It turned, and It was gone, even from their view.

We will meet again. We will all meet again, sometime in the future, where the Thunder Road turns.

Ravenscourt and the mound faded with It, like a dream, and only the village remained.

The Raven and the tribe, as they made their way inland, carrying their rucksacks, their precious few possessions, took one, final look back at the town that had been their brief-home, a collection of empty buildings now fading, returning in full to being the forest it had always been.

They still saw Ravenscourt as it moved through the ether, heading for an unknown destination.

— It's moving, Stacy Larkin stated. — To where, no one can say.

388

It started raining, and it kept on raining, and the many human tribes stumbled and fell into the wilderness, the wilderness, now, once again, such an essential part of their existence.

Thunder cracked the skies. Lightning graced the land, hammering against it like the torrential rain it was.

They hunted again, hunted to survive and experienced its hardship and joy.

It still felt awkward, unreal, difficult to properly utilize.

Martin Keller fell on his knees one day, exhausted, unable to move even his hands, still moving them, still stepping forward, and he started digging in the dirt, in the mud drowning his eyes and hair and skin. He found ants in the ground like he had done millennia ago. He ate. They all ate, starving, ravenous, and they were content, as sustenance filled their system.

And they learned. Slowly they relearned to truly hunt, to gather, to survive. And they taught others, all the others making their way west, fleeing from the rising sea.

Time and space shifted back and forth in the Phoenix's vast consciousness. It handled it with casual ease.

It began slowly, the day after Its first appearance, approaching a fearful humanity like a specter. Planes and satellites attempting to photograph the land to the south, Antarctica, saw nothing but clouds.

– It looks a like a volcanic eruption down there, a pilot shouted into the microphone. – There's certainly enough steam for that.

Scientists studied the heavens, more out of habit than anything else. What they saw scared them more than anything. And beneath all that, they noticed something half-forgotten, a curiosity they once in their youth perhaps had enjoyed.

– *Look* at this. Something is happening on the Moon.

They took turns, looking through the telescope. They watched astounded how the surface of the Earth's satellite darkened and changed, as it seemed to gain substance and texture and color. They saw clouds there, first formed in tiny dots, then spreading.

– We're getting reports from all over the place. People are looking at Venus, at Mars, and Titan, and Europa, and…

Hurricane winds and waves seemed to batter all coastlines at once. People huddled in their cities, their anthills, as the lower coastlines were flooded. Two groups of humans fired at each other with every iota of weaponry and hatred they possessed.

Phoenix walked through New York City. Every human being heard It, saw what happened. Everywhere. In New York the memorial towers, the so-called «freedom towers», the new «World Trade Center» started disintegrating seemingly by itself. Materials shook loose from it and rose at the heavens, disintegrating and falling like dust. People fled from it, and kept fleeing for long, long minutes until everybody had left.

And then it *ignited*, as if it was nothing but flames. Heat burned everybody. Fire rose from the city.

– You are truly idiots, It snarled. – Are you totally out of your mind, completely unable to see what is happening and take independent action?

It played off a message still being repeated across the city, that from the city council and whatever authorities left:

– STAY IN YOUR HOMES AND STAY CALM. THERE IS NO NEED FOR PANIC, NO NEED FOR YOU TO GO ANYWHERE. YOU ARE SAFE. YOU ARE

Phoenix snapped Its fingers, and the mechanical voice stopped everywhere.

Policemen and units from the army kept attempting to keep the masses contained, as they had done so many times before. Suddenly they stopped and froze. They looked down on themselves, saw their uniforms melt off their body.

– You have been the eager servants of the tyrants. You will be oppressors no more. From now on you won't be able to hide behind a symbol, a uniform, a standard. This is your punishment. Pray you will never make me take you to its next level. Crawl back into your cave and be ashamed of yourselves, because you are the lowest of the low of the human beings.

They stared at it, stared at themselves, stared at the wet dogs they had become, the wet dogs they had always been.

– What I am going to do, you sheep, is to re-educate humanity, to eradicate every piece of civilization and its insane influence from your conscious and subconscious psyche. From now on, no worship, no religion is allowed. And you better not insult me by praying to me or worship me. I know every one of you, all six billion, four million four hundred and sixty-five thousand and three of you. I know your actions, I know your thoughts, the very moment you know. I know you better than you know yourself. I will not give you any laws. You will know when you have displeased me. Trust me, you will know…

Several people, police and others fired at the shimmering creature with the few guns they had left. The bullets passed right through it and hit people behind it. They screamed and fell. They crouched in the street, dying, begging for help. No one helped them. Except from stopping the shooting no one seemed to react that much, perhaps because this was trivial compared to everything else happening.

Phoenix lifted Its hand in an obviously redundant gesture. The bullets were pulled out of the wounded, and they healed from one moment to the next. There were wounds, and then there were no more wounds.

– Yes, I am Human, not some distant, aloof god sitting on its throne, enjoying the show. I will enjoy the show, though, as I am right with you, by your side, within you. Now, all you sheep out there, there is a god. A god of vengeance. And trust me, I will make you all human again, even if it kills you, kills you many times.

It stopped a bit, cocking Its head, listening to something they couldn't hear.

– Civilization is gone when there is no more noise of machines anywhere. That time is *now*.

The weapons used by two warfaring groups… stopped working. Just like that. There were bullets left, but nothing worked.

They felt it, they all felt, felt the fundamental change. The noise, the everlasting noise… faded. Faded like a dream. A nightmare of sweat and fear and ugliness.

All over the planet technology quite simply stopped functioning. Nuclear power plants, factories, phones. The intercontinental rockets turned to stockpiles of dead, useless metal, no more dangerous than a pile of twigs. All the hideouts and shelters and refuges made by the rich and powerful collapsed.

In a cellblock, in a prison outside the city of New York Victor Russel looked up. They all looked up, as the cell doors opened.

– It's happening, he said, astonished at first, then again triumphant. – IT'S HAPPENING!

He laughed insanely as he rushed outside, as he ran to freedom.

Prison guards raised their rifles and attempted to fire, but there was nothing, nothing working. So few guards, so many prisoners. They turned and fled. Russel and others chased them, hunted them down, and killed them, with bare hands, with kitchen tools, with anything at their disposal.

– I KNEW YOU TWO COULD DO IT, he shouted. – I KNEW IT LONG BEFORE I MET YOU.

He kicked the man in front of him to a bloody pulp. Similar scenes took place in prisons all over the world.

– Nothing is worse than imprisoning a living being. *Nothing!*

And there was no mercy in the Phoenix's burning eyes.

Fire rose at the sky, even as screams rose and fell.

Everything turned silent. Engines just stopped everywhere. The failing machines were heard for a while, then there was nothing but natural sounds, as it had been on Earth ten thousand years ago. Millions of military personnel laid buried and cold under their hideouts, within their fortresses. Police stations and national assemblies fell apart, and killed almost everybody inside. Factories fell. Huge office buildings crumbled. Everything fell, but what represented the tyranny the most fell first.

Technology didn't work. Many of its foremost users and eager servants were gone with it.

– It's done. Now you have all more or less equal chance of surviving the coming onslaught. Very few of you will, but that's the point. You will have to use your learned skills. Those you already possess or you will have to learn quite a few new, and you need to do it fast.

– How can you do it? One cried, one understanding more than the others. – How can you be so cruel?

– Because every possible alternative is worse, It said simply, almost humane. – And I didn't bring this on. You did. You did, with your suicidal path. Now, reap the whirlwind.

Stunned silence greeted Its words. The woman paled in her tracks.

– But there's no need for you to do it, she persisted. – With your power, you could... run things, teach... us, without destroying us.

Need and hunger were visible in her mind, some of it good, some of it very bad.

– Even if it was desirable, which it is not, it won't work. You see, even the Phoenix would be, have already been corrupted by civilization. So, I am giving in to my rage, sweeping everything clean.

It smiled, and they didn't understand. How could they?

– GOD IS OUR SAVIOR, a man cried out, saliva flowing from his open mouth. – GOD WILL COME AND SAVE US. GOD IS

He died. He just died, just stopped. And everybody saw what happened.

Everybody saw churches, synagogues, mosques, monasteries and every single place of worship around the world catch fire. People gathered in worship were crushed, burned and died. Everyone witnessed how materials loosened and rose from the top of tall buildings still standing, how it turned to dust and fell like rain.

– This is just show and tell. He was among the worst of you. All the others were also eager worshippers, among the most contemptible humans in existence. I could have eradicated billions like him and them this very moment, but I will give the rest of you quite a few chances, give you chances to improve yourselves, to be Human.

Several others fell to the ground, screaming insanely in pain, as they were given fair warning.

The rage was visible in Its form, Its burning eyes. They shivered under the cold stare.

– The coastline cities will go first, drown in the raging sea. Get out or perish. The inland cities will simply fall apart, crumble under its own weight. I wouldn't stay, if I were you.

And they saw it, saw the deluge washing everything away. Fire, water, wind and earth. The black rain fell.

It was everywhere, speaking to every human being on Earth and beyond, including those who had just died, and waited to be born again into the world. It saw their Shadow, their very powerful spirit, their eternal Self. Everybody saw it, saw themselves fully for the first time.

– Yes, Phoenix said. – This is what we have squandered for ten thousand years. This is who we are. This is who we will ever *be*. Fail me, fail yourselves, and I will follow you into the far lands, hunt you down like the sheep you believed yourself to be, but no more. NEVER MORE!

And they saw their own fangs, saw their own claws, and perhaps they learned something, perhaps they would remember, remember who they truly were.

Cars stopped on the highway. Engines failed and even the wheels didn't turn anymore. Boats drifted aimlessly, even more aimlessly at the open sea. People onboard waited for deliverance, but it didn't come.

– I am not Jahavalo, not god, It said. – I have no preferences. I will not help you, any of you.

A woman broke a glass in a museum, picking up a spear, hesitating a bit, before throwing it at the wall. It hit the wall with a loud thud. She felt elation, felt… approval. Nothing more, nothing less.

– Hunters, she said. – We are hunters. This is who we are.

She found a sword, grabbed its hilt, swinging it back and forth, deliberating cutting herself on its blade.

– These will last centuries, she said. – We may be able to make new ones, we may not, but we can use these.

Planes stopped working in midair. Propellers stopped turning.

Planes fell. Quite a few had already landed. But those who hadn't fell and hit the ground hard. Lone pilots, passengers and mice and men died.

– MAYDAY, a pilot screamed into a dead microphone. – WE'RE GOING DOWN. I REPEAT: WE'RE GOING DOWN.

Planes fell, transformed into fire, as the dead payloads of fire hit the ground, and for a while there was noise again, as Fire rose from the Earth.

Everything was jumbled, happening all at once. The past caught up with everyone. The future was now.

A group of people met in a cave deep below the Earth. They walked in silence… until they reached their destination, and the Adversary waited for them.

They stopped, froze in their fear and hatred, and despair as they watched It, as they feared It.

– You'll never be able to destroy God's people, a woman shouted angrily at It. – Our faith will survive, no matter what you do.

– How? It grinned, a vicious grin, a snarl penetrating the deepest recesses of the mind and soul. A grin devoid of humanity, filled with humanity, bursting like a glass filled to the brim. – You won't be able to speak your poisonous words. You won't be able to write it down, to show any of it to your children. Your tyranny will die with you. Within a generation or two it will be Gone. No more christianity, no more islam, hindu, buddhism, wicca, religion never more.

And the incredulity, the absolute horror in their eyes was more than sufficient punishment.

Everybody saw and heard, and many allowed themselves to hope.

Everything fell apart and recreated itself. Everybody was made to experience what It experienced. And they learned. They weren't given any choice. Not if they wanted to survive. And those who died found Phoenix waiting for them on the far side.

Dams broke all over the world, in China, in Egypt, in every place where mankind had attempted to tame nature. The Hoover Dam above Las Vegas broke like dust and the massive flood washed away the city of light.

Heat faded in buildings in the still cold north. Only natural fires would burn. Artificial electricity fizzled and died. The perks and trappings of modern society were cut off one by one.

Civilization… ended.

It ended in guts, pain and blood, like it had to.

Billions died with it. They were killed by the Storm, the countless, unending storms caused by the global heating, killed by heat or drought or rain or hunger and disease. Or in the subsequent chaos and desolation. The struggle for survival was once again a visible force in human life. Humans, once plentiful as ants on the ground once more returned to its natural state, a population size the Earth could feed, could «sustain».

People migrating from the dead cities saw it, saw the sea rise, the waves roll towards the shore, the vulnerable shore.

Scores of people migrated from the dead cities. Some, stubbornly, numb, dead, chose to remain. They drowned in water, as water rolled in from the rising, raging sea, drowned in dust, as buildings of concrete, plastic, glass and forged metal crumbled and fell.

They died in the cities. They died on the road. Bloated, rotting corpses decorated the highways, and the parking lots. New and old diseases raged through the world. Not only did the Pandemonium, the major disease foretold for so long, ravage mankind, but there were several of them. Groups left the cities, left the sick, the dying. One in their group became sick, and they left him, left her, and they died, died one by one, in horrible pain, as blood, puss and poison erupted from their skin, and left the corpses black and dry.

But eventually, finally the diseases faded, for lack of nourishment. The cities had been the worst breeding ground for disease ever existing. Now the cities vanished like smoke.

Coastlines vanished below the sea. The amount of land dwindled drastically, as the years, the decades passed by. Europe no longer looked like Europe. America changed form. The thin line between north and south was severed by an axe of water. Australia dwindled, until there was nothing but a few rocks left. The new, dry land of Antarctica revealed itself, a vast wilderness and islands virtually untouched by human beings.

Roads faded in dust and growth. The paths spreading the cancer vanished beneath the green Earth. The structures not directly touched by Phoenix's machinations eventually also drowned in growth. People passing them years later saw the change, every time they passed it. Surprisingly fast the Earth reclaimed what civilization had stolen.

Where there had been noise, there was now silence. Noise had surrounded the world. Now, in the new wilderness, the new forests appearing everywhere, from the ruins, the ashes of the world, people could hear themselves think. They were able to hear sounds from miles away, differentiating between them with a keen hearing. And the smell, the smell was overwhelming, now, when they were no longer breathing poison. Mountains, once covered in fog, in thick, poisonous pollution, were visible again. Keen eyes spotted game, as a tiny moving spot, valleys away.

Dust fell. Gray faded, as the green returned, as the cancer, the tumor of civilization disappeared from the face of the Earth.

The air, soil and water were clean and fresh. People drank and fed in the night and knew there was no contamination, no more omnipresent poison.

The young girl chased through the underbrush, through the dense forest, lurking on silent feet. Her breasts jumped unbound up and down as she ran. Muscles spilled under her firm skin, on her powerful thighs. She spotted the fat buck somewhere ahead, could smell its fear, its life. She rushed forward, they all rushed forwards, as they threw their spears. The buck died screaming, writhing on the ground as the young boys and girls, men and women stabbed it to death, and they bathed in its blood, and carried their game away. Kyle and Sylvia Warren looked at each other, fire burning in their eyes.

They had grown much the last few years, as they had stretched into their teenage

394

years.

Lil Lith, Nick and Delphi met them in the forest glen.

– We didn't use our powers, Kyle said amazed. – But we could still do it.

– Of course, you could.

Delphi, the adult Delphi, touched the buck, touched its blood, and used it to paint the children's faces.

The ceremony was blissfully short and to the point.

– What is your name? She asked Kyle.

– Kyle of the Warren extended clan, of the Janus Clan, he replied.

– Kyle, it is, she said. – Let it be known, then, that you're welcome.

She greased his hair and painted his face, squeezed his nipples.

– What is your name? She asked Sylvia.

– Audrey, the girl replied, - of the extended Warren Clan, of the Janus Clan.

The older people exchanged looks. This meant that Kyle accepted the role destiny had chosen for him… and Sylvia didn't. Both were good things.

– Audrey, it is, then, Gabi nodded. – Know, then, that you're welcome.

She greased her hair, painted her face and squeezed her nipples.

And later.

- Know that you're welcome, Tommy… Lola… Wes… Stella…

The names echoed through the forest.

– You have passed the test that is not a test, she told them. – You are ready to move on.

The older people, not so much older most of them, saw the pride in their siblings' faces and stance, and felt a certain pride themselves.

- Come, it's time to feast.

The twenty-one ravens flapped their wings, centering on Lil Lith, but yet embracing them all.

They returned to the camp, to their tribe, where there were tall fires and much, much joy. They were welcomed there. They were all welcomed.

The buck was roasted on a spit, and they all participated in its death, its life.

Life permeated their being.

Audrey danced, stars and power and lust in her eyes. Kyle's very visible cock rose, pointing at her.

They danced, all nude or practically nude, only the occasional ornament covering the occasional body, as fancy struck. The Earth was warm, was hot. There was no need for clothes anymore, no need for shame.

Late at night there was silence. No plane passed far above their heads, disturbed the peace.

– No machines, Delphi said. – Not in the sky, not on the ground, not below the ground. We are free, free at last.

Lillith and Delphi stared at the sky, listening to the faint sound of fucking in the camp some corners away. Some trees away, Raven corrected herself.

– Civilization is no longer There, Philip said. – Its everlasting presence has finally ended. It's amazing. It's all gone. Gone!

– And it feels so good. Delphi raised a fist. – I knew it was necessary, but I never thought it would feel this good.

– What is physically built may stand for a while, Lillith said, – but eventually, inevitably, it will fall. What is built in the Shadow, though it may erode… will endure.

The Burning was a fire, touching and constantly changing them all.

– I can feel He and She, Lydia said. – Feel It in my deepest Self.

– «It» is us, Nick said. – Embrace it. It's a part of you… Forever.

They walked a bit, slowly heading back to the small portable village of tents and straw.

– So, how is Andrew and bunch coming along, she asked Betty.

– Excellent, Raven, Betty replied. – I can't teach them much more. I doubt any of you can either.

Raven looked at them all, smiling a bit.

– We are getting restless, are we not? Lillith asked them.

– I would say we are, Nick said, standing there with just a touch of wet at the corner of an eye, enjoying the sounds of the night. – We walk through the forest, the forest without end.

Revealing just a slight choking in his voice.

They felt it, felt the lovemaking, the fucking in the village like a warm, warm breeze on their skin.

The others echoed his words, his sentiment.

A wolf howled somewhere. Everett cocked his head and howled back.

They all did, and the echo from a thousand howls assaulted them and played in their minds.

It faded, lingering forever in their Shadow.

– It is time to move on, Lillith said. – We will teach. That is our mission. We will travel and we will teach, until time once again is.

– And walk? Delphi teased. – I can take us to the moon and back in an instant.

The moon, the bluish, beautiful globe up there, in the sky, awaiting humanity's presence, humanity's lack of touch. Or they would touch, they would always do that. There would always be footprints, to some extent. But they wouldn't conform anything anymore, wouldn't conform themselves.

– Yes, You can, and occasionally, undoubtedly, you will, but not now. We walk, and we teach and explore and learn.

– And Live, Jason greeted her.

– And Live, she repeated softly.

Their fellow tribe members of the wandering Janus Clan, and the moving villagers, the other wandering hunters, greeted them, took their hands and pulled them in between the fires, pulled them into the dance. The wanderers, the nomads danced. The festivities picked up again, filled with joy, tinged with sadness.

It was inevitable. They were human and they were alive. They would always grieve for those who weren't there.

Philip stood by himself, just a second or two, reaching out, not with his hands, but with his entire being, and he felt it, felt the fire. He stopped dancing for just a few moments, and he hardly noticed himself doing so. And… as he smiled two single tears ran from his eyes.

In what had been the Australian desert, there is a place, a circle where nothing will grow, nothing at all.

There are bones there. Human bodies utterly devoid of flesh, uncannily preserved through years and years of storms and floods and cataclysms. Skeleton hands locked in each other's grip. Empty skulls, all the empty sockets staring at the same spot at the center of the circle, where one lone skeleton is reaching for something, something beyond its reach.

And there are ashes, lots of ashes, black and gray and white, dust spreading for the four winds. And no embers, not even the smallest piece of a glow. No fire. No fire at all. It is barren, totally devoid of life.

But around it life is blooming. What had once been a desert was now transformed into a lush forest. The growth was slow at first, a few green spots here, a few others there. But then, as the sand turned to soil, trees and plants began covering the area surrounding the circle in a wide range. Australia, like the world was transformed, but in a few miles in all direction from the circle, Life… *erupted*, in an orgy of growth and blood.

Everybody visiting, visiting the world's one, lone cemetery, briefly, in awe, sensed it, sensed it in their very bones, as much as they could take, before leaving, leaving, but always returning, for reaffirmation, for joy, to perhaps aid the rekindle of fire within themselves, to know beyond belief, beyond doubt what we all are.

It was a giant Hollow, but one that brought forth the best in humanity, not the worst.

Life itself lived in this place.

«As we struggle, as we throw off the chains of tyranny, as we're rejecting The Pyramid and its fundamental injustice, we're looking back… at what… and who we once were. Deep in the ashes of our own fire we give birth to ourselves… Forever»…

Stacy Larkin - ShadowWalk

Legend

Its Reign lasted a thousand years.

They have many names, the Imashaghen, the Wanderers in the Wilderness, the People of Legend, the Janus Clan, the Shadowwalkers, the Forest People, every single one as true as the rest. They lived in shadows for so long before the Reign and still do so in a fashion.

The Phoenix ruled the Earth and its satellites for a thousand years, removing virtually all traces of religion and tyranny and the hierarchy from human life.

But that was just the beginning, the initial spark making all the rest possible. Humanity had become eternal again, had become life again, what *endures*.

For ten thousand years, a brief flash of eternity, a brutal, inhuman Kingdom of Death had dominated human society and almost destroyed all life on the planet. Now, it was gone, and life spread and multiplied anew, returning the gift of nature and freedom, and roaming to the children of the Earth.

In a valley permanently coated in mist, there was a hill, a mound. There was a forest echoing with howls and wails and whispers. At the center of that forest, there was a lake, and at the center of that lake, there was a structure, a house, a castle. Reality shifted and burned within it. The People sought there from time to time, to get confirmation, to remember themselves better and to find what could never be found. The door was always open. The wind chimes chimed every time anyone crossed the threshold. The temple at Fire Lake was always accessible to anyone seeking it.

A redhead female with pale skin, a dark-haired female with dark skin and children that was obviously their offspring greeted the visitors, welcoming them, making them feel at home.

Ravenscourt withstood the test of time. Except for the general sense of age and antiquity, there was nothing even suggesting that the structure would ever crumble and decay.

It would always be there.

Author's comment.

This is it, fellow witches and rebels, the culmination of a work that has been brewing for decades. It began in the fertile mind of a twelve-year-old boy (and even earlier), and culminates here on this night, almost fifty years later, with a man, with a mind more fertile than ever.

I started the actual writing of this book in 2001, and from that moment on, I also started following US politics and society even closer. I spent a lot of time there. It also helped that one of my daughters moved there.

I will hereby apologize to Berry Johnston for substituting him on the list of the finalists in the 1990 World Series of Poker main tournament, though I don't imagine him being too vexed about it. The first woman to truly reach the final table (and taking fifth place) was Barbara Enright five years later.

Much of chapter 7, part 8 is a retelling of chapter 4 and onward of Birds Flying in the Dark… with a twist.

Parts of Shadowwalk are also retold and expanded upon. That book and this one touch each other in quite a few ways and on quite a few occasions. The stories touch and mingle, until becoming one.

The events described in chapter 2, parts 4 to 6 are also described in Dreams Belong to the Night, though altered here and there, both in terms of the events themselves and the players involved in this different, parallel reality.

Some events and destinies in Palestine are altered, mainly because I wanted Yasser Arafat to live, and in order to describe at least the first, major Gaza massacre in 2008 within the context of the story I made it happen more than two years earlier, supplanting «Operation Summer Rain» with «Cast Lead», so to speak. It changes nothing significant. The israeli cruelties described here are merely a small, well-documented selection of what zionists keep doing to the Palestinian people all the time, and not the worst either. Among the atrocities I didn't include are several Palestinian infants being burned alive.

Several other recent historical events are also deliberately changed by the actions of the Janus Clan bringing positive and dramatic changes to the world.

Events, generally speaking happen before they did in «real life», in our worse-off parallel reality.

The world described is better, far better than ours. Far more people join the fight against oppression, against the tyranny ruling humanity and the Earth.

Most science fiction stories set in the future are just present-day stories with a future setting Barring the spaceships and futuristic buildings and stuff, it could just as well happen in the present. I wanted to get away from that, wanted to give people the experience of a story truly set in the future, with truly different circumstances and human behavior.

I would have wanted to publish this novel, the last in the Janus Clan series after the seventh, eighth and ninth, but I don't mind too much. I wanted to make sure I did complete and publish this. The final book in Robert Jordan's Wheel of Time series was written by another author after his death, and the result was just awful.

I have, at least the last ten years a general habit of publishing novels in the order they're written, and I see no reason to depart from that.

I published the first edition of ShadowWalk eighteen years ago, and that story also takes place after that of the first nine. ShadowWalk and Phoenix Green Earth are companion books, really, and should be read together, even though both also works fine as stand-alone stories. Combined, they are one story of 720 000 words. The entire Janus Clan series put together is about 2.2 million words.

This story, in spite of its massive length, like Thunder Road - Ice and Fire had material enough to make it twice as long, make it a million words, but it felt very right to «limit» it to the current length. The story, quite simply, was told.

One Sherwood Forest
2001 – 2021-06-15
The Sherwood Forest isn't a place, but a state of mind.
Printed version ready 2021-09-25

People within and without the circle of the Phoenix in the years before the ascension (People still alive on or close to December 21st 2008):

Ted Warren
Elizabeth Warren

Shuen Parker
Maria Jimenez
Glory Burns
Lee Warren
Carla Wolf
Nick Warren
Linda Cousin
Sally Regehr
Martin Keller
Lillian Donner
Jennifer Woodstone
Betty Morgan
Gabrielle Asteroth
Stacy Larkin
Everett Moran
Jason Gallagher
Loeh
Stewart Warren
Ruth Warren
Ethel Warren
Lydia Warren
Martin Warren
Beth (Bella) Alver
Pearl Warren
Seymour Warren
Michelle Warren
Valerie Musante
Theresa Warren
Kyle Warren (child)
Jill Larkin (child)
Samantha Larkin (child)
Sylvia Warren (child)
Tracy Warren (child)
Tilla Warren (child)
Zoe Warren (child)
Rachel Dalhart (Dalila Warren)
Linsey Kendall
June Warren

Patrick Warren
Morgana Rae
Jeremy Zahn
Karine Lie
Judith Breen
Philip Caine
Udo Beyer.
William Carter Lafayette
Andrea Natchios
Gayle Tadero
Kieron Dane
Travis Nichols
Gregory Leslie Stark
Rick Harding
Charles Warren
Martine Rabelais
Tony Farlani
Giovanni Rossi
Corinne Barbeau
Lynn Fredricks
Marcus Ranford
Joshua Keller
Vanessa Warren
Lynette Alver
Fatou Turay
Ousman Sesay
Jacqueline Manard
Mary Channing
Marcus Ettinger
Ben Morton
Trent Warren
Cat Warren
Troy Warren
Timothy Carson
Shadow
Chini
Nathan Richardson
Chini Richardson
Stevie Stevens

Victor Russel
Kimberly Russel
Floyd McKenzie
Diana McKenzie

Phoenix – the 21:
Linda Cousin
Carla Wolf
Beth Alver
Lee Warren
Glory Burns
William Carter Lafayette
Giovanni Rossi
Morten Falck
Sally Regehr
Michelle Warren
Andrea Natchios
Tony Farlani
Martine Rabelais
Kimberly Russel
Elliott Marsten
Diana McKenzie
Corinne Barbeau
Gregory Leslie Stark
Rick Harding
Jane Morris
Marcus Ranford

The definitely dead (with year of death):

Trudy Warren (2006)
Yvonne Bastian (2006)
Brian Garrett (2005)
Laurie Isherwood (2005)
Stella Carson (1992)
Kelly Regehr (1988)
Michael Warren (1988)
Eric Carr (1987)
Frank Forester (1987)
Iris Carson (1987)
Penelope (Sandy) Middleton (1987)
Jean Gidman (1986)
Jack Warren (1984)
Jonas Bergli (1983)
Mark Stewart (1979)
David Gidman (1979)
Eugene Kendall (1976)

Francis Caine (1976)
Tilla Stevens (1976)
Bob Tremblay (1976)
Regina Forester (1976)
Paul Cornwall (1976)
Kent Farley (1976)
Howard Grey (1976)
Claudia Cornwall (1976)
Hunter Cornwall (1976)
Kurt Meinz (1975)
Peter Clarke (1974)
Ezra Coogan (1968)
Wolf Connors (1966)
Joel Warren (1952)
Virgil Warren (1944)
James Warren (1944)
Lance Powell (1944)
Nancy Warren (1940)
François Stewart (1940)
April Powell (1935)
Sara Woodward (1931)
Desmond Warren (1923)
Susan Warren (1918)
John Warren (1918)
Nell Warren (1917)
Elliott Warren (1916)
Tanya Orbov (1912)
Cynthia Warren (1912)

So when the new-born Phoenix first is seen
Her feathered subjects all adore their queen,
And while she makes her progress through the East,
From every grove her numerous train's increased;
Each poet of the air her glory sings,
And round him the pleased audience claps their wings.

The Phoenix
John Dryden 1631 - 1700

Phoenix Green Earth
Book One

The Phoenix is rising. The green Earth is reasserting itself. After one Storm, another is there to take its place.

Ted knows, Liz knows, now, what to do, with the world, with themselves. They've been wandering for so long, wondering what to do with their lives. Now they *know*.

Now, the Twilight Storm is here.

From the desert, from the ruins of the city called Las Vegas the Phoenix is rising. Phoenix Green Earth, a radical environmental movement is founded, a belief spreading like wildfire among the modern civilization's outcasts, disgruntled rebels hungry for freedom, for life, for a reckoning, a fundamental belief telling them that the present-day world is *wrong*. They know and have done so for a long time, and now, finally they are, they all are, ready to act on that belief, to correct all injustice, all the wrongs, everything screwed up in the world, *come what may*.

So, they leave their homes, leave their semblance of a life, becoming wanderers, joining all the others out there, on the move, on the Freedom Road. They start living and awaken slowly from their long slumber, from humanity's long slumber… and the world awakens with them.

ISBN 978-82-91693-32-3

THE COMPANION NOVEL:

Shadow Walk

The world is changing. They know this, in their core of cores, where everything moves and shifts. Night and fire have followed them all the days of their lives.

What they carry inside has always scared them, always intrigued them...

They have always felt different, apart from the crowd. And here, now, they get the confirmation they have always wanted, always yearned for, that they are truly different, a breed apart. The metamorphosis begins. Their minds, their bodies are changing in shocking and unpredictable ways, as what's on the inside is brought to the outside. And as they themselves are changing they are also changing the world.

Danger awaits them, Life awaits them, in the small, backward New England town. Magick and Mystery may be found beneath unturned stones.

People, young and old, are descending on the small, insignificant town of Northfield, New England.

Boys and girls, students at the school of Life, Seekers, yearning for what's different, what's hidden.

They're seeking within and without, high and low.

And here, in this dusty, remote place they're finding it, turning the stone, finding the strength within themselves to be themselves, to break out of confines, to the world beyond. And in time, after the initial, tentative steps, pushing down paths new and undreamed of.

And the present-day order sees them for what they are... Agents of Change, a threat to any establishment, any imposed reality. The heatwave, the worst in living memory, is nothing compared to the boiling within the human heart. The Indian Summer heralds the twilight of mankind.

ISBN 978-82-91693-12-5

Other published and upcoming novels by **Amos Keppler** from **Midnight Fire Media**:

The Janus Clan - (eleven long chapters about the Wild Man in the modern world, with PGE counting as one):

The Defenseless
The Slaves
Birds Flying in the Dark
At the End of the Rainbow
Lewis of Modern York
The Werewolf of Locus Bradle
The Valley of Kings
Eye in the Sky
The Iron Cage
ShadowWalk
Phoenix Green Earth - Book One
Phoenix Green Earth - Book Two

The Defenseless

The two rivers meet and join in the city of Denver, becoming one...

The two dark brothers, growing up with their sister Linda in a mundane, average suburb, a place well entrenched in modern United States and the world, have since their moment of birth been at odds with the world... and with each other.

Mike and Ted Cousin are not who they are. There is a mystery here, one of birth and upbringing, one of fate. Violence and death, blood and fire follow them all the days of their lives. The fire is resting somewhere inside... waiting for the Spark.

Their parents know something, but are not telling it. The policeman Mark Stewart and their aunt Trudy do, too. Everybody knows something, pieces of the whole, but nobody knows the whole truth, nobody telling it.

The ancient power is returning to the world, a world massively suffering from physical and spiritual poison, on the brink of collapse and a collective tailspin suicide run without its like in human history.

Magick is returning from its long exile. Thus begins the story of the wild beasts rising from their ashes.

The Spark is struck, horrible and terrifying.

First book of ten in the Janus Clan series: Eleven stories of the wild man in the modern world, forty years of wandering, before the Phoenix is rising from its ashes.

Hardcover ISBN 978-82-91693-08-8
Paperback ISBN 978-82-91693-26-2

phoe·nix also phe·nix (fnks).
n.
1. Mythology. A bird in Egyptian mythology that lived in the desert for 500 years and then consumed itself by fire, later to rise renewed from its ashes.
2. A person or thing of unsurpassed excellence or beauty; a paragon.
3. Phoenix. A constellation in the Southern Hemisphere near Tucana and Sculptor.

Mythology of the Phoenix
For mythology fans, the following excerpt was taken from

«The Book of Doors: An Oracle from Ancient Egypt»
by Athon Veggi and Alison Davidson

phoe·nix also phe·nix (fnks).
n.
1. Mythology. A bird in Egyptian mythology that lived in the desert for 500 years and then consumed itself by fire, later to rise renewed from its ashes.
2. A person or thing of unsurpassed excellence or beauty; a paragon.
3. Phoenix. A constellation in the Southern Hemisphere near Tucana and Sculptor.

The wonderful Bennu, with its brilliant plumage, was the sacred bird of Heliopolis. Identified as a heron with its long straight back and head adorned at the back with two erect feathers, the Bennu was later called Phoenix by the Greeks and fabulous stories were told about it.

In Heliopolis, the Bennu bird played a major role in Egyptian mythology, dwelling on the ben-ben stone or obelisk within its sanctuary and revered alongside Ra and Ausar (Osiris). For it was in the City of the Sun where the work of creation began.

The Bennu bird was said to create itself from the fire that burned on the top of the sacred Persea tree in Heliopolis, and in the Metternich Stele, Auset (Isis) says to her son Heru: 'Thou art the Great Bennu who was born on the Incense Trees in the House of the Great Prince in Heliopoli.' (Budge, 1969, vol. 2209)

As the 'soul of Ra,' the sun rose in the form of the Bennu to shine out across the world renewed each morning. But the Bennu was also a manifestation of Ausar (Osiris) and was said to spring from his heart as a living symbol of the god. In the 'Book of the Dead,' there are formulae to transform the deceased into the Great Bennu. Here, the deceased says, 'I am the Bennu, the soul of Ra, and the guide of the gods in the Duat.' In another verse, he says, 'I am pure. My purity is the purity of the Great Bennu which is in the city of Suten-henen.'

For the Bennu is the quintessence of rebirth, it rises from its ashes as the spiritual body rises from the dead physical form, as the new sun rises from the old. It is the new condition reached when the return to life is accomplished, namely the resurrection of Ausar (Osiris).

Herodotus records the Bennu bird -- making its appearance only once in 500 years

-- as coming from Arabia, carrying in its beak an egg of myrrh that contained its father's body. This egg is similar to Geb's egg that was laid on the primordial hill and gave birth to the sun, the egg within which the whole alchemical process of transformation is effected.

When the Bennu became old, he built a nest of incense twigs in the sacred tree, and lay down and died. In Pliny's account, a small worm appeared from his body that metamorphosed into a bird, and thus the Bennu was reborn.

The planet Venus was called the 'star of the ship of the Bennu-Ausar' (Osiris), mentioned as the Morning Star in this invocation to the sacred sun bird.

Most beings spring from other individuals; but there is a certain kind which reproduces itself. The Assyrians call it the Phoenix. It does not live on fruit or flowers, but on frankincense and odoriferous gums. When it has lived five hundred years, it builds itself a nest in the branches of an oak, on the top of a palm tree. In this it collects cinnamon and spikenard, and myrrh, and of these materials builds a pile on which it deposits itself, and dying, breathes out its last breath amidst odors. From the body of the parent bird, a young Phoenix issues forth, destined to live as long a life as its predecessor. When this has grown up and gained sufficient strength, it lifts its nest from the tree (its own cradle and its parent's sepulcher), and carries it to the city of Heliopolis in Egypt, and deposits it in the temple of the sun.

Ovid

As Ovid tells us, the Phoenix comes from Assyria, however, this bird appears in many places at many times.

There are Chinese, Japanese, Russian, Egyptian, and Native American counterparts. (Fêng-Huang, Ho-oo, Firebird, Benu, and Yel respectively). All of these birds are identified with the sun, and are very similar to the bird described by Ovid. The first known mention of this bird was by Hesiod in the eighth century B.C., and the most detailed early account is by the Greek historian Heroditus. He says,

"I have not seen it myself, except in a picture. Part of his plumage is gold-coloured, and part crimson; and he is for the most part very much like an eagle in outline and bulk."

Like Heroditus says, the Phoenix is a large eagle like or heron like bird with red and gold feathers (although the Chinese phoenix has five colours). The bird is also known to have a beautiful song. The bird is supposed to be very long-lived with a life span of, according to various accounts, 500 years, 540 years, 1000 years, 1461 years or even 12 994 years. This is the Phoenix as we know it, the bird that is self-reincarnated from its own ashes.

410

By the fourth century A.D. the phoenix myth had changed so that the mature bird self-immolated after turning its nest into a funeral pyre. After three days, it "rose again". Thus the phoenix became identified with the resurrection of Christ and became a symbol of both immortality and life after death.

One possible explanation for the phoenix myth: some large birds spread their wings over fires so that the smoke kills parasites.

As the bird kept appearing in writing, its origin changed a little. In Pliny's account of the Roman senator Manilius' report of the genesis of the phoenix. He stated that a small worm grew from the bones and marrow of the dead bird. This worm eventually develops into the new bird.

Society's method of crushing opposition:

1. isolate the radicals;
2. "cultivate" the idealists and "educate" them into becoming realists; then
3. co-opt the realists